KU-632-093

Praise for

CONVICTION

'No one crafts a dilemma quite like Jack Jordan ... if you're anything like I was, you'll be swept away on a thrilling ride that starts from the very first page'
JANICE HALLETT

'I thoroughly enjoyed this tightly plotted, moral-dilemma crime novel, which had me on the edge of my seat ... brilliantly written. A true page-turner'
ADELE PARKS

'Whizzes along and drips with detail, with plenty of courtroom drama for those who love watching it on the small screen. Definitely one to take your time with and savour'
BELFAST TELEGRAPH

'More twists and turns than a rollercoaster ... one of the best cliffhanger endings I've read in a long while'
SHOTS

'Electrifying'
CRIME MONTHLY

'Well plotted and with plenty of action, suspense and some fabulous twists, it's a must-read thriller'
MY WEEKLY

'Skilfully mixes courtroom drama with an excellent cat-and-mouse thriller ... Jordan achieves that rarest of feats: a book that satisfies throughout. Not to be missed'
PERSPECTIVE MAGAZINE, **THRILLER OF THE MONTH**

Also by Jack Jordan

Anything for Her
My Girl
A Woman Scorned
Before Her Eyes
Night by Night
Do No Harm

CONVICTION

JACK JORDAN

**SIMON &
SCHUSTER**

London · New York · Sydney · Toronto · New Delhi

First published in Great Britain by Simon & Schuster UK Ltd, 2023
This paperback edition first published 2024

Copyright © Jack Jordan, 2023

The right of Jack Jordan to be identified as author
of this work has been asserted in accordance with the
Copyright, Designs and Patents Act, 1988.

1 3 5 7 9 10 8 6 4 2

Simon & Schuster UK Ltd
1st Floor
222 Gray's Inn Road
London WC1X 8HB

Simon & Schuster: Celebrating 100 Years of Publishing in 2024

Simon & Schuster Australia, Sydney
Simon & Schuster India, New Delhi

www.simonandschuster.co.uk
www.simonandschuster.com.au
www.simonandschuster.co.in

A CIP catalogue record for this book is
available from the British Library

Paperback ISBN: 978-1-3985-0574-2
eBook ISBN: 978-1-3985-0573-5
Audio ISBN: 978-1-3985-2266-4

This book is a work of fiction. Names, characters, places
and incidents are either a product of the author's imagination or
are used fictitiously. Any resemblance to actual people living
or dead, events or locales is entirely coincidental.

Typeset in Sabon by M Rules
Printed and Bound in the UK using
100% Renewable Electricity at CPI Group (UK) Ltd

MIX
Paper | Supporting
responsible forestry
FSC® C171272
FSC
www.fsc.org

Dedicated to:

the Dream Team

PART I

1

Five days until the trial

The thought of a murdered family should make me feel repulsed.
Enraged, even. And yet, I feel the same giddiness one might feel
before a first date; the fervent flap of butterfly wings in my gut.

I sit before the brief for Wade Darling's case, the blood-red
ribbon unspooled on the surface of my desk, eyeing the loose
pages, well-thumbed from when they belonged to Adrian
Whittaker QC. I think of him leaping from the Northern Line
platform before the oncoming tube train and wince. A brilliant legal mind, gone. I met him once, and never would have
dreamed he would be the type. But then who is, until pushed
to their limits?

Just a couple of days ago, I had been green with envy over
this case. Any barrister in their right mind would take it: the
media coverage, the career progression, the recognition from
peers; Queen's Counsel, if they hadn't been appointed already.
It is a dream of a trial, when one looks beyond the tragedy of
the case. I look to my calendar and mentally mark the day.
Wednesday 2 January, 2019: the defining day of my career.

When I was told just yesterday that I had been chosen to
defend, I sat and let the news sink in, knowing this would be

the case to change my career trajectory forever. If only I had more time to prepare. If my client had been charged with a petty crime, it would be easy enough; there is a blueprint to those kinds of cases. I could recite my argument for a client like that in my sleep. But to prepare a defence for a client facing three life sentences, in what is said to be the biggest trial of the year, in a matter of days?

I break away from my thoughts and spot my hands white-knuckling the arms of my chair. I unclench them, flexing my fingers until the blood flows back to the tips.

It has been a long time since I had a physical brief to grip onto, with the justice system finally having reached the digital age. However, the older, more experienced barristers like Whittaker are often stuck in the past, plagued by the superstition that changing one's ways will affect their performance. I get it. It feels right like this, in the same way a painter must feel holding their brush.

I trace the cover with my fingers, savouring the moment. I have advocated in murder trials before, but never one of this magnitude, and with my upcoming fifteen-year anniversary as a barrister, the timing couldn't feel more poignant. Winning the Darling trial will be an automatic shoo-in for Queen's Counsel. Better cases. Better pay. Those two simple letters after my name that I have wanted for longer than I care to remember. And despite the little time I have to prepare, thinking of Whittaker's decades of experience and expertise helps calm my nerves. If I had to choose a case to take over at such short notice, it would be one of his.

I glance over today's front pages fanned out on my desk. The Darlings' house is splayed over every cover, flames roaring from the windows of the sprawling country home. The

Darling murders have graced the headlines for months, and spread through the public masses like wildfire, with everyone from the Scottish Highlands to Land's End forming their own opinions on the case and my client. The truth has been twisted and mangled by their wagging tongues so many times that I know I will have my work cut out for me in bringing them back to the facts. Lies are always so much more enticing.

I pull my copy of the *Metro* from the pile and take a look at my client: Wade Darling takes up the front page, snapped as he was led out of the hospital in handcuffs after he was arrested for allegedly murdering his family while they slept. He is a handsome man, from what I can see of him: pale eyes, chiselled cheekbones, a head of thick blond hair – no easy feat for a man beyond the forty mark. He will certainly be able to woo some of the jury with such good looks on his side, if they can look past his alleged crimes. In the photo, he towers above the officers flanking either side of him, and even in cuffs he has an air of authority. I wonder how he appeared to his family behind closed doors.

I take a deep breath and open the brief, fingering through the newspaper cuttings that have been sliced out with an unsteady hand, and scan the headlines.

HOUSE OF HORRORS: MOTHER AND CHILDREN SHOT DEAD IN FIERY BLAZE

FATHER OF TWO CHARGED WITH DARLING MASSACRE

The horror of the photographs is almost hypnotic. I eye the once magnificent country mansion burnt to a shell, its innards crumbled and collapsed within the wreck; then the aerial shots that the press helicopters took from above as the firefighters were still battling the blaze well into the late hours of the following day, and the day after that, as the thick trail of smoke continued to rise up into the sky for miles. If looked at closely, you can see the corpses of the Darlings' horses, shot between the eyes and left to burn, their remains charred black where they lay in the burnt rubble of their stables. The bodies of the Darling family were found among the mass of destruction. It took almost a week to get them all out; to distinguish their bones from the debris.

I slip the photos of the victims from the brief. Yolanda Darling, forty-two, wife of the defendant; Phoebe, eighteen, daughter of the defendant; and Danny, the youngest and non-binary, just sixteen years of age. All suspected to be victims of an accidental blaze before the signs of arson came to light and the bullets were found in their skulls. They were a striking family, which isn't surprising, what with Yolanda's modelling past. The children shared the same white-blonde hair as their mother, the same stark blue eyes.

Despite not having read the brief from cover to cover, I know the story. It seems everybody does. A husband, father of two, accused of losing his mind and killing his family before setting their country home ablaze. The teens wouldn't have known what happened to them: they were shot dead in their beds as they slept, the entry wounds at the backs of their heads. They wouldn't have smelt the smoke or felt the hot lick of flames, nor would they have heard the shots due to the silencer found on the end of the murder weapon at the scene. Yolanda, however, fared worse. She must have seen or heard something, or been awake at the time of the attack, for she was found under the rubble where the staircase used to be, having sustained gunshots to her right knee, her back, and finally her head. The third and final execution. In my mind, I picture her running for the staircase, her eyes bleared with sleep and her hair tailing behind her. I envisage the first shot to her leg was fired to disable her. The second was to throw her to the ground. The last and final bullet was to take her from this world.

My client was found alive but unconscious from smoke inhalation, lying on the ground floor by the back door in the kitchen where he had crawled to safety. He had suffered second-degree burns to his left hand, and there was gunpowder residue on the other, his family's blood on his pyjamas. The rifle was found beside him, covered in his fingerprints and his alone.

It's a good thing I enjoy a challenge.

As I read through the brief, I find it is far messier than I expected. Whittaker was held in high regard on the legal circuit, and to peek into his world and find it in such disarray is disappointing. By the looks of it, there are even some vital documents missing – a copy of the prosecution's psychiatric examination report of my client's medical history by Dr Samantha Heche, and at a glance, the witness statement from Yolanda Darling's mother, Annika Viklund. To have these missing so close to the trial doesn't fit with my picture of Whittaker at all, and to see Wade Darling on the list to give evidence is even more concerning. It usually works in a defendant's favour to remain silent during their trial and to let us do the talking for them, forgoing the chance for the prosecution to question them in cross-examination. Perhaps Whittaker's mental health struggles bled into his work.

I glance at the name of Wade's solicitor. Eddie Chester, from William and Chase. Although it would have been

Adrian's job to chase the missing files, it is the job of the client's solicitor to acquire all the evidence the barrister needs. As the barrister, it was Adrian's role, and now mine, to be the mouthpiece for the case and form the client's defence to bring before the jury, but it is up to Eddie to source the materials; the man who has been with our client since the first day the police suspected him of the crime, and who knows him best. Which means both Adrian and Eddie failed to do their jobs. I jot down the missing statements to mention at today's hearing.

A swift knock at the door breaks me from my thoughts.

Artie stands in the doorway with a smirk, mischief sparkling in his eyes.

'Good morning, Neve Harper. Or should I say, soon-to-be Neve Harper QC.'

'You can wipe that look off your face. You'll have given Niall an aneurysm by passing the job to me.'

I imagine what Niall Richardson's face might look like when he hears the news of my appointment to Mr Darling's defence. It won't be the first time we have stood on opposite sides of the bench in a trial. We had been at the Bar together before going our separate ways to different chambers, but our competitiveness never fails to reappear when our paths cross.

'I don't know what you mean,' he replies, leaning against the doorframe. 'I simply gave the case to my most promising defence barrister. A bit of healthy competition never killed anyone, did it?'

Arthur Mills – Artie for short – senior clerk and head of chambers, the man who makes sure everything runs smoothly, and who has been a permanent presence in my career ever since I passed the Bar. He is seven years older than my thirty-eight, but has a young, mischievous air about him, as if he is still at university picking his way through freshers and drinking until dawn, puffing on fags like they aren't more than a tenner a pack these days. It is evidently clear upon meeting him that his family's wealth and privilege has meant he has never had to grow up.

'You'll be the most hated clerk in the city this morning. Who'd you have to kill to get your hands on this?'

He taps the side of his nose as he makes his way over to the desk and perches on the corner.

'You sure you can handle it, then?' he asks.

My collar seems to notch closer to my neck, pressing against the ridge of my throat.

'I'm offended you'd ask.'

'I'd ask the same of anyone. You've got less than a week till the trial; no easy feat.'

'That's if the judge doesn't postpone it at the hearing this afternoon.'

'He won't. This case has been delayed too many times, and the public are getting arsey. The CPS won't want people knowing what a complete shambles their judicial system is, will they?'

'We'll see.'

He exhales sharply, his breath laced with the harsh scent of cigarettes, and taps his finger on Adrian Whittaker's case notes.

'Write down anything good before he jumped?'

I flash him a look, and he raises his hands in mock surrender.

'You know me,' he says as he heads for the door. 'I have a knack for crossing the line.'

'Well,' I say pointedly. 'if that's all . . .'

He remains in the doorway with that familiar spark in his

eyes; the sort of smarmy stare a man gives a woman from the other end of a bar, mentally undressing her.

'What do you want, Artie?'

'Nothing,' he replies. 'Just rattling the cage.'

'And why would you want to do that?'

'I've learnt over the years that it pays to piss you off. You're best at your job when you're angry.'

'You're a sociopath.'

He laughs heartily, flashing the dark fillings in his molars. When he recovers himself and sets his eyes on me again, his smile slowly fades.

'All jokes aside – you good?'

He gives me *the look*. The one I always get around this time of year. An offensive amalgamation of curiosity and pity. I feel my guard lock into place.

'I'm fine.'

'You doing the vigil again this year?'

'Like every year,' I reply coolly. I stare down at the brief and pretend to read. 'Will that be all?'

He laughs behind closed lips. 'Yes, miss – I'll be on my way.'

The words swim on the page before me. I try my hardest to concentrate, but I can still sense him standing there, watching me. I know he is smirking without even needing to look at him.

'What is it, Artie?'

I shoot him a look; he is smiling wider now. Forever enjoying a good back and forth. He has always been able to find a person's weak spot, the dagger in a person's side, and twist it. He'd have made a good barrister, if he had ever wanted out of chambers.

'Niall better have his wits about him,' he says. 'All it'll take is one of those glares from you and he'll be shaking like a pissin' dog.'

I listen to him snigger to himself as he heads off down the corridor towards the clerk's office, whistling a playful tune.

When the silence finally returns, I place my attention back on the brief, trying to shake the vigil tonight from my mind. But I can't focus on the words; they become meaningless black blobs, taunting me.

I open my desk drawer, take out my wedding ring from inside, and slip it on. The gold band is cool against my skin after being left in the depths of my desk for days, hidden away along with my thoughts of him. I can barely bring myself to look down at it glinting on my finger and quickly slip it off again, placing it inside the drawer once more. I will put it on before I leave, but for now, all I want to do is forget.

I hunch myself over the brief and begin to read.

2

I sit in the back of the coffee shop at the table furthest from the window, reading over the life of a dead woman as I wait for the man charged with killing her to arrive, when an email pops up in the corner of my laptop screen beside me.

Don't read *The Times*.

It's from Sam, a clerk from chambers. I don't need to ask what the email is referring to. If it had been sent by anyone else or for any other reason, this would have riled me, but I know he means well. They need me to be focused on the trial with no distractions. But of course, I will. I usually avoid all press coverage of my husband, but I feel myself drawn to the story, to him. I type his name into Google followed by *The Times*. The article appears beneath the search bar.

Three years on: the strange disappearance of
Matthew Harper

I click on the hyperlink for the article and hold my breath. There is a photo of him beneath the headline, a professional shot he had taken for work as managing director of a charity for domestic violence survivors, the year before he went missing: his hair had started to grey at his sideburns, with fine lines tracing his olive skin, accentuating his eyes as he smiled for the camera. My husband was handsome. Painfully so.

I haven't looked at a photo of him in the longest time. The sight of him brings up too many emotions that I actively keep down. But looking at him now – at the eyes I would stare into endlessly, at the lips I used to kiss – I feel them slowly crawling to the surface.

Edited into the right-hand corner of the photo is a smaller one: the last known photo of my husband, a freeze-frame shot from a neighbour's security camera capturing him during his final run, his white trainers stark in the darkness of the night.

I cast an eye over the byline of the article.

Delving into the infamous missing person's case that inspired the hit true crime podcast series, crime correspondent Melanie Eccleston returns to the mystery on the three-year anniversary of Matthew Harper's disappearance, and follows up on what became of his Darling.

My stomach pitches at the sight of a single word. *Darling.* Capitalised. A prelude to the link that Eccleston will evidently draw to my life after Matthew's disappearance, and my upcoming case. Sam was right to warn me off it, but I can't keep myself from reading on. I hover my shaking hand over the trackpad and scroll.

... Can a man really vanish into thin air? The disappearance of Matthew Harper enraptured the

nation in 2016, with all our questions unanswered. But of
all those questions, one dominates: if Matthew Harper
is dead, whatever happened to his body?

A man goes for his usual evening run at 8 p.m. on Christmas
Eve and never comes home, the last sighting of him caught by
grainy CCTV footage captured from a property along Western
Road. No witnesses. No trace. All it took for the disappearance
to hit the mainstream was a popular podcast to feature it as
part of their true crime series; the press picked up on it within
days, and soon enough the nation was feverishly gripped,
dissecting my life and grief with gleeful entitlement. Why
would the managing director of a charity, known for his kind
temperament and thoughtfulness, suddenly go missing? Online
forums appeared overnight to untangle the mystery, cult-like in
their devotion to the case and the missing man they had never
met, relaying the story so sensationally that the ins and outs
of my own life soon became foreign to me. Newspaper articles
chased the public's interest, and in turn, the journalists chased
me: the woman known for winning criminal trials who had
found herself trapped within an unsolvable case.

I always do this – describe it like I would the breakdown
of a case. Factual, devoid of emotion. It's easier this way. But
something is different this time; perhaps it was seeing the
photo of him earlier, looking into his eyes lined with his smile,
staring back into my soul from the page, or perhaps it is due
to the vigil this evening.

I reach the clincher of the article and wince.

Neve Harper, a staple figure in the capital's courtrooms,
failed to slow down. While avoiding all press enquiries

and media interest surrounding her husband's
disappearance, she has never shied away from making
sure her clients take centre stage, with her stoic face
featured just a step behind, seemingly conscious of her
better angles so to appear in the best, yet supposedly
coincidental, light. One might argue that Ms Harper
made a name for herself off the back of her husband's
demise, while conveniently refusing to play the victim
so as not to affect her fierce reputation in the courts.
One could even go so far to say that her quiet fame led
to her success in acquiring the infamous Darling trial,
scheduled to appear before the jury on—'

I slam my laptop shut.

Eccleston has never held back, but to cut this deep is a new
low. She chased me for months after Matthew's disappearance,
desperate to be the journalist to crack me open. But once the
gleam on the story waned, she seemed to as well, though not
without making it her mission to smear my character instead.
The anniversary never fails to reignite her grudge.

I look down at my hand, shaking violently where it rests on
the laptop.

*Now is not the time. I can think of him later, at the vigil.
Not before.*

I drum my fingers against the surface of the table. It has been
six months since I had my last cigarette, but at times like these,
I long for my filthy habit.

The bell above the door chimes. The café is a favourite of
mine, small and inconspicuous, hidden down a back street near
to the courthouse. No one would expect to find Wade Darling
here. It is practically empty but for an elderly woman sat alone

at a table by the window, and two solicitors from Murrell and Bergmann sat in a bay to themselves, whom I've known and worked with for almost a decade. When Wade and his solicitor walk through the door, it is impossible to miss them.

Wade enters with his head down and his hands hidden deep within his jacket pockets, his eyes shielded by sunglasses and his shoulders hunched inwards, giving him a sheepish, almost hostile front. His once dashing good looks that have been splashed over the front pages have given way to a man who seems hell-bent on making himself appear invisible. But even with his head down, he towers over everyone in the room.

His solicitor, however, is exactly how I pictured him. Eddie Chester is short, bald, and stocky of build; I can practically see the arrogance rippling off him. The sort of bravado a man adopts to make up for a few inches, either in height or elsewhere. He barks a coffee order at the barista behind the counter and boulders over, grabbing the back of the chair opposite mine and dragging it out with a harsh squeak against the hardwood floor. Wade slips silently into the chair beside him.

'Good morning,' I say.

'Mrs Harper,' Chester says. 'I've heard a lot about you.'

I notice he doesn't mention if what he has heard has been good or bad. He reaches out to shake my hand, and crushes it.

'It's Ms,' I reply, as I take my hand back. My pulse throbs at the tips of my fingers. I turn my attention to my client.

'Mr Darling, it's good to meet you. I'm Neve Harper, and I have been asked to represent you in your upcoming trial, in the wake of Mr Whittaker's passing.'

I hold out my hand. His own is cold and quivering, and his nails have been bitten to the quick. His other hand was burnt in the fire; the skin warped, healed in odd, fleshy waves. He slips it under the table when he catches me looking, and takes off his sunglasses. We meet each other's gaze for only a second. The whites of his eyes are bloodshot, looking almost gruesome against the stark blue of his irises.

'I'm sure Mr Whittaker's passing came as a shock, but please rest assured that you are in very capable hands.'

He nods silently. I clear my throat.

'Thank you both for meeting me here. With the press interest around you, Wade, I thought it best we met somewhere discreet.'

He turns to his solicitor, barely registering my words.

'Do we really have to go through all this again? I went through it all with the last guy.'

'I'm afraid so,' I interject, conscious that Chester has seemingly got Wade's confidence firmly in his grasp. Something I need to change, and fast. 'I have all of Mr Whittaker's notes and have caught up on the hearings you've had to date, but it is important that I hear your version of events from you directly, so I can represent you in court to the best of my ability. I understand you've been waiting a long time.'

'A long time?' he scoffs. 'I've practically been on house arrest for a year. I finally get a court date that isn't pushed back and then my barrister jumps in front of the bloody eleven o'clock train.'

Despite his tactless delivery, I understand his annoyance. These days, trying to get a case to court is almost as likely as winning the lottery. Decades of underfunding. An impossible backlog of cases waiting to be tried; not to mention the barrister shortages due to inhuman hours and insufficient pay, and the legal aid sector virtually at breaking point. If a case is lucky enough to get a date, a defendant and their advocate may arrive in court only to find that delays in the cases before them have knocked them from the schedule. From looking at the brief, Wade's case has been postponed twice.

His face is flushed crimson from the frustration of it all, but when he meets my eyes, his complexion quickly fades to white.

'I'm sorry. I just realised you might have known him.'

'Not very well,' I reply with a polite smile, and check my watch. 'Now, before the hearing later today, we have a few things to go through. First and foremost: do you agree to me representing you?'

Darling looks to his solicitor again. It concerns me how much he relies on him.

'Well, you can't be represented by a dead bloke, can you?' Chester replies with a chortle. 'She's good, lad. One of the best. I wouldn't let you get stuck with the runt of the judicial litter.'

Wade returns his eyes to mine and looks me up and down, assessing me for himself. After a tense few seconds, he nods with a sigh.

'All right.'

'Great,' I reply, with a tight smile. 'So today is a quick meeting before the session with the judge to make sure we are ready to go ahead with the trial as planned, but as discussed on the phone with Mr Chester, we will have a more in-depth conference at your home address tomorrow morning to hear your account of the murders. Do you have any questions for me, before we begin?'

Wade is picking at the hangnail on his thumb, plucking at it between his scarred fingertips until he draws blood. He unfurls another a sigh.

'When is this going to end? I can't have the trial postponed again, I just can't.'

I notice his hands shaking on the surface of the table.

'I can't leave the house because of the press; they've staked out my bloody doorstep. I can't even open my own curtains anymore unless I want to end up on the front page. This has gone on long enough.'

I notice he has centred the ordeal around himself. No mention of his slain family, no mention of grief or justice. Just the inconvenience of being charged. I mentally make a note that this is something we will have to work on, if he wants to win over the jury.

'In an ideal world, we would have more time to prepare for this. I won't lie to you and say that I don't have concerns about taking your case to trial so soon after a change of representation. However, I can only imagine how tough this has been for you, which I plan to make clear to the judge today. If you work with me until the trial, we can be ready. But I must stress, it is only five days away – if you want it to go ahead as planned, I will need your full trust and co-operation.'

We stare at each other across the table, weighing each other up in silence.

'You'll have it,' he replies.

'I'm glad.' I turn to Chester. 'Now I have some questions for you.'

'Me?' he asks, with another of those irritating chortles.

'Yes. Have you worked many murder trials?'

He sits up, puffs out his chest defensively.

'Several,' Chester replies.

'I see. And is it your standard approach to go into trial with vital pieces of evidence missing?'

Wade's eyes widen as he glances towards his solicitor, who is stammering and huffing in his seat.

'What on earth . . . what are you implying?'

'I'm not implying anything,' I reply shortly. 'The brief speaks for itself. We have less than a week until the trial and we are still missing the psychiatric evaluation by Dr Samantha Heche, and a copy of the witness statement from Yolanda's mother, Annika. It's your responsibility to chase the CPS for these documents, correct?'

'It's quite common to have a delay in these sorts of—'

'Not this close to trial, Mr Chester, and certainly not on any case of mine.'

He stares at me blankly over the table, his cheeks growing a deeper shade of pink with each passing second.

'We're not in the courtroom yet, Ms Harper. You're grilling me like I'm in the box—'

'Wade,' I interject. 'What was Yolanda's maiden name?'

'Viklund,' he replies.

'Thank you. And Mr Chester . . .' I turn to him and take in the sight of his gaping mouth. 'Isn't one of your biggest clients the Viklund family?'

The Viklund name isn't one that a lawyer simply glosses over without taking pause; the family probably has the dirtiest money north of the Thames.

A thread of veins throb in the centre of Chester's forehead.

'I don't like what you're insinuating.'

'Again, I'm not insinuating anything.' I slip the document from beneath the brief and place it before the two men. Wade leans in the furthest. 'In the last five years, the Viklund family have paid you almost two point five million pounds for your services. The majority of your company's annual turnover, in fact. That's quite the conflict of interest, wouldn't you say?'

Chester is finally speechless, his mouth ready to catch flies. His whole face has turned beet-red.

'Wade, who recommended you work with Mr Chester?'

'They ... they came to me. Eddie said—'

'I approached him because I was right for the job,' Chester practically shouts.

'Is that so? I know you mentioned you've worked several murder trials just now, but according to public records you've represented just three clients on such a charge in the last twenty-five years. That hardly makes you the best fit, does it? Which made me wonder what your intentions were.'

Wade is looking at me intently. The sheepish man who entered the café has gone; his eyes have come alive, his shoulders are set straight again. I know I have him.

'Wade, if you look over your shoulder, you will see two men in navy suits. They are Antony Murrell and Robert Bergmann from Murrell and Bergmann Associates. They have represented dozens of clients with charges similar to yours, and are the best fit for your case. As your counsel, I recommend you hire them.'

From the corner of my eye, I can feel Chester's gaze on me, mouth agape.

'You can't do this,' he stutters. 'If you think we will ever work with your chambers again ...'

'I don't believe we work much with you as it is, Mr Chester,' I reply coldly. 'And you know full well that it is my duty to inform my client of any concerns I have about his representation, under the Bar's code of conduct.' I stare at him, straight-faced, before turning to our client. 'Wade, this is your decision.'

Chester turns to him, staring incredulously as Wade's eyes remain on mine. I see the faint trace of a smile pulling at the corners of his lips.

'Eddie,' he says. 'You're fired.'

'*What?*'

I nod to Antony and Robert, who stand on my signal and approach.

'Mr Chester, Mr Bergmann here is going to escort you to your office where he will collect everything we need.'

Chester is close to combusting. His cheeks puff and deflate with air as words form and disintegrate in his mouth. He stutters manically, looking between Wade and me, before staring up at the solicitors replacing him. His face is so red that he looks fit to burst.

'You fucking snake,' he spits, pointing a thick, quivering finger in my face.

'One of the best, I recall you saying,' I reply, as the barista comes towards the table with their drinks. 'Eddie here will have his order to go, please.'

Chester stands, huffing and cursing in a nonsensical stream as Wade sits with his eyes on mine, grinning silently.

'No wonder your fella ran for the fucking hills,' Chester shouts over his shoulder, before bustling out of the café.

My cheeks flush from the low blow, deepening further as my client eyes me closely, no doubt wondering about the context of Chester's jab. I clear my throat and fix a thin smile.

'Shall we begin?'

3

I sit at the advocates' bench, lining up my armoury: the brief, my notebook filled with thoughts on the case, and next to it, a fresh yellow legal pad for any notes I need to make during the hearing. Niall Richardson occupies the other end of the bench.

This is the first time I have seen Niall in a year or so. The last time we crossed paths was at Hove Crown Court, working opposite sides of the bench on the Bateman fraud trial. I took home the win, and I can tell by his demeanour in court this afternoon that his ego is still bruised. We have each won two cases against the other; the Darling trial will prove who will come out on top. Since entering the courtroom, we have exchanged nothing more than a cordial nod.

I assess him from the corner of my eye, checking to see if his wig appears more worn than mine, a sign of experience and maturity rather than unkemptness. I take in every wisp of horsehair that has come away from the fray, the staining around the hairline.

Wade Darling is sat silently in the dock, his wide, nervous eyes wandering about the room as he takes in the panelled walls, the white wigs and black robes. Although he would have entered into the dock before, during the hearings preceding this one – the plea hearing, administrative hearings – standing in the dock never fails to remind a defendant of the fate they may face.

The judge's clerk enters, a short young woman with thick-rimmed glasses, and nods to both Niall and me in turn.

'All rise.'

Before we can fully rise from our seats, the judge enters, seeming to glide from the ripple of his robes, and takes his seat with a sharp exhalation.

Judge Douglas McConnell, although big in presence, is small in stature. His wig of grey curls seems too big for him, and his robes, usually making a judge appear authoritative and grand, seem to drown his thin, almost petite frame. But what he lacks in size, his sour expression makes up for. His brow is thick and permanently creased, giving him a menacing glare, even when he smiles.

'Good morning,' he says sharply, waking his laptop with a tap of a key, after arranging his files before him. 'Ms Harper, welcome to the case.'

'Thank you, Your Honour.'

The judge greets Niall and then removes his spectacles, the courtroom falling into silence as he does so. His face grows noticeably sombre.

'I would like to start by acknowledging Mr Whittaker, and what a loss it is to our profession that he is no longer with us.'

Niall and I nod in agreement. Judge McConnell leans forward, lacing his fingers together.

'But despite the very unfortunate circumstances, I must confess my frustration at the thought of a further delay in this case. Everyone in this room will be aware of the level of press interest surrounding the defendant and the upcoming trial, and frankly, it has become rather embarrassing that we keep failing to commit to a fixed date.'

He peers down at us from his perch. Almost fifteen years of standing before judges in the courtroom, and I still have to stop myself from peering up at them like a child being scolded.

'Any further delays to this case and we will fail to find a single juror in England and Wales who hasn't heard of the defendant or the tragedy at hand. So, I would like to make myself clear: this hearing is being held today to make sure there is nothing more that will stand in our way of getting this matter to trial. I sincerely hope this is the case.'

He checks something on his laptop screen.

'Mr Richardson,' he says. 'Is the CPS ready to proceed?'

'Yes, Your Honour,' Niall says coolly.

'I'm pleased to hear it,' the judge replies, almost admonishingly, as he peers at him through his half-moon spectacles. 'Ms Harper. You've been recently appointed to represent the defendant. Have you been given instructions?'

'Yes, Your Honour,' I reply, my voice confident and without waver. 'The defendant has agreed to my representing him, with another conference tomorrow. Unfortunately, Your Honour, I do have some concerns about the timeline of proceedings.'

Judge McConnell's heavy brow lifts swiftly, raising his sagging eyelids to show the whites of his eyes.

'I do hope you're joking, Ms Harper.'

'I'm afraid not, Your Honour. We are less than a week away from the trial, and yet I regret to inform you that we are still waiting for some key documents from the prosecution.'

I sense Niall shooting me a look from the other end of the bench. Judge McConnell's eyes widen.

'Although I'm sure my learned friend has a good explanation for the delay,' I say, giving Niall a quick, dismissive glance, 'without all of the necessary documentation, Your Honour cannot expect my client to receive a fair trial.'

'Indeed,' Judge McConnell snaps, and glares at my opponent. 'What is it that you're waiting for, Ms Harper?'

'A copy of the examination report conducted by Dr Samantha Heche, and Mrs Annika Viklund's witness statement, Your Honour.'

I catch Niall flicking quickly through the brief to the document breaking down the evidence he and Whittaker will have agreed upon prior to my appointment.

It may be the solicitor's job to source the material, but it's our job as advocates to make sure we have all the relevant evidence to bring before the court. It pays for the judge to see my opposition squirm.

'What is the reason for this delay, Mr Richardson?' Judge McConnell asks.

Niall flushes, shame emblazoned on his cheeks.

'I will have to look into this, Your Honour. But I am sure there is a reasonable explana—'

'*Reasonable*? We are set to begin trial on Monday, Mr Richardson – a trial which has been in the making for close to a year, and of which you have had the most time to prepare. Are you honestly telling me that any delays at this point in proceedings can be considered *reasonable*?'

It takes a lot to rattle Niall. He is usually a strong, unwavering figure, propped up by an almost unbearable ego, but looking at him now, he almost looks like a child. The fear has knocked decades from his face.

'No, Your Honour. I can only apologise on behalf of—'

'I want every necessary document sent to Ms Harper by five p.m. this evening, is that understood?'

'Yes, Your Honour.'

He turns his attention to me.

'Ms Harper, you will call my office and leave word to confirm this.'

'Yes, Your Honour.'

He nods swiftly, and looks between the pair of us.

'Is there anything more?' he asks, in a tone that suggests we daren't.

'No, Your Honour,' we reply in unison.

He stands without another word, and we all rise.

I turn towards the dock and give Mr Darling a nod of confidence, who gives me a hopeful smile in return before he is led out. I turn back to my station and pack away my things.

'Off to a great start, aren't we, Niall?' I say once the judge has left the room.

'You could have called me and chased those files,' he replies with a biting tone.

'Yes, I could have.' I finally meet his eye and give him a forced, closed smile. 'See you on Monday.'

I take my case and head towards the doors.

'If you want to play dirty, Neve,' Niall calls. 'We'll play dirty.'

I walk on without stopping, knowing that my indifference will only anger him more.

Glad to hear it.

4

I stare down at the candle shaking in my grip, wondering to myself how it would feel for my lungs to fill with smoke, like the Darlings' had. My flesh turning to gristle from the flames.

I think of Yolanda Darling's soot-coated teeth, her black smile one of the few parts of her that survived the fire. I think of the roof beams that lay atop her rubbled tomb, and the hours it took to free her. The sparks from the industrial saw cutting through steel and charred cinderblocks. The whine of the crane peeling away the layers of destruction.

It could have been me. It could have been any of us. All it takes is to fall in love with the wrong man, like a game of Russian roulette: passing the gun between us and slipping the barrel in our mouths, pulling the trigger one by one until someone gets the bullet.

'*Neve*,' the voice says urgently, breaking me from my thoughts. 'Did you hear me? I said your candle has blown out.'

I stare at my mother-in-law's face, lit aglow by the candle cupped before her. Even in the low light, I can see her eyes, sharp and questioning, as they take in my dazed expression. Her name is Margaret, which she hates, and insists everyone call her Maggie. Her hair is too short for her face, which has tight, pointed features.

I look down at my candle and the smell of the smoke fills my nostrils. I silently scold myself for letting my mind wander and allowing my impartiality to slip. My client is innocent until proven guilty.

I should be thinking about Matthew. I am so used to blocking him out, a coping mechanism I've sworn by these past three years, but sometimes I fear I am too good at it. Burying the guilt, the grief, the pain. Hiding my wedding ring in the depths of my desk.

'I said we should have bought those electric ones,' Maggie says. 'Yours has gone out too, Hannah.'

My stepdaughter, who is stood so close beside me that our arms graze one another with the slightest movement. I wonder if I can still call her that with her father being dead. Or presumed dead, I should say.

'It's too cold out here, anyway,' Hannah replies.

'It's not cold,' Maggie replies with a huff. 'It's mild for January.'

'Well, it feels cold to me.'

'That's because you don't eat enough.'

Maggie looks down at her candle and sighs sharply, extinguishing her flame into a curling pillar of smoke.

'We're not leaving until we've said something,' she says matter-of-factly, and takes the lighter from her pocket.

This is the third year we have done this, more for Maggie's sake than ours. There used to be others; people wanted to feel part of something that first year, spawning a congregation of strangers in the park closest to where Matthew went missing, a mass of candles spread out as far as the eye could see. We'd chosen to hold the vigil on the second of January to avoid his memory getting lost in the celebrations. We needn't have bothered. I think of our deathly quiet Christmas dinner last month, with the three of us around the table, the only sound being the murmuring of the TV in the background and the rustling of the paper hats from the crackers rested dutifully upon our heads, while Matthew's chair sat empty. As for the vigil, the public attention around his whereabouts soon waned, and the numbers inevitably dwindled. With no body to lay to rest, and no grave to visit each year, we stand in Maggie's back garden, cloaked in the evening's shadows.

Hannah and I watch as Maggie clicks the button repeatedly and fails to ignite a flame until she is close to tears.

'Maggie.'

I hold out my hand to take it from her. She meets my eyes, hers shining as the warm glow of her home is reflected in their watery surface.

I light my candle and cup my hand around it.

'Use it to light yours, Han.'

Hannah looks up at me, and I admire her face in the orange glow of the flame: oval in shape, with plump, soft cheeks; large green pools for eyes that betray her every thought, but sharp as a tack despite her young sixteen years. She has the same eyes as her father; they are such a light green that they almost look grey against her auburn hair, the hair she got from her late mother.

Hannah has lived with her grandmother since her mother's death, which happened when she was only a little girl. Maggie browbeat my husband into the arrangement. *A young girl needs a woman to raise her, not a single father who works all hours,* or so she insisted before Matthew and I met. Those closest to Maggie know how better off life is when one agrees to her demands.

Hannah holds her candle to mine, her brow creasing as she concentrates, warmth spreading through my chest as I watch the spark of satisfaction in her eyes when the flame catches. She is the same age now as Danny Darling had been when they were shot in the head. I feel the urge for a cigarette again.

Matthew and I met when Hannah was just six years old, in the park where I walked my dog. Hannah had led her father over to me, wanting to pet Sam. He was an old thing, on his last legs and shook when he had to stand for too long, but his will for life was still strong. As Hannah had petted Sam, giggling as he licked her palm, I looked into the eyes of the man who would become my husband, and smiled.

Maggie holds her candle to Hannah's, the white stick shaking in her grip. We stand in silence with our hands cupped protectively around the wicks.

'I'll start then,' Maggie says, when neither Hannah nor I say a word. She clears her throat behind her fist, shaking with equal vigour.

'Matthew was a good man,' she says, before remembering. '*Is* a good man.'

The embarrassment is contagious. We have all made the same mistake over the years. Is a man really dead without a body to lay to rest, or ashes to spread? But Hannah and I are more forgiving than Maggie would have been, had it been one of us.

'It has been three years since you've been gone,' she continues. 'Three years of calling myself a mother without a son. Three years of wondering where you are. Wondering if you are safe, or if you're . . .'

Her lip trembles. I hate it when Maggie cries; she becomes defensive and callous. I learnt very quickly to stay quiet until the waterworks stop.

'You are missed,' she says finally, gripping tightly to her composure. 'And I love you.'

She nods, like an exclamation mark punching the end of her speech; her stiff upper lip returns.

I look down at Hannah, staring into the darkness deep in thought. She meets my eyes and flushes crimson.

'Love you, Dad,' she utters.

'You have to say more than that,' Maggie says.

'I don't know what to say.'

'Try,' she replies sternly.

Hannah's cheeks turn a deeper shade of pink, and her eyes search the slabs of patio, as if she will find the words at our feet. A lock of hair flits across the bridge of her nose. I tuck it behind her ear and give her a friendly wink when she catches my eye.

'I'll go,' I say.

But as I take a deep breath to begin, I fail to conjure more than Hannah did. The words crowd at the base of my throat, and my thoughts jumble. I can feel their sights on me: Maggie, indignant and unrelenting; Hannah, with those hauntingly familiar eyes.

'We miss you,' I say, forcing the words past my teeth. 'Wherever you are, we miss you.'

My throat is on fire. I swallow hard, and glance down at my candle. It has blown out again. The smoke curls up and stings my eyes.

'I don't know why I bother,' Maggie snaps. 'We won't do it again next year. Clearly it's not what either of you want.'

'People mourn in different ways, Nanny,' Hannah says, quietly.

'Well, a few words for your father wouldn't go amiss. It's the respectful thing to do. The *right* thing to do.'

The tears have formed again, chasing the malice of her words. She snatches the candles from the pair of us, blowing out Hannah's and her own in one swoop, before heading back inside.

Hannah has lost both of her parents: her mother to cancer when she was only young, and her father in her early teens. This should be her moment, done her way, but Maggie has a way of making situations only about herself. Although a small part of me wonders if she is right. Might Hannah be following my lead, burying her emotions when it comes to her father?

I look down at her, her eyes busy with thoughts and feelings that don't reach her stoic face.

'She doesn't mean to be nasty,' I say. 'She loves you very much.'

'I wish we didn't have to do this,' she mutters.

'Then we won't.'

As we return inside, Maggie is tidying up the kitchen, working herself into a familiar state. I try not to invite her to mine if I can help it. She treats it as if it is still her son's home rather than mine, entering with a furrowed brow and eyes busy with criticisms. *Matthew wouldn't live like this. Matthew liked a tidy home. Matthew—*

'Thank you for this evening, Maggie,' I force. The confines of the small, galleyed kitchen makes me want to breathe in the cold night air again. Their company is both craved and unwelcome; the double-edged sword of loneliness that cuts into me whichever way I turn. The thought of home fills me with longing and dread in equal measure.

'Can I stay with you tonight?' Hannah asks me.

'It's a school night,' Maggie says.

'I only have to leave fifteen minutes earlier—'

'You struggle to get out of bed at the best of times,' Maggie quips under her breath.

Hannah looks up at me, those large green eyes enveloping me in guilt.

'Maybe another time,' I say, and stroke her hair. 'I've got some more work to do tonight. I won't be much fun.'

'And I'm sure you have homework to be doing,' Maggie says to Hannah.

She nods and slinks out of the room without another word, leaving just Maggie and me. It is as if Hannah has taken all of the air in the room with her.

'Have a good night, Neve.'

I have outstayed my welcome. She heads through to the living room, small and formal, where Matthew and I visited for many obligatory Christmases. I think of my own sitting room awaiting me: a tight box of a room in my two-up-two-down terrace, with only enough space for the tatty burgundy sofa, which Matthew chose, and an armchair by the sash window, which was mine. Bookshelves frame the chimney breast, home to copious volumes of law books. My home's modest size is both a gift and a prison, depending on the day.

'Can I stay at the weekend?' Hannah asks from the hallway.

'Neve has a big case,' Maggie says before I can open my mouth. 'She won't have time to run around after you.'

I want to tell her not to speak for me, but she's right. All of my time will be taken up by the Darling case until the trial is over.

'As soon as it's done with, you can stay for a week. How's that?'

Maggie opens her mouth to protest.

'Deal,' Hannah replies, and gives me a long, tight hug, as

if to seal the offer before Maggie can pick it apart. I wrap my arms around her and inhale the sweet scent of her hair, a delicious concoction of coconut and youth.

'Come on then,' Maggie says impatiently. 'Your homework won't complete itself.'

I reluctantly peel myself away from Hannah's warmth, and feel the familiar ache return in my chest as I watch her head for the stairs.

Maggie goes to the door, wringing her hands as she goes, visibly uncomfortable at our being left alone. One might think we'd have grown close over the years, but that's not Maggie's style. Her world was her child, and then her grandchild; anyone else is merely someone to compete with for their affection. I follow behind her and slip into my jacket.

'You should get some friends your own age, Neve,' she says as she opens the door. 'Hannah needs to make more of an effort with her peers, but she doesn't seem to see the need when she has you.'

I flinch at the jab.

'I'm not just her friend though, am I? I'm her stepmother.'

'I'm not sure what this situation makes any of us,' she replies. 'But I don't want Hannah sacrificing opportunities to have a healthy sense of normality because she's stuck in the past.'

'No one is asking her to sacrifice anything except you, Maggie.'

Her lips purse together, an exhausted sigh huffing from her nostrils.

'Her father is gone, Neve. And with your connection to us being through him, I wonder if it is healthy to carry this on. Whether we should consider putting some distance between us, for Hannah's sake.'

For Hannah's sake.

I swallow down the hurt. I can almost taste it, a bitter tang lingering on my tongue.

'I will be in Hannah's life for as long as she wants me to be. Goodnight, Margaret.'

I raise the handle on my carry-along case of files and law-books with a sharp snap and slip my bag over my shoulder. Something catches Maggie's eye, and her features sharpen.

'You're not wearing your wedding ring.'

I look down at my left hand, still poised on my bag straps at my shoulder. I'd forgotten to put it on before I left chambers. I shuffle out the door and step out onto to the street with my head down.

'I'm glad to see you are moving on so quickly,' Maggie says from the doorway. Her face is even harder than before, looking down her long, sharp nose at me.

'It isn't like that, Maggie—'

'This will make it easier for Hannah to move on too. She can be led by your example. Goodnight, Neve, and good luck with the case.'

She shuts the door before I can reply. I stand on the quiet street listening as the key turns in the lock on the other side, and glance down at where my wedding ring should be.

That's the thing with being a widow. No one lets you forget it.

⚖

I turn the corner for my street, lined with terraced houses that are all of the same design, with large sash windows that stick in the heat of summer, and chatter like teeth in winter, as the laborious chug of a train calls from the tracks that lie just beyond our gardens. There are cars parked bumper to bumper from the top of the street to the bottom, where St John's Church sits tucked between the rows of houses. It looks strange and out of place, like most churches do in the city nowadays, with housing and skyscrapers built around them. Its bell tower reaches far up into the dark night sky, not a star in sight from the pollution of the city lights. I check my watch: it's close to the hour. The bells will ring out soon. I like to prepare myself, to keep from jumping out of my skin; the bells always seem louder at night.

I fish my keys from my bag as I reach my front door and heft my carry case over the threshold. The house is cold and unwelcoming, and the air clings to the smell of neglect. I need to change the bins, dust the place. But it is so easy to leave these things, living on my own. Matthew hated disorder; it often felt like he was following behind me, clearing mess in my wake. I walk through the ground floor, turning on lamps and shutting the blinds as I go.

I wheel my carry case to the sofa and sink into it with a sigh. Silence rings through the house. I should eat something, but I can't bring myself to cook. I'd meant to grab something before the vigil, but I had returned to chambers after the hearing to work on my opening speech. I wonder if I'm depressed, or if I'm simply set in my unconventional ways. I thrive on order and control in my work, but at home, it is somewhat satisfying to throw organisation to the wind.

I pour a large glass of wine, and play one of my favourite albums to work to: violinist Daniel Hope's *Belle Époque*. I take a sip as the strings begin to play. Matthew and I would listen to it together, drink the same wine, the scent on our breath as we laughed, kissed.

I think back to the vigil. How detached and on guard I had been. Maggie's words from the first anniversary of Matthew's

death echo in my mind, when I had been just as emotionally absent.

You're a cold, cold woman, Neve.

The next song plays, delicately plucking me from my
thoughts. I pick up the brief and have just begun to read when
the power cuts out and I am thrust into darkness. I sit in the
silence with nothing but my heartbeat for company and the
anxious flutter of my breaths. I get up with a sigh and shift
a slat in the blinds: the whole street has gone out. That's the
third time in as many months; it often happens around here in
winter. The cold temperatures damage the underground cables.

Gong.

I jump at the sound of the bells. Ten to mark the hour. It's
the sort of sound that carries through a person, strumming
every muscle and nerve.

To hell with this, I think, and down my wine before heading
up the stairs for bed. *All will be right in the morning.*

But as I reach the landing, listening to the bells ring out
along the street, I know the reason for the knot of unease in my
gut: a grown woman shouldn't be afraid of the dark.

I brush my teeth and crawl into bed, the faint scent of Merlot
still tainting my breath, and listen to the now silent street. But
the bells continue to echo in my mind. I wasn't even afraid of
the dark as a child; it was a fear that grew on me as an adult.
When I learnt of all of the terrible things that we humans do
to one another, once the lights go out.

5

I wake to the smell of bleach and the undeniable sense that something is wrong.

I am not in my bed, but hunched over, naked in the dark. I can feel the cold air nipping at my bare flesh. My hands are burning as if they are on fire, but there are no flames, just darkness and the racing patter of my heart. There's something else, too. A creaking sound piercing the gloom, turning my skin to goose flesh.

Creak. Creak.

I breathe deeply and the ammonia hits the back of my throat. I cough and gag it back up, a string of drool webbing from my bottom lip to the floor. I wipe my eyes and mouth and stare aimlessly about me.

The darkness is so thick that I can barely make anything out. But the more I rouse from my slumber, the more I begin to spot small, indistinct details creeping through, shadows darker than the rest.

My knees are burning against the carpet, the flesh hot and sore from friction burns as if I've been dragged. The smell of bleach is unbearable; I blink back tears and sniff to keep my nose from dripping. I can just make out enough of my surroundings now to know that I'm at home: the banisters running along the stairwell, the pictures hanging on the walls. The door to my bedroom sways on its hinges with a breeze, and beyond it, the curtains billow at the open window.

Creak. Creak.

I reach for the banister, my palm on fire and wet with slime, and get to my feet. I must have been hunched over for a while, for my back seizes as I attempt to straighten it, and I release a brief whimper as it threatens to give. Through the dark, I reach for the light switch where I know it to be, my fingers dancing clumsily along the wall, until light bursts above my head. I clench my eyes shut, before slowly opening them again, peering at the scene.

My hands are red raw. The flesh has cracked between my fingers and around my nails, and there are raised, red patches where the bleach has burnt through the skin.

The carpet is completely ruined. A yellow pool lies before me where the bleach has sucked the life out of the once grey fibres, glittering with bubbles where I must have been scrubbing with the sponge that is hidden beneath a mass of white foam. A bottle of toilet bleach lies on its side in the mess. I pick it up to find it practically empty but for a few last dregs swishing at the bottom of the bottle, before dropping it to my feet.

I head to the bathroom at the other end of the hall, quickening my pace as my whole body begins to sting unbearably, trying not to cough up the ammonia that has followed me and lodged at the back of my throat. I turn on the shower and thrust myself beneath the ice-cold spray with a gasp, until the shock subsides and the burning slowly begins to cool. I stand there and let the water run in sheets before my eyes, the bleach bubbling around my feet before swirling down the drain, as it finally washes away the daze of sleep, and everything becomes clear.

I am sleepwalking again.

6

Four days until the trial

I sit swaying from side to side with the motion of the tube, convinced that I can still smell the bleach on me. I had stayed in the cold shower for almost an hour so I wouldn't have to face the mess I'd made in my sleep. There is nothing more I can do but pull the carpet up and replace it, but there is an odd sense of shame attached to the act: rolling up the ruined carpet and bagging up the bottle with the same embarrassment as a bed-wetter might feel bundling up their soiled sheets.

I haven't sleepwalked in a while. Months, in fact. A childhood habit rediscovered in my adult life, which became unbearably familiar after Matthew went missing. I would wander night after night, waking up in the strangest of places, wondering where I was or how I'd ended up there. A therapist I was encouraged to see after Matthew's disappearance suggested I was looking for him in my sleep. I stopped seeing her after that.

I try to think of the case, but my mind inevitably returns to last night, my mind wandering as my legs had the night before. I look down at my red, angry hands, irritated from the bleach and the cold. There is no doubt that Matthew's vigil spurred my sleepwalking; it has always been exacerbated by stress.

There is something debilitating about my nighttime habit. It takes me straight back to my childhood when I would wander the hallways and rooms of each of my foster homes, waking up in varying degrees of distress, depending on how those I lived with chose to deal with it. Some shouted at me, shook me awake. Others would try to guide me back to bed, whispering encouragement as we went. But no matter how they reacted, they all got sick of me in the end. It wasn't long before I was shipped off to the next home, and the home after that, forever becoming another fosterer's problem. They say sleepwalking can be hereditary, but I wouldn't know anything about that.

All of that was so long ago now; I have moved on, made something of myself, and have found family in Hannah and Maggie, as dysfunctional as we are. And yet, my habit never fails to draw up that empty twang in my chest, the same sensation I'd felt as a child as I wandered the halls of strangers' homes.

I drag myself back from the past, and focus on the task ahead. Today is the day that I will hear the story of the Darling murders straight from the horse's mouth. I wince at my choice of words, remembering the photographic evidence of the fried remains of the Darlings' horses. Yesterday's conference had been administrative in nature; now it is Wade's chance to explain his version of events, and my opportunity to think of how I will defend his case in court. I must think of how the prosecution might spin things in their favour, create retorts to each in an endless back and forth until one of us finally misses; a fucked-up game of judicial tennis.

The tube begins to slow and my stop appears on the digital screen. I reach for the nearest rail and get up as the station approaches. The entire time, I feel that strange sensation one feels when one is being watched: skin prickling, hairs standing on end. I glance down the carriage and lock eyes with a man staring at me behind his reflective sunglasses. He doesn't look away in embarrassment or falter under my gaze. His eyes remain locked on mine; I can't see them behind the lenses, but I know they are upon me. I feel their hot, almost unbearable intensity.

Looks like someone read Eccleston's article.

The tube comes to a stop, and I depart with my head held high, refusing to look back at the man as I pass the window. Not that I need to look at him to know. I can feel his eyes, watching me as I go.

⚖

'Can I get either of you a drink?'

Mr Darling's mother, Marianne, stands in the doorway to the modest dining room. She is unusually chirpy for the mother of a man charged with killing his wife and children. I suspect it's denial, and wonder to myself if she believes her son's plea of innocence, or if late at night her mind drifts to the possibility of his guilt. It wouldn't surprise me if she secretly suspected him; I have watched mothers stand by their children despite all kinds of monstrous acts.

Antony Murrell is sat beside me, dressed in an impeccably pressed suit and smelling of expensive aftershave, his dark hair perfectly coiffed. We will combine our expertise to construct Wade's defence: Antony will be the one to find the evidence we need, and I will be the one to deliver it in court. I have worked with him on other cases over the years, and it feels good to have a shorthand with someone on a case like this.

'Tea for me, thanks,' he says. 'Milk, no sugar.'

'Me too, thank you.'

She nods with a faint smile, wringing her hands in a slow, methodical rhythm, and turns to her son.

'Tea, darling?'

From the other side of the dining table, Wade shakes his head without a word. Marianne nods and drifts silently towards the hall.

Wade appears to be a broken man. His hair is unwashed and kinked from sleep. His eyes are puffy and bloodshot. I watch as he runs a hand across his mouth, stubble bristling audibly against his palm. He is still wearing his wedding ring. I wonder if he will still be wearing it three years on, or if like me, he will hide it away.

'Thank you for seeing us today, Wade,' I say. 'I know it has been a long process for you, but we should be on the straight and narrow very soon.'

He nods glumly, and the room descends into silence. This isn't a good sign. I need as much information as I can get in anticipation of the trial, but by the looks of him he is in the tight grip of a depression. The glimmer of hope I saw in his eyes at our meeting yesterday morning has long gone.

Wade's mother enters with a tray of tea.

'Thank you, Marianne. Could we perhaps get a coffee for Wade?'

She places the tray down on the table, each cup jittering against their saucers in her shaky grip.

'That's a good idea,' she replies, and glances down at her son. 'Wakey, wakey, Wade!'

She laughs nervously and waits for him to respond, with an eagerness in her eyes that catches my heart. Another reason for her chirpiness, I realise: she is trying to make up for her son's silence; keeping up appearances while he crumbles. When he doesn't lift his sights from the table, her smile slowly fades, and she slinks out of the room again.

'I know you went through your version of events with Mr Whittaker, but it would be really useful for us to hear of the night in question first hand.'

'Like you said,' he says gruffly, 'I've already gone over it.'

Antony and I share a glance, the silence of the room ticking on. By the look in his eyes, he has the same concerns as I do. Our client appears to have given up.

'We need to make sure your version of events is the same as before,' I say. 'And I need to be familiar with the details to defend you to the best of my ability. Reading back over Mr Whittaker's notes won't be the same as hearing them from you directly. It's important we have every bit of information in our arsenal. Like I said yesterday, it wouldn't be wise to go into this unprepared, particularly with only four days ahead of us before the trial. I will feel confident in going forward if you can assure me you'll co-operate.'

Still he sits, shoulders slumped, eyes down. His lack of fight not only concerns me, it infuriates me. I control the urge to reach over the table and shake some sense into him.

'Thirty years,' I say, abruptly.

He looks up at me with those sad, bloodshot eyes.

'I'm sorry?'

'Thirty years – that's the sentence you're likely to serve before you can appeal, if you're found guilty. If you don't want that to happen, I urge you to co-operate. It is in your best interest to do so. Let us fight for you.'

We stare intently at each other over the table. His eyes slowly come alive again with flickers of anger. I don't care if his motivation to help himself is spurred by his disdain for me; whether he likes me or not is irrelevant. Pussyfooting around him like his mother won't keep a guilty verdict at bay.

Marianne returns with a mug of coffee and the same inappropriate smile chiselled onto her face.

'Thanks,' he says to his mother, slowly tearing his eyes from mine. 'Give me five minutes.'

He takes the mug of coffee and heads out the room and up the stairs. We all listen to the floorboards creaking under his weight from the floor above. Pipes gurgle from somewhere in the house.

'It's been very tough for him,' Marianne says. 'What with losing Yolanda and the children, and then being accused of doing something so heinous . . .' Tears spring to her eyes. Her sadness seems to be forever present, veiled just beneath the surface. 'It's been difficult for him.'

'I'm sure it has been tough on you all.'

Her smile is polite and tense, her jaw locked to keep the tears at bay.

'He won't be long,' she says. 'I'll be in the kitchen if you need anything.'

When she turns the corner for the kitchen, I notice the smile has fallen, and in its place is the saddest expression I have ever seen.

'I thought we agreed to go in slowly on the walk over,' Antony says when we find ourselves alone. We had planned our approach as we headed for Wade's address: a rented three-bed house, tucked away in a new-build cul-de-sac. Photographers sculked outside the property for a glimpse of him, snapping shots of Antony and me as we headed up the drive.

'We weren't going to get anything out of him in that state.'

The floorboards creak again above our heads, as a clatter comes from the kitchen.

'So, he's looking at thirty years?'

'Perhaps more. Three counts of murder with a firearm, and arson to boot. I wouldn't be surprised if the judge felt pressured to make an example of him, what with all the public interest.'

We fall into a comfortable silence, listening to Wade move about upstairs, the scent of Antony's aftershave lingering in the air. I look about the room. There are quite a few personal touches, despite the short time they have been at the property, having moved to the city to be close to the Bailey for the trial.

On the wall is a family photograph of Wade and the victims. The children were young; it must have been taken five or so years before their deaths. They have that innocence to them, where life has yet to taint them, and puppy fat at their cheeks, both with the trademark white-blonde hair they inherited from their mother. Yolanda was beautiful. She doesn't seem to be wearing make-up in the photo, exposing her spotless skin, exquisite bone structure, perfectly straight teeth. But despite her striking features, they bring a sense of melancholy and revulsion, for the bones and teeth were the only things they found of her.

I had been so transfixed by the photograph that I hadn't heard Wade make his descent. He stands in the doorway, having combed his hair and pulled on a white shirt, and his face looks fresher, tinged pink as if splashed with cold water. He follows my line of sight to where I had been looking as he entered, and his face falls. His eyes drop to the floor.

'Mum,' he calls.

We hear the hurried patter of her footsteps.

'Yes dear?'

'Take that down please.' He nods to the picture frame on the wall. 'I can't . . . I can't talk about it with them looking over me.'

Marianne's expression falls as his had. Silence thrums through the air.

'Yes, of course. I didn't think.'

She slips the frame from the wall and takes it with her into the other room, the glass of the frame coveted closely to her chest. I wonder if Wade will let her hang it up again once we're gone, or if the reminder is too much to bear.

Wade sits down with a curt nod.

'Ready.'

'Great,' I reply. 'Let's get started.'

7

'I woke up, choking. That's the first thing I remember.'

His face grew ashen the moment he thought back; his eyes glassy and distant. Antony and I are silent, conscious of allowing him the room to speak. When he fails to continue, I clear my throat.

'What else do you remember?'

'It was the physical reaction that I remember taking in first. The smoke had filled my chest, my throat. My eyes were streaming and I was covered in sweat from the heat. And the room ... Everything in the room was bathed orange from the fire outside the windows. The stables had been completely engulfed, which had spread to the neighbouring trees. I thought ...'

He shakes his head.

'What did you think?'

His throat bobs as he swallows.

'I thought I had woken in Hell.'

Wade appears to be back there, eyeing the blaze outside the windows in a trance. His right lid twitches every time he mentions fire, and when I look closely at his face, I see that he's sweating, as if he is back in the inferno.

'What do you remember next?'

'I tried to call out for them, but my voice was too hoarse; I couldn't get the words out. I made my way to the hall from the living room.'

'Why were you sleeping in the living room?' Antony asks.

Wade flashes Antony a look, irritation etched between his brows as he is pulled from a memory.

'Yolanda and I had had a deep conversation before bed, and I wanted space.'

That will be a point to the prosecution. Having an argument just before the murders will be firm grounds for suspicion. I want to dig deeper around this, but am conscious of going too hard too soon. This is a point I will certainly come back to.

'So you stepped into the hall . . .' I say.

'Yes,' he replies. 'That's when I saw the intruder.'

'Can you describe him to me?'

'It was hard to see from the smoke.'

I skim through the brief for the blueprints of the house, and place my finger on the doorway he speaks of. The house is nothing but a burnt-out shell now, set for demolition after the trial. But looking at the blueprint, I imagine how it used to be: the Darlings running up and down the stairs, sitting down to eat Sunday roast in the dining room facing the grounds. I wonder what Wade sees when he looks at the blueprints. Whether he sees the good memories or the bad. Life or death.

'We have the floorplan here.' I trace my finger from the living-room doorway to the stairs, and back again. 'There is only six, perhaps seven feet between them. You couldn't make out anything at all, from such a close distance?'

'Like I said,' he says pointedly. 'It was almost impossible because of the smoke. Not just the smoke in the air – it had stung my eyes. It felt like pins had been pierced into them. They wouldn't stop streaming. But if you were to put a gun to my head . . .'

I stiffen at his choice of words. It's a strange description to use. Even more strangely, he doesn't seem to notice the connection. I remind myself it's a common figure of speech. But the fact that it didn't register with him rattles me.

'I would say he was about my height, and he appeared to be wearing all black. He was wearing a mask or a scarf across his nose and mouth, and a hood over his head. He was holding my rifle.'

'You knew it was your rifle immediately?'

'No, only later. As I said . . . it was difficult to see. He stopped at the bottom of the stairs, and we stared at each other for a few seconds. I asked who he was – shouted it at him – and he dropped the gun and ran for the front door. I had locked it before going to sleep, but it was wide open. He bolted out into the night before I had even grabbed the gun.'

Anthony leans forward.

'He dropped the rifle? Gave you a weapon to potentially injure him with? Why didn't he shoot you too?'

His right eyelid spasms again.

'Clearly it was part of the plan to frame me, because I picked it up, putting my fingerprints all over it. I ran to the door but he was nowhere to be seen.'

I think of the photo of the murder weapon tucked inside the brief, covered in my client's bloody handprints from where he handled the gun after discovering the bodies.

'What did you do next?'

'I turned back for the stairs.' He pauses, holding his breath. 'I knew I was going to find something bad, but I didn't know what. Or maybe I did and I didn't want to believe it. The intruder had come from upstairs, where my family had been sleeping.'

I watch his throat move as he swallows. His eyes sheen over.

'There was blood on the stairs. Not a lot, just droplets. They must have dripped off him as he was heading for the door. But the higher I got, the more I found. The drops turned to streams. The streams to pools.'

He glances at me briefly, before his eyes fall to the table top. I could see the horror in them, the fear. His hands start to shake, and he subconsciously picks at his nails.

'You knew it was blood the moment you saw it?' I ask.

'No, not completely. I failed to make the connection, or maybe I was in denial from the shock. The only thing lighting my way was the fire roaring on the other side of the windows, making the blood appear black. I just remember the cream carpet was completely soaked. It was wet under my feet. Warm.'

He makes a grimace, as if remembering the feeling. This rings true. The first responders found him barefoot, noting the soles of his feet were red with what would turn out to be his wife's blood.

I watch his Adam's apple rise and fall. His face has grown paler.

'There is a curve in the staircase. It was the feature that made Yolanda fall in love with the place. I remember when we went to view it for the first time. She stepped into the foyer, saw the grand, curved staircase, and looked at me. She was in love. We both were.' He looks down at his hands, his jaw clenching as he grits his teeth behind closed lips. 'When I made the turn on the stairs . . . I found her.'

There is a tense silence. From the outside, it would appear that I am giving him time to collect himself, gather his thoughts. But in truth, I am watching him. Analysing every minute reaction that the memories bring up, to decipher if he is telling the truth or spinning a lie: the muscle twitching at his temple, the tears pooling in his eyes. His whole body is shaking now.

'She was lying on her back on the staircase ... looking up at me.'

His voice breaks, and two tears fall simultaneously down his cheeks.

'How was she lying on the stairs, Wade?' I ask softly.

'Head first, her feet closer to the top. Her nightgown had ridden up, and I could see the gunshot to her knee.' He covers his mouth; his jaw clenched tight on either side of his face. 'Blood had soaked through her chest from the shot to her back. And her head ...' A whimper slips out, and he clenches his fist tighter, his teeth harder. 'Her hair was soaked with it. Her face ... her beautiful face ...'

All the colour has drained from his complexion. For a moment I fear he might be sick, but I push on. It was difficult enough to get him to open up. He might not allow us a second time.

'What did you do when you found her?'

'I sobbed, and held her. She wasn't stiff – she was floppy, deadweight. I cradled her. Checked her pulse, although I didn't need to. She was dead, I knew she was – but it was like I couldn't believe what was right in front of me. I kept telling her to wake up.'

She wouldn't have been stiff so soon after death. The rigor mortis would have taken at least an hour to set in. I immediately think of questions the prosecution would ask him, if he were in the witness box. If his wife was shot and fell on the staircase, why didn't he wake from the noise her body would have made? Did he really fail to hear the intruder enter through the front door and pass the open doorway to the living room on his way to the stairs?

He wipes tears from his face with the brutish rub of his fingers. Fresh streams fall in their place.

'I knew then my children were dead too.'

'How did you know that?'

'The house was on fire. Their mother was dead. Had they been alive, they would have called for me. Tried to escape. The only reason for the silence in the house was that they were dead too.'

He takes a deep, heaving breath, and sighs it out of him. He wipes his face again, this time on his shirt sleeve.

'I tried to move her to the landing, but she was so heavy and slippery from the—' he stops. When he speaks again, his voice is hoarse. 'I didn't want to drop her. I got up and went down the hall to the children's bedrooms. I was covered in Yolanda's blood. My hands were black, and my clothes felt wet. Their bedroom doors were open. They always closed them, and had before bed that evening. I was crying.'

His pulse is racing, I can see it beating in his neck and the forked vein at the centre of his forehead. His chest is motionless with a held breath.

'They had both been shot through the head in their beds . . .'

He exhales and instantly doubles over as if from a physical blow, and sobs into his hands.

'Let's take a break for a moment,' Antony says. When I turn to face him, I notice his eyes shimmering with unshed tears.

I nod and clear my throat. I am sat in a room with two men, one sobbing, the other trying to compose himself, while my eyes are bone dry.

Perhaps it's because I'm good at keeping the barriers in place for the sake of professionalism. Or maybe it's because of my own pain, my own guilt. And if I open that door . . .

You're a cold, cold woman, Neve.

I dig my fingernails into the back of my hand to keep the memories at bay. But however hard I try, I can't rid my mind of the thought of him, as if Matthew is sat on the other side of Wade, staring straight back at me.

$$\text{⚖}$$

After a fifteen-minute break, we are back at the table ready to proceed. Wade looks wearier than when we started. His eyes are swollen and red again, and I can sense the depression clawing him back into the sorry state we first found him in. I need to get more details out of him before he completely shuts down again.

'Thank you Wade, we are almost done. After you had discovered the children, what did you do?'

I note that I sound cold, almost clinical, but I can't give him room to fall apart again.

He closes his eyes with a sigh. Emotionally preparing himself. When he opens them again, he is back in the past, those bright eyes jaded with pain.

'I don't know how long I was up there, holding each of them in turn. The smoke . . . it had made me drunk, almost. I was dizzy and disorientated, and came round in Danny's bedroom when the windows smashed from the heat and glass showered down on us. I didn't want to leave them behind, and contemplated bringing them all into the master bedroom so we could all ... be together. The only thing that kept me from closing my eyes again and succumbing to the smoke was the thought of the intruder getting away with their deaths.'

I imagine them all lying on the Darlings' marital bed. Faces frozen and pale like porcelain dolls, with Wade nestled among them, waiting for release.

'When I returned to the hall, the fire had grown. The smoke made it impossible to see. The air was completely black with it, and the floor was scorching hot from the fire burning below. I got down to my hands and knees and crawled for the stairs. I had to pass Yolanda. One small mercy was that I could barely see her through the tears and the sweat from the heat. I made my way down on my hands and knees, slipping on the ...'

He looks down at his hands with such a pained grimace that I wonder to myself if he sees his wife's blood there, and in what capacity. Literal? Figurative? Perhaps both.

'The fire was ripping through the ground floor. In the living room, the sofa I had woken on was completely ablaze. The walls were blackening where the fire was burning through from the other side. The path to the front door was blocked by flames. I could barely breathe and coughed so hard that I retched. All I could keep thinking was that I shouldn't be alive. I shouldn't be living through this.'

Antony goes to say something, but I stop him with a subtly raised hand, lifting it slightly from the table top. Wade is on a roll, remembering beat by beat. I don't want to pull him out of it until he's done.

'I made my way down the hall towards the kitchen, crawling on my front, completely flat to the floor. The whole time I could smell fuel, and realised I had put my hand in a pool of gasoline. That's when I saw the door to the cellar and my gun room was open.'

I imagine the fire creeping inside and licking each of the unspent bullets. It takes over two hundred degrees Celsius of heat to set off a bullet, according to my research. I imagine how the gunpowder would have exploded over and over, sending metal shrapnel in every direction. According to the records, Wade had around five hundred rounds stored in the gun room. Not surprisingly, that wing of the house all but burnt to the ground.

'In your statement, you said the gun room was key-coded.'

'Yes. I made sure it was secured before going to sleep. Always do. So whoever opened the door knew the access code, and knows me well enough to have chosen my favourite rifle.'

He looks down at the burnt flesh on his hand. His fingernails have grown back in abnormal shapes, small little half-moons hidden deep in the flesh of his gristled fingers.

'I crawled through the open doorway of the kitchen. It was completely ablaze, but I couldn't turn back. There was a clear path to the back door, but I was losing consciousness. I could feel myself drifting. The room was getting dark. I must have passed out and come to again, because suddenly I was screaming.'

He clenches his scarred hand into a fist, the warped flesh growing taut from the strain.

'Why were you screaming?'

His brow creases as if in pain.

'My hand was on fire.'

He puts his injured hand in the other and massages the scars with his thumb in small rotations.

'I managed to get to the back door and open it before I slipped unconscious. The next thing I remember I was in hospital, where I had been in a coma for two days.'

He finishes his story with a mighty sigh, and the breath seems to drain the life out of him. When he meets my eyes, I see how utterly exhausted he his.

'Thank you, Wade. I know that must have been difficult for you.'

His gaze alters in an instant. He looks at me with such rage that I flinch.

'How could you *possibly* know?'

Antony tenses up beside me, and my cheeks flush.

'How could you possibly know how it feels to hold your family dead in your arms? To wake up in hospital and learn that your entire world has burnt to the ground? Tell me, how on earth could you relate to that?'

His face has grown red with rage, veins snaking from his forehead to his temples. I can feel Antony squirming at my side, eager to jump in should I drop the ball with my response.

'I apologise if I offended you, Wade. That wasn't my intention. I only wished to commend you for going through this again – I can only imagine how hard it was for you.'

His expression softens. I move the brief towards me, eager to change the subject and take back control.

'Firstly, I need to recommend that you don't give evidence during the trial. I noticed you're on the list of witnesses. It might seem counterproductive not to speak in your own defence, but you have us to do that for you. If you give evidence in court, you give the prosecution the chance to cross-examine.'

'The last guy didn't seem to have a problem with it,' he says. 'I'm saying my piece. That's the end of it.'

Why would Adrian have agreed to something like this? It's not just bold, it's reckless.

'This will make things harder for us—'

'I'm giving evidence, Ms Harper. I won't change my mind on this.'

Antony and I share a defeated glance. We'll try and tackle this again later.

'The other issue we have is, the only evidence to suggest that there was an intruder in your house that night is your statement. There were no vehicle sightings we could tie to the area for means of the intruder's transport, no positive identifications of the man you describe. For all intent and purposes, you could be plucking the idea of the intruder from thin air.'

'It doesn't change the fact that I'm telling the truth.'

'No, but it does make it harder for us to convince the jury. As you can imagine, anyone can commit a crime and blame it on a person that no one else can verify. Unless of course, you believe there is someone in your life who meant you and your family harm, who had the motivation to carry out the murders that night. Who might have known the keycode to your gun room, like you said. The Viklund family are known for their illegal activity. Do you think that could have played a part?'

'No. The Viklunds would know who had done it if that were the case; it wouldn't be playing out in court.'

'So you don't know of anyone who might have done this,' I retort.

'I do,' he replies.

Antony and I look to one another. Wade has never named another possible suspect before, unless both Antony and I missed it in the brief, which I doubt.

'Who?' I ask.

The silence echoes through the room again, thrumming like a pulse.

'My former business partner, Alex Finch. He lost everything, just as I had. Money, the business, his wife was leaving him. But I had something he wanted and could never have.'

'And what was that?' Antony asks.

The seconds draw out, the only sound being the tick of a clock behind our heads. Wade sighs again, and meets my eyes.

'My wife.'

8

Antony and I sit in silence at the back of the wine bar where we have claimed a quiet nook as our own. The table between us is covered with law books, witness statements, pathology reports and police interview minutes, and empty cups from our last round of coffees, before we finally went for a bottle of red wine to share. When the waitress had brought it over, she caught a glimpse of the photograph exhibiting the blood on Wade's clothes and turned completely white, before I tucked it out of view.

Antony's lips are stained burgundy from the wine, his brow furrowed while he reads over the notes Eddie Chester and Adrian Whittaker had written up on our client's last movements in the days leading up to the murders.

Wade's revelation about his business partner continues to echo in my mind, but the sceptic in me refuses to rest. Why would he wait to share this fact, if it would prove he has been wrongly accused of murdering his family?

Wade was arrested at the hospital six days after the murders, and brought in for questioning, with the police interview detailed in notes included in the brief. Wade refused to speak until he had legal representation, answered no comment thereafter, and was held in custody until he was granted bail the following day. The only public comment he has made since his arrest was his written witness statement issued to the courts when he was represented by Chester and Whittaker. I read over it for the umpteenth time, familiarising myself with his account on the page, which I must follow to the letter in my defence. His account hasn't changed since this original statement: each beat matches up with the details he relayed today during the conference, except for the revelation about Alex Finch. Wade's motive for concealing such information will have to be highly credible if we are to get it past the prosecution and the judge at this point in proceedings; otherwise, it will appear to be nothing more than a desperate attempt to escape the charges.

The prosecution case against my client is strong. The murder weapon is registered in his name and covered in his fingerprints. The blood of the victims was on his clothes and person. They have their suspected motive: Wade had a mental breakdown due to his financial struggles and planned to kill himself as well as his family to escape the situation he had put them all in, with specialist witnesses to back up their claims. I begin to read over the witnesses the prosecution plans to bring before the jury. We can expect to hear accounts from Yolanda's mother, the first responders on the scene, the detective on the case, the ballistics expert. The list goes on. They are going to paint the picture that our client fell into a deep depression after the closure of his business and murdered his family in a case of familicide. The definition of the word has been printed out and clipped to the page.

Familicide: the murder of one or several members of one's own family, often resulting in murder-suicide.

I am re-reading Wade's medical history and his use of antide-pressants, which the prosecution are bound to use against him to fit their agenda, when Antony breaks me from my thoughts.

'How did his business fall apart again? In a nutshell.'

I take a sip of wine and sigh, my breath tasting of Merlot.

'The company sold a particular pump for swimming pools for which they created the design and owned the patent. After many years of success, they began to spend more than they made, taking out a string of loans that never got them out of the red. To make things worse, they dipped into the employee pension fund to try and bail themselves out, and by the looks of it there is even potential evidence of insider trading on his business partner's side. That'll be a whole trial of its own once this is over.'

'Right. And this business partner of his, Alex Finch. What was his role again?'

'Finance director and member of the board.'

'So essentially, he was the man to spot these problems both before they began and as they arose?'

'Theoretically, yes, but I suspect they both have a cross to bear.'

'What's the history between Wade and Mr Finch?'

I flick through the paperwork to refresh my memory, as my head spins from the pages of facts.

'They met at university and went into business together in 2006. Wade was the man with the knowhow about the product and would be the man to sell it and build their clientele, while Finch was to grow the business around it and source the funds.'

'So if we want to skewer Finch, we need to find out if he was the one who authorised the money being taken from the employee pension fund, and created the downhill spiral for the success of the business. Paint him as a man set on destroying Mr Darling's life: his business, his financial security, and finally, his family.'

'There will be a paper trail, I'm sure. If it has anything to do with Finch, as Wade suspects, we have our alternative suspect. But we'll need to secure his motive too.'

'We could paint Finch as a lover scorned?' he asks. 'For wanting Yolanda but not being able to have her?'

'That could work, but we'll need more from Wade on what happened between them. The only way we are going to get the suspicion off him is to have someone else to pin it on. If we're going to find the evidence we need to back up this claim, Wade needs to lead us in the right direction.'

'Isn't it too late to admit evidence?'

'Not if it's key to giving the accused a fair trial. I'll threaten to push the trial back to assess the lead should it not be accepted; then the judge will have to accept anything we have if he wants the trial to commence as planned.'

Whittaker did none of this while Wade's case was under his charge. He had had the case for months, but as I read and re-read through the brief, I can't see which direction he planned to take it. No alternative suspects, no alibi or character witnesses to offset the prosecution's suggested motive. I feel that same pit of disappointment twist in my stomach.

What on earth was he thinking?

'So as for our witnesses,' Antony says, picking up a document from the table. 'We have Mr Finch; the nurse who disclosed the news of their deaths when he woke from his coma; the pathologist to analyse the bloodied clothes to prove it was deposited when he discovered the bodies, rather than being evidence that he killed them ... Then there's Wade himself, if we can't persuade him otherwise. But out of all of them, Finch is the one who could be the most damning for the prosecution's case?'

'Yes. Although I must confess, I'm concerned about the timeline we have to nail this. Three full working days to focus on it isn't long at all.'

'You think we should push for more time?'

'The judge would fight it with every breath in his body, but if we prove it will impact Wade's right to a fair trial, we could sway him.'

'But if we can nail Alex Finch to the cross then we have our defence, right? The police didn't interview him, from what either of us can see. They suspected no one else but Wade. If we find out more about Alex Finch and Wade Darling's relationship, and Finch's alleged infatuation with Yolanda, we'll have him as a key suspect the police missed, and rip their investigation from under them. Then we could really win this thing.'

Antony's excitement shimmers in his bloodshot eyes.

'You think we can get what we need in that time?' I ask. 'Because if we turn up on Monday and try to push the trial on the day, the judge will make it impossible. We'll need to do it before nine a.m. Monday morning or not at all.'

Antony thinks it over, chewing on a fingernail until I hear a faint, bone-like crack. He nods once, conviction in his eyes.

'We can do it.' He pauses, taking me in. 'You don't seem convinced.'

I sigh, rubbing the bridge of my nose.

'There's one thing that's troubling me. Wade has had a year to mention Alex Finch's obsession with Yolanda, which had it been investigated, might have rendered his trial obsolete and sent the police scrambling for new suspects. He could have saved himself all of this grief, but has only done so now, right before the trial. Why?'

I watch his eyes moving busily as he tries to think of an answer.

'Wade is essentially suggesting that he's sat on this information for a year,' I continue. 'Unless he had an extremely good reason for doing so, it will look like he's making a last-ditch attempt to lay the blame at someone else's feet.'

Antony returns to biting his nail, and it takes all of my willpower not to intervene, tap his hand away like an adult might do to a child.

'We have the conference with him in the morning,' he says. 'We can apply pressure then, get more out of him. I'll look into his business partner some more too and see what I can find. Wade said Finch's life had fallen apart, just as his had. That'll be just as much motive to suspect him, just as the police suspected Wade.'

'Sorry to disturb you,' the waitress says, breaking us from our thoughts. 'But we close in ten.'

'Christ, have we been here that long?' Antony checks his watch. We have been at it for hours. The glass frontage of the bar is black with the night sky. 'Thanks, I'll take the bill.'

I slug back the last dregs of wine and begin to tidy up my paperwork, slipping it all into my trusty carry case, as the sense of unease continues to gnaw away.

'I've got a gut feeling about this,' Antony says as he tidies his side of the table. 'If we nail Finch, we'll win this. I just know it.'

I smile, but inside, my stomach churns with apprehension. I don't know what it is: it's not a thought, but a feeling. The sense that something isn't quite right.

'Don't worry about why he took so long to tell us,' he says, reading my face. 'We'll get an explanation tomorrow.'

⚖

I rock with the motion of the tube, listening to it grind and clank against the tracks. The dark tunnel passes on the other side of the window, with its soot-covered wires snaking along it like veins.

The carriage is freezing, but riding the Metropolitan Line is a godsend compared to the likes of the Bakerloo Line, which I take to get to courthouses on the south side of the river. The former is fresh and open, where one can walk from one end of the train to the other and watch as it tails around the bends; and the other, its carriages older than I am, covered in black grime with gang tags carved into the plexiglass, and seats that one must peel away from when they reach their stop.

The tube is almost empty. Most of the passengers got off at King's Cross, then Farringdon. Just a few nightly stragglers remain dotted along the train: a woman with plastic bags at her feet that chime with wine bottles, muttering to herself in a way that sets my hackles rising; a young couple huddled close together, laughing at something on one of their phones; and a man at the far end, dressed in black sports gear, a coat and cap, and sunglasses shielding his eyes.

I close my own and let myself move with the train, my head and spine bobbing as if in water, when my carry case knocks into my knee with a sudden kickback of motion, and my eyes spring open, my mind back on the trial.

In tomorrow's conference, I hope to discover the link between Finch and Yolanda. With the trial fast approaching, I won't be afraid to push Wade for the answers we need. I think back to his dishevelled appearance on the other side of the table. When he had spoken of the fire, sweat had broken out along his forehead. When he described finding his family, the pain welled in his eyes, shivered in his bottom lip. And still, he allowed himself to be wrongly accused of their murder, withholding the information on Alex Finch until now.

Why?

I close my eyes again and think of the scene, blow by blow. Fourteen rifle shells were found about the property. All of the horses and show ponies were shot with the silenced rifle before the family were violently laid to rest. I imagine the smell of gunpowder in the air, the nervous shuffle of the horses in their stables as they waited for the end of the rifle to reach them, the thud of their bodies against the straw. Then the gasoline, thick in my nostrils, and the spark of the lighter scratching in my ears, before the dark November night was set ablaze and the full moon was hidden behind the smoke.

I open my eyes with a sigh. Is Wade Darling innocent? Is he guilty? It isn't my job to know; to feel. I am not hired to decide who is right or wrong. That is for the jury to decide. Something I remind myself of every time I take on a case that makes me question my moral compass. I mustn't even allow myself to wonder, in case it impacts my impartiality – I cannot afford to form a grudge against the man whose only chance of a fair trial rests firmly on my shoulders.

The death of the Darlings, and the thought of the empty house that awaits me, makes me think of Matthew. He usually creeps to the forefront of my mind when I find myself alone. I had been emotionally detached during the vigil; I was practically gritting my teeth through it. I wonder if Maggie and Hannah spotted my cold front. Guilt fills my gut, sloshing from the rocking motion of the carriage, as I attempt to bury the thought of him again.

The tube slows and judders to a stop at Liverpool Street. The doors open with a mechanical whine and the young couple depart, followed by the lone woman trailing off behind them, clinking and chatting to herself as she goes. The doors shut behind her and we return to the dark depths of the tunnel.

I start to get myself together as the end of the line approaches. A short walk from Aldgate to Whitechapel and I'll be home. Sometimes I take the District Line to take me straight there, but on nights like this, when my mind is weighted down by work, I crave the fresh air to clear the fog; to feel the night breeze against my pores after so many hours in the stale air of chambers and courtrooms.

A shadow catches my eye: the man dressed in sports gear is heading along the train. It is just the two of us now, and I suspect he will be heading further up the carriage to make a dart for the station exit to avoid the extra walk along the plat-form. The closer he gets, the more he seems to tower over me; his trainers must be a size thirteen. But instead of passing me by, he sits in the seat directly opposite mine, slipping off his sunglasses and smiling, smelling of cigarettes and Brut.

I stare at the man. Dark-haired and broad-shouldered, with pitted olive skin that's wrinkled around his eyes. I sigh quietly to myself, hardening against the man's presence, my face sour-ing; it wouldn't be the first time I was hit on while on the tube.

'Hello, Neve.'

The use of my name makes me pause. We stare at each other wordlessly, rocking in sync with the carriage, as my heart rate slowly begins to climb. I wonder if he is a former client. By the intense glare of his eyes, I must not have won his case.

'You don't know me, if that's what you're thinking,' he says, as if I spoke aloud. 'But you will.'

I glance up at the rolling train sign towards the ceiling. *The next stop is Aldgate, where this train terminates* moves across the screen. I slowly reach into my jacket pocket for my keys, slipping one between my fingers as my pulse pounds feverishly at the tips.

'That won't be necessary,' he says, nodding towards my pocket, and opening his coat with his free hand. The other is hidden within. Pointing the handgun at my gut.

'We have some things we need to discuss,' he says. 'Where shall we start?'

I pry my eyes away from the end of the gun. My heart is racing so fast that I feel sick; my stomach coils.

'I know . . .' His smile breaks open, flashing jagged, yellow teeth. 'Let's start with how you murdered your husband.'

I stare down the dark, endless eye of the gun. One tug of the trigger. One bullet. That's all it would take. He whips his aim until it is pointed directly at my heart, and I brace myself with a jolt, waiting for the bang, the blood. The gunman laughs to himself behind closed lips.

I have met many criminals in my time in the courts. Nine times out of ten, the people I defend are sad, lost souls who never stood a chance at any other way of life, and ignite pity rather than fear. It's the small percentage of criminals I'm afraid of – the remaining one after the pitiful nine. The type who laugh as they point a gun at a stranger's chest.

We stare at each other in silence and sway with the motion of the carriage, but his aim never strays. My eyes sting, too terrified to blink; to take my eyes off him for even a millisecond.

Let's start with how you murdered your husband.

My heart drums against my ribs. My airways slowly seal shut. I sit before him, practically choking on my own breath, as his words sink in. The man stares at me from the other side of the carriage, watching me with a smile.

He knows.

I think of ways I could try to escape, and imagine myself dashing towards the nearest exit. But I have too many belongings, too many layers, whereas he is free to move at a second's notice. I wouldn't stand a chance. I clench the keys until metal teeth dig into my palm, thinking of all the places I can jab him if I need to: the base of his throat, his eyes, his groin. The entire time, he is smiling at me, the gun unwavering in his grip.

'If it's money you want—'

'It isn't,' he replies.

I try to swallow, but shock has leeched my mouth dry. I lick my coarse lips and glance up to the CCTV camera between the doors on either side of the carriage.

'They won't see the gun, not from here.' He wags it tauntingly from side to side where he hides it at his hip. 'They'd only know what happened when it was over.'

I imagine my chest cracking open with the bullet. Blood exploding against the window at my back; soaking into the fabric of the seats. I wonder who would have to clean up the mess.

'Then do it,' I hear myself say, voice shaking. 'If it's not money you want, if there's nothing I can do or say to stop you, then just do it already.'

He throws his head back and laughs, the sound carrying all the way down the empty train.

'They said you had balls,' he says. 'Suppose you have to, to kill a man like you did. Tell me, did the police ever suspect you?'

'I don't know what you're talking about—'

'Oh, I think you do.'

Adrenaline surges through me. I feel the need to grip onto something, but stop myself. Even through my terror, I know I mustn't look weak. The whole time, I ask myself the same question over and over, the words swirling in my mind in an endless, dizzying loop.

How could he possibly know?

We sit without a word between us, rocking with the carriage to the clanking, grinding sounds of the tunnel.

The transport police will be able to see his face through the CCTV now that he has removed his sunglasses, won't they? If he kills me, they'll find him. My death won't have been in vain. But from the angle of camera, his cap will be covering his features. I glance at the dark tunnel on the other side of the window, praying for the platform to appear; witnesses waiting for us beside the track. But of course, there won't be. Aldgate is the end of the line, and this is the last train of the night.

'Look, if you've got something to say, then say it,' I stammer. 'The train is about to pull up at any minute.'

He grins, seeming to like the fight in me. A man who enjoys the game. Despite the fear clouding my mind, I can't shake the niggling thought that I recognise him from somewhere. It's not so much his face or his height that I remember, but his eyes. He has the sort of stare that peels off one's clothes, one's skin, until it is peering into your soul. I recognise him in a flash: this is the same man who had watched me during my tube journey en route to Wade's address this morning.

He has been following me.

'You're defending Wade Darling in his upcoming trial,' he says.

So that's what this is about. He says this as a statement of fact rather than a question, and I sit waiting for the next blow, failing to see how the case might be connected to what I did. I was so careful; I didn't tell a soul, leave any trace. The only people in the world who know of my husband's murder are this stranger and me.

I look at the man, desperately trying to decipher his possible motive, looking for the slightest tell: the twitch of his mouth, a gleam in his eye. I wonder if he is a distraught family member of the victims, or perhaps a disgruntled shareholder of Mr Darling's bankrupt company. He could even be a crazed follower of the story, with no personal connection at all. The thought of sitting across from a man obsessed causes sweat to break out beneath my blouse.

'Big gig for you this trial, I'm sure . . .'

The tube will be pulling up at the last stop any minute now. I could kick off my shoes, sprint as hard and as fast as I can until—

'. . . It's a shame what happened to his previous counsel, isn't it?'

My thoughts stop dead. His eyes narrow as he smiles knowingly.

'Adrian jumped . . .' I say. 'He took his own life.'

'I can tell you what his last words were before the train hit him, if you like?'

Winding rivulets of sweat slink down my ribs from each pit.

I imagine the scene: Adrian Whittaker innocently standing back from the tracks as he waits for the tube home, when a strange man thrusts him into the oncoming train from behind, feeling nothing but the stranger's hot breath against the nape of his neck and rough palms thrust into his spine. There one minute; gone the next.

Bile spits up my throat. I stare at Whittaker's killer, gripping my hands together in my lap until every drop of blood is squeezed out of them.

'Why on earth would you want to kill Mr Whittaker—'

'For the same reason we're sat here tonight. You have something valuable, something I want, and I have something of yours you want to keep hidden. So, I'm going to offer you a trade.'

I sit in my shock, wondering how the evening has transformed into this. I had been getting the tube home, a journey I have taken so many times. I had been slightly tipsy from the red wine when I sat down in my seat. Now I am stone cold sober.

'And what about Adrian? Why didn't he get to trade?'

'He did,' he replies. 'But he didn't want to play along.'

I stare at the man's unwavering smile, each of his crooked teeth. The ridges between them are stained with dark tar from cigarette smoke.

'W-what . . . what do you want from me?'

'Wade Darling mustn't get off,' he says seriously, the amusement gone from his eyes. 'He is to go to prison for a very long time.'

He tightens his grip on the gun, his palm rasping against the handle. His finger moves slowly towards the trigger. My heart skips so violently that a wave of nausea rips through me.

'I can't throw a trial,' I stutter. 'I have a duty—'

'But you also have a dirty little secret, don't you? One that you're desperate to hide.'

His smirk makes me feel ill. He could be bluffing, waiting for me to assume too much; watching as I dig my own grave. I know from my experience in the courtroom how easy it is to twist a story with just a few facts, spin a narrative until it points in the direction you want.

'The people I work for,' he says. 'They have a way of bringing buried secrets out into the open. They don't take kindly to being told no. Adrian Whittaker thought he could outsmart them. That would be a fatal mistake on your part.'

'Who do you work for?'

'You know full well I won't answer that,' he replies. 'You'll lose the trial, Wade Darling will go to prison, and you can keep your sordid secret to yourself.'

Despite the terror, I almost scoff at his arrogance.

'You make it sound easy.'

'It would have been easier, had you not pulled that trick with Wade's solicitor. Eddie Chester's role was to help you lose the case. You'll have your work cut out for you now, but that's your affair. I'm just the messenger.'

That's why Eddie had approached Wade. He will have purposefully failed to deliver those files to help, rather than hinder.

I nod towards the gun.

'Well, if you're planning to kill me, it won't matter, will it?'

'Who said this bullet is meant for you?' His smile widens. He draws out the silence between us, staring so deeply into my eyes that the sounds of the tunnel fall into the ether. It is just him and me, swaying lightly from side to side, staring into each other's souls. 'Hannah's a pretty girl.'

I had never fully believed one's blood could turn cold until Hannah's name left his lips. His words hit me square in the chest, the utterance of her name lodging a breath in my throat.

Hannah.

I grip the keys tighter, trying to keep myself in my seat while eyeing the soft skin at the base of his throat. I could lunge forwards, end this. But the reality of the situation pins me to my seat in fear.

This man hasn't just been watching me. He's been watching Hannah too.

'If you hurt her—'

'Nothing will happen to either of you if you make the trade. You can be angry with me all you want, but her fate isn't in my hands – it's in yours. The same goes for that little secret of yours . . . you decide what happens now.'

The tube starts to slow. The man clicks the safety on his gun and slips it into his waistband. It's only then that I allow myself to soften; my head is throbbing from contracting every muscle in my body. The Messenger returns his sunglasses to the bridge of his nose, and my reflection stares back at me, hued green from the coloured lenses. I look gaunt with fear, almost as though I have aged a decade between Liverpool Street and the end of the line.

'So,' he says casually. 'Guess you've got a decision to mull over, eh? I'd make sure Wade Darling goes to prison, because it's him or you. His freedom or yours. And then there's sweet little Hannah, of course . . . You'll be of no help to her behind bars. Who knows what could happen to her.' He looks me up and down with those predatory, infringing eyes as he rises to his feet, somehow even taller and broader than before. He could crush the life out of me if he wanted to. I jolt at the sound of a tired voice coming over the tannoy announcing we have reached the end of the line.

'And what if I go to the police, and tell them what happened here tonight?' I stutter. 'What then?'

He stops at the door as the tube pulls up at Aldgate Station with a squeal of the brakes. The doors open with a hiss and whoosh of stale air. He stands at the threshold, watching me. The smirk returns to his lips.

'Then your secret will be out in the open,' he says. 'And I'll pay a visit to sweet, sweet Hannah.'

He pats the gun at his hip and gives me a wink, before slipping away as suddenly as he appeared.

10

I am sitting in the empty train carriage, staring at where the gunman had been. The silence of the station on the other side of the open doors is ringing in my ears.

Guess you've got a decision to mull over, eh? It's him or you. His freedom or yours.

I had been on the train home, a journey I have taken over a hundred times. I am familiar with every jut in the tracks, recognise the faces of frequent passengers and the stops they call home. Now the familiarity of the journey has been ripped from under me and I don't recognise it at all. My blouse has stuck to my back with sweat, and my palm is indented with deep, purple craters from gripping onto the keys.

I hear a man's voice and a bolt of fear rips through me. The conductor is staring in at me from the platform edge.

'I said it's the end of the line, love. Gotta get off.'

'Sorry.'

I take my carry case and step out onto the deserted platform in a daze. All there is to be heard is the cooling thrum of the tube train as it winds down, and the distant whisper of traffic calling down the stairs from street level.

I am the only passenger. The man from the tube is nowhere to be seen.

'You sure you're all right, love?'

I jerk again. The conductor is approaching me, his brow creased with concern.

I catch my reflection in the framed tube map behind him. My face is as white as a sheet and my eyes look empty, as though a piece of me is missing; just like the woman from the tube had appeared as she muttered to herself, bottles clinking at her feet. I manage to force enough composure to reply.

'I'm fine, thanks.'

I drag my case towards the stairs and take it by the handle as I ascend, gripping onto the rail like a lifeline, the conductor's eyes burning into my back as I go. I'm swaying from the shock, rather than the drink I'm sure he suspects.

I reach the top of the stairs and pass in a haze through the barriers. The evening chill seeps in through the open station from the street.

I step out into the night and take a deep breath of fresh air. The panic hits me as soon as it fills my airways.

Let's start with how you murdered your husband.

Tell me, did the police ever suspect you?

Hannah's a pretty girl.

I hide myself away in the nearest doorway; it feels like there is a foot crushing down upon my chest, pressing my ribcage against my organs.

The people I work for, they have a way of bringing buried secrets out into the open.

A single word makes my heart jolt.

Buried.

I raise the handle on my case and break out into a sprint, my

case jolting against the uneven pavement and kicking the backs
of my heels as I race for home.

They know where I buried him.

⚖

I turn the corner for my street and lurch violently as my heel
cracks beneath me, snapped in two like a wishbone. I stumble
out of my shoe, kick off the other with a huff of breath. I can't
remember the last time I ran as fast or as far as this, and stop to
catch my breath as the muscles in my legs spasm from the strain.
The church sits at the other end of the street. Witnessing my sins.

I'm almost home.

I snatch up my shoes, chuck them in the carry case, and run
along the street as I hunt for my keys, stray stones digging into
the soles of my feet. My hands are shaking so violently that I
can barely hold the key to the lock as I reach the front door.

'Evening, Neve.'

I flinch at the sound. My neighbour, Lucinda, is stood
outside her door with a bin bag in her grip. She has wiped off
her make-up and slipped into a baggy sweatshirt and jogging
bottoms, her hair tied up in a messy bun. Very different from
her work attire, selling commercial real estate. Her smile fades
as she takes in the state of me.

'What on earth happened to your shoes?'

I look down at my feet and see blood stained between my
toes. I must have stepped on glass.

'Long story,' I reply, and fit the key into the lock.

'Your foot is bleeding—'

'I'm fine.'

Leave me alone. Please.

Any other time I would stop to chat, but tonight I can't get free of her quick enough. She isn't my friendly neighbour, but a hurdle. I open the door and take my first step inside.

'Are you sure?' she asks, her voice an octave higher.

'Yes,' I snap curtly, and hike my carry case up the step. I slam the door shut behind me and sink against the door.

I heave for breath, my heart hitting the wood at my back like a jackhammer. Lucinda is a nice, thoughtful woman, and on any other night I'm sure she would say the same for me. Now I will have set off alarm bells. I can't help but think like a barrister: should tonight become pivotal in a case against me, Lucinda will remember it.

Something wasn't right. She was scared and bloodied, and completely barefoot. She looked like she was running from someone, or in a hurry to get somewhere.

I will have to make an excuse and extend my apologies. Cover my tracks. I have spent these last few years trying to appear as the perfect neighbour to avoid any suspicion after Matthew's disappearance. To keep people from noticing the blood on my hands. I can't screw it up now. But the thought of more lies makes my throat tighten. Lies upon lies upon lies. The secret I have kept all these years, the guilt I have kept inside. The Messenger has dragged them out into the open.

Maybe I deserve this.

I should feel safe now I am home, but it is as though Matthew is here, waiting for me. I can smell him, feel him. As the memories draw in, I almost expect him to call out my name.

I peel off my jacket, drag on my nearest pair of shoes, and bolt through the living room for the kitchen. The chicken I left out this morning to defrost is sitting in its saucer in a pool of defrosted ice, tinged pink with blood. It was just another morning, nothing unusual or exemplary, with no notion of what was to come. I scramble at the lock on the back door, throw it open, and sprint.

Stray locks of hair stick to the sweat beading at my temples, and the sky has started to spit, but all I can think about is what lies ahead. The grass is damp with the night, licking at my ankles. I imagine Lucinda watching me run into the darkness from her window.

When I returned back inside, I caught sight of her running down the garden from my window, despite the dark and the rain. I have never seen her like that before. It was as if she had lost her mind.

I clamber over the wire fence separating the lawn from the train tracks, and wince as it claws at my inner thighs. Long, jagged rips run down my inseam.

I stand before the moonlit rails, my thighs smarting. The tracks stretch along the back of the terraced houses and go on for miles. I peer at my watch. The next train is in five minutes or so, passing the back of my house at quarter-hour intervals.

The stones between the tracks move and dislodge beneath my feet, and I stop before the small patch of woodland on the other side. The past comes to me in violent flashes.

Thwack.

I hear Matthew's head crack open.

Thwack.

Blood splatters against my face.

Thwack.

He's near dead, but I keep on hitting.

Thwack. Thwack. Thwack.

I haven't been here since, but the memories are as fresh as if it were yesterday. The smell of blood creeps into my nostrils. Nervous sweat slinks down my sides. Seeing it, hearing it, it's enough to make me sick. The guilt feels solid, swelling in my abdomen; a meaty black mass inside of me. I'd vomit it up if I could; stick my fingers in my mouth and prod the back of my throat until it was steaming on the cold ground.

I head into the darkness, making my way through the small knot of trees, drifting between the past and the present in my mind.

Thwack.

Twigs and undergrowth crack beneath my feet.

Thwack.

I count the trees, following the mental map inside my head.

Thwack. Thwack. Thwack.

I freeze when I reach it, and my knees buckle. I catch myself against the nearest trunk.

Someone has marked the tree with an aerosol paint can, the colour red as blood. X marks the spot.

I drop to my knees before the tree with a crunch from the undergrowth, my husband's body buried directly beneath me. I scratch helplessly at the red paint until my fingertips are bloodied and torn and bark has dug beneath my nails. Rivers of tears snake towards my jaw as the church clock tower strikes the hour, each gong of its bell calling through the darkness.

They know what I did. They know everything.

11

Three days until the trial

I ride the Metropolitan Line, listening to the jarring squeak of people's shoes after getting caught in the rain, the rustle of wet anoraks. The sort of sounds that make one's teeth numb. I grit them together and look down at my shaking hands.

I cut my fingernails right back to the beds after breaking them against the tree. There are still splinters dug deep into my fingertips, littered with small cuts where I managed to tweeze out others. After I had found the mark on the tree, I ran back inside, saddled myself with supplies, and returned to the scene, scrubbing at the trunk until the air reeked of chemicals and I had bleached the life out of the bark; its dark brown shell turned off-white, like bone. As for the cut on my foot, thankfully it only needed a plaster. I close my eyes and try to calm myself.

I spent the night pacing, unable to sit still in case my panic took hold and consumed me entirely. But nothing helped me escape *the fear*. The fear that no matter what I do, the truth will come out in the end, as if I had buried a bomb among the trees rather than a body, and any minute it will blow my life to smithereens. It has been ticking for three long years; the persistent backdrop to my every thought.

Guilt tugs at me. The consequences of one wrong act ripping through those closest to him and changing their lives forever. People often said my husband adored me in ways they had never seen before. And then I took a golf club and ground his skull into the hallway floor.

I am woozy with exhaustion, and my jaw throbs from grinding my teeth through the night. My first instinct was to run. I didn't know where. I didn't know how. It wasn't a logical train of thought, but visceral. I can feel it even now, twitching incessantly in my legs.

His freedom or yours.

Sweet, sweet Hannah.

When I sat in the aftermath of what I had done, dripping with my husband's blood, my first thought was to call the police and confess. Pay the price for my sudden burst of rage. I picked up my mobile phone, the screen bloodied in my grip, and pressed one nine, then the other, my thumb shaking over the third. I paused. If I confessed to what I had done, I wouldn't just lose my job, my freedom. I would lose the only family I have ever known. Hannah and Maggie would never speak to me again, and I would have no one else in the world.

Now, their love is bittersweet. When Hannah looks at me, I shiver with shame. I took away the person she loved more than anyone else in the world, and here I am, taking that affection as my own, to fulfil my desperate need for a family. I thought the toll would only be against me; that if Hannah and Maggie didn't know what I'd done, we could carry on with my secret buried deep within me. But now the price is to be paid in the form of the Messenger, putting Hannah's safety in jeopardy because of me and my lies.

How did they discover what I did? I left no trail of where to look or how to find him. I did the deed alone, in the dead of night. Even the police couldn't find him, with their countless searches and sniffer dogs, which had been fooled by the rabbit carcass that I'd found by the tracks and buried just above his grave to throw off the scent.

Now my secret has finally been dug up.

Wade Darling mustn't get off. He is to go to prison for a very long time.

My stomach pitches at the memory of his low, menacing tone.

The client conference is within the hour. I am expected to sit before my client while quietly planning how I can twist his case and condemn him. I place a hand on my stomach to keep it calm. I can't throw the case for my own gain, however desperate my circumstances may be. The sense of duty is engraved in me. There is right, and there is wrong; black and white. There is no grey area to use to one's own advantage, or the justice system would collapse like a house of cards. Pull one rule away, and the whole thing topples.

I can't call the police either. They pose just as much of a threat as the Messenger. I might as well be handing myself into their charge and leaving Hannah to fend for herself.

The only person I know who could possibly help me is dead. Adrian Whittaker went through this very dilemma: he had the same ultimatum, the same goal thrust upon him. I wonder what secret he had that the Messenger held against him. We all have skeletons in our closets. But not all of us have them buried at the foot of the garden.

If I don't do this, they'll hurt Hannah, and everyone will know.

I think of all the heinous things they might do to her,

imagining all the possible ways she might die in gruesome, heart-skipping detail, all the while wondering why. Dying not for her sins, or her father's, but mine.

I wonder how I would throw the trial, if I had to. When I took the case, the possibility of losing the trial seemed almost inevitable: no other suspects in the police investigation, only his fingerprints on the murder weapon, the severe depression he experienced leading up to the murders. But after working with Antony last night, we have found our path to redeem him: Alex Finch could be the perfect scapegoat to completely undermine the police's investigation and have the case thrown out. So if I were to sabotage the trial to save Hannah and myself, I would have to keep that from happening. I'd have to somehow stop Antony from chasing the lead he is so keen to secure.

The carriage feels hot and tight, and I struggle to catch my breath where I am trapped between the passengers on either side of me. I dig my fingernails into my thighs.

Who does the Messenger work for? Who would go to these lengths for a conviction?

Just like when I work a case, I immediately think of the person's motive. Whoever the Messenger works for, they want Wade Darling to pay for his alleged crimes. By law, my client is innocent until proven guilty. His fate isn't their decision to make, nor is it mine. It is down to the jury and the jury alone. Whoever the Messenger works for clearly isn't willing to take that chance.

The Viklunds. It has to be. Not only are they related to Yolanda and her children by blood, they have the criminal means to master something like this. The family seems to evade the criminal justice system at their own will. Police charges are dropped. Court cases fall through and never appear before a judge. If they have Eddie Chester in their pocket, I am sure they have many others in the profession who can be bought into doing their bidding. Or maybe they have more people like me, forced to trade in secrets.

If we pushed back the trial, I would have more time to try and get out of this situation, try to find another way to protect Hannah and still give my client a fair trial. Keep the world from knowing what I did.

I can't decide what to do now. I need time to think, to breathe, and get through this conference.

I hear my stop announced over the speakers and take hold of the railing to steady me as I get to my feet. As I approach the doors, the hairs on the back of my neck rise to attention, sensing something that stops me dead in my tracks. The heat of someone's gaze prickling on my skin.

The Messenger.

My entire body goes cold. I feel like a doe stood in the crosshairs of a rifle, waiting to be blown away. He will look like an average tube passenger to everyone else. He had appeared that way to me before he approached. He wears dark jeans and the same large trainers, a black tee and hooded sweatshirt. That black cap covering the grey. He blends into the commuter crush perfectly. No one would suspect he is holstering a gun at his hip. The tension is so thick between us that everyone else inside the carriage fades into nothing but wet, rustling shapes.

The doors whizz open and I force my way onto the platform, pushing through the maze of hot, slick bodies as I yank my carry case behind me. A woman yelps as it jostles over her foot.

I shoot a look over my shoulder and scan for his face among the scrum. I wonder what they would do, if he shot me now. I imagine the crowd parting like the Red Sea as my body slumped to the ground, a brief beat of silence before the screams began echoing through the tunnel. If the shot didn't kill me, their panic would. Crushing me beneath the stampede. Boots breaking my ribs. High heels piercing my face.

'Can you stop pushing me?' the man in front spits, his face scrunched into a snarl.

The stairwell leading to the ground level is hot and airless. Almost as if the walls are creeping inwards and pressing us into one mass of flesh. I stumble on the steps as the crowd moves upwards and scramble for the railing, but I can't reach it. My lungs continue to shrink, and shrink.

We reach the escalators, and I latch onto the black railing, my pulse pounding in my grip. As we pass halfway, I steal a look over my shoulder. He is stood on the escalator too, with just seven people between us, that knowing smirk carved into his face.

I scramble for my phone as I near the end of the escalator and rush towards the barriers, almost slipping on the wet, tiled floor, scanning my e-pass at the nearest gateway. The confirmation beep seems to take a lifetime. I stand, shaking and silently pleading for the barriers to part. When they finally open, I rush through them before being yanked back with such violence that I let out a yelp, and whip around. My case is stuck between the barrier doors. I pull at the handle furiously to try to dislodge it, until hair falls in my face, and my cheeks flush hot.

'*Miss*, don't do that!' the ticketmaster says from the other side of the barrier. The passengers on the other side are all glaring at me, tutting. Two teenage girls are laughing at me. He taps his card against the reader and the doors open. I almost lose my balance as the case gives, and whip around without thanks, looking for the Messenger. Waiting to see his face smirking out at me from the crowd.

I step out into the pouring rain. A shoulder knocks me to the left. A briefcase hits the back of my knee from the right. I walk blindly as the rain falls in my eyes, fighting my umbrella that quickly turns inside out with a gust of wind. Exhaust fumes from the road scratch at my throat and my lips taste of rust from the rain. I am just about to hide in the nearest doorway when I feel a large hand grasp onto my arm. I tear myself free with a cry and spin around.

It's Antony.

'Christ, sorry. I didn't mean to scare you. Are you all right?'

I must look horrendous: panicked and breathless, my shirt and blazer soaked through, hair plastered to my face. He is completely dry under his umbrella, and always looks and smells so clean, but for the cigarette burning between his fingers. There is not a hair out of place in his dark brown quiff. I look about me, but the Messenger is nowhere in sight.

'You all right?' he asks again, holding his umbrella over the both of us. His aftershave fills my nostrils.

'Fine,' I force out, and nod towards the tube. 'It's too hot down there.'

'Tell me about it. It should be illegal, cramming us all together like that. Like cows in a bloody cattle car.'

He catches me looking down at his cigarette.

'Want one?' he asks, before taking a drag.

You have no idea.

'I quit,' I mutter absently.

'Good on you.' He takes one last puff and crushes it underfoot. 'Let's get a cab. We can catch up on the case on the way.'

He stands at the kerb and flags one down to a quick

succession of horns from disgruntled drivers, taking my carry case and opening the door for me in one swoop. I clamber inside and sink back into the seat, before peering out of the window at the bustle of people leaving the tube. A mass of faces, void in the eyes, zombie-like in energy and formation. That's when I see his eyes peering out at me from behind the blur of passers-by. The Messenger is stood in a doorway of a closed-down butcher's shop. Watching me. Smiling.

Antony slams the door behind him, breaking me out of my trance with a jolt.

He gives the driver the address before turning to me with a grin. My heart is still racing, but there is an element of relief, being safely away from the Messenger and ending his pursuit. It takes all of my focus to meet Antony's eyes.

'I was up all night looking into Alex Finch. Wade was telling the truth about Finch's life falling apart. Not only were his personal finances hit hard by the failure of the business, but his marriage broke down, too: Mrs Finch asked for a divorce *three days* before the murders.' His eyes glitter with excitement as dread seeps through me. 'Once we find out how far Finch's obsession went with Wade and Yolanda, we'll have a motive that practically mirrors the prosecution's accusations of Wade Darling, and undermines the police investigation pinned against him.'

This is why I suggested Mr Darling hire him. Antony is ambitious, meticulous. He gravitates towards a challenge, rather than buckling beneath it. It's exactly what I want in an acting solicitor. That is, until now.

I must stop Antony from asking Mr Darling too many key questions about Mr Finch until I come up with a plan. But how can I possibly avoid it, when that is the very purpose of this client conference?

If I can't stop Antony from progressing with the trial, I will have to stop it completely. I need to persuade our client to request more time. I'll have more of a window to find a way out of this.

As the cab pulls away, I peer out the window towards the butcher's shop in search of the Messenger, but he is nowhere to be seen.

12

As we get out of the cab outside the Darling residence, Antony asks again if I'm all right. I tear my attention from the lone photographer stood twenty feet from the drive, snapping photos of us, the camera's lens seemingly blinking with each shot.

'I'm fine,' I reply, forcing a smile. 'Just tired. Late night working on the case.'

He nods, seemingly placated, and we head up the garden path. Every window at the front of the property is shielded by drawn curtains and blinds, keeping out prying eyes and the photographer's zoom lens. It adds a melancholic air to the property, as if the Darlings' sadness pulses behind the glass. Plants in flowerpots that Marianne would have bought to brighten up the place have been left to die in winter, their old stalks slinking down the sides of each pot like brown, withered vines.

I wish my lie to placate Antony had soothed me too. I wish I was merely tired, rather than absolutely terrified.

All I need to do is persuade Wade to delay the trial, so we have more time to prepare. I am not leading him astray.

My heart thumps wildly against my ribs as Antony knocks on the front door.

At least, not yet.

'Don't dive straight in about Mr Finch,' I say. 'It's clearly a touchy subject for him and we don't want him to shut us out.'

Before Antony can reply, Marianne Darling answers the door, which pulls against the security chain as she peers through the gap. As soon as she recognises us, she shuts the door to unfix the chain and opens it wide, making sure to stand near-flat to the wall to avoid the photographer, before shutting it again.

'He's been out there every day for the past two weeks,' she says, as she peers through the peephole. 'He doesn't say a word. He just stands there, staring at the windows in the hope we'll open the blinds and give him a shot. You should see him when he sees a twitch of the curtains or hears the squeaky hinge of the front door. Jumps up like a dog hearing the chime of its dinner bowl. Greedy little—' She clears her throat, seemingly remembering herself and the company she's in, and turns back to us. 'I can't wait until all of this is over.'

Her naivety is almost endearing, if not concerning. Her son is embroiled in one of the biggest criminal trials to have taken place in the last ten years, and yet she speaks of it as if it will all float into the ether the moment the trial ends. She hasn't thought of the stream of articles that will keep the story alive, both online and in print, raking it over year after year. Photographers will want photos of her and her son for decades to come. *Where Is Wade Darling Now?* The headline reads in my mind. There will be documentaries commissioned. Podcasts rehashing old ground. YouTubers relaying the story to creepy music in the background, to a demographic the papers will have otherwise missed. This isn't a blip in their lives they will leave behind them. They are wrapped up in a legend that is set to be told and retold long after they have gone.

'How is Wade today?' I ask, noticing the slight shake to my voice.

I catch a brief flicker of sadness in her eyes at the mention of his name.

'He's doing fine,' she replies, unconvincingly, her eyes falling anywhere but on mine. 'Let's go through.'

Marianne guides us along the hall to the dining room we had occupied the day before. Wade, however, is nowhere to be seen.

'He didn't get much sleep last night,' she says, when Antony and I both turn to her after finding his seat empty. 'I think yesterday drained him. He's been sleeping this morning to catch up. Please,' she signals to the tray on the table. 'Help yourself. I'll go and get him.'

Antony and I take our seats in silence. The room is stuffy and artificially hot from the central heating, making my skin itch mercilessly beneath my clothes. Sweat begins to break above my lip.

If Antony succeeds in getting the details on Alex Finch from Wade this morning, we've effectively got his route of defence: we'll have a man the police failed to suspect, an investigation that was pinned against our client from the start. With enough details, and evidence to back up Wade's claims, I will have the opportunity to create doubt in the jurors' minds.

You must be sure that the client is guilty, beyond a shadow of a doubt.

Doubt. It's a defence barrister's main weapon in their arsenal. And Antony is set on delivering it.

It's all happening too fast. The trial is just days away. The defence argument is almost formed. Things are aligning at the very moment I need them to stall. My heart races.

Hannah's a pretty girl.

I think of the Messenger's tone, the sly smile curling up from the corner of his lip.

I just need a bit more time.

'You don't look well,' Antony says beside me, breaking me from my thoughts with a jolt. 'You're all sweaty.'

What is he thinking? What does he suspect? Can he sense my guilt, see the fear in my eyes?

Just as Antony opens his mouth to speak again, Marianne returns.

'I'm sorry,' she says. 'Wade says he isn't feeling up to it today. He's too exhausted.'

I have to fight back my sigh of relief. Antony, however, looks fraught.

'I can only imagine how hard this is for him, but with the greatest respect, we don't have much more time. If Wade wants to win this trial, he'll have to push through.'

I can see he is sweating too, but for different reasons to me. I had been panicking at the thought of the trial moving forward, whereas he seems fearful of it stalling. Two people supposedly on the same team, fretting over the loss of deeply opposing objectives.

'I'm sorry,' she replies. 'It's just not possible today. You'll have to come back tomorrow.'

'Tomorrow . . .' he stutters. 'We don't have time for this, Mrs Darling. If we don't ensure a strong defence, your son will go to prison for up to three decades or more. It's imperative—'

'Would you excuse us a moment, Mrs Darling?' I ask.

Antony stops, his mouth open. Clearly he had hoped I would echo his thoughts.

'Of course,' she replies. 'There's no rush. Please ...' she signals the tray again. 'Do help yourselves.'

When Marianne leaves the room, the air becomes stifling again. Antony looks at me with his eyes darting up and down, trying to read my expression.

'We can't force the words out of him,' I say. 'We need him to work with us, but pushing too hard could mean he shuts down. We can't afford for that to happen.'

'We don't have time for this,' he spits under his breath. 'He either talks now or he's off to prison. You know that.'

'Or there's another option.'

'What's that?'

'We could delay the trial.'

'*What?* You heard what the judge said. No more delays.'

'McConnell won't be able to refuse, if it's conditional on the client getting a fair trial.'

'I can't believe you're considering this. We practically have the information we need to back his defence. All he needs to do is tell us what we need to know and I can hunt down the necessary evidence—'

'But he's *not* telling us, is he? We can't force this out of him, Antony. That's not how this works. We will give him a day. Visit again tomorrow and try to get him to talk. But if we don't, I'm meeting with the judge to push the trial. If we can't defend him, we have no business trying to represent him in court.'

Antony sighs and wipes his face with his hands, his pale skin flushing with blood. I wonder how late he was up last night.

'Fine. We'll give him one more day. In the meantime, we can

do some further digging to make his defence airtight. We're close to cracking this, Neve. I can feel it.'

That's what I'm afraid of.

Marianne walks back into the room.

'We'll be back tomorrow morning to speak to Wade then,' I say.

'Yes, I'm sure we can make that work.'

'It's important you do,' Antony says, as we get up from our seats and approach the hall. 'If he doesn't talk to us, he's looking at a long time behind bars.'

'I'm well aware of that, Mr Murrell,' Marianne says, prickling at his tone. 'I'll do my very best.'

We walk down the hall and through the front door, back into the cold, grey day.

I have twenty-four hours to figure out what the hell I am going to do.

I sit down in the wine bar, nestling in the corner of the room in a high-back leather chair, with a pile of paperwork on the coffee table before me, and reluctantly order a pot of tea rather than something stronger.

I had returned to chambers after Wade failed to appear for the conference, but soon found myself feeling caged, pacing back and forth like a lion before black, cylindrical bars. It's the sort of fear that sucks the air from one's chest, paralyses a person to the spot. After no more than an hour, I'd had to get out of there, and was only able to draw a deep breath when I turned the corner of the street, far enough away from my chambers with its inscription in the stone above the front door: *Lus est ars boni et aequi*. 'The law is the art of goodness and equity.'

I was completely unprepared this morning, going into the client conference; my only saving grace was Wade's inability to speak with us. I won't be granted the same mercy again. Next time, I must be prepared. Which means I have to work out what the hell I'm going to do.

I pick up my legal notepad, the yellow paper shining up at me, but all I can do is stare down at the pristine page as each of my fears runs through my mind.

I need to focus, treat this approach with the same emotional disconnection that I would any other case.

I take a deep breath and begin.

My first goal is to push back the trial and buy myself more time. If I can keep Wade from answering Antony's questions about Alex Finch, so that Antony is unable to paint him as a suspect the police missed, then I will have the grounds to request the delay. We can't go to trial without a sufficient defence. But Antony won't make that easy. In fact, I'm positive that he will make it virtually impossible; I won't be able to keep him from chasing his lead indefinitely. If I want to delay the trial, I will need to focus on Wade himself; sow seeds of doubt in his mind about our not having had enough time to prepare. That the risks of going forward as things stand will make a guilty verdict much more likely. Outnumber Antony two to one. I remember how broken Wade had seemed yesterday, unwashed and melancholic, and then this morning, when he refused to appear at all. He's clearly lost the will to fight for himself.

What if he doesn't want to push the trial back and fight for his freedom? What if he has truly given up? That would work in my favour of course, if Antony wasn't by my side, eager to continue with the set date. But if I can't stop Antony from pursuing his lead, and I can't persuade Wade to agree with pushing the trial back, we will be headed towards disaster.

I sit back in the chair, my mind spinning in dizzying circles, and take a deep breath.

If Wade won't fight for himself, his mother will. Perhaps I can get Wade to delay the trial through her. Two routes of attack. I write down Marianne's name on my pad and scribble down my thoughts.

I feel slightly buoyed by my first plan of action, until my thoughts return to the Messenger. I hear his gravelly voice in my ears, remember the smirk pulling at the corner of his lips. Dread slowly fills me up again.

Even if I give myself more time to figure out what to do about my situation, how can I possibly get out from under this stranger's grasp? I don't know for sure who employed him, or what I can possibly do to make it all go away except to go through with the Messenger's demands. And who's to say there won't be something else they want from me, after this? Another reason to hang my crime over my head, keeping Hannah in danger? Who's to say this will ever end?

If I want to escape my predicament for good, I need to find out who the Messenger is, and more importantly who sent him. If I find out who they are, and I'm able to push the trial back, I might be able to find a way to stop this before proceedings commence. But I know I can't possibly do this alone. I need someone removed from the business, yet knowledgeable. Dependable, while asking as few questions as possible. In short, I need a miracle. Stress pulses at my temples. I knead them forcefully, as if the pressure will force out the answers I need. A name springs forward in my mind. Fredrick Hurst, private investigator and former client.

It has been five years since Fredrick and I last spoke, and as I pick up my phone and scroll through my contacts, hoping I still have his number stored, I fear he might have new contact information; maybe even quit the business after he was dragged through the courts. I click on his name and type out the text, the phone quivering in my grip.

Fredrick, it's Neve Harper. Is there any chance we

could meet? Preferably somewhere where we'll be
lost in a crowd.

Having two plans of action makes my furled shoulders ease
slightly. But I know the worst task is yet to come, one I cannot
put off any longer.

I look down at my tea, which I have inadvertently left to cool
without taking more than a sip. I raise my hand to beckon the
waiter and order a medium glass of Merlot, then call him back
to request a large glass instead. For this next task, I'll need it.

My heart begins to drum inside my chest. I flick over a new
page to jot down the next stage of my plan, sick to my stomach
at the thought of what I am about to consider.

I must premeditate how to throw the trial if all else fails.

The thought of even considering it makes me flare with guilt.
My main role in the courtroom is to ensure my clients get a
fair trial; I'm the mouthpiece for the defendant, essentially the
one person in the room who is unilaterally on his side. Then
there are the moral aspects within me: what is right, and what
is wrong. What is good, and what is evil. I don't miss the irony
of this; a killer pondering their morals.

Just when I think I cannot bring myself to plan such a
betrayal, I think of Hannah. Her youth, her innocence; all the
years that lie before her. She mustn't fall to harm because of my
actions. The conflicting goals tug at me from within.

*This is only a last resort. I'm only doing this as part of a
back-up plan.*

But despite my attempts to quell my fears, it's tough to even
fathom such an act.

It's hardly worse than murder.

The waiter returns with the glass of Merlot, and I take it

with a trembling hand. I should have ordered food to go with it. I can't remember the last time I ate; this trial has completely devoured my appetite. I take a large sip and poise the tip of the pen on the page.

If I'm going to sabotage the trial without being detected, I will have to appear to be following our plan to the letter. Which means I have to essentially perform two roles at once. I must be both efficient and inefficient, supportive and deceitful.

I write down a list of the witnesses both for the prosecution and the defence, detailing their purpose while drinking the wine heartily as I go. Names peer up at me from the page, and as I take them all in, it's difficult to escape the lives hidden behind my scrawled words. This job can devour a person's soul if they're not careful. It becomes frighteningly easy to see a list of names like this as mere words on a page; to see witnesses, defendants and victims as nothing but pawns in the game. But as I look at them now, wondering how I can twist their testimonies to my advantage, I realise the magnitude the repercussions of my actions will have upon them. My actions won't just affect Wade Darling. There are multiple necks on the chopping block. I go through the list of the prosecution's witnesses to assess what evidence they will bring.

First, the prosecution will call Yolanda Darling's mother, no doubt to paint a picture of the woman she was before meeting Wade, and the ins and outs of their married life. To show the jury that the victims are more than just photos beneath the headlines: they are children, grandchildren, confidants. Rebutting testimonies like these is tough enough at the best of times: if I go in too intensely, the jury will think me heartless and calculated, but if I approach my questioning too softly, their stories could well win over the jurors. Antony won't suspect any wrongdoing on my part if I tread too lightly here, but he will expect me to go in for the kill with the next witnesses.

The crime scene personnel will be called next: the first responders who attended the scene, followed by the detective on the case, Detective Inspector Markus Hall, the witness I'm most concerned about. If Antony manages to get information on Alex Finch, I will be expected to decimate DI Hall's character and the integrity of his investigation, question repeatedly why he failed to consider other suspects in the case, until there are enough holes in his testimony that the jury will lose confidence in his version of events. This is usually my strongest skill; I've been known to have detectives leave with lumps in their throats after I'm done with them. There is no way I will be able to avoid questioning him like this; my motive would be far too clear. Which means, if I'm going to question him in the way Antony, Wade Darling and the press will expect, I will have to sabotage our case in a different way. I will have to find something else conclusive on my client that helps him fit the crime. I pick up my wine glass to take a sip and find it empty, as my phone vibrates on the surface of the coffee table.

Fredrick
Of course. Blackfriars, platform 1, 4pm?

I stare down at the message. Once I follow this path, there's no going back. I will be putting my plans into action. They won't just be ideas or scribbles on a notepad. I will be preparing to commit an act that is wrong on every ethical, moral and legal level. I lean back into the chair and close my eyes with a sigh.

I don't even know if I have to go through with it yet. I'm

*just assessing all of my options. I mustn't make myself sick
over this, not yet.*

But my plans aren't just hypothetical, not when I must
actively hunt for evidence to disarm my own client's case, even
if I don't use what I find; the act will have been performed. I
need Fredrick to discover who the Messenger is and who he is
working for, but that's not all. I have another job for him. One
I will have to fall back on, should all my other options fail. It
is the only way to keep Hannah safe, and keep my secret from
getting out.

My phone shakes in my grasp. I look to the empty wine
glass, wishing there was enough for one final sip for courage,
before typing out my reply.

See you then.

As I collect my things and get ready to leave, I think of the
Messenger. It's all well and good employing Fredrick to find
out more about this man, but I'll need to take other measures
to keep him from using my crimes against me. He knows of the
body, but there will be more he has yet to find, more pieces of
evidence he could pin against me.

I walk towards the door, trying not to sway, and silently
make up my mind.

I need to destroy the murder weapon.

14

I stand on the platform at Blackfriars Station, perched on a bridge across the River Thames, and look out at the city. The sun has almost set, giving everything it touches a burnt, orange hew. Tower Bridge, the Shard, St Paul's Cathedral, they are all set ablaze by the sun's rays, as the darkening waters of the river slip beneath the platform.

The last time I met Fredrick Hurst, he was my client, after he had been charged with stalking by the man he had been paid to investigate. I got him off swiftly, with no case to try. He had been invasive, yes, but all within means of the law. It shouldn't have been taken to trial in the first place; a civil lawsuit maybe, but certainly not criminal. After the win, Hurst had said he would help me if I needed anything in return. I never thought I would have to cash in the favour at the time, but I'm grateful for the opportunity now.

The glass of wine I had has worn off, all but for the hollow, uneasy feeling in my legs. I could have done with another glass to calm my nerves. As I stand waiting for Fredrick to arrive, the request I have to ask of him gnaws away at me. Asking for help with discovering the identity of the Messenger and his employer is one thing, but to ask for information on my own client to potentially use against him is quite another.

From the corner of my eye, I see a figure approaching. Fredrick walks with conviction. A man with a purpose. He has shaved his head since I last saw him, and he looks skinnier than I remember, thin about the face and shoulders. But his height, standing at around six-five, gives him a commanding presence, as his long black coat billows behind him. He doesn't smile when he reaches me; he's not a smiling man.

'Ms Harper,' he says. 'A pleasure.'

'It's good to see you,' I reply, meaning it. 'Managed to stay out of trouble?'

'If I hadn't, you'd have been the first person I called.' He does smile then, or at least his version of one: the slightest rise to the corner of his mouth.

'You said you wanted to see me. This about a case?'

'Sort of.'

A train pulls up at the platform, and I turn back towards the view, staring through the plates of glass giving view to the city. I don't speak until the passengers have departed and dispersed, and the train pulls away from the platform again.

'I'm working the Darling trial.'

He whistles through his teeth.

'He did it then?'

'What makes you say that?'

He arches his brow.

'Only the worst people need the best lawyers.'

'You're not painting yourself in a very good light there, Fredrick.'

He gives me a wink. I release a heavy sigh, and cast my eyes towards the view again.

'I'm not sure how much I can say.'

'Whatever you tell me doesn't leave this platform.'

A rush of warmth flushes through me. It feels so good to be able to lumber this on someone else, even if most of the detail is missing. I won't tell him everything, but I can tell him enough, and for a minute or two I won't be alone. I look about me and find the platform empty.

'I'm being blackmailed. Someone wants me to throw the trial to ensure Wade Darling is found guilty. A man is threatening me on someone else's behalf. The only person I can think of who could be responsible is someone from the Viklund family. My client's deceased wife – the murder victim along with her two children – her maiden name is Viklund.'

Fredrick falls quiet as soon as I utter the name. In the reflection of the glass, I spot his chest deflate with a sigh. A shiver runs through me as a breeze ripples along the platform.

'And this blackmail,' he says. 'I assume the consequences of not following through are—'

'Bad.'

'How bad?'

Whoosh. Thwack.

Hannah's a pretty girl.

I swallow hard and meet his eyes.

'Really bad.'

'And you can't go to the police?'

I shake my head, and feel the sudden surge of panic return. It is as if talking of it aloud has made me finally realise how bad my situation is. I can't turn to the police for help. I can't forgo the Messenger's demands; he killed the barrister before me who tried that. The train tracks at my back feel too close all of sudden.

Fredrick doesn't ask me why, and I know then that I have made the right decision in contacting him. Anyone else would want to know what the Viklunds had against me, why I couldn't call the police. But Fredrick allows me to keep my cards close to my chest.

'And you know they'll go through with it, if you don't comply?'

'Adrian Whittaker, the lawyer who worked the case before me—'

'The chap who jumped in front of a train?'

It had hit the news due to his stature, but still, it surprises me that Fredrick knows of him.

'He didn't jump.'

My voice comes out hoarse, the fear gradually choking me. Hurst nods solemnly.

'What do you need me to do?' he asks.

'I need to know who the Messenger is, and who is employing him. Maybe there is something I can use against them in return – blackmail for blackmail. Anything at all to give me some leverage. You know, I'll keep their secret if they keep mine.'

He shakes his head.

'If it's the Viklunds we're talking about here … they don't work that way. The only people who know their secrets are either within their close circle, or they're dead. Adrian Whittaker is proof of that.'

He is being gentler than usual. The hard man who doesn't smile, softening beside me. I wonder if he has a child, a partner. What his life looks like once he hangs up his coat of an evening.

'What does this man look like?'

'He's tall, perhaps six-two, six-three. White, late-forties, acne scars on his cheeks. Deep voice. He was wearing a sports cap, hooded sweatshirt and jeans when I met him.' I pause for thought, realising I've just described tens of thousands of men in London alone. 'I'm sorry, that's probably not much help.'

'I'll do some digging around, and see what I can find. I'll look into the Viklunds first. I'm sure that'll lead me to him.'

'What sort of fee would you take for a job like this?'

He waves me away.

'Pro bono. That's what you guys say, isn't it?'

'You really don't need to do that.'

'I know.'

We fall silent. The lights have flickered on above us, and beyond the glass the sun has set; the Thames is black but for the city lights reflecting in its waves, with only the last few embers of light shining on the glass Shard, the very tip of St Paul's dome.

'What is it they have against you, exactly?'

My mind darkens with memories of the past. My monstrous crimes; the endless list of sins I've committed. I wonder if he would still help me if he knew what I have done.

'They know something about me – something I've done. It was years ago, and no one knows but me; at least, that's what I thought. It isn't something they could have discovered recently; it had to have been when it happened, but that means they would have to have been watching me before they even had a need . . . when the Darlings were alive.'

He nods.

'People like the Viklunds like to have influential people in their pockets to call on should they need them. Most can be bought, but others . . . they need a push.'

'So, there's a possibility they've been watching me?'

'Like I said, you're one of the best. They would want you on side. All they had to do was keep an eye on you and wait for you to trip up; to give them something they could use against you later.'

'But they didn't choose me for the case, not initially.'

'You probably weren't the only person they kept an eye on.'

So they had been watching Adrian too. I wonder how many others they have kept tabs on. Do they sit in the public gallery, watching us at work, picking us out like they are at a cattle auction? They will have enough people on their list in case I don't comply, like Adrian failed to do. Back-up after back-up.

'Let me see what I can do. When do you need to hear back?'

'The trial starts Monday.'

'I better get to work then.'

We stand before each other, unsure what the proper etiquette is to wishing farewell to the private investigator who is your last hope, and for him, a dead woman walking. He touches my arm and gives it a gentle squeeze.

'You're tough, Neve. Remember that.'

I have one last thing to ask him. The request that, once uttered, cannot be taken back. This will set the wheels of my deception in motion. Even if I find a way to evade the Messenger's conditions without throwing the trial, I will have to live with the fact that I did this.

'There's one more thing.' I slip a file from my carry case. 'I need you to find information on someone.'

I can't bear to look him in the eye in case he sees the shame within mine. He takes the file and peeks at the first page. His demeanour changes when he reads Wade Darling's name.

'What kind of information?'

I have to practically force the words from my mouth.

'The damning kind.'

I still can't bear to meet his gaze, to glimpse the disapproval in his eyes.

'If he did something bad in his past, I need to know of it. If he ever raised a hand to a spouse, failed to gain consent in a sexual act, conned anyone in business. Even a speeding ticket. I need to know of every mistake he's ever made.'

'Why would you want to know about something like that? To bury it?'

I don't answer. My silence, it seems, is telling.

'I see,' he says.

I finally look at him then, terrified I've lost his support, taking his confidentiality a step too far.

'So you'll do it?'

He looks deeply into my eyes. Perhaps he is assessing if I am someone he should trust; if I am a good woman in a bad situation, or whether I'm simply bad to the core.

'I will.'

He heads off the way he came without another word, the coat billowing behind him as he goes, as I process what I have just done; the betrayal I have set into motion. It is as though I have taken the first step off a ledge, my foot dangling above an unknown abyss, as I silently pray not to fall.

I return to an ice-cold house and reluctantly shrug off my coat, rubbing my arms to get my blood racing as I turn on the heating. The radiators crackle to life, with the familiar sound of the boiler purring from the kitchen. It isn't long before Fredrick's words drift back into my mind.

Families like the Viklunds like to have influential people in their pockets, to call on them should they need them. All they had to do was keep an eye on you and wait for you to trip up; to give them something they could use against you later.

It's likely the Viklunds have been keeping tabs on me, but how? Just the thought of them lurking nearby without my knowledge makes it feel like my home has been violated in some way, like an unwanted touch. Just like when Matthew went missing, and the crime scene investigators searched about the house in their crisp white suits, rifling through every drawer and cupboard, opening every book on the shelves in the hope something incriminating fell out. They pulled the sofa cushions apart, yanked out their innards and stuffed them back haphazardly, peered behind every picture frame on the wall. But they didn't find anything to help discover what had happened to Matthew. Not even a single trace of blood.

Whoosh. Thwack.

I scrunch my eyes shut as the memory comes. The scene in my mind is bathed in red: blood splatters, a pool at my feet, swipes of it sprayed violently up the walls from the swing of the club, all unravelling as the church bells chimed and I stood above my husband's body, wet and dripping with him, club in hand.

I used to think I would be useless in a moment like that. But despite my shock, my legal knowledge and need for damage control crept through. I thought back to cross-examining a forensic crime scene investigator about blood traces, or lack thereof, at a crime scene. She explained that when a suspect used a chlorine-based bleach product to clean up a crime scene to cover their tracks, blood still remained, even after multiple applications. However, when oxygen bleach was used, it eradicated all traces. Environment-conscious homeowners using the more natural counterpart have no idea they are using a product that could help them clean up a murder scene without a trace. It even smells less potent, further disguising when excessive amounts are used. But what I didn't know was that, while I was scrubbing away at the evidence, the Viklunds were somehow watching my every move.

The doorbell rings, ripping through the silence in the house. I slowly make my way towards the door and slide back the cover on the peephole. Hannah stares back at me, fidgeting on the doorstep from the cold.

I turn the latch and shiver as the evening breeze slips into the house. Hannah looks up at me from the street. Tears shimmer in her eyes.

'Han, what's the matter?'

She promptly bursts into tears, covering her face with her spare hand. In the other is a black duffel bag filled to the brim. I usher her inside and shut the door behind her.

The Messenger. He's approached her, like he accosted me. That's my first thought. I think of the places I should have jabbed him with my keys when I had the chance. The soft skin at the base of his throat. Those dark, repulsive eyes.

Hannah sniffs back tears as she dashes the streams from her cheeks with her sleeve.

'Nan and I . . . we . . .'

She can't seem to catch her breath, huffing for air between words.

'Give me all that and sit down.'

I take her bag and coat, placing the duffel at the foot of the stairs and her coat on the banister, and sit beside her on the sofa. Her face is blotchy and red.

'We had an argument,' she says. 'Nan is such a bitch.'

You're telling me.

'What happened?'

She takes a deep, shuddering breath, before sighing it away and looking down at her lap, picking at a loose thread on her sleeve until the fabric bunches.

'She said we shouldn't see you anymore because Dad's gone. That we were holding onto you for all the wrong reasons. That . . . that keeping you in the fold wouldn't keep Dad's memory alive.'

A twang of pain nicks at my chest. I knew Maggie was cold, and knew what she thought of mine and Hannah's relationship, but I didn't foresee her stooping this low. Actively trying to pry us apart.

Maggie knows they are the only family I have.

'She feels threatened, Han, that's all. We're close; it must be hard for her at times.'

'Why are you sticking up for her?' she asks, brow furrowed.

'I'm not. What she said was wrong, and hurtful. But that doesn't mean things have to change between us if you don't want them to. I want you in my life for as long as you want me in yours, and no one can change that. Not even your nan.'

Her expression softens, her shoulders lowering, and I think of her as a six-year-old again, giggling as Sam licked at her. How Matthew and I looked at one another over her head. If only we had known what lay ahead. We'd have bolted in opposite directions.

'Did you run away?' I ask.

'She knew I was coming here, if that's what you mean. I told her I would rather be with you than her.'

I glance towards the home phone and see the flashing red dot of the voicemail inbox. Maggie will have filled it to capacity with her angry ramblings, no doubt. When I look back to Hannah at the other end of the sofa, I see the nerves have returned, that same desperate hope flickering in her eyes again. I know what's coming before she even opens her mouth.

'Can I stay here for a while?'

I look into her eyes, which are the spitting image of her father's. It is almost as if Matthew is staring back at me from the other side of the sofa. A memory resurfaces in a sudden flash: Matthew's death stare, his eyes locked with mine in a lifeless gaze.

'How long were you thinking?'

Tonight, she looks and seems far younger than her sixteen years. Sometimes, she almost appears as a grown woman in the way she holds herself, but as she sits on the sofa with her cheeks flushed from the cold and her eyes as wide as a doe's, she looks more like that little girl again.

'Not forever,' she replies. 'Not yet anyway. I thought maybe we could . . . try it?'

We haven't even set foot in the courtroom, and already the Darling trial has taken over my life. I don't know how I could possibly juggle having Hannah waiting for me at home, what with chambers calling for me to sit at my desk until the early hours working on the case. And if the Viklunds are watching me, having Hannah stay here could put her in danger, couldn't it? Staying here could put her in harm's way. But with Hannah in front of me, the Messenger's threat against her feels all the more real now, like a living, breathing thing, watching us from the corner of the room. I would be able to keep a close eye on her, if she were here.

I can't let anything happen to her.

Her eyes fall to her lap, her throat bobbing with a nervous swallow.

'It's okay, I get it.'

'No,' I reply quickly. 'I want you here, of course I do. I was just thinking how we could make it work with my trial.'

Hannah quickly springs to life. 'You wouldn't even know I was here. I have school, and homework, and a bunch of my friends live nearby. I cook for myself when Nan is out, and I wash up every night. I'll clean up after myself and I promise I won't get in your way.'

My heart breaks at the excited tone of her voice. If only she knew who I truly am. What I am. A monster to fear, rather than a stepmother to love. If she knew of what I did, she would hate me more than anyone else in the world.

'Let me speak to Nan. Why don't you go and run yourself a bath?'

She jumps up eagerly, as if I might suddenly change my mind, and heads for the stairs.

I had decided too quickly. I should have put her off, thought about this more thoroughly. This trial, and the task I've been given to destroy it, will be enough to drive me crazy in the coming days. Having Hannah here, greeting me each morning, sharing the sofa of an evening, the very physical embodiment of my guilt looking me directly in the eye? It will be enough to push me over the edge.

But helping her is the least I can do, after what I've done.

'Erm, Neve?' Hannah calls from upstairs. 'What's that?'

'What's what?' I shout back.

'That.'

I climb the stairs, wondering what she could have found. Living on my own, I could be – or should I say *used* to be, what with Hannah staying here now – careless about where I left things, with no one around to see them. When I reach the top of the stairs and see Hannah standing in the hall, my heart pitches.

She is staring down at the mess I made of the carpet during my sleepwalking episode.

I had cleaned up as much as I could, after I scrubbed the burning bleach from my body, but the carpet could in no way be redeemed. There is a large yellowish-white pattern all over the hall floor.

Hannah looks at me, awaiting my answer.

'Oh, that. I spilt a glass of wine and accidentally used bleach to try and clean it up. Made more of a mess than I'd started with. I've been meaning to pull that up.'

'Oh, well . . . you don't have to do it now,' she says, as I get to my knees and start pulling the carpet from the hem. 'I just wondered what it was, that's all.'

I pull the edge of the carpet free with a grunt, hearing the fibres rip from the tacks keeping it down, and pause when I spot chips and dents in the floorboards beneath. I'd made them with the golf club, whacking the floor on the odd time I missed Matthew's head.

'You're right,' I say, and push it back down with shaking hands until it lies flat. 'I'll do it another day.'

'Are you okay?' she asks, her tone tinged with concern.

I feel dizzy, have done ever since I saw the marks I made with the club, as if all the blood has drained from my head. All the blood had drained from Matthew's too, in this very spot.

I grab the banister to get to my feet.

'I'm fine, you go and run the bath.'

As soon as the bathroom door shuts behind her, I drag the rug from my bedroom and out into the hallway, and place it over the stain. It covers most of it, with only the odd yellow splash creeping out from the sides. Another reminder of everything I've done.

I must be more careful, now that Hannah is staying here. God knows what else she could find.

⚖

I am sat up in bed working on the case, pages of the brief fanned out before me and scrunched-up yellow pages from my notepad strewn across the bedspread, while listening to Hannah unpacking her things on the other side of the wall. The more she makes this house her own, the less it feels like home to me. I have grown so accustomed to the silence, my own familiar way of things. Now I feel myself treading carefully when I walk, keeping myself covered in case she steps into the room without knocking.

This was a mistake. I never should have allowed her to stay.

Maggie hadn't taken it well on the phone. I barely said a

word before she began shouting down the line at me. It went this way for most of the call before she finally hung up, cutting me off mid-word.

Sitting across from Hannah this evening has made my situation all the more urgent. The Messenger's threat of harming her had been terrifying but almost otherworldly, as if it were nothing more than a frightening hypothetical. Now she is here, sharing the same rooms, breathing the same air, making the threat dangling above our heads feel overwhelmingly real. I have been going over my plan for the witnesses ever since, looking for ways I can navigate each cross-examination with my main objective in mind. My eyes are burning from lack of sleep, and I occasionally feel the pull of my lids as my brain desperately tries to rest.

I have worked far longer than I should have, and not just because of the approaching conference tomorrow morning, but in fear that when I close my eyes to end the day, I will sleep-walk again. I think of Hannah finding me, how frightening it would be.

A yawn rips from my mouth. I collect up the pages of the brief and tidy them away in defeat, throwing the discarded balls of yellow paper to the floor for the morning. I can't stay awake forever. I pause when I see the details of one of the notes I'd written: *destroy club tomorrow*. I rip it into as many pieces as I can and pile them on the bedside table, before switching off the light. I lie in bed trying not to think of the sounds it made, the mess it left behind. My heart races at the thought of seeing the murder weapon again, feeling its cool metal neck.

Whoosh.

Thwack.

Crack goes his head.

I wince and turn over in bed, lying in the dark as I listen to Hannah go about her unpacking. All the while, she has no idea what danger I have put her in.

She shouldn't be here, it just isn't safe.

Eventually, I hear her head towards the bathroom to get ready for bed, then return to her room with the quiet click of her door, as she too settles down for the night.

I slip out of bed, take the chair from my dressing table, and jam the back of it beneath the door handle. Only then am I able to close my eyes to sleep.

⚖

I wake with a gasp and the call of the church bells.

The cold night air sucks into my chest. My skin is speckled from the elements, the icy breeze billowing the few clothes I have on. I look about me, blinking away the confusion, but all I see is darkness.

Gong.

Gong.

Gong.

I am not in my bed. I am standing, barefoot, my toes almost blue against the dark earth. I am wearing nothing but night shorts and a cotton vest, and a cardigan that is inside out, whipping against me as the wind picks up. My cheeks are wet where I have been crying, tears I have no memory of shedding. My eyes slowly adjust to the dark, and slowly but surely, I realise where I am.

I am stood before Matthew's grave.

My chest heaves up and down as I eye the untouched earth at my feet. The cold air burns my throat. Tears fall as the panic takes hold and I look about me, only to find the dark night's shadows each way I turn, all except for the train tracks

gleaming beneath the moon. Beyond the fence, my lawn spar-
kles with dew. All the lights in the house are off but for the
kitchen, where I must have lit the way before leaving the house
in the middle of the night. The bell tower peers over the roofs,
its last chiming bell echoing through the night.

The hyperventilation doesn't slow. The panic doesn't ease.

Hannah.

I rush towards the fence, the stones among the tracks digging
into my naked soles, and straddle over to the other side. My
feet slip on the wet grass and leave footprints along the patio as
I reach the back door, which I had left ajar, squeaking faintly
on its hinges.

The house is freezing, the air damp with the outside chill. I
creep inside, clicking the door shut behind me, and look about
me for any mess I might have made in my sleep. The number
of times I have gone about supposedly tidying, putting files and
books in the oven, the washing machine running with an empty
drum, pyjamas soiled with urine where I'd gone without properly undressing. That's if I'm lucky. The bad nights are when
they are linked to my past: waking up surrounded by bleach,
or stood above my husband's grave.

I sway up the stairs, still blinking away sleep, and creep
towards the door to Hannah's bedroom by the light of my own,
where the chair lies on its side and the door has been left wide
open. My grip shakes on the handle, and the internal springs
stretch loudly as I push down. The hinges creak with the movement, light from across the hall moving with the motion, until
it illuminates her peaceful, sleeping face.

I release a heavy sigh as I shut the door quietly and creep
back to my room, picking up the chair and replacing it by my
dresser as I go. I know I won't get another wink of sleep. The

stress of my wandering will fester within me, and I'll only toss and turn fitfully until dawn. The clock on my bedside table tells me it has gone three in the morning.

I slip into my dressing gown, pick up the work that I'd left beside my bed before sleeping, and take it downstairs with me. As I pour myself into the trial, I try to ignore the relevance of where I had woken up; my subconscious leading me to my worst deed, and the biggest problem I have yet to solve.

Matthew.

16

Two days until the trial

If someone tells you not to think of something, what do you immediately think of? It's the same with sleepwalking. You tell yourself you won't, that you have control over your own autonomy. And then you wake up in the cold, in the dark, far away from your bed, not knowing how you got there or what you've done.

Before this trial, I hadn't sleepwalked in a long time. I'd had a bad relapse after Matthew's death, but as the months passed, the sleepwalking slowly began to ease. The specialists said my sleepwalking could have been triggered by the trauma of my childhood, lacking a stable home, which became a pattern with stressful life events thereafter. I couldn't sit for an exam, or start a new job, or go on a first date without spending the night wandering. Now the trial is bringing it out of me again.

I stand in the garage on the small lot tucked away a few streets from my house, waiting for the beep from the machine charging up the battery of my old trusty Audi. Matthew and I bought it for driving out of the city at weekends, or for when we had business meetings or trials outside of London. The

garage is musky and smells of damp, its asbestos-clad structure
covered with thick tendrils of spider webs.

I had left the house at six this morning. I couldn't bear the
thought of Hannah's face, excited at the thought of us living
together, in case she saw my dread staring back at her. Instead,
I took the coward's way out, leaving the spare house keys on
the breakfast table with a note and twenty pounds in cash,
telling her to text me if she needs me. On my way out, I had to
step over the morning paper on the doormat, where Wade and
I stare up from the roll; another of Eccleston's articles about
the case that I can't bring myself to read.

I stand listening to the whir of the battery charger, trying
and failing to calm my frantic heart. I'd dressed in casual
wear for this morning's deed: a plain grey sweatshirt, old dark
jeans that are an inch too loose, and dirty trainers, a navy cap
covering my face. My suit hangs in a carrier in the back of the
car with my heels in the footwell, ready to change into after
the deed is done.

Soon enough, I will be holding the weapon that killed my
husband. A Callaway 'Big Bertha' golf iron: clad with black
carbon at the tip, its steel spine reaching just below my ribcage. The last time I felt the cool metal in my hands was the
morning I cleaned off the blood, bleaching the club within
an inch of its life. Just the thought of it brings the memory of
the whistle it made as it cut through the air. The crunch the
head made as it met Matthew's. The tuft of his hair that was
stuck to the tip.

Whoosh. Thwack. Whoosh. Thwack.

I bolt towards the bucket on the tool shelf and vomit. Dust
billows up into my eyes, and my throat and teeth sting with
each retch, but all I can focus on is the horrendous sounds the

club made. The battery charger beeps three times before falling silent, and I rest against the wall, breathing in the dust, the scent of damp and stomach acid.

After the murder, I knew I had to do three things. Hide the body. Clean up the crime scene. Conceal the murder weapon. The body came first – and what a night I chose to do it.

As the night sky was lit by fireworks ringing in Christmas Day, flashes of colour exploding from a neighbour's garden, I tried to concoct a plan. I couldn't drag the body to the car; the streets were teeming with drunken stragglers, and front doors were forever opening and closing with partygoers. Even if I parked right outside the house, there would have been too many opportunities to be stumbled upon.

I couldn't leave the body and wait for a better opportunity either. I knew it wouldn't be long before it started to smell. Foul gases and rotting flesh attracting bluebottles. We have all heard the horror stories of neighbours complaining of a bad odour seeping through the walls, only to discover a body on the other side.

My best chance was the woodlands just beyond the train tracks. I had to wait for the Midnight Mass service to end, and for the partygoers along the street to finally go to sleep, but it seemed like the safest option, at least in the short term. That's what I thought to myself at the time. But he has lain at the foot of the garden ever since, taunting me whenever I dare to peer through the window.

I grab the bucket and retch again.

When I'm finally done, and my stomach has nothing left, I stand on shaking legs to tidy away the battery charger and climb behind the wheel. It has been a long time since I sat in this seat. The memories Matthew and I shared are pressed into the sagging leather; each scratch and scruff on the dashboard. The markings have completely worn off the gear stick from his strong grip. I turn the key in the ignition and the engine stutters to life.

He is so present in here. I can smell his aftershave as if he were next to me. My hands shake at the wheel, and I grip tightly, until my palms rasp against the leather. I turn on the radio to distract myself, and freeze as soon as I hear it.

Our song.

I'd clicked on the CD player rather than the radio. I smack the butt of my palm against the power button, and kill the song mid lyric.

Love of my life, you've hurt me . . .

My heart is thumping wildly, my palms slick with sweat at the wheel as I am met with a rush of emotion. Tears spring to my eyes and I blink them away.

I need to destroy the club. Chances are, the people who work for the Messenger will be looking for it too, as they did with the body. I can't allow them to hold another thing over me.

I press the button for the garage door and lower the window for a breath of fresh air. The cool morning breeze drifts in, sending a shiver down my spine. *Someone just walked over my grave,* Matthew used to say.

I wonder what he would say to me now.

⚖

I sit in my car outside the storage unit, forcing myself to take deep, slow breaths.

I had been a mess throughout the drive, convinced I was being followed. My tired eyes would clock the Messenger in every car tailing behind mine, spot him in the men eyeing me from the path as I drove by. I must have seen his face a hundred times, my heart jumping in my chest with each perceived sighting.

The lot is the perfect place to keep something hidden. It is a forty-minute drive from home and set back from the main streets, with only an MOT garage and a vacant building waiting to be let for its neighbours. I chose this place for the self-service access that is available during out-of-office hours: a key fob for the secured entrance, and a keypad for each respective storage unit.

The cold morning breeze sends a shiver right through me. Another person crossing my grave. The storage unit looks small from the outside, but beyond the entrance lobby is an endless corridor, leading to door after door of strangers' belongings, each with their own story: deaths, new beginnings, long-kept secrets. I press the fob key against the reader beside the door and step inside.

To my relief, the security protocols seem to be the same. I sign in at the desk, using an initial for my first name, and my maiden name for my second. *N. Norton*. The door leading towards the storage units squeals on its hinges as it opens, sending a high-pitched echo down the long, cold corridor. It still has the same metallic smell, the unwelcoming chill. A corridor of secrets, hidden away under lock and key.

Each step I take echoes against the metal doors; they're the roller kind, similar to the shutters one might see drawn over shopfronts after hours. I count the units as I go, waiting for number 34 to appear, as my body instinctively tugs at me to turn in the other direction. I pass units 30 and 32, breaking out in a cold sweat as I reach mine.

The first time I came here, the murder was still fresh. It had been hours, rather than years. I could still smell his blood on me despite my scrubbing, hear the screams as though they were happening at that very moment. My hands stung from the bleach, my skin flushed and angry, cracked between my knuckles and around my fingernails. I press the numbers into the keypad beside the door.

2-4-1-2

The keypad beeps and flashes green, and I reach down for the handle, pulling it upwards with a deafening clatter as I rise to my feet, the metal rolling above my head until it reaches the top and the corridor falls silent.

The rolled-up rug lies alone in the centre of the room.

I am shivering from the adrenaline and the cold. My whole body seems to be repelled by the sight, squirming like a strand of hair before a flame. But I can't tear my eyes away.

I step inside the unit, drag the door down behind me, and crouch before the roll, feeling the edge of the rug in my grip. The underside feels as rough as I remember; the same material that gave me friction burns as I lugged it from the car. It had been with us in every one of our homes, a hand-me-down from Maggie. We made love on this rug, spilt drinks during parties, with no notion of what it would be used for in the end.

I place my palms flat on the roll and push, watching it unfurl along the length of the unit in a cloud of dust. I cover my mouth and nose and cough as it hits the back of my throat. When it settles, I turn back.

The golf club lies inside.

I blink back the memories, and despite my better knowledge, I reach for it, my hand quivering before me as I lower it towards the club, but as soon as I graze the cold metal with my fingertips, I flinch as if I've been stung and roll the rug up again.

The rug is heavier than I remember. When I try to lift it, my back almost gives. I had been fuelled by adrenaline when I brought it here; I would have done anything to make the ordeal end. I lumber it up with a groan, and hold it before me in both hands.

After I've sealed the door behind me, I carry the rug back up the corridor and out of the lot to the car, and drop it in the boot with a *thunk*, before hiding away in the safe confines of the car. I close my eyes and listen to the loud, anxious rasp of my breaths, feel my heart pulsating feverishly in my chest. I only meant to store it here for a week or two, to give me time to figure out what the hell I was going to do with it; its presence here has hung over me like a black cloud ever since.

Hindsight, they say, is a wonderful thing. I have regretted using the club ever since that night. You can't burn metal, or hide such a long, awkward thing. But I didn't think of the aftermath. The only thing I can remember knowing in that moment was that I wanted him dead.

I wipe the sweat away from my face, and pinch at my sweatshirt to peel the fabric from my damp ribs. I've done the first part of the task.

Now I just need to destroy it.

⚖️

I drive at a crawl towards the car park of the tip, pull up in the nearest spot and cut the engine. There are already a number of cars parked up, but to my relief I can't see any queues, meaning I can quickly slip in and out before crossing paths with too many people. But there will still be witnesses who could recognise me.

I have to look normal, act normal. Just like everyone else here.

I lower my cap, slip on my sunglasses, and get out of the car, retrieving the rug before setting off.

Can I dump the club and rug together, or do I need to rid myself of them separately? As I step through the main gates, I eye the large, towering containers of waste, with steel staircases and platforms to stand upon, each with its own particular contents. I scan each of them as I pass, looking beyond the rows of disused fridge-freezers and washing machines reflecting the morning sun off their white, dented bodies, until I spot the sign for metals.

I lumber the rug under my arm to rest on my hip, and cross the potholed forecourt for the metal disposal. There are other people here, emptying an array of junk from their vehicles; dead, brown Christmas trees added to an already toppling mound.

I approach the staircase and latch onto the railing, trying to stop myself from glimpsing the ground below through the metal grating, getting further and further away the higher I climb. The rug grows heavier, burning the muscles of my thighs, my back threatening to give.

I reach the container and look down at the gleaming, rusting metal within. I hoist the rug onto the lip of the container, and pause. My heart is racing; not just from the exertion, but the fear.

It's the club, it's brought out the worst in me. I can't stop thinking of the night I held it in both hands, past and present bleeding together. I am stood before the container, but in my mind, it's Christmas Eve. I listen to the church's bell tower ringing in Midnight Mass, matching the swing of my club.

Gong. Thwack.

Gong. Thwack.

Gong. Thwack . . .

The cheers of my neighbours brought me round as midnight rang, and I paused with the club above my head, blood splattered on my face, in my mouth. Fireworks burst on the other side of the windows, flashing us in reds, whites and blues. My husband's once beautiful face beaten into pulp beneath me. The wet meat of him reflecting each burst of light.

I snap back to the present at the sound of my name, my stomach plummeting at the familiarity of the voice.

The Messenger is stood tall, looking down at me where he stands on the other end of the platform by the stairs. He wears that same, dark grin on his face.

I blink furiously, half convinced that my paranoia is playing tricks on me. But it's him. It's really him.

'Good morning,' he says, and nods towards the rug. 'I think you have something that belongs to me.'

How did he know I would be here? How did he follow me without me seeing him?

As my heart races and my thoughts jumble, he reaches out for it, grazing the back of my hand with his leather glove; it feels like cold, wet skin, sending a shiver of revulsion through me. As he moves towards me, I see two men stood at the bottom of the steps.

He tugs lightly, but I don't unfurl my grip. His breath is warm, and his closeness is both terrifying and strangely intimate.

'Remember what happened to Adrian Whittaker. I suggest you don't make the same mistake.'

Hannah's a pretty girl.

I close my eyes to bury my reluctance, and let him prise the rug away. I open them again and watch helplessly as he walks down the metal steps with the rug held securely under one arm.

I stand in silence as the Messenger and the men head off into the distance, and I am left empty-handed, with my heart in my mouth.

They knew exactly what I would do. They know every step I plan to make before I even make it.

But how?

I sit on the tube, slowly piecing together how I had played right into their hands.

If they had known where I buried the body, they must have been watching me for a long time, but clearly, they hadn't known where I kept the murder weapon until I led them right to it. As far as I'm aware, I haven't been followed since yesterday morning; they must have wanted to lull me into a false sense of security, to feel bold enough to collect the club and lead them directly to it. Perhaps they were following me all day, but they didn't want me to know it; conspicuous when it pays to be, and hot on my heels when they want me to know that I have nowhere to run. I must assume they are following me everywhere I go now. That everything I do, everything I say, will be scrutinised.

I am only a few stops away from my next conference with Wade. Despite my nerves, I am far more prepared than I was yesterday, even if my 3 a.m. start and this morning's events have robbed me of energy. I take a deep breath and close my eyes, and remind myself of my plan. My main goals of the meeting are to keep Antony from asking too much about Alex Finch, and persuading Wade, and his mother if necessary, to push back the trial so I have more time.

The tube stops at the next station, and as we pull away again, my phone buzzes with a text from Antony.

Hey, just saw you on the tube. See you in a sec.

I glance around me for the Messenger among the passengers, suddenly paranoid that I'm being followed again. Then it hits me.

My phone.

I'm furious not to have thought of this before now. The amount of stalking cases I've worked on where the defendant has used their victim's phone as a means to follow them. But it's something so outlandish that I would never have dreamed it would happen in my own life.

I stare down at the phone in my grip and unlock the screen, swiping anxiously through the apps. There are the usual suspects: social media, email and photos, the running app I haven't opened in months. I scroll through the pages of apps scanning for anything that might grab my attention, and pause.

The *Find my Mobile* app.

I didn't even think of it. It's one of those apps that I downloaded with my new phone and then immediately forgot about, only needing it if my handset went missing. It tracks where my phone is at all times in case I lose it. If they were able to hack into it, could they track my every move? Or worse, might they see everything I type, hear everything I say?

I need to talk to Fredrick.

'Neve—'

I jolt in my seat.

It's Antony. The tube has started up again, but I had been so engrossed in my own thoughts that I hadn't even realised.

'Christ, you're rather jumpy at the minute, aren't you?' he

asks, looking down at me with a playful grin on his face. He is dressed in a checked grey suit and a camel overcoat, his polished leather shoes matching the satchel bag at his hip. In his hands are two takeaway coffee cups.

'Latte no sugar, right?' Antony says, passing me a cup as he sits down beside me.

'Thanks.'

Antony looks about us at the near-empty carriage before returning his attention to me.

'I've done some digging on Alex Finch. He is definitely a factor in the Darlings' downfall, but get this: the police never even spoke to him.'

A man sat further down the carriage has taken out his phone from his pocket and is tapping away at the screen.

Is he relaying everything we say?

No. I'm being paranoid.

'Definitely?' I take a sip of coffee. 'You sound confident.'

'I am, and you should be too. Finch was all over the paperwork for Wade's business. Signing off on the big decisions that would come back to bite them; even seemed to be the driving force behind the Ponzi scheme they had going, according to the paper trail. Hell, Finch might even have been leading Wade along too for all we know, and keeping the dirty dealings under wraps. The third-party companies suing them for unpaid fees name both Wade Darling and Alex Finch on the complaints, but it seems Finch was a big part of why the business went under, if not the main catalyst.'

'That doesn't mean he killed the Darlings.'

'Not outright, no, but it certainly plays into the obsessive, jealous angle, doesn't it? From looking at the copy of the company's books we have on file, Finch used to do his job well.

The company wasn't failing when he began his dodgy business tactics, which means he's either a greedy son of a bitch, or—'

'Something happened to make him change tack.'

'Exactly,' he replies. 'It all happened in the year leading up to the murders.'

My heart is racing. He has sunk his teeth into this case and is refusing to let go.

'And you said his ex-wife filed for divorce three days before the murders,' I say, thinking aloud. 'Which suggests they would have had marital problems during that year too. It sounds like Wade was right when he said Finch's life was falling apart.'

I have to give it to Antony, the idea sticks. Wade said Finch wanted everything he had, but the one thing he couldn't have was his wife. If Finch's world was crumbling around him, and he snapped under the pressure, perhaps the murders were his way of exacting revenge.

'But why wouldn't Wade mention it sooner?' I ask. 'What does his ex-business partner have on him?'

'Got to be something bad.'

'But what's worse than your family being murdered, and being framed for it?'

'I'm determined to find out.'

While I have been sleepwalking, taking in teenage runaways and trying to destroy murder weapons, Antony has found a way to spin the prosecution's argument in favour of our client. The very thing that I cannot afford to happen, if I have to go through with what the Messenger demands.

'Good work,' I mutter, and look up at the tube map; the next stop is ours.

'You don't seem too pleased,' he says.

'Only because I know you won't like my plan B.' He stares

back at me, waiting. 'Look, I know you want to run with this trial, but if we don't get what we need from him, I'll be urging him to push it back.'

He goes to speak, but I cut him off.

'I'm not ushering him into the dock if the defence case isn't ready, and nor should you.'

'Of course not. But if we *can* get the information, if it's right there, on the tip of his bloody tongue, we've got to try and push for it, no?'

'Right. Except it's his job to give us instructions, not the other way around. We can give him the best legal advice, but that doesn't mean he has to take it.'

He looks away, and we rock with the carriage in silence as the seconds tick away from us. The tube begins to slow, and our stop appears on the other side of the window.

'You're right,' he says finally. 'I know you are. But let me try and get this out of him. If we know the truth, we can make sure we get the evidence we need to help him win this thing.'

He looks at me, pleading with his eyes like a dog for a scrap, as the tube comes to a stop.

I never should have chosen you for this trial, I think to myself.

'Let's hope he's willing to play ball.'

⚖

'No,' Wade says from the other side of the table.

Antony and I sit in silence, in the same seats as before. I can feel him practically twitching beside me.

'Why not?' I ask, staring him down. He says nothing, crushing Antony's hopes to dust.

'Wade, whatever you're holding back could be the very thing to help you avoid being found guilty,' Antony says.

'There will be another way,' he replies, crossing his arms.

'There isn't,' Antony says. 'If you want to avoid being sentenced for these crimes, this is your chance.'

'Then I'll go to prison,' he snaps. 'I told you, I'm not talking about this any further.'

Why wouldn't he? What could he possibly be hiding?

Poor Antony. He must have been up half the night digging this up.

Wade sits, stoic and defiant. I look down at my notes for ways to lead him off the topic.

'I think what would be good to do today is go over the days leading up to the murders. How you were doing as a family, how your marriage was going ... how you were feeling, in the final days. You were depressed due to the closure of your business, is that right?'

'Do we really have to talk about this?' he snaps.

'The prosecution is going to use your depression as a reason for committing the murders. They will paint you as a man who lost his mind and saw red. I need to know as much as possible to accurately convey the true nature of your experience to counteract their narrative.'

He chews on his bottom lip and looks away, his eyes on the window. He stays like this for some time, seemingly transfixed. Finally, he speaks.

'That last week before the murders was ... dark. I had learnt we were being sued by multiple suppliers for unpaid invoices, and I knew I had nothing to give them; I couldn't even afford my lawyer. Everything I had built for myself and my family was crumbling before my eyes. I knew I would have to file for bankruptcy, and what that would mean for the future. No reputable bank or business contact would lend me the start-up money to build another business off the back of something like this.'

'Did your wife know about the business?'

'No. I was too ashamed.'

'So she had no idea about your financial predicament? Hers too, essentially, what with you being the provider for the family?'

'She knew nothing. I tried to buy myself some time, to fix things without having to worry her. I borrowed money to keep the accounts full so she wasn't any the wiser. But as our situation got worse, I knew I couldn't hide it from her anymore. It was only a matter of time before word spread to our group of friends, and I wanted her to hear it from me. But I didn't get the chance.'

Silence falls upon on the room.

'How were Yolanda and the children during this time?'

'Yolanda was aloof,' he replies. 'My depression was like a dark cloud over us. They were used to me taking care of things, and for the first time I couldn't. I was failing. We all felt lost and disconnected, like a house full of strangers.'

'In what way was Yolanda aloof?'

His face softens as he thinks of her.

'I think she was purposely stepping on eggshells around me. She knew I was in a bad way, and didn't want to tip me over the edge. My mood swings were ... irrational.'

'Were you ever angry with her?'

'Not in an abusive way, if that's what you mean.'

'I wasn't insinuating that at all. We're on your side, Wade.'

The lie makes me break out in a sudden rush of sweat. I feel the heat prickling the skin of my back, speckles forming above my lip.

He softens slightly, his shoulders lowering from the tensed hunch he had them in.

'Yes, I was angry, but not about anything logical. The depression ... it made every small task impossible. I could barely string a coherent thought together, so if my family so much as spoke to me, I snapped, or became tearful. It was an impossible situation to put them in.'

'But it wasn't your fault, Wade,' Antony says. 'It was the depression, not you.'

Wade's eyes sink to his lap. I wonder if he believes that.

The mood swings, the walking on eggshells – these give the prosecution many opportunities to paint him in a darker light. A man to be feared, rather than helped.

'I barely spoke in the final days leading up to their deaths. I hid away in my office, trying to soften the inevitable blow of the business closure. I would go for walks in the woods, hunt.'

'With the murder weapon?'

His eye twitches. 'Yes.'

Antony sits forward in his seat. I can see by the eagerness in his eyes that he is done with my deflections; he's ready to return the questioning to Alex Finch.

'What about your business partner? What communication did you have with him in those last days?'

Wade straightens in his seat.

'It's important we know of anything the prosecution might bring up in court.'

He crosses his arms and looks to the window.

'Why were you sleeping on the sofa the night of the murders?' Antony asks, his tone more desperate than before. 'Had you and Yolanda argued?'

'No, actually. We had reconciled. We'd gone through a rough patch.'

'What kind of rough patch?' Antony asks.

Wade stares out the window again, shutting himself down. I can practically feel the heat of Antony's anger bubbling away inside of him.

'Had you thought to tell Yolanda about the finances then?' I ask.

'I wanted to, but we had just reached a good place; I couldn't bring myself to tell her and ruin the progress we'd made.' His eyes glaze over. 'It would have killed me to see the look on her face when I told her.'

I look down at my notes. It's time I presented the idea of pushing the trial to him. I take a deep breath and am just about to speak when I'm cut off.

'Wade,' Antony says abruptly. 'I'm going to put it to you straight because we don't have much time. At present, it looks like the jury won't be on your side. If you know something that could help us – could help *you* – you don't have long to tell us. On Monday, the prosecution is going to paint you as a monster. A liar. A killer. A failed husband, father and businessman. It is going to be character assassination. They are going to insinuate that you killed your family to hide the shame of your failed business. They will take every opportunity they can to make you seem like the ghastliest man that has ever stepped into the courtroom, and at present, you're gifting them the chance. If we don't have all the information to counteract their claims, it's highly likely that the jury will believe them and consider you guilty.'

Antony stands.

'It's your life, your freedom. We will do whatever you

instruct. But if you change your mind, and you decide to be open with us – to fight for yourself – then get in touch. Otherwise, we will see you on Monday for the trial.'

Although his speech is similar in sentiment to what mine was to be, I am left feeling a lingering sense of unease. His words run the risk of inspiring Wade into action, rather than delaying him. I assess Wade intently, looking for the slightest flare of provocation in his eyes. He remains in his seat as Anthony heads for the door, strides down the hall and out into the street.

'I'm afraid he's right,' I say. 'It doesn't look good for you, Wade. I think we may need to consider requesting to push back the trial to a later date. I said we could work towards the set trial date during our first meeting, but only if you worked with us. Pushing the trial seems to be the only other way to give us more time to prepare your defence. If there *is* another way to tackle this, we'll need time to prepare.'

Marianne is stood listening in at the kitchen doorway, pale with angst. When Wade doesn't look up at me or register my words, I rise to my feet as Antony had.

'Mrs Darling,' I say softly as I reach her. 'The wisest thing Wade can do at this stage is agree to push the trial. Right now, we don't have enough to defend him – if the trial commences on Monday . . .'

'They'll lock him up,' she replies, her voice thick with dread.

I nod, and give her a sympathetic smile, before taking one last glance at Wade. He is sat at the table in silence, staring down at his burns. I almost will him to make the right decision, wishing my eyes could burrow into the back of his skull and see what he is thinking, what decision he plans to make.

My freedom depends on it.

18

I stand on the dock, waiting for the 18.56 RB2 river bus from Westminster Pier on which I am to meet Fredrick.

I pull my coat closer to my body, as the chill of the breeze bites at me through my clothes. The journey from Westminster to Embankment only takes five minutes, so he can't have much to tell me. Perhaps he has found something that he doesn't want to get caught up in, and he has asked me here to withdraw his support. I know I wouldn't want to get caught up in this voluntarily.

I trace my finger along the edge of the cigarette packet hidden in my coat pocket. I had bought them after the conference with Mr Darling before returning to chambers to work on the case, the need for relief clawing at me from within, but still, I can't bring myself to spark one up after abstaining for so long. But the temptation continues to whisper its sweet encouragements in my ears.

'Screw it,' I mutter, and pull the packet free. I peel off the cellophane, pick out the silver foiled paper covering the cigarettes, and breathe in the fresh, familiar scent of them. I prise one free with my teeth and cup my hand around the lighter, inhaling deeply. The first hit goes straight to my head, and for a brief few seconds, I feel nothing but bliss.

The river is black with the night but for the bursts of colour

rippling in its waves from the London Eye, illuminated purple
and stark against the evening sky. Behind me, Big Ben towers
over Westminster, clad in unsightly scaffolding, and beside it,
Westminster Bridge carries the bright lights of city traffic from
one side of London to the other.

The night is ice-cold. If someone were to fall in the water,
they'd have hypothermia in minutes. I have always thought
that would be the worst way to die. It's often said that burning
is the ghastliest end, but if you're lucky, the smoke gets to you
before the flames. Cold water stabs at you, slows your blood,
numbs your legs until you can't kick to keep afloat, and slip
silently below the surface.

After planting the seed into Wade's and Marianne's minds
to push back the trial, and having Fredrick working to free me
of the Messenger, I feel I should be experiencing an element of
control. But that same adrenaline-fuelled restlessness plagues
me, and as soon as I returned to chambers I spent the rest of the
day obsessively going over each of the prosecution's witnesses
and planning how I could twist their evidence to suit my best
interests over those of my client, as I battled the guilt within
me with each and every turn. I stand at the dock, shoulders
slumped and eyes hooded, exhausted from the endless fight.
At least Hannah is at a friend's this evening; her text said she
wouldn't be in until after dinner.

The river bus appears slowly from beneath Westminster
Bridge. I smoke my cigarette to the filter as the boat drifts
towards the pier. Fredrick is already aboard, waiting for
me. I had called him from my work phone at chambers and
explained my suspicions about the Messenger tracking my
phone, warning him not to contact me through my mobile
anymore, which is turned off at the bottom of my bag.

There are five or so people waiting to get on the boat. Londoners unsteady on their feet after sinking a few too many drinks. I wonder where they have been, and where they are all off to; it's easy to imagine everyone has it better than you: better jobs, better relationships. But in this case, it must be true. I can't imagine anyone here being in a worse situation than mine.

The boat docks and we head aboard. I cross the gangplank, eyeing the black, chopping water below, and almost feel it tugging at me, beckoning me down, before stepping safely onto the deck.

I walk along the row of seats towards the prow of the boat and recognise Fredrick sat with his head down, halfway along. He doesn't look for me as we board, and I continue to the front as he instructed and take a seat by the window.

The boat grumbles into motion, and we set off along the Thames at what feels like a snail's pace. The city passes us by. There aren't too many people on board, just straggles of passengers riding alone, some suited up, others casual. Everyone is dotted about to give each other space, a luxury rarely permitted on the underground. I hear the crack of a drink can; the man two rows behind me takes a glug of a pre-mixed gin and tonic.

After a minute or so, I feel the rustle of Fredrick's coat against mine as he sits down beside me, the scent of oaky after-shave filling my nostrils.

'Good evening,' he says, his breath visible in the air. 'Couldn't have got yourself into this trouble during the summer?'

His nose and cheeks are red from the cold. He is dressed in the same black overcoat, buttoned up to the navy scarf wrapped tightly at his neck. His shaved head is covered by a black flat cap, his hands hidden in leather gloves.

'Out of my hands, I'm afraid,' I reply, and force a smile.

I hear the man behind us slurp from his can of G&T, and have the sudden urge to reach around and snatch it from him, guzzle it down until there are two bubbling streams of it seeping from either side of my mouth.

'You were right about the source,' he says, speaking low. 'The man who accosted you works for the Viklunds. They've worked together for some time; he seems to be their go-to man for things like this.'

A part of me doesn't want to know who the Messenger is, to put an identity on the man. It makes him seem more real. A man with a history. I don't want to think of him as human; he would have been a baby, a child, an uncorrupted soul until something happened along the way to turn him into the monster he is now. But despite my reservations, my curiosity gets the better of me.

'Who is he? The Messenger?'

'Leon James. A nasty character with a charge sheet as long as your arm.'

'That makes me feel better,' I quip. 'What has he gone down for in the past?'

'Extortion. GBH. And he's rumoured to have committed far worse.'

'It's fitting, at least.'

'I'm sorry not to have better news. But it's good to know who you're dealing with.'

I don't know what I had been expecting. Of course he would be a dangerous man. I think of the gun he pointed at my chest the day we met.

'And the Viklunds? Are they as bad as the rumours suggest?'

He nods solemnly, which tells me they are even worse.

'I'm still looking into them, but they have connections throughout the city. I can't imagine you're the only one being . . . exploited like this. The Viklunds don't have any one means of business – if there's a way to make a living from a crime, they play a part in it.'

Despite the conversation, my thoughts drift to Fredrick himself. I wonder if he has cottoned on to what I've done. I am known for my husband's disappearance just as much as my legal work. Perhaps he looked further into me too, when he was digging into the Messenger. Maybe he can see right through me. See the blood dripping from my hands.

'I don't know what to say. Thank you, I suppose.'

'This is just the first step,' he says. 'I'll dig around, see if I can get wind of anything more that might be able to help you.'

'Thank you.'

I turn my attention to the window and admire the lights of the city. The night suddenly feels colder; my bones ache with it, and my teeth chatter behind my lips. I clamp my gloved hands between my thighs.

The boat begins to drift from its course towards the side of the river as Embankment comes into view.

'And the other thing we discussed?' I ask, my eyes straight ahead. 'Anything there?'

'Yes,' he replies. 'Something I think you'll be able to use.'

He doesn't say what I might use it for, and for what outcome, but in a few simple words, it's clear he knows of my motives: preparing for the last resort, to use Wade as my sacrificial lamb.

He hands me a file. The cover is blank, with no hint of what might be inside.

'I'll get off here, you leave at the next,' he says. 'I'll call you when I have more.'

'Thank you,' I say, meeting his eyes. 'Do you have enough time? The trial begins on Monday.'

'It'll have to be,' he replies. He places his gloved hand over mine, and gives it a comforting squeeze, to the sound of squeaking leather. 'You're not alone in this, all right?'

I hadn't realised how alone I had felt, until I heard those words.

'Thanks.'

He gets up as the boat pulls up at Embankment.

'I'll see you soon,' he says, and gives me a comforting wink.

The night feels colder just a few miles up the river. The wind carries an arctic chill, bringing water to my eyes; the sort of cold that makes one's skin ache. I look for him on the shore over my shoulder as the boat pulls away, and see him standing at the dock, giving me a nod. Behind him, the view of the city glows.

I turn back to the file in my lap. It seems so inconspicuous, and yet it seems to burn into my thighs with all the possibilities it might hold. I lift the cover and begin to read, my face slowly draining of colour as I take in the potential evidence I could use to damn my client, if I choose to put it in the wrong hands.

What Fredrick has given me isn't a mere spanner in the works, it's explosive. If this were sent to the prosecution, they may well have won the case before it has even begun. It is perhaps the best hand I could have been dealt.

I just pray I don't need to use it.

I sit in my armchair in the living room with the new evidence on my lap and a glass of wine in hand, wondering how I could possibly bring myself to unearth this against my client.

I was wrong before. It isn't explosive evidence. It's nuclear. No defence barrister would be able to dodge this bullet. This information wouldn't just smear Wade Darling's character. It would implode our entire route of defence.

I drink the last gulp of wine in my glass and assess the prosecution's case laid out before me. This would be the evidence needed for them to win, no questions asked. It would give credibility to every one of their claims, but had been buried so deeply that even they struggled to find it. The question I have now is: do I use this to my advantage, or bury it as far down again as I can?

My guilt rears up, closing about my throat in a chokehold.

It hasn't got to that point yet. I mustn't drive myself mad over something I might never have to do.

But as I open my eyes again and stare down at the evidence laid in my lap, I know the odds of avoiding the Messenger's demands aren't exactly in my favour. I jolt out of my thoughts at the sound of Hannah's voice.

'You okay?' she asks from the sofa, remote in hand. 'You look really pale.'

I force a tight smile.

'I'm fine. A bit stressed. Nothing wine won't help.' I get up with my empty glass. 'Want anything?'

'I'm good.'

I head into the kitchen and brace myself against the counter for a moment, trying to stop my head from spinning with thoughts.

If I sent this to the prosecution, I would be destroying a man's life. Stealing away any chance of a fair trial. It's grossly unjust. It would make me despicable.

But what if it's the only way to protect Hannah, and keep my secret? What then?

I pour myself a generous glass of red wine. I'll need to sleep tonight, and this will help to keep my mind from wandering.

I step back into the living room and pause.

Hannah is up from her seat, peering over my paperwork sprawled across the footstall before my armchair.

'What the hell are you doing?'

Hannah jumps at the cutting sound of my voice and spins around.

'I was just . . . curious.'

She steps aside as I march over to my armchair and snatch up the files. She'd been glancing at the document Fredrick gave me.

'This is confidential information. That's really not on.'

'I was interested what you did in your job. I'm sorry, I didn't know—'

'You did know, Hannah. You wouldn't have waited until my back was turned if you didn't know it was wrong.'

I take the files and the glass of wine with me towards the stairs.

'Lock the doors before you come up. I'll see you in the morning.'

I march up the stairs, the wine glass shaking in my grasp.

I wake standing in the dark.

The room is pitch black. So dark that the air before my eyes appears thick enough to run my hand through. I am naked. I can't see myself, but I feel the nip of the cold room all over my body, gooseflesh running up my thighs and across my buttocks, raising the hairs on the backs of my arms. Through my fear, I feel the whisper of pain: my teeth are ringing, and the skin on my wrist feels like it has been burnt.

The rush of blood pulses in my ears, my thoughts running in a muddled, anxious loop.

It's happening again it's happening again it's happening again.

My eyes slowly acclimatise to the dark, colours peering through the shadows, forms and shapes breaking through the wall of black. There is movement before me. Twisting. Turning. The realisation of where I am hits me suddenly, like a fist in my gut.

I am not in my room. I'm in Hannah's.

My body shakes, my aching teeth chattering together. I am stood above Hannah's bed, watching her. Through the darkness, I can see her milky white skin, her eyes closed with sleep.

I back away, tripping over a piece of clothing that has been left on the floor, and stumble. Hannah stirs, her limbs unfurling beneath the sheets. I watch in terrified silence where I am flat against the door. She sits up, squinting to see through the dark. I don't breathe. I don't think. The only lifelike thing about me is my rampant pulse screaming from beneath my skin.

Seconds pass, feeling like minutes. I listen to her breaths, sleepy and ragged, before she groans and turns, flopping down on the bed again. When her breathing slows, and I know she has returned to sleep, I edge open the door and click it shut behind me.

In my room, my bed is messy and unmade where I threw my covers off in my sleep. The restraint I had tied to my wrist to fix me to the headboard is on the floor: a fabric belt from a jacket in my closet. No wonder my teeth hurt; I had gnawed myself free, the fabric frayed where I'd bitten at the knots.

I get back into bed, shivering beneath the covers, and bind my wrist to the headboard so tightly that my fingertips swell with blood.

I mustn't let this rule my life again. It's just the stress of the trial; things will calm down as they did before.

But as I try to return to sleep, one question niggles through my brain.

Why had I been standing above Hannah's bed?

20

One day until the trial

The trial is so close now that I can practically smell the wood panelling on the courtroom walls, hear the creaks of the jurors' chairs. I glance up at the clock on the wall of my office in chambers, the seconds ticking away from me as the hand whirls around the face.

Breathe. Just breathe.

I close my eyes, resting back in my chair before my desk. I'd managed an hour's sleep, perhaps two, interspersed between nightmares that made me wake with a violent jolt each time, tugging at my restraint, in fear I had been walking again. I woke the final time to the sound of my name, and Hannah's pale, frightened face peering through the doorway to my dark room, asking if I was all right.

I was dreaming of murdering your father.

I imagine Hannah in the witness box, relaying my tossing and turning to the court, adding her name to the ever-growing list of prosecution witnesses that could be used against me at trial: the neighbour, the stepdaughter, the solicitor, the client. But there is a way out of this, something I hadn't allowed myself to even think of, until meeting with Fredrick. That's if

I can bring myself to do something so despicable as sacrifice a man's life for my own.

My thoughts return to Hannah. Last night had been too close a call. The memory of waking up beside her bed, staring down at her through the darkness, is enough to bring up the taste of bile.

She can't stay another night. I need her to go home.

I pick up my work phone with a shaking hand and dial Maggie's number. She answers on the fifth ring.

'Maggie, it's Neve. Don't hang up.'

She sighs at the other end of the line. 'What is it? I was about to go out.'

'It's about Hannah.'

'Of course it is,' she says, with an exacerbated huff. 'I expected this.'

'Expected what?'

'It was only a matter of time before the shine of having Hannah all to yourself would wane. It's not as easy as it looks, is it, looking after someone other than yourself?'

'It isn't that, Maggie. The case is taking over, and I'm not able to be around as much as I'd like. Come the trial, I'll barely be at home at all.'

'So you want me to take her off your hands?'

'I wouldn't put it like that.'

'The answer's no. You both made your bed – made me the bad guy, ganged up on me – now you need to lie in it.'

'This isn't a pissing contest, for Christ's sake. This is about her care. My job—'

'Your time is not more precious than anyone else's. You chose to come between Hannah and me, and these are the consequences. When she's had her fun, she'll come home again.

You wait and see. But I'm not going to be made out to be the bad person here by demanding she does.'

I go to respond, but she cuts me off.

'Now if you'll excuse me, I have to go out.'

She ends the call before I am able to utter another word, and I am left listening to the endless tone shrilling in my ear. I replace the phone back on the dock with a sigh and rub my tired face.

'Sleeping on the job?'

I jolt up in my chair. Artie is stood in the doorway leaning against the frame, his smirk slanted across his face.

'No,' I snap. 'I was thinking.'

'Let me take a load off then. Fill me in. What's your argument for Mr Darling's case?'

'I'm not really in the mood, Artie.'

'Oh come on,' he says, and perches on the edge of the desk. 'You know old Artie likes to be kept in the loop.'

He peers down at me in his usual way, before glancing over the open law books on my desk. He wants to know how I'll defend my client. Except, I hadn't been looking for ways to defend him. I had been researching ways to condemn him. The last thing I need is Artie picking my plan apart.

My work phone rings. I briefly hope it's Maggie, calling to change her mind, and fumble for the receiver.

'Yes?'

'Neve. It's Antony.'

'Antony, good morning.' I wave Artie away, who chuckles to himself and gives me a salute, before heading for the door.

'I've heard from Mr Darling,' Antony says. 'He wants to speak to us at midday.'

I hold my breath, willing him not to utter the words I know are coming.

'Oh?'

'He wants to talk about Alex Finch.' I can practically hear him grinning down the phone. 'I think he's going to tell us something important.'

My heart sinks.

'Right,' I say, and cough nervously. 'I'll be there.'

I hang up the phone and sigh into my hands.

This is it. The moment I've been dreading. The point where Wade reveals his hand, and I have to deliver my own in response. Whatever he is about to tell us, I won't be able to keep Antony from asking all the questions he's wanted to about Alex Finch, which will be a direct chance for us to show the police investigation in a suspicious light. That's unless I blow it out of the water with the truth about Mr Darling's past.

I take a deep breath, hold it in my chest, before finally letting it unfurl.

I don't have to do anything yet. All I have to do is listen to what he has to say.

But deep down, I know. I know that whatever he is about to put to us will push me to act; to defend me, defend Hannah.

It will come down to him or us.

⚖

Antony and I sit across from Mr Darling in the same seats as before.

Wade looks more prepared this morning. He has dressed and showered ahead of time, shaved off his stubble, styled his hair, put on a crisp white shirt and dark jeans. He looks ready. Almost as if he has an objective of his own for this meeting.

I try to keep the panic suppressed, smothered behind a

professional smile, silently willing him not to take us down a path from which we can't return.

'Thank you for coming,' he says, in a low, serious tone. 'I'm sorry I haven't been more open with you during the past few meetings. I had my reasons, but now I see it's the only way.'

He glances at his mother, and I wonder what they talked about in our absence. I had hoped Marianne would urge him to push back the trial, but clearly it backfired. Instead, it seems she has talked him into opening up. I sit before him, bracing myself for the inevitable blow.

He takes a deep breath.

'I didn't want to talk about Alex Finch, not because of our business dealings, but because of my family. My wife, in particular.' He looks down at his hands, lacing them together on the table top. 'I told you that Alex Finch wanted my wife. But what I didn't tell you was that, for a time, she wanted him too.' He clears his throat, averting his eyes momentarily before meeting mine and mine alone. 'They had an affair.'

My heart jumps with the blow. If Alex Finch was sexually involved with Yolanda, and their relationship went sour, it takes the heat off Wade as the sole suspect. His defence just grew remarkably stronger.

You stupid fool. You've damned us both.

The silence has ticked on, with neither Anthony nor I saying a word. Anthony is the first to speak.

'Why didn't you tell anyone about this before?'

'I didn't want to give the prosecution a motive for murder,' he replies, matter-of-factly. 'And I didn't want my wife to be disgraced before the nation. She would die all over again if she knew that people knew of her indiscretion. They would judge not only the type of woman and wife she was, but what kind of mother she was. Our children were her world. I couldn't do that to her, even after everything she had done to me.'

'You didn't want to give the prosecution a motive,' Antony repeats. 'As in, if you disclosed that your wife was having an affair with your business partner, you would have had cause to kill them?'

'That's one way the prosecution could have spun it, yes.'

I am still sat in silence, unable to bring myself to speak, to force encouragement from my lips when all I want to do is beg him to take back the words. To undo the mayhem he has unknowingly caused. He has hooped his own noose without even knowing it.

'Can someone else confirm this?' I say, my voice strained. 'I find it odd that the police didn't find evidence of the affair during their investigation.'

'My former business partner, for a start.'

'And if he denies it?'

'Then the evidence will speak for itself.'

He reaches for the empty chair next to him, and lifts a wad of pages from the seat and puts them on the table.

'Their phone records.'

Antony and I stare down at the files in disbelief.

'Alex ordered new work phones for our employees and added two extra plans to the order, so that he and Yolanda could contact one another without being caught. The police didn't find Yolanda's, what with it being incinerated in the fire and the phone plan being on the business account under a different name. If they looked through Alex's work phone, they wouldn't have found anything. Although I don't believe they looked into him much at all. They suspected me from the very beginning.'

I look to Antony; his eyes are bright with hope.

'May we see them?'

He hands over the documents, a fat wad of pages containing hours and hours of communication. This couldn't have been a mere dalliance. This was a long, committed relationship. I turn the first page and begin to read.

'The affair started three years ago,' Wade says. 'Alex and I would go on group holidays with our families. Their kids, our kids. It worked well for a number of years. Perhaps some of our best memories were on those trips. It was the trip to Alicante that they first slept together. They did it right under our noses. Emily, Alex's wife, was pregnant with their third child at the time. Their full-blown affair began on our return.'

Antony reads out a text message, dating back to 2017.

'Come to the office. W's out. I want to fuck you over his desk until you come all over my—'

He clears his throat and looks up, cheeks flushing, before continuing to read in silence. I watch as Wade tries to compose himself after what he has just heard. He takes a deep breath and sighs it from his nostrils.

'We went on one last holiday after that. They had been together a year by then. They were at it like rabbits, according to the text messages. They were messaging one another while we were all sat around the pool. Feeling each other up beneath the table in restaurants, the same table where our children were sitting.

'It was in 2018 that things got more complicated. Alex wanted more. He said he would leave Emily, his wife, and that Yolanda should do the same to me and the kids, so they could be together openly. He would leave the business, start his own – likely planning to take half our clientele with him, knowing him. But Yolanda didn't want that. This was in August, a few months before the murders.'

I skim towards the month. The texts are noticeably colder. Alex is sending far more, while Yolanda responds with short, sharp replies.

> Meet me at the usual place and time.

> *No. I love my husband*

> Sure seemed like it when you were fucking me.

> What would W think of that? That I had you more times in a year than he had? Doesn't sound like love to me

> *Stop. I love my husband. My children.*

> Or what? Usual place. 8pm.

'He became obsessive,' Wade says. 'Alex doesn't like being told no. He was a nightmare to have as a business partner, in that respect. And Yolanda learned the same lesson.'

He relays the story calmly, but beneath the surface, I can see the rage. His jaw flexes whenever he says Alex's name.

'How did you find out?' I ask.

'A member of staff brought these records to me during the annual audit in 2018,' he says. 'She found the phones on the bill but couldn't trace them to any of my employees, so she looked a little deeper and saw the content. Due to their unprofessional nature, she raised her concerns.'

'And you knew it was your wife?' Antony asks.

'Yes.' He clears his throat. 'The initials they used for themselves, and for me and Emily; the way my wife's accent worked into her text messages. Alex's usual pushy tone he uses across the board.'

'And how did you react?'

His eyes fall to the surface of the table.

'I was devastated. Angry initially.'

'When you say you were angry,' Antony says. 'How did you express that?'

'I didn't. I was at work, at my desk, staring through the glass partition to Alex's office across from mine. He smiled at me, and I forced one back.'

Tears fill his eyes. He blinks them away, swipes them from his face with the back of his hand.

'Did you tell Yolanda that you knew of their affair?'

'Not for a long time. I didn't want her to leave me. I hoped she would get tired of the game they were playing, and eventually come back to me.'

A client discovers his wife and business partner have had a three-year affair right under his nose, and instead of expressing anger, he lets them continue. His business partner allegedly ran their business into the ground and stole his wife, and he is only mentioning this now, in the final days before the trial. No matter how well he expresses his story, a jury won't believe it. Not unless Alex's motive for murder eclipses his.

'What do you believe happened the night your family were killed?' Antony asks. 'Who do you think the masked figure was?'

He sits quietly in contemplation, as if he is choosing the right words before he opens his mouth.

'Alex Finch ruined my life. He took Yolanda away from me, he destroyed my business, and then he took what mattered most of all: he killed my family in cold blood, and left me alive. To take the fall, yes. But I know Alex – he would have wanted me to feel this agony. Alex Finch is responsible for this – I would bet my life on it.

'The man I saw in my house. The man who knew the code to the front gates and to my gun room, the man who knew my favourite gun, and the rooms where my family and I slept ... He is the only person who could have done this.'

Antony and I stare at him from the other side of the table, stunned by the bombshell.

'What would his motive be, to destroy your life like this?' Antony asks.

'He has always wanted what I had. When I got a girlfriend, he got one too. When I proposed to Yolanda, he proposed to Emily the month after. When Yolanda and I had Phoebe, he and Emily began trying. When I decided I wanted to start my own business, he worked his way into it until it was his too. We have been best friends since we were at university; I just thought he was insecure and competitive – I didn't realise how obsessed he was until it was too late. He had stolen my wife, driven my business into the ground after running it like a fuck-ing Ponzi scheme and keeping me away from the books. And before you ask why I didn't insist on seeing them, on keeping a better eye on my business – I didn't because I trusted him. I trusted him with my life.

'Alex grew up in a world where he was never told no. He got what he wanted his whole life. Yolanda was probably the first person to truly reject him.'

'And your children?' I ask. 'Why would he hurt them?'

'He knew that would hurt me the most.'

I take a sip of water, needing a minute to process my thoughts. The glass shakes in my hand. He thinks he is saving himself by telling us this. But in actuality he is digging himself a deeper hole and dragging me down with him. I return the glass to the surface of the table.

'The most important question here is why you waited until now to expose this. You don't owe him or your wife anything, after they betrayed you. I say this because it could appear that you're using Alex as your scapegoat just before the trial starts. So why did you wait so long? Why should the jury believe you?'

His eyes flicker, perhaps with a memory.

'When I discovered the gravity of the situation – the affair, the state of the business – I plunged into a deep depression. My whole life had turned out to be a lie, and there was one sole man responsible. Alex sat at the seat of the fire like a cancer, eating away at everything I loved. I didn't tell anyone this because I knew how it would make me look, if it was brought up in court.

'Three days before the murders, I invited Alex to come hunting with me. We went into the woods and walked a while. He was on edge; he must have sensed that I knew what he and Yolanda had been doing. I had called him out to the woods to tell him everything I knew: the affair, his part in the failure of the business. Everything. I wanted to hear it from him, but before we could get into it, he tracked the buck I had been after for months – the most beautiful thing you've ever seen. I didn't want him taking another prized possession from me.

'He tracked it to the edge of woodland, and as we walked, space grew between us, approaching the buck from both sides, before stopping and raising our guns. I remember it so vividly. I could see his breath in the air each time he exhaled, the rosy tip of his nose from the cold. He raised his gun, aiming between the trees. And I raised mine. Towards him.'

I brace myself, trying not to let my reaction show. His eyes have become razor-focused as he recounts the tale, as if he is peering at his target in the crosshairs of his rifle.

'Alex caught sight of me in the corner of his eye, and we stood like this for what felt like hours. I knew what he had done, and he knew he had reached the end of the road. He had taken everything from me, or so I thought at the time, before the murders happened. And yet I couldn't bring myself to do it. However much I wanted him to pay for what he had done to me, no matter how much I wanted him gone – I couldn't do it. I raised the gun and shot in the air. He practically jumped out of his skin, and the buck scarpered. We walked back to the grounds in silence, and before he left . . . I said something I would regret.'

'What did you say?' Antony asks, engrossed in the tale.

'I said if he ever came near me or my family again, I wouldn't hesitate. I would kill him on sight.'

The room thrums with tension. It is so quiet I can hear the faint nasal breaths from Antony at my side, hear a clock ticking from another room.

'That's why I didn't mention it until now,' he says. 'I threatened to kill him, with the very gun that would be used to kill my family three days later. My lawyers at the time, Eddie and Adrian, advised me to submit no comment. But the longer I went without mentioning it, the more I realised I would look like I was spinning a lie if I were to bring it up so late in the process. But now I know the country will think me a killer either way.'

Of course. Adrian and Eddie Chester would have led Wade down the wrong path, knowing how guilty he would look should he bring up the only thing that could exonerate him later.

A single thought makes me break out in a cold sweat.

Is Wade innocent?

'Alex Finch wanted everything I had,' Wade says, his voice hoarse. 'And when he couldn't take it for himself, he made sure to take it away from me.'

We sit, reeling in the silence. My guilt grows at the thought of his innocence. He trusts me to save him, to do the right thing, and the entire time I have been thinking of ways to save my own neck. But as Antony and I look at one another, I know he has had the same revelation as me.

Adrian missed something crucial when he was appointed to the defence. He had wanted to bury this because he saw it as a way for them to undermine the police investigation, providing a strong defence for Mr Darling. He saw his ultimatum as black and white, but what lies before us now is the most beautiful shade of grey.

To Wade's confusion, I smile.

He doesn't know it, but he might have just saved us both.

21

I stride down the street from Mrs Darling's address, tuning out the sound of Antony's incessant chatter as he matches my stride, jittery with adrenaline. I had thought the evidence proving Wade Darling's innocence would make my objective harder. Now I realise how wrong I was.

'This evidence of the affair with Yolanda,' Antony says. 'It throws everything the police have concluded into question. It shows how little they have searched for other suspects. This isn't just an oversight, it's a failed police investigation, which means—'

'There is a chance I could call for the case to be thrown out.'

'Exactly,' he beams, grinning wildly. 'It's perfect. Fucking perfect.'

I feel so on edge; the excitement is electric. But my anxiety has me doubting this sudden possibility of freedom. Could it really be so simple? The Messenger said I had to lose the trial – but I wouldn't need to if there was no trial at all. Wade and I could *both* walk free.

'Is the evidence admissible at this point?' Antony asks.

'The judge won't throw this out, it's too strong. The fact that the police didn't investigate Alex Finch as a suspect means the prosecution cannot definitively prove the investigation has been thoroughly carried out. They cannot prove, without a shadow of a doubt, that Wade committed the crimes.'

Hearing me say the words aloud makes the opportunity seem all the more tangible. I have the overwhelming need for something sugary and full of carbs, and try to think back to when I last ate.

'But what if the judge does reject it?' he asks. 'There is so much media attention around this. To then have it thrown out right before commencement after so many delays . . . the courts would be made a fool of.'

He's right. Every pair of eyes in the country is on this case. It's mentioned every night on the six o'clock news, featured on every newspaper front page. The growing uproar from protestors and women's rights groups. One can't pass a newspaper stand without having Wade Darling's face stare back at them.

'Then I will have to make my argument completely airtight,' I reply, a nervous rasp to my voice. We stop at the fork in the road. 'I need you to look into this former employee who found the call records – we'll need her as a witness if the case goes to trial. The judge would be hard pushed to not admit a new witness at this stage if he plans to press ahead with the prosecution's case the way it is.'

'Got it,' he replies, nodding excitedly. 'When will you call the judge?'

'I'm going to do it right this second.'

He grins, visually exhilarated by the prospect ahead. I can't help but smile back, and take the pack of cigarettes from my pocket.

'Thought you didn't smoke anymore?' he asks through a smirk.

'This close to trial, all bets are off.'

We part ways as I head east towards the tube station, my pace growing faster and faster, dragging on the cigarette as I go. This is my get-out clause. I won't need to sabotage the trial because there won't be one. I can lay the blame at the judge's feet, telling the Messenger that it was orchestrated without my knowledge, that the Viklund family could appeal, and get the case back to court. Only I would make sure to be long gone by then.

I don't want to lose my life in London and the career I've built, to lose the only family I have ever known in Hannah and Maggie, but I won't be able to stay here waiting for the Messenger to reappear. I'll need to cover my tracks, find a way to keep Hannah safe, and then get the hell out of this city.

But first things first. I slip my phone from my pocket and scroll for the number of Judge McConnell's office.

'I'm sorry, Your Honour. But I thought it best to bring this to you immediately.'

The judge stares at me from behind his desk. He looks angry, resentful even, but as the information sinks in, his shoulders sag and his eyes close with a heavy-bodied sigh. He slips off his glasses and pinches the bridge of his nose.

Calling a judge into work over the weekend doesn't set up one's chance of success in one's argument well, but with the trial looming, it is the only chance I have to bring the new evidence to light. Despite his frustration at being torn away from his Sunday plans, I can see the necessity of the meeting settling in.

Niall is sat in stunned silence beside me. I can feel him practically vibrating with rage at my pulling the rug from under him. I had sent the damning phone records electronically to his chambers shortly before the meeting, knowing full well he wouldn't have time to read them; his clerk might not have even opened the email yet. But had he done his due diligence, he wouldn't have been caught out. His ego thought he had the win in the bag.

'I'd like to see the phone records,' Judge McConnell says.

I pass the wad of paper over the desk, hole-punched and arranged in a binder.

'I would like to see them too, of course,' Niall adds sharply.

'I sent them to your chambers electronically, but here is a physical copy for you.'

I pass another copy towards him, and watch his cheeks burn red. He isn't a man who reacts well to being duped, and I can see the words he wished he could call me burning in his eyes.

We sit in the silence of the judge's chambers, with nothing but the tick of the clock and the soft, whistling nasal breaths of the judge as he reads.

Sat before the judge, I feel my confidence in my plan begin to waver. Suppose he won't throw the case out to protect his own hide? He'll want to be on this case as much as Niall does – the notoriety, the cemented reputation. Dismissing the case certainly won't carry the same merit. There is right and wrong of course, but in the end, we are all walking, talking egos, wanting our moment in the spotlight.

This has to work. It is the only arsenal I have.

My palms grow damp in my lap, and I fight to wipe them dry in case either of the men see. Sat beside me, Niall is flitting through the pages of the text messages, the paper sounding like a cracking whip with each violent flick. His breathing grows faster and shallower the more he reads.

Judge McConnell drops the binder on the surface of the desk.

'For crying out loud.'

His professionalism slips only briefly, as the credibility of the evidence hits him. He shuts his eyes for a few seconds, emits a sigh, and opens them again.

'Am I to believe you didn't have these tucked away for this precise moment before the trial?'

'Some trick,' Niall adds.

'No trick,' I reply. 'Just a scared client who has finally opened up with the right counsel.'

'What sort of man tries to bury evidence that could get him let off bloody murder charges?' Niall asks with a scoff.

I turn my eyes to the judge, refusing to reply. If Niall wants to know the answer to that, he'll need to discover it when cross-examining my witnesses, if he gets the chance.

'I might ask you what sort of police investigation doesn't uncover a lousily covered-up affair and a clear alternative suspect to boot,' Judge McConnell rebuts.

Niall and I both sit in silence, waiting for the judge to continue.

'This isn't . . . ideal,' he says. 'In fact, it's a bloody nightmare. The CPS will look like a laughing stock. The press and the public will inevitably go mad.'

'And an innocent man will go free,' I add.

'Don't push it,' he snaps, and sighs once more, his eyes falling on the binder of text messages on his desk. 'I will need to think about this.'

'Of course,' I reply, and turn to glance at Niall. He can't even meet my eyes any longer. His hands are curled into fists in his lap.

'We will go ahead as planned tomorrow unless I say otherwise,' Judge McConnell says. 'My office will leave word in the morning.'

'Yes, Your Honour,' Niall and I reply in unison.

The judge glances towards the door and back again – our time is up. As soon as we step out of the judge's office, Niall is on me.

'That was so fucking dirty, Harper. You could have given me a heads-up.'

'If you'd done your job properly, I wouldn't have had to.'

His face boils red, cheeks the colour of pigskin.

'He won't pull it,' he says, stepping so close to me I can smell his breath. 'You really think he'll dismiss the trial, after all this time? Right before it's set to start? He'd look a fool, we all would.'

'Not all of us.'

He is practically shaking now, his livid eyes set firmly upon mine. I can't say it doesn't please me to see him so rattled. He is one of those men who need to be knocked down a peg or two every so often to keep them falling victim to their ever inflating ego.

I watch as he storms off towards the doors, and huff out a relieved sigh.

McConnell has to throw out the trial. He'll look like a crony if he doesn't.

All I have to do now is wait.

'Ms Harper?'

I open my eyes. The judge's clerk is stood in the doorway of the office.

'Sorry, I have a man on the phone for you. He said he's been trying to contact you at your chambers, but keeps missing you.'

'Who is it?' I ask.

'A Mr Hurst.'

Fredrick.

'You can take it in my office.'

'Thanks.'

I follow her inside, my palms tingling by my sides. What could be so urgent for him to call me through the judge? The clerk holds out the phone, and I rest it to my ear.

'Neve Harper.'

'Neve, I'm glad I've tracked you down.' I had expected his usual cool tone, but there is an unusual buzz of excitement to his voice. 'I've found something.'

I arrive at the decided meeting spot, a bench looking out at Tower Bridge on the north side of the Thames, and find that I am the first one there.

The air is sharp, and the evening is dark with that unmistakable tang of winter on the breeze, similar to burning cinder. The path along the river is quiet. Only the odd person passes me by. The majority of the time I am alone, watching the bustling city reflect its light in the chopping river. Fredrick, however, is nowhere to be seen.

I wait for ten minutes, then fifteen. The chill of the bench has leached into my thighs until I am shivering beneath my coat, and the sound of my chattering teeth fill my ears.

My phone makes me jump. I had meant to turn it off, to keep from being followed. I silently curse myself as I slip it from my pocket. It's Artie.

'How's my favourite barrister?' he asks when I answer.

'Busy,' I reply.

'I'm sure you've got time to run an update by me, after your not-so-subtle brush-off this morning. I'll get one of the lackeys to go and get you a coffee tomorrow if you're nice to me.'

I warm to his playfulness and lean back in my seat.

'Well, if you must know, I might have just successfully ended the trial before it's even begun.'

There is a beat of silence before he speaks. When he does, the playfulness has gone from his tone. 'What do you mean?'

'I mean, the CPS screwed up. The police investigation ignored a clear alternative suspect in the murders, placing all of their bets on our client, and the CPS failed to spot it. I ran the evidence by the judge and he's contemplating whether to throw the trial as we speak.'

'What evidence?' he asks.

'Text messages between the defendant's business partner, Alex Finch, and the defendant's wife Yolanda, revealing an affair. She ended it – to his dissatisfaction – and then there's the clincher: Finch's wife filed for divorce just before the murders. A motive for his business partner to enact revenge is just as strong as the case of familicide against our client, and the police failed to investigate it. At this point there's no case to try, it shouldn't have even got this far.'

Artie doesn't react like I might expect. I had expected him to laugh, or speak through his usual grin. But the silence rings out on the other side of the phone.

'Don't you lot run anything by me anymore?'

'I thought you'd be pleased.'

'Well, it's hardly a victory, is it? All this momentum, fizzling out at the last second due to what, a technicality? It's a win by default.'

'Well, I'm sorry if the defence of my client's best interests is disappointing to you, Artie, but I have to say I didn't really consider your score card when I was weighing up the thought of striking three life sentences from my client's future. What's the problem? Put a bet on us for the win, did you?'

'I'm not saying it wasn't the right decision, miss – you know best – but these big decisions, surely you'd want to run it by one of us before jumping into action?'

'Who's the advocate for the defendant, Arthur, me or you?'

He clears his throat.

'You are, miss.'

'Would you like the job instead?'

'No, miss.'

'Then I suggest you let me get on with it.'

I hang up the phone and sigh the frustration out of me. Whatever I do, whatever I say, I have a man giving me his two cents. If it isn't Antony, it's Artie. If not the judge, then Niall. There is Wade, and then there is the Messenger. The only man I truly want to hear from is Fredrick, and he is still nowhere to be seen.

I check my watch. Almost twenty minutes late. As long as I've known him, he has always been on time. My imagination runs rampant, thinking of all the things that could have held him up.

Stop panicking. He said he'd be here, so he'll be here.

I turn off my phone and dislodge the battery. There had been nothing from him, but then there wouldn't be, with the risk of the Messenger keeping track of me. What if Fredrick has left me a message at chambers changing the location? What if I got the time wrong? My thoughts continue like this, round and round, my shoulders knotted with nerves.

I wait until thirty-five minutes have passed and my fingers appear almost blue, until I cannot bring myself to wait another minute more.

Maybe he's found something about the Viklunds that scared him off.

I walk back the way I came and towards the main road, my

eyes down and bracing myself from the cold. That's when I see the flash of headlights behind me, and look up.

That must be him.

I sigh with relief, and instantly feel my heart begin to calm, as I pick up the pace and head towards the roadside. I reach the driver's window and watch the glass lower.

The Messenger stares back at me.

'Get in,' he says.

⚖

Thirty minutes have passed by the time we enter the abandoned industrial estate. I am sat in the back of the Messenger's car, with a large burly man squeezed in beside me. In the front sits another man, with the Messenger behind the wheel. No one has said a word since I got inside the car.

The estate sits a stone's throw from the Thames. A landscape of grime and discarded oil drums, bronze with rust, with the teasing gleam of central London in the distance, which is quickly enveloped by the fog creeping in from the water; I can smell it on the breeze from the driver's open window: the faint lingering scent of salt and scum.

The buildings have been graffitied and vandalised, and every pane of glass has been smashed. As the car turns in, the headlights cast over the glint of broken bottles and rusting beer cans, the red beady eyes of pigeons peering through the windows from their perches in the rafters. The car moves at a crawl over the potholes pitted in the tarmac, making my racing heart jolt out of sync with each jutter.

I hear a thud from the boot behind my seat. It isn't the first time I've heard this sound. Every few minutes, I feel the sensation against my back; hear it at each stop light as we squeal to a halt. I think of a cannister of fuel rolling back and forth, sloshing its stink into the fabric. Or maybe it's a gun and a shovel chiming against one another in a morbid death call.

I should have run.

The car passes warehouse after warehouse, driving at a crawl towards the water's edge. As we get closer, two men appear through the mist, stood before a dock that slowly peters out into the fog. They are dressed entirely in black, their faces void and their eyes seemingly on me, piercing through the windscreen to where I sit in the back seat, crammed between the door and the wide-shouldered stranger. The view of the city has been engulfed by the fog.

I feel my bladder clench. My kneecaps are chiming together like teeth and my pulse is so fast that a wave of nausea ripples up my throat. Fear has a scent to it: the salt of sweat, tinged with something sweet and rotten. I taste it in my mouth, smell it on my breath.

The car pulls to a stop and rocks back and forth with the shifting weight as the doors open and close. I am led out roughly, the man's grip pinching at my arm through my sleeve, but I don't make a sound. Despite the terror coursing through me, I have the overwhelming need for them to think me stronger than I am.

The air smells of rotten fish and pollution, and at my feet, oil shimmers in the puddles in the pitted concrete ground. As we near the men, I feel the mist wet my face.

The Messenger stops in his tracks and turns to face me, that familiar smile cutting into his cheeks.

'Do you know why I brought you here?'

I hear another bang from the boot of the car and think of the cannister of fuel, the gun and spade.

I shake my head.

'Let's remind her,' he calls behind us.

I hear the boot door open. The click of the lock and the air-pressured whine of the mechanism as it rises. It is hard to see through the slips of mist drifting in our path, but I hear a bang, a grunt. Shadows move amid the fog. And then they appear.

Fredrick is dragged into view by the two men the Messenger and I made the journey with, his feet trailing beneath him. His hands are zip-tied in front of him and his eyes are wide with shock. I have never seen someone so pale. I know in an instant that I have killed him by bringing him into this. More blood on my hands. Adrenaline courses through me with such ferocity that I feel it tingling all over my skin, in my eyes, my tongue. When Fredrick parts his lips and coughs, blood splutters down his chin. The banging I had heard had been him, locked inside the boot. So close yet out of reach.

'Still not sure?' the Messenger asks with a grin. 'Do you remember what I told you about Adrian Whittaker? About him trying to outsmart us?'

I try to swallow, but my mouth is bone-dry.

'... Yes.'

The Messenger thrusts me towards the dock, the shock of it forcing all of the air from my lungs. I find my footing and look out at the mist.

'Walk,' the Messenger says.

So I walk. I head into the fog in a death march; the dock creaks with each step, the cold brown water lapping around its pillars, spitting up through the cracks. I can hear the Messenger behind me; the calm pattern to his breathing. The planks are so rotten that I fear each slab of wood will give beneath my feet, and I can feel the dock shifting with our weight. Ahead is nothing but a thick wall of mist, until I approach the end, and shadows appear, black shapes morphing into silhouettes. Two more men stand at the edge, with indecipherable objects at their feet. I slow as I see them, and feel a prod in my spine as the Messenger urges me on. At their feet, I realise, are concrete cinderblocks and chains.

My heart leaps. I instinctively step back, only to turn and meet the Messenger's chest with a thud. I feel the heat of him, the thrum of his heart beneath his clothes. His musk gets stuck in my nostrils. Behind him, Fredrick is being dragged along the dock, his feet strumming against the planks until they pass us and reach the edge, and he is thrust down to his knees. He is eerily silent, as if he too is trying to appear braver than he is. Death chops in waves before him, and still, he doesn't beg. He doesn't ask why. He stares off into the fog as the men jostle about him, looping the chains around his torso, through his bound limbs and over his neck.

'He didn't know . . .' I stutter. Fear has me in a chokehold. The words come out strained. 'This was all my doing. He didn't know what I was getting him into—'

'Neve,' Fredrick warns, urging me into silence. One of the men punches him in the back of the head. I yelp at the sound of the brain-juddering thwack, and bite my lip to stop myself from speaking in case I cause him more pain.

The chains rattle as they criss-cross around Fredrick's body, as the waiting water chops incessantly. The cinderblocks are pushed to the very edge of the dock.

I want to tell them to stop, to allow me a moment to catch my breath and think of ways to reason with them. But as I go to speak, the words lodge in my throat. I'm too terrified to utter a word, even as I beg my lips to part.

The two men drag Fredrick to his feet, and I look up at the

Messenger towering by my side. He meets my eyes with a grin. This is my opportunity to say something, to stop this from happening. But just as I finally part my lips to speak, and as a desperate croak slips up my throat, he turns away and with a nod of his head says, 'Do it.'

The men kick the blocks from the edge.

'No!'

Fredrick is yanked from the dock. A quick flash, and then he is gone. The dark water envelopes him whole.

The Messenger grabs the nape of my neck and propels me towards the edge, a splintered scream bursting from my lips. I am led with my head down, hair whipping into my eyes, until my face is held directly over the water where Fredrick fell.

He is going to make me watch.

The water is choppy and wild, bubbles rising from Fredrick's lungs, but I can't see him through the filth in the water, only the tips of his fingers breaking through the surface as he tries to claw himself up and draw breath. But I know that beneath, he will be staring up with those stark blue eyes, kicking and thrashing helplessly against the chains.

'This is what happens when you don't listen,' the Messenger whispers.

The bubbles grow scarcer and scarcer. From the thrashing in the water, I sense Fredrick's movements slow. I wait as life leaves him, and his body falls still, until finally, it's clear he has passed, lolling against the pull of the chains beneath the surface. My tears splash silently into the water.

I am shaking violently from shock, as if in spasm. I can't stop staring at the surface, imagining those lifeless blue eyes staring back at me.

Then they start fitting chains to me.

I am thrust upwards, and the chains looped over me, through me. My hands are yanked behind my back and tied. I always thought I would beg for my life. Kick and scream and bite. Do all I could to live. But I am frozen to the dock, staring out at the shifting mist, as silent tears run down my cheeks and the chains tighten and tighten, pinching me where they meet at my chest, my back, my thighs.

'Did you think we wouldn't find out about your little trick, trying to have the judge throw the trial?'

The metal weighs me down, and the blocks are moved towards the edge of the dock. I hear a sound, like a puppy's yelp, or a distant siren, and realise it came from me.

How could he possibly know that? I was so careful.

The realisation hits me square in the chest, voiding my lungs of air.

It's over. It's really over.

'You still have a choice,' he says from behind my back. 'You can still get yourself out of this. Wade Darling or you and Hannah, remember?'

I stand before death, biting the flesh of my cheeks to keep from crying out.

Him or us.

Whoosh. Thwack. Whoosh. Thwack.

'Do it,' the Messenger says to the men.

I feel their hands on me; a hard snatch of the chains. They are so strong that I am practically lifted off my feet, waiting to be thrown. I gasp in the mist.

'I'll do it!'

The hands yank me back, and my legs give. I slam down onto the planks. My head knocks against the wood without my hands to break my fall.

The Messenger reaches down and snatches the chains at my back, lifting me up so my ear meets his lips.

'Next time,' he whispers. 'It will be your sweet little Hannah.'

He drops me again with a thud, my brain rattling in my skull. As the men begin unfastening the chains from the blocks, I look down through the cracks in the planks at the chopping water below, imagining Hannah staring up at me. Thrashing silently until the life leaves her eyes.

The day of the trial

I wake up to the sun beaming through the window. I hadn't drawn the curtains before sinking into bed. At least, that's what I guess happened. Everything is a blur. My last memory was of lying on the dock as the chains were pulled from me. I don't remember the journey home, nor slipping my front door key in the lock. Hannah was there, I know that much. I can remember flashes of her, the smile slipping from her face, her lips moving but her words not reaching my ears. *I don't feel well*, I remember saying. But not before knocking back two straight brandies. For the rest of the night, I dreamt that I was drowning, staring up at the Messenger where he stood on the dock above. But as far as I'm aware, I didn't wander in the night. There's that mercy, at least.

I am fully clothed, with my feet still firmly in their heels. The sun is hot on my face, and I squint to look about for my phone. Three missed calls. Voicemails. All from the judge's office. My heart jumps in my chest as I scramble up to a sitting position. I wasn't in my right mind and didn't set an alarm – it is almost nine. I should be in court preparing to begin trial in an hour.

I rub my eyes furiously to rid them of the yellow orbs from the sun and play the voicemail.

'Ms Harper, this is Nicola Bennett calling from Judge McConnell's office. I'm calling regarding the Darling trial set for commencement this morning. Please give me a call back as soon as you can.'

I hang up and bring up the call log on the screen, noticing how the phone shakes violently in my grip.

Personal reputation or not, McConnell can't go ahead with the trial with such an oversight in the police investigation. If we proceed, he must know I could push for there being no case to try, when it comes to the end of the prosecution's case. I wonder which he would find more humiliating in terms of the press.

The judge postponing the trial is my only chance to get out from under the Messenger's hold on me. To form a plan to protect Hannah and me, before the trial recommences again. Otherwise, I have no other choice but to proceed with his demands. Last night was proof of that. I press the phone to my ear and listen to the dialling tone, my heartbeat echoing in the other.

When Nicola answers the call, I notice immediately that she sounds tired and stressed. Her voice is an octave higher than usual.

'Nicola, it's Neve Harper returning your call.'

I hear her sigh with relief on the other end of the line.

'Ms Harper, I was worried I might have missed you. Thank you for calling me back.'

She clears her throat as I wait with bated breath. Whatever comes out of her mouth will determine my fate. Sweat breaks out all over me. I sit in wait, feeling the warm trickle of it running down my ribs.

'Yes, the Darling trial. Judge McConnell has considered your evidence and—'

There is a muffling at the other end of the line, and a distant, tinny voice muttering in the background. My heart is lodged in my throat.

Come on, come on, come on.

'Ms Bennett?'

The line clears.

'Apologies, Ms Harper, it's a bit manic this morning. The press is calling off the hook about this, we can barely keep our phone lines open.'

I sigh silently and rest my head against the headboard. My heart is beating so violently that I can barely focus on my breathing.

'Neve,' she says, in a tone I can't distinguish. 'The judge has decided to proceed with the trial.'

It hits me like a blow. I close my eyes as the panic rips through my every nerve.

Nicola has continued talking, but I've not registered a word, catching only her last sentence.

'. . . it seems someone leaked the possibility of a mistrial to the press.'

Niall.

It was a genius counter-move. The only thing that could have kept the judge from dropping the trial would be to throw his reputation to the wolves of the press. By having them threaten to slander his character and reputation before he'd made the call on whether to proceed, it would almost definitely affect his judgement and overall decision.

I imagine Niall getting the same news, the inevitable grin sweeping across his face.

'Right,' I reply, trying to compose myself.

'Sorry, Neve – it was a close call.'

'Thanks.'

I hang up and sit in silence.

We are going to trial.

The fear crushes down upon my chest, until I am shaking from head to foot, and tears wet my eyes. I force myself to breathe, taking small sips of air.

It's Wade's freedom or mine.

A knock at my bedroom door jolts me from my thoughts.

'Come in,' I force.

Hannah's face peers through the gap in the door.

'Are you okay?' she asks. 'You looked really bad last night.'

Her complexion is pale, and her eyes are wide with worry. I would feel guilty for troubling her, did my fear not have its hands wrapped about my neck, squeezing the life out of me.

'Fine,' I reply. 'Shouldn't you be at school?'

'I don't feel good either,' she says, her voice turning child-like, almost baby-ish. 'Maybe I have the same bug as you.'

I doubt it.

I don't have the capacity to take this on; I don't have the mental space to call the school and report her sick, nor jump through any other hurdles they might put in my way. If she wants to play truant, I'll let her.

'I'm running late,' I say, and clamber out of bed. 'Do I need to call and let them know? Or will they get the message if you don't show?'

'Don't worry about it,' she says.

So I don't. I grab my towel from where I'd let it dry on the radiator and head towards the bathroom when I hear a knock at the front door. Hannah and I both freeze.

'Are you expecting anyone?' I ask.

She shakes her head.

I pass her for the stairs, my heart hammering as fast as my feet, as the knocking picks up again. I reach the bottom, notice how bad I look in the mirror above the mantle. My hair is wild from sleep, with dark circles framing my eyes. I don't look like myself, but like a creature. Wild. Dangerous.

The knocking starts up again.

I open the door. A man dressed in an orange fluorescent jacket stands before me. My eyes drift from his face to the name of the company he works for above his breast. *Thameslink.* On the other side of the road, another man in the same jacket knocks on the door of number forty-five.

'Yes?' I ask.

'Sorry to disturb you, madam. We're just doing the rounds to confirm the railworks commencing this week.'

I stare at him, a piercing whistle screaming down both ears. *Did he just say . . .*

'Madam? I'm confirming the railworks behind your property.'

'W-what railworks?'

'We sent a notice to each resident last month.'

'No you didn't,' I stutter angrily.

'We delivered them by hand, madam. This is just a courtesy call to confirm—'

'I didn't get a letter,' I repeat, as if that will change anything.

'I'm sorry for that, madam. Perhaps you thought it was a piece of junk mail?'

As if that matters now. The taste of bile is rising up my throat. I raise a shaky hand to it.

'What . . . what works are you doing?'

Whoosh. Thwack. Whoosh. Thwack.

'We will be laying a new track alongside the existing line.'

'But surely there isn't room—'

'We've had permission to remove the trees on the far side,' he says. 'This was quite the hot topic last year. There was a meeting with the local residents. Have you lived here long?'

I have gone completely cold.

'Yes. I ... was distracted. I have a demanding job. When does this work commence?'

'Today, madam—'

'*Stop calling me madam!*'

His eyes widen, and his colleague across the street peers over his shoulder at the commotion.

'When will you be removing the trees from behind my address?'

'This will be the first task, but I'm afraid it would be difficult to estimate when—'

My mind is reeling so fast that I can barely pin a thought down. Only one persists: Matthew, rotting in the ground. I stare at the man in a blind panic.

'Apologies for any inconvenience, mada—' he stops himself with a nervous cough, before trundling off to the house next door. I click the door shut.

The body.

They are going to unearth the body.

PART II

The Prosecution

Day One

24

The weather is ice-cold. The sort of air that feels wet with each breath. Londoners pass me by in a huddle of rustling coats and coiled scarves as I stand before the Old Bailey, looking up at the ray of sunlight breaking through the clouds and beaming upon the Bailey's dome, illuminating Lady Justice where she stands in all her bronze-gilded glory. A sword in one hand, scales in the other. She represents blind justice: fairness, honesty, integrity. Everything I do not.

I don't think I truly realised what I am to face until now. Before hearing the news about the trial this morning from the judge's office, there seemed to be a window of hope where I thought I might still wriggle out of it. A point where a clear route of escape would open up before me. But time has run out, Fredrick is dead, the trial is about to begin, and now of course, there's the matter of the body.

I have always feared this day would come.

When I had buried him there, it was not with the notion that it would be forever. He was too close to home, literally and figuratively, and if he were found, fingers would inevitably point towards me. But once the deed was done, I couldn't find the strength to go through with it again. Now I fear I have left it too late.

The panic is sudden and overwhelming. I clench my fists to ground myself.

I can't think of that now. I must tackle one problem at a time.

My other problem stands before me. I peer up at Lady Justice, gleaming from her perch.

I have never knowingly lost a case before. Never jeopardised a client's fate for my own. Not just because I love my job, but because I'm tied to a strict view of right and wrong. This is my comeuppance for tipping the scales. The consequences of my crime.

The evidence I have against my client is nestled safely in my carry case. It is as if I can feel the weight of it, the pull of my guilt. But whenever it becomes too much, I think of Hannah, and my fear for her safety drowns out everything else. I must find a window in the day to deliver the evidence to the prosecution. I say this to myself factually, devoid of emotion, but as soon as it comes time, I know the fear will grip me, for once I do this, there is no going back. The trial will only end one way.

The press has crowded before the doors. They won't have caught Wade, who was escorted into the building by Antony earlier this morning, but they will expect me to give them something. After Matthew's disappearance, the press and I agreed on an unspoken rule where I would discuss my work but not my personal life. To deny them now would be inviting them to dig deeper into me rather than my client, picking at my life like vultures.

I take a deep breath, my exhalation unfurling in a cloud.

I can do this, I think to myself, in the hope that I'll believe my own lie. *Because I don't have a choice.*

I cross the street towards the doors, bracing myself as the press catch sight of me and begin their onslaught.

There is no going back now.

⚖️

The inside of the Bailey is essentially two worlds: the past and the present. On one side, you have the original building. The same doorways the likes of Myra Hindley and the Krays passed through to face their crimes. Decades of bloodshed tried and sentenced; British history that has bled into the walls. The other side is modern and cold, where the juror chairs don't squeak and the panelled walls on the courtrooms still smell fresh. I can't help but see the similarities between my surroundings and my life. The present ever plagued by the past.

I pass through the building for the de-robing room, listening to the echoes of my heels on the cold hard floor, when I hear the hard clap of footsteps growing louder behind me.

'It appears your trick of attempting to throw the trial didn't go according to plan, Harper,' Niall says behind me, stopping me in my tracks. 'Sorry about that.'

I turn to face him and see the victorious grin on his face. Humility is something Niall never quite mastered.

'Your plan worked though, leaking it to the press. I suppose I owe you congratulations.'

'You can save your congratulations for the end of the trial,' he replies. He steps closer, the smell of coffee lingering on his breath. 'Your theory of the second suspect won't stick – you know that, right?'

With so much at stake in my life, Niall's competitiveness seems childish in comparison. I watched a man die last night. Now I stand before another, watching as he strokes his ego, playing a trivial game of back and forth. I long to care about nothing but the win; to have nothing more at stake. To have this burden lifted from my back. I turn to leave and feel a tug on my arm.

'Are you still playing dirty?' he whispers. 'Any more tricks up your sleeve?'

Having a man so close to me, lay his hand on me – it makes my skin crawl. I cannot help but think of the rough, calloused palms of the Messenger thrusting me towards the dock's edge to watch Fredrick die.

I snatch my arm away, and turn without giving him a response, my stomach somersaulting as I quicken my pace towards the ladies' room.

I push my way into the bathroom and stop before the mirror, waiting to discern if I am alone. All the cubicles are free, and the only sounds to be heard are the incessant drip from the furthest tap, and the quick rush of my breath.

I was too distracted to check how I looked this morning, too terrified to care. But as I stare into my reflection, I wince at the sight of the woman staring back at me. I am deathly pale, and my prominent cheekbones almost make me look gaunt in this lighting. The life has been drained from my eyes.

Despite the trial before me, my mind returns to the body. I can see it in my mind, rising from the earth tangled in tree roots as they are clawed from the ground to make way for the new track. It's one thing to bury a body in plain sight when you have to, but to gamble twice, and do so again, seems far too reckless. But now I have no choice. It's not *if* I will move the body, but *when*.

I have no other choice.

But of course, I do. I could pay for my crimes. I killed my husband, and with murder comes the consequences. I of all people should know that. But then having my life and those I love at risk muddies the water. It isn't just about me paying my price, and Wade receiving a fair trial – it has become something so much bigger. I think of Hannah – so innocent, so pure. So much of her life has yet to be lived. I deserve to pay for what I have done, but Hannah deserves to live. I cannot condemn us both. The Messenger's threats seem all the more real after Fredrick's death. I remember the thrashing of the water as he bucked against the chains, the bubbles from his lungs slowly dissipating on the surface of the water until he went still. I look down at my shaking hands. More blood is upon them now. I might not have fixed the chains about him, or thrust him from the dock. But I killed him. I dragged him into this mess, and now his body is at the bottom of the Thames. I scrunch my eyes shut at the thought of the wild, chopping water. The memory of the Messenger's grip on my neck burns into my skin. I rub the same spot and sigh heavily.

I am so sorry, Fredrick.

My watch ticks quietly at my wrist, the seconds counting down to the commencement of the trial. To the decision I must inevitably make.

The door to the bathroom opens. I straighten up, reach for the tap, and begin washing my hands.

'Good morning.'

I jolt at the sound of his voice. The Messenger stands by the door, the smirk firmly on his face.

'You shouldn't be in here,' I hear myself say.

He releases that vile, smug laugh I've come to expect of him. The arrogance seeps from him, exuded from every sound and movement.

'That's the least of your worries,' he replies, and steps closer.

He doesn't stop until he is behind me, and we stare at each other through the mirror. I can smell his breath as it cascades down upon me: minty fresh, with a hint of tobacco smoke lingering beneath.

'I just wanted to check in on you, after last night,' he says through a smile. 'My buddies didn't think you'd show. They were sure they'd need to man the airports, but I told them you'd come. I said you had the biggest pair of balls on a woman that I'd ever met. I was right, of course.'

I say nothing and look down to turn off the tap when his hands latch onto my head and snap it upwards, until I am staring back through the mirror. His fingers are laced in my hair, the tips digging into my temples and cheeks.

'You understand what will happen if you fail, don't you?' he whispers. 'I've made myself clear?'

His hands squeeze tighter around my head. I can feel the pressure burning into my eyes, my pulse drumming against his palms. His fingers pull at my hair until tears creep into my vision.

'But I suppose prison is the least of your concerns, isn't it? What with young Hannah. Such a pretty girl.'

'I'd kill you,' I whisper.

He cocks a brow. 'Do your job, and nothing will happen to either of you. You have my word.'

'Your word,' I spit. A single tear snakes from my eye, running off his thick, meaty finger. 'I said I'd do it, didn't I?'

'Just making sure you haven't lost your nerve.' He kisses my crown tauntingly, and a wave of nausea rips through me. 'It doesn't look like you have long, either ... not with those rail workers setting up shop behind your house. How long till they dig up your dirty little secret, do you think?'

I feel my entire body stiffen.

Christ, he really does see everything.

'And hey ... if you ever feel yourself wavering in court, or you find yourself forgetting what's at stake, all you have to do is look towards the gallery – I'll be watching.'

The door opens and he quickly drops his hands.

'Oops,' he says to the woman at the door. 'Wrong room.'

He steps out, giving me a wink over his shoulder as he goes.

The woman gives me a concerned look. I nod that I'm okay, and wait until she has used the bathroom and left again before I bolt to the nearest cubicle and vomit.

I wipe my mouth, check myself over in the mirror, and take a deep breath.

My decision is clear to me now. No hope jading my objective. No last-minute saves. I am alone in this, with one objective and one alone: protect Hannah. Even if the consequences are monstrous to me.

Then there is the matter of the body.

I can't deal with this all at once. At the Old Bailey, I will concentrate on the task at hand. Only when I have clocked off will I let myself consider what else is in store for me.

It's time to meet Antony and our client before the trial begins, to go over our plan of action and give our reassurance before making our way to courtroom one.

Then, I will destroy our case from within.

25

Wade Darling is waiting for me at the other end of the corridor, in conference room three.

It's simple enough to concoct a plan for oneself; play out scenarios, set goals. But to execute a plan that is detrimental to another person, all while looking them in the eye, is not so simple at all. I am stood at the top of the corridor, willing my legs to move.

Think of Hannah. Think of the body. Think of what happened to Fredrick. This is why you're doing this. It's us or him.

As the pit of worry grinds into my stomach, I pick up my phone and fire a quick text to Hannah, asking about the progress that's been madewith the railworks, before thrusting my phone back in my bag.

I walk down the corridor as if on autopilot, heading towards conference room three, as my heart rate climbs with each step, and pause before the door, frozen by the prospect of the task that awaits me on the other side.

It's us or him.

I raise a shaking fist to the door, my pulse thundering in my ears, and knock.

'Come in,' Antony muffles behind the door.

Inside, it is a tight cubbyhole of a room, with barely enough space for the desk in the centre of it. There are no windows, no art on the walls. Just a tight, airless space. Both of the men are looking up at me expectantly, waiting for me to join them; Wade is sat on one side of the table, Antony on the other. I take the seat beside Antony and bid them both good morning.

'How are you feeling, Wade?' I ask.

'I've been better.'

He has looked better too. He must have been up the whole night, for he is paler than I have ever seen him, with dark rings around his eyes.

I am about to destroy this man beyond repair.

I dig my nails into my thigh to keep the guilt from engulfing me.

'Well, after our conference yesterday, we have good reason to believe we will win this case,' Antony says. 'We have a game plan now, one that we're all determined to see succeed.'

Antony sits tall and composed, speaking with a firm, reassuring tone. I have known him long enough to be aware that, behind his professional façade, he is as excited as a boy. I peer down beside me. His right leg is restless with anticipation, juddering up and down. I sit forward to speak so I appear engaged, rather than downright terrified.

'I will run through how the day is going to go, Wade, and then I will break down how the trial is set to commence. Then you can ask us any questions you may have.'

Wade nods wordlessly, peering down at his cupped hands on the table. He has begun to trust us more, or at least become more comfortable. When my eyes are drawn to his scars, he doesn't hide his hand beneath the desk like he would have in the beginning. Back when I deserved his trust, before I had been dragged into doing the Messenger's bidding.

'So, this morning will start with the empanelling of the jury. There will be a jury panel of about fifteen or sixteen potential jurors, and twelve names will be called. Before they take their oaths, the names of the witnesses will be run by each of them for any juror to declare if they have a connection with any of the people named – if they do, they will be replaced by one of the remaining members of the public from the jury panel. Once the jury is assembled, you will have a chance to object to any particular jurors, should you recognise their name or face for example, to ensure you have a fair trial. They will then be sworn in, and the trial will commence.

'The advocate for the prosecution, Niall Richardson, will deliver an opening speech. He will describe what their argument is for charging you, and explain how they intend to prove your guilt to the jury. They will state their case, list their witnesses, and try to persuade the jury with as many buzzwords as they can cram in. Then it will be my turn to give an opening speech, to counteract their claims and defend your case.

'Once the opening speeches have been made, the prosecution will call each of their witnesses. They will question them to elicit the answers they need to condemn you, but I will then cross-examine each of the witnesses to poke holes in their state-ments and create doubt in the jurors' minds. The prosecution has the harder job here – they must prove to the jury that you caused your family's deaths, beyond a shadow of a doubt. Our sole purpose is to create that doubt.

'At the halfway point of the trial, when the prosecution have delivered their case, the roles will be reversed. I will call the witnesses speaking in your defence, and question each in turn to help deliver their statements. The prosecution will then cross-examine each witness to create doubt, as we will have with theirs.

'Once this is complete, the prosecution and I will each give a closing speech, and the jury will be sent off to deliberate and decide upon their verdict.'

I look at Wade on the other side of the table, and see a glint of trust in his eyes. My heart plummets.

'The prosecution's argument,' Antony says, 'is to push the notion that you murdered your family. They will call witnesses to try to assassinate your character, imply your mental health struggles were your motive. They will do everything they can to create this image of you, but please do keep in mind that we expect this, and that you have Neve on your side, who will cross-examine each of their witnesses to disarm each of their claims.'

I force myself to nod.

You have Neve on your side, he'd said.

'When will you mention the affair?' Wade asks me.

'Once we've reached the middle of the trial, and it is our turn to call witnesses. We want the prosecution to dig their own grave, before we seal it shut behind them.'

I flinch at my poor choice of words, and the thought of Matthew's body being discovered by the rail workers stops me mid-flow. I cough nervously.

'They will have based their entire argument on you as their sole suspect. Then we can deliver the blow to undermine their entire case, with the truth of the affair. Our evidence of a potential second suspect will prove they didn't consider any other option, thereby delivering an incomplete and biased investigation.'

Wade nods slowly, drinking the information in. The

room feels unbearably hot. I can feel my skin prickling with approaching sweat; my chest is incapable of drawing anything but shallow sips of air.

I haven't lied to Wade, not yet. I have explained exactly how the trial will go. What I have failed to tell him is that, before the prosecution has delivered their case, I will have sent the evidence I have against him to their quarters, and as soon as it is admitted into evidence, the countdown to the end of the trial begins. I will look to be on his side, fighting the good fight, but when we least it expect it, the evidence will be revealed, and the defence case as we know it will be blown to smithereens.

I give him a tight smile.

'You have nothing to worry about, Wade,' I say, delivering my first lie.

He nods again with a grateful smile, his throat bobbing with a nervous swallow. Antony checks his watch.

'I say it's about time we go win this thing.' He gives Wade a comforting squeeze on the shoulder. 'Let's do this.'

We all rise from the table and file out. I let Antony lead the way, trying not to let my nerves show as I decide when I will send the damning evidence to the prosecution. I will let the morning play out: the summoning of the jury, the opening speeches, the first witness or two, and as soon as we have our first break, I will send the evidence to the prosecution, and ensure Hannah and I get out of this in one piece.

When we part ways and I am alone, I check my phone for any word from Hannah on the rail works.

I have no new messages.

My robe is trembling around my legs where I sit at the advocates' bench. Facts I thought I had embedded in my mind and been able to recite on my walk to the courtroom are gone, lost to the pages of my notes again. It will be my fifteen-year anniversary as a barrister come spring, but as I stand in the courtroom, I feel my throat burn with the same nerves I felt when prosecuting in my first trial. The wig on my head is already starting to itch, and the collarette around my neck has tightened like a noose.

The jury has been selected and the judge has introduced the case. What lies before us now is the trial itself.

The court is deathly quiet but for the odd rustle of pages and scrape of chairs. The chatter from the public gallery has fallen to a whisper, after the buzz of excitement that stalked today's onlookers to their seats. I half expect to hear the rustle of popcorn or spot the the glint of opera glasses pointed in my direction, taking in every thread and fold of my robes.

Niall stands to deliver his opening speech, exuding the sort of confidence that is earned, not faked. His white wig has yellowed over the years, now the colour of a smoker's fingers; years of experience and respect stained into the horsehair.

'Members of the jury, the case we are about to set before you is centred around one family: the Darlings.'

Niall stands with his spine straight and his head high, his eyes set firmly on the jurors' bench. His projected voice echoes off the panelled walls.

'The Darlings, it seemed, had everything. An adoring, close-knit family, with the big beautiful house, the fast cars, millions in the bank, horses' stables, and acres of land with a private woodland. It is an awe-inspiring story of one man working to the bone for everything he ever wanted, and bestowing it on those he held dearest. But this story, members of the jury, is a lie.'

Niall pauses for dramatic effect. He isn't a classically handsome man: his hairline is slowly receding beneath his wig, and his nose is slightly crooked, with his chin too large for the rest of his face. But his eyes have a way of transfixing anyone they settle on.

'In the early hours of Saturday the seventeenth of November 2018, the defendant's wife, Yolanda Darling, and their two children, Phoebe and Danny Darling, died in a fiery blaze at the family home. Initially, it appeared to be a tragic accident. But once the smoke had cleared, a far more sinister story emerged.

'What had once appeared to be an accidental tragedy quickly became a murder inquiry. Phoebe and Danny Darling, eighteen and sixteen respectively, had been shot in the head in their beds while they slept.

'Yolanda Darling, too, had been shot. She was found beneath the rubble of the staircase, with forensic evidence revealing that she had been shot three times: in her leg, in her back, and finally, the fatal blow to her head. Three members of one family, wiped out in a single night.'

As the jury sits transfixed, waiting on tenterhooks during each of Niall's dramatic pauses, the room is eerily silent.

'This wasn't a spur of the moment attack, members of the jury. This was a carefully planned execution. The fuel used to ignite the fire was stored in an outhouse on the defendant's property. Every horse was shot dead in their stables before the structure was purposely set alight. The gates to enter the property had been bolted shut to prevent anyone coming to help. This wasn't just a case of arson, or a man covering his tracks – this was complete annihilation, with only one man's fingerprints on the murder weapon. It is these crimes that we are here to try before you, and it is Wade Darling – husband . . . father . . . provider – who is charged with their murders.'

Niall leaves a beat for effect, allowing time for the jurors to glance from the bench to the dock, disgust and curiosity flickering upon their faces as they look to Wade behind the glass.

'During this trial, you will hear from an array of witnesses. You will hear of Yolanda Darling's distress at her husband's mental health decline, of Mr Darling's sanity spiralling rapidly during the closure of his business, and the near-obsession he had with guns and hunting. You will hear from Yolanda Darling's mother, who was the last to see her alive, other than the accused. You will hear from the specialists who led the investigation and assessed every angle of the crime: the fire, the gunshots, the remains. And finally, you will hear from a criminal psychologist who specialises in domestic abuse cases that end in murder.'

He pauses at this. His insinuation is irrevocably clear.

'According to the law, a person is guilty of murder if they unlawfully kill another person with the intention to kill or cause grievous harm. We, the prosecution, must prove that, one: the defendant killed the three victims, and two: that the defendant intended to kill them while committing these violent crimes.

'It is the Crown's case that Mr Darling, after falling into a deep depression and losing everything he had built for himself and his family, murdered his wife and their two children to conceal the truth of his failures from them for eternity – that his pride was more sacred to him than those he was supposed to cherish most. And it is with our evidence during this case that we will prove this to you.'

Niall's eyes wander over the jury. The art of a good opening speech isn't just a matter of relaying the evidence of one's stance, it is a testament to the power of storytelling. Speeches in court are ways to grip the jury with your tale: pull at their heartstrings, deliver open questions they will be left to answer. It is our best chance to persuade the jurors to take our side. Niall has executed his well.

He sits down on the other side of the bench, straightening his robe as he does so before throwing me a quick glance. He doesn't smile, but his eyes glint knowingly.

Now it is my turn. I stand on my side of the bench, my legs quivering beneath my robes. My mouth has dried with fear. I reach for my water glass, and spot the violent tremor running through my hand. Courtroom one is freezing, being in the older part of the Bailey, but I know I can't blame my trembling on that. The room is so quiet that the knock of my glass against the top of the bench echoes against the panelled walls. I clear my throat and begin.

'Members of the jury, I am Neve Harper, the advocate representing Wade Darling during this trial. My learned friend has just given you his terms for my client's charge, and the ways he intends to prove this to you. I will now break down the issues with the prosecution's statements, to ensure you have all of the facts.'

I peer down at my notes. The words swim on the page as my head goes light. I push my feet into the floor in attempt to ground myself, and take a deep breath before returning my gaze to the jury.

'Firstly, there is the matter of circumstantial evidence. In this case, we the defence will show you, the jury, that the evidence the prosecution is to provide for Mr Wade Darling's alleged guilt is inadequate to *categorically* prove he is responsible for the crime. For example, the evidence that will be provided to insinuate my client's guilt includes the discovery of his fingerprints on items that originated from his home – possessions that would already bear his fingerprints due to them belonging to him.

'Two, there is the matter of the prosecution using Mr Wade Darling's experience of depression in this case. We will explain that the defendant's depression was due to his circumstances – a combination of personal struggles and financial changes, two entirely relevant causes for depression. According to the Priory Group, a leading provider of mental health services, approximately two hundred and eighty million people in the world have depression. Demonising a person's mental health diagnoses to insinuate their role in a triple homicide leads us down a dangerous path, for which we will hold the prosecution to account.

'And finally, there is the matter of the police investigation. In our rebuttal of the prosecution's case against my client, we will provide evidence to prove the police actively pursued my client as the perpetrator of the crime, without exploring any other suspects.

'My role, as the advocate for the defence, is to ensure that the facts you receive from the prosecution can withstand interrogation and can be used to prove my client's guilt beyond a shadow of a doubt. Our evidence will prove to you that you cannot.'

I nod to the judge and take my seat. The room is ear-splittingly silent. I reach for my glass of water and clamp my hand upon it in a desperate attempt to keep it from quivering. Despite the numerous eyes that are set upon me, there is one pair I think of. One man who knows what the rest of the room do not. I glance towards the public gallery, and see the Messenger staring back at me. Next to him sits a man who appears taller than everyone else on the row, with tanned, wrinkled skin, and white tufts of receding hair. His eyes are an icy blue, and I know who he is as soon as I meet them. They are the same eyes as Yolanda's, staring out from the front pages.

Mr Viklund.

Judge McConnell bows his head towards Niall at the other end of the bench. It is time for the prosecution to call their first witness.

Niall stands.

'The prosecution calls Annika Viklund.'

27

As Annika Viklund is led to the witness box, she walks as all grieving mothers do: slow and lethargic, as though the life has been sucked out of her bones. Despite this, and her family's reputation for criminal undertakings, she appears glamorous and together. She glimmers with jewellery and her white hair is perfectly set. But her eyes are as hard as her husband's, staring at me from the gallery.

She reaches the box and stands before the court, giving her oath with a delicate tone and soft Swedish accent, the threat of tears ever wavering behind her words.

Yolanda Darling had the same eyes as her father, but her face belonged to her mother. They shared the same button nose, the same high cheekbones and plump bottom lip. Annika is dressed formally in an all-black fitted suit as if in mourning. I wonder if she knows what her husband has orchestrated, if she too has a part to play in the corruption of the trial.

Niall stands at his end of the bench, and introduces himself, before asking her to confirm her name.

'Annika Viklund. Yolanda's mother.'

'I can only imagine how difficult this must be for you and your family, Mrs Viklund,' Niall says. 'So I will make this as brief as I can. When was the last time you saw your daughter, Yolanda?'

The room falls silent. It is so quiet that when Annika opens her mouth to speak, I hear her intake of breath.

'The day before she died,' she utters. 'At her home.'

'What was the reason for your visit?'

'Yolanda and I were close,' she says. 'We would talk every day on the phone, see each other once a week, sometimes more if we could. She was quite isolated in the countryside, so I liked to keep in touch as often as I could. But leading up to her death, we had spoken less and less, and I was worried.'

'What were you worried about?' Niall asks. His tone is soft. A noticeable charade, to anyone who knows him. But to the jury, he may seem sincere. The kinder he is, the crueller I will seem when it is time to cross-examine.

'She had become noticeably withdrawn,' Annika says. 'I know my daughter, and when she wants to hide something, she retreats into herself. She was never a very good liar, or at least, not a good enough liar to fool me. I only had to hear or look at her to know something was wrong.'

'So when you went to visit your daughter on Friday the sixteenth of November 2018, you thought something was amiss?'

'Yes. Our conversations had been getting shorter and further apart. She was worried about Wade.'

'What was worrying her about the defendant?'

Her eyes flicker, as if she is about to look up at the dock and meet Wade's eyes. She looks to the bottom of the witness box instead.

'He had become depressed.' She pauses. 'We know now that it was due to his business failing, but Yolanda was kept in the dark about that. All she knew was that her husband was going downhill, and she didn't know why or how to help. It affected them all, as a family. Yolanda and the children seemed to be walking on eggshells, waiting for him to snap.'

'Waiting for him to snap,' Niall repeats, glancing at the jury. He waits a few seconds, allowing the thought to sink into their minds.

'Was the defendant at the property during your visit?'

'No, he was out hunting, and the children were at college. It was just Yolanda and me. I was relieved, as I wanted to get to the bottom of what was happening.'

As Annika gives her evidence, I watch the jury for their reactions. Every one of them is transfixed by her story. They will have no reason not to trust her, the mother of the deceased.

'What did you think of the defendant's hunting?'

'My husband partakes in the sport, so I'm used to it. But over the years, Wade became almost obsessed with it. His collection of firearms grew, he spent thousands upon thousands on them. He would go on hunting retreats, was a member of several hunting clubs in the county. It got to a point where it would seem strange not to see him with a rifle of some kind. He would clean them, pull them apart to put them back together again, read books about them, talked about the guns he wanted next. There was a buck in the area that he obsessed over; he wanted to shoot it and mount its head above the mantel. I'm not sure he ever got it.'

A gunman waiting to snap. That's what Wade looks like, in the eyes of the jury.

'Tell us about your visit to see Yolanda on the sixteenth of November 2018.'

'I arrived at about noon, and I could tell she was in a bad way before I even saw her. Her voice over the intercom at the

front gate was quiet and lacking her usual cheer. When I drove
up to the house and she opened the door, I could have cried at
the sight of her. She looked utterly drained. She was very pale,
and had lost a lot of weight. Her eyes, her smile; the light inside
of her had vanished.

'As soon as I asked her if she was all right, the tears came
bursting out. Hers first, then mine. We went into the living
room. I didn't even take off my coat or my shoes, I was so
eager to hear from her. I got the sense she was finally going to
open up to me.'

She stops briefly to compose herself, closing her eyes.

'What did she say?' Niall asks softly.

Annika opens her eyes again, blinking the water from them.

'She told me of Wade's depression. He was barely speaking
to any of them by this point. Not in a callous way, she said – he
would try to play the part. But he was utterly broken, and she
was growing scared of what he might do.'

'Scared of what he might do?' Niall repeats.

'To himself,' she replies. 'That's what I thought she meant
at the time. Now, I'm not so sure.'

I stand from my side of the bench.

'Your Honour, I'm not sure speculation of this nature
is helpful.'

Judge McConnell nods to me in response, before turning
to the witness.

'Stick to the facts of the matter please, Mrs Viklund.'

She nods dutifully, her cheeks pink, and looks to Niall at the
other end of the bench, waiting for him to proceed.

'And was Wade hunting during all this?'

'Yes, he would go off for hours. She was a bag of nerves
every time he left. She said that whenever she heard a gunshot,

she feared it might have been one he bestowed upon himself. I think it was the first time she truly said aloud what it felt like to live in their household. She had been staying strong for Wade, for the children, keeping up airs and graces. But she was finally letting down her guard.' Her eyes flick upwards towards the dock, and her expression curdles with a grimace; venom seeping into her eyes. 'And then he came back.'

'The defendant?'

'Yes.'

'How did the defendant's return change things?'

Annika tears her eyes away from the dock. Her hands are held in fists at her sides, her knuckles white.

'It changed everything. Yolanda steeled up again, rushing to tidy her appearance, before inviting him to join us and making us all tea. I sat with them in the kitchen, watching them pretend that everything was fine, wanting to scream at them both to address what was going on, but they were so wrapped up in their lie. Lying to me, to each other . . . to themselves.'

'How did the defendant seem to you, during all this?'

'He was his usual upbeat self: attentive, making jokes. But beneath the surface I could tell something was wrong. They both looked like they had aged a decade. I wanted to try and get her alone again, but she made her excuses. I don't think she felt comfortable lowering her guard with him home. So I left.'

Tears come to her eyes. She tries to compose herself, her lip wavering.

'When I hugged her goodbye . . .' Her voice breaks. 'I hugged her as if it would be the last time. I just . . . *knew*. I don't know how. Perhaps it was a mother's instincts. But I felt as though I was about to lose her for good. I told her I loved her, got in my car, and drove home. I cried the whole way. I woke up that

morning to the police at the door. They came to tell us of the
fire at the house, and that Yolanda and the children hadn't
been found. And I knew then that my premonition had been
right. I think about the moment I left that house every minute
of every day, wishing I had insisted upon her coming with me.
We could have collected the children and I could have brought
them home, where it was safe.'

'Safe from what, Mrs Viklund?'

The question hangs in the air. Her eyes flick towards the dock.

'From *him*.'

We all sit, watching as she stares at the man accused of
killing her daughter and grandchildren. Tears slip down her
cheeks until she finally bursts into a sob.

'Thank you, Mrs Viklund,' Niall says. 'I know that will
have been extremely difficult for you.' He looks to the judge.
'Nothing more from me.'

It is a tricky business, cross-examining the mother of a
victim. Come on too strong, and I will look bullish and callous, but tread too lightly, and I could allow the power of her
testimony to sway the jury. It is even harder when the mother's
husband is sat in the public gallery, with a figurative sniper
pointed at my back.

I stand at my end of the bench.

'Mrs Viklund, I'm Neve Harper for the defence. I am so
sorry for your loss; I will make this quick.'

She nods curtly. Her eyes are steely towards me, and I
wonder if it is because I am defending Wade, or because like
her husband, she knows she has control over me. The Viklunds,
pulling my strings.

'I would like to highlight some of the areas of the testimony
you just gave. You mentioned the defendant's enjoyment of

hunting, and described his collection of weapons as "obses-sive". You also told us that your husband also hunts, correct?'

'Yes,' she replies sharply.

'In fact, your husband went hunting *with* the defendant on numerous occasions, didn't he?'

'Yes . . .' she says, her stare deadly. 'They were family.'

'How many weapons does your husband own?'

She shrugs her shoulders.

'I'm not sure.'

'That many?' I reply with a cocked brow.

Annika gives me a look of warning.

'No, I was not implying that. I'm just not sure.'

'You must have some knowledge. An estimate is fine. Three guns? Four?'

'About ten.'

'Not much less than number owned by the defendant?'

She sharpens her glare.

'Less than half, I think you'll find.'

'But more than the average hunter would own, yes?'

'Perhaps.'

'So, in your opinion, would it be fair for someone to tar your husband with the same brush, because of his hobby? Suspect him of a crime due to this sport?'

'Without context, no.'

'Thank you. And lastly . . . you said your daughter changed when the defendant returned home during your visit. Said that you believed she "didn't feel comfortable lowering her guard around him". Correct?'

'Yes.'

'You were both talking about him at the time, isn't that right?'

'Yes.'

'About something very personal to him?'

'Yes.'

'With that in mind, isn't it possible that this is why your daughter's demeanour changed when he returned? So not to hurt his feelings?'

She purses her lips.

'Mrs Viklund?'

'Perhaps,' she says, her tone sharp.

'So would it be fair to say that it was your *perception* that Yolanda was uncomfortable around the defendant, rather than uncomfortable about discussing the *subject* in the defendant's presence?'

'Well, yes, it was my perception. But I do wish to remind you that I was actually *there*, Ms Harper. I felt the tension between them, I witnessed their dynamic with my own eyes. You weren't.'

'Thank you, Mrs Viklund.' I look to the judge. 'No further questions.'

I take to my seat, not daring to turn around to see Mr Viklund's expression, as he and his wife meet each other's eyes.

We break late for lunch, but I can't eat a thing. As I pace outside the Bailey, puffing on cigarette after cigarette, all I can think about are the rail works, of how much closer they are to finding Matthew with each breath I take.

How long does it take to uproot a tree? Or a dozen trees? I wonder where they will start, how much time I have to play with before they reach him. I wonder what his body will look like after three years. How much of him will still be flesh, and how much of him will be nothing but bone.

I open my text messages again. Still no response from Hannah. What if they've found him already, and she is with the police right now? Would she text me back if she thought I was the one who put him there?

Calm down. If she's truly sick, she's probably sleeping. Or maybe she's skiving and is out and about with friends. There will be an explanation. Even though I've never seen her without her phone in her hand.

I pace back and forth, faster this time, my mouth sapped dry from nerves.

I need to move him tonight. I cannot risk leaving it too long and returning home to a crime scene beyond the tracks, or the police officers meeting me at the doors to the Bailey. But how am I going to do this under Hannah's nose? And where on earth would I bury him?

I need to drive out of the city, as far as I can get.

Then of course, there is the matter of the trial.

Above my text to Hannah is the last text I sent. It was to Johnny, the errand boy we use at chambers. He is to meet me to collect the file on my client's past and deliver it directly to the prosecution. The first thing I did when the judge announced the break was run to the bank and withdraw the money to cover Johnny's fee, along with a large tip to keep him quiet. I can't have anyone knowing this evidence came from me.

Once I do this, there is no going back.

The body. The trial. The body. The trial. My thoughts spin in an endless, panic-inducing cycle. Each task is so overwhelming that tears of desperation sting at my eyes.

I drop my cigarette to the ground, toying with whether to light another despite the sickly taste in my mouth and tight, breathless chest, when I come face to face with the Messenger.

'Mr Viklund wishes to speak with you.'

⚖️

I walk silently through the streets towards the meeting point, passing St Paul's Cathedral in a daze until I reach the Thames. Before me is the Millennium Bridge, where I am to meet Mr Viklund. I stare at its metal Jurassic spine jutting out from the walkway. Beyond it, on the other side of the river, the Tate Modern's brick mast towers up towards the overcast sky. I look to the right towards Blackfriars and think of Fredrick. We had stood just there, uttering the Viklund name. Now I am about to meet with the man himself and Fredrick is dead.

Mr Viklund is waiting for me in the centre of the bridge, staring out at the view of the city.

I slowly make my way across. The wind is strong today, and the bridge trembles beneath my feet as I walk. People pass me by, in their own little worlds. I wish I could trade places with one of them, steal their lives, wear their skin as my own, and disappear.

When I am mere feet away, Mr Viklund turns to me, his expression stoic. But his eyes seem to be forever vengeful. I had felt them burning into me from the public gallery during the trial proceedings, and I feel the heat of them again now. I force myself to hold his gaze.

'We don't have long,' I say, as I reach him and stand at his side. He looks out at the Thames snaking through the city, slipping beneath Southwark Bridge, then London Bridge, to Tower Bridge in the distance. 'And it's important we aren't seen together.'

'Then I'll make it quick.' His voice is deep and authoritative, with the same Swedish accent as his wife. When the wind blows, I catch the scent of his aftershave, potent and masculine.

'I'm sure you think what is happening to you is unfair,' he says. 'And that the predicament I have put you in is unjust. But I would like to offer you another take on the matter.

'My son-in-law – your client – took my most precious gift away from me. He murdered my child, and killed both my grandchildren. He lost his business, and as punishment, destroyed everything around him, and then had the audacity to save himself. This man you have been hired to defend deserves nothing more than to rot in a prison cell, to never breathe the scent of freedom again. Death is too good for him. Too merciful. I will not allow any other verdict but guilty.'

He tears his eyes from the water and looks at me. I can't help but squirm beneath his gaze.

'You are not the victim here, Ms Harper. You murdered your husband, as Wade killed my family. If you expect remorse from me for putting you in this situation, you will not get it. I don't care why you did what you did. Only that it can be used to get what my family deserve. And if you don't . . .'

He looks out to the Thames again, his eyes steeling, until they appear as grey as the water.

'The world will discover what you did, and you will go to prison for the rest of your life. But it won't end there. I will personally make sure that everyone you love will pay the price. You will lose loved ones, as I have lost mine, and you won't be able to do a thing about it, whiling away your last days behind bars and wire fences, as the guilt and the grief eat away at you, knowing that you could have saved the people you lost.'

He looks at me again, his eyes watery. I am not sure whether it is the chill of the wind, or the talk of his family. But as he talks of my demise, I can see the rage in them too.

'I have friends in all sorts of places, as I'm sure you know. And I can assure you, your time in prison would be unbearable. You'll be wishing the UK still orchestrated hangings, when I'm done with you. And when you're old and grey, and have had the life crushed out of you, you'll die alone, without dignity or redemption. I have many incarcerated friends who like to fashion knives out of toothbrushes and visit their victims in the showers. They won't stop until the water runs red and the life leaves your eyes.' His stare penetrates into me, until every one of my muscles twitches and squirms. 'Have I made myself clear, Ms Harper?'

I nod slowly.

'Yes, Mr Viklund.'

'Are you sure? Because you didn't seem to hold back when cross-examining my wife this morning.'

'I'm sure.'

The corners of his mouth rise slightly, followed by a brief nod of his head.

'Good.'

He looks back to the water and watches it for a while, the violence of the current, the algae on either side of the bank a glimmering emerald in the sun.

'I want you to know I'm serious about this task, Mr Viklund.'

I slip the file from my bag and pass it to him. He looks down at it suspiciously, before taking it slowly from my grasp.

'What is it?'

'The evidence I am sending to the prosecution to sabotage my client's case.'

His eyes flicker with something I can't pin down. It's not quite pride, or amusement. Perhaps he is impressed. He opens the file and begins to read, the pages fluttering in his grip from the breeze.

'This will ensure that whatever I say in defence of my client, we will lose the case. I will need to keep up appearances, looking to be doing my job while sabotaging it from afar. Just like I had been when I was cross-examining your wife. Do you understand?'

He is silent for a moment as he continues to read of his son-in-law's history. I see the corner of his mouth turn upwards with a smile, before he shuts the file and returns it to me.

'Perfectly,' he replies.

'Because I don't want you, or your . . . colleague, to be concerned if I appear to be going against what we've discussed.'

'Message received.' He drops his eyes to the file. 'When will you be delivering this evidence?'

My phone vibrates in my pocket. I long for it to be from Hannah, to put my mind at ease. I slip it out and peer at the screen. It's the errand boy. He has arrived at our meeting place, on the corner of Carter Lane, a small winding back street close to the Bailey.

'Now.' I clear my throat and look about me. 'I'm doing everything you're asking of me, Mr Viklund. I really hope you'll keep your word, about not harming me or those I love.'

'You'll remember the agreement, when all of this began,' he says. 'You were told it was a trade of sorts, correct?'

'Yes.'

'Well then. Fulfil your part of the agreement, and the trade is complete.' He takes his eyes off the view. 'We'll be watching to make sure you do.'

⚖

The errand boy is perched on his bicycle, waiting for me on the corner of Carter Lane, occasionally looking about him for my arrival before returning to his phone screen.

I stop in the nearest doorway and slip the file in a large envelope, with Niall's name written on the front of it in large black capitals, which I had scrawled in the Bailey's de-robing room the moment I found myself alone.

I still have time to do the right thing. I could turn around now and be done with it. Face the consequences of my crimes. Sacrifice my freedom for my client's right to a fair trial. But Mr Viklund's words whisper in my mind, my heart rate climbing at the sound of his deep, crackling voice. *You will lose loved ones, as I have lost mine, and you won't be able to do a thing about it.*

A bout of panic ripples through me. This task Mr Viklund has laid at my feet goes against everything I have ever known as a barrister. It is everything that our society deems wrong. And yet, I have no other choice. If not for my sake, then for Hannah's. For Maggie's. I have put them through enough. But beneath the duty to protect them whispers my own selfish greed. If the truth of what I have done was exposed, I would lose the only family I have ever known. Clinging onto the family of the man I killed, to keep them as my own. The twisted nature of it makes my stomach lurch with shame.

I check the time, trying to concentrate on the ticking hands while my pulse drums loudly. The break is almost over. If I don't do this now, I will lose my chance. Any later and the judge may well refuse to admit the evidence out of principle.

It's now or never. Us or him.

I take a steeling breath and walk towards the boy. He looks up at me with a smile and the casual nod of his head.

'All right, miss?'

'Hi Johnny. Thanks for this.'

He gives me another of those boyish nods.

'It's going to the Old Bailey, right?'

'Yes. The recipient's name is on the front. You remember what I said?'

'It didn't come from you.'

'That's right. That part is really important.'

I pass him the envelope of cash first. A tip larger than his fee, paying handsomely for his discretion. He knows I've paid him more from the thickness of the envelope, and breaks into a beaming smile.

'Whatever you say, miss.' He shoves the envelope of cash inside his jacket before zipping it shut. 'You got the package?'

I hold the top of the envelope, just poking from my bag. I still have time to change my mind, to choose another path. But time is forever against me. I can practically hear the seconds ticking away, matching the beat of my heart.

It's now or never.

I lift the envelope free and pass it to him, my heart jolting as the paper parts from my fingers.

'Cheers miss. I'll drop you a text when it's delivered.'

He cycles off, standing on the pedals to build momentum, before zipping down the street.

It's done.

29

As the trial recommences and the judge enters the courtroom, I stand at my end of the bench feeling sick with anticipation. The prosecution will have had the new-found evidence for just fifteen minutes before we returned to courtroom one. Fifteen minutes to read through the file and gather their argument to add it into evidence for the case against my client. Johnny confirmed the package had arrived before I had even returned to the Bailey. I can see it in the way Niall stands restlessly at his side of the bench. When he peers down towards me, he smiles knowingly, no doubt anticipating his surprise reveal, with no notion that I was the stranger who planted the information. Antony catches his triumphant glare where he sits before me at the solicitors' row and turns to face me with a questioning expression. I shrug my shoulders to feign ignorance and look down at my files.

After welcoming everyone back to court, Judge McConnell looks to Niall to call back his witness to the box. Only the prosecution and I know what's to come next.

'Your Honour, before we begin, there is a matter I would like to address.'

I feel Antony's eyes as he turns back to me. I don't look back at him, but keep my focus on the judge, my face poker-straight.

'And what matter is this?'

'Fresh evidence has come to light, Your Honour, which we wish to have admitted so the jury have all the relevant facts.'

The judge raises his hand, silencing him instantly. 'I would like the jury dismissed before you go any further, Mr Richardson.'

'Yes, Your Honour.'

The jurors file out, an air of confusion and intrigue about them, as they glance to one another and head for the door. The public gallery seems to have woken up, talking to each other in hushed whispers. I look towards them, and find Mr Viklund staring back at me.

Once the jury has been dismissed, the judge returns his attention to Niall and me.

'You're aware you had the chance to submit your evidence prior to this trial, Mr Richardson? This is how proceedings are set for every trial. I can't think why this should be any different.'

The adrenaline must be surging through Niall at this moment. A piece of evidence that, if admitted, will land him the trial has just fallen into his lap without him lifting a finger. I can imagine he feels like the luckiest barrister in the world. And me, the unluckiest.

'Yes, Your Honour. Unfortunately, we were not made aware of this evidence until this afternoon. We cannot disclose evidence to the court in advance if said evidence isn't available.'

The judge sighs and slips his spectacles from the bridge of his nose, and begins to rub them clean with the sleeve of his robe.

'And what is this evidence you speak of?' he asks.

'It is to do with the defendant's medical history.'

'You were given this by the defence during the preliminary proceedings, were you not?'

'Not this evidence, Your Honour. This was not featured on his medical file; the health matter in question was dealt with privately, which one can only assume was to keep the evidence from his medical records—'

'You can save your assumptions, Mr Richardson. I am quite capable of forming my own judgement without your assistance.' He sighs again, before replacing his glasses upon his nose. 'I would like to see this evidence.'

'I would also like to see it, Your Honour,' I say from my side of the bench.

The judge nods dismissively, reaching out for the file as it is brought to him, and begins to read while another copy is brought to me. I look down, scanning it as if I wasn't the person to drop the file into the prosecution's lap, before passing it to Antony. I watch his shoulders tense up as he reads, and look with bated breath towards the judge. His eyes follow the words on the page, reading the history that will inevitably damn my client to a life in prison. All done by my hand.

The air in the room thickens, and the time creeps on, the faint ticking of a clock or a watch being the only backdrop to the judge's turning of the pages. He closes the file, exhaling deeply through his nostrils.

'Court will be adjourned for the day so I can consider this matter. I will have my decision on admission by the morning.'

The judge stands, and Niall and I follow suit, the creak of benches and squeak of chairs sounding through the room. Antony looks up at me, wide-eyed with confusion.

'Don't worry until we have to,' I say quietly. 'We will have a conference in the morning after I meet with the judge and go from there.'

I look towards my client in the dock, taking in the grey-pale skin of his face, and give him a deceptively supportive nod.

He doesn't know it, but I have just sacrificed his future for my own.

⚖

I return home to find myself alone, and yet I still feel that unfamiliar thrum in the air; there's a sense to the place now that I'm not the only one living in it, finding Hannah's presence wherever I look: her coat on the peg, a pair of shoes that aren't mine, a mug left on the coffee table, sticky at the rim with tinted lip gloss; the subtle, lingering scent of her girlish perfume in the air.

I need to see the train tracks.

I stride through the house without removing my shoes, and as I step into the kitchen, I spot a note on the breakfast table from Hannah: she is out with a friend and will be home for dinner.

So much for being ill.

I stand at the back door and stare through the glass past the garden, which is dark with the evening's shadows. Even from here, I can see the progress the workers have made. The trees at the bottom of my house are still standing, but by the long line of those felled before them, they will undoubtedly be the next to go.

I'm not sure how much time I have until Hannah returns. But I do know that if I want to retrieve the spade I used to bury Matthew without being seen, this is my window to do it.

When I was dealing with the aftermath, covering my blood-stained tracks, I knew that if I wanted a good chance at getting away with the murder, I needed to keep each damning item apart. The body at the bottom of the garden. The murder weapon hidden in storage. I wonder what Hannah would say if she knew that the spade I used to bury her father was hiding directly above our heads.

I head up the stairs and cross the landing, taking the long hook from the airing cupboard as I pass and using it to open the loft hatch, guiding the door open until it dangles on its hinges, its squeal echoing up through the hatch and into the darkness.

I drag down the ladder and climb up into the cold, dark loft, shivering as the draught greets me. I turn on the torch on my phone and clamber in.

The last task I had to cover my tracks was to hide the spade I used to bury him. I knew the police would search my premises. So, I found the next best thing.

I make my way towards the brick wall separating next door's property from mine and crouch down towards the right-hand side where I'd loosened the bricks. I begin lifting them free, stacking them beside me until my fingertips are gritty with orange dust. Lucinda's loft is filled to the rafters with boxes and bin bags of belongings heaped on top of one another; old files stacked bare and speckled with damp. She can't know half the things she has in there. Which works in my favour.

When the gap is big enough, I reach in, feeling blindly in the darkness, my fingertips collecting dust and cobwebs, until I feel the rustle of the black bin bag hidden behind a tower of boxes, and the cold metal of the spade within. I drag it forwards, edging it bit by bit so as not to send Lucinda's things toppling down upon me, and guide it through the gap. I sit with it in my lap, breathing heavily as dust tickles my throat.

Even through the bag, I can smell the earth that once coated the spade. It's impossible of course, after scrubbing it as thoroughly as I did, and the amount of bleach I used. But the weight of it in my hands instantly reminds me of all the gruesome details that haunt me to this day.

I am just putting the last few bricks back into place when I hear my name called from beyond the hatch.

Hannah.

I cock my head, and hear her footsteps on the stairs.

'What're you doing?' she asks from the foot of the ladder.

'Looking for something, I'll be down in a minute.' I blow a lock of hair from my face with a hot huff of air. 'Pre-heat the oven for me, would you?'

'Okay.'

I stay deathly still, listening as she heads back down, not daring to move again until I'm sure she's out of sight. When I hear the sound of the television downstairs, I crawl across the boards with the spade rustling in the black bin bag, dangle my legs over the open hatch, and slowly reach out for the first rung of the ladder. The metal creaks beneath my weight. I try to think of a place to hide it until nightfall, a place where Hannah won't find it. The longer she stays here, the more comfortable she seems about the place. It wouldn't surprise me if she spent her time alone in the house finding all of its nooks and crannies, looking for things her father left behind.

I've just reached the landing when I hear Hannah on the stairs again.

'Neve?' she asks.

I impulsively bolt into my bedroom, scanning furiously for a place to hide the spade, before dropping to my knees and thrusting it beneath the bed. Hannah appears in the doorway as I get back to my feet, and I pretend to collect something from the bedside drawer.

'What's up?' I ask. I find a Lipsol inside the drawer and play the part by running it across my lips.

She nods towards the ladder. 'Do you have anything of Dad's up there?'

She looks and sounds so childlike as she says this. It fascinates me how she can flit between a child and a young adult with just the flick of her lashes, the variable tone of her voice.

'What sort of stuff?'

She shrugs.

'I don't know. Photos, maybe? Of him as a kid, me as a baby, that sort of stuff?'

My heart sinks. I have been so caught up in my own dilemma that I hadn't considered how big of a deal this temporary move must be for Hannah. She stayed at weekends of course, and school holidays, but this was very much mine and Matthew's space that she came to visit, rather than a place to call her own.

'I'm sure I do. How about you make us dinner and I'll have a look up there.'

Her face softens, and a smile slowly curls the corners of her lips.

'Okay. What would you like for dinner?'

'Surprise me.'

She nods, the smile still firmly on her face, and turns back for the stairs.

'You're feeling better then?' I ask.

Right on time, she coughs.

'I had to meet a friend to collect homework, still feel rough. I feel worse at night.'

'Right,' I say, not buying it for a second. 'Well, we'll see how you feel in the morning then.'

She nods and heads for the stairs, and as I listen to the reassuring creaks of the floorboards, I sit down on the edge of the bed with a sigh and close my eyes, trying to calm my racing heart.

⚖

I sit in the armchair in my living room, watching the clock on the wall approach midnight. Once Hannah had gone up to bed, I snuck out of the house and moved the car to the church car park, closest to the wire fence separating the grounds from the tracks, ready to transfer the body to the boot. All I need to do is collect the spade from beneath my bed, and make my way towards the tracks.

I watch the seconds pass on the clock, my nerves jumping with each tick. If I'm going to do this without being caught, I need to do so in the dead of night, where there is less chance of being spotted. I have dressed in black from head to toe to blend into the shadows.

I have dreaded this day from the moment I buried him. Now I have no choice: it's time to dig up the past and face what I did.

The clock nears ten seconds, nine . . . My chest grows tight. As the clock strikes midnight and the church bells sound, the memories hit me.

Gong.
Thwack.
Gong.
Thwack.
Gong.
Thwack.

They say you can't outrun trauma, that you must deal with it. But what might be a possibility for other people isn't an option for me; I cannot go to a therapist without confessing my crimes. In a strange way, I have accepted the notion that this will stay with me forever. That this eternal prison I have made for myself is the consequence of my actions. The punishment for my sin.

The clock ticks and ticks. Another minute has passed now, and the bells have stopped ringing.

It's now or never.

I force myself to get up and creep up the stairs, avoiding the areas I know creak underfoot. The higher I get, the faster my pulse climbs, echoing in my grip on the banister.

I reach the top and slowly tiptoe by Hannah's room, before stopping at a sudden sound.

The door opens slowly.

'Can't sleep either?' Hannah asks, child-like again in her soft, hopeful tone.

I pause at the door, torn. I can't do this while Hannah is awake. Her room faces the tracks; suppose she heard a sound as I was digging, and peered out from behind the curtains?

I steel myself on the landing, feeling the opportunity slipping from my grip.

'No,' I reply. 'I can't sleep either.'

Day Two

I wake to the sound of the rail works blaring on the other side of my bedroom window. The whine of the chainsaw ripping its teeth through the trunks of the trees.

I thought I would have more time. I would never have imagined that the workers would begin removing the trees on the first day of the project. When will they dig up the stumps, the roots? As soon as they do, they will bring Matthew's body with them. I think of the smell of decay hitting them, followed by their horrified faces as they spot a rotted hand creeping out from the earth.

There are many other trees they have to take down before they get to that stage. I can go back tonight, and continue with the plan.

But the doubt continues to chip away at me. *What if. What if.*

I shower and dress without thought or focus, methodically moving from task to task, all the while thinking of both the trial and Matthew's body. I stop before the bathroom mirror and stare at my paled complexion.

Today, I will find out if the judge has allowed the evidence I fed the prosecution to be added to the case. If he does, I will have to live with the fact that I sold a man down the river to save myself. But if he doesn't, I will have to find a whole new way to protect Hannah and my secret. The thought of going back to square one hits me with such a bout of fear that white blots fill my vision. I force myself to breathe.

Once I have met with the judge, I will need to meet with Antony and our client, and continue spinning my web of lies, before it's back to court where I will cross-examine Yolanda's mother, and question the detective leading the case.

As for tonight, I will meet Matthew again.

My stomach threatens to lurch; I run the tap urgently and gulp down water from my cupped hand.

I'm so sorry, Matthew.

I force the guilt down and leave the bathroom to continue with my tasks. Once I've blow-dried my hair and stepped out of my bedroom onto the landing, I hear a cough from behind Hannah's door. I knock briefly and peer inside. The curtains are drawn, the night still thriving inside her room.

'You still feeling rough?' I ask.

She coughs again for effect.

'Yeah,' she replies croakily. 'Can I stay at home one more day?'

Her presence in the house while I'm out makes me feel nervous, but it would help to have her here, to keep an eye on the rail works. If something happens, I can stay ahead of the curve. The works continue to clamour outside.

'All right, but keep your phone on you and text me back when I message you, okay?'

'Okay.' She eyes me through the gloom. 'How come you're so stressed about the train tracks stuff?'

I am immediately grateful for the gloom so she cannot see my face. I have been so panicked, and clearly I have been acting out of sorts, showing my cards.

'Not stressed,' I force. 'Just overwhelmed. This case is a lot;

coming home to mayhem is the last thing I need. Makes me feel better to think it'll be over soon.'

I venture in, tripping over a crumpled garment on the floor, and kiss her forehead, which to her defence does feel warm beneath my lips.

'I'll be back for dinner. Be good while I'm gone.'

I force a smile and shut the door, knowing that if I'm going to move the body with Hannah in the house, I will have to do something to make sure she isn't able to witness it.

I will have to do something bad.

⚖

The tension in conference room three is stifling and immediate. Antony, it seems, was up much of the night, no doubt analysing the evidence to try to conjure a strong rebuttal. By his faint smile in greeting, it doesn't appear he has found one.

Wade is sat on the other side of the table. The depression we had witnessed in earlier conferences is more evident than ever. He is dressed in the same suit as before, and a freshly ironed shirt, no doubt by the hand of Marianne. But his hair shimmers with grease, and his eyes appear utterly vacant, as if he doesn't know or recognise me, disassociating from the situation he has found himself in.

I did this.

I sit down with a held breath, trying to keep my composure.

'Good morning, Wade. How are you?'

A beat of silence takes over the room, the ring of it echoing off the windowless walls. Just when I think he isn't going to respond, his lips part.

'I wish people would stop asking me that.'

His voice croaks with despair. The man is becoming a mere shadow of who he once was.

'The new evidence from the prosecution has shocked us all, Wade,' I lie. 'I would be doing you an injustice if I said it wasn't pretty damning to our case. Your past ... it gives the prosecution a chance to paint what happened to your family as an escalation of previous acts.'

I wonder if he is even listening. He has disassociated again, staring into oblivion with his eyes set vacantly upon the surface of the desk.

'But we won't give up,' I continue. 'Antony and I have a strong argument for calling the police investigation into question. Even if the prosecution succeed in persuading the jury to see a link between your past and the crimes against your family, we can argue that other avenues went unexplored. This isn't over.'

'Isn't it?' he croaks. 'The prosecution team contacted my mother this morning. They've called for her to be a witness ... to talk about what happened.'

Antony sighs at the blow.

'Why didn't you tell us about all this, Wade?' he asks. 'We could have tried to prevent it from ever reaching court.'

'An innocent man doesn't think of the ways he may be seen as guilty,' he replies. 'I didn't think it was relevant to the truth.'

Wade rises from his chair suddenly, towering above us both.

'I want a minute alone.'

'We'll be right here, Wade,' Antony says, his words cut off by the shutting of the door. When the room falls quiet, Antony is the one to break it.

'When will they bring the evidence, do you think?'

'Their specialist witness Dr Heche is their last. I suspect they would plan to call Marianne just before Heche.'

'We're fucked, aren't we? I tried to find ways to counter-act the evidence, to keep it from being added. But it's killer,

isn't it?' He leans back in his chair, his hands upon his head.
'Fuck.'

'We've got our angle to pursue too, Anthony. If we create
enough doubt, their evidence might not stand as strong. Let's
reconvene prior to their specialist witness, to think of a way
around this.'

'Do you think the judge will agree to it? The new evidence?'

I hope so.

'I don't know.' I let the words sink in, hoping he will begin
to accept the defeat, to allow me to send our client to the cells.
'But whatever happens, we have a strong argument too.'

Neither of us sounds convinced. Our client has given up, and
our opposition's evidence casts a deep, dark shadow over our
defence case. I've pulled the rug from under them both.

Now I just need to pray the judge makes the decision I
need him to.

⚖️

The judge enters, and everyone in the room stands. I try to
distinguish his decision from his demeanour: the way his eyes
stay downcast, the slow, tired way he walks. He looks to Niall
first, then to me, and bids the court good morning, before we
take to our seats. He turns towards the jurors' bench.

'Members of the jury, while you were called out of court
yesterday afternoon, a matter of fresh evidence was brought to
my attention. I called the day's proceedings to a close to consider this new evidence, and make my decision as to whether
it should be admissible at such a late stage in the trial process.
There is a manner in which we must conduct criminal trials,
with numerous preliminary hearings long before you are
called, to decide which evidence will make its way to court,

which witnesses will take to the box to give their statements. It is unusual, but not impossible, for late evidence to be added to a case.'

He looks down at his notes, before returning his attention to the jury.

'Reasons for accepting late admissions of evidence are tied to the importance of the evidence at hand – how important it is for you, the jury, to know of what is enclosed, so you can make your fair and honest verdict with all the facts to hand.'

He turns his attention to Niall, then me.

'That is why I have decided to accept this into evidence.'

Antony's head bows, and the press row shuffles excitedly, as murmurs break from the public gallery. I turn to meet Mr Viklund's eye, who is peering down at me. He gives me an imperceptible nod, before I turn back towards the judge, but not before glancing at Wade in the dock. He looks just as he had when I first laid eyes on him: his shoulders concaved to make himself smaller, his eyes towards the floor. He looks utterly defeated. A defeat orchestrated by me, the one person in the room he should be able to trust.

I stand before the judge, squirming with the rush of conflicting emotions; guilt and relief filling me up like oil and water. I have betrayed my profession, my morals, my dignity. Condemned a man to save my own hide. But it also means Hannah and I will be safe.

'We will now continue with proceedings.'

Niall stands. 'Thank you, Your Honour. The prosecution calls Rita Cummings.'

31

As the second witness takes her oath, Niall stands at the other end of the advocates' bench and asks for her to confirm her name for the court.

'Rita Cummings,' she replies.

Cummings stands straight but nervous, her hands knotted together before her and her eyes wide and alert, taking in the room and the people staring back at her.

'Thank you for coming here today, Ms Cummings. You're a paramedic, is that right?'

'That's correct. I've been a paramedic for close to nine years.'

Her years in service are painted all over her face. Her expression is warm yet tired, her eyes padded from sleepless nights.

'You were called to the Darlings' address during the early hours of Saturday, the seventeenth of November, is that right? Can you tell us how the evening unfolded?'

She takes a deep, resolute breath.

'I was on the night shift, my second in a row, with my colleague Sam. We had just finished escorting a patient to A&E when the Darling case was assigned. We were the closest to the scene.'

'What was your first instinct, when you were alerted to the incident?'

'It was called in as a house fire with four people known to

live at the address. By the sound of the description, the fire was severe. These aren't nice calls to receive. There isn't much we can do while the fire is still going, so we have to wait and hope that survivors are pulled from the blaze. The firefighters were en route when we arrived at the address just after half three in the morning. We were the first on the scene.'

Niall leaves a deliberate pause. *The scene.* I imagine the jury painting a picture of it in their minds. The fire burning wildly, curling up towards the night sky; the opulent gates of the country home lighting up blue from the ambulance's lights.

'And when you arrived, what did you find?'

'The fire could be seen from half a mile up the road. It had to have been about fifty feet in the sky. We could see the flames above the entry gates, and the shrubs and fences surrounding the property. It was clear to me that the fire would be fatal to anyone trapped inside, and I began to set my expectations.'

Niall allows a long, drawn silence to unfold in the court-room. The jurors shuffle awkwardly in their seats.

'When you and your colleague arrived, did you enter the grounds of the property straight away?'

'No.'

'Why not?'

'The entrance gates had been bolted and padlocked shut.'

Niall pauses for effect again, glancing at the jurors as he does so.

'Padlocked shut,' he repeats. 'From outside the property, or inside?'

'From the inside,' she replies. 'My colleague called it in to make the firefighters aware, who weren't too far behind. My colleague and I pulled the ambulance out of the drive to keep the gates clear. The fire team arrived with bolt cutters at the ready, and made their way into the property. We pulled in behind them.'

'What were your first thoughts about the entrance gates being locked from the inside of the property?'

The witness pauses, wringing her hands before her.

'In my mind, the only reason the gates would be locked from the inside was to keep us from gaining entry to help those trapped inside . . . or to keep those within from escaping.'

The courtroom falls silent. A nervous cough sounds from the public gallery.

'What did you see when you got inside?'

'When we reached the end of the drive, the east side of the property had been completely engulfed. We parked up and got our equipment ready. It didn't seem possible that anyone would survive; our preparation was purely protocol. I was shocked when the firefighters said they had found someone alive.'

'And who had they found, Ms Cummings?'

'The defendant.'

Chairs creak as those in the room turn to glance at the dock.

'Could you describe the condition the defendant was in?'

'The patient was brought to us by the firefighters, and we immediately set him up with oxygen to combat the smoke inhalation. The patient was unconscious, and had second-degree burns to his left hand. He was dressed for sleep – a navy pyjama set, and his feet were bare and bloodied.'

'Was it his blood, on his feet?'

'No,' she replies. 'I inspected both soles for wounds to treat, but found none. The blood came from someone else.'

'Was there any other blood on his person?'

'Yes. His uninjured hand was also bloodied, but again, there were no wounds to signify the blood was his. His pyjamas were soiled with it, too. Neither my colleague nor I noticed at first, until I touched the fabric to attach the ECG pads to check his heart, and pulled my fingers away to find them wet and red.'

'The blood was still fresh?'

'It had dried on his hand and both feet, but his clothes were still damp with it, yes.'

'And was the defendant conscious during this?'

'No, but he was stable. My colleague treated the burns to his hand, and we set him up on oxygen and left the premises quickly, calling it in so we could be replaced, in case any further survivors were found.'

'Is it usual for only one ambulance to attend a scene of this magnitude?'

'We were particularly stretched that night.'

'Thank you, Ms Cummings. That will be all from me.'

Niall sits, and the attention of the room turns to me. The witness is stood in the box, waiting for me to pick her testimony apart, and now the nuclear evidence has been delivered, I can, but however efficiently I cross-examine the prosecution witnesses, the evidence Fredrick secured will blow it all out of the water. I stand on my side of the bench.

'Ms Cummings, my name is Neve Harper, acting for the defendant. In your nine years of service as a paramedic, have you come across patients bearing another person's blood in the past?'

'Yes. Plenty of times.'

'In what kind of scenarios did these instances occur?'

Ms Cummings looks away, thinking back. 'Usually, it's when one person has harmed another; the perpetrator is often covered in their victim's blood. Other instances might be during an emergency situation, in which one person may have attempted to help another who was injured.'

'Like a house fire, for example?'

'Yes, for example.'

I give her a forced, deceptively comforting smile.

'So, would it be fair to say that, in your opinion from nine years of service, it would be wrong to jump to the conclusion that a patient covered in another person's blood automatically means they caused harm to that person?'

She blushes in the box.

'It's not my job to judge a patient, but to treat them.'

'Thank you, Ms Cummings. And in your training to become a paramedic, were you taught about placements of blood on a person? Did you study forensic science?'

'Like a crime scene investigator might, you mean?'

'Yes.'

'Well, no. I'm not an investigator. I treat patients.'

'So, your professional opinion of this case, which you are here today to give, is simply that your patient – the defendant – was discovered with traces of blood on him that were not his own.'

'Yes.'

'And you have just acknowledged that it is not your role or expertise to assume where that blood might have come from, in terms of a motive? It's your job to look for wounds to treat, rather than to investigate the origin, or make assumptions of a person's involvement, correct?'

'Y-yes,' she replies nervously.

'Thank you.' I look to the judge. 'No further questions.'

32

After the lead firefighter was called to the box to give his statement on the deliberate nature of the fire and the time it took to extinguish, the prosecution calls their last witness of the day, Detective Inspector Markus Hall.

DI Hall is a tall, broad figure. The sort of man that commands a room just by being in it. His heavy brow appears to be constantly furrowed, and his buzz cut makes him appear more like an army sergeant than a detective. He steps into the box and gives his oath, before the prosecution guides him through his history with the force. Twenty-two years since he joined the police, nine years as an inspector. Building character, securing credibility in the eyes of the jury.

'When I was assigned to the case, the home itself wasn't safe to investigate; the fire was still going at this point, so it was down to my team and me to interview those closest to the Darlings to try and gauge the status of the relationships between the victims, and if there was any reason to suspect foul play.'

'And was there?' Niall asks.

'Yes. It was clear from the first responders' statements that the fire had been started deliberately.'

'Deliberately,' Niall repeats. 'Which elements of the case drew you to this conclusion, in particular?'

'The gates to the property were locked shut with a chain and padlock. The gates were electronically powered and showed no sign of fault after inspection, so the only conclusion that could be drawn for the gates being chained shut were to keep the victims from escaping, and the first responders from intervening.'

'Was the padlock used to lock the gate fastened from outside or inside the property?'

'They were locked from the inside.'

DI Hall responds to each of the questions with calm confidence, stating the naked facts without emotional embellishments, which only seems to make the testimony all the more impactful. In the corner of my eye, I can see Antony, fidgeting nervously in his seat.

'Was there anything else to suggest foul play?'

'Yes. The fire appeared to have been ignited purposely in particular places to ensure destruction. There were puddles of gasoline found around the property. The canister was discovered on the forecourt.'

Niall instructs the jury to view their evidence packs. Inside is a series of photographs. If one looks closely at the picture of the main house and stables, the charred figures of the horses can be seen lying in the wreckage, their heads removed and taken to the pathologist's office to assess the bullet tracks through their skulls.

'Were there any suggestions at this point who the perpetrator might have been?'

'Yes,' he replies confidently. 'When we discovered Mr Wade Darling's fingerprints on the canister, he quickly became our first suspect. His fingerprints were also found on the murder weapon, which was found beside him by the firefighters when they discovered him.'

'Did the rifle exhibit anyone else's fingerprints or DNA, other than that belonging to Mr Wade Darling?'

'No. Just his.'

The courtroom falls quiet.

'Was that all the evidence you had to suspect the defendant?'

'No,' the inspector replies. 'There was more.'

'*More?*' Niall exclaims. It takes all of my strength not to roll my eyes at his faux dismay. 'What other evidence did you have?'

'The property had CCTV.'

The press bench creaks as each journalist leans in eagerly. The gallery is deathly silent.

'Members of the jury will now be shown a portion of this footage.'

The old, rickety trolley is pushed in, with the TV mounted on top. The tension builds as the room waits. There have been photographs, articles and third-party testimonies, but this is the most visceral glimpse the court has had into what happened on the night of the deaths. They will see the fire burning. The shadowy silhouette of the gun against the backdrop of fire.

The black screen bursts with colour as the footage plays.

The position of the camera shows the front of the property, with a view of the forecourt, and beyond it, the garages and horse stables. What appears to be a male figure enters the frame, dark with the night but with the unmistakable shadow of a rifle in one hand. As the minutes roll by, we watch him enter and exit the garage, returning with the bright red canister in his grip. He approaches the stables, rests the canister on the ground, and approaches the first door. A flash of white light bursts from the gun and reveals a glimpse of the scene:

the man stood with the rifle, pointed inside. He goes along the line of stables, the jury watching with ashen faces, as he sloshes the fuel from the canister inside, up the walls, the doors. The fire envelopes the stable in what seems like seconds, and the flames roar to life, lighting up the forecourt, as the man crosses towards the house and enters with the fire erupting behind him.

The footage stops and Niall clears his throat.

'Detective Inspector Hall, can you confirm the identity of the person in this footage?'

'We believe this is the defendant, Mr Wade Darling. As can be seen in the footage, this figure is familiar with the property: he knows where to retrieve the fuel canister, for example, and walks with purpose and conviction. We can also see the gunman holds the rifle with his right hand. The defendant is also right-handed. The figure in the footage also appears to be the same height, ethnicity and build as the defendant.'

'Is there any evidence to indicate a third party committed these crimes?'

'No. There is no sign of forced entry to the property, no CCTV or visual sightings of vehicles different to those owned by the Darling family. There was no other DNA evidence on the murder weapon, or the petrol canister, other than Mr Darling's.'

Niall appears to check his notes; an old advocate's trick to allow a witness statement to settle in the minds of the jury.

'And to clarify,' Niall asks. 'Who owned the murder weapon?'

'The rifle was bought and registered by the defendant.'

'Was this his only weapon?'

'No. Mr Darling owned a significant number of firearms. He had a gun room in the property to store his collection, which is worth over twenty thousand pounds.'

Niall allows the witness's last words to reverberate around
the quiet courtroom, as the onlookers do the maths. The sum
my client spent on firearms is likely to be more than some of the
jury could ever hope to spend in a lifetime on a mere hobby. A
good tactic, to reveal my client's alleged obsession and greed.

'Thank you, Detective Inspector Hall. No further questions.'

Niall takes to his seat.

'I'm afraid we've met our time limit for the day, Ms Harper,'
Judge McConnell says. 'We will reconvene tomorrow morning
for cross-examination.'

After the judge has left, Antony sighs heavily, his shoulders
sinking. I peer along the bench towards Niall, who undoubtedly has had a fantastic day in court. He gives me a playful
wink, and I look away.

'Don't worry, Antony,' I say in hushed tones. 'We'll skewer
him in the morning.'

'Yeah. Shame the judge had to give the jury the entire bloody
night to think over everything the detective said, though.'

He packs up his things quickly, looking towards the dock
as Wade is led out.

'I'll go and give him a pep talk. Let's meet later and plan our
attack on the new evidence.'

'I'm sorry, I can't tonight. Let's each work on it and reconvene tomorrow.'

'Neve, come on. We need to nail this. What could possibly
be more important?'

We stare at each other, unblinking.

I have to dig up my husband's body.

'I don't really think that's any of your business, is it?' He
flinches at my sharp tone. 'I'll see you in the morning.'

Antony sighs disappointedly. 'Fine. Tomorrow it is.'

As I watch him leave the court, I wonder how different I will be, come the morning. While the rest of the courtroom sleeps, I will be facing my biggest fear. Staring my worst sin right in the eyes.

Matthew.

33

The first thing I notice when I step out of the Bailey is how much the presence of the press and protesters has grown. Among the camera flashes and heckling photographers, they pace with their picket signs, chanting about Wade and his alleged crimes. I spot a blown-up photo of Yolanda Darling bobbing above the growing crowd, her eyes crossed out in red paint, a bloody handprint at her throat.

I forge on with my head down, my eyes blotted from the flashing lights, and stumble when a woman with a sign shoves through the photographers to reach me.

'Like cosying up to women-killers, do you? You make me *sick*!'

I feel the spray of saliva on my face, the heat of her words. A scuffle breaks out as the photographers shove her back, and I dart around the corner as fast as I can, but no matter how much distance I put between the crowd and me, I can still hear the shouts, their chants sing-songing in my head.

I dig around my bag for my phone, desperate for an update from Hannah. What if all of my worry was in vain? Perhaps they've found him by now, and this is already over. The lit screen shakes in my hand as I tap in the security code.

Hannah
Definitely made headway. Can't see any trees from
the window. What time will you be home? X

She sent that two hours ago, and I think of all the things that
might have happened between then and now. I imagine police
officers sat in my living room, awaiting my return to take
me in for questioning, with Maggie pacing the kitchen after
ordering Hannah to stay upstairs until I've been taken away in
cuffs. Maggie would make sure we never saw each other again.
Although, should Hannah discover what I did, all the lies I've
told, I'm sure she wouldn't need persuading. I feel that empty
twang in my chest, the same one my sleepwalking brings, and I
think back to being that little girl, wandering about strangers'
homes in the night, looking for her mother.

I fish my cigarettes and lighter from my pocket and light one
hungrily, as I think of my next steps. The nicotine seeps into my
bloodstream with the first hit and I exhale in a slow, relieved sigh.
I smoke the cigarette to the filter as I head for the tube station.

As I uncork the wine and bend down to check on the pizza in the
oven, not trusting myself with anything more mentally taxing,
I listen to Hannah padding around upstairs, the sound of life
within the house still foreign to me. She hadn't showered all day,
instead lying on the sofa tangled among blankets. I order her up
the stairs to get washed before dinner, and as soon as I hear the
water running, I bolt out into the garden towards the tracks.

The trees are gone. Every single one. All that remains are
the stumps in the earth, their roots still intact. No holes in the
dirt. He's still down there, waiting for me.

I return to the house and make my way upstairs. I slip the tablets from my bedroom drawer before returning to the kitchen, just as the shower turns off.

I couldn't sleep for weeks after the murder, replaying every swish of the club, every crack of my husband's skull. The warm splash of his blood spraying my face, the soft skin at my neck. Everyone around me thought it was grief that was eating away at me rather than guilt, and the doctor prescribed zopiclone sleeping tablets, which helped for a time, although she almost hadn't let me have them when I admitted to drinking heavily to get to sleep.

You mustn't mix this medication with alcohol, or it will intensify the effects. If I prescribe these, I need to know you won't drink.

I pour the crushed tablets into the wine glass and stir it in. The rioja appears to envelope the mixture whole.

'Smells good,' Hannah says.

I jump at the sound of her, picking up the wine glass as I turn.

'Here we go,' I say, and hold out the glass.

Her eyes gleam, reaching for it slowly, as if my offering is a trick to catch her out.

'Seriously?'

'You're old enough to have a drink with dinner. You like red wine?'

'Totally,' she replies quickly, her eyes fixed on the glass in her hands. I can tell she's never tried the stuff. But even if she doesn't like it, I know her teenage willpower will have her finish the lot.

I raise my own and eye her over the rim as I take a sip. She does the same, trying to hide a grimace.

'Gets easier to stomach the stuff the more you drink,' I say with a wink, before turning back to the stove. My smile drops instantly, and the guilt coils in my wine-filled gut.

It's the only way.

I listen as she takes a seat with a sigh and forces down another gulp.

'You feeling better?' I ask.

'I think so. I've slept a lot.'

'Ready to go back to school tomorrow?'

'Maybe.'

The oven timer goes off, and I remove the pizza and chips, both brown around the edges.

'Are you sure there's not anything else bothering you? Not making you want to go to school?'

She is silent as I cut the pizza into slices and place them on each plate.

'Han?'

I turn with both plates, placing one before her, and take to my own seat. She takes the ketchup bottle from the centre of the table.

'I'm fine.'

'That was convincing.'

She sighs, dipping a slice of pizza into the puddle of ketchup, moving it around rather than eating it.

'I don't really like this time of year.'

My heart drops. I take a piece of pizza and force myself to take a bite, despite losing my appetite too.

'Of course, you don't. It's tough.'

'Does it get easier? The whole grieving thing?'

I take a sip of wine to buy some time, and watch as she does the same. She had been sipping while my back was turned; nearly half the glass is gone now.

'I don't know. I hope so.'

We eat in silence, chewing and sipping at the wine. It usually takes thirty minutes to an hour for the tablets to take full effect, but when mixed with alcohol, it should take only half that time. She covers her mouth as she yawns.

'Have you heard from Nan?' I ask.

'She's not talking to me.'

'That can't be easy either.'

'You know what she's like.'

Her eyes look glassy now, and her words sound more drawn out than before, her lips and tongue growing lazy. What if mixing it with wine is too much for her system? Christ, what if she went to sleep and never woke up?

She takes one last sip, and I spot some of the undissolved tablets poking up from the dark pool at the bottom of her glass. I leap forward and snatch it from her hand.

'This was a bad idea,' I say as I head to the sink and throw the last dregs down the drain. 'You're not well, this won't help.'

'I'm fine,' she slurs, her eyes heavy.

A pang of guilt hits my chest. It's working much sooner than I thought.

Christ, what am I doing?

'Eat the pizza, it'll sober you up a bit.'

She yawns again, her mouth thrown wide, showing her wine-stained tongue.

'I'm not that hungry.'

'Eat it all, Han, or we won't have wine with dinner again.'

I watch anxiously as she chows down on the last of the pizza, ketchup on her chin and melted cheese on her fingers. Her eyes get hazier. The panic grows in me the drowsier she becomes.

You need her to stay asleep. You can't do what needs to be done without this.

She finishes the last mouthful, yawning widely.

'Why don't you have a lie-down, watch TV in bed?' I say. 'Perhaps you still aren't one hundred per cent.'

I expect her to fight me with it still being early in the evening, but she nods slowly.

'Yeah, okay.'

'I'll come and check on you.'

She rises from the table, swaying slightly, and heads for the stairs.

I sit with my guilt, waiting ten minutes, fifteen. When I don't hear any sign of her, I creep upstairs and pop my head into her room.

She is out for the count.

34

I decide to wait until midnight again to be sure that Hannah and most of the street are asleep, to limit the chances of me being seen, and spend the hours beforehand almost obsessively checking on Hannah: feeling her breaths on the back of my hand, making sure she's lying on her side. Now I sit in my armchair, waiting for the clock on the mantel to strike twelve. The arm turns around the dial, shuddering with age as it crawls towards twelve. The church bells ring out on the other side of the window.

It's time.

I head for the back door and step out into the night. The air is cold and thick, the sort of chill that clears the skies of clouds and reveals the stars. I stop in my tracks, my breath white on the air, and look up. I almost wish I was up there floating in the nothingness, where the guilt or repercussions couldn't reach me.

I continue my journey towards the end of the garden, shivering beneath my coat and gripping onto the handle of the spade. The trees have been sawn down, leaving nothing but a trail of stumps, their cream-coloured centres illuminated beneath the moon, as far as the eye can see. The train tracks reflect the night sky too, the moonlight glinting in the steel of the rails.

I hike myself over the fence, taking extra care not to knock the spade and alert anyone to my presence, and cross the track. I have already moved my car to the small car park wrapped around the church, right beside the fence that separates the grounds from the tracks. I look at the distance I will have to drag him, all the way along the tracks, following the length of the road from my house to the church. It's either that or drag him through the house.

When I reach what used to be the woodland edge, I close my eyes and think back to when there were trees, counting my way through the trunks, and open my eyes.

There is no going back now.

When I buried the body, I had been reeling from shock, moving on autopilot to get through the trauma of the night. I wasn't myself, but a raw, animal version of myself. But now, three years on, I must retrieve him with a sound mind. I will see and feel everything.

I stand before the stump and look around me. My heartbeat quickens. Without the trees, I am stood in plain sight. The row of terraced houses has a direct view of me. The majority of windows are dark with the night, but for the odd yellow glow emitting from hallway windows, the odd bedroom lit up behind the curtains. Hannah's, of course, is pitch black.

If I don't dig him up tonight, the rail workers will.

I poise the spade and stare down at the earth beneath my feet. How decomposed will he be now? He won't be a mere skeleton, not yet. But he would have begun to decay. His teeth and nails falling out, his skin waxy and slipping from his bones. I blink the fear back.

Just do what needs to be done.

I raise the spade and make the first crunch in the earth. The winter weather has made it almost rock solid. I raise the spade, and thrust with all my might. *Crunch*.

I push down on the handle, bringing up a pitiful amount of dirt, and close my eyes with a defeated sigh.

I am going to be here for hours.

⚖

An hour has passed. I have sweated so much beneath my coat that my clothes have stuck to my body, and locks of hair have plastered to my face. Every muscle throbs with pain. I'm so exhausted that I could cry for thinking about it if I dared to stop for too long, so I keep digging and digging.

The earth is practically frozen solid, but once I prepared a flask of boiled water from the kitchen and poured it over Matthew's grave, steam rose in white, whistling curls, and the water sank into the earth, softening it enough to break through. I have followed the shape of the grave as I remember it, thinking back to the way I laid him down: his head towards the tree, his feet facing east.

I thrust the spade down and stop when I hear a different sound. It isn't the earthy crunch, but a familiar rustle, and beneath it, a meatier thud.

Matthew.

I had buried him in the carrier my wedding dress came in. It was the only thing I had that was big enough to store him in; the closest thing I could find to a body bag. That night, as I dragged it out of storage in the loft and removed the dress, I'd found a small dried flower stuck in the netting of it that had fallen from my bouquet. I remember sitting among the rustling white fabric, my husband's body lying bloody in the hall as I twirled the dead flower between my fingers, tears running silently down my face.

I get down on my hands and knees, digging at the dirt with my gloved hands, and slowly reveal the dress carrier, its corner poking out from the earth. But I can barely see through my tears and the fog of my breath.

Even through the bag, I can smell him. The scent is rotten and musky, like that of a dung beetle, its tang so sharp that it catches at the back of my throat and lingers there, clinging to every drop of spit.

I look about me anxiously and towards the row of houses, looking for any silhouettes stood at the windows. But I see no one. As far as I'm aware, I am alone.

I have cleared most of the earth now. I can feel the shape of his body within the bag, as cold and hard as the earth. Will his eyes have rotted away? Those beautiful, captivating eyes that Hannah inherited? I clench mine shut at the thought of her, forcing myself to focus, and dash the last of my tears away.

I'm so sorry.

The roots have bound themselves around the bag, claiming him. I try to tug him free, but I can't dislodge him alone, and stagger to my feet. Loose earth slips from my knees. My head is spinning, but there are no trees to rest upon to catch my breath. I stand, swaying in the night, begging myself to focus.

You're almost done.

I lift the spade and try to wedge it beneath him to use as leverage. I lower the spade, watch the bag rise slightly, repeating the motions until I hear a dreadful sound.

A rip.

The smell hits me, suddenly and with force. It infiltrates my nose and throat, seeping through my airways. I lunge away from the grave as I cough and gag, landing on my hands and knees as strained, dying sounds retch up my throat. It is the most putrid scent I have ever known. It burns my eyes, coats my tongue and teeth. I spit against the mud in my desperation to clear it, but still it remains.

I rise up and sit on the ground, catching my breath, and see the scene before me. Piles of dirt, the abandoned spade gleaming beneath the moon, the shadowy grave. I look down the tracks, at the long distance I must drag him. I can't move him with the tear in the bag, the smell is strong enough to rouse even the deepest sleeper. The sort of scent that claims the air.

I'll duct tape it shut. Then all there is left to do is move him.

I check my watch. It is almost two in the morning. Just over five hours till sunrise, seven hours until I'm back at the Bailey.

I get to my feet, my entire body throbbing with stress, smoothing the piles of loose dirt over the bag to keep him hidden while I'm gone, and cross the tracks for home in search of duct tape for the bag, and wire clippers for the fence.

I had lied to myself before, when I said it was almost over with. For this is only the beginning of a long night ahead: once I have pulled the body free from the earth, I will have to bury him all over again.

⚖️

I turn the corner sharply and hear the thump of Matthew's body hitting against the side of the boot.

I flinch at the sound, sending shivers of pain through me. My muscles are so tense that it hurts to move; every time I glance in the rear-view mirror, a splice of pain shoots up my neck.

It had been a nightmare moving the body. It was so heavy despite decomposition, and there had been no other way to move him but to drag him alongside the tracks, before finally having to tug him over them, hearing the thud of him falling from each rail. Next was the fence. I'd had to cut at the wire and drag him beneath, looking about me with every snip. A trail of mud and grass leads from the fence to where I had parked my car, and I lugged him into the boot with sweat dripping into my eyes and hair sticking to my lips with each heave for breath, before attempting to conceal the trail I left in my wake.

I drive out of the city towards the outskirts, forever looking behind me for the Messenger or one of his men following behind, while trying not to think of what I saw when duct-taping the bag shut. As my eyes watered from the stench, and I gritted my teeth to keep from breathing it in, I saw a flash of him. The yellowed, mummified flesh of his hand. His wedding ring mottled into him.

I will bury him in the woods at Low Valley Wood outside of East London. There are miles of trees, which will be completely empty but for the woodland creatures, and no witnesses to stumble across me. Matthew and I had taken Hannah there when she was younger. I continually force the memories of the visit out of my mind: holding his hand, Hannah running gaily before us, her auburn hair shining copper in the sun.

I take the next left and drive down a long, straight road. The further out of London I go, the thinner the range of buildings become. To my right is an open field, and to my left, a hedge grove. I check the time at the dash: it's gone three.

The steering wheel begins to shudder beneath my grip. Slow at first, before the vigour grows and the headlights begin to flicker. A beeping sounds from the dashboard: the battery light flashes at me in strobes.

'No ... *No, no, no!*'

The engine splutters as it slows, and the lights grow dimmer and dimmer, until the car falls silent and I am drifting to a stop towards the roadside. I lift the handbrake and sit in the darkness, with no sounds to be heard other than my short, panicked breaths and the violent thud of my heart.

My phone is at home to keep the Messenger from tracking me. I am alone, in the middle of nowhere, with my husband's body decaying in the boot, with less than four hours to go until the sun rises.

I stare silently at the pitch-black road beyond the windscreen.

35

I have been stationed on the side of the road for over an hour, and not one other driver has passed me by. The night is impenetrably dark, and the inside of the car is as cold as the outside; even in here, I can see my breath on the air. The windows have fogged up, and my lungs crackle and wheeze as I breathe in the wet chill.

This is the only time it would have been beneficial to have the Messenger following me, for it wouldn't do him any good to have me caught either. But I seem to have evaded them, on the one night I need them. I go to check the time, remembering that I haven't got my phone on me, and the dashboard is as dark as the night.

What the hell am I going to do?

I get out of the car to get my blood moving, rubbing the arms of my coat, and light a cigarette, looking out across the fields at the miles of sprawling void. I had wished to float in nothingness, hadn't I? Although these weren't the circumstances I'd had in mind.

Something catches my eye, and I whip my head to the left.

Headlights appear in the distance.

I stare at the two taunting orbs, growing in size the closer they get, my heart rate climbing as the seconds tick by. What sort of character would be on the road at this sort of time? I know I should move for the car, but I am quite literally like a deer in headlights, watching as the vehicle gets closer. Should I flag them down for a jump-start, or hide and hope they pass without seeing me? A potential witness to my crimes.

There will be more passers-by when the sun rises.

Before I have time to act, the car begins to slow and pulls up before mine, our front bumpers facing one another on the side of the road. It's a beaten-up old Ford, with its trusty engine sputtering like a tractor. I can only see the silhouette of the person behind the wheel, and listen as the ignition is turned off, followed by the click of the driver's door. I drop the cigarette to the ground.

'You all right, lass?' The man asks. He's an older gentleman, his white hair crisp against the night, his tone warm and thoughtful.

'I-i-it's my battery,' I reply, my teeth chattering around the words.

'Poor mite, you must be freezing. Need a boost?'

I nod. 'Please.'

He steps closer with a kind, fatherly smile.

'You got the cables by any chance?'

I pause, unsure. My uncertainty must be all over my face, for he speaks again.

'You might have some tucked away in the spare tyre bed in the boot, with a car like that,' he says, pointing towards the rear. 'Let's have a look.'

'*No,*' I reply. The man stops in his tracks, his smile falling in an instant. 'I'll look. God knows what I've got back there.'

I feign a laugh and head for the rear of the car, shaking from the cold and the fear. Will he be able to smell the body from where he stands? What if the tape has been knocked loose from the bumps in the road? My mind is bombarded with questions as I take each step, the road crunching underfoot.

I have to appear as normal as I can.

'Thank you so much for stopping,' I say through chattering teeth. 'I thought I was going to be out here all night.'

I take the key from my pocket, jumbling in my shaking fingers, and crouch at the boot to try to slip it into the manual lock. It's so dark I can barely see my own hands.

'No problem, least I could do. You need some light?' he asks. He begins to approach, pawing for his phone.

'No, no,' I say, raising my hand. 'I'm good, thank you.'

I wrestle the key against the lock, listening to the metal scrape, all under the man's watchful eye as he appears to edge closer. I can't have him standing beside me as the door opens. The fear of being caught has me fumbling with haste; sweat breaks out beneath my coat.

'Are you sure you don't need—'

The key slips inside, and I turn it roughly, a relieved, white breath huffing from between my lips.

'Got it.'

I stand up and slowly lift the boot door.

The tape has remained intact, and yet the smell still hits me. I try to keep the disgusted expression from my face, but the potent scent makes my eyes water. My gut squirms beneath my coat.

'Corr,' the man says, sniffing the wind. 'You catch that? What's that God-awful smell?'

I blink the water from my eyes.

'Maybe it's field fertiliser,' I stutter.

'Bit early for that, pet.'

The body lies over the well where the spare tyre is stored.

I reach in and try to shift it, but with my strained arms shaking and useless, the weight of him seems immovable. I blow a lock of hair out of my face and heave against the bulk of him. The well's cover appears slowly with each shove.

Matthew's inside here, a voice whispers in my head. I imagine him twisted from each movement, his limbs bent, face frozen in an eternal, quizzical look.

'Christ love, what you got in there, a body?'

I bolt up and stare at him over the roof of the car. The smile drops from his face.

We stand in the dark, the arctic breeze howling between us.

'It . . . it was a joke, darlin'. No harm meant.'

I couldn't appear more suspicious if I tried. I cough to clear the panic from my throat and force a laugh. The sound is inauthentic and awkward.

'Sorry. The cold . . . I've lost my sense of humour.'

I give the body one last shove and lift the latch with a shaking hand, fighting against the weight of the body bag, shifting him enough to clear the way.

'Got it,' I say, as I reach in for the cables.

The man steps forward to retrieve them, so I yank them free and slam the boot shut just as he turns towards the rear of the car. I hold out the cables in my shaky grip.

'Thanks so much again for your help.'

He smiles, although it is smaller than before. Forced.

Christ love, what you got in there, a body?

'Course,' he says, heading towards the front of the car. 'Can't have you out here alone, can we? God knows who's about.'

I smile tightly. The irony is not lost on me.

I'm the most dangerous thing out here.

'I'll pop my bonnet and get them on. You should be able to pop yours from under the steering wheel somewhere; a small catch in the footwell.'

I silently resent him giving me instructions about my own car, but truth be told, I wouldn't have known had he not said. This was more Matthew's car than mine. He knew where everything was, was the one to change the oil and all the other tasks. As I head towards the driver's side, I fear I can still smell the body on the air.

I open the driver's door and use my lighter to search about in the dark, enjoying the faint warmth of the flame against my face, and pull the lever. When I close the door behind me, the man is already lifting the bonnet of my car and fitting the cables.

'Sorry love,' he says from beneath the bonnet. 'I never introduced myself. I'm Andy.'

'Nice to meet you.'

I hear a metal clang from beneath the bonnet.

'What's your name then?' he asks.

Why does he want to know that?

He could have jotted down the registration number plate when he pulled up. Will he think my behaviour odd, and look up the reg plate when he gets home? He could find out my address that way, couldn't he?

He steps out from under the bonnet and glances at me, awaiting my answer.

'Amy,' I lie.

'Nice name. Same as my niece.'

As the silence falls between us, I can't help but think of the testimony he would give at my trial.

I found her on the side of the road in the middle of the

night. She looked cold and scared, but it wasn't long before she started acting . . . oddly. She was reluctant to let me see inside the boot, and gave me a false name. I knew she'd lied because I'd seen her on the front page of The Times.

Andy blows hot air into his hands before rubbing them together for warmth.

'What brings you out here so late then, love?'

He's not doing anything wrong. He's just making light conversation. I'm being paranoid.

'I was staying with some family, but needed to head home for work tomorrow. How long does it take to recharge a car?'

He gives me a quizzical look. I force a smile, but I'm clearly on edge.

'We leave them like this for a few minutes, then I'll run my engine for another ten, then we'll turn off both cars and wait a minute before disconnecting. Hopefully your car should start after that, no problem.'

Ten whole minutes of talking to this man.

'Great.'

We fall into an uncomfortable silence. The treetops swish with the icy wind. My eyes stream from the chill of it. I'm sure I can smell the body from here.

'What do you do?' he asks.

I shouldn't have mentioned work; I practically asked for this question to be put to me. He stands rubbing his hands together, eyes on mine.

'An accountant,' I lie. 'What about you?'

He laughs. 'My niece Amy, she's an accountant too.'

I force one back. 'Small world.'

'Really is. You must currently be in hell with tax return season,' he says.

'Oh yes,' I force. 'So what is it you do?' I ask, trying to shift the conversation from me to him.

'Retired copper,' he replies.

My heart drops as I try not to let the shock show on my face. Of all the people who could have stopped to help.

'Been off the force a few years now. Haven't shaken the sense of duty yet though, as you can tell.'

No wonder he has been asking so many questions. He clearly senses something is amiss. Would he know what a body smells like, from his time on the force? Is that why he made that joke about the boot?

'Shall we turn your engine on now?' I ask.

'You really are keen to get home,' he says with a chuckle, and heads towards the driver's side door.

'Just cold and tired,' I reply.

The engine grumbles awake, and we stand in the cold, listening to it chug to life. Not a single other car has passed since he arrived.

'Your phone die, or something?' he asks.

'Sorry?'

'Your phone. Did it run out of battery? I'm surprised you didn't call anyone.'

'Oh. I planned to charge it from the cigarette lighter on the dash, but never got the chance. So, ten more minutes you said?'

My insistence only makes me seem more suspicious. I can see everything I say piquing his curiosity. His eyes are no longer kind, but inquisitive, looking me up and down, scanning the car as if to remember details later.

'Eight and a half by now,' he says. 'You'll be on your way in no time.'

The cold has seeped into my bones. No matter how much I pull my coat around my frame, or rub at my arms, the chill remains. The skin on my face is starting to burn from the ice-cold wind.

'You shouldn't be out this late at night without a phone, y'know,' he says. 'Never know who's about.'

The irritability bites back before I can stop it.

'Yes,' I snap. 'But we all make mistakes, don't we?'

His expression falls. I don't know the man, and despite his kind act of help, I dislike him. I hate his questions, his prying eyes.

'I wasn't telling you off,' he says. 'Just some advice from an old man.'

'Right.'

'Sorry, I've got a daughter about your age. It's the dad in me.'

And the copper, I bet.

I begin to pace back and forth, partly to keep myself warm, but also to keep him from studying me, in the hope that a moving target is harder to remember than a still one.

'So what have you got rattling around back there?'

I stop in my tracks.

'Excuse me?'

He nods towards the boot.

'You said you had to sift through stuff.'

'Is that really any of your business?'

He raises his eyebrows and shrugs.

'I just meant ... I can give you a list of things that would be good to have in the car, should something like this happen again. Bottled water, blanket, battery-operated phone charger—'

'This won't happen again.'

I pace some more, faster this time. It mustn't be much longer now. Six minutes? Five?

'Christ, what *is* that smell?'

A copper would know what a corpse smelt like. If he hasn't pinpointed it yet, I have no doubt he will. If not here, then when I'm gone. The recognition clicking like a switch in his brain.

'Sewage, maybe,' I say.

'Nah, whatever it is, it's dead.'

'Roadkill then,' I reply smartly. 'How much longer?'

He gives me a look. The smiles have long gone. Now he is frowning at me.

'Are you sure you're all right?'

What do I do if he doesn't give up?

I think of him opening the car boot and seeing the body bag inside, the smell hitting him like it had me.

What would I do then?

He is still staring at me, awaiting my answer.

I hear the swish of the golf club. *Whoosh. Thwack.* Then an intrusive thought, a horrible one. I think of taking the spade from the back of the car, raising it through the night air, and cracking the back of the man's skull.

'Look, I'm really grateful you've stopped to help, but I'm cold and I'm tired, and in the nicest possible way, I don't know you. Being out here alone with a strange man is putting me on edge.'

A light sparks in his eyes. One of recognition and relief.

'Of course ... I'm sorry, I didn't think.' He runs his hand through his thin whisps of white hair. 'Why don't you sit in the car, warm up a bit?'

I get behind the wheel and shut the door behind me, but even here, behind metal and glass, I can sense him watching me, trying to figure me out. Why had he joked about there being a body in the car? The smell is in here too, drifting through the back seats. I cover my nose and mouth with my scarf, but it seeps through the fabric.

After a few more agonising minutes, he knocks on the glass and opens the car door.

'Right, start your engine for me. Let's see if she plays ball.'

I turn the key in the ignition, and the lights appear on the dash.

'It's working,' I say. 'Thanks for your help—'

'Hold your horses,' he says. 'Let's check the engine too.'

I turn the key further and listen to the engine spit and grumble, eventually coming to life.

'Let's give it a minute, then we should be done.'

'Look,' I say, desperately. 'Let's not. I should be getting home. But thanks for all of your help, it was really kind of you.'

'Want me to fit the cables back in the—'

'*No* . . . I'll take them in here with me.'

We turn off our engines and he removes the cables. I rock with the car when he slams the bonnet shut, and gives me a nod.

'Thanks again for your help.'

'No problem,' he says, passing me the cables through the window, without the smile he had greeted me with. 'Get home safe, Amy.'

I start the engine again, praying it runs. When it grumbles to life, I lift the handbrake and speed off, spitting stones behind me, glancing in the rear-view mirror as I go.

The man is stood in the road, watching as I drive away.

It is early morning by the time I have dug the new grave, but the sky is still dark with the night. All I can see are the shadows of the trees, the odd bit of moonlight breaking through the treetops, and the white fog of my breath.

I reached the woods around five thirty in the morning, and dragged the body from the boot and down into the woodland verge with tears of pain and exhaustion blurring my eyes, my hands shaking and numb to the bone despite the gloves. I barely remember digging the grave. I dissociated from the act, thrusting the spade into the hard earth on autopilot. Had I thought about it, I would have wept from the work I had yet to do, and the pain screaming all over my body. My back has blown from dragging Matthew, twinging every time I raise the spade and bring it down again. Whenever I thought I was nearing the end, I quickly realised the grave was too shallow, and had to set about digging once more. As I dug, a fleeting thought crept into the forefront of my mind.

Give in. Give up. Call the police, and this is all over: the trial, the hiding. The guilt.

But it's not just my life at stake. I kept digging, and digging, muttering my motivation repeatedly beneath my white breath.

I'm doing this for Hannah.

When the grave is finally deep enough, I grab onto the edge of the body bag and tug with the last of my energy, lugging it into the grave until it lands with a lifeless thud. It's a snug pit, just big enough to have him lay down with each edge pressing against him: the top of his head, the flats of his feet, his arms pressed against his sides.

My husband.

My darling.

My victim.

I check the time: I have to be at the Bailey in under three hours. I won't get a single wink of sleep. I could cry for thinking of it, longing for my bed, but I deserve every wincing pain, every second of exhaustion.

I pile the loose earth onto him, listening to the rustle as it hits the bag, until soon enough he is out of sight. I pat the loose earth with the spade, then walk over it to pack it shut, before disturbing it with the shovel again to hide my footprints and dragging fallen branches and loose undergrowth across the grave. I stumble back and assess my work. Matthew's new resting place blends in with the terrain as though I were never here.

I claw myself up the dark verge, every muscle in my body spasming from excessive use, and my head is pounding from lack of sleep and water. When I reach the top, I check the road. No headlights. Not a sound. I stumble to my feet and turn around to look at the scene, trying to remember the exact spot where I buried him. Counting the trees, looking for landmarks. Something I never dreamt I would have to do again. But if I have done this right, I will never have to come back.

I let myself inside the car, quivering violently from exertion. I am covered in dirt: my black clothes now soiled brown, and when I catch my reflection in the mirror, I see how earth has stuck to the tear tracks on my face. My eyes are bloodshot and empty. The interior light slowly fades, plunging me into the darkness again.

I turn on the headlights, ignite my last cigarette in a shaking hand, and pull away.

Day Three

36

I am cleaning the earth from the spade when the phone rings.

I stand at the kitchen sink shaking violently from exhaustion, before summoning the energy to retrieve the phone.

'Hello?'

'What the *hell* do you think you're playing at?' Maggie barks down the phone. 'The school just called and told me Hannah hasn't been in for days, and there's been no word on her absence.'

The ferocity of her tone makes me jump; I'm nothing but a mass of nerve-endings, which shoot and fire at the slightest sound.

'Hannah didn't feel well—'

'Every teenager says that. Unless they're on their last legs, you send them in, for Christ's sake. And you didn't think to call the school to let them know?'

'I've been busy with the trial—'

'Right, well you insisted on coming between Hannah and me and playing the role of her guardian, so I expect you to bloody well act like one. Send her into school this morning – I don't care if her head is hanging from her neck by a thread. Understand?'

'Yes, Maggie.'

She hangs up the phone, and I stand listening to the endless tone. I don't know how long I stay like this, transfixed in a sleep-deprived trance. I am roused again by a car horn sounding outside and glance at the clock on the wall.

Hannah.

The memory of what I did to her the night before hits me. I had been so caught up with my task and the body, that drugging my stepdaughter, the most important person in my life, got lost among the many other sins I have committed.

I make my way upstairs, my heart beating wildly in my chest, and conceal the spade beneath my bed, before slowly opening the door to Hannah's bedroom.

Hannah is still fast asleep, her hair as wild as a nest, with spittle shining at the corner of her mouth.

'Hannah, you awake?' I creep through the gloom and open the curtains. 'You'll be late for school.'

She rouses languidly, the pull of the drug trying to drag her back down. Her eyes search the room for me, and when she speaks, her mouth and tongue are lazy around the words. My heart leaps with guilt.

I'm so sorry.

'I don't feel well—'

For once, she may well be telling the truth.

'You look fine, come on. You've had enough time away from school.'

'But—'

I turn at the door and give her a look.

'No buts. Your nan has just given me a bollocking down the phone after the school called her. I can't deal with this during the trial, Han. Please.'

She sits up in bed, staring up at me through a mess of hair

and eyes bleared by sleep. But when she takes in the sight of me, her gaze turns to a look of fear.

'Are you okay? You look . . .'

As she stares at me in wonder, I glance at my reflection in the mirror on the wall. I look horrendous. My eyes are bloodshot and puffy. My hair is knotted, with a stray bit of dirt above my ear where I tucked my hair out of the way. I look like I've been dug up myself.

'I'll be fine once you're up and on the way to school.'

I stand before the Bailey, trying to muster the courage to step inside. I have showered the night away, but I can still smell the body on me. It's almost as if it's become a part of me, burrowing into my skin and rising from me with the slightest movement.

Today, the prosecution will bring more experts to the witness stand: there is the cross-examination of Detective Inspector Hall, the ballistics expert and the pathologist. Then there will be Wade's mother Marianne, before the prosecution will rest their case with the key and final witness, Dr Heche.

The press outside the Bailey seems even more excitable today, and the papers had been even more damning this morning. The protestors too have grown in number, pacing back and forth, their chants fogging before them in the cold air, their signs waving from side to side with each step, with uniformed police outside the Bailey keeping watch.

Among the crowd, I see a face looking at me, staring out from the others who are otherwise watching the front of the building: Melanie Eccleston. The smirk is undeniable. I try to steel myself as she approaches, to ready myself for whatever game she is set on playing.

'We need to talk,' she says, the smile still plastered to her face.

'Melanie, with the greatest respect, I don't have the time or the energy to deal with you.' She reaches into her bag as I talk, retrieving a high-end camera from inside. 'If you're after a lead, you're going to have to find it another way—'

'Oh, I have my lead,' she replies, and turns the camera screen towards me.

I peer down at the screen with a frown, trying to work out the photo she's showing me.

What I find hits me like a punch.

I cover my mouth with a shaking hand.

It is a photo of me, dragging the body bag from the tracks to the boot of my car in the church car park.

She presses a button and the screen shows the next image. It is of me hoisting my dead husband's body into the boot, struggling beneath the weight of him. Another, where I am looking up towards the bell tower as the clock struck and the sound boomed above my head; my face clearly identifiable as I stare up in the path of the full moon.

It was so dark last night. I thought I was alone, I didn't see any movement, hear any noise. But Melanie must have been there, staking out the house. Waiting for me to trip up.

I straighten and meet her gaze. She is stood so close to me that I can feel the warmth of her breath.

'I think we should have a chat, don't you?'

She heads down the street, away from the Bailey, not needing to glance behind her to check I will follow. She knows I will.

⚖

Melanie leads me to the coffee shop where I first met Wade Darling. The room is the same: near-empty and dimly lit from its position in the back street, shielded by the high buildings. The usual barista is making our drinks behind the counter. But despite the similarity, my life couldn't have changed more since the morning I met my client. Could that really have been only a week ago?

We sit down in the booth by the window. Melanie is practically jittering with excitement as she shrugs off her coat.

'You look shattered,' she says. 'Late night?'

Her face is straight, but she smiles with her eyes, a mischievous glint that tells me she's enjoying this.

The barista brings over our order, and I look down at the drink before me: a frothy latte that I'm not sure I can stomach. But the smell of coffee calls to me, the need for caffeine aching in my bones. I lift the mug to my lips and gulp.

'We don't have long,' I say. 'I need to meet with my client.'

'Yes, about that. What's your game plan, exactly? I mean, you're not exactly hitting it out of the park. That new evidence is said to be pretty damning.'

I give her a long, hard stare.

'If you think I'm going to give you anything – on or off the record – you're dumber than you look.'

She smiles.

'I can't say I blame your poor performance. You seem rather . . . distracted.'

'Cut the foreplay. What do you want?'

'An explanation, for a start.'

'I don't owe you anything.'

'Not me personally, no. But what about the public? After all these years of searching for your husband's whereabouts . . . don't you think they have the right to know?'

'That's quite the assumption.'

'What? That you were dragging your husband's body into the back of your car?'

The accusation sits between us like a held breath.

'Can you confirm there was a body in the bag, Melanie?'

She smiles wider and reaches for her camera again, sifting through what seems to be dozens of photos.

She holds it before me again. I lean closer, my heart beating wildly, and pause.

Melanie hadn't just taken photos of me in the church car park. She had staked outside my house all night and snapped photos of my return. In the photo, the sun is just beginning to rise. I look pale and exhausted, and I'm covered in mud: my clothes are soiled with it, with stray swipes on my face. I look like a feral animal with glassy, dilated eyes.

'How do you explain these, Neve? You didn't return with the body bag, and you were covered in mud. There's only one conclusion the police will come to . . . I'll be writing my story and backing up these photos as soon as I'm home, and will file it first thing in the morning, along with these.' She waves her camera from side to side, tauntingly. 'Hell, I'd have written it last night if I could have, but I've had just as much sleep as you.'

I feel myself grow dizzy, and grip the side of the table.

'That is, of course, unless you can give me something better . . . I doubt you can – breaking Matthew's missing persons case will be the best story of my career. But I'll give you the chance.'

I stare at her from across the table, a grimace of loathing set upon my face. She doesn't intend to give me a chance at all. She will be filing that story and those photos whatever I give her. She is hanging this over me, giving me a glimpse of hope, before snatching it away.

She checks her watch.

'Best get going if I want to get a good seat.' She slips the camera back into her bag. 'I'll wait to hear of your decision regarding my story. In the meantime, I'll be deciding which photo will look best on the front page. There are just so many good ones ...'

She stares at me from the other side of the table with an almost violent curiosity; a smirk creeps across her face. 'You and Wade make quite the murderous pair, don't you?'

⚖

I hide in the furthest cubicle in the women's bathroom and sit on top of the seat with my knees held tight to my body.

I don't know what to do. Now Melanie has these photos, it won't be long until the whole world knows. I think of Hannah and Maggie's faces paling as they take in the sight of me on the cover of *The Times*, dragging Matthew's body to the boot of my car.

I need to tell the Messenger.

Melanie knowing this will lessen the Messenger's hold on me. She will be just as much of a threat to him and Mr Viklund as she is to Hannah and me. If the truth were exposed before the trial is over, they will never get what they want.

But telling the Messenger would be effectively killing her.

I toy with the thought silently. If there were any time to intercept, it would be now. She hasn't written her story yet; she hasn't backed up the photos. All we'd need to do is destroy the camera and all traces would be gone, as though this never happened.

But I can't shed any more blood. I have accumulated enough guilt to last me a lifetime.

I stare at the dirty grouting between the tiles on the floor, blinking away the tears of frustration that blur my vision.

But what if it's the only way to keep Hannah safe?

Despite my desire to hide away, I check my watch and leave the cubicle, fixing my messy appearance in the mirror before reaching down into my bag for my wig and placing it on my head. I remember the first time I tried it on, the pride I felt. All of my youthful hope for the future. The naivety and innocence that is lost to me now. My beliefs in right and wrong had been so concentrated, sacrosanct.

Now I stand here, breaking every vow.

Melanie is good at what she does, but by dangling her win in front of me, she has made one fatal mistake.

She has given me time to stop her.

37

'Christ,' Antony says when he meets me at the door of conference room three, and steps out into the corridor. 'Are you all right? You look . . .'

His sentence trails off as he looks me up and down.

'Thanks.'

'Sorry, I just mean . . . I can't look much better.'

Thankfully, he doesn't. Despite his usually kempt appearance, his eyes look almost as bloodshot as mine. But he certainly won't be as tired. My entire body thrums with pain: every joint throbs, every muscle has been pulled taut.

'Were you up all night digging too, then?'

I flinch at his choice of words.

'Yeah. Not much luck.'

He sighs and shakes his head. 'I couldn't find much either. Damn the judge for admitting this so late.'

'We still have a strong narrative with the skewed police investigation. If we hammer this home as hard as we can, we are still in with a chance. I'll do my very best, Antony.'

'I know you will,' he says, and pats my shoulder. The guilt knots tighter in my chest.

'How is he?' I ask, nodding at the door to the conference room.

'No better than yesterday. Surely, we can't let him step into the box like this? He's in the grip of a depression and the prosecution's new evidence relates to just that. We'd be playing right into their hands.'

'And say what: "The defendant can't give evidence because of the depression the prosecution has just lambasted him for?". No, we've got no choice but to stick this out and try to save face. He's expected to stand in the box tomorrow. We can't back out now.'

He runs his hands through his hair, the smell of fresh, nervous sweat creeping from his open blazer.

'I thought we had this in the bag. I really did.'

'It'll be close to the wire, but it's not over yet.' I give him a soft smile. 'Come on.'

Wade is sat at the desk in his own vacant world, staring in a trance at the surface of the table. I wonder if he is thinking of his family and the past, or the unknown nature of his future. Whether he will walk away a free man or live the rest of his life behind bars.

'Good morning, Wade,' I say, as we sit before him on the other side of the table.

'When will this be over?' he asks, his voice croaking as if they are the first words he has spoken since the day began.

'The prosecution's case will likely end today, if there aren't any delays. Then it will be time for us to deliver ours. As for today's proceedings, we will start with my cross-examination of Detective Inspector Hall. It's a crucial part of our case, in terms of causing doubt in the juror's minds.'

'Until the prosecution tell them about my past.'

'We still have time to get them on side, Wade—'

'Let's just get this over with.'

He stands up from the desk and heads for the door, which clicks shut before we have even risen from our seats.

⚖

Detective Inspector Hall seems as serious and composed as the day before, and unlike me, he appears to have slept well, with no worries gnawing away at him. No bodies to bury in the dead of night.

I rise at the other end of the bench, my back threatening to give. As I set my tired eyes upon the detective in the witness box, I am sure I can feel the Messenger's gaze on me from the gallery, lasering into the back of my head. Not twenty feet from him, Melanie sits, watching me with an amused smile.

I break out in a sweat beneath my garb and clear my throat to begin.

'Detective Hall, I am Neve Harper, for the defence. I have a few concerns about the statements you gave yesterday afternoon.'

I give him a long stare, building my authority in the minds of the jury. He meets my eyes confidently, having done this so many times before. I look down at my notes.

'I would like to start with the gates to the property. You said you believed they were locked from the inside. How were they operated?'

'The gates were controlled from the main house, via a control panel in the hallway of the property.'

'I see. So, if the defendant wanted to keep the first responders from entering, is there a way he could keep the gates locked using this control panel?'

DI Hall picks up the glass of water before him. 'Yes, I suppose,' he replies, before taking a sip.

'So, what need would the defendant have for a chain and padlock?'

'I don't quite understand the question.'

'*If the defendant wanted to keep the gates locked*,' I repeat sternly, 'why would he not control them from the main house? Why would he fit a padlock and chain, which could easily be cut through, when the gates' pre-existing security system would have easily kept anyone from entering? Arguably, it's their sole purpose, no?'

He glances briefly towards the jury, before returning his gaze to me.

'It is my belief that the chain was applied in case of any breach of the system by the police, and to keep the victims from getting to safety.'

'Your *belief*,' I repeat. 'The fire service cut through the chains relatively quickly, didn't they?'

'Yes.'

'So in retrospect, would it not be safe to say that getting hold of the supplier of the electrical gates at three in the morning to override the system would have taken far longer than using a pair of bolt cutters to sever the chain?'

'When put that way, yes.'

'What other way is there? It suggests that this would be the action of someone without such access, wouldn't it?'

'I don't follow.'

'A third party is far less likely to know the gate system to achieve this – which I believe is quite a complex array of numbered codes – and is therefore likely to employ other measures of locking the gates, such as a padlock and chain?'

'Perhaps. But as I said, the gates were locked from the inside.'

'Ah, yes, my next concern.' I look down at my pad for some

time, pretending to scour my notes to prolong the silence, as I wonder what the Messenger and Mr Viklund might be thinking in the gallery. Am I being too efficient for their liking, despite the trap I've set? 'You have stated the person responsible for fitting the chain could not exit through the front of the property. Is there any other way in or out of the grounds?'

'No.'

'No? A person couldn't climb any one of the perimeter fences or walls?'

'There were no signs of that occurring.'

'What signs would you expect?'

'Damage to shrubbery, scuff marks on walls. Footprints in the earth.'

'The weather was cold with it being winter, and the ground was rock solid. That would make it incredibly difficult for the perpetrator to leave footmarks behind them, surely?'

'Difficult, but not impossible.'

'What about the woodland at the rear of the property, could that not be used as a route to escape?'

'Again, it wouldn't be impossible.'

'I think the word you're looking for is "yes", Detective Inspector Hall.' I give him a pointed look, before continuing. 'So, when you mentioned there were no visuals of cars not belonging to the Darlings near the property on the night of the murders, could it be that the assailant made their way on foot?'

'That is not what we believe to be the case.'

'There's that word again.' I turn to the jury, meeting the gaze of the older woman with the pink rinse, the younger man with tattoos creeping from the collar and cuffs of his shirt. 'Detective Inspector Hall, can you categorically confirm the man in the CCTV footage is Mr Darling? Or is this just another one of your *beliefs*?'

DI Hall continues to stand tall and composed, but his cheeks appear more flushed than before. I'm rattling him.

'The man in the footage matches the defendant's description in height, ethnicity and stature,' he says. 'The rifle and the petrol canister the figure is holding only have the defendant's fingerprints on, with no DNA found at the scene not belonging to him.'

I look towards the clerk.

'Can we please see the footage once more, from' – I look down at my notes at the time stamp I jotted down – 'two minutes and twenty-three seconds?'

As the clerk rolls out the television set, the wheels on the trolley squeaking across the court, I wonder if this is a step too far. The move I am about to play is a strong one, one that Antony will expect me to play, but the Messenger might prefer I bury.

I have to keep up appearances.

For the first time, Hall appears uneasy. We all wait in deathly silence as the footage is rewound before stopping at the desired time, when the figure is firing the gun into the stables.

'I have two questions for you, Detective Inspector Hall. One: can you categorically confirm from this footage that the man we see here is my client?'

He stares at the screen, his eyes moving busily.

'It's a yes or no question, DI Hall.'

'No,' he replies gruffly.

'And why is that?'

He flashes me a look; his resentment for me is clear in his eyes, and I wonder if he ever has women holding him accountable, not least with an audience.

'The footage isn't clear enough.'

'Thank you. And now my second question.' I point towards the television screen. 'Do you see what the figure has on their hands?'

He squints to make out the footage from the witness box.

'I have a CCTV still printed, if that's easier for you to see, Inspector Hall.'

'I can see fine,' he replies, the deep crow's feet framing his straining eyes telling me otherwise.

'Then please, tell me – what does the figure have on their hands?'

He spots them and swallows. I watch his Adam's apple jump up his throat.

'Gloves.'

Over my shoulder, I hear muttering from the public gallery.

'You stated that both the rifle and the canister belonged to the defendant?'

'Yes.'

'So then we can rightly assume that his fingerprints would already be on each of those items?'

He clears his throat.

'Yes.'

'So is it fair to say that if a third party were to handle these items while wearing gloves, they wouldn't leave any finger-prints behind?'

The muscles of his jaw flex on either side. His chest deflates with a sigh.

'Yes, that's fair.'

I hear the scurry of pens from the jurors' bench.

'One last question, Inspector Hall: did you consider anyone else in your line of enquiry, other than the defendant?'

He looks far more nervous now than he had at the start of my questioning. I have taken his testimony, his whole investigation in fact, and shaken it until each thread he so carefully laid has come unravelled. I glance at the jury – their interest is well and truly piqued, hanging off my every word.

Perhaps I have gone too far.

No. All of this will change when they learn of the prosecution's new evidence.

I spot speckles of perspiration gleaming above his lip as he opens his mouth to speak.

'We were confident with the evidence collected that the defendant was responsible for the crime.'

'I'm glad to hear you're a man confident in your convictions, but that doesn't answer my question. Did you consider any other lines of inquiry when investigating the deaths?'

He closes his mouth, considers his answer for a moment.

'DI Hall . . .'

'No,' he replies reluctantly.

'Your focus was entirely on my client?'

'Yes.'

'Thank you. No further questions.'

The mood of the room has changed dramatically; the air buzzes with angst and trepidation. From the podium, Judge McConnell looks at me with a neutral expression, but his eyes gleam approvingly. And just to the side of me, sat in the front row of the press bench, Melanie watches with a smile.

The Messenger's smirk, however, has gone. I catch sight of him in the gallery, and his piercing eyes lock onto mine. Beside him, Mr Viklund rises from his seat and storms off towards the exit.

I return my gaze to the witness box, trying to ignore my

heart leaping wildly behind my ribs. With a single glance, I know I will pay for what I have just done. I told Mr Viklund I had to keep up appearances. But perhaps in my exhausted state, I forgot my true objective.

Niall rises once more.

'Quick question, Detective Hall. In terms of the defence's theory as to why the gates to the property were physically chained shut as opposed to being programmed to stay closed – is it fair to suggest that Yolanda and the children would have also known how to operate the gate system and make their escape, unless a chain was put in place?'

I stand to object to Niall's clear line of speculation, but Hall answers him before I can open my mouth.

'That is a fair suggestion, yes.'

Niall nods.

'Thank you. Nothing more.'

38

I lean against the wall outside of the Bailey and exhale a sigh of smoke.

After Inspector Hall, the prosecution called the forensic pathologist to break down the cause of death, followed by the ballistics expert who detailed how the shots were fired, confirming the weapon, the range, the trajectory of each shot, to back up the pathologist's claims. As each new witness was called, I felt the intensity of Melanie's attention from the press bench, her excitement practically radiating off her, as the time I have to intervene ticked away in my ears.

Ever since Matthew's disappearance, and my refusal to satiate her hunger for an exclusive interview, Melanie has had me firmly in her sights, waiting for her moment to take her shot. Last night, I gave her that opportunity. Hell, I might as well have been posing for her. Once the final witness has finished giving evidence and court has adjourned for the day, Melanie will leave the Bailey and my opportunity to intervene will be lost.

I rub my eyes, listening to the dry squeak of them beneath my curled fingers, and pop some painkillers I found in the bottom of my bag and swallow them dry, in the hope of easing my aching back. The only thing keeping me upright is the constant surge of adrenaline pumping through me.

I jolt at the sound of the Messenger's voice. He stands just a few inches from me. We meet each other's eyes, and I drag on the cigarette to buy myself some time.

'Care to explain what you're doing in there?'

I stare up at him, my heart racing.

'I explained to Mr Viklund that I had to keep up appearances—'

'Oh, is that what you call it? Because it looks like you were playing both sides of the fence. I'm sure I remember telling you what would happen if you didn't do what was asked of you. Do you need reminding?'

'No,' I stutter. 'Besides . . . we have a whole other problem.'

He scoffs. 'We?'

'Yes, we.'

His smile falters.

'What kind of problem?'

The words crowd in my throat. Once I say them, I cannot take them back.

This will kill her.

But if I don't tell the Messenger, she will destroy me and put Hannah in harm's way.

It's her or us. Just like Wade's case.

'Well?'

I stare up at him, take a drag on my cigarette, and sigh the smoke out of me, before crushing it underfoot.

'Someone knows what I did.'

Now it is the Messenger's time to pause. He looks at me closely, his gaze flicking between my eyes and mouth.

'Who?'

'A journalist.'

For the first time since knowing him, the Messenger looks nervous. His smirk falls into a grim line.

'And how did they find out?'

'Does it matter?'

He stares at me intently, his cool eyes burrowing into mine until a shiver runs down my back.

'She has incriminating photos of me on her camera. It's in her bag—'

'It sounds like your problem, not mine.'

'I think you'll find this is your problem too – she plans to file the photos along with her story with the newspaper in the morning. If I'm arrested before the end of the trial, this would have all been for nothing. Neither of us will get what we want.'

Despite his eyes twitching, busily thinking of his next move, his expression doesn't change. I listen to his incessant chewing of the gum rolling around in his mouth, the smell of peppermint so strong that my stomach churns.

'Name,' he says gruffly.

'If I tell you, what will you do—'

'I said give me a name.'

We stare at one another, knowing what will happen the moment I tell him. Men like the Messenger, they don't solve problems, they eradicate them. He steps closer, as if to force the name from my lips.

'Melanie Eccleston, from *The Times*,' I blurt out.

He nods once.

'I'll deal with it.'

He turns back for the building, leaving as quickly as he appeared. I stand frozen against the wall and consider running after him, telling him that I made a mistake, that I was wrong. That it wasn't Melanie I saw after all. But instead, I stay rooted to the spot, knowing that it won't make a difference.

I sealed her fate the moment I uttered her name.

39

'The prosecution calls Marianne Darling.'

The tension in the courtroom is palpable, as Marianne steps into the box. She is shaking from head to toe, and the first thing she does is glance to me for reassurance. I give her a soft smile, but it does nothing to stop her shaking. When she takes her oath and confirms her name, she is asked to speak up to be heard.

'Can you please tell the court how you know the defendant?' Niall asks.

She glances up towards the dock, her eyes glassy.

'I'm his mother.'

Heavy murmurs break out in the gallery. This is the killer evidence they have all been waiting for, the piece of my client's past that could potentially tip the scales. The judge asks for quiet.

'Mrs Darling,' Niall begins. 'I will keep this brief. I am particularly interested about your relationship with your son in the autumn of 1999, and the events that unfolded. Can you confirm how old your son was at the time?'

She swallows, her throat bobbing delicately above her necklace: a thin row of pearls.

'Twenty-four,' she replies, croakily.

'Thank you. And he lived with you at that time, is that right?'

'Yes. He had been to university, and then returned home for a while.'

'Why was that?'

She reaches down for her cup of water, which quivers violently as she brings it towards her lips.

'Mrs Darling, can you answer my question, please?' Niall asks this like he is lightly admonishing a child. She places down the cup again.

'He wasn't well.'

'In what capacity was your son not well?'

She glances up at her son, her expression pleading.

I'm sorry, her eyes say.

'He was experiencing depression.'

Niall allows for a pause, giving the jurors and the press time to connect the dots.

'Was this the first time your son had had a depressive episode?'

'No, but it was his most severe.'

He looks down and begins to recite from his notes.

'The symptoms of severe depression are described by the Mind organisation as the following: "down or tearful; agitated and restless; isolated; finding no pleasure in life; no self-confidence or self-esteem; hopeless and despairing; suicidal". Would you say your son's symptoms fitted this description of severe depression, as you referred to it?'

She nods solemnly. 'Yes.'

'Your son was suicidal?'

'Yes.' The word escapes from her lips in a clipped, pained fashion. Her eyes are glassy, reflecting the lights when she flicks her glare towards Wade in the dock.

'I see. And what treatment did he seek for this?'

She presses her lips firmly together, rolling them against one another to dissipate her nerves, but it almost looks as if she is desperate to keep the truth from coming out of her.

'Mrs Darling?'

'His father and I paid for him to stay at a psychiatric rehabilitation facility in Torquay in the autumn of 1999.'

'What was the name of this facility?'

'The Lodge.'

'Thank you.' Niall instructs the jury to turn to their evidence packs, where they find the admission sheet for The Lodge. The date and Wade's name are present at the top. 'And prior to the defendant's admission to the facility, how long had he been experiencing this depressive episode?'

'About six months.'

'I see. And what made you seek treatment for him at this point? Was there a deciding factor?'

Marianne looks to me, then the judge. She parts her lips and stutters.

'I-isn't there the matter of c-c-confidentiality here?'

'For his psychiatrist or doctor perhaps,' Niall replies. 'But not you. You have sworn under oath to tell the truth and nothing but the truth in court here today. So please, elaborate on what motivated you and your husband to have your son admitted to The Lodge in the autumn of 1999.'

She blinks back tears and bites down on her bottom lip. A clerk steps forward with a box of tissues. The courtroom waits in deafening silence as she dabs her eyes.

'My son's depression had been worsening for many months,' she says. 'And in October of '99 . . .'

She stops, pressing her lips together again.

'What happened in October '99, Mrs Darling?' Niall asks.

She sighs defeatedly, and closes her eyes.

'He tried to take his own life.'

Niall nods slowly, coaxing the damning information out of her.

'Can you please tell the jury *how* your son attempted suicide?'

Marianne sniffs back tears, dabbing the tissue in the corner of both eyes.

'He . . . tried to shoot himself.'

The gallery comes alive with whispers, and those on the press brench are practically salivating. I avert my eyes for a moment, racked with guilt at the sight of Marianne's pain.

'You and your husband found him as he was about to take his life, didn't you?'

I look back and spot a tear sliding down her cheek. She dabs at it furiously, leaving stray pieces of white tissue behind.

'Yes.'

'And you both stopped him from harming himself, isn't that right?'

She nods reluctantly. 'Yes.'

'Please explain to the jury how this unfolded.'

She looks to me for help, her bottom lip quivering. The judge peers down at her.

'Answer the question please, Mrs Darling.'

She nods up at him before looking down at the tissue in her hands, teasing it out of the scrunched-up ball she has made in her fist.

'We pleaded with him not to go through with it, but he was adamant. So my husband tried to wrestle the gun from him.'

'Did your husband succeed in getting the gun, Mrs Darling?'

She sniffs back tears again.

'No.'

'What happened?'

Silence. Her eyes are on the tissue in her hands. She reminds me of her son, the way he looks down rather than meeting me in the eye, when he must discuss a subject he doesn't like.

'You are under oath to tell the truth, Mrs Darling . . .'

She nods, her eyes remaining downward.

'To . . . to make my husband stop trying to keep him from going through with it . . . Wade grabbed me.'

'He grabbed you?'

'He wasn't going to hurt me,' she insists, looking up to meet his eyes; her voice is the loudest it has been since her evidence began. 'It was just a way to stop my husband from taking the gun.'

'How did Wade grab you?'

She pauses, her breathing loud and panicked. The tears are falling freely now, with the tissue tearing to pieces in her grip.

'He held me from behind. He had an arm across here.'

She moves her arm about her neck.

'Did Wade ever point the gun at you, Mrs Darling?'

She looks at Niall, her jaw trembling. Tears well in her eyes.

'Yes.' A gasp sounds from the gallery. 'But not because he wanted to hurt me, but because he was hurting so badly himself, and couldn't bear to be stopped. I-I-I . . .' She takes a breath to compose herself. 'Wade let me talk him round, and I was able to take the gun from him. He was crying out for help . . . my husband and I knew that.'

'You knew that when he pointed the gun at you, Mrs Darling?'

Marianne stares at him, dumbfounded at how to respond.

'No further questions.'

The courtroom comes alive with murmurings from the press bench and the gallery. I turn to look at Wade in the dock: he stares at his mother, tears streaming down his face. Before me, Antony's shoulders look as tense as rock.

Me. This is all because of me.

The evidence I planted is finally out there, on public record. I should feel relieved, but all I feel I guilt, barely able to draw air in my lungs from the weight of it.

The parallels between my client's past and the present-day case are scarily aligned. Both times, my client had a mental breakdown. Both times resulted in gun violence, only this time it ended with three homicide victims. Now, the prosecution can use Wade's history to insinuate his guilt in his family's deaths due to his past, and their star witness who specialises in familicide will be able to use this to show how my client's personal history with mental health and firearms would have followed the textbook route to gun violence in domestic violence disputes.

I gave them the evidence they needed to corroborate every one of their claims.

The judge calls for silence in the court and looks to me.

I stand up. 'Good afternoon, Mrs Darling. I understand this must be incredibly difficult for you. I only have a few questions, and then we will let you go, okay?'

I take a sip of water, trying to put the distance of time between Niall's questioning and mine. Marianne takes the opportunity to do the same, before taking a couple of deep, calming breaths.

'Why did you decide to seek private treatment for Wade's depression in 1999?'

Marianne sniffles, dabbing her nose with the battered tissue.

'We didn't want this blip in his life to affect his future in any way.'

'How might experiencing depression or suicidal thoughts have affected his future?'

'Well, the stigma of course. The judgement around those who experience mental health problems is often so cruel and unnecessary. Most of us experience it at some time or another, don't we? I have. My husband did. Most of my friends. It's normal, but treated so abnormally. I didn't want anyone judging him for something he couldn't help. If we had gone through the usual route, his struggles and his stay at The Lodge would have been on his medical record.'

'I see. And could you explain to me your understanding of suicidal behaviour?'

She glances behind me, towards the dock, a fleeting look at her son. Her baby.

'Well . . . it's when a person thinks of taking, or attempts to take, their own life.'

'Does it mean a person wants to harm others?'

'*No*. They only want to harm themselves. It isn't about violence; it is about escaping the agony they feel. This is what I mean about stigma around mental health. My son would never hurt anybody. He just wanted to be free.'

'So, you don't think your son was capable of murdering his family?'

'Never. He loved Yolanda and the children more than anything in the world. He never so much as got in a fight on the school playground as a child, for Christ's sake. Violence isn't a part of him. He is sensitive, and caring, with a big heart. I think that's why he gets depression in the way he does. Sensitive people suffer the most in this dreadful world.'

I pause, allowing her heartfelt words to bleed into the jurors' minds, knowing full well that they won't mean a thing, with the prosecution evidence that has just landed in their laps.

'Thank you, Mrs Darling. No further questions.'

I sit down in my seat, exhausted, deflated, my body throbbing with pain, and sigh.

It's done.

40

In the courtroom, the air is thick with anticipation. It is time for the prosecution's key, and final, witness.

Criminal psychologist Dr Samantha Heche enters the witness box.

Heche stands, calm and collected, her dark hair pulled away from her face. She gives her oath, and Niall begins with questions about her education and professional expertise, spoon-feeding the jury with her supposed superiority on the subject, due to her speciality being that of familicide for the last twelve years. When she explains the term for the jury, the whole court falls still: *the act of killing one's own family.*

As Niall asks her more and more questions to build her integrity before the jury, my tired mind drifts towards the press bench. Melanie isn't anywhere to be seen. The Messenger, too, is missing from the gallery. I haven't seen either of them since the break in proceedings. My heart pounds beneath my robes.

'What led you to specialise in familicide, Dr Heche?' Niall asks, breaking me from my thoughts.

'It is one of those crimes that stops you in your tracks when you hear of it: an entire family gone, and usually by the person who is supposed to love them most. Beneath my horror and concern, I was immediately fascinated by how a person could do such a thing. I wanted to understand why it happened, in the hope of better preventing it.'

Niall speaks clearly and precisely, so every syllable projects about the room.

'From all you have learnt in the last twelve years, could you please explain to the court the nature of familicide?'

'Of course,' she replies with a smile, before turning her attention to the jury. 'In these kinds of cases, we so often know how familicide ends, but for a long time, no one knew how they started. Until about thirty years ago, familicide was grouped in with domestic violence, and not seen or studied in its own right. We now understand more about the complexity of these cases, and the theory of how they come to be.

'Most often in familicide cases, it is a family unit with a heterosexual couple at the centre. The perpetrator, whom we will call the annihilator, is usually the male in the equation, and often there are no outward signs to suggest anyone is in danger. Many annihilators are considered upstanding members of society, with successful employment and close relationships with family and friends. They aren't usually known to police or have criminal records, with what could be deemed as good upbringings and backgrounds. This, it seems, adds to the shock factor of the crime, as this sort of character might not be what one expects.'

'How does one determine a risk of familicide before the fatal event?' Niall asks. 'How can, say, a person be seen to be at risk of annihilating their family?'

'To assess the risk of the crime occurring, we need to assess the environment that the perpetrator and victims are in, which could be deemed to motivate or trigger the annihilator. Over years of study, we have determined the different types of family annihilators, and the differences between them are down to what *motivated* them to commit the crime.

'For example, an annihilator may be motivated by a need for revenge, or experiencing an uncontrollable rage – say, during a divorce, or a child custody battle, or infidelity. These characters usually show possessiveness towards their spouse and children, and exert authority within the home. The victim putting an end to the relationship with the annihilator or leaving the family home can trigger the crime.

'Then there is what we call the "civil reputable" killer, studied and coined by author and specialist Neil Websdale. This type of killer annihilates their family out of a distorted sense of altruism. Their identity is highly dependent on their family unit and economic status, and should anything put them at risk – say, financial ruin – the annihilator murders their family in the belief that they are saving them from shame and hardship. This perpetrator often takes their own life after the killing spree. But whether deaths are caused because of possessiveness and control, or pseudo-altruism, it is clear that all offenders of this crime have a sense of ownership over their families, and a grandiose sense of self, believing the family will not survive without them.'

When Dr Heche has finished, I look about me, spotting the horror on the jurors' faces; the way the press remain transfixed on the specialist witness. There is no movement or sound from the gallery. If I closed my eyes right now, the silence might well convince me that I'm entirely alone in the court.

'You were asked to assess this case, is that right?' Niall asks.

'Yes,' Dr Heche replies.

'And with your twelve years of expertise in this area, what did you find?'

She pauses, seemingly choosing her next words with care.

'Although it is not for me to determine whether the defendant did or didn't commit the crime, I have assessed the factors surrounding the case, and assessed the relevant factors surrounding the defendant that could be seen to relate to a case of familicide.

'In my opinion, should the defendant be responsible for the crimes, Mr Darling would fit the criteria of the altruistic annihilator. Annihilators of this kind are typically highly educated, the provider for their family, and have underlying mental health issues and self-destructive tendencies. They will usually have a history of depression.

'From my analysis, Mr Darling was suffering from severe depression due to his financial status and the looming closure of his business. He kept this a secret from his wife, children, employees – from all who knew him, except for his business partner who shared in his troubles. He also collected firearms, and shooting and hunting were his main hobby. With the severity of his financial state, and his history of depression alongside his role of providing for his family, his ownership and frequent use of firearms – which is statistically the most-used weapon in familicide cases – these are potential triggers to cause a person in such a position to annihilate.'

Niall pauses, and looks at the jurors one by one.

'Thank you for your time, Dr Heche. That will be all from me.'

The witness stands tall, seemingly pleased with herself. I rise to cross-examine.

'Dr Heche, you said yourself that you cannot prove that Mr Darling did or did not kill commit the crimes he has been charged with, correct?'

'Yes, that's right.'

'So to be clear, the information you've given us today is nothing more than you sharing your opinion on a hypothetical scenario?'

She gives me a tight, almost patronising smile.

'I think my expertise can be considered a little more in-depth than that.'

'I'm sure you've worked very hard, but you didn't answer my question. You assessed this case on the hypothetical scenario that Mr Darling is guilty of the crimes, correct?'

'Correct.'

'So, if he is found to be not guilty, your analysis will be rendered obsolete? As an incorrect theory?'

Heche clears her throat.

'My analysis is based on many years of research in the field, and a multitude of familicide cases.'

'Which one might call a theory, Dr Heche.' I look down at my notes. 'You said that you look for indicators in a person's life or behaviour to assess whether they are likely to annihilate their families. You mentioned depression, financial insecurity, is that right?'

'Yes, those were a couple of the factors I mentioned.'

'Do you believe that every man who happens to suffer from depression due to the loss of his business and financial security is then automatically likely to kill his family?'

'No, of course not.'

'Is depression a likely outcome to one losing the business they have spent years creating?'

She pauses.

'I'd say it's quite a common response. Yes.'

'In fact, wouldn't one be *expected* to experience depression in these circumstances?'

'It would be a likely outcome I imagine, yes.'

'Thank you, Dr Heche. Nothing more from me.'

Once Dr Heche has been led down from the witness box, Niall turns to address the judge.

'The prosecution rests,' he says, before returning to his seat.

The weight of dread briefly lifts from my shoulders, allowing me to catch a rare deep breath. I sigh it away as discreetly as I can, closing my eyes for a stolen second. That is, until I remember what is still before me.

There is still the rest of the trial to go. Now, I must navigate the task of being seen to lead my client's defence, while sabotaging it behind his back. The prosecution may have concluded their case, but my task is only just beginning.

The dread returns, pummelling me in an instant.

I turn and glance towards the public gallery to see the Messenger has stepped back into the courtroom. When I catch his eye, he stares back at me, and gives me a nod.

I know in an instant he is referring to Melanie.

41

I arrive at my front door utterly exhausted, weighed down by my guilt. I don't have the luxury of lowering my guard when I return home. Not with Hannah watching my every move. If I were alone, I would crawl into bed and sleep until daybreak. Instead, I have to plaster on a smile and pretend my life isn't falling apart. That Melanie Eccleston wouldn't have died today, if it weren't for me. I imagine what might have happened to her as I slip the key in the lock.

I step inside and drop my bag in horror.

Hannah is in the middle of the living room. She has pushed the coffee table aside, pressed it against the back wall, creating a vast space to move in. I heard what she was doing before I saw it: the sound of a golf club hitting a ball, followed by a rattle as it enters the cup at the other side of the room.

She turns to me with a smile, which instantly falls when she sees my face.

'Stop.'

I march forward and snatch the club from her. The feel of the metal in my hands shocks my palms. *Whoosh. Thwack.* I smell his blood, feel the splatter against my face.

'I'm sorry, I—'

'Where did you get this?' I only realise I am shouting when she flinches from the spray of my words.

'I . . . I went in the loft. You said some of Dad's stuff was up there and—'

'So you went rifling around in places you don't belong? Taking things that don't belong to you?'

I can't hold the club anymore. It physically hurts to touch it, as if the metal is scorching hot. It isn't the murder weapon, of course, the Messenger took that. But it is from the same set that belonged to Matthew. I take it to the foot of the stairs and lean it against the wall, wiping my palm against my thigh as if it is dirty. On the counter by the stairs is a large stack of photo albums. She has clearly been going through them again today, when she said she would be at school. There is one loose photo to the side – it's one of Matthew, Hannah and me. Matthew stares at me from the photograph, smiling gaily. Tears creep from my eyes.

Whoosh. I hear the crack of his skull. *Thwack.* The pop of a tooth being knocked from his mouth.

'I didn't think you'd mind. I thought—'

I can't stop the tears now. They keep coming, and coming. I cover my face with both hands and sob silently into my palms.

'I'm sorry . . .' She's crying too. 'I didn't think you'd mind. He was my dad – it's my stuff too.'

She barges past me, and I hear the ruffle of her coat. I uncover my face as she is snatching up her bag.

'Where are you going?'

'*Home.*'

She grabs at the door latch, sniffing back tears of her own. I know I should stop her, to try and explain and apologise. But instead, I watch her go, jumping as the door slams shut.

⚖

My home is a stranger to me now. Has been since I first raised the golf club above my head and swung. Whenever I dare to sit in the quiet without a case brief to distract me, the memories seep in: the incessant swing of the club, the thuds, the splatters, my screams lost among the noise of the church bells tolling on the other side of the window. Tonight, however, I do have a distraction.

Hannah is gone.

I sit in the armchair in the dark, the very place I have sat for hours, and think of the pain in her eyes as I shouted at her, the shock of my anger. She had every right to go through her father's things, and nor would it have been a problem had I not got so many secrets to hide.

I sit in the living room, listening to the silence ringing through the house, joining the tick of the clock in an ear-splitting chorus, and imagine Melanie Eccleston floating lifelessly at the bottom of the Thames beside Fredrick, chains about her body with her feet hooked to a concrete cinderblock, the camera loaded with incriminating photos waterlogged on the riverbed beneath their swaying feet.

No one foresees becoming a murderer, do they? When a person thinks of the future, they think of love, careers, hopes and dreams. I certainly didn't foresee I would be capable of killing a man. Even after murdering and burying Matthew, I didn't foresee I would be capable of doing anything like that again. And yet here I am, with Fredrick's blood on my hands, and Melanie's fate sealed by my lips. I haven't just killed one person now. In my attempt to save my own neck, I have killed three.

My body trembles beneath the blanket I have draped over

my legs. I can feel myself breaking; the grip I thought I had on the situation has unfurled, and with it has come all of the pain I had worked so hard to smother; the memories, the guilt. A violent split between who I was before, and who I have become, and an insurmountable sense of loss. I sit among the panicked thoughts, wondering how I got so lost. How I became a woman with so many people's blood on her hands.

I am a monster.

Sleep seems like a stranger to me now. Sleepwalking. Digging up bodies in the dead of night. I can't remember how long it has been since I've had an unbroken rest. My body aches for it, whining from each joint and knotted muscle.

I hobble upstairs to the bathroom and turn on the shower, slowly undressing as the room fills up with steam. As I grip the basin to steady myself, I look up at my reflection, watching the exhausted, broken woman in the pane as the glass slowly fogs up. My sins and lies have leeched the life from me, leaving my skin slack and grey, my eyes tinged pink and puffy, framed by deep, dark circles. I stare at the woman in the mirror, and fail to recognise the person staring back at me.

I step beneath the water and stand there until my skin blushes red from the heat, allowing tears of exhaustion to snake down my cheeks.

I need to sleep. My sins, my dilemma, the looming second part of the trial, Hannah; they will all have to wait until the morning.

⚖

For the first few seconds when I wake, I'm not sure where I am. I sway on my feet in the dark, dizzy and disorientated as my teeth chatter violently in my mouth from the cold.

Gong

Gong

Gong

The bells are so close, striking above my head in a deafening chorus.

The tower looms over me, obstructing the path of the moon. I am stood before the church steps, as if my sleeping mind has brought me here to confess my sins. My bare feet feel frozen against the ice-cold ground, glittering with frost, and my frantic, nervous breaths escape from me in short huffs of cloud.

I blink furiously to acclimatise myself to the darkness, and pull the clothes I have on closer to my body: a coat I don't remember putting on, pulled over a small slip nightgown, and nothing more.

Gong

Gong

Gong

The bells. They shouldn't be ringing out more than once. And yet they keep ringing and ringing to the count of three.

I turn and stagger towards my home. Do I have my keys? I rummage around in the pockets of the coat, but find nothing more than scrunched-up tissues. Thankfully, I can see the door was left ajar. I walk as fast as I can, as if trying to outrun the bells, and shut the door firmly behind me. I wrestle out of the coat and let it drop to the mat as I rest my head against the door, trying to calm my shivering teeth. That's when they start up again.

Gong

Gong

Gong

The sound can't be coming from the bell tower. The tolls only sound once to mark the hour. And yet, they are still as loud as if I were stood before them. Which means they can't be coming from the tower. The sounds are inside my head.

Am I going insane?

I try to take deep breaths, in through my nose, out through my mouth, as I lean against the door. It is just a bad dream, I tell myself.

I pinch myself and feel a stabbing pain in my flesh.

I'm awake.

I open my eyes and turn for the stairs – I just need to get back into bed and close my eyes – when I catch something in the corner of my eye: a figure of a man.

It's not real, I tell myself, as I begin to shake. *It isn't Matthew. He's dead.*

Before me, Matthew is in the living room, putting a golf ball into a cup. He looks up at me and smiles.

Gong

Gong

Gong

I cover my ears as tears fill my eyes. The memory is gone; the living room is dark and empty again. But the bells keep sounding. The deep, groaning tolls blaring against my eardrums.

'Shut up!'

I stagger up the stairs, each toll of the imaginary bells so loud and disorientating that they throw me off balance.

This isn't happening. I'm asleep. It's just a night terror. I'll wake up any minute.

I can smell bleach in the air, feel the aroma stinging at my eyes, and beneath it, the metallic tang of blood.

It's just a night terror. I'll wake up soon.

Please
Please
Please wake up
I reach the landing and freeze.

Matthew is lying in the hall in a pool of blood. His head is concaved, his beautiful face crushed. The walls are splattered with him. The golf club is lying by his side, gleaming wet and red in the path of the moon shining through the window.

Gong
Gong
Gong

Sobs heave out of me. I turn blindly for my bedroom door, dashing away the tears, only to find my hands slathered in hot blood. I stagger blindly into bed and hide beneath the white sheets. They are blood-soaked, just as I found them when I woke to find my whole world had changed, three years ago.

This isn't happening
This can't be happening

I roll up into a ball, my cries silenced by the ever-ringing bells. They grow louder and closer together until they become one long, deafening howl.

I cover my ears, begging for them to stop, and scream as loud as I can, when—

⚖

I wake up with a jolt, sitting bolt upright in bed.

My chest is hammering with my heart and glistening with beads of sweat. My nightdress is completely soaked through. I can still hear the bells, but they are not tauntingly close, as if trapped in my head, but where they should be on the other side of the window. I check the time: it's 3 a.m.

It was 3 a.m. when I found Matthew dead.

I rip away the sheets and get out of bed, desperately trying to draw air into my lungs. I head for the window and throw it open to gasp in the nightly chill. The cold air pinches my cheeks, rousing me from my nightmare, and I stand heaving it in until my heart slowly begins to calm.

I'm safe. It was just a night terror.

Once I have caught my breath, I head back towards my side of the bed, and take the pack of diazepam I keep in my bedside drawer. I pop two tablets into my palm and drink them down with the water on top of the night stand.

I can't keep living like this. The secrets. The lies. They are finally catching up with me. So many people have been hurt by what I've done. Matthew. Fredrick. Melanie. Who else has to die for me to protect my secrets? Will it be Hannah next?

I think of all I have done to keep my past hidden, all of my lies, the deceit. Conning a client. Digging up a body. I watched a man drown right before my eyes, and destined Melanie to the same fate.

I can't keep doing this. Not for Hannah. Not for me. There has to be another way to keep her safe, so this can end.

I sit up and head towards the window again, inhaling the fresh night air into my lungs. My eyes fall on the earth before the tracks where Matthew's resting place used to be.

It's time that I stopped fighting the inevitable, and face all that I have done.

42

24 December 2016

I've always hated Christmas. As a child, I never really had one. Each year would be spent with a different foster family. I never celebrated with any of them more than once before I was ferried off to the next.

So as an adult, I can't help but resent the obligatory enjoyment the season demands: the sickeningly enthusiastic songs playing repeatedly on every radio station and in every shop, the dry turkey and the paper hats from the crackers. Then there is New Year, with its fireworks and obligatory kisses, or lack thereof, at midnight. It's a time that demands joy, when for some of us it is the most difficult time of year, inherently reminding us of what we don't have, rather than what we do. This is all topped off by the duty to improve oneself from the first day of the new year. Drink less. Eat better. Quit smoking. Try to last with the new depressing regime until at least the end of the month.

I'm just tired, I tell myself, as the bitter thoughts form within me. *Things always seem worse when I'm tired.*

I haven't slept much this week; the sleepwalking has been relentless. I enjoy the festivities more when Hannah is here, but what with her staying at her mother's parents for Christmas this year, and Maggie staying with my brother-in-law, the whole thing seems like a forced charade. I sit on the sofa with a glass of wine, watching a re-run of a sitcom Christmas special, as Matthew practises his putting, knocking the golf ball into the cup at the other side of the room, the faint smell of sweat from his evening run drifting off him with each movement. The sound of the club making contact with the ball makes my eye twitch and twitch.

The sleepwalking began again last month, triggered by work stress from all the cases continuing to pile up on my desk. Murder. Rape. Theft, after theft, after theft. It had been over a year since my last sleepwalking episode; I came down the next morning to that familiar pitying look on Matthew's face, and I knew it had started up again. It has struck almost every night since, whittling away my energy until I feel like a shadow of myself.

It could be genetic. Drink less caffeine, cut out alcohol. Try to form a good sleep routine. Work on managing stress and anxiety. That's what every so-called sleep specialist has told me. Hypnotherapy, CBT, I've tried it all. I sigh heavily and take a sip of wine; I'll be damned if I won't have a glass on Christmas Eve.

The house is in disarray from the redecorating project we have given ourselves over the Christmas break. Paint pots, a ladder and footstool, the floorboard sander; belongings hidden under old bedsheets.

I look at my husband, his brows knitted together with concentration as he looks from the ball to the cup, and putts. I love him, tremendously so. He is perhaps the most thoughtful man I've ever known. When he isn't putting that fucking ball, at least.

I flinch each time the metal club connects with the ball, brace myself for the irritating rattle as it enters the cup and makes my teeth chime. I love him with every part of me: I love his heart, his smile, his eyes. His soft, tender hands. But if he putts that ball one more time, I am going to fucking scream.

Matthew senses me watching him and looks to me, a smile growing on his face. How can he look at me like that, after all these years? So much love in his eyes despite all the burdens I carry, how difficult I can be.

'You're knackered, aren't you?'

I force a smile. 'Exhausted.'

'Why don't you go up to bed? The telly will be naff anyway. I'll call Hannah in a bit and then I'll come up and join you.'

'You sure?' I ask, my tone tinged with relief. 'That won't make me horrendously boring?'

He comes over and kisses my hair. 'You could never be boring.'

I tug his T-shirt as he goes to pull away, and bring him closer to me. Our lips meet. Soft, familiar, tasting of wine.

'You're an amazing man, you know that?'

'I try,' he replies with a wink, kissing me again before returning to his game.

As Matthew putts the ball with the same wince-inducing sounds, I head up the stairs for bed, silently praying that tonight is the night I sleep straight through. But even as I lie in bed, I can hear each tap of the ball echoing up from the floor below, chipping away at my hold on myself; a chisel working its way into a crack until I finally burst open.

Please, for the love of God. I just want to go to sleep.

⚖

I release a hot, ragged scream.

I am holding a golf club above my head and straddling a man in the dark.

I don't know where I am. I don't know what I'm doing. Only that I'm terrified. A church bell is sounding from somewhere; a deep, sombre song that makes me flinch with each note.

A swirling shriek of noise screams from behind me, terrifying me in the dark, followed by an explosion of colour on the other side of the window. The man kicks out beneath me, tugging violently at the clothes covering my chest. He shouts something through the noise, and I feel his hand lunge for my neck. I swing the club back and bring it down with a scream as the church bell rings out.

Gong.

Thwack.

Gong.

Thwack.

Gong.

Thwack.

The church bells stop ringing after twelve tolls to ring in midnight, and I pant for breath, my face and body splattered with blood, the metallic taste of him in my mouth. Fireworks light up the sky on the other side of the window, bathing us in red, blue, white. With each flash, I see more of my surroundings. I'm on the landing. The walls are painted with violent swipes of blood, sprayed along the ceilings. My clothes are covered in it. Below me is a man. His face is mangled; wet, fleshy pulp flashing with each explosion. The hand that had been tugging at me releases its grip, and falls to the floor with a lifeless thud, as a ragged breath bubbles out of his mouth, and I spot the wedding ring on his finger.

I recognise that wedding ring.
And then everything goes dark.

I wake up in bed, my eyes flickering open to the distant sound of the bell tower.

The nightmare I had comes back to me all at once. The blood. The violence. The terrifying confusion I'd felt, totally at a loss as to what was happening, and the horror I'd felt as I recognised Matthew's wedding ring, just before I woke.

My heart is pattering fast in my chest at the thought. I've never had a dream so visceral in my life. I instinctively reach for Matthew on his side of the bed so that I can pull in close to him, feel his warmth and kiss the nape of his neck in sweet apologies for thinking such a vile thing, even if it was against my will. I paw his side of the bed blindly.

Matthew isn't there.

I frown in the dark, and perch on my elbow to peer at the clock on the nightstand.

It's just turned three.

Where the hell is he?

And then I feel it. The wet, sticky substance on the sheets.

I reach for the lamp on the side, flick the switch, and freeze.

Blood. So much blood. It is splattered across the white bedding in violent splashes. There are lashes of it up my arms; my hands are smothered in it.

The headboard begins to shiver against the wall from my violent shaking.

'Matthew?'

My voice echoes through the open doorway, followed by

nothing but silence and the incessant racing of my pulse pounding in my ears.

I peel back the sheet, feeling where it has stuck to me with blood. I am completely covered in it: frenzied splashes dashed across me in all different directions. The skin on my face feels dry, and I reach up to inspect it with my fingertips and find more there, dried on me in flecks.

I stumble out of bed, flattening myself against the wardrobe doors, unable to shake the fear throttling the air out of me to make sense of the scene.

'Matthew?' I call, and look to the open doorway, longing to hear his reply. He had a nose bleed in the night, that's what he'll say. He has just gone downstairs for supplies to clean up the mess.

A minute passes with no response. Then another.

I force myself away from the wardrobe door and walk shakily into the hall, heading for the stairs to call down to him, when I step in a wet spot on the carpet.

I look down and see dark blood soaked into the carpet.

This isn't happening this isn't happening I'm still dreaming

I reach a quivering hand towards the light switch on the wall, and flick on the light.

That's when I see Matthew, lying in the same spot he had in my dream. His face is crushed as it had been. The blood is splashed up the walls in the same frenzied pattern. The golf club I'd held is beside him, smothered red with blood, the end tufted with skin and hair.

My knees buckle and I hit the floor with a thud, as a scream works up my throat. I clamp my hands over my mouth and bellow.

I stare at his body; the animalistic groans claw out of my chest and the tears leak from my eyes, as the truth slowly sinks in.

It wasn't a dream.

PART III

The Defence

Day Four

43

Imagine going to sleep and dreaming up the most terrifying moment of your life. A dream where you're in the dark, fighting against an unknown assailant, struck by the instinctual need to protect yourself. To fight and hit and scream, pummelling the man to death to the call of the church bells ringing out Midnight Mass. You wake up with a pounding heart, relieved to escape such a dark, imaginary place. Then you realise it wasn't a dream at all. You wake with no recollection of what led you to such violence, and no control over your own autonomy. No clarity. No answers. All you have is the bloody aftermath and your husband's body ground to a pulp on the hallway floor.

The aftermath is almost as much of a blur as the violence. I wasn't thinking logically, but instinctively. People often imagine how they would act in a desperate situation such as this. I can see them now, watching a crime drama on the television of an evening, shouting profanities at the protagonist as they take the wrong turn. If they were me, they would do everything right. They would call the police. They would contact a lawyer. They would act rationally. Perhaps that sort of response might be expected of me because of my work. My entire role is to be concise, controlled, level-headed. But the truth is, there is nothing rational about waking up to find you have murdered your husband. You cannot think clearly as you wash your loved one's blood from your face, with little memory of how it came to get there but for flashes in a dream.

There was a brief moment in which logic prevailed: as I knelt beside Matthew's body, I began to type out the number for emergency services. The first nine, then the second. Then I thought of Hannah. She would hate me for what I had done. How could she not? I would not only lose the love of my life, but the only family I have ever known, the same family I had craved ever since I can remember. I would be thrown in prison for something I would never do while awake, punished for an act I never wanted to commit, with no one missing me on the other side of the prison walls.

So, I acted irrationally.

I buried the body. I bleached every wall and surface, ripped up the carpet and bleached the stained boards below, before sanding them down, and laying the new roll of carpet myself, after painting the walls and ceiling. I hid the club, the spade. I tried to hide the memories within me too. As the whole street celebrated Christmas, I spent three days working to cover my tracks, redecorating the hall as we had planned, making sure nothing looked out of place, all the time concocting my lies while I worked. If I had done the right thing and called the police, I wouldn't be in this position now.

Matthew and I had an argument, that's what I would tell the police. I packed a duffel bag of his clothes, toiletries and medication, and placed them in the boot of his car. I told the police I thought he had left to stay at his mother's the night of our argument, which was vacant while she was away with family, and it was only when I finally picked up the phone three days later and Maggie asked to speak to him that I realised he hadn't been seen for all that time, and I discovered his bag in the car. The three days he was supposedly missing gave me time to cover my tracks, to work on my alibi as closely as possible, digging myself a deeper hole the more I plotted, until I saw no way out but to continue on with my lies. I worked to conceal my husband's murder while those around me were distracted with Christmas celebrations; holding their loved ones close as I buried mine.

And the rest, as they say, is history.

Now I am here, finally paying for what I have done; all of the mayhem I have caused thereafter. Fredrick, Melanie: more blood, which would never have been shed had I faced the consequences of what I had done. I would never have met Melanie – her obsession with the missing person's case wouldn't have been born. I wouldn't have met Fredrick at Blackfriars Station on that cold winter's day. I would have never met Wade Darling, or been sucked into the Messenger's game.

My mind spins as I think of all the lies I have told. Lies, upon lies, upon lies. It's easy for a person to lose who they are among them after so long; fact and fiction bleeding together as one. Because once made, the lies can never stop being told. That is, unless I finally tell the truth.

Before I make any plans, I need to make sure Hannah is safe from the Messenger, should he retaliate. I reach for my phone and call Maggie.

'Yes?' she asks pointedly.

'Is Hannah okay?' I ask.

'She left your house in tears. What do you think?'

I bite down on my lip. Now is not the time to argue with her.

'Maggie, I need you and Hannah to get away for a bit.'

'I'm sorry?'

'You both need to leave London. Just until the trial is over.'

She scoffs. 'And why on earth would we do that?'

'Because those close to me are a security risk right now.'

She pauses.

'At risk from who?'

'People are very invested in this trial, and they won't like it if my client succeeds. They may want to retaliate. If you won't do this for me, please – do it for Hannah.'

As my words sink in, I cradle the phone to me, silently willing her to shed her usual stubbornness and to listen.

'This all sounds a little dramatic . . .' she says.

'It isn't.'

She falls quiet again. I stand listening to my pulse racing in my ears.

'Perhaps you could stay with your sister,' I say.

'I'll decide where we go, thank you,' she snaps. But my racing chest eases with relief; she is considering it.

'So you'll do it?'

I listen to her breathing on the other end of the line.

'For Hannah, yes.'

She hangs up the phone and I close my eyes, rub my temples.

Hannah will be safe.

I look at the clock on the wall. I haven't long before it's time to lay out the defence's case. Before Wade himself steps into the box. Hannah will be safe now, at least for a while, until I plan my next steps. But first, I must focus on the matter at hand.

It's time I set the record straight and give my client the fair trial he deserves.

It's time I stop running from my past, and pay for the consequences of my crimes.

44

Wade enters the witness box, pale and visibly shaken as he gives his oath. Every pair of eyes will be on him: judging him, condemning him. They have heard of his alleged crimes in gruesome detail; many will have decided on his guilt before he has even opened his mouth.

I stand in the courtroom feeling surprisingly calm, despite the course I am about to take. The Messenger sits behind me in the public gallery, expecting me to condemn my client. I wonder how much time will pass before he realises I have changed tack. How long it will take for him to set the wheels in motion to expose my crimes.

Wade raises the plastic cup of water to his lips, the liquid jumping about until it drips from the rim.

'I understand that this is going to be very difficult for you, Mr Darling, so I will go through this as quickly as I can. It is not easy to stand where you are today. Do you need more water?'

I want him to appear almost child-like in the eyes of the jury. He is someone who needs attention and care; the polar opposite of the man they will have imagined he'd be after hearing of his alleged crimes.

He shakes his head. 'No, thank you.'

I look down at my notes, allowing this idea to take hold: he is not the monster they imagined. The tension drags out until it is unbearable. What I am about to do will change everything. For my client's case. For me, and the objective I have been given by the men staring into the back of me from the public gallery. Once I do this, there is no going back.

I brace myself and look up towards the witness box.

'When did you learn of your wife's affair with your business partner, Mr Darling?'

Several gasps break from the public gallery, muttered conversations breaking out until the judge has to call for quiet. During the commotion, I glance towards Niall at the other end of the bench. The smirk has been wiped from his face. I daren't look behind me towards the Messenger.

Wade clears his throat, and the room falls silent.

'About six months before the fire,' he says. 'An employee raised concerns about two mobile phones on the work plan that didn't appear to be assigned to any particular employees. She had accessed the call logs as the representative of the company who had organised the phone plan, and discovered ... unprofessional messages.'

'What constitutes unprofessional messages, Mr Darling?'

He looks down at his hands, his cheeks blushing pink.

'They were of a sexual nature.'

A nervous cough from the gallery. It never surprises me, the reactions the mention of sex in court will bring. We talk about blood, murder, a ream of injustices, and yet sex is what makes the British public the most uncomfortable.

'And who did these phones – these messages – belong to?'

'My wife, Yolanda, and my business partner, Alex Finch.'

I turn to my attention to the jury and ask them to open their evidence packs. As they turn the pages, I pick up my copy of the call log and read the text messages aloud.

'"I want to fuck you on top of his desk" Alex wrote on the fifteenth of September, 2015. Yolanda replied three minutes later with, "There is glass, people will see." To which Alex replied immediately, "I want them to see." Whose desk are they referring to in these messages, Mr Darling?'

'Mine.'

The room is hanging off our every word.

'How did this make you feel?' I ask softly.

'I was devastated.'

'Were you angry?'

'Yes. I think anyone would be.'

'Did you ever think of hurting Yolanda, for betraying you?'

'*No*,' he replies sternly. 'I was angry for the children's sake, and I was deeply hurt, but I'm not that kind of man.'

'What did you do then, when you discovered their affair?'

He pauses, emotion welling in his eyes.

'I just . . . let it happen.'

'You didn't say anything to your wife or Mr Finch?'

'No. I had to protect my children and my business. I couldn't let their affair destroy everything we had. They were being reckless; one of us needed to hold the fort.'

'That's very admirable of you, Mr Darling.'

I take a moment to collect myself as I flush hot beneath my robes. Whenever I ask a question, I think of Mr Viklund in the public gallery, planning on how he will make me pay for this. I fight the urge to dab at the sweat gathering beneath the rim of my wig.

'How did keeping this secret impact you? Knowing the affair was going on right under your nose?'

'I fell into a deep depression. However hard I tried to hold things together, I could feel myself losing my wife, and the business was failing under our broken leadership. Through it all, I hoped and prayed that Yolanda would see sense. That whatever phase she was going through would pass. That she would come back to me.'

'And did she?'

He smiles softly.

'Yes, she did.'

Another pause. A juror shuffles noisily in their seat, the wood creaking beneath them. I can see Wade's testimony is getting under their skin; many of their faces have softened towards him.

'When did this reconciliation happen?' I ask.

His smile falls.

'The night of the fire.'

You could hear a pin drop in this room. The pluck of a hair, popping in the silence.

'You reconciled the night Yolanda and your children died?'

'Yes. The business was going under, and our marriage seemed to be hanging by a tether. I had been trying to hold down the fort, hoping things would work out in time, but things were too far gone. I had planned to confront her, but I didn't need to. She came to me and confessed to the affair, and that it was over. She wanted to try and make our marriage work.'

'And you took her back?'

'Without question.'

I look to the jury, make eye contact with the front row, before returning my attention to Wade.

'You didn't hold anything against her? You didn't at least give her a hard time?'

'Things were already hard enough. I was just relieved to have her back. I felt so alone with the failing business, and having my wife back made me feel stronger; I felt I could face what was to come with her by my side. However, I needed time. I had agreed to reconcile, but I needed to take it slow.'

'Did their affair end amicably?'

'It was clear to me that Alex Finch was angry at her for breaking it off.'

'What made you think that?'

'He sent her threatening text messages.'

I ask the jury to turn to the evidence packs to see the messages for themselves, sent the week of the murders. I pick up my copy and read aloud.

'"You will have nothing, Yolanda. Wade will leave you. You'll be broke. Your kids will know you're a whore who fucks her husband's mates. You'll die of shame when I'm finished with you." Can you confirm this is a text message you found on the phone archives, sent to your wife by Mr Finch?'

'Yes.'

I leave a purposeful pause, allowing the tension in the courtroom to rise before my next question.

'What happened on the night of the murders, Mr Darling?'

He takes a moment to compose himself, closing his eyes as he takes a deep breath.

'Yolanda and I had reconciled after dinner, when the children had gone up to their rooms. It was relatively late. She asked if I was coming to bed with her, and I explained I needed time. She looked hurt but understood. However, I did go upstairs to check on the children. Danny was asleep, so I pulled their door to, but Phoebe was awake on the phone. I kissed her goodnight. She asked if I was okay.'

And what did you say to her?'

'I said . . .' His eyes sheen over. 'I said everything was going to be better from now on. In fact, I *promised* things were going to get better . . . and then . . .'

His voice breaks with the encroaching tears.

'Take your time,' I say, almost at a whisper. The courtroom is hushed now, each sniffle and whimper echoing about the room.

'I planned to sleep in one of the spare rooms, but decided to watch TV for a while, as I was too distracted to sleep, after everything Yolanda and I had discussed. I had a couple of drinks to take to the edge off, and ended up falling asleep on the sofa in the living room.'

'And what happened next?' I ask, my words echoing against the walls of the deathly silent courtroom. 'What happened when you woke up?'

A single tear slips from his right eye. He dashes it away.

'I saw the flames.'

I stare at the jury, noticing how many of the men have cast their eyes downward; two of the women are teary-eyed. The press bench watches him hungrily.

I turn back to my client and smile softly.

It's time to ask the questions Antony first put to him, during our conferences in Marianne's home. To have him guide us through the night he found his wife dead on the stairs, his children eternally sleeping in their beds. The open door to the gun room, passing out only to wake up with his hand on fire. But before I begin, there is a question burning to be asked, one I know will have Niall bolting from his pew to object to Wade's inevitable answer.

'Mr Darling: what do you believe happened that night?'

By the quick flash in his eyes, I know he has spotted the

opportunity I have given him. He utters his next words as quickly as he can.

'I believe Alex Finch murdered my family.'

Niall shoots up from his seat. 'Your Honour—'

'Strike that from the record,' the judge demands among the noise of the court, stating that the jury are to forgo the comment when assessing the case.

But as I give my apologies to the judge, we all know it's too late. Words can be struck from the record, but not from the heart.

I turn slowly, stealing a look towards the gallery, and see the Messenger staring back at me. His usual smirk is nowhere to be seen, and a hateful stare is in its place. Beside him, Mr Viklund glares at me, his skin boiled red with anger.

They know whose side I'm on, and they know it isn't theirs.

I turn back towards the judge, trying to calm my racing heart.

Whatever happens, Hannah will be safe.

45

'How long have you participated in hunting, Mr Darling?'

Niall's first question comes hard and fast, making Wade visibly brace.

'My father hunted. It was something I grew up doing.'

'What do you like about it?'

Niall asks this as if inspired by curiosity. His tone is soft and upbeat. But I know that all will change when he decides to go in for the kill. Wade seems to sense it too.

'I like the calm. The quiet. I have to focus on the task at hand. It helps to clear my mind.'

'That's a nice sentiment, Mr Darling. But I think you're missing one crucial element. You like the control it gives you, don't you? The power.'

'There is an element of power, but no, that's not what draws me to it. There is the calm, followed by the exhilaration of hitting a target.'

'Exhilaration after a kill, you mean?'

'It could be clay shooting,' he says, flustered. 'It doesn't have to be a live target.'

'You predominantly hunt live prey, correct?'

'When we moved to our last address, I used to hunt in the woodland. The wildlife there. Pheasants and deer. It made sense.'

'And what would you say gives you the biggest thrill? A clay pigeon or a live target?'

I stand to object.

'Your Honour, is this line of questioning entirely necessary?'

The judge peers down his nose at me, then Niall.

'It's relevant, Your Honour,' Niall says from the other side of the bench.

'I'll allow it.'

Niall smiles as I return to my seat. 'Thank you, Your Honour.'

Wade thinks of his answer. If he says the latter, he will be painted in the light Niall wishes him to be seen in: a blood-hungry killer. But if he says the former, the jury will assume he is lying.

'The latter.'

'Taking a life?' Niall asks.

'Hunting live targets, yes.'

Niall makes sure to glance at the jury before returning his attention to my client.

'And you find that exhilarating?'

'Your Honour,' I say, standing again. 'I'm failing to gauge the point of this line of questioning other than to antagonise my client.'

'There is a point to make, Your Honour,' Niall says in rebuttal.

'Then please,' Judge McConnell replies, 'make it.'

He clears his throat. 'Yes, Your Honour.' Niall checks his notes, seemingly rattled, his cheeks flushed. 'I'll move on to my next question – Mr Darling, could you tell the court how many guns you owned, at the time of the murders?'

'Twenty or so. Perhaps more.'

'You don't know how many you owned?' he asks incredulously.

'I had participated in the sport for many years,' Wade replies. 'I bought more guns as my skill progressed. Money wasn't an object at that time.'

'I'm sure even you'd agree that that's rather excessive. Does one man really need over twenty firearms?'

'Some people collect cars. Others buy watches. I liked guns for my sport.'

Surprisingly, Wade seems calmer than before. Although he is still shaking, he holds himself well in the box, and is speaking clearly. He knows the importance of this. He's doing much better than I had anticipated.

'Did you have a favourite weapon in particular?'

The room falls quiet. It seems everyone knows where Niall is taking this line of questioning. The tension pulses in the air, like a heartbeat.

'Yes, it was the Tikka T3x Compact Tactical Rifle.'

'This was the weapon used to murder your wife and children, correct?'

Wade swallows. 'Yes.'

Niall calls for the jury to turn to their evidence packs. I reach the page in question at the same time as the jurors: it's a photo of the murder weapon covered in the victims' blood.

'This is the rifle in question, yes?'

Wade is looking intently at the image, seemingly transfixed.

'Mr Darling?'

'Yes,' he replies.

'You had a secured gun room in the property, didn't you? The place where you kept' – he makes a show of checking his notes – '*roughly* twenty weapons?'

'Yes.'

'Who else knew the code to this room?'

'I was the only person with the code. But I didn't make a habit of hiding it around people I trusted. Someone could have seen me enter the code.'

'That's convenient, isn't it? You were the only person who knew of the code, but someone just *might* have made a note of it?'

'It's the truth,' he replies. 'However convenient.'

Niall leaves a pause. I know from watching him work before that he is preparing to begin his onslaught. Until now, he has been working to paint Wade into a corner. Soon my client won't have anywhere else to turn.

'Did you ever leave the gun room unlocked?'

'No. It's important to keep them secure for licensing purposes.'

'And was it locked the night of the murders?'

'Yes.'

'Were the front gates to the property also locked?'

'Yes.'

'And the front door?'

'Yes.'

'Were all doors to the property locked?'

'I don't remember checking the back door. As I said, I passed out on the sofa. I usually check that before going up to bed.'

'So, let me get this straight,' Niall says. 'The entrance gates were locked, the front door was locked, and the gun room was locked, but you expect the jury to believe that an unknown stranger managed to waltz in, pick up your favourite rifle out of the twenty others you own, and murder your entire family in cold blood?'

I sit, tapping my leg silently, fighting the urge to object. There is a balance to be had with objections, and advocates must choose their windows wisely. Object too little, and the prosecution may walk away with the win. Object too much, and I could frustrate and alienate the jury, who want to hear the story. If I continuously halt my client from speaking freely, they may wonder what we are trying to hide.

The room is unbearably quiet, and the air is stifling. Sweat is speckling across Wade's face. A drop slips down his temples.

'Like I said, the back door might have been unlocked. It's perfectly possible for someone to have scaled the exterior walls to enter the grounds.'

'Someone could *possibly* have scaled the walls ... the back door *might* have been unlocked ... other people *might* have witnessed you keying in the code to your gun room ... an unknown gunman was allegedly in the property at the time of the murders, *despite* no concrete evidence of this other than your testimony ... Do you see my concern here, Mr Darling? A lot of your story rests on convenient possibilities and uncertainties. Where are the hard facts in all of this?'

Wade finally gives in and wipes his brow on his blazer sleeve, which comes away dark with sweat.

'The fact is,' Wade replies, 'the police didn't pursue any other suspects for this crime. They fixated on me, despite my insistence of a third party inside my home, holding my gun. They failed to interview or suspect anyone else other than me. There isn't more evidence because the police failed to investigate any other possibility other than their desired outcome.'

'There *are* hard facts in this case, Mr Darling,' Niall continues. 'Only, they don't back up your claims. The property was locked up, according to your own testimony. Only you knew the code to your gun room. Your fingerprints were the only prints found on the gun – your favourite gun, by your own admission. You were found covered in your family's blood. You say that you and your wife reconciled on the night of the murders, but other than your testimony, do you have any proof of this? Is there anyone else who can corroborate *any* of your claims?'

Wade stands silently in the box, chewing on his bottom lip.

'No,' he says finally.

'So, for all we know, your wife might not have wanted to reconcile at all; she might well have suggested you separate. Is that fair to say?'

'No. The text messages between my wife and Alex Finch prove she didn't want to stay with him.'

'But that doesn't automatically mean she wanted to stay with you either, does it?'

Wade stares, open-mouthed. He is starting to crack under the pressure. The sweat continues to slip down his face. I would object if I could, but I don't have the grounds. It's a question he will have to answer on his own.

'You were hoping, praying – in your own words – that your wife would end the affair,' Niall continues. 'What you didn't expect was for her to leave you too, right?'

'That's not true.'

'Yolanda wanted a fresh start. To get away from the toxic men who had been pulling her every which way. But you wouldn't let that happen, would you?'

'You've completely twisted this, sir.'

'You were severely depressed, in mountains of debt. The world you had built for your family, and the role of provider you had so proudly taken on, had crumbled. You had failed them and yourself. You had nothing but your wife and children, and then they decided to leave you too, didn't they?'

'That's not what happened—'

'Isn't it? Then why did your wife have three tickets booked for a flight to Sweden the following day?'

A gasp from somewhere in the room. Antony whips around to face me, his bewilderment mirroring mine. I flick furiously through the brief for the agreed evidence list.

'S-s-she and the children had planned that weeks before,' Wade says. 'To visit family. I couldn't go because of the state of the business; I had to stay to try and fix it.'

'But can you prove any of this?'

'It's what happened!'

'I'm sorry, Mr Darling, but all we have is your word. Because it seems to me that your wife was finally planning to leave you, and take the children with her. And that's what finally made you snap, isn't it?

'You had lost your money. Your business. Your status. Your mental health. Your best friend. All you had left was your wife and your children. And they were leaving you too, weren't they?'

'*No*.'

Niall begins to instruct the jury to turn to their evidence packs for the plane tickets when I stand, my finger pressed to the list. The tickets aren't there.

'Your Honour. This evidence was not agreed upon prior to trial.'

Judge McConnell looks towards the other end of the bench.

'It was, Your Honour,' Niall injects. 'I have it confirmed right here—'

The judge raises his hand. 'We will dismiss the jury before going any further.'

Niall and I stand in tense silence as the jury files out. I can tell he is furious at my stopping him, just as he was hammering home his point.

'Continue, Mr Richardson,' McConnell says.

'It was agreed upon and submitted into evidence before Ms Harper joined the case, Your Honour. My learned friend then agreed to this list in our last hearing before this very trial.'

'The list I agreed to does not contain any evidence regarding plane tickets, Your Honour—'

The judge shakes his hands dismissively to silence us both.

'Let me see what you have,' he says, reaching out for both forms, as the judge's clerk begins to search his notes on the case. She places it open on the correct page before him. He looks back and forth among each list. 'You're right, Ms Harper – the evidence in question is missing from your list. But it's not missing from Mr Richardson's or mine, which was agreed upon by you in the hearing before commencement, you'll recall.'

'Respectfully, Your Honour, I can't have agreed upon evidence I didn't know existed until this afternoon.'

The judge contemplates the files, his frown knitted deeply between his brows.

'Under the circumstances, Mr Richardson, we will have to strike this from the record. This is clearly an oversight that was missed during the changing of hands between the previous counsel and Ms Harper.'

I see Niall go to protest, before remembering his place, nodding in agreement while his cheeks flush.

The judge instructs his clerk to deliver to me a copy of the correct list, and calls the jury back into the courtroom. Antony grins at me before returning to face the witness box.

'The evidence you have just heard has been struck from the record,' the judge tells them. 'You must not consider this when you gather to deliberate.' He turns to Niall. 'Did you have further questions for the witness?'

'No, Your Honour,' he replies, jaw tensed. 'No further questions.'

46

I try to shake Niall's words from circling my mind while Wade steps down from the witness box.

Why did your wife have three tickets booked for a flight to Sweden the following day?

That is a question I would like answered, too.

Judge McConnell had put the missing evidence down to a clerical oversight, but there is much more to it than that. I received the brief that very day of the administrative hearing before the trial, after the list of evidence had been agreed upon months before. Which means someone had to have purposely led me astray like this; omitting the tickets from my list of evidence before I had a chance to lay eyes on it. I had thought Adrian Whittaker hadn't planned for the trial ahead of him, but perhaps he did after all. Maybe this omission was his last act of betrayal against our client before being thrust in front of the oncoming train.

It seems to me that your wife was finally planning to leave you, and take the children with her. And that's what finally made you snap, isn't it?

My heart is racing, and racing.

Antony and I certainly could have created a defence for this, had we been given the chance. If our theory is correct, and a third party like Alex Finch wanted to harm Wade's family, this would also be their last chance to act; the trigger that could have caused them to snap. As for Wade's testimony, he did well. Much better than I initially feared. He came across as genuinely pained, forthright and, ultimately, human. He will be so much more relatable to the jury now than he had before. But as I stand from my bench and call Alex Finch as our next witness, one question continues to linger in the forefront of my thoughts.

Why didn't Wade mention the plane tickets to us?

Finch steps into the witness box and takes his oath.

He is dressed in what appears to be an expensive pin-striped grey suit, a crisp white shirt, and navy tie. I imagine his shoes and belt are made of expensive Italian leather, and that his cologne costs a small fortune; I can smell it all the way from the advocates' bench. He looks like the sort of man whose ego depends on wearing expensive things.

This is my chance to give my client the fair trial he deserves. No holding back, no second-guessing. If I am to show the jury the skewed nature of the police investigation against my client, it's now. I won't stop until Finch has dug himself a hole he can't climb out of.

As he gives his oath and I ask him the preliminary questions, he speaks clearly, without nerves.

'How long have you known Mr Darling?'

'We met in the first year of university,' he replies.

'I see. And whose idea was it to go into business together?'

He frowns as he appears to think back.

'I can't remember, it was too long ago. I think we had always toyed with the idea, but we decided to take it seriously about fifteen years ago.'

I nod along as he talks, allowing silence to build between us before asking my next question.

'How long had you known Mr Darling's wife?'

A twitch under his eye. The first sign of distress I have spotted since he entered the box.

'Pretty much as long as Wade. I was there when they met, back in 2007.'

'I see. And when did you first have *sex* with Mr Darling's wife?'

His jaw drops. The court is deathly silent.

'Was that around the same time, too, Mr Finch? Or did the sexual element to your relationship with your best friend's wife come later?'

He stops. Swallows. He glances nervously at the dock where Wade stands, before throwing a quick glimpse at the jury. He can't have known that the affair had been brought to light before his turn in the box. He will have been kept away from the public gallery until it was his turn to speak.

Finch looks around, meeting the stares of the room.

'Why are you asking me that?'

'Because Yolanda Darling is dead, Mr Finch, and we are here to discover why.'

I ask the jury to turn to the text messages in their evidence packs, and pick up my copy of the page for the witness. The clerk steps forward and hands it to Mr Finch.

'Can you confirm these are messages between you and the deceased, Yolanda Darling, dated thirteenth of August 2017?'

He reads through them, the worry growing on his face the more he reads. I take it upon myself to read them aloud.

'"I'm going to fuck you in his bed. Make you come where he sleeps." These are your words, correct?'

He looks up from the paper, which shakes in his hand. His whole face is flushed now, whether with anger or embarrassment, I can't quite tell.

'Answer the question please, Mr Finch,' Judge McConnell says from his podium.

'Yes,' he forces.

'And when you refer to wanting to "fuck" the victim where "he sleeps" and in "his bed" ... Who are you referring to?'

He swallows, his Adam's apple bobbing against the collar of his shirt. His tie suddenly looks too tight, like a noose.

'Wade,' he replies hoarsely.

'You wanted to "fuck" the deceased in Wade's bed? Make the deceased "come" where Wade sleeps?'

'Yes,' he bites. 'I've confirmed that already.'

'I see. Had your relationship with Mr Darling changed by this point? In your statement, you spoke of being inseparable since your first year of university, but in your messages, you appear to hold him in contempt.'

'We were still close.'

'And yet you chose to pursue a sexual relationship with his wife?'

I hear a creak from the other end of the advocates' bench.

'Your Honour ...' Niall says, as he stands.

Finch isn't Niall's client, but he might as well be; if I successfully highlight the police's poor investigation, Niall's case comes apart at the seams.

The judge gives me a look of warning for badgering the witness.

'Apologies, Your Honour, I'll rephrase the question.' I return my gaze to the box. 'When did the affair with Yolanda Darling begin, Mr Finch?'

He swallows, eyeing me suspiciously.

'The summer of 2015, I believe. I can't remember the month. June or July.'

'And when did it end?'

He falls quiet. The silence becomes deafening.

'Mr Finch,' I say, sharply. 'When did your relationship with Yolanda Darling end?'

'The week before.'

'Before what, Mr Finch?'

He looks at me, shaking with what appears to be loathing.

'Before she died.'

The tension stretches, swells.

'Who ended it?' I ask.

He pauses, chewing on his bottom lip, as if trying to keep back his reply.

'Mr Finch . . .'

'Yolanda did.'

I glance at the jury. Their faces are awash with hostility towards the witness, and a sense of exhilaration bolts through me. It feels so good to be doing what I'm best at, despite the threat of harm that awaits me. Throughout this trial, the power I am so used to having has been within another's control. To have it back, even if only for a short while, brings an overwhelming sense of relief.

'How did you take her decision to end things?'

'I wasn't thrilled about it, obviously.'

'For the sake of doubt, Mr Finch, let's assume that nothing is to be deemed obvious during your testimony.'

His eyes, set firmly upon on mine, glitter with hatred. I wonder if it's because of my questioning, or because I'm a woman.

'Your wife left you upon discovering the affair, correct?'

'Yes.'

'And what date was this, exactly?'

'The fourteenth of November.'

'Three days before the murders?'

'Yes. Although I don't see how that's relevant to—'

'I'll decide what's relevant and what isn't, Mr Finch,' I reply, before allowing the room to fall quiet again. Stretching out the silence as long as I can before the blow. 'Where were you the night of the murders?'

Niall jumps up from his seat.

'Your Honour, the witness has not been charged with a crime, nor is he on trial—'

'I'm merely establishing where he was on the night the crimes took place, Your Honour.'

McConnell contemplates this from his pew, staring at me over his half-moon spectacles.

'I'll allow it,' he replies finally.

Niall reluctantly sits back down.

'Thank you, Your Honour.' I turn to the witness box. 'Where were you the night of the murders, Mr Finch?'

'I was at home, in bed,' he replies.

'Was your wife in bed with you?'

'No. I was in the spare room. But she and the children were home.'

'Could they corroborate that you were at home all night?'

'Yes.'

'You can prove this?'

'How would you expect me to prove that?' he asks sharply.

'I believe that means you can't prove it, Mr Finch,' I reply. 'And to confirm, these are the only witnesses who can attest to you being at home the entire night? Your family members who were asleep in different rooms to you?'

He stares at me, practically shaking with rage, his cheeks bright red, as Niall shoots to his feet.

'Your Honour, my learned friend is clearly making insinuations here.'

The judge nods and turns to me.

'I think you have established where the witness was, Ms Harper.'

'Yes, Your Honour.'

I turn to Mr Finch. He looks far less confident than he had when he stepped into the box. Perhaps one of my most treasured moments in a trial is looking into a witness's eyes and seeing the fear of the unknown staring back at me. The fear that, at any moment, I could change the course of our conversation, and their lives, to the point of no return.

I take a deep breath, treasuring the adrenaline pulsing through me.

'Here is my concern, Mr Finch. My client has been accused of killing his family due to a breakdown after the collapse of your joint business. But from where I stand, you've lost an awful lot too, haven't you? You *also* lost your business, your livelihood. Your marriage broke down, just like Mr Darling's. Your mistress left you. You destroyed your relationship with your longest, oldest friend. It seems you too lost everything you held dear ... Were you angry that Yolanda ended the affair with you and returned to Wade?'

'I was ... disappointed.'

I ask the jury to turn to their evidence packs, and give them time to reach the right page.

'Were you expressing your disappointment when you sent

the following to the victim: "Your kids will know you're a whore who fucks her husband's mates"?'

'I was upset, and sent messages that I regret.'

'"You'll die of shame when I'm finished with you." Is this one of the messages you regret?'

He clears his throat, his eyes flicking towards the jury before returning to me. 'Yes.'

'I see. And were you ever interviewed by the police about your whereabouts during the early hours of the seventeenth of November, 2018?'

'No.'

I give him a look of contempt, before turning my attention to the jury, making sure my last question sinks in.

'No further questions.'

I sit down on my pew, my heart racing, as Antony turns to me with an exhilarated smile, which I can't help but match. But as I treasure the sense of approval from Antony, knowing I've achieved exactly what we needed to, the dread slowly creeps in. I have met the objective I set out to achieve by exposing the affair and painting Finch as a suspect the police missed. Now, I must pay the consequences. I stare ahead, unable to bring myself to turn towards the gallery and meet Mr Viklund's eyes.

47

I hide away in the chambers at the Bailey, preparing for the last few witnesses for the defence. With Wade and Finch complete, following Niall's cross-examination of him before the break, we only have three more witnesses to go before the trial is wound down: Wade's former executive assistant, the pathologist to confirm the blood found on his person, and the nurse who told him of his family's deaths. Then all there is left to do is give our closing speeches before the jurors go off to deliberate. If all continues to run smoothly, we could even arrive at the jury's deliberation by tomorrow.

I wonder if I will make it till then.

Mr Viklund and the Messenger must have gauged that I am working against their wishes by now. Defending my client's case to create a sense of credibility in the eyes of the court is one thing, but essentially suggesting the witness may be responsible for the crime rather than my client is something else entirely; it is clear from my tactics today that I am working on behalf of Wade's best interest instead of theirs.

I push the fears for myself aside momentarily and focus on my client. The case we have laid before the jury for his innocence is strong: we have dismissed a key piece of evidence with the plane tickets, which would have been a killer move for the prosecution. We have humanised Wade in the witness box, making it so that his giving evidence actually worked in our favour, rather than against us. And then of course, there was the decimation of Alex Finch's character, creating doubt around the police investigation and their charge against my client. It was virtually impossible for Niall to deliver a cross-examination to match. After my interrogation of Finch, Niall was stuck as to where to go. He couldn't paint my client as an abuser by asking Finch questions about their marriage without a heavy dose of hearsay, which I shut down each and every time. He couldn't have the jury see Wade as a bad businessman, without dragging the witness into that very same category, what with him being the financial director and heavily responsible for the funds that got their business into trouble. After twenty minutes of attempting to refute our argument, Niall sat down, defeated.

I think back to the close call we had with those plane tickets, and stare at both of the evidence lists: the most recent copy, and the original from the brief I was given. The tickets are clearly on the approved list of evidence, but they're missing from mine; the only difference between each of the forms. Could I have really had an older copy? Or did someone make sure I didn't know of it ahead of time, hoping to trip me up?

I raise half a sandwich to my lips before placing it back down again, unable to stomach it. I am running purely on coffee and adrenaline.

'Ms Harper?'

I look up and find a clerk from the Bailey's chambers stood in the doorway.

'There's someone asking after you.'

The possibilities run through my mind, none of them good.

'Who is it?'

'Tinsley Adams. She's the personal assistant for a gentleman named Fredrick Hurst.'

My heart jumps at the name. I immediately think of him tied up in chains, staring up at me.

'She's here?' I ask.

'Not in the building, miss, she's on the phone and waiting outside. What shall I tell her?'

I close my laptop and begin to tidy away my things.

'Tell her to meet me at St Bride's Church.'

I have no idea why she might want to meet me. Perhaps she knew that Fredrick and I had been working together and wants answers. But it's the possibility that she has some information for me that makes me hurry. Fredrick had said he had found something that day. Whatever Tinsley has to say, I need to hear it.

⚖

St Bride's is a small church set back from the road, not far from the Bailey. It's a hidden gem among the bustle of the city, accessible through a set of black iron gates, and a courtyard overshadowed by trees. I'm not a religious person, but I have escaped here in the past between trial adjournments, when the buzz of the court became too much and I needed quiet. That is, until Matthew's death. I haven't set foot in a church since.

I make my way inside, admiring the tall, arched ceilings, the gold detailing and panelled pews. My footsteps echo across the black and white tiled floor to where Tinsley is sat waiting for me.

Tinsley is younger than I imagined. Although in hindsight, perhaps I should have guessed; her name seems youthful, modern. She has long blonde hair, straightened to death with visible split ends. She doesn't smile as I sit down beside her.

'Tinsley?'

She nods. 'Thanks for meeting me.'

Despite her age – twenty-four, twenty-five – she has the confidence of someone older, instantly taking control of the conversation.

'Fredrick is missing,' she says bluntly. She pauses as if to gauge my reaction. Perhaps I'm being paranoid.

'I'm sorry to hear that.'

She gives me a long look, as if she is trying to figure me out. After what feels like a long time, she reaches into her bag and removes a file.

'I found this on his desk when I was looking through his office. He'd left a note, asking for it to be passed on to you. Good thing he did, with him going missing and all.'

Almost as if he knew what might happen, I think to myself.

Her tone makes me wonder again if she is suspicious of me, wondering if I know more than I'm letting on, or whether it's just her blunt, monotone delivery.

'What is it?' I ask, with a nervous wavering to my voice.

'I'm not entirely sure,' she replies. 'But . . . I wouldn't broadcast that you have it, if I were you.'

I nod and take the file, noticing how it shakes in my grip, where it had been still in hers.

'Thank you for bringing this to me.'

She nods once and rises from her pew.

'Good luck.'

I watch her as she leaves, her heels clacking against the cold tiled floor, the sound echoing up to the eaves.

Once I am alone, I open the file and read.

⚖

It's the list.

I stand on the tube station platform, thinking of the names printed in the file Tinsley gave me. Fredrick had found the list of names the Viklunds have collected to call upon should they need them.

High-up police officials, members of parliament, lords, judges. It could be mistaken for a list of who's who in London.

Then I reached a name I never would have imagined I'd find. It was one of those moments you can't quite believe, doubting yourself despite the truth staring up at you in black and white.

Artie Mills, Senior Clerk of Whitehall Legal Chambers.

I then had to go through the remainder of the day in court with his name rolling around in my mind, questioning Wade's former personal assistant to confirm her discovery of the work phones used between Yolanda and Finch during their affair.

Does Artie know what the Messenger is doing to me? Or worse, did he have something to do with it? He was the one who got the case for me, after all. He had shown no guilt as he handed it over. He had been his usual, chipper self. Maybe that doesn't change the fact that he's implicated in this. But I've known him for practically my whole career; he was a mentor of sorts. The anchor to keep me from drifting. The colleague I could always count on.

You'll be the most hated clerk in the city this morning. Who'd you have to kill to get your hands on this?

He'd said nothing, just tapped his nose playfully.

Perhaps I don't know him at all.

Once the trial ended for the day, I returned to the court chambers immediately, the lamps on the desks around me shutting off one by one as the other barristers left, until it was just me and the brief bit of light beneath my desk lamp. If I were to leave the premises at the end of day, I was far more likely to bump into the Messenger or Mr Viklund. It was better to wait until dark.

The station is practically deserted. I stand back from the edge, swaying on my feet from exhaustion, battling my anxiety at the thought of being alone on the platform, open and exposed.

I need to sleep; I am practically drifting off where I stand. But I know my memories of the night before will continue to haunt me. I glance up at the tube timetable rolling across the screen. My train is only a minute away.

That's when he appears, snatching me roughly from behind.

'Did you really think you'd get away with it?'

I stand, frozen in the Messenger's tight grip, his large hands clamping down on both my arms. I hadn't seen or heard him approach; perhaps Adrian Whittaker didn't either. I should have left for home when there was a crowd, instead of waiting until now when I have no one to help me, and no witnesses.

The train is approaching, clangs of metal echoing through the tunnel. A strangled sound creeps up my throat. His grip tightens.

'You can't say I didn't warn you,' he says close to my ear. 'You remember how Adrian Whittaker died, don't you? You remember who pushed him?'

The train appears around the bend.

'I wonder what your husband will say, when you see him again?'

I feel his grip tighten, and his body shift. I try to scream but no sound comes out, even as I am forced forward, my feet skidding across the tiles, air stuck in my throat. My feet teeter over the yellow line running along the platform edge. The sound of the train clangs in my ears. The rush of air. The grind of metal. Just as the train approaches, he thrusts me forward.

The train passes an inch from my nose, my hair whipping against my face in a frenzy, dizzy as the passing carriages blur before my eyes. I feel his breath against my ear again.

'One last chance, Harper. Or it'll be Hannah on the tracks.'

His hands release me, and then he is gone. The tube pulls to a stop and passengers pour out, the crowd moving about me like a rock in a river, as I stand frozen to the spot.

Day Five

48

I wake up with a lurch.

For a brief moment, I'm not sure where I am. I had expected to find myself in my bed, legs tangled in the sheets and my alarm blaring on the bedside table. But instead, I am curled up in my chair in my chambers. The morning light beams through the window, hot on my face, dust floating in its path, as the memory of how I ended up here slowly returns.

After the Messenger's trick at the tube station, I had been too afraid to go home. I had boarded the tube in a trance and sat down, watching platform after platform pass me by, realising how close I had been to death. I had felt it as the train brushed so close to me, sensed the heavy mass of metal. I tasted it in the polluted air, smelt it on the Messenger's breath. I'd stared death straight in its face and managed to walk away. When I arrived at the stop for chambers, I got off instinctively, too deeply in shock to think beyond putting one foot in front of the other.

Today is the day. The last day I have to defend Wade Darling's case before the jury goes off to deliberate. There are only two more witnesses to enter the box, and then it is time for closing speeches from Niall and me. After that, it is down to the jury. The case will be out of my hands.

I think back to what the Messenger said during our first meeting: it is my client or me. The choice has always been there, dangling over me like a blade, but despite all I have done, I have silently hoped that I could save us both. I had initially chosen what I thought was the right path for Hannah and me – to keep her safe, and hide my sins – by putting my client in jeopardy. But the thought of Hannah being somewhere far from the Messenger's reach, and my truth finally being out in the open, makes me feel a strange sense of calm despite the fear. This laborious secret will be lifted from my shoulders, and the truth will be out there: I will pay for what I have done. And even though I am likely to be sentenced to prison for a very long time, in an odd way, I'll be freer than I am now, wandering in the open. But there is one last thing I must do. Hannah will have to come back to London after the trial, and I want to ensure it is safe for her when she does.

My eyes fall on the file Tinsley gave me, poking out of my bag. The list of names. I slip it from my bag and place it on the desk.

As a defence barrister, it is my job to pinpoint my opposition's power, and use it against them. Anticipate their every move, and remain one step ahead. This list is Mr Viklund's power. I just have to find a way to use it to my advantage.

A knock sounds at the door.

'Yes?' I ask, frantically smoothing down my hair and wiping my eyes.

The door opens, and Artie appears.

'You're in early,' he says, the same usual smirk on his face. 'I thought you'd want to hear the good news.'

He chucks a print-out from *The Times*' website, an online

article posted this morning about Melanie Eccleston's disappearance. My stomach turns.

'Won't have to worry about those front page stories now, will you?'

Rage seeps into me like venom. It must show on my face, because his smile falls.

'Sit down,' I say.

'Everything all right, miss?' he asks tentatively.

'You tell me.' I nod towards the file Tinsley gave me. 'Open it.'

He looks down at the file on the desk. I watch closely as he opens the cover, and his expression changes.

'I think it's about time you told me the truth, Artie.'

He swallows. His eyes flick from the file to me, his gaze awash with pity.

'I'm sorry,' he says gravely.

'I don't care if you're sorry. I want to know what you've done, and more importantly, why.'

He looks like a different man. His usual chipper bravado has gone; the man who sits before me looks smaller, older. I wonder, after all these years, if I am seeing the real Artie Mills for the first time. The man behind the bravado. He closes the file and returns it to the desk. He looks at me for a moment before releasing a heavy sigh.

'When I started my career, I did so with a bullseye on my back. Only I didn't know it. My boss was under Viklund's thumb. His name was on this list, and as his most promising clerk, he added mine too.

'That's how the Viklunds work. They get those under their control to recruit the next generation. Once they receive a name, they look into you – into your past, your family, your lovers. Every aspect of your life. If they don't find anything to exploit, they watch and wait until you slip up.'

'How did my name end up on this list?'

I know the answer, but I need to hear him say the words. He looks at me across the desk; there isn't any way he can back out of this now. The only thing left to do is confess.

'When it was my turn, I had to give the names of my most promising barristers. You were my best.'

He watches me, waiting for my reaction. Perhaps he is expecting me to cry, or scream in rage. Fling the files from the desk. But I just sit, watching him.

'So, for all these years, you have known this would happen?'

'I didn't have a choice.'

'We all have choices to make. You *chose* to make this happen to me, so you could protect yourself.'

'So were you, at the beginning of the trial.' He stares at me, a glimmer of resentment flickering in his eyes. 'That killer piece of evidence didn't just magic itself out of thin air, did it?'

My cheeks blaze with shame.

'Question is,' he says. 'What are you going to do now? Don't think they won't follow through with their threats, because they will.'

'Yes, I know all about what happened to Adrian Whittaker.'

'And yet, you're still planning to play the hero. You'd sacrifice yourself for a man who killed his family?'

'You don't know that he did it – none of us do. I won't be like you; I won't sacrifice someone else's freedom to save my own.'

'Let's see where that moral compass gets you. A prison cell, if you're lucky. Death if you're not.'

'At least I'd be able to sleep at night. You're looking pretty tired over there, Artie.'

He looks down at his lap, a quiet sigh unfurling from between his lips. I wonder how long they have been threatening him, and what secret they might be using against him. By the look of him, they've been in his ear a lot longer than they have mine.

The truth dawns on me.

'The evidence list,' I say. 'You tampered with it, didn't you? You made sure I wouldn't know about the plane tickets until it was too late.'

Artie averts his eyes.

'You'd fired Eddie Chester, who was employed to help you lose the case. I was aiding you in his place.'

'By stitching me up?'

'By taking some of the burden,' he replies.

I hone my eyes on him, taking in his glum, self-pitying face.

'Do you know what they have against me?' I ask.

'No,' he replies. 'Nor will I ask. I hope you pay me the same mercy.'

I scoff at the word. 'Mercy.'

He gets up without a word and heads for the door, slowly, painstakingly, as if he is desperately trying to muster a way to fix the mess he has made.

'I'm sorry, Neve,' he says.

I stare back at him, watch as a shiver runs down his spine from the coolness of my glare.

'Goodbye, Arthur.'

I watch him until he clicks the door shut behind him, before returning my attention to the list.

This is his power. Now I just have to make it mine.

49

I stand in the courtroom, convinced I can hear the chants of the crowd waiting outside. The police presence outside the Bailey is unprecedented compared to the cases I've worked on in the past, as if the public can sense the end of the trial looming and each wants a piece of it.

Wade, Antony and I had our final conference first thing, before the last few beats of the trial. It was clear that Wade hadn't had a wink of sleep. No one can truly know how exhausting it is to have one's fate hang in the balance like this; to have strangers decide your fate. But I know. My fate has been dangling right beside his, and worse, I've been made to decide which one will fall.

The jury looks drained. They have absorbed so much information in such a short space of time. So many conflicting testimonies pulling them in opposite directions. One can almost see the burden thrust upon their shoulders, dragging them down until they slump.

I break from my thoughts to a silent courtroom, and find Judge McConnell looking at me from his podium – it is time for me to call in my next witness.

'The defence calls Dr Allison Fadden.'

Forensic scientist Dr Fadden stands in the witness box.

'You were tasked with analysing the blood found upon Mr Darling, is that correct?'

'That's right. The evidence was collected from Mr Darling's person and his clothes, a pyjama set.'

I instruct the jurors to turn to their evidence packs, listening as pages flip in the otherwise silent court, until they reach the photographs of the blood-soiled pyjamas Wade had been wearing. Their eyes come alive at the sight of the blood. His clothing was soaked in it. What originally had been a set of navy pyjamas appear deep burgundy. There are grazing strokes on the fabric by his clavicles from Yolanda's hair as he held her, but from the chest down, the clothes are completely soaked through, pooling at the front of the pyjama bottoms where he had positioned himself beneath her and held her body to his.

'Dr Fadden, from your analysis, can you determine whose blood this was?'

'Yes. The majority was found to belong to Yolanda Darling, but there were also traces from both of the children, Phoebe and Danny.'

'Thank you. And have you determined how the blood was deposited onto Mr Darling's clothes and person?'

'Yes. The smaller deposits to the defendant's face, and the fabric of his night shirt by his shoulders, indicate close contact with the victim. An embrace, for example. As for the blood found on the defendant's soles, this implies the defendant walked through an area where the blood was present, with fibres that match that of the carpet that had been present in the hallway and on the stairs.'

All of this matches Wade's testimony of finding and embracing Yolanda on the stairs.

'And what of his clothing? What do the blood deposits indicate?'

'This indicates that the blood was allowed to settle for a time, rather than a quick transference.'

'Can you elaborate on that?'

'Well,' Dr Fadden says. 'The blood could have been transferred to the clothing if, say, the body had been resting against him for some time.'

'Like an embrace?'

'Yes.'

'Thank you. And from your analysis, does the evidence indicate the wearer of these clothes inflicted violence on the victims?'

'There were no patterns to indicate the person wearing this clothing was responsible for the violence inflicted, no.'

'Thank you. No further questions.'

I take to my seat. Niall stands abruptly for cross-examination.

'Dr Fadden, I'm Niall Richardson, the prosecutor in this case. Using your scientific analysis, is it possible for a person to commit a crime in one outfit, and then change into another?'

His patronising tone hangs in the air. Dr Fadden straightens her posture, her chin rising.

'Well, yes. But I don't work with hypothetical scenarios, Mr Richardson. I analyse evidence, not the lack of.'

'Then perhaps we can discuss the evidence of gunpowder residue on the defendant's hands. From your analysis, can you tell when this was deposited?'

She nods. 'The gunpowder residue found on the defendant's hands would indicate the traces were left that same day.'

'And the residue matches the ammunition used to kill victims Yolanda, Phoebe and Danny Darling?'

'Yes.'

'Thank you. Nothing more from me.'

Niall takes to his seat as I shoot up from mine.

'One last question from me, Dr Fadden: can you determine the gunpowder residue was left during the hours that the victims were shot? Or is it possible that the deposits were made earlier in the day, when Mr Darling was out hunting, using the same gun and same ammunition?'

'I cannot determine that the deposits were left during the time frame of the murders, no.'

'Thank you. No further questions.'

I take my seat, and glance along the bench where Niall sits at the other end, nervously tapping his foot beneath the desk.

50

When the last witness is called to the box, I am overcome with both relief and dread in equal measure. The end is in sight. But in this story, there is more than one ending. Whether the completion of the trial brings an end to my freedom or my life, I'm not quite sure. I can't bring myself to fathom the outcome; only that this must, and will, end.

I rise from my seat and call the last witness.

One can always tell a trial is coming to a close by the air in the courtroom. It buzzes with anticipation. The last witness is Christine Vinson, a nurse at Queen Elizabeth Hospital where Wade was treated after the murders. It is to be a short exchange, with only a few key facts to confirm for the jury. It often feels anticlimactic to end a case like this, after such a long, drawn-out trial. One expects it to finish with a bang. Niall and I will save that for our closing speeches.

Christine Vinson takes her oath and answers my preliminary questions with nervous assertion. Her voice is as mousey as the colour of her hair; sweet, tender. Traits that I hope will inspire the jury to plead not guilty – a woman as timid as this wouldn't defend a killer.

'You treated Mr Darling during his stay in hospital, is that right?'

'Yes,' she replies, an anxious rattle to her voice. 'The patient was in a coma for the first two days. I spent my time checking his stats, bathing his wounds, helping with sanitary care. That sort of thing.'

'Were you there when Mr Darling woke up?'

'I was,' she replies. Her face softens with the memory. 'I was re-dressing his burns, and when I looked up he was staring right at me.'

'And how did he appear to you?'

She swallows, and glances up at the dock.

'Terrified.'

'Did he say anything when he woke up?'

'Yes. The first thing he asked was where his family was. If his wife and children were okay. He just kept saying his wife's name. *Yolanda. Yolanda.*'

I pause, letting the name linger.

'What did you say in return?'

She rubs the back of her hand nervously, her gold rings catching the light. 'I said I would get the doctor, but he took my hand as I turned to leave. That will have caused him great discomfort from the burns, but he still didn't take his eyes off me. He said he needed to know immediately.'

The silence in the courtroom thrums like one, collective heartbeat. Ms Vinson takes on a grave expression.

'I told him there had been a fire, and his family hadn't yet been found.'

'And how did Mr Darling take this news?'

'He ... bellowed. That's the only word I can think to describe the sound. It wasn't a scream, or a shout ... just pure pain. I've never heard a sound quite like it before.'

'If you had to describe your patient in that moment with a single word, what would it be?'

She considers this for a while, wringing her hands before her, her teeth chewing on her bottom lip.

'Heartbroken.'

'Thank you, Ms Vinson. That will be all from me.'

She nods, a small triumphant smile curling at the corners of her lips at surviving her testimony, which quickly falls when Niall stands for cross-examination.

'Nothing from me,' he says, and returns to his seat.

A sound from the back of the courtroom sends heads turning towards the dock.

Wade is sat behind the glass with his face in his hands, wracked with sobs he is trying to smother. When he lowers his hands, and sees the room staring back at him, his tear-streaked face blushes red.

I stand silently and address the court.

'The defence rests.'

I lower myself to my seat, lightheaded with exhaustion. All the witnesses have been called. The cross-examinations have been completed. We only have the closing speeches left, before the jury deliberates. The task I had thought impossible is almost over with. My heart flutters angrily in my chest.

And then what? I think to myself, as I feel the hot, searing gazes of Mr Viklund and the Messenger from the gallery.

Hannah will be safe, I remind myself, as I keep my head down, refusing to look.

The break goes by in the blink of an eye. I smoke two cigarettes in quick succession, before hiding away in the loos, pacing back and forth until someone enters, which sends me scurrying back towards the courtroom doors.

The day passes as though I am in some sort of trance. Scenes unfold before me, but I have no memory of them. Hours tick off the clock in what feels like fleeting seconds. The closer we get to the end of the trial, the more my fear grows. I both crave the end, to finally be free of it, and dread it in equal measure, for the consequences of my actions await me.

All that matters right now is that Hannah is somewhere safe, and I do right by my client.

The judge begins the proceedings quickly, the exhaustion just as evident on his face as those of the jury. Niall gives his closing speech first, speaking of his case as though it were black and white, as though he holds the answers to the week-long question of my client's guilt.

The court has taken his views, digested them. I watched every juror as their thoughts glinted in their eyes, disgust and confusion etched in their expressions. Niall might be arrogant and self-assured, but he is also a good lawyer. His closing speeches rarely fail to potentially sway a jury.

And now it is my turn. The last hurdle, before my client's case is out of my hands, and both our fates are sealed.

I think of all the events that have brought me here to this moment, and all that I have done. My life changed within a single tube ride. My bones ache with the memory of thrusting the spade into the earth, the weight of my husband's body pulling at my muscles as I dragged him through the woods, the smell of him getting caught in my nostrils. I think of all the lies I've told. The sleepless nights I've had. The danger I have put people in. The deaths I have caused. The list of my sins seems endless. But now I am finally doing the right thing, whatever the consequences may be for me. There is only so much guilt one person can live with before they reach their limit, and as I stand at my bench with the jury's eyes upon me, I know I have reached mine.

Whatever lies ahead for me, I will accept it.

I clear my throat. The sound echoes about the silent room.

'Members of the jury, in the late hours of the sixteenth of November, 2018, Wade Darling fell asleep on his sofa after reconciling with his wife, who'd had an extramarital affair with Mr Darling's business partner. Despite his business failing, his money running out, and while experiencing a deep, debilitating depression, Wade had reason to hope that things would get better. Instead, he woke up to his house burning to the ground around him.

'Coughing and terrified, Wade's first thought was of his family, and he made his way from the living room to the hall. That is when he came face to face with a masked intruder holding Mr Darling's gun in gloved hands. After the intruder escaped, Wade put his own safety aside to search for his family. He found the love of his life, dead on the stairs, shot in the leg, back, and finally her head. He sobbed and cradled her, inadvertently covering himself in her blood, as the world they had built together smouldered around him. Then he found his children, dead in their beds, shot as they slept. Wade Darling fell asleep on the sofa with hope, and woke to find his entire world had been ripped out from under him.

'Members of the jury, I want you to imagine waking up in the middle of the night, disorientated and dazed, to your home burning to cinders all around you. I want you to imagine that, upon searching for your family, you find an armed intruder coming down the stairs from where your loved ones sleep. Then, I would like you to imagine finding your spouse and your children, shot dead. The entrance gates have been chained shut. Every way out is blocked by flames. And despite falling unconscious and suffering severe burns, you survive. You survive against all odds. Only, upon investigation, your version of events is not believed. The police accuse you of the murders, despite all the other unexplored avenues the investigation could have – and should have – taken. I want you to imagine being made to sit in court and listen to twisted versions of events, as an untrue picture of you is painted before a jury. What would you do? What *could* you do?'

I pause, looking at the jurors one by one.

'The Crown must build their case on evidence, but as this trial has shown, the evidence is lacking or easily discredited. The Crown's main points of evidence are thus: Wade Darling suffers from depression. This is not grounds for a murder conviction. This depression was due to his wife's affair with his long-time friend and business partner, and the closure of his business. Is this such an outlandish outcome? Does a person experiencing depression automatically mean they are to be suspected of murder?

'Then there's the fact that Mr Darling's fingerprints were the only prints present on the murder weapon. But we have seen the CCTV footage, and know the figure holding the gun was wearing gloves, thereby removing any possibility of a third party's fingerprints being left behind. Mr Darling's fingerprints would be on the rifle regardless of a crime taking place.

'As for the gunpowder residue on the defendant's hands, the Crown wish for you to believe this is proof that Mr Darling murdered his family. What they omitted to tell you is that Mr Darling had used the weapon earlier that day, which would easily explain the presence of such residue.

'Members of the jury, the Crown want you to believe that

because the weapon belonged to the defendant, and because he was the main bearer of the code to his gun room, that he must have committed these crimes. But someone close to him could have learnt of the code to gain access for themselves. The same person who would know which weapon was most frequently used by the defendant. The same person who would know that there was fuel on the property, and knew where each of the family members slept.

'It is up to the Crown to prove to you – beyond a shadow of a doubt – that the defendant committed these crimes. But instead, the Crown has submitted to you an imperfect, incomplete argument, born from a spectacularly problematic investigation, in which the police failed to consider if anyone else could have been responsible for the crime. What you must decide now is whether the Crown's case is enough to submit a guilty verdict. Your decision will ultimately decide whether the defendant is allowed to grieve his family in peace, and for the case to return to the police for a thorough investigation, or whether Mr Darling will go to prison for crimes he did not commit, and the unknown, undiscovered intruder will be allowed to walk free.

'You are not here to decide upon a verdict based on your emotions, but upon the evidence that has been presented to you. And it is up to you to ensure that the Crown's case has convinced you of the defendant's guilt without a *shadow of a doubt*. So I ask you, when the evidence is assessed on the basis of hard, cold facts: can you honestly submit a verdict of guilty?'

I stand in the silence, analysing the jury one by one, before returning to my seat.

As the judge begins his speech to the jury before sending them away to deliberate, I sit with the realisation that my part in the trial is over. What will happen to me now, I can't say.

Only that in some way or another, it will be deserved. It's time I stopped running and paid the price for my past.

Once the jurors have filed out to begin their deliberations, the air in the courtroom shifts. The press bench busies with anticipation, journalists eager to type up the stories burning at their fingertips. From the back of the court, a clerk hurries from the judge's doorway, his robe swishing at his feet with his hurried steps. He whispers in the judge's clerk's ear, and I watch as her face changes. Her eyes flick towards me, before returning to the clerk, and nodding.

My stomach drops – I know they bear bad news before I have even heard a word of it – and shoot my eyes towards the gallery. When I look to the Messenger, that familiar smirk creeps across his face, and my heart contracts.

'Ms Harper,' the judge's clerk says, having approached the bench. 'We have a message for you. I'm afraid it's of an urgent nature.'

'What is it?' I ask.

The clerk swallows nervously.

'There appears to have been an accident, miss,' she says.

By the look in her eyes, and the pity in her tone, I know.

I know she's talking about Hannah.

51

It takes me over an hour to get to the hospital. Throughout the journey, I replay the scene in my mind, trying to divulge more information. But the clerk only knew so much.

What kind of accident?

A car accident, miss.

The accident didn't just involve Hannah. Maggie was behind the wheel. I wonder if they had been heading out of town when it happened, as I had suggested. When I was stupid enough to think I could go against the Messenger, and still keep them safe. The clerk knew nothing of their condition, just that the accident had happened, and that it was urgent enough to call me. Mr Viklund's words have haunted me ever since.

I will personally make sure that everyone you love will pay the price. You will lose loved ones, as I have lost mine, and you won't be able to do a thing about it.

I rush through the entrance doors, and look about me wildly for the reception, approaching the desk out of breath and sheened with sweat.

'I need to find someone,' I blurt out.

The receptionist holds her finger up at me, signalling me to wait, a phone cradled between her ear and her shoulder. I

reach over the desk and press the button at the base to discon-
nect the call.

'Hey! You can't just—'

'This is *urgent*. I need to find Hannah and Margaret Harper.
They were in an accident.'

The receptionist stares at me, anger darkening her eyes,
before slowly admitting defeat. It must be clear by my demeanour that I won't give up until I get the answer I need. She types
the names into her computer.

'Miss Hannah Harper is in the children's ward,' she says,
and then her expression softens. 'Mrs Margaret Harper is
currently in surgery.'

In surgery. Oh God, oh God.

'Thank you.'

I rush off down the corridor, eyeing the signs for the children's ward. The receptionist hadn't said Hannah was in the
children's ICU. That must mean she's okay, mustn't it? At least
relatively. I rush towards the ward, my heart racing so fast that
I feel dizzy. I try to enter the ward, but the doors are secured
shut, so I bang wildly on the pane of glass until a disgruntled
nurse appears in view and heads towards me. She presses a
button on the wall.

'I need to see Hannah Harper.'

'Visiting hours—'

'I am going to see Hannah right now,' I interject. 'You can
either take me to her, or call security to try and stop me. But
regardless of what happens, I'm not leaving until I've seen her.'

She seems to weigh up her options, clearly taking my conviction into consideration, and how much hell I might kick up
if she tries to turn me away.

'She's just been in a car accident and she's all alone,' I plead.

The nurse's expression softens.

'This way.'

I follow behind her anxiously, wishing she would walk faster. Every step she takes is too slow, too small. We pass sickly children and exhausted guardians, who are nothing but a blur to me. My mind only focuses when Hannah comes into view, lying in a bed by the window, tears shimmering on her bruised face.

I rush to her bedside, looking her over for plaster casts, bandages, stitches. Her face is swollen and bruised, and she has two black eyes. The more I look at her, the more damage I see. Her nose is cut and swollen; her lips indented with scabs where her teeth must have sunk into the flesh upon impact. Her face crumples with approaching tears.

I sit down on the seat the nurse brings to the bedside, and take her hand. It's cold and shaking. 'What happened?'

She cries for a while, too tearful to get out the words. As her face contorts with her tears, the graze on her cheekbone begins to ooze.

'We were driving to Auntie May's. Nanny said we needed to take a break from the city ...'

She stops to try and catch her breath.

'Take your time, sweetheart.' I stroke the back of her hand, feel the rush of her pulse beating beneath the skin.

'We didn't get far from home before it happened. We were heading down the hill from King's Street. Towards the lights.'

I picture it. A steep hill, the kind that makes your stomach turn as you cross the hump before the drop. The lights are positioned at the bottom before the crossroads. I close my eyes with dread, knowing what will come next.

'The brakes weren't working. Nanny kept pushing but ...'

She heaves for breath between sobs. 'But we kept going faster. And faster. The lights were red, and ...'

The speed would have been increasing rapidly with the gradient of the hill. Forty miles an hour. Fifty. I imagine the car careening through the traffic at the crossing. The pile-up that followed. Smashed glass and crushed metal. Blood. Screams.

'I looked over to Nanny, but ... she wasn't there anymore.'

... everyone you love will pay the price. You will lose loved ones, as I have lost mine, and you won't be able to do a thing about it.

This is all my fault.

I wipe away my tears. 'I'm so sorry this happened to you.'

'Is Nanny all right?' she asks, her eyes wide with hope. 'I keep asking, but—'

Maggie will be on the operating table right now. There will be a tube down her throat. A scalpel cutting into her.

'I'm not sure. But I will find out, okay?'

We sit in silence for a while, unsure what to do, what to say. As I hold on to her hand, feeling her pulse calm, I am struck with the overwhelming need to hold her and never let go. Most of the pain Hannah has experienced in her short life has been because of me.

'I'm sorry about what happened between us,' I utter quietly. 'I wasn't angry with you, I was overwhelmed with work, and trying to juggle everything. Your father's belongings ... they bring emotions up, and I have to try and keep them down.'

'I know,' she says, with a sniffle. 'I take things too personally. It's so easy to feel like I'm not wanted. I don't have Mum, or Dad, the two people who should be there. I know I can be a bit much sometimes.'

She's too young to be saying these things, feeling these things. I reach out and kiss her hand.

'*I* need you – I really hope you know that. And so does Nanny. You are so deeply loved by us. What happened between us, it was just a bad moment. It doesn't mean we don't love or need each other.'

A smile tugs at the corner of her lips.

'A bad moment. Yeah.'

I reach up and stroke her hair. She closes her eyes, and lets me lightly dab at her tears.

'I'm not going anywhere.'

The sound of my phone ringing makes us both jolt. The nurse approaches the bed before I've even got it out of my pocket.

'No phones—'

'Yeah, okay. One second.'

I wait until she leaves before looking down at the screen. It's Antony.

'I have to answer this really quickly,' I say, and give her hand a gentle squeeze. 'But I'll be right back.'

As I make my way out of the ward, I know what Antony is going to say before I even take the call. I feel sick with dread as I press the green button to answer.

'Antony?'

'Neve.' He sounds excited, anxious. My heart begins to race. 'We need you back here.'

I hold my breath as my heart races.

No. It's too soon. It's not even been two hours.

Antony breaks my train of thought.

'It's time.'

52

I rush from the tube station to the Bailey, adrenaline coursing through me, my heart in my mouth. It had started to rain while I was underground; the pavement is dark and slippery, and I have to squint to protect my eyes, as my hair grows heavy and drips down the nape of my neck.

I shouldn't be doing this. I should be with Hannah, holding her hand, waiting for news of Maggie's surgery. My heart tugs at the thought of Hannah in bed alone, while my head begins to wonder what lies ahead of me.

The jury must have a question about the case. They can't have reached a verdict so soon.

Don't think of it. Just get there.

But it's all I can think about. Maggie in hospital, Hannah in tears. All because of this trial. Now it is about to come to a close. So many fates hanging in the balance.

I turn from the road towards the Bailey, slipping momentarily on the wet surface as I move too fast, and stop at the corner.

The crowd outside is the biggest I've seen for one of my trials. The road has been cordoned off, and protesters outnumber the police officers at least ten-to-one. A maze of bobbing signs and contorted, angry faces. The red paint on some of the signs has run from the rain, flowing like blood. The press is stationed before them: camera crews, photographers, camped out under anoraks and umbrellas that amplify the rainfall as it ricochets against them.

An officer sees me stationed at the corner and ushers me over. I follow his lead, allow him to escort me to the door. It only takes a second for someone to clock me. The shouts start, the chants begin, questions bellowed from the press as their cameras flash, and flash, and flash.

⚖

The courtroom thrums with expectation. Nervous mutterings from the public gallery, fidgeting from the press bench. In the dock, Wade stares out, pale with fear. His fate will be determined with the simple uttering of one word or two. But he's not alone. My fate hangs on the same, dwindling thread. I anticipate the deafening snapping sound in my ears. Wait for the inevitable fall.

The jurors file in with their heads down. None of them glance towards the defendant, nor Niall and me at the advocates' bench. In these few, passing seconds, it's sometimes possible to gauge a jury's verdict: a kind glance towards the defendant, a knowing smile to the winning barrister. But none of them look up or make eye contact. We will find out with the rest of the room.

The usher speaks to the judge's clerk with bowed heads and hushed tones. I watch them, trying to read their lips. Niall and I share a look from each end of the bench, our only act of solidarity, before returning our gaze to the usher. Then the clerk nods to the usher's words. The clerk signals to us in turn.

We have a verdict.

It's almost over. The hell of the trial, the sleepless nights, the panic, the violence. All of the lies. But I can't settle, and I daren't allow myself to feel relief. Once this is over, a new challenge awaits Hannah and me. One that I cannot see myself getting through unscathed.

I don't care what happens to me, as long as she is safe.

The judge enters the room, and we all rise, taking to our seats again once he is in place. McConnell addresses the court, but I can't hear a word. I can only hear the sound of my heart pounding in my ears. I take a deep breath to compose myself as the jury is read the indictment, and the jury foreman stands.

'Has the jury reached its verdict?' the clerk asks.

The foreman is a man in his late fifties, too tanned with sun spots on his balding head and deep-set wrinkles around his eyes. He parts his lips to speak, revealing crooked smoker's teeth.

'Yes.'

A palpitation knocks against my ribs. I grit my teeth together until I'm sure I'll hear a crack from inside my mouth. I have tried to do the wrong thing, then the right thing. But neither will serve me. Not completely. I finally realise that now. Whatever the verdict, I was never going to win.

The room is perfectly still, with not a single sound nor movement. Those on the press bench are sat forward in their seats, practically dragging the words from the foreman's mouth. Family members hold hands in the public gallery for support. Outside the Bailey, the crowd waits. Poised to cheer in celebration or chant with rage.

'And do you, the jury, find the defendant guilty or not guilty of count one on the indictment?'

The room is absolutely silent. The air itches with impatience, with dread. But beneath it all, fear thrums. Lives are about to change irrevocably. We all hold one, collective breath.

'Not guilty.'

My jaw drops as the two words hit the room all at once.

Did he really just say—

A scream from the gallery rips through the room, making everyone jump. My heart leaps in my chest. It's Wade's mother, sobbing with relief. Behind her, Mrs Viklund is crying, but for the very opposite reason: Wade Darling has been found not guilty of murdering her daughter.

The clerk goes through the indictment, asking the foreman for the jury's verdict on each count. Each time, the answer is the same.

Not guilty.

Not guilty.

Not guilty.

A mess of conflicting emotions thrash within me, as the room continues to explode with noise and the judge has to shout to be heard. Tears of both relief and fear bite at my eyes, as my breaths grow shallower each time I inhale.

I just gave my client the fair trial he deserves, and helped him walk away a free man. Even if it meant risking everything I myself hold dear.

I blink back the tears and turn to Wade in the dock, who looks fit to faint. His eyes and mouth hang wide, water pooling in his eyes. He looks to me, as if he can't quite believe his ears.

I turn my attention to the public gallery.

Mr Viklund and the Messenger are forcing their way out. I can see by the flushed, red skin on Mr Viklund's neck that anger has consumed him.

Wade Darling may be free, but my verdict has yet to be cast.

All I can do now is wait.

53

Wade, Antony and I make our way into the nearest conference room. Even from here, the heckles can be heard from outside the court. The news of Wade's acquittal has reached the baying crowd. I imagine them pacing, their picket signs bobbing above their heads, spit flying from their mouths as they chant.

Usually, a client would rush into the arms of their loved ones after a not-guilty verdict has been called, but Wade had exited the dock in a trance, visibly overwhelmed with shock. When he met my eyes, I found them pleading.

Get me out of here. I can't face them. Not yet.

I understand the feeling. I cannot bear the thought of what comes next: head in the guillotine, waiting for the blade to drop. I shuffle into the conference room behind the men, silently grateful for the respite. Antony, however, sits with a confused expression on his face. He had expected to cheer and celebrate. Instead, we settle at the table in silence, while Wade sits with his eyes closed, trying to breathe through the panic visibly throttling him from the inside. Then his tears start to fall. This isn't the behaviour of a free man.

'Why don't you give us a moment, Antony?' I ask.

He looks to me, the confusion deepening on his face, before nodding and exiting the room. As soon as the door clicks shut

behind him, Wade opens his eyes. I wince as I stare into them.
I have never seen so much pain. Without even a word, I know. I
realise where the pain manifests. I recognise it in myself. It's not
the realisation that his family are still gone despite the ordeal
being over, or the fear of the media circus awaiting him at the
bottom of the court steps.

It's guilt.

My heart sinks.

Wade Darling killed his family.

He sees the click in my mind, the awareness seeping into my
face. His expression crumples.

'I'm sorry,' he whispers. Tears flow silently down his cheeks.

'Why?' I ask, as if there is a simple answer to the question.
'Why did you do it?'

He covers his face and cries a while, as I sit imagining the
scene. Wade, holding the gun. Wade, carrying the canister.
I imagine his children asleep in their beds, as the man who
brought them into this world stands above them, cocking his
gun to take them away again. Yolanda would have known it
was him. Seen him raise the rifle in her direction. Felt the burn
of the gunshots to her leg, her back. The last, merciful gunshot
wound to her head to end the pain.

Wade lowers his hands. He looks like a broken man, drowning in self-pity.

'I don't know,' he replies finally.

'Yes, you do,' I reply curtly. 'This is your only chance to
unburden yourself. As soon as I'm out of those doors, you're
going to have to live with this for the rest of your life. I suggest
you seize the opportunity.'

He notices my difference in tone. How much colder
it sounds.

'My world had crumbled,' he says. 'I couldn't ... I just couldn't take it anymore.'

He looks down at his lap.

'I wrote notes to each of them. Saying goodbye, that I was sorry. I was going to go into the woods and shoot myself. But I couldn't stop thinking about how selfish it was of me to leave them in the mess I had made.'

'So you decided to kill them?'

'I don't know who that man was that night, the man who did those things ... I wasn't in my right mind. It was like someone else took over. I looked down at the gun in my hands, and I ... just started shooting.' Tears fall again; his bottom lip quivers like a boy's. 'I didn't see red ... I didn't see anything. I was numb. I was blind. I was ... a monster.'

He sobs into his hands again, and I can't help but feel repulsed at how weak he is. How selfish. But I have no right to judge him, not after what I've done. There are two monsters sat at this table. And yet, I cannot stop hating him. Perhaps I hate the killer part of him with such ferocity because I loathe the killer within me.

'Why not confess?' I ask. 'Why hide it?'

I ask from my own guilt of doing the same. Of trying to move on after my horrendous deed. For claiming my victim's family as my own. For not wanting to be alone.

'I couldn't ... I couldn't do that to my mother.'

But deep down, I know he's lying. He did it for the same reason I did. Survival. Self-preservation.

'Come on,' I say, sitting up in my seat. 'The crowd won't go away, however long we hide. It's time to face them. It's time to face what you've done.'

He looks up at me like a scorned child. He knows that once

we part ways, we will never see each other again, and that he has lost the ally he once had in me. That after this is over, he is on his own.

He wipes his face and takes a deep breath as I lead him towards the door.

It is time for us both to face the repercussions of our crimes.

⚖

The crowd erupts as we approach the steps outside the Bailey. Cameras flash. Journalists immediately begin shouting questions, their microphones thrust towards us with a series of logos printed on them. *BBC. ITV. Channel 4. Sky News.* Behind the journalists, the protestors push against police, who have formed a line between them and us, their red faces screaming in our direction. The police have a canine unit with them today, too. German Shepherds whining with excitement on their leashes.

I lead the way down the steps towards the waiting journalists and clasp my shaking hands before me. Wade stands in the centre, with Antony and I flanking either side of him. I clear my throat, and the crowd hushes, the microphones edging closer.

'We are delighted with today's verdict,' I say. 'This was an incomplete, imperfect case against an innocent man, held together by circumstantial evidence and fantastical theories that could not withstand interrogation.'

The protestors bellow at the words; the angered faces I can see are practically foaming at the mouth. I continue to speak, but I can barely be heard over their taunts.

'Today, Mr Darling gets to—'

'*MURDERER!*'

'—return to his life, and the police must now look into who truly—'

'GUILTY! GUILTY! GUILTY!'

'—killed the Darlings. In the meantime, we hope this result will allow Mr Darling time to grieve, and for the public to—'

It all happens in a brief, dizzying second. The protestors break free from their cordon like water from a dam. The police shout with their batons raised, pushing back but failing to make ground, as the dogs are freed of their restraints and run towards the protestors. I hear a bark, a scream.

The police are too preoccupied with the protestors to see him. The man rushing forward, rage painted on his face. Mr Viklund looks at me, hatred boiling within him. He has something in his hand. Black, metal. I only compute it's a gun when he aims it towards us. The Messenger is chasing after him, but Mr Viklund is too fast. I barely have time to draw breath before the gun fires.

The sound explodes in my ears, as something hot splatters against my face. Blood. Wade Darling's blood. I look to him, blinking furiously as it drips down into my vision. The bullet hit him straight in the eye and tore through the other side of his head. He twitches, bubbles of blood forming on his lips, before falling to his knees, flailing slightly, and landing on his back on the steps with a deafening crack.

Another shot. Another. I instinctively drop to the floor. There is more blood down here. It is pooling out of Wade's eye socket and the back of his head, painting the steps red and seeping beneath me and into my clothes. Something is cutting into my palm. I raise my hand and inspect my wet, glistening skin. My brain tries to tell me it is a rock, or stone, rather than a piece of my client's skull. I look to him and see his other eye is staring lifelessly into mine, the pain I had seen in the conference room blown away.

Antony crouches on the other side of him, eyes wide with terror. The crowd is screaming. The police scrum in a high-vis knot around Viklund where one of the dogs is attacking his ankle, ripping the flesh to ribbons as he screams. Among the rushing crowd I see the Messenger, choking on his own blood on the ground where a stray bullet must have clipped the side of his neck. I just catch sight of his hand falling limp from where he'd held the wound, when I feel hands upon me. It's Antony, pulling me up and dragging me inside. We stumble to our feet and run, dripping with our client's blood, leaving a warm, red trail along the foyer's tiled floor.

54

Four months later

'Do you think he did it?'

Hannah's voice tears me from my thoughts. She is sat on the other side of the garden table, her hair lit bronze from the beaming sun. The weather seems miraculous after the torrential rain last night that threatened to wash half the city away. It had been the worst storm the south of the country had had in four years, blowing down trees and flooding residential streets further out of the city. Now we're sat in the sun, as if it never occurred at all.

In the distance, I can hear Maggie preparing tea, the high-pitched ding of the teaspoon whirling around china mugs. Hannah flicks a stray piece of lettuce onto the lawn that had fallen from her lunch plate before the table was cleared.

'Wade Darling,' she says. 'Do you think he did it? Killed his family?'

She has asked me this question a lot since the shooting; I think she is trying to work out if he deserved to die. She had seen the video footage plastered all over the internet, along with the rest of the country. Saw Wade's blood hit my face before he fell lifelessly to the ground. I wonder if her knowing me makes it all the more real somehow; these weren't just characters in a trial – she watched her stepmother narrowly miss a bullet to her head.

'The jury determined he wasn't,' I reply.

'But what do *you* think?'

When I lie in bed at night, I often think about the fact that I am the only living person who knows of Wade Darling's guilt. Bound by client confidentiality, his confession added another skeleton to my closet.

'I don't think,' I reply. 'It's not my job to decide who's guilty and who's not. My only task is to defend their case and ensure they get a fair trial.'

'But what if he didn't *deserve* a fair trial?'

'That's not how it works, Han. People convicted of crimes are innocent until proven guilty. Imagine you or Nanny were charged with a terrible crime, and the one person who has been hired to defend you thought you didn't deserve to have your case heard? Wade was deemed innocent in the eyes of the law.'

Hannah rolls her eyes. 'But you must have a *theory* about his potential guilt, at least—'

'Hannah, that's enough,' Maggie snaps as she steps through the back door with a tea tray. 'You'd give a parrakeet a headache with all that chatter.'

Maggie hobbles towards the table, her weight shifted to her good leg. She broke her hip in the car accident, and has yet to fully bounce back. She is still as grouchy as ever, but with a difference: it seems she has finally let me in. It only took a decade.

I had moved in with them for almost a month to help Maggie around the house after the crash. It was harder for her to dislike me when I was the one who cooked her meals, helped her to the loo in the middle of the night. By the end, she was almost fond of me, and her biting digs had turned into playful jabs. Hannah, of course, had loved me being there, and Maggie had reluctantly agreed that she could stay with me every other weekend. At least something good came out of all this.

It was good to have time away from home too. When I returned, the rail works had been completed. The trees were a distant memory, the trains were running again, and Matthew was gone. At least his body was. His spirit, his essence, it seems to have worked its way into the walls, whispering at me whenever it's quiet. Nor will I ever escape the church bells. Even when I have finally found the courage to pack up the house and move on, I know the sound of them will follow me, calling to me in my dreams.

Maggie places a mug of tea before me. I'd been about to make my move, but turning down small acts of kindness like this from Maggie seems impossible. I'm forever waiting for her to retract her openness, to shut me out again. Not that I wouldn't deserve it, after everything I've done.

'You've got to work today, you said?' Maggie asks.

'On a Sunday?' Hannah interjects.

'Just a meeting,' I reply, refusing to let my dread show. 'Nothing exciting.'

'I'm surprised you continued with the job after all that business to be honest with you,' Maggie says, waving her hand in the air, as if the shooting were nothing more than an inconvenience.

I had thought of quitting after the trial. Not because of Wade's death, although perhaps that would have been wise, but because of the damage I had caused trying to save my own neck. For a brief while, I had decided to take justice into my own hands, sway a trial at the expense of my client for my own benefit. There should be no grey area when it comes to justice – only black and white. Guilty and not guilty. For a time, the lines had blurred, and boundaries were crossed. I'd taken a break after the trial to look after Maggie, and when I finally returned to chambers, under a new head of chambers after Artie made his departure, I sat at my desk and opened my emails. I would look at a case brief, and know if I was up to the task. That was my plan. It had taken me less than a minute to be sucked in again.

Being a defence barrister is all I know.

'It's complicated,' I reply with a smile. 'Besides, what else would I do?'

'You could teach,' Hannah says.

'She hasn't the patience for that,' Maggie quips. 'She'd need a job where you're paid to argue, be stubborn.'

I smirk, knowing this is as close to a compliment as I'll get from Maggie.

'A traffic warden then,' Hannah says, and bursts into laughter.

'No, no. I couldn't bear to wear that uniform. I'll stick to my wig and robes, thanks.'

I glance down at my watch and sigh. I can't put it off much longer.

'I'd best get going.'

Hannah accompanies me to the door, with Maggie trailing close behind. I give Hannah a squeeze, inhaling her sweet scent. Maggie and I haven't got used to hugging yet, but to my surprise, she gives me a brief embrace with a sharp pat on the back before pulling away.

I've finally earned her love.

If only I deserved it.

'Don't work too hard.'

'I'll try, thanks.'

'Who are you meeting anyway?' Hannah asks. 'Is it a new client? Anyone exciting?'

'No, no one exciting,' I reply, as my heart begins to race at the thought of him.

I had secretly hoped that I would never have to lay eyes on Mr Viklund again.

⚖

I wasn't sure what emotions or reactions Viklund might claw out of me when I saw him again. The last time we looked into one another's eyes, he'd had me at gunpoint. Would seeing him bring it all up again? I stand in the queue for the visiting area of the prison, my mouth sapped dry with nerves.

Mr Viklund was deemed too dangerous to be released upon being charged and was refused bail. He is to wait in prison until his trial. The barrister in charge of his case had pushed for a manslaughter charge rather than murder, citing loss of control, but the plea bargain was denied. Viklund is to plead not guilty to murder, and have the manslaughter charges added to the indictment. It is up to the jury to decide which charge fits his crime. I don't pity his barrister, and wonder if it's someone with a secret like mine. I didn't notice the barrister's name in the list Tinsley gave me, which I had checked over repeatedly after learning of the appointment in *The Times*.

The visitors are filed in one by one, directed to tables by a sour-faced guard.

I had almost ignored the visitor request. I could have ripped it up, burnt it. But I knew that if I didn't see him now, he would send someone to make me reconsider. Despite the invitation giving off the appearance of a choice, I know I have none, that I never truly did, from the moment I met the Messenger.

I reach the front of the line and am instructed to head to table seven by the gruff guard.

Despite being in prison, Mr Viklund hasn't changed one bit. He doesn't look to have lost a wink of sleep over the ordeal. But then, with all the power he has, I am sure he has many friends here. In fact, he probably rules the place, telling the inmates when to jump and how high. At least, that's what he must think.

My angst heightens as I approach the table, my heart racing as his cold blue eyes take me in. I drag the seat out from under it, the metal legs scraping against the lino floor, and sit before him.

'You came,' he says.

'I assumed you would have sent someone to convince me if I hadn't.'

His smile seems to agree with me.

'How's freedom?' he asks, a touch of resentment in his tone.

'Fine. How's prison?'

He smirks at my slight, but I know his smile isn't one of amusement; he would reach over the table and knock me down if he could get away with it.

'Just fine, thanks.' He stares at me, his glare piercing and unrelenting. 'Although I don't plan on staying long.'

'You're being represented by Nathan Lane, I hear.'

'Know him?' he asks.

'Afraid not. But I hear he's good.'

'Shame. I don't want good – I want the best.'

'If you want legal advice, it's best to ask your lawyer.'

'It's not advice I'm after.' The smile returns. 'Tell me, when no one came for you after the shooting, did you think you'd got away with it?'

My cheeks flush, but I keep my composure, swallowing down my nerves.

'You didn't strike me as the sort of man to let go of a grudge too easily,' I muster.

'That's wise,' he replies. 'I haven't forgotten what you did, in the trial. How you changed sides. Got him off. Hell, I wouldn't be here if you hadn't, would I?'

'I didn't pull the trigger, Mr Viklund. You did that on your own.'

On the outside, I appear confident, together. But beneath the table, I dig my nails into my legs until I'm sure I've drawn blood. I try to tell myself he's just a man, no more special than anyone else in the room. But that is difficult to believe, after he spent so long with my life held in his palm. All while I waited anxiously for him to clench it shut and grind my entire world to dust.

'Ah,' he says. 'High and mighty, eh? And there was me thinking I was among friends, in that regard.' He leans closer. 'I heard you got a look at that list of mine. Did you think I'd let someone wander around free with information like that rolling around in their skulls?'

I stare into his eyes, and he mine. We sit in the uncomfortable silence, with only the quietened chatter of the other tables around us.

'What do you want from this meeting, Mr Viklund? If it's to taunt me, you've accomplished your goal. If there's nothing more—'

I go to stand, and his smile vanishes.

'You know there's more. Sit down.'

I return slowly to my seat.

'My trial is coming up,' he says. 'I need the jury to decide I'm guilty of the lesser charge to reduce my sentence.'

'I'm sure Mr Lane will do a fine job.'

He looks at me with a vindictive glint in his eyes.

'Mr Lane won't be representing me during the trial, Ms Harper. You will. That's the thing about the list ... Once you're on it, you never get off.'

I'd been anticipating this was the reason for the visit request. In fact, I'd been banking on it. A smile crawls across my face. I see his confidence quiver like a flame behind his eyes.

'Yes, the list,' I reply, as he stares at me, seemingly perplexed by my smile. 'I knew you wouldn't give up, Mr Viklund. It's not in your nature. But it's not in mine, either. Unfortunately, I think you've forgotten that it's my job to anticipate my opponent's next move. Counteract every possible attack. To do that, I need to find their point of power and use it against them. Yours, as we know, is the list. That's why I decided to form a list of my own.'

I pause like I would in the courtroom, letting the tension mount. His brow knits together with confusion.

'I didn't use blackmail, obviously. Not like you. There wasn't any need for that. Everyone on my list has something in common: they were all wronged by you.'

He huffs a laugh, albeit nervously.

'You got a death wish, have you, girl? I could have you shot before you've even reached your car.'

'I've worked in courtrooms for almost fifteen years, Mr Viklund. I know a bluff when I see one. Wasn't it you who shot your right-hand man in the neck? As for the rest of them, word on the street is your business has gone deep underground without you at the helm. Laying low until the fanfare around you settles. If you wanted to hurt me – if you had the *power* to hurt me – you would have done it by now. But they've thrown you to the wolves, haven't they?'

'I didn't have you killed because I have a use for you, remember? No point killing an asset.'

'I'm afraid I won't be defending you in your trial, Mr Viklund. Because there isn't going to be one.'

His face pales. As I lay in bed at night imagining this moment, I had expected him to flush with anger, to mutter threats under his breath. But he's not angry. He's scared.

'My list is comprised from yours. Remember when you threatened me, on the Millennium Bridge? About your friends in prison, waiting for their right moment to strike, as soon as you gave the word? Well, I have friends you've wronged in these settings too. In this very room, in fact. They want you off their backs just as much as I want you off mine.'

He peers around, scanning the other prisoners sat before their visitors.

'Bullshit,' he spits.

'I guess we'll have to wait and see, won't we?'

I watch as his expression changes, until he almost looks like a scared little boy. I lean in and keep my voice low so only he can hear.

'I'd sleep with one eye open from now on, Mr Viklund.'

I rise from my seat, only this time he doesn't try to stop me. He has shrunk in his chair, his shoulders concaved, making him look smaller, frailer. A man who is only powerful when he has a group of violent men behind him. A group of men who turned on him on a dime.

I head for the exit without looking back, a small, triumphant smile pulling at the corners of my mouth.

⚖

The smile continues to tug at me until I am back in the car park, and slip a cigarette between my lips. I've cut down, close to quitting, in fact. And now I've dealt with the hold Mr Viklund once had on me, the weight that has been resting on my shoulders inevitably feels lighter; now, the need for my vice feels almost trivial.

I head to the car and sit behind the wheel, turning the key in the ignition to lower down the window, and blow clouds of smoke towards the stark blue sky as the radio hums quietly in the background.

I should feel free at this moment. Vindicated, even. I have finally dealt with the man who threatened to hurt me and those I love the most. But perhaps that's because vindication is for the innocent, and when an injustice has been righted. I can't possibly feel that. Not after I have gotten away with murder.

Matthew. Fredrick. Melanie. They are all dead because of me. I could still turn myself in – do the right thing – but still, I push the deed back, and back, and back, too terrified to lose Hannah and Maggie; to lose my career, and step into the dock myself, staring out at the courtroom from the other side of the glass. I would never be allowed to try a case again. I would never smell Hannah's sweet, youthful scent. If I told the truth of what I have done, what or who would I have left? My conscience would be clear, and yes, a wrong would be righted. But then what? A good person can make mistakes, make bad decisions – I didn't mean to kill Matthew; I adored him with every bone in my body – but can a good person continue making that same bad decision? Or does that make them bad?

I take one last drag on the cigarette and flick the end under the neighbouring car.

Maybe I am a bad person after all.

I turn the key in the ignition and the engine grumbles to life. The radio comes on again and I turn it up as a song comes to an end, and the news segment begins. I am just pulling out of the space when I hear the broadcaster reading a news bulletin. The engine stalls and I brake sharply.

> The body of a man was discovered in Low Valley Wood earlier today, said to have been unearthed by a flash flood in the area after the storm that wreaked havoc across the South East for much of the night.

As the broadcaster continues with the news headlines, I sit in stunned silence, white-knuckling the wheel and only managing to muster one, desperate thought.

They found him.

Acknowledgements

It's true what they say: writing a book really does take a village, and I have many people to thank for bringing this book to life.

Firstly, my agent, Madeleine Milburn, for being the best champion an author could ask for, as well as the amazing team at the Madeleine Milburn Literary, TV & Film agency: Rachel Yeoh, Liv Maidment, Esmé Carter, Valentina Paulmichl, Georgina Simmonds, Liane-Louise Smith, Hannah Ladds, and many more. Thank you for all you do for your authors.

At my publisher, Simon & Schuster, my first thanks must go to editor Bethan Jones, who signed me back in 2020 and launched *Do No Harm* with unrivalled passion and vision, and worked on *Conviction* with me before flying the nest. Thank you for your invaluable feedback, which made this book the best it could possibly be. It was a dream come true working with you, and although I was and am so sad to have lost you as an editor, I am equally happy to be able to call you a friend.

My next thanks go to Katherine Armstrong, who has taken over the role of editor seamlessly. Your long list of editor-author friendships gained during your time in publishing is a testament to your talent and character, and I am so excited to work with you and join this list.

The Dream Team thanked at the front of this book not

only includes my agent and editors above, but also the truly phenomenal marketing and publicity teams I'm so lucky to work with.

First, I want to thank Richard Vlietstra and Sarah Jeffcoate. I am beyond lucky and spoilt to have both of your brilliant minds as part of Team Jordan. Your enthusiasm, passion and dedication are utterly infectious. To my publicist, Harriett Collins: thank you for being truly amazing at what you do. You make the intense role of publicist look utterly effortless.

I also owe additional thanks to the following people at Simon & Schuster: Craig Fraser, Clare Hey, Suzanne Baboneau, Ian Chapman, and everyone who played a part in launching *Do No Harm* and *Conviction*. I also wish to thank my copy-editor, Sally Partington, and Georgina Leighton at Simon & Schuster, for catching the pesky errors that slipped by me and helping to make the prose that bit tighter.

As always, I wish to thank Waterstones Colchester for their phenomenal support and commitment to making sure my books reach their readers, and to whom I owe much of my success due to their professional and personal support. To the team past and present: Jon 'The Bitch with the Pitch' Clark, Helen Wood, Violet Daniels, Liv Quinn, Joe Oliver Eason, Karl and Chloe Hollinshead, and Mark Vickery. And also to Karl Nurse of Waterstones Chelmsford, who we sadly lost in 2022. He was the kindest man, who dedicated 25 years to Waterstones. Rest in peace, my friend. I also owe special thanks to Gaby Lee and Bea Carvalho for their amazing support and kindness, and to booksellers around the country supporting my books – you are amazing.

To my main support system, my family and friends: thank you for your continued support through the good times and the bad and for never letting me give up. I wouldn't be the writer I am today without the following: Sandra and Carl Jarrad, Pamela and Tony Jordan, Martin Chester, Abbi Houghton and Anna Burtt.

To authors, bloggers, bookstagrammers and early readers for your support, quotes and reviews of this book (with special shoutouts to Stu Cummins and Lex Brookman) – I cannot tell you how much your support means to authors like me.

I would also like to thank Christine Vinson for bidding on having their name featured in this book, as part of the auction in support of Ukraine, founded by Sally over at @whatsallyreadnext on Instagram. Thank you both for creating and supporting such an amazing cause.

Lastly, I would like to thank *you*, the reader: thank you for picking up this book, and for making my dreams come true – I hope you loved it, and that you enjoy my other books, as well as the books yet to come.

DO NO HARM

'Chilling and perfectly paced' **Sarah Pearse**

**My child has been taken
And I've been given a choice . . .
Kill a patient on the operating table
Or lose my son forever.**

The man lies on the table in front of me.
As a surgeon, it's my job to save him.
As a mother, I know I must kill him.
You might think that I'm a monster.
But there really is only one choice.
I must get away with murder.
Or I will never see my son again.
I've saved many lives.
Would you trust me with yours?

'A belter of a thriller with proper breathtaking,
pulse-racing levels of tension' **Louise Candlish**

'Had me on the edge of my seat' **Nadine Matheson**

'An absolute rollercoaster, you won't be
able to put it down' **Holly Seddon**

'Brilliant. Relentlessly tense' **Lesley Kara**

AVAILABLE NOW IN PAPERBACK, EBOOK AND EAUDIO

SIMON &
SCHUSTER

CATHY KELLY

Past Secrets

HARPER

Harper
An imprint of HarperCollins*Publishers*
77–85 Fulham Palace Road,
Hammersmith, London W6 8JB

www.harpercollins.co.uk

This paperback edition 2008
9

Copyright © Cathy Kelly 2006

Cathy Kelly asserts the moral right to
be identified as the author of this work

A catalogue record for this book
is available from the British Library

ISBN 978 0 00 7268658

This novel is entirely a work of fiction.
The names, characters and incidents portrayed in it are
the work of the author's imagination. Any resemblance to
actual persons, living or dead, events or localities is
entirely coincidental.

Set in Sabon by Palimpsest Book Production Limited,
Grangemouth, Stirlingshire

Printed and bound in Great Britain by
Clays Ltd, St Ives plc

All rights reserved. No part of this publication may be
reproduced, stored in a retrieval system, or transmitted,
in any form or by any means, electronic, mechanical,
photocopying, recording or otherwise, without the prior
written permission of the publishers.

This book is sold subject to the condition that it shall not,
by way of trade or otherwise, be lent, re-sold, hired out or
otherwise circulated without the publisher's prior written consent
in any form of binding or cover other than that in which it
is published and without a similar condition including this
condition being imposed on the subsequent purchaser.

Mixed Sources
Product group from well-managed
forests and other controlled sources
www.fsc.org Cert no. SW-COC-1806
© 1996 Forest Stewardship Council
FSC

FSC is a non-profit international organisation established to promote the responsible
management of the world's forests. Products carrying the FSC
label are independently certified to assure consumers that they come
from forests that are managed to meet the social, economic and
ecological needs of present and future generations.

Find out more about HarperCollins and the environment at
www.harpercollins.co.uk/green

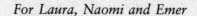

For Laura, Naomi and Emer

CHAPTER ONE

If a road could look welcoming, then Summer Street had both arms out and the kettle boiling.

Christie Devlin had lived halfway up the street for exactly thirty years in a small but exquisite red-bricked house that gleamed like a jewel in a necklace of pretty coloured stones.

Summer Street itself was curved and ran for half a mile from the crossroads where the café sat opposite a house which had once been a strawberry-ice-cream shade and was now a faded dusky pink.

From the moment Christie had seen the graceful curve of the street, where maple trees arched like kindly aunties over the pavement, she'd known: this was the place she and James could raise their family.

Those thirty years had gone in a flash, Christie thought on this beautiful late-April morning as she went about her chores, tidying, dusting, sweeping and wiping.

Today the sun streamed in through the windows, the house seemed filled with quiet contentment and Christie didn't have to go to work. She loved her job as an art teacher at St Ursula's secondary school, but she'd cut back her hours recently and was relishing the extra free time.

Her dogs, Tilly and Rocket, miniature dachshunds who had clearly been imperial majesties in a previous life, were sleeping off their morning walk on the cool of the kitchen tiles. The radio was playing quietly in the background and the old steel percolator was making the rattling death throes that signalled the coffee was nearly ready. All should have been right with Christie's world.

And it was – except for a niggling feeling of disquiet. It had been simmering in her subconscious since she'd awoken at six to the joyous chorus of birdsong outside her bedroom window.

'Happy Anniversary,' James had murmured sleepily when the alarm went off at a quarter past and he rolled over in the bed to cuddle her, to find Tilly squashed between them. The dogs were supposed to sleep on their corduroy bean-bags on the floor, but Tilly adored the comfortable little hollow in the duvet between her master and mistress. James lifted the outraged dog and settled her at his other side, then moved closer to Christie. 'Thirty years today since we moved in. And I still haven't finished flooring the attic.'

Christie, wide awake and grappling with the intense feeling that something, somewhere, was wrong, had to laugh. Everything was so normal. She must be imagining the gloom.

'I expect the floor to be finished this weekend,' she said in the voice that could still the most unruly class in St Ursula's. Not that she had ever had much trouble with unruly students. Christie's love of art was magical and intense, and transferred itself to most of her pupils.

'Please, no, Mrs Devlin,' begged James, in mock-schoolboy tones. 'I don't have the energy. Besides, the dog keeps eating my homework.'

Panting, Tilly clambered back defiantly and tried to make her cosy nest in between them again.

'The dog would definitely eat the homework in this house,' James added.

2

Christie took hold of Tilly's warm velvety body and cuddled her, crooning softly.

'I think you love those dogs more than you love the rest of us,' he teased.

'Of course I do,' she teased back. Christie had seen him talking adoringly to Tilly and Rocket when he didn't think anyone noticed. James was tall, manly and had a heart as soft as butter.

'Children grow up and don't want cuddles, but dogs are puppies for ever,' she added, tickling Tilly gently in her furry armpits. 'And let's face it, you don't run around my feet yelping with delight when I get home from work, do you?'

'I never knew that's what you wanted.' He made a few exploratory barking noises. 'If I do, will you whisper sweet nothings to me?' Christie looked at her husband. His hair was no longer a blond thatch. It was sandy grey and thinning, and he had as many fine lines around his face as she had, but James could still make Christie smile on the inside.

'I might,' she said.

From the bedroom floor, Rocket whimpered, wanting to be included in the fun.

James got out of bed and scooped her on to the duvet beside her mistress, whereupon Rocket began to smother Christie in kisses.

'I hope I get to come back as one of your dogs in my next life,' he remarked, heading to the bathroom for his shower.

Christie shivered. 'Don't even speak like that,' she said, but she was talking to a closed door.

Thirty years in this house. How had the time passed so quickly?

'I love it,' she'd told James that first day, as she stood, pregnant with their second child, Shane, outside number 34, a house they could only afford because it required what the estate agent hilariously described as 'a wee bit of renovating'.

'You're sure you don't prefer the mock-Tudor heap seven streets over?' asked James, holding tightly to little Ethan's hand. At the grand old age of three and a quarter, Ethan's current favourite hobbies included trampolining on his bed and wriggling out of his parents' grasp to fling himself in danger's path.

Christie had arched a dark eyebrow at her husband.

The heap's front garden had been tarmacked while the back garden contained two fierce dogs who hadn't responded when Christie instinctively reached out her hand. There was a sinister brick-sized hole in one of the upstairs windows and when James had casually asked the estate agent why there was no gun turret complete with AK47 peeking out, Christie had had to smother her laughter.

'Call me old-fashioned,' she told James, 'but I somehow prefer Summer Street and this house.'

Despite the obvious dilapidation, the very bricks of number 34 seemed to glow with warmth, and the stained-glass oriel window over the graceful arched porch was in its original condition.

From where they stood, the Devlin family could see the Summer Street Café with its aqua-and-white-striped awning and paintwork. On the pavement outside stood white bistro chairs and three small tables covered with flowered sea-blue tablecloths that looked as if they'd been transported from a Sorrento balcony.

On the same side of the street as the café there were terraced houses; then a couple of slender detached houses squeezed in; eight small railway cottages, their classic fascia boards traced with delicate carvings; then a series of redbricks including theirs; five 1930s bungalows and, finally, a handful of one-storey-over-basements. The other side of Summer Street was lined with more terraced houses and cottages, along with a tiny park: two neatly kept acres with a colonnaded

4

bandstand, an old railway pavilion and a minuscule fountain much loved by the pigeons who couldn't bear to poop
anywhere else.

The maple trees that lined the street were flanked by
colourful border plants, while even the doors to the dizzying
variety of houses were painted strong bright shades: cerulean
blues, poinsettia scarlets, honeyed ambers.

Christie would always remember how James had responded
when she'd said she loved the house. He'd put the hand that
wasn't holding on to Ethan around hers and squeezed.

'Then we've got to have it,' he'd said.

They hadn't even looked inside.

When Christie told astonished people afterwards that
they'd decided to buy 34 Summer Street without crossing the
threshold, she'd explained that you knew when you were in
the right place. Homes were about more than actual walls.

'You can't go far wrong with a well-built redbrick,' James's
brother said sagely, put out by all this talk of feelings.

And indeed, the house was beautifully proportioned even
though it was sadly down at heel, like a genteel lady who'd
fallen on hard times but still polished the doorstep every
morning even when she could barely afford milk for her tea.

But James and Christie knew it was more than decent
proportions or the welcoming width of the copper-coloured
front door that had made up their mind. Christie had simply
known it was the home for them and James had learned to
trust his wife's instincts.

When she, James and Ethan moved in a month later, they
were the proud owners of a ramshackle four-bedroom pile
with one bathroom, nothing resembling a usable kitchen and
a butterfly sanctuary for a garden.

In those days, there was no three-storey apartment block
at the bottom of the street and no unneighbourly huffing
about parking since most families were lucky to own just one

car. But it was also before the park was given the primary-coloured playground equipment where small children roared with both delight and temper, depending on how the arguments were going over whose go it was on the slide.

Christie used to take Ethan and Shane to the park to play. Now, she walked Rocket and Tilly along the neatly trimmed pathways. Her two beautiful granddaughters, Sasha and Fifi, had been wheeled into the park in their buggies, and Sasha, now two and a half, loved hurling herself at the fountain as if she was about to leap in. Just like her dad, Christie thought fondly.

Ethan had always had so much energy. He'd thrown himself into life at full tilt from his very first breath. And he'd adored Summer Street.

'We'd better get the mower out,' James had observed that first day as Ethan ran into the garden, whooping with excitement, his blond head almost disappearing in the long, wild grass. The van they had rented to move their belongings was parked on the drive and a few friends were due round to help shift all the heavy stuff. But for the moment, the small family were alone. 'It's like a jungle out there.'

'It's like a jungle in here too,' Christie had said wryly, looking up at the corner of the kitchen where a particularly murky black bit of wall stood out amid the peeling cat-sick-yellow plaster. 'Please tell me there wasn't that much mould on the walls when we viewed. We should have got the infectious diseases people to survey the house instead of an architect.'

'You think we'll be eaten in our beds by a noxious house fungus?'

Christie smiled affectionately at her husband, who'd given their son both his blond hair and sunny disposition. The pride of finally owning their own house shone in James's eyes, noxious fungus notwithstanding.

'Probably. Now, are you going to rescue Ethan, or am I to

6

shift my five-months-pregnant bulk out after him?' Tall and normally slender, she'd carried Ethan easily with a neat little basketball of a bump that was unnoticeable from behind. This time round, her slender figure was a distant memory and she felt like a giant stretch-marked pudding, equally enormous whichever angle she was viewed from.

Her sister Ana reckoned it was second baby syndrome, where all the muscles gave up the ghost. But Christie knew that her inexplicable cravings for huge bowls of deep-fried banana with ice cream hadn't helped.

'I'll go and rescue him, o Massive One,' James said, laying a hand on her swollen belly. 'I don't want you so tired out that you don't have the energy to christen the house with me tonight.' He grinned suggestively.

A laugh exploded out of Christie. The exhaustion of pregnancy meant she was asleep by nine most nights and not even a vat of aphrodisiacs could rouse her. But then she relented, seeing the look of hope on her husband's face.

'Back massage first,' she bargained. Why her back should be an erogenous zone, Christie didn't know. But feeling James's supple hands kneading away her aches always got her in the mood for love.

'Deal.'

The upside of living in such a wreck of a house was that Christie didn't have to worry about Ethan crayoning on the walls, though he was an intrepid mountaineer so she spent much of her time rescuing him from various pieces of the second-hand furniture which was all they could afford. The downside of the house was that it seemed to take for ever before the damp was banished and they could eat a meal without a bit of ceiling falling on to their plates.

Now, a lifetime later, Ethan was thirty-three, Shane was almost thirty and Christie was a grandmother twice over.

The long dark hair she'd worn in a loose ponytail all those years ago was now cut to jaw length and waved, its cool silvery white highlighting the warmth of her olive skin and dark, winged eyebrows.

She still wore a delicate flick of eyeliner, which gave her eyes a magical tilt at each olive green corner, but had swapped the block of cake eyeliner she'd grown up with for a modern miracle liner pen. She liked embracing new things, believing that living too much in the past made a person look their age.

The kitchen wasn't showing its age, either. Currently on its third incarnation, it had been decorated in brightly coloured chic, then antique pine and was now showcasing modern maple. Many woman-hours of hard work had turned the garden into a honeytrap for lazy bees, which moved from one variety of lavender to another in the height of summer.

Now, in the last days of April, the old French rose that Christie had been nurturing to sweep over the pergola had produced its first decent crop of antique white flowers with a musky, amber scent. Her garden was so sheltered that her roses bloomed at least a month before they should and she could smell their fragrance from the open window as she stood rinsing the breakfast dishes at the sink.

Scrubbing at some stubborn crumbs of toast glued to a white plate, Christie tried to rationalise the niggling anxiety in her head.

Anniversaries brought up old memories, that was all it was, surely.

Christie had been so lucky these past thirty years. Blessed, almost. There had only been that one time in her married life when it had all nearly gone wrong, and, like catching a falling glass before it hit the floor, Christie had averted the disaster. There was a tiny crack left behind from that time, but nobody except Christie could see it. That couldn't trouble her now, could it?

No, she decided firmly, as she slotted the clean plate into the drying rack. That was all in the past.

She knew she was blessed. James was as good a husband as he'd been when she married him. Better, in fact. They'd grown closer as they'd grown older, not apart, like so many others did. Christie knew plenty of people her own age who'd stayed married and had nothing to show for it except spite and old wedding photos. They bitched and bickered and made everyone around them uncomfortable. Why bother? Christie wondered.

Wouldn't it be better to be happy on your own instead of coupled off in sheer misery? She liked to think that if she and James fell out, God forbid, they could end it with dignity and move on.

'I bet you wouldn't,' her sister Ana had pointed out mischievously once, at the end of one long night on the small terrace in the garden when the wineglasses were empty and the conversation had turned to what-ifs.

'There wouldn't be a bit of dignity involved. I bet you'd stab James with your secateurs one night, bury him under the rhubarb and act delighted when it turned out to be a good crop!'

'Ah, Ana,' said James, feigning hurt. 'Christie would never do that.' He paused for effect, looking round the garden his wife adored. 'The lilac tree needs fertilising, not the rhubarb. That's where she'd bury me.'

'You're both wrong,' said Christie amiably, reaching out to clasp her brother-in-law Rick's hand. 'I'm going to bury James right here, under the flagstones, then Rick and I are going to run off into the sunset together.'

'As long as I get this house,' Ana said, getting to her feet, 'the pair of you can do what you want.'

It was a beautiful house, Christie knew. One of the loveliest on Summer Street. Christie's artistic talent had made it just as beautiful inside as outside.

'If Mum and Dad could see this place,' Ana said wistfully as the sisters hugged goodbye in the hall where Christie had black-and-white photos of the family hung alongside six watercolour paintings of irises of the kind that she used to sell to make money during the early days of paying the Summer Street house mortgage.

'Dad would hate it,' laughed Christie easily. 'Too arty farty, he'd say.'

'Ah, he wouldn't,' protested Ana, who at fifty-four was the younger by six years. 'He'd love it, for all that it's nothing like the house in Kilshandra.'

Kilshandra was where they'd grown up, a small town on the east coast that was never a destination, always a place cars drove past en route to somewhere else.

'No, it's not like Kilshandra,' Christie murmured and the fact that it was nothing like her old home was one of the best things about it.

Thinking of the past made the anxiety tweak again. She didn't want to think about the past, Christie thought with irritation. Get out of my head. She'd spoken out loud, she realised, as the dogs looked up at her in alarm.

The dishes done, she poured a cup of coffee to take into the garden while she went through her list for the day. She had groceries to buy, bills to pay, some letters to post, a whole page of the by-the-phone notepad filled with calls to return . . . and then she felt the strange yet familiar ripple of unease move through her. Like a thundercloud shimmering in a blue sky, threatening a noisy downpour. This time it wasn't a mild flicker of anxiety: it was a full-scale alert.

Christie dropped her china cup on the flagstones. Both Rocket and Tilly yelped in distress, whisking around their mistress's feet, their matching brown eyes anxious. *We didn't do it, we didn't do it.*

Automatically, Christie shepherded them away from the broken china.

'You'll cut your paws,' she said gently, and shooed them safely into the kitchen. Dustpan in hand, she went outside again and began to sweep up.

Her whole life, Christie had been able to see things that other people couldn't. It was a strange, dreamy gift: never available on demand and never there for Christie to sort out her own problems. But when she least expected it, the truth came to her, a little tremor of knowing that told her what was in another person's heart.

As a child, she'd thought everyone could do it. But there was no one in her deeply religious home whom she could ask. Something warned her that people might not like it. Her father prayed to centuries-dead saints when things went wrong, ignoring them when all was well, but he disapproved of the local girls having their fortunes told and hated the Gypsies' gift of sight with a vengeance. Her mother never ventured any opinion without first consulting her husband. Opinions that Father didn't approve of meant his black rage engulfed the house. So Christie had learned to be a quiet, watchful child. Her six elder brothers and her baby sister made enough noise for nobody to notice her, anyhow. And as she grew older and realised that her gift wasn't run of the mill, she was glad she'd kept it quiet.

How could she tell people she'd known the McGoverns' barn was going to burn down, or that Mr McGovern himself had set fire to it for the insurance money?

The first time she even hinted at her gift was when she was nineteen and her best friend, Sarah, had thought Ted, handsome with smiling eyes and a blankly chiselled face like Steve McQueen, was the man for her.

11

'He loves me, he wants to marry me,' said Sarah with the passion of being nineteen and in love.

'I just have this feeling that he's not being entirely honest with you. There's something a bit two-faced about him,' Christie had said. It was a flash of knowing that Ted didn't love Sarah and that there was someone else Ted made promises to.

'I don't believe it,' said Sarah angrily.

Christie noted the anger: there was a lot of truth in the cliché about shooting the messenger.

It transpired that Ted had indeed been seeing another girl, one whose family had money, not like Sarah or Christie, who came from a world of hand-me-down clothes and making do.

'How did you know?' asked Sarah when her heart was broken.

'It sort of came to me,' Christie said, which was the only way she could explain it.

The closer the person was to her, the fuzzier it became. For herself, she could never see anything. Which was probably as it should be. Except that today, for the first time ever, she'd had a horrible feeling that the premonition of gloom was for herself.

In the pretty kitchen with its bunches of herbs hanging from the ceiling, a place where Christie always felt perfectly happy, panic now filled her. Her family. Something awful must be about to happen to them and she had to stop it. Yet, the feeling had never been like this before. She'd never, ever seen any harm coming to her sons or James.

There was the day thirteen-year-old Shane had broken his collarbone falling from a tree, and Christie had been on a school trip to a gallery, explaining the gift of Jack B. Yeats to twenty schoolgirls.

When the frantic St Ursula's secretary had finally reached Christie, she'd cursed her own inability to see what mattered.

12

How could she not have seen her own son in pain? What use was her gift if it only worked for other people?

This morning, within ten minutes, Christie had phoned her two sons to say a cheery hello, she was thinking about them and her horoscope had said she was going to have an unfortunate day, and she thought it might extend to them, so not to walk under any ladders.

Finally, Christie phoned James, whom she'd only said goodbye to two hours before as he headed off to the train station for a meeting in Cork.

'Is everything all right, Christie?' he asked carefully.

'Fine,' she said, not wanting to transmit the intensity of her fear to him. 'I felt a bit spooked, that's all. It's thundery here.' Which wasn't true. The sky was as blue and clear as the single oval sapphire in her antique engagement ring. 'I love you, James,' she added, which was entirely true. And then the signal on his mobile phone went, the connection was severed and Christie was left with her feeling of terror still beating a tattoo in her chest.

She left a message on her husband's mobile phone: 'I'm fine. Off shopping now, phone me later and tell me if you're able to get the earlier train. I love you. Bye.'

James worked for a government environmental agency and had worked his way up the ranks so he now held a senior position. He travelled round the country a lot, and Christie worried that the endless trips were getting too much for him. But James, still fired up wanting to be busy and to make sure that everything was done properly, loved it.

By ten, Christie was on her way along Summer Street with her shopping bags in her hand, trying to put the fear out of her mind. On the three days a week when she worked at St Ursula's, she turned left when she walked out of her garden gate. Today, she'd turned right in the direction of the Summer Street Café.

13

It was a pleasant time of day, with not much traffic. The stressed morning drivers were at their offices and Summer Street belonged to the locals again. Many of Christie's original neighbours were gone, but there were some who'd lived on the street nearly as long as the Devlin family.

Like the Maguires, Dennis and Una, possessors of a series of clapped-out cars and gloriously oblivious to the outrage of their current next-door neighbour who clearly felt that a car with that many dents in its paintwork should not be parked beside her gleaming BMW. The Maguires had one daughter, Maggie: a good kid, Christie recalled. Tall, shy, always polite, hiding her prettiness behind a heavy veil of carroty red curls as if she needed a retreat from the world. She'd never been in Christie's art classes but, like many of the girls on Summer Street, she'd had a crush on Shane. Lots of girls had. It was that combination of tousled blond hair and a slightly cheeky smile. He was a few months older than Maggie – extraordinary that they could both be thirty now – and indifferent to her pubescent longing.

'Just say hello to her,' Christie said, exasperated that Shane couldn't see that even a few words from her idol would make a difference to this shy girl.

'Ah, Mum, she'll only think I like her. Get real, would you?'

'What does that mean?' demanded his mother. 'Get real? I am being real. I'm saying show a bit of kindness, Shane. It doesn't cost you anything, does it?' Her voice had risen up the scale.

'OK,' he muttered, realising his mother was off on her high horse about how goodness and kindness filled your soul with happiness. It was a sweet idea and all, but it didn't work with girls, did it? 'I'll say hi, right?'

'And be nice.'

'Should I propose as well?'

14

Maggie lived in Galway now and Christie hadn't seen her for ages.

But the adult Maggie had lived up to the early promise Christie had seen in her. She was truly stunning-looking, her hair darkened to glossy auburn, her face a perfect oval with silvery cobalt-blue eyes, wide expressive lips and the translucent skin of the pure redhead. Yet she didn't appear to be aware of her beauty. Rather the opposite, in fact. Christie sensed that Maggie Maguire was still hiding her real self.

'She's doing so well,' Una Maguire said every time Christie asked. All those years ago, Una had been red-haired, too, but now the red was a faded strawberry with fine threads of grey. She was still beautiful, though, with the fine-boned face her daughter had inherited. 'Maggie's going out with this fabulous man. He's a lecturer in the college and she's in the library research department now. They're made for each other. Living together for three years and they have a beautiful apartment off Eyre Square. No sign of them getting married, but young people don't bother with that these days.'

'No, they don't,' agreed Christie easily, who understood quite plainly that Una longed with all her heart for her only child to be settled down with a husband and children.

They'd gone on their separate ways, Christie sure that Una had no notion of what she'd really seen in Una's heart.

Along with learning about her odd gift, Christie had learned that mostly people didn't want you to know their deepest, darkest secrets. So she kept her insights to herself unless she was asked.

Ten yards ahead of her, Amber Reid shot out of her gate at number 18, long tawny-gold hair bouncing in the telltale manner of the newly washed. Amber was seventeen, in her final year at St Ursula's and undoubtedly one of the stars of Christie's class.

Amber could capture anyone or anything with her pencil,

15

although her particular gift was for buttery oil landscapes, wild moody places with strange houses that looked like no houses on earth. Even in a large class, Amber stood out because she was so sparky and alive.

An unfashionable pocket Venus shape, with softly curved limbs and a small, plumply rounded face, her only truly beautiful feature was that pair of magnetic pewter eyes, with the ring of deepest amber around the pupils. She'd never have been picked as one of the school's beauties, the languorous leggy girls with chiselled cheekbones. Yet Amber's vivaciousness and the intelligence of those eyes gave her an attractiveness that few of the teenage beauty queens could match. And the artist in Christie could see the girl's sex appeal, an intangible charm that a photographer might not capture but an artist would.

Christie knew that unless St Ursula's had been evacuated for some strange reason that morning, Amber should be in school. And yet here she was, trip-trapping along in achingly high heels and a colourful flippy skirt that flowed out over her hips – unlike the institutional grey school uniform skirt that jutted out in an unflattering A-line. Amber was holding a mobile phone to her ear and Christie could just overhear.

'I'm just leaving now. Has anyone noticed I'm not there? MacVitie's not got her knickers in a twist over the absence of her best student?'

Mrs MacVitie was the maths teacher and Christie doubted that Amber, who was typically left-brained and hopeless at maths, was her best student. Favourite, perhaps, because it was hard to resist Amber, who always paid attention in class and was a polite, diligent student. But not best.

She must be speaking to Ella O'Brien, to whom she was joined at the hip, and Ella obviously told her that no, the St Ursula's bloodhounds had not been alerted.

'Sweet. If anyone asks, you think I was sick yesterday and

16

it must have got worse. I phoned in earlier and told the school secretary I was sick but, just in case, you back me up and say I'm puking like mad. It's true,' Amber laughed. 'I'm sick of school, right?'

Christie wondered if Faye, Amber's mother, knew what her daughter was up to.

Faye Reid was a widow, a quiet, businesslike figure who'd never missed a school meeting and was utterly involved in her daughter's life. Even though they lived on the same street, Christie didn't see much of Faye. She kept herself to herself, head down, rushing everywhere, clad in conservative navy suits and low-heeled shoes, with a briefcase by her side. There was such a contrast between the butterfly beauty of Amber who had the best of everything and caught people's eyes, and her mother, who always appeared to be rushing to or from work, trying hard to keep the mortgage paid and food on the table. A person didn't need Christie's gift of intuition to see that Faye's life had been one of sacrifices.

'She's one of the most gifted students I've ever taught,' Christie had told Faye two years before, shortly after Amber arrived in her class. 'Any art college in the world would love to have her.'

And Faye's face had lit up. Christie had never seen a smile transform a person so much. Faye was defiantly plain beside her daughter, overweight to Amber's curved sexiness and with her brown hair pulled severely back into a knot that only someone with the bones of a supermodel could get away with. Faye Reid didn't have the supermodel bones. But when she smiled that rare smile, she suddenly had all the charm of her daughter and Christie caught herself wondering why a woman like Faye, who could only be forty, lived such a quiet life. No man had ever been seen kissing Faye a wistful goodbye on the doorstep. Her clothes, the discreet earrings and low shoes that screamed comfort – they were like armour.

17

It was as if Faye had deliberately turned her back on youthful sexiness and hidden behind a façade of plain clothes.

Christie wondered if she could see more . . . but suddenly, it was as if Faye Reid had abruptly closed herself off and Christie could see nothing but the woman in front of her.

'Thanks, Mrs Devlin,' Faye said. 'That's what I think too, but I love her so much, I thought I was totally biased. Every parent thinks their kid is Mozart or Picasso, don't they?'

'Not all,' replied Christie grimly, thinking of some of the parents she'd met over the years with no belief in their kids whatsoever.

Her comment apparently touched a chord with Faye and the smile vanished to be replaced by her more usual, sombre expression. 'Yeah, you're right,' she said, nodding. 'There are always a few who don't appreciate their kids. Nothing that twenty years of psychotherapy wouldn't cure.'

Up ahead, Amber said a cheery 'byee' into her phone. Christie knew that the correct teacher response at this point would be to catch up with her and ask what she was doing out of school. But suddenly Amber broke into a run, high heels notwithstanding, and was gone down the street before Christie could move.

Christie shrugged. Amber was a good student, hardly a serial absentee. She and Ella had never been part of the school's wilder cliques and had both managed to move from adolescence to young womanhood without any noticeable bursts of rebellious behaviour.

There might be a perfectly good reason for her absence today. And Christie herself knew that you could learn plenty of things outside school as well as in.

When she'd been young, she hadn't done everything by the book either.

Yet again, Christie thought about the past and the places she'd lived. The house in Kilshandra with bitterness and

18

misery engrained into the wallpaper so that she'd barely been able to wait till she was old enough to leave. The bedsit on Dunville Avenue where she'd met so many friends and learned that she didn't have to hide her gift. And Summer Street, where all the best things in her life had happened.

She could remember what the young Christie had looked like when she'd moved to Summer Street – long dark hair drawn back in a loose ponytail, always in jeans and T-shirts – and she could remember how lucky she'd been, with a kind husband, enough money so they weren't in debt, with one beautiful, healthy child and another on the way. Yes, the years on Summer Street were the ones she liked to remember.

But there were other times she'd like to forget.

The strange feeling came through her again and despite the warmth of the morning, Christie shivered.

CHAPTER TWO

Amber Reid was concentrating so fiercely on getting to the bus stop in time that she hadn't noticed Mrs Devlin walking along Summer Street behind her. This was despite her intention to watch out for anyone who might sneak to her mother about her appearance out of uniform on a school day.

'We're going on a field trip,' Amber had planned to say blithely should the need arise, though the final-year students at St Ursula's didn't have time for field trips this close to the all-important state exams. And even if they did, what sort of field trip would require her best high heels – Oxfam spindly sandals revitalised with bronze paint – a sliver of a silk camisole and a flippy skirt, all topped off with the curious and fabulous silver tiger's-eye pendant she'd recently found buried in her mother's bottom drawer? The pendant was a mystery. She'd never seen her mum wear it. Faye dressed in boring suits and was resolutely against making the best of herself, no matter what Amber said. The pendant was so not 'her'. Amber was still wondering where her mother had come by such a thing. She didn't like to ask, because Mum would be hurt that she had been snooping. But it was odd of her to keep it hidden because they shared everything.

Well, not everything. Amber felt a splinter of guilt pierce her happy little cocoon. Today was a secret she couldn't share with her mother. It wasn't the first time she had concealed something. Mum was so square, so protective, that on the rare occasion that Amber had done anything outside her mother's rigid code of what was acceptable, she'd had to fib a little. But the current secret was certainly the biggest.

Ella had phoned just as Amber slammed the front door behind her.

'Ring me later and tell me how you got on, won't you?' Ella begged.

'Promise.'

'Wish I was bunking off,' Ella grumbled. 'I've history in ten minutes and I haven't finished my bloody essay on the Civil War.'

'Sorry, I did mine and I could have lent it to you so you could use some of my ideas,' Amber apologised. She loved history and the words flowed effortlessly from her pen to the page. Although how she'd written her essay last night was largely a mystery, as she'd been consumed with excitement thinking about today.

When she'd said goodbye to Ella, she broke into a run so as to race past the Summer Street Café in case of neighbours lurking within.

A minute later, she was at the bus stop on Jasmine Row, just in time to catch the 10.05 bus into the city, and Karl.

Karl. She whispered his name to herself as she gazed dreamily out of the windows on the top deck. Karl and Amber. Amber and Karl.

It sounded just right, like they were destined to be together.

Destiny had never been a concept Amber had held much faith in up to now. Just a few weeks away from her eighteenth birthday, and a month from the hated exams, she felt that she was in charge of her own life.

So she'd only been half paying attention when Ella read their horoscopes that fateful Friday at lunch. Horoscopes were fun but hardly to be relied on. Mum always insisted that Amber was responsible for herself and that life should not be lived on the word of what some astrologer had dreamed up for that day.

Mum was firm that Amber should never follow the crowd or do anything just because of someone else's opinion or because 'everyone else is doing it'. It was a lesson Amber had followed very well up to now.

'Crap for Aries, as usual,' muttered Ella, reading hers quickly. '"Rethink your options but don't let your enthusiasm wane." What does that mean? Why doesn't it ever give us hints on what's coming up in the maths paper? Now that would really be seeing the future.'

They were eating lunch on the gym roof – strictly forbidden but the current cool spot for sixth years – plotting their weekend and how to fit exam study in around at least one trip to the shopping centre to flip through rails of clothes they couldn't afford. All study and no play made you go mad, Ella insisted.

'Yours is better. "Single Taureans are going to find love and passion. Expect sparks to fly this weekend."'

'Sparks at the football club disco?' Amber roared with laughter at the very ridiculousness of this idea. It was the same big gang of people she'd known all her life and you couldn't get excited about a bunch of guys you'd watched grow up. Where was the mystique or the romance of that?

'Patrick?'

'Too nice. He'd want to walk along with his hand in your jeans pocket and yours in his and discuss the engagement party. Gross.'

'Greg's cute.'

'He called me Chubby Face once. No way.' Growing three

inches taller in the past year meant Amber had gone from being childishly plump to womanly and voluptuous. The addition of honeyed streaks in her rich brown hair meant that all the boys who'd previously talked to her like a clever younger sister suddenly sat up and took notice.

This new power over guys was heady and Amber was still testing it, gently. But she wanted to go somewhere more exciting than the football club disco to do so. Somewhere, beyond the confines of Summer Street, the football club disco and St Ursula's was Life with a capital L: pulsing, exciting, waiting for her.

'You're getting so choosy,' said Ella. 'You fancied Greg last year.'

'That was last year.'

'Should I get more highlights?' asked Ella, pulling forward a bit of the long, streaky blonde hair that was almost mandatory in sixth year and examining it critically. 'Your highlights look great but mine have gone all dull and yellowy.'

'Use the special shampoo for blondes,' said Amber.

'It costs a fortune. I bet your mum buys it for you. Mine wouldn't.' Ella was indignant. Because there were only the two of them, Amber's mum bought her everything she wanted, while Ella's, with three older sons as well, could hardly do the same thing.

'I'll give you some of my shampoo,' offered Amber. She knew how lucky she was and always shared any goodies with Ella. That's what best friends were for. 'Now, tomorrow night.' The pewter eyes gleamed. 'Not the football club disco, please.'

'Well . . .' Ella began. 'We could try something different.'

'. . . Something bad . . .' Amber shivered deliciously. 'Let's try to get into a grown-up club. Come on, in a few months, we'll have left school and we'll be the only people in our class to have never done anything interesting, Ella. Everyone else has gone to clubs they're not supposed to be able to get into, except us because we're the sensible ones. I'm fed up being sensible.'

Sensible was nice when you were thirteen and adored by all the teachers, but less so when you were nearly eighteen. The girls who never had their homework done and never got top marks in exams seemed to be having all the fun now, which seemed like an unequal division of spoils.

'Me too,' Ella breathed. 'And I've just thought how we can do it.'

Amber's eyes glittered. 'How?'

This feeling of dissatisfaction had in fact been incubating for weeks. Fed up with studying for exams and stifled by the pressure-cooker atmosphere at school, they felt the need to do something wild and rebellious for the first time ever, but their options were limited.

Most of their pocket money went on clothes or their mobile phone top-up cards, so they had little cash left over for wild behaviour.

Smoking was considered cool by some of the older girls, who insisted that it kept them thin, but cigarettes were too expensive to be more than a rare treat. Alcohol was easily available, like hash and ecstasy, but Amber's mother had a nose like an airport sniffer dog and could smell badness anywhere, so coming home drunk or stoned was hardly an option. Faye would have had a fit and grounded her for a month, not to mention being hurt by her daughter's behaviour, which would, in turn, make Amber feel bad for failing her beloved mother.

And that was the crux of the matter: their family unit was just two. Two people who adored each other, two people who'd gone through it all together, who protected each other from the world. But sometimes, that could be a burden too.

At least Ella had three brothers who could share living up to their parents' expectations: Amber had the weight of her mother's hopes and dreams resting squarely on her shoulders alone. And unlike Ella's parents, who seemed to understand that their kids eventually tested their wings and flew the nest, Faye Reid still seemed to think that she and Amber would be together for ever.

'What's the plan?' Amber asked now. 'Where are we going? Nowhere round here, surely? There's nothing but boring pubs.'

'Exactly. So forget about round here.' Ella grinned excitedly. 'Marco's going into town to a club tomorrow night, and if we went with him, we could get in without being carded.'

Marco was Ella's middle brother and they both realised he was their best bet for an illegal excursion. Her eldest brother wouldn't dream of taking two schoolgirls into a city night-club, while her youngest brother was too square to go at all. But twenty-three-year-old Marco, who had his own late-night show on a small radio station and went to all the coolest places, just might be persuaded to take them with him.

'Where?' asked Amber.

'Highway Seven.'

'That's twenty-ones and over.' It was hopeless. Doormen were up to speed on the best fake IDs. Amber and Ella didn't even have fake IDs. All the best clubs were over twenty-ones only. They'd be busted before they got in the door.

'Yeah, but there's a gig on there tomorrow night, some new band Marco's going to check out for his show,' Ella explained. 'He'll be on the guest list and he'll be going in the back door of the club, so the bouncer will let him in no hassle, and if we're with him . . .'

'. . . We'll waltz right in,' laughed Amber gleefully. 'You are one clever chick, Ella O'Brien. But how do we get Marco to take us in the first place?'

'Bribery and corruption.' Ella had thought it all out. 'We'll twist his arm this evening after school.'

Marco looked a lot like Ella: dark eyes, pale skin and the

25

same dark hair as she'd had before she discovered peroxide. Easy-going to a fault, he wasn't keen on taking his little sister and her friend out with him.

'In your dreams,' he said.

'Mum would go mental if she knew you'd had that huge party in the house when the rest of us were in Kerry at Christmas,' Ella said, all wide-eyed innocence. 'The one where the neighbours called the police. You'd be chopped liver if she ever found out. You know what she's like about not upsetting the neighbours . . .'

'How did you hear about that?' demanded Marco and then slapped his forehead and groaned. 'You didn't know, did you? You were just guessing.'

'Oh, Marco, we knew about the party,' Amber said, exasperated. 'We were only guessing about the police, but we found some guy's coat under Ella's bed, along with a lot of empty Heineken cans and a condom.'

Marco blanched.

'It's not as if Ella put the beer cans there. We never drink beer. We prefer wine or vodka,' she added, hoping to sound worldly-wise.

'Can't you go out with your own friends?' Marco begged, not even commenting on the wine or vodka remark. It seemed like only last week his sister and her friend had been sobbing their hearts out over guinea pig funerals in the back garden and winning badges for Guides.

'Think of it as community service for deeds previously unpunished,' Amber pointed out. 'We won't be any trouble. Once we're in the club, you can forget about us. We can look after ourselves.'

'OK, you're nearly eighteen and you know everything, right?' he said sarcastically.

'I've a yellow belt in karate,' Amber said, assuming what she hoped was a karate stance, though it was years since

26

she'd set foot on a dojo. Her mother's insistence on self-defence lessons had been fun when she'd been ten, less so when she hit puberty.

Marco sighed. 'Close combat is not the answer to all situations in life. The most dangerous guys in the club probably won't ask you to arm wrestle, Amber. Understand?' He looked at both girls as sternly as he could. 'I don't want to have to come home at two in the morning and tell Mum and Dad that I've lost you two. Or worse, tell your mother, Amber. She'd rip me limb from limb.'

Amber's mother had always made Marco a bit nervous. There was something steely in Mrs Reid's gaze, as if she was warning him that she had his measure.

'We're not kids,' growled Amber. 'We're coming. It's no skin off your nose. You only have to get us in.'

'Well, you'll have to watch your drinks,' sighed Marco, knowing when he was beaten. 'There are guys out there who'll slip a date rape drug in your glass and, well . . . you don't have any experience. You don't know the half of it.'

'You're a wonderful brother.' Ella gave him a hug.

'This is a one-off deal,' Marco insisted. 'OK? And you've got to behave yourselves.'

'Of course,' said Amber, who had absolutely no intention of behaving herself. She could do that in the football club.

The truly difficult part of the plan was lying to her mother about where she and Ella were going that night. They decided that, because of Faye's ultra-vigilance, they'd stay at Ella's that night after their alleged trip to the disco. Having gone through it all before, Ella's parents were definitely more relaxed about their daughter's behaviour.

'Mum will check we're home, but if I put pillows in the beds, she'll think we're there,' Ella said.

Amber thought of how her mum never slept until Amber was back after an evening out. How many nights had they

27

sat up on Amber's bed on her return, Mum listening as Amber recounted her triumphs and disasters?

Then, she brushed the feeling of guilt away. It was only because Mum was so protective that she had to lie. She wasn't a kid any more. She didn't want to hurt Mum's feelings but she had to move on and Mum must be made to understand that.

Getting into Highway Seven worked precisely as Ella had predicted, although Amber only felt her breathing come right when they were deep inside the club, far from the stern eye of the doorman. In spite of her outward nonchalance, she was nervous. She and Ella might have sunbathed on the forbidden gym roof and smoked a few illicit cigarettes, but they were strictly homework-on-time girls in other respects. This was breaking into new territory, both exciting and scary at the same time.

Dark, moody and almost vibrating with bass-deep music, the club was crowded with bodies, perfume and a sweet smell that Amber knew was marijuana because even the football club wasn't trouble-free.

'Er . . . what do you want to do now?' asked Marco, wondering how he'd got lumbered with this situation. Thankfully, the two girls looked old enough to fit in, but hey, they were still his little sister and her friend. He had a bad vibe about the whole thing.

'We're fine,' Amber said airily.

'Yeah, you go off with your mates. We're cool,' Ella added, matching her friend's unconcerned look.

Marco shrugged, but he looked relieved. 'If you're sure . . .'

'We're sure.' Both girls nodded.

Amber scanned her surroundings idly, her body moving gently to the music. Ella adopted the same laid-back hauteur.

Marco was no match for them. He was fooled.

28

'Text me if you need me,' he said, then turned and was swallowed up by the crowd.

On their own, Amber and Ella clutched each other and shrieked, all pretence at being cool gone. Nobody heard them over the pumping beat. 'We're here,' they screeched and did their own little war dance.

'Loos,' gasped Amber, taking Ella by the hand.

In the toilets, they re-adopted adult cool while Amber applied a line of smoky kohl around the rims of her eyes like she'd seen in a magazine. The effect was startling: her beautiful eyes seemed larger and more hypnotic than ever.

'You really do look twenty-one,' sighed Ella, pausing in the act of applying another coat of sticky lip gloss.

A woman rinsing her hands at the next basin glanced at them.

'Thanks!' said Amber. 'I'm actually thirty-two but my plastic surgeon is a miracle worker.'

The woman left in a hurry and they creased over laughing again, high on their own daring.

They had enough money to order one drink each, which they'd have to make last all night, and they stood at the bar, nursing their vodkas, trying to look as if they'd been here a million times before and were bored with it all.

Behind her calm façade, Amber was enthralled, watching everyone, envying them the way they all seemed to fit in.

In a corner cordoned off by velvet rope sat a dozen people drinking champagne. All beautiful, having the time of their lives, utterly at home. One slender brunette in faded, sequin-decorated jeans was holding court, talking and laughing, while everyone else watched her with evident fascination. In that one second, Amber longed to be just like her: part of the scene instead of watching enviously from the sidelines.

Then, one of the guys saw her watching them, a guy with dark cropped hair and stubble that was probably five o'clock

29

shadow at ten in the morning. His gaze was so intense Amber looked away in embarrassment. Shit, how gauche to be caught staring hungrily like a schoolgirl.

She did her best to stare anywhere else, but she really wanted to look back at the guy and drink him in. She'd never felt that connection before, that instant buzz from another human being, the feeling that she knew him.

But who was she kidding? He was probably only staring at her because it was obvious she and Ella were out of place. She'd thought they looked old enough but perhaps they didn't and the guy was wondering what a kid was doing there.

'Nobody's bothering to chat us up,' moaned Ella beside her.

'It's early yet,' said Amber with more enthusiasm than she felt. Perhaps Marco had been right and they should have gone out with their own friends, but the football club would seem so tame after this. After him.

'Are you lost?' said a low voice.

Amber swivelled round. The dark, crop-haired man stood beside her, staring at her with intense blue eyes. Every nerve in her body quivered into alertness, though she tried to stay calm.

'Lost? No.' She shrugged, hopelessly trying to adopt the laid-back aura of the brunette in the VIP section.

'You weren't looking for someone?' he asked. His voice was soft and deep, a man's voice, not a boy's.

Amber shook her head.

'I thought you were looking for me,' he added, 'and you've found me.'

Amber just stared at him, concentrating on breathing.

Chat-up lines for her usually consisted of the guy asking what class she was in at school. This approach was wildly different. Amber felt her spine lengthen, some new instinct making her stand up straighter, yet slightly closer to him.

'I wasn't looking for you,' she said, nonchalant. How was she doing this? She'd never spoken this way before, like a heroine from a film. 'I was watching people. I'm an artist: I like watching people.'

'You draw them, then?'

Amazingly, he didn't spot that she was making this up as she went along. Buoyed up, Amber lowered her eyelids and gave him a sultry gaze she'd rehearsed in her bedroom in front of the faded line of her childhood teddy bears.

'If I like the shape of them and the look of them, I might draw them,' she replied coolly.

'And me? Do you like the look of me?' he asked.

It was noisy, so he'd moved till he was very close to her and, despite the gloom of the club, she could see that his face was moulded like a beautiful Renaissance statue: a straight, proud nose, flaring cheekbones, a finely planed forehead and a mouth so sensitive it would take a sculptor months to get right. Tightly cropped brown hair and a filament-thin cotton shirt flattened against his lean body took him into the modern era, but otherwise, he was like the historical princes of art that Amber had grown up admiring.

'I like the look of you very much,' she breathed, not bothering to be cool any more.

And he smiled at her, revealing an endearing dimple on one side of his mouth and perfect white teeth. Amber forgot about everything else in the world except this fabulous man. She wanted to touch him, kiss him, feel him wrap his arms around her and press his body against hers for ever. This, she thought, was love at first sight.

Karl was in a band, he told her. She introduced him to Ella and he led them over to the VIP area.

Ella squeezed Amber's hand in delight as they were ushered past the velvet rope, but Amber was too engrossed in Karl to sense Ella's message of 'Wow! Look where we are now!'

31

Some of Karl's as yet unsigned band were among the group. The rest, the ones who'd undoubtedly got everyone into the VIP area in the first place, were a band with an album that had just been released, the ones Marco had come to hear.

'The Kebabs, of course I've heard of you! My brother came to hear you play. Tell me, you do, like tours and stuff?' asked Ella, fascinated, as she was handed a glass of champagne.

As Ella listened to stories of life on the road, Amber barely heard a word. She was conscious only of Karl sitting beside her, with an arm loosely around the back of her seat, his leg casually close to hers.

She didn't want to hear about anyone else, only Karl.

'What do you do in your band?'

'I am the band,' Karl shrugged as if it was obvious. 'I write the songs, I sing, I play lead guitar. The band is me.'

'You're an artist too.' She smiled and took his hand, tracing the lines on it with sensitive fingers. 'I could paint you.'

'I could write a song about you,' Karl said, touching her face with his other hand.

Their faces were inches apart now, Karl was drinking in every inch of her, his eyes travelling from her tawny hair, past the softness of her jaw down to the firm, high curve of her breasts highlighted in the tight little T-shirt she'd borrowed from Ella.

'You're so sexy,' he whispered. His eyes roamed lower, past her waist to the rounded curve of her hips and along her jean-clad legs. For once, Amber didn't bother trying to lift one thigh up so her leg looked thinner. There was no mistaking the fact that Karl liked her the way she was, and that was headier than any alcohol she could have drunk.

'Get a room!' shouted someone to them, and everyone creased up laughing.

Amber and Karl didn't hear the jest or the insistent throbbing of the club music: they were locked into their own beat,

32

aqua eyes in a lean face staring fiercely into grey-and-amber eyes in a gently rounded one, the red stain on each of Amber's cheeks owing nothing to her make-up.

They moved at the same time, Karl's arms winding around Amber's waist, her hands spreading out to feel the heat of his torso through the thin shirt. Before her fingers had a chance to revel in the fine muscles of his back, his mouth met hers and they were kissing. It was unlike any kiss Amber had experienced: Karl's tongue snaked into her mouth with practised ease, banishing the memory of every St Bernard slobber of a French kiss she'd ever had before. They melted against each other, his hands cupping her face, her hands raking through his hair. The heat of their bodies burned through their clothes. And long afterwards, when Amber was again capable of thinking, she realised that this was what love was all about.

As the morning bus lurched along into the city, Amber sat on the top deck in her finery and thought of how much had changed in the past two weeks. She had been a kid then, but now she was an adult.

An adult with an adult relationship. Or at least, she'd be properly having an adult relationship soon. Today, she was meeting Karl to take him home where they'd have the place to themselves all day. There was no privacy in the poky flat he shared with five other musicians. In her bedroom on Summer Street, there would be as much privacy as they needed. Briefly, Amber thought of how she'd explain it all to her mother if she arrived home early from work. She could imagine Faye's horrified face, and how hurt she'd be to have been lied to. But Amber flicked the thought away. She'd worry about that later. Everyone had secrets, didn't they?

CHAPTER THREE

Twice a week for the past six months, Faye Reid had taken an early lunch and walked a mile to the swimming pool complex near her office. The brisk walk past the mirror-windowed buildings of the docklands was soothing. Striding along the pavement, away from the incessant phones and the beehive drone of the busy recruitment company where she worked, she listened to music, watched seagulls swoop and dive towards the river, and relaxed.

Today, she had Billie Holiday on her portable CD player. Billie's golden voice told of men who'd left and Faye thought how wonderful it was that, no matter how many times she heard Billie, it always sounded as if the guy had just that second gone, the screen door still banging behind him.

Music talked to Faye. Sound was the most evocative sense for her and the first few bars of a song on the radio could take her right back to where she'd been when she'd first heard it. She herself had a softly husky singing voice that few people had ever heard and could repeat a melody after only hearing it once. When she'd been Amber's age, she'd always been singing but she rarely did now.

For music could be a curse too. There were still some

songs she couldn't listen to, songs that would break her heart because of the memories they brought to life.

Billie Holiday songs thankfully, for all their pain, didn't fit into that category.

'It's lovely and everything, but it's kind of depressing, Mum,' Amber had pointed out the previous weekend about her mother's love of exquisitely melancholy jazz.

'Some of it is,' Faye agreed, trying to see things from her daughter's point of view. It was an unseasonably warm Saturday for the end of April and they'd spent the afternoon in the garden, Amber keen to start a dusting of golden tan on her face.

With the iron discipline Faye brought to every area of her life, the housework in the Reid household was always up to date. But when it came to gardening, she didn't know weed from plant. Occasionally, she wished she was more like Christie Devlin who'd created an exquisite all-white garden at the front of her house. Faye had never seen Christie's back garden, had never seen the inside of the Devlins' house, actually, because they barely knew each other in spite of living mere doors apart for ten years, but she'd have bet that it was just as beautiful, with frothy roses and trailing blooms that flourished under Christie's magic hands.

On this particular Saturday, Faye wore a tired pale-pink polo shirt over cheap loose-fit jeans that did nothing for her shape, and was trying to uproot any weeds she could identify. It all looked weedy to her. Surely that big thing that looked strangely like a marijuana plant couldn't be a flower? Although since she'd thrown those packets of wildflower seeds every which way last year, it was hard to tell. That would be a fine advert for sensible single parenthood, wouldn't it: a hash plant in Faye Reid's garden.

She grinned. If there was any illegal vegetation in her garden, nobody would cast aspersions on the arch-conservative Mrs

Reid, the very model of a career-minded widow with an equally model teenage daughter. Faye had worked very hard to reach that place in the local psyche. She'd learned that a single woman bringing up a child needed to be beyond reproach. Nobody would ever have cause to accuse her of trying to steal their husband or of letting her daughter run wild.

'I like songs like "Respect",' Amber went on. She was lying on her tummy on a rug on the lawn, her feet in the air and a school book propped up in front of her. 'Not sad ones where everyone's depressed, like no guy will ever look at them again 'cos they messed it up the first time.'

Faye paused in her weeding.

'You've got to remember, Amber, that the old jazz and rhythm-and-blues songs are from another age, when life was different and women didn't have the same opportunities we have today,' she said, wiping her hands on her jeans so she could clip a few strands of light-brown hair back. Faye didn't bother with her hair much: shoulder length, wavy and undyed for many years, it got washed, tied back firmly and treated to conditioner when she had the time, which wasn't often. 'They didn't have contraception, any hope of equal pay or equal rights in lots of things. So it might sound depressing to you now,' she explained, 'but they were brave. I think they were feminists in their own time because they sang when it wasn't considered a decent job for women. They didn't have what we have now. Girl power hadn't been invented then.'

'Yeah, I know that, but why do all the women hang around waiting for the lover man to turn up?' Amber wanted to know, abandoning her book with a speed that showed she hadn't been that engrossed in revising maths equations. 'The women do all the waiting in these songs and in the old movies. If a guy doesn't respect you, he's going to walk all over you. They're waiting for him to make it right. It's so passive. You don't need girl power to see that.'

'You and Ella have got to stop reading the therapist's sections in women's magazines,' Faye groaned, but she was smiling. 'I thought you were going to study art, not psychotherapy.'

'Ha ha. All I'm saying is that some people want to be rescued and that's, like, not going to happen.' Amber's small face was determined, her chin lifted to signify that life would have to take her on her terms, and not the other way round. Faye felt the familiar clammy grip of a mother's anxiety on her heart. Amber was full of energy and hope, for all her careful studying of women's magazines' problem pages.

What if one day, despite all Faye's efforts at protecting her daughter, someone or something destroyed that energy and hope?

'My little suffragette.'

Amber looked pleased. 'I like to think so,' she said, 'only I'm the modern version. No chaining yourself to the railings involved. I'm glad it's different now.'

Faye said nothing. It was hard to tell a seventeen-year-old with her whole life ahead of her that heartache and loss crossed every century, women's rights notwithstanding. She sat back on her heels, tired from gardening. If only she could wave a wand and conjure up a lovely garden: then she'd take care of it. But creating it was another matter.

Her house was one of the smallest on Summer Street, the first of the eight railway cottages lined up in a terrace like an illustration in a Victorian picturebook. The painted front doors – theirs was teal blue – carved fascia boards and perfectly square windows were like something a child would draw.

Most of the cottages had been extended at the back. Faye's extension had made the kitchen bigger, creating a T-shaped upstairs attic bedroom for Amber, and taking the already tiny garden down to shoebox size. It had a small block of mossy lawn, flower beds on either side and a rackety garden shed at the bottom.

'I can't imagine Gran waiting for a man to fix what was wrong,' Amber added, 'and she grew up when it was different. I mean, she takes the car to get it fixed, not Stan. She's a real role model. I tell all the girls in school about her and they think she's amazing. They think you're amazing too, Mum, because you don't take crap from anyone.'

'No,' said Faye, ignoring the use of the word crap and wondering if that would be her only epitaph. *Here lies Faye Reid, who never took crap from anyone.* It wasn't what she'd hoped she'd be remembered for when she was younger, but it certainly fitted now. When she'd been Amber's age, she'd wanted to be thought of as exciting and glamorous, a mysterious woman loved by many men. Teenage dreams were funny in retrospect, weren't they? She'd bet that Amber would never imagine that her mother could think like that. Before Amber had been born, Faye had been a very different person altogether, not the cautious, dowdy mother she'd become.

'Nor does Gran,' Amber went on. 'And not everyone her age is like that. Ella's grandmother makes them all run round after her like headless chickens since she had her heart operation. Ella's terrified her grandmother is going to end up living with them. She says they'll all have to be on drugs to cope. I'm glad Gran's not like that.'

Faye's widowed mother, Josie, had got married again a few years previously to a widower who understood that his new wife had got too used to the independence of almost twenty years of being on her own to ever be under a man's thumb again. A retired teacher with boundless patience, Stan was a calm breeze to Josie's cyclone of activity. Josie ran her local meals on wheels, while Stan was the Martha to her Mary.

'Your gran was on her own for a long time so she had to learn to take care of herself,' Faye said absently.

'Like you.'

'Yes, like me.'

'I was thinking.' Amber swung her legs back and forth. 'About Dad being dead and Granddad being dead, and now Gran is married to Stan and, well . . . When you go to heaven, how do they work it out if you've had more than one husband? I mean, if Stan dies and then Gran dies, who does she live with in heaven – Granddad or Stan? It's a problem, isn't it? They never talked about that in religion classes. Just that we'd all be happy but how?'

'Your gran's probably not planning on shuffling off to meet her maker just yet,' Faye said, startled.

'I know, I can't stand the thought of her not being here.' Amber shuddered. She was very close to her grandmother. 'But how does it work? Like if you met someone and Dad's up there waiting for you. He's still only in his late twenties, and then you come and you're this old lady, but you've got another husband who's waiting too, because women live longer than men, so he's there first. Do you see what I mean? Reincarnation sounds better,' she added, 'because then you're not all going to be in heaven at the same time. It makes more sense.'

Faye had a sinking feeling in the pit of her stomach, the same feeling she always had when Amber talked about her father. The long-dead and beloved dad who was reduced to a photo in a frame, a misty figure who never did anything wrong, never shouted or discussed tidying up her bedroom. Never said no to a mobile phone or the purchase of a miniskirt of belt-like proportions. The dead could do no wrong.

'I hope Dad's waiting for you in heaven, though. That's nice. I like to think of that.' Amber smiled. 'For your sake, really. So you can be together again, like in *Titanic*. Although the woman in that was really old at the end, and then when she joined them all on the ship, she was young and back being Kate Winslet. Which was a bit convenient, wasn't it? Does that mean you get to be at your best in heaven, like twenty-one, even if you're very ancient and falling apart when you die? I think it's a bit too convenient.'

Faye breathed an inward sigh of relief at this rapid turn in the conversation. It meant she didn't need to discuss the concept of Amber's father waiting patiently for her in heaven. Not that he'd have waited. Patience had never been one of his virtues.

It was because saying he was there already would be a lie and now that Amber was older, it was getting harder and harder to lie. Adults lied to children all the time, little white ones for their own good. But time had turned Faye's white lie into a giant black one and now she couldn't stomach repeating it any more.

'I think the whole problem with heaven is that nobody really knows anything about it,' she said, copping out. 'You're supposed to believe even though you don't know.'

Amber grimaced.

'That's what the whole faith thing is about,' Faye added, feeling she was on shaky ground here. 'Believing when you don't know for sure.' Like you've always believed me, she thought guiltily. 'You could ask Stan. He studied theology.'

'The thing is, you have one person who's right for you, your soul mate, the one who's waiting for you,' Amber said. 'But if they die, how can you meet another soul mate? There's only going to be one person who makes you feel complete, who you can't wait to see and talk to, right? Isn't there? People say that, anyway,' Amber added hurriedly. She bent her head to her book again.

A few more minutes passed by and Faye tugged listlessly at a couple of weedy plants, obsessing over her daughter's vision of her dad happily waiting in heaven for Faye to turn up. Amber never needed to know, did she?

'Ella said something totally crazy the other day, Mum.' Amber broke the silence.

40

'She said that maybe you have to pretend not to be independent and that's what men like. That's crap, isn't it? Why should you pretend? I told her, Ella, you have to be you.' Amber was earnest, sounding like a much-married matron explaining the ways of the world to a teenage bride.

'That doesn't sound like Ella.' Faye knew her daughter's best friend as if she were her own daughter. Like Amber, Ella was clever, sweet, responsible and had never caused a moment's trouble in her life. 'What's come over her?'

'Giovanni's new girlfriend, that's who,' Amber went on. 'Dannii. With two i's and little hearts over each of them. The hearts are very important. She's messing up Ella's head and saying that the reason Ella and me don't have boyfriends is because we're too clever and too independent and guys don't like that.' Amber snorted dismissively.

Giovanni was Ella's youngest brother and Faye had heard about this new girlfriend enough times for alarm bells to tinkle gently. Giovanni was in his second year in college, handsome like all Ella's half-Italian family, and Faye knew Amber had a mild crush on him, despite the fact that she said he was boring. The appearance of an actual steady girlfriend was certainly a catalyst for Amber to realise this. Faye wouldn't have minded if her daughter's first serious boyfriend was someone like Giovanni: someone she knew all about and approved of.

'Dannii's OK-looking, I suppose,' Amber conceded, grudgingly, 'but she's a pain and she's round Ella's house all the time talking this crap. She's doing business studies, Mum, right, and when she's with Giovanni, she behaves like she's had her brain sucked out. You don't get into business studies in college if you're a moron, so I don't know who she's kidding. Well,' she added gloomily, 'Giovanni appears to be falling for it. Big dope. Dannii told Ella that Giovanni's a really hot guy. You can't say that to your boyfriend's little sister! *Your brother is so sexy*. Yeuch. That's disgusting. I can't stand her. She hasn't a clue about anything.'

Faye said nothing for a while. She gazed at her work so far. She'd definitely pulled up some genuine flowers along with the weeds. How was it that carefully planted flowers could be ripped up easily, while unwanted weeds needed incredible force to shift them?

'If you act stupid with a guy, he's only going out with you because of how you look,' Faye said eventually.

'Exactly what I said,' Amber pointed out. 'Oh, I suppose Ella was only thinking out loud. She couldn't act dumb, anyway. She's going to come top of our year in the exams.'

Talk of the exams made Amber stare wearily down at her maths book again. 'That's not love. Love is different. If any guy's only interested in what a girl's like on the outside, then he's not what you want, is he?'

It was half question, half statement.

'That's what I think,' Faye said decisively. This was safe ground: she'd been telling Amber to appreciate her worth all her life. 'If he doesn't love you for who you are, then he's not the right person for you. Have you and Ella met any hot guys?' she asked lightly. She'd love to ask if Amber thought she might fancy Giovanni.

'No,' said Amber hastily. If her mother hadn't been so busy being thankful at the change of subject, she might have noticed just how hastily Amber had spoken. But Faye didn't notice. She was pulling at weeds and she didn't see the hint of red on her daughter's cheeks.

'Summer Street is not exactly awash with hot men my age.' Amber fanned herself with her book as if the sun was responsible for the heat suffusing her complexion. 'Ella's road is just as bad. The whole neighbourhood's full of nerds and middle-aged men with beer bellies who suck them in when we walk past.'

42

Savage but accurate, Faye thought with a smothered laugh. Amber and Ella's teenage beauty made them a stunning pair, Amber all tawny hair and those spectacular eyes contrasting with Ella's flashing dark Italian looks. Though they'd never have believed it, they were gorgeous – a scary prospect when you were the mother of one of them. But Amber was so sensible. Faye had taught her well. How not to make mistakes, how not to be led by other people. Except, Faye thought, she'd never explained to her daughter how her mother knew these lessons were so important.

'The people from number 42 have sold up,' Faye said breezily. 'Who knows, a handsome father-son combo might have bought it.'

'Doubt it. But hey, if you're right, you could go out with the dad. Wouldn't that be great?' Amber was delighted. 'You could come home and tell me all about it. And I'd laugh and warn you not to let him get past first base on the first date!'

Faye grabbed a nettle by mistake and gasped with pain.

'Ouch. That was stupid,' she muttered lamely.

'It's a serious subject, Mum,' Amber said gravely. Just to show how serious, she sat up cross-legged and gazed at her mother, her face solemn. 'I know how much you've given up for me but I'm an adult now and you can have your life back. I'll be going to college. You need to do your own thing.'

The little speech sounded like one Amber had been working on for ages and Faye almost grabbed the nettle again for the comfort of physical pain against this shocking emotional stabbing sensation. She was meant to be urging Amber gently into the world, not the other way round.

Seventeen-year-olds were supposed to be too involved with their own problems to notice their mothers'. If Amber was urging her to get a social life, she must be a total basket case. Well, Faye's own mother thought so, too.

'Come on, Faye, don't bury yourself. You're not dead yet,'

43

Josie had said many years before, and it had triggered the one big row between them since before Amber was born.

'Leave me alone to live my life my way! You don't know what I want,' Faye had said furiously.

She'd never forgotten what her mother had said. Josie hadn't understood at all. This life with Amber wasn't being buried: it was living peacefully and contentedly without the interference of any man.

'I'm just saying think about it,' Amber went on. 'I'll be gone and I'll worry about you, Mum. I won't be here so much and you'll need to keep busy. And I don't mean doing overtime,' she added sternly. 'I mean having fun. Getting out. Going on dates. Grace would love to set you up on a blind date at one of her dinners, you know she would. Sure, you'd probably meet a few men you'd hate, but you never know, you might find romance.'

Lecture over, she went back to her maths book, leaving Faye feeling that their roles had been reversed. She'd been the one receiving the lecture on life from her daughter.

Amber's remarks had been running through Faye's head since Saturday afternoon.

Climbing the steps to the swimming pool complex, Faye wondered, was this all normal teenager stuff: get a life, Mum, because I'm going to and I don't want to worry about you. Or was there something else?

Faye went into the women's changing room, switched off her music and changed into her plain black swimsuit quickly. She did everything quickly and efficiently.

'Economical and precise,' Grace said, which was high praise indeed because Grace, Faye's boss in Little Island Recruitment, turned efficiency into an art form.

'Economical and precise or obsessional?' Faye wondered from time to time when she was interviewing in her office

44

and saw candidates staring at her pristine desk with everything exactly at right angles to everything else. A cluttered desk meant a cluttered mind and Faye had never had time for a cluttered mind.

But didn't it signify an obsessional mind if you arranged all your paperclips to lie lengthwise in their compartment in the desk organiser?

She stowed her navy skirt suit in a locker and pulled on a swimhat. She never looked at herself in the mirror like some women in the changing room, anxiously making sure they didn't look awful in clinging Lycra or admiring a physique honed by laps.

At the age of forty, and carrying probably two stone more than she should, Faye was no fan of mirrors. They lied. You could be scarred to bits on the inside and look beautiful outside.

She walked out of the changing room, shivered under the cool shower for a moment, then slipped into the pool's medium-fast lane where she pushed off into the water.

The Olympic swimming selectors were unlikely to be calling on her any time soon, but over the last six months she'd worked her way up to swimming sixteen lengths each time and she knew she was getting faster, no matter how unprofessional her forward crawl. She felt more toned too but that wasn't the primary reason for the exercise.

What she loved about swimming was the solitude of the pool. Even if the lanes were full and every noise was amplified by the water, when her head was down and her body was slicing through the pool, she felt utter peace.

This was her time, time for Faye alone.

Six months previously, when she'd paid for the swimming complex membership, she'd realised it was the first time in seventeen years she'd indulged herself in something that didn't directly benefit Amber. Even the CD player she used was an old one that Amber had discarded when she'd saved up her pocket money for an iPod.

The money she'd spent on the membership fee could usefully have gone somewhere else. Amber would need a whole new expensive kit for art college, and there would surely be trips to galleries abroad. There never seemed to be enough money for all the things Faye thought Amber should have.

But the pool had called to her.

'I wish I was into swimming,' Grace had begun to say on the days that Faye took an early lunch.

Grace and her husband Neil ran the recruitment company together. Grace regularly said they couldn't have done it without Faye, and Neil, who actually worked very little, was smugly convinced its success was all down to him.

'Swimming sounds so easy, swim, swim and the weight falls off,' Grace had said.

Faye grinned, knowing that Grace liked the idea of exercise and the results that exercise provided but wasn't that keen on actually doing it.

'Is it better than running, do you think?' Grace went on. 'I'd quite like to run but I've weak ankles. Swimming could be the answer.'

'You'd get bored in a week,' Faye told her. Grace was a chataholic and got anxious if she hadn't had at least four friends phone her a day in between her hectic schedule of business calls. 'There's nothing sociable about swimming. You put your head into the water and plough on. You can't hear anyone and you can only see what's ahead of you.'

It was like praying, she often thought, although she didn't say that to Grace, who'd have thought she was abusing recreational pharmaceuticals. But it seemed like that to Faye – here it was only you and God as you moved porpoise-like through the water, nobody else.

'Really? No *Baywatch* male lifeguards?'

'I haven't noticed any,' Faye said drily.

'Well, who needs a *Baywatch* lifeguard anyway?' Grace said.

Which was, Faye knew, her way of moving on to another line of conversation. Because Grace, although happily married, had many fantasies about a muscle-bound hunk who'd adore her. It was strange when Faye, who'd been on her own for most of the past seventeen years, went out of her way not to notice men at all. She was with Billie Holiday on the whole men issue: they were too much trouble. And she'd learned that the hard way.

Lunchtimes could be busy in Little Island Recruitment because that was when staff from other offices got the opportunity to slope off, march into Little Island, relate the sad tale of their current employment and discuss the possibility of moving elsewhere where their talents would finally be appreciated. But today when Faye arrived back from her swim, damp-haired, pleasurably tired out and dressed in her old reliable M & S navy suit, reception was empty except for Jane behind the reception desk.

'Hi, Faye,' said Jane cheerily and held up a sheaf of pink call slips. 'I've got messages for you.'

The office was very high-tech and designed to impress. Nobody could fail to be dazzled by the glass lift, the stiletto-crunching black marble floors, or the enormous modern-art canvas that dominated the reception. Faye thought the picture looked like what two amorous whales might paint if they'd been covered in midnight-blue emulsion and left to thump around for a while on a massive canvas. But having an artistic daughter, she understood that this was probably not the effect the artist had anticipated.

'People are scared of modern art,' Grace said gleefully when the painting had first been hung.

47

'It can be intimidating,' Faye pointed out bluntly. 'But this one's a bit dull, to be honest.'

'Perhaps you're right,' sighed Grace. 'But it says we've arrived. We've come a long way from that awful dive of an office we started out in, remember.'

Faye remembered. Ten years ago, Faye had been broke after a series of dead-end jobs, and was desperately trying to get her foot on an employment ladder that didn't involve late-night bar work. She'd been so grateful to Grace for taking a chance on her in the fledgling recruitment business she had made sure Grace never regretted it. Nobody in Little Island worked harder than Faye. The two had forged a professional friendship that grew stronger every year.

'The ex-barmaid and the ex-banking queen, who'd have thought we'd make it?' Faye used to say, smiling. She didn't let many people past her barriers, but Grace was one of the few. What if Grace was a social butterfly, was married to the obnoxious Neil, and could air-kiss with the best of them? Despite all that, she was a real person. True, kind, honest. Faye trusted her, which made Grace part of a very small and exclusive club.

'You should say "ex-beverage administrator",' Grace chided. 'Besides, you should have been running that bar. If you'd had the childcare and the opportunity, you would have been.'

Grace knew Faye's history and how she'd worked in dead-end jobs so she could take care of Amber herself. She knew most of Faye's secrets, but not all.

Faye took her messages, walked past what was now dubbed 'Flipper Does Dallas', went up to her office and got ready for the afternoon meeting.

At three in the afternoon, on Mondays and Wednesdays, there was a staff meeting in Little Island Recruitment. Grace said it kept everyone in touch with what the whole company was doing.

48

They'd been holding it for nine years and it was a marvellous idea because it made every single member of staff feel both personally involved in the company and valued by it.

'We're only as good as our last job,' Grace would remind the staff at the meeting, where there was always a buzz of conversation, until the apple and cinnamon muffins came in. 'This is the think tank where we come up with ideas to improve what we do.'

The staff all believed the idea for the meeting had been Grace's. After all, she'd been a banking hotshot for years before starting up the agency, and could write a book on how to get ahead in life.

It could be called Who Moved My Emery Board? joked Kevin who was in charge of accounts. Grace's nails were things of beauty: ten glossy beige talons that clacked in a military tattoo on the conference-room desk when she was irritated.

Clack, clack, clack.

In fact, Faye had suggested the staff meeting shortly after she joined.

Grace felt that some benign presence had been on her side the day Faye walked into her life. Grace may have been the one with the financial acumen and the qualifications as long as her fake-tanned arms, but Faye was the one who'd made the agency work.

On this afternoon, nineteen members of staff sat around the conference table and worked their way through the agenda.

Today's meeting focused on the few sticky accounts where the jobs and the jobseekers didn't match. There were always a few. Little Island had an ever-growing client roster, with just three companies who created the problems, people for whom no applicant was good enough and who went through staff faster than Imelda Marcos went through shoe cream.

Chief among the difficult clients, known as VIPs, in-house code for Very Ignorant People, was William Brooks.

It was wiser to transfer a call from him by saying, 'It's Mr Brooks, one of our VIP clients,' and risk being overheard, than to say, 'It's that horrible bastard from Brooks FX Stockbroking on the phone and I'm not talking to him, so you'd better.'

William Brooks, the aforementioned company's managing director, was yet again looking for a personal assistant. This was his third search in six months, the previous two assistants having decided to leave his employment abruptly.

Little Island also supplied temps, and only that morning, Faye had been on the phone to Mr Brooks's current temp who said she was giving it a month more, 'Because the money's so good, Faye, but after that, I'm out of here. He's a pig. No, strike that. Unfair to pigs.'

'We have no PAs on our books that will do for him.' Philippa, who was responsible for Mr Brooks, scanned through the file wearily. 'Out of last week's interviews, we found two wonderful candidates and he doesn't like either of them. I don't know what he wants.'

'I do. He's after a Charlize Theron doppelgänger who can type, operate Excel and doesn't mind picking up his dry-cleaning or listening to his dirty jokes,' said Faye.

'If such a person existed, she wouldn't want to work for a fat, balding executive who goes through secretaries faster than I get through Silk Cut Ultra,' Philippa said with feeling. She hated William Brooks. The only person who seemed to be able to handle him was Faye, who somehow made William rein in the worst parts of his personality and who stared him down into submission. Philippa wished she could glare at men in the steely way Faye did. Mind you, the steely gaze seemed to scare guys off too, because in the years Philippa had known Faye, she'd never had a man around. She couldn't

50

imagine Faye with a guy, anyway. There was something about Faye, something about the look on her face when the computer repairman came in and flirted with everyone in the office, which suggested Faye was one of those women who had no interest in men.

'It's a prestigious account,' Faye pointed out gently. 'We've made a lot of money out of Brooks FX and having them as clients looks great on our prospectus. William is the fly in the ointment but it would be sensible to work with him.'

Recruitment was a delicate balance. Finding the right person for the right job didn't sound too hard in principle, but, as Faye had discovered during her ten years in the industry, it could be impossible in practice. The right person in the right job might suddenly realise that her boss (sweet on recruitment day) was a control freak who insisted on just two loo breaks a day, didn't allow hot drinks at the desk in case coffee spilled on the keyboard and thought that paying a salary meant he owned her, body and soul.

'The right PA for William Brooks exists,' Faye said. 'And we'll find her.'

'Only if someone comes up with a PA robot,' muttered Philippa. 'They won't complain if they get their bums pinched.'

'He's pinched somebody's bum?' This was news to Faye. Difficult clients were one thing, sexual harassment was another.

'Well . . .' Philippa squirmed. She wasn't supposed to say. The second assistant they'd placed with William had phoned her up in tears.

Faye looked grim. 'Tell me. Chapter and verse.'

Philippa told her and gained some satisfaction from the steely look on Faye's face.

'You'll talk to him?' Grace asked warily, also seeing the look.

'I'll talk to him,' Faye agreed.

The women around the table grinned at each other. Mr Brooks was about to be taken down a peg or two. If only they could witness it, but they wouldn't. Because Faye was so famously discreet.

After the meeting, Faye poured herself another coffee and shut the door to her sanctum.

She loved her job. Recruitment suited her perfectly because it was about placing the right person in the right job and to a woman who liked the towels in her airing cupboard folded just so and in the correct place, it was very satisfying indeed. People were not towels, but life might have been easier if they were.

Over the years, she'd discovered that the main skill was interviewing potential employees and working out whether a certain job and company would suit them. With no training whatsoever, Faye turned out to be a natural at it.

'It's like you can work out precisely what sort of person they are from just twenty questions,' Grace said admiringly.

'Yes, but you've got to know which twenty questions to ask,' Faye said. She was justifiably proud of her ability, if a little amused. It was odd being successful in business by seeing through people's façades to the character within, when the biggest problems in her private life had come from being unable to do just that.

'It's easy to suss people out when you're not involved with them,' she added. 'You might never have met them before but it's possible to gauge fairly soon whether someone is hard-working, easy-going, anxious, a team player, whatever.'

In the early days, they only recruited secretarial staff and the competition was vicious, but the combination of Faye's talent and Grace's business savvy meant the company took off. Then, there would have been no question of dropping difficult clients: they needed everyone they could get. But not any more, as William Brooks was about to find out. Recruitment was a small business where everybody knew everybody. Faye phoned a couple of her old colleagues, now with other agencies, and asked what the word was on William Brooks. Fifteen minutes later, she hung up the phone a lot wiser.

After a moment or two of deep thought, she dialled the number for Brooks FX. She was put straight through to Mr Brooks, probably because he thought she bore news of a suitable PA with the required Miss World physique.

'Well,' he snapped. 'Found anyone?'

'I'm not sure Little Island is the right recruitment agency for you,' Faye began blandly.

'What?' He was instantly wrong-footed, she knew. Few agencies could afford to turn down business.

'As you know, we work with Davidson's and Marshal McGregor.' She named the two biggest stockbroking firms in the country, both of which could buy and sell Brooks FX with the contents of their petty cash boxes. 'And we have excellent relationships with both those companies, but you do appear to have peculiar requirements, Mr Brooks.'

'I'm exacting, that's all,' he snapped. 'You've been sending me morons. Call yourselves a recruitment agency . . .'

'You're more than exacting,' Faye interrupted, feeling cold rage course through her. She'd planned to do this the official way, but it was clear that Brooks needed the unorthodox approach. 'Let's put it this way, Mr Brooks, if we were offering sports massages, I believe you'd be the client insulting our therapists by asking for a massage with a "happy ending".'

'What?' exploded out of him again, and Faye grinned to herself. 'Happy ending' was code for a massage with sexual services included, the sort only available in red-light districts.

'How dare you . . . ?'

Probably nobody had ever talked to William Brooks this

53

way. She knew his sort: a bully. And, importantly, she now knew some even less pleasant things about him.

'We have our reputation to consider too, Mr Brooks,' Faye went on, the vein of ice evident in her tone. 'And we've been hearing stories from the staff we've placed with you, stories that neither of us would like to hear repeated. You see, we place temps in the equality agency too, and with some of the city's top legal firms, and we can't have any hint of scandal associated with our company.'

'What are you implying?' he roared.

'We've placed a lot of staff with Wilson Brothers too,' Faye went on. 'They're one of our best customers and actually handle our legal affairs, so if there was any, shall we say, unpleasantness, we'd naturally go to them.'

This time, there was an audible indrawn breath at the other end of the phone.

Wilson Brothers was a law firm where the senior partner just happened to be William Brooks's father-in-law. The unspoken message was that Mr Wilson would be fascinated to learn of his son-in-law's fondness for touching up his assistants.

'How about we pretend we didn't have this conversation, Mr Brooks,' Faye went on, 'and we'll resume our search for a PA for you. However, if and when we do find one, I shall be in constant communication with her and I assure you, I expect any Little Island person to be treated with the utmost respect and dignity. I'm sure you agree that bullying and sexual harassment cases can be so messy and time-consuming?'

'Oh, yes,' blustered William Brooks but the fight had gone out of him. 'I'll talk to you again, Mrs Reid,' he muttered and hung up.

Result, thought Faye, leaning back in her chair, relieved. She knew that what she'd done was unethical and that Grace would have had a coronary had she overheard, but sometimes the

54

unorthodox approach was required and this time, thankfully, it had worked. She'd never had a problem thinking outside the box when it came to business. And being tough was second nature to her now.

Some people thought it was being hard-nosed, but it wasn't: it was self-preservation.

She'd tried to instil that and a sense of personal power in Amber.

'You are responsible for you,' Faye used to repeat mantra-like. 'It's not clever to be led by other people or to do what you don't want to do, just to fit in. You have the power to do and be anything you want and to make your own choices. Believing in yourself and in your own power is one of the most important things in life.'

'Ella's mum says to behave like a little lady, not to hang around with rough boys in the park and that if a stranger tries to get you into a car, to scream,' Amber reported when she was younger and her friends thought Faye's 'be your own boss' mantra was cool. 'But Ella thinks your rules are better. I told her you were a feminist because you never let anyone walk all over you. It's because Dad's dead, I said. You had to be tougher because we were on our own.'

Faye spent an hour on paperwork, then returned her emails, by which time her eyes were weary from staring at the screen. She fetched another coffee, shut her office door firmly, kicked off her shoes and lay down on the couch for a few minutes. She was tired today. The reason still worried her. Amber had woken her up at three the night before, talking loudly to herself in her sleep, saying, 'No, I will not!' firmly.

Faye had stood at her daughter's door in case this middle-of-the-night conversation became a nightmare, but it didn't. Amber muttered 'no' a few more times before turning over and falling back into a silent sleep.

Amber had been prone to nightmares when she was a

small child and Faye, who couldn't bear to think of her darling lonely and frightened in her bed, would carry the pink-pyjama-clad little girl into her own room.

Having your baby sleep with you when you were a lonely, affection-starved single mother was probably against every bit of advice in the book, Faye knew. But she needed the comfort of her little daughter every bit as much as Amber needed her. The sweetness of that small body, energetic little limbs still padded with baby fat, gave Faye strength. No matter how tough life could be, she'd go on for Amber. Her daughter deserved the best and Faye would provide it, no matter what.

'Mama,' Amber would mutter in her lisping, babyish voice, and fall into a deeper sleep, taking up half the bed by lying sprawled sideways.

'Mama, how did I get here?' she'd say in wonder the next morning, delighted to wake up in her mother's bed. And Faye would cuddle her tightly and they'd giggle and tickle each other, and the nightmare would never be mentioned.

Now, Amber didn't have nightmares, just the odd restless night when she had a lot on her mind, like exams or last year's school play where she was in charge of painting the scenery and used to sit up in bed murmuring about more Prussian blue paint for the sky.

She was probably suffering from the most awful exam stress, Faye decided, as she sipped her coffee. There were only weeks to go, after all.

If there was anything else worrying her daughter, she'd know, wouldn't she?

Except that recently, she was beginning to think it was easier to understand total strangers searching for the perfect job than work out what was going on in her daughter's mind.

CHAPTER FOUR

One hundred and fifty miles away, Maggie Maguire didn't know what impulse made her go home that afternoon instead of trekking off to the gym. Karma? Fate? Destiny twirling a lazy finger in the human world?

Unexpectedly getting off work early meant she could have had a rare meander around Galway's shops before taking her normal Wednesday evening Pilates class. But some unknown force made Maggie walk past Extreme Fitness, bypass the lure of the bohemian boutiques, and go home to the apartment she shared with Grey. A modest third-floor flat, it was her pride and joy, especially since she'd gone ahead and painted the tiny cloakroom's wall tiles a mesmerising Indian Ocean blue.

'You can't paint tiles,' Grey had said, lounging against the door of the cloakroom, barefoot and jean-clad, as Maggie sat on the floor and read the instructions on the tin. Grey had the sort of shape that lent itself to lounging: long, long legs, a lean torso and an elegance that made women stare, admiring the swept-back leonine hair, strong, patrician face and intelligent eyes that were the same colour as his name.

'You can. It says it right here.' Maggie peered at the instructions, her nose scrunched up. Her auburn hair was held up with a big clip, but bits still straggled wispily round her freckled face. Maggie could have used cement as a hair product and red wisps would still have escaped to curl around her face.

Grey said he loved her hair: it was unruly, wild, beautiful and unpredictable. Like her.

After five years together, Maggie believed him, even though his last three girlfriends before her had been Park Avenue-type blondes with sleek hair, sleek clothes, push-up bras and shoe collections organised by Polaroid. Maggie's shoe collection was organised by age: old cowboy boots at the back of the wardrobe, new ones at the front. Her clothes were rock chick rather than chic, faded Levi's being her must-have garment. Being boyishly slim, she didn't have enough boob to fit into a push-up bra. And nobody looking at her pale freckled face with the silvery cobalt-blue eyes that showed exactly what she was thinking could have imagined Maggie having even a grain of Park Avenue Princess hauteur.

Alas, she'd have loved to be such a creature: icily cool without a hair out of place, and could never see that her wild russet beauty and eyes that belonged to an ancient Celtic warrior queen were far rarer and more precious than high-maintenance blonde glamour.

'And this is the last bit of beige in the whole place. It's got to go,' she'd added, opening the tin of paint and breathing in, as if the salty tang of the sea would drift out, scenting the air with memories of a foreign beach.

They'd bought the apartment two years ago and the previous owners had been keen on beige, beige and more beige. It was like living in a can of mushroom soup, said Maggie, who'd grown up in a quirky house on Summer Street where her bedroom had been sky blue with stars on the midnight-blue ceiling. Dad had been going through his planetarium phase and the stars had been in their correct places too. Ursa Major and Ursa Minor would not be the wrong way round when Dennis Maguire was in charge.

The cloakroom in the Galway apartment was the last room Maggie had painstakingly redecorated. Now it was all cheery blues and whites, like a small beachside restaurant from their last holiday, a glorious, special-offer week in the Seychelles. Holidays had been off the agenda for the past few months as they were broke but Maggie had an almost physical longing for the feeling of sweltering sun toasting her skin while her toes wriggled in sand.

We need a break, she thought as she stepped out of the lift on to their floor. Sun, sand and no conversations with irritated students when they'd discovered that the very book they needed for that night's rush-job essay on Greco-Roman funerary practices wasn't in its place.

Grey was a politics lecturer and Maggie was one of six librarians in the vast, modern Coolidge College library, a job she loved because it allowed her mind to wander over many varied subjects from medicine to literature. The downside was that pre-exams the stress levels of the students went up and people who'd spent six months working on the formula for the perfect Long Island Iced Tea to fuel a party suddenly required actual research materials for their courses. And Maggie was the one they got mad at when the research material in question was booked out by someone else.

'But, like, I need it today,' a radiantly pretty brunette girl had said only that morning, slim fingers raking through her hair, which irritatingly made her look even better. What hair product did she use? Maggie wondered briefly but didn't ask.

Instead, she said, 'I'm really sorry but I can't help you. We've only two copies and they're both booked out every day for the next week. You've got to make arrangements in advance with some textbooks.'

'Well, thank you very much,' snapped the girl sarcastically.

59

'You've been a great help, I must say.' And she marched off in high dudgeon.

'You can't win 'em all,' commiserated her colleague Shona. 'Still, she's not like the back of a bus, so she can always sleep with her prof if the going gets tough.'

'Shona! That's so sexist. I thought you were reading *The Female Eunuch*?'

'I did and it's marvellous, but I'm on to the new Jackie Collins now. I know Germaine Greer wouldn't approve, but I'd have slept with my prof if it'd have improved my degree,' countered Shona wistfully. 'He was sex on legs, so it wouldn't have been a hardship.' Shona's degree had been in European Literature. 'When he talked about the Heart of Darkness that was in all of us, I swear, I felt a shiver run right down my spine into my knickers.'

Shona was, in fact, happily married but she was an irrepressible flirt and batted her eyelashes at every passing cute guy, despite many weary conversations with the head librarian about appropriate behaviour in the workplace. 'Just because I've eaten doesn't mean I can't look at the menu,' was her motto.

Fortunately her husband Paul, whom she adored and would never cheat on, was merely amused by all this.

'Professors don't have sex with students, except in the fevered imaginations of people like you,' Maggie retorted. 'Besides, she's in third-year history. Have you seen Prof Wolfowitz? Brilliant, yes. Beddable, no. He is totally bald except for that one eyebrow. Every time I see him, I want to pluck a few of the middle hairs out and give him two eyebrows instead of one.'

'Maggie, Maggie,' sighed Shona. 'The eyebrow is immaterial. Sleeping your way to success has precisely nothing to do with how good-looking the powerful person is. You may wear scuffed cowboy boots and a tough attitude, but you're Haven't-a-Clue Barbie at heart. You don't have a calculating bone in your body – apart from the one hot Dr Grey Stanley puts there, of course.' Shona laughed like a drain at her own joke.

Maggie groaned. She was used to Shona by now. They'd become fast friends from the moment they'd met on Maggie's first day in the library, where she discovered that her new friend's second degree subject was indubitably Teasing: Honours Module. Now Maggie leaned over and swatted Shona on the arm with her ruler. 'Brat.'

'Haven't-a-Clue Barbie.'

'Slapper.'

'Oh, thank you,' Shona said, pretending to preen. She was impossible to shock. 'Shona O'Slapper, I like that. Now, can you swap shifts with me? I know you're on till six tonight, but I'll do it and you can go early if you'll do tomorrow afternoon for me? You could spend another hour honing your body in Extreme Fatness,' she wheedled. Shona had accompanied Maggie to the gym once and hated it, hence the new name.

'Are you and Paul going out?' inquired Maggie.

'I'm providing a shoulder to cry on,' Shona informed her. 'Ross has broken up with Johann.' Ross was a hairdresser who lived in the apartment below Shona and Paul, providing the perfect opportunity for Shona's fag-haggery and giving Paul a chance to watch football on the television while she and Ross sat in the apartment below, rewatching old *Will & Grace* episodes and bitching happily.

'He's inconsolable, even though he whined all the time they were going out about how insensitive Johann was and how he didn't like Nureyev.' Nureyev was Ross's beloved pet, a lop-eared rabbit, who was spoiled beyond belief and had his own Vuitton bunny carrier as well as a purple velvet collar with his name spelled out in diamanté. He lived in luxury in Ross's Philippe Starck-style kitchen and was house-trained to

61

use a cat litter box. 'Nobody's ever truly gorgeous until they dump you, right? We're partying to get him over it.'

'On a Wednesday?'

'Woe's day, sweetie, as the ancient Danes would say. It's apt.'

'Who's looking after Nureyev?'

'We're going to leave the Discovery channel on for him. He loves all those shows about meerkats.'

Maggie was still laughing at the idea of the rabbit sulkily glued to the television when she got to her own front door and pulled out her keys.

The mortice lock was undone. Grey must have got home early, she thought with a smile. That was good, they could have a blissfully long evening together. Good call, Maguire, she thought as she let herself in. Sometimes a girl's gotta know when to miss stretching on a mat so she can stretch on a bed. And for all of his intellectual cool, Grey knew some pelvic contortions the Pilates teacher had never taught. It was funny though, Grey was supposed to be at a meeting – perhaps it had been cancelled?

'Shouldn't be too late, honey,' Grey had said on the phone earlier. 'You've got your class tonight so I'll pick up Thai food on the way home.' Grey believed in sharing cooking duties, although he preferred takeout to actual slaving and stirring with wooden spoons.

Inside the apartment, Maggie heard muted noises coming from the apartment's lone bedroom. Grey must be watching the TV, she thought, and, shedding her possessions as she went, handbag on to the floor, jacket on the couch, she crossed the small living room, went down the hall and pushed their bedroom door open.

The door was still swinging open when Maggie stopped on the threshold, frozen.

Grey was on the bed, naked and lying underneath a woman, also naked.

The woman's hair hung like a silken curtain, erotically half covering a lingerie-model body with a hand-span waist and high, perfect C-cup breasts.

Three mouths opened in surprise. Maggie twisted her head sideways to try to get the scene to make sense. It was like a clever illustration in a psychoanalyst's office, a bizarre, mind-bending scene designed to make you question everything you knew: what's wrong with this picture?

Well, Doctor, that's our bed with our duvet tangled up on the floor, and my side table pretty much the way I left it this morning with a book open on it. And there's the photo of me and Grey outside the cathedral in Barcelona, but in the bed, there's this strange blonde girl with an unbelievable body arched over my boyfriend who has – well, had – an erection. And there really is no other explanation for this apart from the obvious.

'Maggie, I'm so sorry, I never meant you to see, I wouldn't hurt you for anything,' Grey said urgently, wriggling out from under the blonde girl so fast that she squealed.

Maggie didn't answer him. She couldn't. She just stared in disbelief.

Politicians were supposed to be excellent at wriggling out of embarrassing situations. Perhaps Grey taught that, too, along with analysis of world power structures and globalisation.

Bile rose in Maggie's throat and she turned without a word and ran to the tiny cloakroom she'd decorated with such pride. Student. That girl had to be one of Grey's students. Someone who'd possibly stood in the college library and looked calculatingly at Maggie sitting at the research desk, pleased to realise that her rival was older. Perhaps wondering what Grey saw in thirty-year-old Maggie with her tangle of wild hair when he could have a twenty-one-year-old with a silken mane like a hair commercial, and a va-va-voom figure with the peach-bloom skin of youth.

Students were always getting crushes on Grey. The two of them joked about it, because it seemed so funny, despite Shona's stories. Grey was miles away from the image of a fusty academic with woolly hair, badly fitting jackets and mismatched socks. When they had first met, five years previously, when she was finding her feet in the city, Maggie herself had found it hard to believe he held a doctorate in political science. At a start-of-term college party, he'd stood out among the soberly dressed professorial types. He wore jeans, and, around his neck, a couple of narrow leather coils from which hung a piece of obsidian that glittered like his cloudy grey eyes. Maggie had heard of Dr Grey Stanley, a brilliant thinker who'd resisted attempts by various political leaders to advise their parties and who was the author of several widely read articles on the state of the country. Nobody had mentioned how jaw-droppingly handsome he was.

'Hey, Red,' he'd said, tangling long fingers in the tendrils of her auburn hair. 'Can I get you a glass of the vinegar that passes for wine round here?'

Maggie, tomboy extraordinaire whose shoulder-length hair was one of her few concessions to femininity, would normally have given the death glare to any strange guy who dared to touch her. But this man, all heat and masculinity so close to her, made it hard to breathe, never mind shoot murderous glares. She exhaled, suddenly glad she'd worn the black camisole that hung low on her small breasts, the fabric starkly dark against her milky white skin. Her skin was true redhead type, so white it was almost blue, she sometimes joked.

Grey stared at her as if milky white with a smattering of tiny freckles was his favourite colour combination. The party in a draughty hall on the Coolidge College campus was full of fascinating, clever people with IQs that went off the scale, and he'd chosen her. Even now, no matter how many times

64

Shona told her she was beautiful and that Grey Stanley was lucky to have her, Maggie shook her head in denial. It was the other way round, she knew.

'Maggie . . .'

As she slammed the cloakroom door shut and slid the lock, she heard Grey's anxious voice outside. He rarely called her Red any more. Red was the girl he'd fallen in love with, the feisty redhead who was fiercely independent, who needed nobody in her life, thank you very much. She was so different from the Park Avenue Princesses, she must have struck him as a challenge he couldn't resist. But five years of coupledom had surgically removed her independence and now, she realised, she had become like a tiger in a zoo: lazily captive and unable to survive in the wild.

She leaned over the toilet bowl and the cloudy remains of her lunchtime chicken wrap came up. Again and again, she retched until there was nothing left in her except loss and fear.

She was the old Maggie again, the one who hadn't yet learned to hide her anxiety under an armour of feistiness. Stupid Maggie who'd never imagined that Grey would cheat on her. Just like Stupid Maggie from years ago. It was a shock to feel like that again. She was so sure she'd left it all behind her. The memory of those years in St Ursula's, when her life had been one long torment of bullying, came to her. She'd had four years of hell at the hands of the bullies and it had marked her for ever. Now she was right back there – reeling from the shock, sick with fear.

When she could retch no more, she sank on to the floor. From this unusual vantage point, the bathroom had turned out well, she realised. The colours were so pretty and it was so carefully done. Even Grey had said so.

'You're wasted in the college library,' he'd laughed the day she finished it. 'You should have your own decorating business.

The Paint Queen: specialising in no-hope projects. Your dad could consult.' Grey had seen and admired the planetarium ceiling in her old bedroom in the house on Summer Street.

'Lovely,' he'd said and joked that her parents were sweetly eccentric despite their outwardly conservative appearance.

Grey's parents were both lawyers, now divorced. He'd grown up with money, antiques and housekeepers. She couldn't imagine his French-cuff-wearing father ever doing something as hands-on as painting stars on the ceiling for his son. Or his mother, she of the perfect blonde bob, professionally blow-dried twice a week, breathlessly explaining about winning €75 in the lottery and planning what she'd do with the money, the way Maggie's mum had.

'My parents are not eccentric,' Maggie had told Grey defensively. 'They're just enthusiastic, interested in things . . .'

'I know, honey.' Grey had been contrite. 'I love your mum and dad. They're great.'

But it occurred to her that Grey had been right. Her parents weren't worldly or astute. They were endlessly naïve, innocents abroad, and they'd brought her up to be just like them. Blindly trusting.

She put her head on her knees and tried not to think about anything. Numb the brain. Concentrate on a candle burning. Wasn't that the trick?

There was noise outside in the hall, muffled speech, the front door slamming. Grey's voice, low and anxious, saying: 'Maggie, come out, please. We should talk, honey.'

She didn't reply. He didn't try to open the door but she was glad it was locked. She had absolutely no idea of what she'd say to him if she saw him. There was silence for a while.

After half an hour, he returned, sounding harder this time, more lecturer than contrite boyfriend. 'I'm going out to get us some Thai takeout. You can't sit in there all night.'

66

'I can!' shrieked Maggie, roused to yell at him with an unaccustomed surge of temper. How dare he tell her what she could and couldn't do.

'You *can* stay in there all night,' Grey said patiently, in the voice he used to explain difficult concepts to stupid people at parties, 'if that's what you want to do, but you ought to come out and eat something. I won't be long.' The front door slammed again.

Gone to phone his nubile student, perhaps? To say that Maggie would get over it and then it would be business as usual.

We'll have to use your place instead of mine.

Grey mightn't like it so much if he had to bonk his lover in some grotty student digs, though. He liked the smooth crispness of clean sheets, a power shower and wooden floors where you could comfortably walk barefoot without wondering how many other zillions of people had walked barefoot on it before, shedding flakes of dry skin. He'd been brought up in luxury. Before she'd met Grey, Maggie had known nothing of the world of Egyptian cotton sheets with a 400-thread count. To her, sheets came in only two varieties: fitted and flat.

Maggie stuck her ear up against the door and listened. Nothing. She unlocked the door, came out and looked around the apartment, thinking that it no longer looked like the home of her dreams, only an identikit apartment trying hard to be elegant and different, but still looking exactly like its neighbours.

Everything she had achieved had been done on a budget, from the bargain basement African-inspired coffee table to the Moroccan silk cushion covers she'd bought on a street stall and which were now woolly with loose threads. Despite the kudos of being an ultra-clever doctor of studies whose lectures were always packed, Grey wasn't paid well.

The library paid less. But Maggie was used to not having money. She'd grown up that way. Making do, managing: they were the words she'd lived with as a child. There had been great happiness in her home, for all the lack of hard cash and the shiny new things some of the other girls had. Money wasn't important to her. Love, security, safety, happiness were. She'd tried so hard to make their home beautiful, the heart of their love. What a waste of time that had been.

Sinking down on the low couch, still numb, she wondered what she should do next. Storm off? Or wait for Grey so she could rage at him that since he'd cheated, he should be the one to go.

Maggie's Guide to Life didn't cover this one.

He'd tell her not to be stupid. She could almost hear him saying it, in measured tones that made any argument he laid out sound entirely plausible.

Honestly, Maggie, listen to yourself. There's absolutely no point in being hasty. Think about this, don't give in to some primitive emotional response. It was just sex.

Just sex. One of Grey's endlessly philosophising colleagues had probably written a paper on the subject: how *just sex* was occasionally justifiable. If the partner in question was away; if the potential bonkee was particularly gorgeous; if nobody would ever know.

Even with her eyes open, Maggie could still see Grey and the blonde on her bed, imagine it all: the blonde's moans of pleasure as she rose to orgasm; Grey saying: 'Oh baby, oh baby, that's so good.' The words he murmured to Maggie, her words. But they'd never be truly hers again.

Although there was nothing left inside her stomach, Maggie felt she might be sick again. No, she wouldn't wait for him to explain it to her. Grabbing her handbag from where she'd dropped it so happily what felt like a lifetime ago, she ran out of the apartment. If she was somewhere else, a place where every single ornament didn't remind her of Grey, she might be able to work out what she'd do next. A bus was coming down the road, the bus to Salthill where she could walk on the beach. Without hesitation she ran to the stop and got on.

CHAPTER FIVE

On Summer Street, the sun had shifted in the afternoon sky. Christie Devlin's back garden was bathed in a golden glow that lit up the velvety roses and turned the cream-coloured trellises a glittering white. It was the sort of afternoon Christie loved.

James had phoned to say he'd caught an earlier train and should be home by seven instead of nine. The postman had arrived with a late-afternoon bounty of the gadget catalogues Christie loved to devour at night, picking out useful things she'd buy if she could afford them. The dogs, too tired of the heat to clamour for another walk, were content to lie in the shade of the kitchen door, dreaming happily, two sets of paws twitching.

Sitting on her tiny terrace with a cup of iced tea, Christie was supposed to be marking art history essays for tomorrow morning, but she couldn't concentrate.

The heat, the glory of her garden, James coming home early, none of it mattered. Nothing except the fear that sat hard and stone-like in the pit of her stomach, telling her there was something very wrong.

*   *   *

In her kitchen seven houses away, Una Maguire was standing on a chair looking for a spare tin of baking powder in the larder cupboard beside the fridge. She'd decided to bake a Victoria sponge for the church fair and there had been only a scraping of powder in the old tin.

'Dennis, have you been at my cupboards again?' she yelled good-humouredly at her husband. It was a joke. As their daughter, Maggie, was well aware, Dennis Maguire barely knew how to open the cupboards in the kitchen and his only domestic duty was washing and drying. He never put away the dishes he'd dried. Una did that.

For years, it had been Maggie's job in the production line of washing and drying, but she was long gone with her own life, and the duty fell to Una again.

'Never touched them,' Dennis yelled back from the living room where he was putting the final touches to the model of a Spitfire that had taken two weeks to complete. The construction was entirely accurate: Dennis had checked in his *Jane's Aircraft Guide*.

'Don't believe you,' teased back Una, over-reaching past a pack of semolina because she was sure she'd seen the red metallic glint of the baking powder tin. With a swiftness that surprised her, the chair tilted, she lost her footing and fell to the floor, her left leg crumpling underneath her.

The pain was as shocking as it was instantaneous. Cruelly sharp, like a blade neatly inserted.

'Dennis,' whimpered Una, knowing that she'd done something serious. 'Dennis, come quickly.'

In the comfort of her bedroom at number 18 Summer Street, Amber Reid lay in her boyfriend's arms and heard the sound of the ambulance droning up the street to the Maguires' house. Amber had no interest in looking out the window to see what had happened. The world didn't exist outside

71

the tangled sheets of her bed, still warm from their love-making.

'What are you thinking?' she asked Karl.

She couldn't help herself, even though every magazine she'd ever read said that this sort of question was a Bad Idea. She didn't think she was a needy person, but there was something about this intimate moment after lovemaking, that made her want to know. She'd been a physical part of Karl. She wanted to be inside his head too, inside for ever, always a part of him.

'Nothing. Except how beautiful you are.'

Karl shifted, laying his leg over hers, trapping her.

As fresh heat swelled in her belly, Amber realised that there was nothing more erotic than the feeling of naked skin against naked skin. Just lying there after the most incredible lovemaking was almost beyond description.

She ran questing fingers along his powerful chest, feeling the curve of his muscles, the sensitive nubs of his nipples, so different from hers.

She'd seen men's bodies before, but never fully naked except on a canvas or on a plinth carved from finest Carrara marble. And marble felt different from the warm, living beauty of a man's body beside hers, inside hers. Desire rushed through her veins again. Why had nobody told her love-making could be like this? All those talks about pregnancy, AIDS and being emotionally ready, nobody had said how utterly addictive it all was.

'We should get up,' Karl said. 'It's after six. Your mother will be home soon.'

Half six, Amber had said. Her mother ran her life on a strict schedule. Half six home, change out of her office suit by 6.35, dinner on the table – pre-prepared from the night before, obviously – by seven.

Amber used to love the comfort of their evening routine.

It made home seem like a refuge. No matter how much life changed in the outside world, her mother put dinner on the table at seven. But lately, Amber found herself telling Ella that when she moved out of home, she'd never have a schedule as rigid as her mother's as long as she lived. Life was about being a free spirit, not a slave to the clock or the powers of good kitchen cleaning products, or having to hear the oft-repeated phrase 'a good education and you can go anywhere, Amber'.

Right now, education suddenly seemed so boring. Her mother's view of life was stifling and there was no escape from it. And Mum would hate Karl, who was a free spirit, would hate his intrusion into their tightly run lives. It wouldn't be the two of them any more. It would be a different twosome, Amber decided firmly: her and Karl.

She slithered over until she was astride Karl, her long tawny mane a tangle over his lightly tanned shoulders. 'We don't have to get up,' she said, smiling. 'We've ages yet.'

There was so much they could do in that precious twenty minutes.

'And if my mother arrives home early, you can always hop out the back window and climb down the flat roof of the kitchen.'

Her mother was still paying off the credit union loan for the kitchen extension, a fact that often brought a worried look to her face.

Money: that was another subject Amber never wanted to worry about again, along with timetables and exams. Karl was going to be a famous musician and they'd have loads of money. Enough to pay off her mother's debts, enough to buy anything Amber wanted.

Just once, she'd love the thrill of shopping and never looking at the price tag. Wouldn't it be glorious to spend without worrying or feeling guilty over it?

'The neighbours will call the cops if they see a strange bloke hop out of your bedroom on to the kitchen roof and down the lane.' Karl put both hands around her waist and splayed his fingers.

Amber was proud of her tiny waist. She'd inherited her mother's hourglass figure, although, thank God, she hadn't inherited her total lack of interest in looking good. Her mother wouldn't have been seen dead in the clothes Amber wore: slivers of vintage fabric that barely covered her breasts, low-rise jeans that revealed more than a hint of bare skin. Mum just never bothered making herself look good or showing off her waist.

Amber arched her back as Karl's fingers moved up to cradle her ribcage. She didn't want him to go. They had plenty of time.

'Everyone's at work or cooking kids' dinners,' she said, feeling sympathy for anyone engaged in such boring duties. 'Nobody will see you.'

There was only one person on the street who might possibly know she had phoned in sick to school and might wonder at her having a strange guy in the house, and that was Mrs Devlin.

Amber approved of Christie Devlin, even if she was old and, therefore, should be totally wrinkly, boring and incapable of remembering what it was like to feel alive. For all Christie's silver hair, she had a way of looking at Amber that said she knew what was going on in the girl's head. Scary. Amber wondered if Christie would know by looking at her that Amber had just had the most incredible sex of her life.

Losing-her-virginity sex. She'd nearly done it eighteen months ago, with cute but dopey Liam, who was a friend of Ella's youngest brother. She'd called a halt to the proceedings just in time. Liam's hand was burrowing into her jeans and she'd realised that she was about to have sex with a guy just to see what it was like rather than because she would die then and there if she didn't.

A woman had the right to say no at any point, her mother had said in one of her talks about sex.

'Whaddya mean, you don't want to after all?' demanded Liam, who clearly didn't agree with Amber's mother on the whole issue of coitus interruptus.

'I mean no,' said Amber. 'No means no. Got it?'

And although Liam hadn't spoken to her since – not a big worry – she was glad she'd said no when she did. Imagine having to live your whole life knowing you'd lost your virginity to an ordinary guy like Liam when you could have the memory of a man like Karl Evans?

This was sex with a man of the world, a twenty-five-year-old man with a future. He was her future. She was going to travel the world with him and discover life, with a big L. She'd be eighteen in less than three weeks. She could do what she wanted then. Nobody could stop her.

'So you'll come with us?' he asked, returning to the subject they'd discussed earlier, before they'd fallen into bed. 'If we're going to work with a producer in New York, we'll be gone at least six months. I'd hate to be away from you. I couldn't bear that.'

'I'd hate to be away from you too,' Amber answered, stroking his skin with exploring fingers.

This was love. Pure contentment flowed through her veins. Karl was so crazy about her that he wanted her to travel with his band to America to record their album.

He needed her, he said. He'd been writing songs like a man possessed since they'd met. 'You're my muse,' he'd said.

And Amber, who'd been told all her life how talented and special she was, believed him. She and Karl: they were the twosome now.

As the ambulance carted Una Maguire and her frantic

husband Dennis off to hospital, Amber gazed at her lover with shining, besotted eyes and imagined all the wonderful times they'd have. Her mother would flip when she discovered Amber wasn't going to art college after all, but Amber was an adult now, wasn't she? She could do what she liked. That, surely, was the point of all those years of 'you have the power to do what you want' conversations. Amber would do what she wanted and although she hated hurting her mum, Faye would have to live with it.

Faye left work early so she could dash into the mini-market near home and pick up a few last-minute bits. They were out of basmati rice and she'd defrosted a home-cooked vegetarian korma the night before.

Ordinary rice wouldn't work, it had to be basmati.

Near the checkout, she dallied briefly by the ranks of magazines and papers. She loved the interior decoration magazines but they were all so expensive, so she didn't splash out very often. But she felt weary this evening, and the house felt lonely when Amber was upstairs at her desk bent over old exam papers. Faye could do with a treat. Finally choosing a magazine with a supplement on bedrooms, she looked down and her eye was caught by the lead story in the local free newspaper.

Developer's Deal With Council: 25 Apartments in Summer St Park

She picked it up and moved to the checkout.

'They must have got it wrong. They can't be talking about the park here, opposite my house?' she said to the cashier.

'That's the one,' the woman said, scanning the groceries. 'Shame to rip up that lovely little park. I don't know how they get away with that type of thing. There won't be a

76

bit of green left around here if the developers get their way.'

'But it's tiny,' Faye protested. 'And surely nobody's allowed to buy an actual park?'

A queue appeared behind her and Faye was in too much of a rush to stop to read the story, so she stuffed the paper into the top of her grocery bag and left. In her car, she read it all quickly with mounting horror.

The pavilion in the park was falling down and the council had decided to sell it, and the half-acre of land that accompanied it, to a developer in return for the developer building another park and a community centre on a sliver of waste ground a mile away.

'We're not tearing up the park,' insisted a council spokesperson. 'The park is staying. The pavilion was never part of the park. People just thought it was. We've every right to sell it because we can't afford to renovate it and it's dangerous, besides. Summer Street will still have its park.'

Except that it will be half the size and have a dirty big apartment block cutting out the sun, Faye thought furiously.

She drove home angrily. Amber would be just as annoyed to hear about this, she loved that little park. Honestly, why did things have to change all the time?

The evening walkers were out in force when Maggie left the beach at Salthill and got the bus back into the city. The bus was only half full and she sat a few seats behind a group of schoolgirls still in uniform.

Half listening to their chatter, she stared listlessly out the window. She'd come to no conclusions because she couldn't think about Grey. Her mind refused to cooperate, racing off on ideas of its own. She had to work late the next evening instead of Shona. Were they out of coffee? Should she and

Grey go to see the new Pixar film? Anything was better than thinking about what had just happened.

From the depths of her handbag, her mobile phone rang. On auto-pilot, Maggie retrieved it, saw that her father was calling and clicked answer.

'Dad,' she said, managing to sound bright. Her entire world hadn't just crashed and burned, no. All was well. Faking happiness – wasn't that what communicating with your parents was all about?

'What's up, Dad?'

'Hello, love, it's your mum.'

Maggie's hand flew to her chest.

'She's in hospital, she's broken her leg.'

A breath Maggie didn't know she'd been holding was released. 'I thought you were going to tell me something terrible,' she whispered, cupping her forehead in one hand with relief.

'It is terrible,' he went on. 'Your mother insisted they did a bone density scan in the middle of it all, and it seems she's got osteoporosis. The doctor says he doesn't know why she hasn't broken bones before.' Her father had to stop talking for a moment and gulped. 'I don't know what to do, Maggie. You know how your mum copes with everything and all, but she's taking this badly. She keeps saying she's fine but she's been crying. Your mother crying.'

He sounded shocked. Una Maguire could see the silver lining in every cloud and had taught her daughter that a smile was easier to achieve than a frown. Mum never cried, except at films where a child was hurt or the dog died.

'Maggie, I know it's not fair but could you come home for a couple of days ... ?'

Maggie could imagine her father standing obediently outside the hospital entrance, not using his mobile phone

78

inside as per the instructions on the hospital walls, even though nobody else obeyed them.

Dad, with his wide-open eyes, his few strands of hair and his endearing inability to deal with daily life to the extent that Maggie felt he ought to wear permanent L-plates. Dad, who'd never seen her mum cry over anything.

'I'll be home tomorrow,' she said. 'Don't worry about a thing.'

It was, after all, the solution to everything.

You're running away, said a voice in her head: a voice that sounded remarkably like Shona when she was in Dr Phil mode. Shona loved Dr Phil and felt that America's favourite television doctor's principles could be applied to every life situation.

Are you doing the right thing? Ask yourself that. Would you advise a friend in a similar situation to do what you're doing? Will running away solve your problem? Dr Phil asked all the right questions and so did Shona.

No, no and no. Maggie knew the answers. But Dr Phil hadn't the benefit of Maggie Maguire's Guide to Life.

Don't stuff your bra to make your A-cups look like B-cups. Boys won't get close enough to notice but nasty girls from school will. Nobody wants to be No-Tit Maguire for a whole month, as Maggie knew from experience.

Guys who say things like 'I've never met anyone like you' are not lying, exactly, but probably don't mean it the way you think they do.

Maggie had a new piece of advice to add to the Guide:

When in doubt, put your running shoes on. Nothing will improve but at least you don't have to stare your defeat in the face on a daily basis. And if you can't see it, surely it can't be there?

In a trendy little internet café close to the apartment, she ordered a latte and a session on the web. Flicking through flights to Dublin, she found one that left the following afternoon, giving her time to pack as well as to negotiate with the library for emergency leave. When she'd booked it, she knew there was only one more big task left: to go home and say goodbye to Grey.

Goodbye Grey, I'm going and we're selling up so you'll have to take your jail bait somewhere else from now on.

No, too bitter.

Bye, Grey, I'm going home to Dublin for a while to think. You cheating son of a bitch.

Again, too bitter.

Maybe she ought to stick at *Goodbye, Grey.*

When she got back to the apartment, Grey and the remains of a Thai meal were both in the living-room area. Maggie didn't feel even mildly hungry.

The words 'You lying, cheating bastard' ran round in her head like a washing machine on final spin.

'Hello,' she said. See, not bitter.

'Honey.' Grey leapt off the couch and went to touch her, but the frozen look in Maggie's eyes stopped him. They stood several feet apart, staring at each other, misery on both their faces.

'I am so sorry,' Grey said, and he sounded it.

He honestly was sorry. But sorry that he'd had sex with a stunning blonde student or sorry he'd been caught? Bastard.

'I love you. You might not believe that, but I do.'

'Then why did you do it?' Maggie asked. She hadn't meant to ask anything, had meant to tell him bluntly she was going home for a while. But the question had shot out of her mouth before she could stop it.

Grey's gaze didn't falter, she had to give him that. 'I don't know,' he said dismally. 'She was there, I could have her ...

it sounds dumb, but I still love you, Maggie. You're different, special.'

The spinning washing machine still kept rattling out 'lying, cheating bastard' as Maggie struggled to make sense of Grey's words. Her heart was broken and this was his sticking plaster?

'She was there? Is that your only excuse, Grey? She was bloody well there? If I'm so special, why would you even want to make love with someone else whether she was there or not? If I'm so special, then you wouldn't want to look crossways at another woman, never mind screw one in our bed. IN OUR BED!'

He looked taken aback at this. Maggie was not a shouter.

'It wasn't making love, it was sex. It's not what you and I have. That's . . .'

'Don't tell me,' she snapped, 'special.' Infidelity must have a previously undetected side effect of robbing people of their linguistic skills. Even Grey. She had never known Grey to run out of words before.

'I'm not explaining it correctly,' he began.

'Oh yes, you are, and it still doesn't make sense. You're the one who says he's logical, I'm supposed to be the klutzy one who forgets her bank card numbers and can't program her mobile phone.' Maggie knew her voice was rising but she couldn't help it. If Grey was tongue-tied, her word power was on 110 per cent. 'So how can you come up with such an illogical explanation? If I'm so different and special, you shouldn't want sex or love with anyone other than me. Simple. QED. That's what I thought I was getting when we moved in together: fidelity, monogamy, no threesomes. Did I miss the briefing where you said we'd sleep with other people? Or were you just lying through your teeth when you said that I was the sort of woman you wanted, not a pneumatic blonde like all your previous girlfriends?'

'I wasn't lying and I do believe in fidelity, really,' Grey

said helplessly. He sat on the edge of the armchair, running a hand through his hair. He had such long, sensitive fingers, like a pianist, fingers that could elicit a ready response from Maggie. He still looked handsome and desirable, with sexily rumpled hair as if he'd been so lost in his books he had forgotten to comb it. Maggie, who spent all her time surrounded by books, had always found this combination of brains and beauty utterly captivating. She could totally understand Ms Peachy Skin wanting to sleep with him. Grey was gorgeous, clever, and powerful within his sphere, all wrapped up in one package.

Just not faithful.

'I love you, Grey, I don't look at other men,' she said. 'I don't think about anyone else but you, I almost don't see anyone else but you. If there was anyone else there, if Brad Pitt and George Clooney and Wesley Snipes and anyone else you can think of were there for the taking, you know what?' She paused. 'I'd still say no.'

'I know, I'm sorry, so sorry.' The long piano-player's fingers ran through his hair again and for a flicker of an instant, Maggie thought of his hands running through the girl's hair in the throes of passion, twisting it and pulling gently like he did with Maggie.

'I love your hair,' he'd mutter when they were naked together. Maggie almost never cut it now. Grey loved its length lying tangled on the pillow as he hung over her, cradling her face before he kissed her. He thought she was feminine and sexy, things Maggie had never felt in her life until he'd come along and made her feel them. Now he'd taken all that away.

When her mother or Shona or other people said she was beautiful, she didn't believe them. They loved her, they were being kind to her. But when Grey said it, she had believed him. He made her beautiful because she glowed from being with him.

82

That he had so much power over her made her feel helpless now. Going back to the sort of woman he'd had before her made it a double betrayal – a blonde with curves that Maggie would never have. She felt so hurt that she wanted to hurt him too.

'You're lying. You're not sorry, only sorry I got home early and ruined it all. You screwed her. In. Our. Bed,' she said slowly. 'That's not love and respect.' She paused. 'Were there others?'

A strange look touched his face briefly, a look of sheer guilt, and it was gone so quickly that only someone who loved his face and knew it in every mood would have noticed. But Maggie was that person. She noticed.

'No,' he said. She didn't believe him.

The armchair seemed to rise up to greet her. Collapsing into it, she hugged her knees to her chest, a gesture that said 'keep out'.

There had been others, of that she was sure and she wasn't strong enough to hear about them. Her mother was ill, crying and not coping. Her father was asking for her help. Maggie's world was topsy-turvy.

'Just tell me, what's so hard about fidelity?' she whispered, afraid she knew the answer.

It had to be her fault. This confirmed what she'd known all along. She'd always felt lucky to have Grey, astonished that he was with her.

Someone like Grey could manage faithfulness with other people, with one of those icy blondes, but not with her. For one of those women, the right sort of wife for a man with a political future in front of him, he'd have got married. But Maggie obviously wasn't the right sort of wife for him. She was an experiment between the Carolyn Bessette Kennedy types, the trophy women. She wasn't worth giving up other women for. That was what this was all about.

The demons of anxiety and the self-doubt she'd grown up with rushed back howling into her mind and it was as if they'd never been away.

'I'm sorry, Maggie, I swear this will never happen again, never.' He looked up at her but Maggie was away in her head, remembering the years when she'd lived with a permanent clench of anxiety in her gut.

Sunday nights were the worst, when the weekend was careening to an end and Monday loomed, Monday with Sandra Brody and her taunting crew who'd made it their mission in life to destroy Maggie Maguire. Maggie had never done anything to them but that didn't appear to matter. Maggie was the chosen scapegoat. Daily verbal torture and cruel tricks were her punishment. The self-loathing – because it had to be her fault, hadn't it? – felt just like it did now.

'I'm sorry, Maggie,' Grey repeated. 'I don't know why I did it. I wouldn't hurt you for the world.'

'Really?' she asked with a bitter laugh. Why was he bothering to pretend? She'd prefer it if he told her the truth: that he loved her but just not enough. She wasn't quite good enough.

'You're different, Maggie,' Grey began and sat at her feet, pulling both her hands from around her knees, trying to make her hold him. 'I love you, I never meant to hurt you. I am so, so sorry. Can't you forgive me?'

She whisked her hands away, but he laid his dark head on her chair, pleading, imploring. It would be so easy to reach out and touch him, make it all go away and start again. Go on holiday, sell the apartment, move somewhere else, anything to paper over the crack. Maggie felt her fingers reach out, an inch away from brushing the softness of his hair.

Marriage – that would be the ultimate Band-Aid. A sign that they were together despite it all. Her mum would love it if she got married. Poor Mum, always hoping for the fairy-tale ending for her daughter. But Grey had never discussed marriage with her. Perhaps she wasn't worth that, either.

Maggie's hand stilled on its way to his hair. She could forgive Grey, she could forgive him almost anything. But then it would happen again. Other women, who'd work at the university and pity her, understanding that a prince like Grey wouldn't be satisfied with just one woman. That was the price a woman like Maggie had to pay to be with a man like Grey. Why hadn't she realised that there was a trade-off, a price?

She pulled her hand away. She couldn't pay that price.

Suddenly, her running shoes seemed very inviting. Even home, the confines of Summer Street where her life had never been storybook perfect, was better than this.

It was familiar, somewhere she could lick her wounds. Shona and Dr Phil were probably wrong about running away. Now, staying was the hard option and running was easy.

Christie had cooked a beautiful goulash by the time she heard James's key in the lock.

Goulash in honour of her dear Hungarian friend, Lenkya, who'd once said, 'You can kill a man or cure him in the kitchen.' This had been nearly forty years before, when Christie's culinary expertise extended to making porridge or boiling eggs.

'Cooking is the heart of the home and is the place where the woman is queen,' Lenkya pointed out in the husky Hungarian accent that would have made the phone book sound fascinating, should she ever want to recite it.

Lenkya had lived below Christie in a house on Dunville Avenue that contained a veritable warren of bedsits.

'If you can kill in the kitchen, I'll end up in the dock for murder,' Christie had said merrily.

She was dark-haired then and when she and Lenkya walked the half-mile to Ranelagh to buy groceries, people often mistook the two women with their flashing dark eyes, hand-span waists and lustrous curls for sisters.

'You should learn to cook,' said Lenkya, who could rustle up the tenderest stew from a handful of root vegetables, a scattering of herbs and a scraggy piece of meat. 'How have you never learned before this? In my country, women learn to look after themselves. I can grow vegetables, raise chickens, kill chickens, pouf –' She twisted both hands round an imaginary chicken's neck. 'Like that. If you are hungry, you soon learn.'

'My mother cooked for all of us, my father, my brothers and sister,' Christie told her. It was harder to explain the family dynamics which meant cooking was the only power her mother had ever had. Under Christie's father's thumb all the time, it was only when Maura was in front of her stove that she was in charge. If it was possible to kill or cure a man in the kitchen, Christie wondered how her mother had resisted the impulse to kill her overbearing husband.

James hadn't known Lenkya well, but he'd been benefiting from her cooking expertise ever since. Food was all about love, Christie knew now. Feeding your family, giving them chicken soup when they were sick, and apple cake to take away the bitterness in their mouth when they were lovelorn: that was how you could cure them. Love and healing flew out of her kitchen into her home. Her life was nothing like her poor mother's and she had no need of killing.

'Hello, Christie.' James put his arms round her and held her tightly. He smelled of the train, of dusty streets and other people's cigarette smoke. He looked, as he so often did these days, tired and in need of a long, long sleep.

'Hard day?' Christie took his briefcase and jacket, resisting the impulse to push him up to their room, tuck him into bed and make him stay there until the exhausted look had gone from his face.

'Ah no, fine,' he said, removing his shoes and pulling on the old leather slippers he kept on the second step of the stairs. 'The trip takes it out of me, I don't know why. I'm sitting on the train half the day, not driving, so I should be in fine fettle.'

'Travelling is exhausting,' Christie insisted. 'There's a difference between sitting in your own armchair at home and sitting on a train at the mercy of leaves on the track, worrying about missing your meeting.'

'I'm hardly Donald Trump,' he joked.

'He has a limo, I'd say, so he's not at the mercy of the leaves.' Christie handed her husband a glass of iced tea. 'And someone else to drag his briefcase around after him. How did the meeting about the emissions go?'

'We're getting there. But one of the people was sick today, so there's a chance we'll have to go through it all again.'

'For heaven's sake,' exclaimed Christie. 'Surely if they're sick, they have to catch up with the rest of you, not the other way round.'

'You know how it works, love,' said James. 'For some people, the more meetings there are, the better. Then nothing actually gets done, but lots of minutes are typed up and the department's accounts' people are kept busy printing out expenses cheques for tea and coffee. Global warming won't kill the planet: bureaucracy will.'

He followed her into the kitchen and sat down on a low stool to pet the dogs, who'd been clamouring for love since he arrived.

He normally knelt on the floor to pet them, she knew. His hip must be bothering him again. Not that James would ever say so. Christie knew many women with husbands whose flu symptoms were always at least on a par with Ebola, if the patient was to be believed. She was the lone dissenting voice with a husband who never magnified his illness to the power of ten, which worried her because James could be having a heart attack in front of her and he'd probably say he had 'a bit of an ache' and that a moment sitting down would cure it. How could you look after a man like that?

'Now, what was that all about this morning?' he asked when Tilly's inner ears had been rubbed to her satisfaction and Rocket had snuffled wetly all over his shoes to establish that no other dogs had been admired that day.

'What was all what about this morning?' said Christie, feigning innocence.

'You know, the phone call when I'd only just left the house.'

'I was having an anxious day, that's all,' she relented. 'Sorry, I didn't mean to worry you but I had this awful feeling that something bad was going to happen to us.'

James pulled her over on to his knee and the dogs whimpered in outrage. This was their time for cuddling, not Christie's. Tilly stormed off to her bed to sulk.

'You can't take my weight on your hip . . .' Christie began. She knew it was stiff, she could see from the way he'd been walking that morning.

'Oh, shut up about my bloody hip, woman,' James said and held her tight. 'I love you, you daft creature, d'you know that? I love that you still worry about me.'

'Yes and I love you too, you daft man,' she replied. 'Even if your hip is aching and you won't mention it.'

'It's only a twinge.'

'I don't believe you. You'd be in agony, and you'd still say it was only a twinge. You're not impressing anybody with your stoicism,' she said crossly.

'It's not agony.'

'If your arthritis is playing up, it's not good to have me on your lap,' she said.

James laid his head against her cheek. 'The day I can't manage to have you on my lap,' he said, 'get them to shoot me.'

'They couldn't shoot you,' Christie murmured, hugging him. 'You're an endangered species.'

'Like the dodo?'

'The poor dodo's been and gone, sorry. You're more of a white tiger: rare and special.'

'You say the nicest things,' he replied, his lips close to her cheek.

'Impossible man,' sighed Christie, kissing him on the forehead and getting up. 'I made goulash.'

'Lenkya's recipe? Great, I love that.' James sat down at the table expectantly. 'Whatever happened to her? She hasn't been in touch for years, not since Ana was involved with that artist fellow and they were all here for the big exhibition in Dawson Street. Remember that? How many years ago is it?'

Christie opened her mouth but no sound came out. Fortunately the phone blistered into the silence and she leaped to answer it.

It was Jane from the Summer Street Café, with news that poor Una Maguire had been carted off in an ambulance after a fall.

'I knew you'd want to know,' said Jane, 'and that Dennis might not get round to telling people.' Which was a kind way of saying dear Dennis would be too flustered to brush his teeth and might need some hand-holding. Christie was good at that: calm in a crisis.

'I'll pop a note through their door telling him I'll drop in on Friday and to phone me if he needs anything before then,' Christie said and Jane hung up, knowing it was all taken care of now that Christie Devlin knew.

'Looks like your feeling of gloom was right after all,' James said as they sat down to their goulash. He'd opened a bottle of lusty red wine to go with the stew, even though it was only midweek, and they stuck pretty much to the wine only at weekends rule.

'Yes,' said Christie, thinking of the Maguires and how Dennis would cope with being the carer instead of the cared for. 'That must have been it, after all.'

But she wasn't telling the truth. Whatever dark cloud had moved over her head was still there, looming, promising bad things to come.

And James had mentioned 'that artist fellow' of Ana's, Carey Wolensky, who'd turned out to be one of the most famous painters of his generation. When James had carelessly referred to him, Christie had felt a shiver run right through her. She didn't believe in coincidence. Everything happened for a reason. There were tiny signs of the future everywhere and only the watchful spotted them. First her anxiousness, now this mention of a man she wanted to forget. Christie was scared to think of what it might all mean: her past coming back to haunt her. Why now?

CHAPTER SIX

The next afternoon, Maggie's suitcases arrived together on the carousel. They looked shabby among some of the classier travellers' bags from the Galway to Dublin shuttle.

She hauled them off the belt with some difficulty, having murmured, 'No thanks, I'm fine,' to the man who'd leaped to offer to help the tall redhead in the trailing pale suede coat.

Her eyes were raw with crying and she kept her head down as she spoke, embarrassed by how she must look. The man probably felt sorry for her; thought she was one of those care in the community patients who rattled because of all the Xanax bottles in their pockets.

Maggie didn't need anyone feeling sorry for her today. She felt sorry enough for herself.

The first piece of luggage was the heaviest, a wardrobe-on-wheels affair that was fit to burst, only a bright purple strap preventing its internal organs splurging out over the concourse. An orange 'heavy item' sticker hung from the handle. The second was a hard candy-pink case that was a dead weight even when empty.

Grey used to joke that it had been cursed by so many

baggage people, it had probably developed magical powers itself.

'If our plane ever goes down, the pink case will be the only survivor, you wait and see,' he'd laugh.

Fresh misery assailed her at this thought of Grey and the fabulous holidays they had saved up for and shared before they'd bought the flat.

They'd never go away together again. Not when she'd be watching like a jailer every time he tipped a beautiful waitress or glanced at a woman on the beach. Only a fool would trust him again. Maggie was not going to be that fool. Last night she'd packed and said they'd talk later, trying to delay the inevitable argument in case she gave in.

'Would you like me to sleep on the couch?' Grey had asked, and she wanted to whisper: no, lie next to me and hold me. Tell me it'll be all right, it was a mistake, that you'll make it better.

'Yes, sleep on the couch,' she said, finding the strength from somewhere to say it.

We'll try again, I know you love me, her heart bleated.

But her head had to do the talking. Leaving this way was easier, because if she stopped and thought about actually losing him, about not sharing her life with him, Maggie was afraid she'd relent. And her head told her that staying would destroy her, in the end.

Gulping back a fresh batch of tears, she grabbed Cursed Candy Pink and shoved it on to the luggage trolley behind Wardrobe, ignoring the interested gaze of the man who'd tried to help her. She wished he'd stop *looking* at her. Honestly, what was wrong with people? Couldn't a person cry in public?

On top of the trolley, she dumped her handbag, a banana-shaped black leather thing that held everything, and cleverly deposited the most vital bits right at the bottom, thus deterring both purse-snatchers and Maggie from locating her money in shops.

She wheeled her trolley hopefully past the special mirrored section, holding her breath.

On those girls-only holidays to Greece, in the pre-Grey days, the others had always trooped through customs happily clinking contraband bottles of ouzo and Metaxa brandy, while she (the only one who'd actually read the customs bit of paper about only importing 200 fags and giving notice if they'd been loitering near goats) was the one to have to unpack her case in public.

Today, fortunately, the customs people behind their two-way mirrors resisted the impulse to go through Maggie's blameless luggage.

Then she was out into arrivals, into the spotlight, where hundreds of eager people scrutinised and rejected her as they searched for whichever special person they'd come to meet so they could wave their welcome home placards, wobble their helium balloons and scream 'hello!!!'

It brought home to Maggie that she had no special person any more. The person for whom she used to be special had cheated on her. God, it hurt.

Trying to look cool, as though she didn't care, she was thankful when her mobile rang and she could busy herself answering it.

'We're home from the hospital,' said her father happily. 'Where are you, love? Are you nearly here yet? Will I boil the kettle? Your mother can't wait to see you.'

Maggie felt the usual dual burst of affection and irritation reserved for conversations with her parents. The plane had only just landed, for heaven's sake. She'd already given Dad the details and told him to add another fifteen minutes for normal plane delays. Unless Clark Kent was bursting out of his Y-fronts in a telephone box nearby in order to whisk her off home at supersonic speed, she wouldn't reach Summer Street for another three quarters of an hour at least.

'Not quite, Dad,' she said, keeping her tone cheery. It was only because he cared. 'I've just come through arrivals.'

'Oh, right then. You'll be here in . . .'

'Less than an hour,' she said. 'See you then. Bye!'

She stuck the phone back in her jeans pocket and tried to ignore the feeling that the walls were closing in. She was back home. Back with nothing to show for five years away in Galway and the Maguire family clock – always at 'Where were you? Why didn't you phone? We were worried!' – was ticking once again.

Maggie manhandled all her worldly goods towards the door and the taxis. It was too late for the if-onlys but she went through them all the same – if only Grey hadn't screwed someone else, if only she hadn't witnessed it, if only he'd realised how much he loved her and pledged undying faithfulness instead of saying he couldn't help himself. If only she wasn't so stupid to fall for someone like him in the first place.

That's what it all came back to: her stupidity. An intelligent woman would have known that Grey, who could have had any woman, would one day stray. An intelligent woman would have got out before this happened. An intelligent woman would have made it calmly clear long beforehand that straying wasn't an option and that if he did, their relationship was over. For such a woman, Grey would have agreed.

But not for Maggie. For all that he'd said she was special, that he didn't want a pert blonde, he'd lied to her.

Now all she had to do was work out what to tell her parents. With luck, she'd have some peace on the ride home to adjust and get her story straight. They didn't need her in tears right now, with her mother in such distress.

* * *

94

'. . . So you see, what the politicians don't realise is that if you have a system with toll roads, it's the people like myself who are paying for it . . .'

'Right, I see.'

The taxi driver's monologue was only stemmed by having to negotiate the tricky box junction just before St Kevin's Road. Since picking her up at the airport, he'd been talking at high speed about the price of property, chewing gum on car seats and now toll roads. Maggie hadn't felt able to interrupt. It would have been rude and in the grand scheme of things, there was no excuse to be rude, was there? Her mother's training had kicked in as usual.

Maggie was the one who got stuck with bores at parties, charity muggers in the street, and sweet bewildered people who wandered into the library for warmth and who ought to have been thrown out. She was too kind and too polite to say no or ignore people.

'That's what I said to that woman politician. I said: that's my opinion, Missus, and if you don't like it, don't get in my cab,' the taxi driver went on. 'Was I right to say it?' As with all the other questions he'd posed on the forty-minute trip, he didn't pause for a reply. 'I was right, you see. Nobody stands up to these people. Nobody.'

The taxi turned the corner, driving slowly past the Summer Street Café where people sat outside at the small tables, looking as if they hadn't a care in the world. Mum and Dad loved the café, loved the buzz of meeting people there. Mum would listen to all the gossip and pass it eagerly on to Maggie, forgetting that she'd lived away for five years and didn't know all the people they met.

Maggie, who didn't know all of the people in her Galway apartment block and clearly didn't know her boyfriend at all, had learned that the wild-eyed Mrs Johnson was off the sauce after failing the breathalyser test one night and losing her licence, that Amber Reid, the teenage girl who lived alone with her mother – lovely woman with a big job but never too busy to bake cakes for the Vincent de Paul fundraisers – was going to art college and would be a big star one day. Christie Devlin said she was a marvellous artist, and Christie would know, wouldn't she? Look at those lovely paintings Christie had done for Una's sixtieth. Maggie knew that the carrot cake muffins in the café were now sugar-free; oh, and she knew that Jane and Henry in the café had hired this lovely Chinese waitress.

'Xu her name is, although we call her Sue, because it's almost the same. Came all the way from China by herself, brave little thing, and not knowing anybody here. She'd put us to shame,' Mum had said. 'Learning English and working at the same time, and not knowing a sinner here. It must be terrible hard to leave your country and start again.'

Maggie loved the way her mother was so interested in people. Maggie used to be like that too, she realised, before she met Grey and became so wrapped up in him that she had no space or time left for anyone else. Yet how could she be totally involved with him and still not see the obvious? Love wasn't just blind, it was lobotomised.

In the back seat of the taxi, her thoughts miles away, Maggie realised they'd passed the third of Summer Street's maple trees and suddenly they were slowing down outside her house.

'Number forty-eight you said?' the driver asked.

'Yes, thanks,' she replied.

She scrabbled in her bag to pay him.

'Cheer up, gorgeous,' he said, beaming up at her from the window, 'it might never happen.'

True to form, Maggie managed a smile.

'See ya,' she said. There was no way she was going to tell him it had already happened.

She turned and stared at number 48. Home. It was one of the 1930s houses, white with dark beams painted on the front gable and diamond-paned windows. Part of the house was covered by the bronzed leaves of a Virginia creeper that had science fiction film capabilities to regrow no matter how often it was pruned back to the roots.

Maggie felt the years shrink away. Home made her feel not entirely like a child again but as if still under the influence of all the old childhood problems.

Her father met her at the gate, dressed up in his going-into-the-hospital outfit of navy blazer and tie, but still comfortingly familiar. When he put his arms around her, Maggie snuggled against him like the child she once was, even though he was shorter than her and as skinny as ever.

'It's so lovely to have you home,' he said. 'Thank you for coming. I know it's a lot to ask, but thank you.'

'How could I not come?' admonished Maggie, pulling away briskly. If she let her reserve drop, she'd sob her heart out. Better to be brusque and not give them a chance to ask after Grey. She'd tell them later, when she – and they – felt stronger.

'How's Mum?'

'Much better today.' Her father's face brightened. 'She got an awful shock, you know. It was all so quick. One minute we were here, the next, she'd passed out with the pain. I thought she was dead, Maggie,' he added, and he looked so forlorn that Maggie had to take a deep breath to steady herself.

'Where is she?'

'Where do you think?'

The kitchen at the back of the house was certainly the heart of the Maguire home. A cosy room which had been decorated at a time when there was no such concept in interior design as using too much pine, it was the room Maggie felt she'd grown up in.

Sitting in an armchair at the table (pine) with her plastered leg up on a kitchen chair (pine), watching the portable television that was perched on the *Little House on the Prairie* dresser (distressed pine), was Maggie's mother, Una.

As tall a woman as her daughter, she was just as slender but with faded red hair instead of Maggie's fiery curls. Their faces were very similar: perfect ovals with other-worldly cobalt-blue eyes and wide mouths that were always on the verge of a smile. But whereas Maggie's smile was tremulous, anxious, Una's was the all-encompassing beam of a woman who embraced life. Now Una sat listlessly in the chair, as if breaking her leg had taken the strength out of all her bones. Beside her was the crossword, nearly finished.

'I've left the hard ones for your father,' Una said, which was the standard and affectionate lie in the Maguire household.

Dennis was no good at crosswords. A champion at the Rubik's Cube, and deeply sorry when that had gone out of fashion, he was marvellous with gadgets, figures and magazine quizzes where you had to work out which tetrahedron was the odd one out.

But words defied him.

'What'll I say?' he used to beg Maggie when he had to write the only birthday card his wife didn't write for him.

'To Una, happy birthday, I love you so much, Dennis,' was Maggie's usual suggestion.

It was what she'd have liked written on a card to her. Grey, for all his eloquence, hadn't been much good at cards either, although Maggie had kept every single one he'd given her.

Mum hugged Maggie tightly, then somehow managed a final squeeze and whispered in her ear: 'We're so glad you're here, Bean.'

Bean or Beanpole was her nickname, so given because she'd been long and skinny as a child.

'Like a beanpole!' her cousin Elisabeth used to say joyfully.

Elisabeth, also tall but with Victoria's Secret model curves instead of Maggie's racehorse slenderness, was never called anything but Elisabeth.

While Dennis bustled off with Maggie's suitcases, Una told her daughter that the osteoporosis was advanced.

'They can't believe I haven't broken anything before,' she said finally. 'It's a bit of a miracle, and at my stage, I could end up breaking bones with just a knock against a bookcase.'

Maggie was shocked. 'Oh, Mum,' she said. 'That's terrible. Dad said it was osteoporosis but he never said it was that bad.'

They heard Dennis coming back.

'I don't want him to know everything,' her mother went on. 'It'd only worry him and what's the point of that?'

'He ought to know, Mum.'

'Ah, why? It won't be good for his heart if he's watching me every moment worrying about me. I'll be fine.'

Maggie's father came back into the kitchen.

'What'll we have for dinner?' said Una breezily. 'I can't wait for a decent meal. Your poor dad is doing his best but he can only do soup and rolls. How about a roast? I fancy beef.'

'Roast beef? Is there beef in the fridge?' Maggie asked.

Her mother looked blank. 'I don't know, love. I can't get near the fridge. But look. Or you could go to the shops. The car's there.'

At that instant, Maggie began to feel panicky. Everything was more serious than she'd thought.

Her father wasn't exactly one of life's copers. He'd never been able to cook, and viewed both the iron and washing machine as arcane specimens, beyond his ability. Her mother had done everything in the Maguire household.

And yet here she was, expecting Maggie, who had just arrived, to know what was in the fridge, not to mention to feel confident hopping into a car she had never driven before and going to the supermarket. Maggie had passed her driving test when she was a teenager but she'd never owned a car and could barely remember the difference between all the pedals.

Had breaking her leg broken something else in her mother too?

'Mum,' Maggie said, feeling horrendously guilty at not being able to do this simple thing in a family crisis, 'I can't drive. You know I can't.'

She looked into the fridge. There were several big chill-cabinet cartons of soup, half a pack of butter and eggs. Nothing else. 'We shop from day to day,' her father added helpfully. 'I'll stay with your mother.'

Maggie shut the fridge. She was in charge. She wondered how this had happened. She was not qualified for this. Her mother was the one who was in charge.

'You'll be able to go, won't you?' Una's voice quavered slightly.

With frightening clarity, Maggie saw that their roles had swapped. One cracked femur and she was the parent.

She had no option.

'I'll do a shop right now,' she said firmly. 'The mini supermarket will have everything we need. I'll walk.'

Speedi Shop on Jasmine Row had been open from dawn to dusk since Maggie had been in infant school. More expensive than the proper supermarket a mile away, it was always busy but there were never any long queues at the checkouts, mainly because Gretchen, the owner, didn't encourage chitchat. She was, however, an interrogator of Lubyanka

100

standards and Maggie had always felt that Gretchen was terrifying. She didn't smile much and when she did, her forehead and face remained static, as if filled with Botox, although it was hard to imagine Gretchen spending the money on such a thing. Beauty, a bit like politeness, was a waste of time in Gretchen's book.

She was there behind the counter when Maggie arrived at the checkout, her basket spilling over with the makings of a roast dinner, shop-bought apple pie and ice cream for pudding.

'Maggie Maguire, a sight for sore eyes. Long time no see. I thought you were living in married bliss in Galway.'

Maggie translated this bit of faux politeness in her head: *fancy seeing you here, and is it true you're not married at all but still shacking up with some fellow who clearly won't marry you?*

'Home for a few days,' said Maggie, aiming for the happily unconcerned approach. Had Gretchen X-ray vision? Could she see that Maggie's man had cheated on her? It wouldn't surprise her if the answer was yes. 'And I'm not married, actually, I've a long-term partner.'

Translation*: I am a fulfilled woman who has made interesting life choices and wouldn't be bothered getting married when I could live the free life of a modern feminist unshackled by silly old wedding vows.*

'Right.' Gretchen nodded appraisingly and began to scan Maggie's groceries. 'You remember my Lorraine, don't you? You were in the same year in school. Lorraine's living in Nice, married to this gorgeous French pilot, Jacques, with three kids and a live-in nanny. You should see their house: Jacuzzi, pool, bidet in every en suite, the lot.' *I don't buy your story*, said her eyes. *Long-term partner, my backside. Now Lorraine, she's a success story. She has it all: fabulous husband, children, everything money can buy. She's not home with her tail between her legs at the age of thirty with no ring and no kids either.*

'How wonderful for her,' Maggie said, adding a large bar of chocolate to the basket to comfort herself. 'Lorraine always knew what she wanted, didn't she?' She snatched back her shopping and shoved it into a bag. *Lorraine was a hard-nosed little madam and she was always keen on self-improvement without doing any actual work. Like stealing other people's homework or hanging round with the class bullies.*

'Bye, Gretchen, have to rush.'

On her way home with the grocery bags weighing her down, Maggie passed the time by trying to remember who lived in the various houses on Summer Street. Many of them were still owned by the people who'd lived there when she was a child, like the Ryans, who bred Burmese cats and never minded the neighbourhood children coming in to coo over the latest batch of apricot-coloured kittens. Or sweet Mrs Sirhan, who'd looked eighty when Maggie had been small, and now must be unbelievably old, but still went for her constitutional every day, up the street into the café for a cup of Earl Grey with lemon.

There was a sign on the park gate: 'Save Our Park', written in shaky capitals on a bit of cardboard, and Maggie idly wondered what the park had to be saved from. But the sign-writer hadn't thought to add that bit of information. Rampaging aliens, perhaps? Or people who didn't scoop the dog poop?

The old railway pavilion was her favourite part of the park: she'd played in it many times during her childhood and it was easy to imagine it as a train station, with ladies in long dresses sobbing into their reticules as handsome men left them behind, sad stories behind every parting. There hadn't been a train that way for many years.

The train tracks were long gone, too. Maybe that was the lesson she needed to learn: nobody cared about the past. Her misery over Grey would mean nothing in a hundred years.

It was ten before Maggie managed to escape to bed and to her private misery. She'd left her mobile phone unanswered all day and when she finally checked there were seven *where are you?* texts from Shona, along with two missed calls and one *I am so sorry, please answer your phone* text from Grey.

Yeah, right, Maggie thought furiously, erasing it. One lousy text and a couple of phone calls. What an effort that must have been. Feeling angry with Grey was easier than giving in to feeling hopeless and alone. If she let go of the anger, she'd collapse under the weight of the loneliness.

She unwrapped the giant bar of milk chocolate she'd bought and dialled the only person in the world, apart from Shona, who might possibly understand: her cousin Elisabeth. Despite coming up with the nickname Bean, Elisabeth was one of Maggie's favourite people.

Elisabeth was tall, athletic, had been captain of the netball team and was wildly popular at her school, a fact that had often made Maggie wish they'd gone to the same one. She might have protected Maggie. She was now a booker in one of Seattle's top model agencies and incredibly, despite all these comparative riches, she was a nice person.

It was eight hours earlier in Seattle and Elisabeth was on her lunch break, sitting at her desk with her mouth full of nuts because she was still doing the low-carb thing.

'How are you doing?' asked Elisabeth in muffled tones.

'Oh, you know, fine. You heard about Mum's accident?'

'Yes, Dad told me.' Her father and Maggie's were brothers. 'You don't sound OK,' she added suspiciously.

Elisabeth picked up tones of voice like nobody else. Certainly nobody else in the Maguire family, who all had the intuition of celery. 'What's up?'

'I told you.'

'I mean what else?'

'You can hear something else in my voice?'

'I spend all my life on the phone to young models in foreign countries asking them how they are, did anybody hit on them and are they eating enough/drinking too much/taking coke/ screwing the wrong people/screwing anybody. So yes, I can hear it in your voice,' insisted Elisabeth.

'I caught Grey in bed with another woman.'

Silence.

'Fuck.'

'I didn't know you were allowed to say that outside Ireland any more,' Maggie remarked, in an attempt at levity. 'Everyone on your side of the Atlantic nearly passes out when they hear it, when here, it's a cross between an adjective and an adverb, the sort of word we can't do without.'

'Desperate situations need desperate words,' said Elisabeth, then said 'fuck' again followed by, 'Fucking bastard.'

'My sentiments exactly.'

'Is he still alive?'

'He has all his teeth, yes,' Maggie said.

'And they're not on a chain around his neck?'

Maggie laughed and it was a proper laugh for the first time all day. Elisabeth was one of those people with the knack of making the unbearable slightly more bearable. With her listening, Maggie didn't feel like the only person on the planet to have been hurt like this before.

'No, they're still in his mouth. I did think about hitting him but he was attached to this blonde fourteen-year-old at the time . . .'

'A fourteen-year-old!' shrieked Elisabeth.

'Metaphorically speaking,' Maggie interrupted. 'She's probably twenty or twenty-one, actually. Gorgeous, from the angle I was looking from. Which was really a bummer. I mean, if she was ugly and wrinkly, I might manage to cope, but being cheated on with a possible centrefold doesn't do much for your self-confidence.'

'Oh, Maggie,' said Elisabeth and there was love and pity in her voice. She'd long since given up trying to boost Maggie's self-esteem, although having a beautiful cousin with a skewed vision of her gorgeousness was perfect training for working with stunning size six models who thought they were too fat and faced rejection every day. 'I wish I was there to give you a hug. What did you do?'

'Dad phoned about Mum, so I left to come here. Ran away, in other words, which is what I'm good at.'

'You haven't told them.'

'No. Couldn't face it.'

Maggie heard muffled noises at Elisabeth's end.

'Sorry, I've got to go. Call me tomorrow?'

'Sure.'

Maggie looked at her suitcases waiting patiently to be unpacked. It was hard to feel enthusiastic about moving back into her childhood bedroom. All she needed now was one of those big doll's heads that you put eye make-up on, her old Silver Brumby books, and she'd be eleven again.

She'd read so much as a child, losing herself in the world of books because the outside world was so cruel. And yet she hadn't learned as much as she'd thought she had: books taught you that it would work out right in the end. They never envisaged the possibility that the prince would betray you. They never pointed out that if you gave a man such ferocious power over your heart, he could destroy you in an instant.

She finished her bar of chocolate slowly.

If everything had been different, she'd have been at home now in her own flat with Grey.

Without closing her eyes, she could imagine herself there: sitting on their bed, talking about their day, all the little things that seemed mundane at the time and became painfully intimate and important when you could no longer share them. Like waking up in the night and feeling Grey's body, warm and strong beside her in the bed. Like leaning past him at the bathroom sink to get to the toothpaste.

Like hanging his T-shirts on the radiators to dry. These things made up their life together. Now it was all gone. She felt betrayed, broken and utterly hollow inside.

She was back in her childhood bed with nothing to show for it.

CHAPTER SEVEN

Mrs Devlin's art classes were different from any other lesson in the school, agreed all the girls in the sixth year. For a start, Mrs Devlin herself was not exactly your average teacher, although she was older than many of the others. Even her clothes bypassed normal teacher gear, whether she wore one of her long honey suede skirts and boots with a low-slung belt around her hips, or dressed down in Gap jeans and a man's shirt tied in a knot around the waist. Compared to Mrs Hipson, headmistress and lover of greige twinsets and pearlised lipstick, Mrs Devlin was at the cutting edge of bohemian chic.

Most of all, the girls agreed, it was her attitude that made her different. The other teachers seemed united in their plan to improve the students whether they wanted to be improved or not. But Mrs Devlin, without ever exactly saying so, seemed to believe that people improved themselves at their own rate.

So on May the 1st, with just weeks to go to the state exams and with the whole teaching body in a state of panic, Mrs Devlin's assignment to her sixth-year class was to 'forget about the exams for a moment and paint your vision of Maia, the ancient pagan goddess who gave her name to May and who was a goddess of both spring and fertility'.

'As today's the first of May, it's the perfect day for it.'

She stopped short of pointing out that the exam results probably wouldn't matter in a millennium. Not the way to win friends and influence people in a school. 'You've all been working so hard with your history of art,' Christie added as she perched on the corner of the desk at the top of the class. She rarely sat down at the desk during art practicals, preferring to walk around and talk to her students: a murmured bit of praise here, a smile there. 'I thought it might be nice to spend one hour of the day enjoying yourselves, reminding yourselves that art is about creativity and forgetting about studying.'

The class, who'd come from double English where they were re-butchering *The Catcher in the Rye* for exam revision, nodded wearily.

The most art they got to do these days involved colouring in their exam revision timetables with highlighter pens – generally a lot more fun than the revision itself.

'Maia is the oldest and most beautiful of the seven stars called the Seven Sisters, or the Pleiades,' Christie continued. 'The Pleiades are part of the constellation of Taurus, which is ruled over by Venus, for those of you interested in astrology. Maia is around five times larger than our sun.'

It was such a sunny morning that flecks of dust could be seen floating on shafts of light filtering in from the second-floor windows. St Ursula's was an old building, with decrepit sash windows and huge sills perfect for sitting on between classes and blowing forbidden cigarette smoke out into the netball court below.

'In art, spring is represented, as you know, by the sense of sensuality and passion,' Christie went on. 'Can anyone remember any artists who painted spring in such a way?'

'Botticelli,' said Amber Reid.

Christie nodded and wondered again what Amber had

been getting up to on Wednesday. The way she'd been dressed and the joy in her step made Christie damn sure that Amber had been on her way to some illicit activity.

'Yes, Amber, Botticelli is a good example. Remember, girls, artists didn't have television to give them ideas, or films. They looked at their world for inspiration and got it from nature. Keep that in mind during the exam, they were influenced by their times. By war, poverty, nature, religion. As we discussed in art history last week, religion is important as an influence on artists. Remember the puritanical Dutch schools with their hidden messages.

'Today's the pagan festival of Beltane, which is why May is called Bealtaine in Irish, and it's a celebration of spring, warmer days, blossoming nature and blossoming of people too. Of course, the Church wasn't too keen on pagan festivals, but they're part of our history too, so it's interesting to know about them. You paint, I'm here if you need me.'

The class were silent as they considered painting a fertility goddess. At St Ursula's in general, sexuality was given a wide berth by the teaching staff. Even in sex education classes, the concept of passion was diluted, with scientific words like 'zygote' giving students the impression that it was a miracle the human race had gone on for so long considering how boring procreation sounded.

'Is it true that Titian only painted women he'd gone to bed with?' asked Amber suddenly, her eyes glittering.

Christie had a sudden flash of knowledge: a picture of Amber and a dark, moodily dangerous young man came into her mind, entwined on a childhood bed doing grown-up things. Christie knew exactly what Amber had been up to the day before. She blazed with burgeoning sexuality. To embody Maia, Amber just needed to paint a self-portrait.

Christie felt a rush of pity for poor old Faye who probably hadn't a clue that her teenage daughter had just taken one

109

of the giant steps into womanhood. Having sons was definitely easier than daughters, she thought gladly. Sons were rarely left holding the baby.

'So I believe,' said Christie carefully. 'Paint, Amber,' she whispered, 'don't talk.'

'I swear Mrs Devlin'd bring in nude life models if she was let,' groaned Niamh to Amber. Niamh was struggling with art in general and was sorry she hadn't done home economics instead. How was she going to embody a fertility goddess? Couldn't they please do a still life instead – a couple of bananas or a nice simple apple?

'I wish she did bring in nude models,' said Amber, glaring at Niamh. 'It's impossible to learn to draw people properly with their clothes on.' At least in art college, she'd be able to study line drawing properly with nude models . . .

But she wasn't going, was she? She was going to New York with Karl, before the exams, and she had to tell her mother all this, and soon.

'It's not as if you haven't seen a man with no clothes on, Niamh,' added the girl on the other side of Amber with a wicked grin. 'You've been going out with Jonnie for a year now, don't tell me he's kept his boxers on all this time.'

It was Niamh's turn to grin. 'He's worth drawing, all right. And he's got a bigger you-know-what than all those Michelangelo statues!'

The back of the class dissolved into filthy giggles, but were sure Christie, who was walking sedately around the art room, couldn't have heard the remark.

Silvery-white hair was a fabulous disguise, Christie thought as she managed not to smile. Schoolgirls appeared to think that white-haired equalled deaf, which meant she overheard all manner of things she mightn't have heard otherwise. These girls probably would have been stunned to think that their esteemed art teacher had made the same jokes once, a lifetime ago, when she was as young and when men's heads turned to look at her.

Young people always imagined that sex and passion had been invented by them. Christie fingered the gold and jasper scarab necklace that James had once bought for her in a market in Cairo, and smiled.

When you were over the age of sixty, if you hinted at a moment of wildness in your youth, people smiled benignly and imagined you meant a reckless time when you'd sat in a public bar and drank a pint of Guinness when such a thing was frowned upon. But she'd known plenty of passion. Still did. Being a stalwart of the local church didn't mean she was dead from the neck down, no matter what the youngsters thought.

That holiday in Cairo had been before the children were born, when she and James had been able to take advantage of a cheap week-long trip. They'd sighed with pleasure over the treasures of the Egyptian Museum by day, and lay in each other's arms in their shabby hotel by night with the overhead fan not quite doing its job.

Despite that, they'd made love every night, caught up in the sensuality of Cairo with its iconic sights, and the heady perfume of the spice markets.

The heat was an incredible aphrodisiac, James said, on the last night of their holiday, as he lay back against the pillows, sated, and watched his wife standing naked in the moonlight in front of the hotel-room mirror.

'Just as well we don't live here all the time, then,' Christie teased, admiring the necklace that lay between her full, high breasts. 'I love this,' she said, holding it tenderly. 'Thank you.'

'You do understand that I'll want to rip your clothes off every time you wear it?' he asked.

'Even in the supermarket?'

111

'We'd probably have to wait till we got to the car park,' he amended. 'Wouldn't want to bruise the avocados.'

'How about we introduce a one-hour rule? Once you notice the necklace, we have one hour to get to bed.'

James grinned lazily. 'Sounds good to me.'

No, she thought now, watching her class concentrating on their drawing boards: young people thought that old age was at best fifteen to twenty years older than they were, and reckoned your life was over once you hit forty. They'd learn one day.

Christie had no teaching in the period before lunch, so she headed for the staff room to mark the art history revision test the fifth years had handed in earlier. St Ursula's staff room was in the original, 1940s part of the school, surrounded by small classrooms with creaky wooden doors, crumbling parquet floors and thick walls that you couldn't hammer a nail into. The staff room itself was the biggest room in this section of the building and, in the fifteen years she'd worked in the school, Christie had decided it had a routine about it, an ebb and flow rather like a sea.

There was the calm of half past eight in the morning, when Christie sat at the long veneered table with its decoration of mug rings and drank green tea while she mentally prepared for the rest of the day.

By 8.45, the staff room would have filled up, the teachers all business, fuelling up on murderous coffee from the large catering tin.

By late afternoon, the tide had swept steadily out and no amount of coffee could raise the energy of the staff as the clock ticked on towards four and freedom.

Once, when an Italian teacher – Gianni, a man who looked as if he'd love to whip you off to bed and teach you how to roll your 'R's properly – had arrived to teach languages, there had been talk of buying a proper coffee-making machine.

112

'This ees muck, this coffee,' Gianni would say when he caught the rest of the teachers listlessly spooning brown dust into their mugs. 'If we had a proper machine, then you would have coffee worth dreenking.'

A coffee machine collection had been started, not to mention a few diets, but then Gianni had decided that he missed the Italian climate too much, and had gone home to Florence.

Christie, who'd been immune to Gianni's Paco Rabanne-scented charms and wasn't as heartbroken as the rest of them by his abrupt departure, suggested they buy a small television with the coffee machine fund.

'Not to watch junky soap operas on,' insisted Mr Sweetman, who taught English.

'What's wrong with soap operas?' demanded Mademoiselle Lennox, French.

'You're both so busy, you probably won't get to watch much but the lunchtime news,' Christie remarked gently and there was much muttering in agreement.

The news, yes, that's what they'd watch. Keeping in touch with current affairs was vital, Mr Sweetman agreed.

The television was now a much valued part of the room, with the channel screening *Who Wants to Be a Millionaire* repeats being the favourite. Mr Sweetman was currently top of the league having got to the quarter of a million question four times, with Mrs Jones, physics and applied maths, in second place.

Today, the TV was off, though, and only Christie and Liz, who taught home economics and biology, were there. Christie pulled the uninviting pile of essays towards her.

She'd only had two classes that morning, but she felt tired because she'd slept so badly, waking three times in the clammy grip of a cold sweat after nightmares, one particularly horrible one involving a sea of giant black spiders which burned people

113

they touched. She often had vivid dreams – the downside of her gift of intuition. But giant spiders? Very strange.

Eventually, she had stopped trying to sleep and did her best to lie quietly, eyes closed, amusing herself by imagining how useful the inside of her head might be to a roomful of psychiatrists.

Some people left their bodies to medical science – she might leave her brain because there was definitely something weird going on in there.

'Are you all right, love?' James had murmured drowsily at half five when Christie had given up on the psychiatrists, slipped out of bed and pulled on her jeans and a T-shirt.

'Fine, I'm fine. You go back to sleep, pet,' she'd replied, gently pulling the pale-blue sheet over his shoulders.

James's nightmares had to do with losing his job or not having money to buy food for his family. Christie had long ago decided that he could do without hearing about her horror movie versions. Now her eyes felt gritty with tiredness and the nagging sensation of doom was still there.

'Christie, how are you?' A voice interrupted her thoughts.

Liz, the other teacher, plonked herself and her 'You don't have to be mad to work here but it helps' mug down beside Christie and the untouched pile of essays.

'Busy?' she said, obviously hoping the answer would be no.

Liz was in her early thirties, attractive with dark curly hair, and had been a big hit with the pupils since she'd arrived at the school the previous September. She'd replaced eccentric Mrs Cuniffe who'd been at St Ursula's for over twenty years and refused to be in the same room as a microwave because of a story she'd heard about a man cooking his liver by accident. Eventually, this had made her position as home economics teacher untenable and Liz had arrived to take her place.

'I'm not really busy,' fibbed Christie. 'How are you?'

'Fine,' Liz began and stopped herself. 'Awful. Sorry.' Her eyes brimmed. 'I only wanted to say hello, not burst into tears.'

Christie reached into the tapestry bag that served as her briefcase, rifled a bit and came up with a pack of tissues.

It transpired that Liz was in love with a man who loved her back but felt it was all moving too fast, and perhaps they should see other people.

'He said he needs time,' wept Liz helplessly. 'We've been going out for a year. He's never mentioned this before, why does he need time? I don't know what to do, Christie. I love him. My sister says I should send him packing but she's never liked him. She thinks I'd be better off without him. He says we're still going to my brother's wedding as a couple, so it can't really be over, can it? What should I do?'

The hardest questions were often simplest, Christie thought. Stay and hope, or walk away to start again?

'I can't tell you what you should do, Liz,' she said gently. 'Only you know that.'

'But I don't.'

'Close your eyes and tell me what does it feel like in there?' Christie gestured at the place on Liz's chest where her heart resided.

Liz obediently closed her eyes and instantly her face lost some of its tension. Her shoulders slackened.

'I think it's over. He's being nice by saying he'll go to my brother's wedding with me and he thought it was all fun between us until I mentioned that I wanted a baby.' She snapped her eyelids open and stared at Christie in misery.

'Then it's over,' Christie said gently. She hadn't seen the future for Liz, she'd merely let Liz reach out and think the unthinkable herself.

'You're right. I was kidding myself, wasn't I? I think I always knew he wasn't in it for the long term,' Liz said sadly.

'I kidded myself because I wanted it so much. Looking back, I can see it all now and I should have done everything differently.'

'Looking backwards is a terrible thing,' Christie added, smiling. 'With the benefit of hindsight, there are lots of things we should have done and didn't, and vice versa. But we learn from them and do better next time.'

'You're being kind,' Liz whispered, getting up. 'I bet you've never been as stupid as me. You think before you act, Christie. I blunder along and convince myself that everything's fine when it's not. I only wish I could stop myself doing that. I wouldn't be in bits now if I did.' She bent to give Christie a small hug. 'You're very good for listening to me. I know why everyone says you're wise. You really are.'

The room was filling up again as lunchtime arrived. Liz took her cup and her folder and left Christie sitting at the table, frozen in thought.

For all the noise going on, all the chat about the third form's behaviour that morning and the traffic being a nightmare, Christie might as well have been sitting in a room all on her own. She heard nothing, except Liz's words. You think before you act, Christie.

Because there had been a few times when she'd acted before thinking, and one time in particular that haunted her. One stupid, awful thing she'd done and regretted ever since.

She thought she had put it out of her mind, filed in the memories best left forgotten box, and had tried to forgive herself ever since. And recently she had been thinking of it again and again and it was as red and raw as if it had all happened yesterday. How was it that she hadn't been wise then, when Ana had been involved with Carey Wolensky and the world had been a different place? And why did the memories of that time keep sneaking into her mind, so many years later? She simply didn't know.

116

Shane phoned her that afternoon as she walked home.

'Mum, I've something to tell you,' he said, after the how-are-yous.

Even in late-afternoon sun as she stopped on the footpath on Summer Street, Christie felt the shadow of fear over her again.

'Yes,' she said, dry-mouthed, thinking of all the terrible things that could happen to her beloved son.

'Janet's pregnant. We didn't want to tell anyone until she was three months gone and then, the other day, we thought she was having a miscarriage but she didn't and it's all fine.' Pride and joy sounded in every one of Shane's words.

It really was like having a great weight lifted from her. The fear fell away. 'Oh, Shane,' was all she could say. 'Oh, Shane, my love, I am so happy for you both.' She leaned weakly against a garden wall, her eyes focused on the park opposite where children played and dogs barked. Thank you, thank you, God, she prayed silently.

'That's the best news I've heard in a very long time,' she said. 'It's wonderful. I'm so happy for you both. How is Janet? Tell me everything.'

'Delighted, and so relieved after we thought she was going to lose the baby.'

Christie's mind flashed back. It was then the insight had started – something was about to go horribly wrong. She'd been right. Her grandchild had almost been lost from the world.

'She's had a scan, though, and everything's fine. You can see your third grandkid in a speckled black-and-white picture. We got one for you and Dad. Could we come over at the weekend and give it to you both?'

'I can't think of anything I'd like more.' Christie sighed with pure happiness. 'Shall I tell your father or did you want to phone him yourself?'

'I'll tell him.'

He sounded so like James at that moment: proud daddy-in-waiting, that Christie felt overwhelmed with the emotion of it all. She was so, so lucky.

'Let's have Ethan and Shelly and the girls over too, and maybe your Aunt Ana. Just a small family gathering on Sunday afternoon, not a party in case you think it's bad luck, but just us celebrating the baby getting this far. If you think Janet would like it?' Janet loved the Devlin family get-togethers but she might not be up to even a small one right now and Christie was never one to bulldoze.

'That'll have to be a few weeks away,' Shane said eagerly. 'We're going to a house-warming this weekend, and something else the next weekend, but I'm sure Janet would love a little party. It nearly killed us both not telling anyone. Well, Janet told her mum when she thought she was miscarrying . . . I'm sorry, it's not that we were leaving you out, Mum . . .'

'Shane, you know me better than that,' Christie admonished. 'Girls tell their mothers more, it's the way of things. And I'd be some piece of work if that vexed me. Now, if we have the little party the Sunday after next, why don't you ask Janet's mum to come too?' she urged. Janet was an only child with a widowed mother. 'We'd love to have her here.'

'You're a star, Mum,' Shane said. 'Hey, you'll be up for babysitting, right?'

'Count me in,' Christie said fervently.

At home, humming happily as she thought about the good news, she spent an hour and a half cooking, then filled a basket with dishes for Una and Dennis Maguire. She hadn't heard yet that Maggie was home, and Dennis didn't know one end of the kitchen from the other. If it was left to him, the pair of them would starve. So Christie had made a huge stew, enough for two days, some chicken soup with her own

118

home-made stock, and a dozen fat floury scones. Then she hurried up Summer Street to see Una.

'Christie, how lovely to see you,' said Una when Dennis led Christie into the kitchen.

'And you too.' Christie laid down the basket, pulled up a chair and sat beside her old friend, laying a comforting hand on Una's.

'This is terrible, Una. Such bad luck. How long will you be in plaster?'

'Six weeks,' said Dennis, hovering in the background anxiously. He was sorting out papers for recycling, a job his wife usually did efficiently, while he was getting in a muddle.

'Five and a bit now,' corrected Una. 'The doctors and nurses were lovely; said I'd be right as rain.'

This was clearly said for Dennis's benefit. Christie had felt the fragility of Una's bones as she'd touched her: instead of strength, she'd felt a spider's web of bone, fragile, tissue-thin. Christie had a sudden flash of the gleaming wheels of a wheelchair in her mind and she hoped, as she often did when she saw something sad, that this was only one out of many possible futures. Her hand patted Una's in a gesture of understanding and their eyes met in complicity.

'Dennis, you know, I believe I didn't shut the front door properly behind me,' Christie smiled at him. 'Perhaps you should check . . .'

'No bother,' he said, getting up. 'I have to put the rubbish out anyway and sort it out. It's the recycling collection next week instead of normal rubbish and I've got to tie up all the newspapers with string.'

'Is it *that* obvious I'm worse than I'm letting on?' Una said when he'd bustled off.

'Only to me,' Christie replied. 'What did they really say?'

'I wish I had your gift,' Una sighed. 'It must be great to know things, to see what's up ahead, although I don't know

119

if I'd have liked to see this.' She looked morosely at her leg in its plaster cast.

'My gift?' asked Christie, genuinely surprised. She still rarely talked about what she could do. And she'd certainly never talked about it with Una. Not everyone approved of the concept of visions and she'd never wanted to be labelled a dotty old dear.

'You see things, don't you? My mother had a friend like you, she read the cards for us when I was younger.'

'I don't read cards,' Christie said. 'I think I had it engrained in me as a child that the Church didn't condone anything like that, but you're right, I do see things sometimes. Not so much the future, as what might be. I can't see for people close to me,' she added quickly, in case Una asked her what her future held. 'If I could see everything, I'd have seen that you knew!'

'You can see when people are lying, though?' Una asked perceptively.

Christie nodded. 'It's more intuition than anything,' she added, which wasn't entirely true. 'I knew you weren't as well as you said. What did the doctors say?'

'It's osteoporosis, quite advanced,' Una said. 'My mother had it, you see, so I pushed them to do a bone scan in the hospital, although they kept going on about how I could have it done later, and I insisted. Seems it's a miracle I haven't broken things before. I'm going to have to be careful now or I'll be like a mummy in a film, all bandages trailing after me.'

'How's Dennis coping?'

'Maggie's back, so she's looking after us both,' Una pointed out.

'And is she well?' asked Christie warmly.

'Great,' said Una with pride. 'She's just nipped off to get the papers and something for dinner. Although she needn't have bothered now you've come with food. She's so good to

120

us, you know, Christie. Dennis phoned her from the hospital on Wednesday and she was on a plane yesterday, quick as anything. She's a great girl. I just wish she'd settle down like your two lads. But you can't make them do what you want, can you? Still, she's happy and that's the main thing, isn't it?'

'Yes,' said Christie, resolving that now wasn't the moment to tell her friend the news about her daughter-in-law's pregnancy. 'Shall I make a fresh pot of tea?' she said, indicating the tea-cosied pot that sat on the table.

'Go on,' said Una. 'Milky tea is one way of getting more calcium into me. Far nicer than those awful tablets they have me on. You should have a bone scan done, you know. It's our age, unfortunately.'

'I know,' said Christie, rinsing the teapot and automatically tidying up around her. Dennis's newspapers caught her attention. There were Sunday supplements from weeks ago jumbled up with daily papers open at the crossword pages and she organised them neatly into a pile while she waited for the kettle to boil. Una was telling her about the hospital and the steam from the kettle was building as Christie threw the last paper lightly on to the heap. Before the newsprint landed, the small headline caught her eye:

Polish Artist's First Irish Show in 25 Years

Christie caught the countertop to stop herself swaying. It was only a small story and she pulled it towards her, hardly daring to read it. Carey Wolensky was coming to Ireland next month for an exhibition of his work, including his most famous paintings, the Dark Lady series.

Much prized by the world's richest art collectors and quite unlike all his other work, the Dark Lady paintings are Wolensky's mysterious masterpieces.

121

Before Christie could rip the story from the page, she heard Dennis come back.

'Christie, don't bother with those,' he said, scooping up the pile of papers. 'I'll put them out with the bins.'

He carried them off and Christie was left staring into the neat shrubbery of the Maguires' back garden, barely hearing what Una was saying. She was thinking of Carey Wolensky, her darling younger sister's one-time boyfriend, the man who'd almost destroyed everything. He was coming back into their world and, even now, he could devastate their lives.

Now, at last, Christie knew for sure what her feeling of doom had been about.

CHAPTER EIGHT

Motherhood was harder than marriage, Grace realised, as she admired the art portfolio that Faye had just purchased, at great expense, for Amber's forthcoming eighteenth birthday. At least with marriage, you got time off for good behaviour and could duck out when the going got tough. But motherhood was never-ending and was clearly designed to make you a selfless person. Like when you spent more than a week's wages on something for your kid.

'She'll love it,' Grace said, thinking that if she ever bought anything of supple leather that expensive, it would be hanging off her arm right now with a discreet label inside proclaiming that it was handstitched lovingly by people at the Tod's leather goods factory. Still, that was Faye for you: the only exquisitely dressed thing in Faye's house was Amber. 'Any art student would kill for it.'

'Do you think so?' Faye asked anxiously.

She'd just spent a fortune buying the portfolio from the most expensive art shop in town because she wanted her darling Amber to have the very best of everything when she started art college.

Basically nothing more than a large wallet for transporting

drawings and paintings, it wasn't the most important bit of art college kit. Amber had an old plastic portfolio that could have done her perfectly well. But this large zippered folder was a thing of luxury and it would be nice for Amber to have a beautiful creamy leather one. Except, maybe Amber would have preferred a black leather one. Who knew? The fact that she'd once admired a cream leather one might mean nothing now.

She could have totally changed her mind, in the way she'd announced the night before that she might start having a quick dinner before Faye came home, so she could retreat to her room to study.

'If I eat earlier, I sleep better,' she explained.

'You've got to eat properly,' Faye had said, motherly hackles raised.

'Mum.' Amber dragged the single syllable out in exasperation. 'I'm not anorexic or bulimic or anything. I like to eat early, that's all.'

'OK,' agreed Faye, deflated.

It was mid-May, the exams were looming ever closer and it wouldn't be fair to complain that she missed mealtimes together, the only time the two of them could really talk these days. Amber was under a lot of strain, she looked tired too from all that studying, with violet circles under eyes that looked wildly alert.

Faye had never seen her work so hard, locked in her room for hours every evening, sometimes emerging pale at ten to say she was going to sleep and not to bother going in to say goodnight.

That was what worried Faye most: her daughter not wanting to talk to her. They'd been so close for so long, had managed to bypass most of the awfulness of adolescence, only to end up with this coolness between them over Amber's exams.

For the past few weeks, Amber had barely spoken to her

and seemed lost in her own world. Was she *that* worried about failing?

'I can see your mind whirring,' Grace warned, interpreting Faye's look incorrectly. 'Stop already. She'll like it, OK? If she doesn't, she's being . . .'

She'd nearly said *rude* but stopped. The childless should not criticise other people's children; that was the eleventh commandment and came right before the twelfth, which was not to criticise how other people put their own lives on hold for the said children. When she saw how Faye had given her life over to Amber, Grace felt glad that her own biological clock had never started the fabled ticking.

She'd known Faye for ten years and among all the things she'd learned about her – like the fact that Faye was incredibly clever, yet liked hiding her light under a bushel, and was the only single woman Grace knew who genuinely had no interest in finding a man – foremost was the fact that Amber was Faye's reason for living.

Surely that wasn't right. Were children supposed to be the only thing in a woman's life? Grace was sure her other friends with kids had more fulfilled lives than Faye.

'If she doesn't like it, it might be a fashion thing,' Grace amended, 'but the natural look is very chic.'

'I'm sure she'll love it,' Faye agreed, thinking that she no longer knew any such thing.

The catch on Amber's window had finally given in and broken. She'd jemmied it so many nights when she crept in well after midnight, pushing the window up and praying it wouldn't creak and wake her mother. Burglary must be easier than people thought: nobody had stopped her or even appeared to notice her late-night climbs in and out of her bedroom window.

'I don't know how you've got away with it,' Ella remarked.

She and Amber walked to school together most days,

although they were getting later and later, as Amber was finding it hard to drag herself out of bed.

'Your mum must be losing it if she hasn't noticed that you're not in your room at night. So,' Ella added, 'what did Mr Luverman do with you last night? Spill.'

'I wish you'd stop calling him that.' Amber didn't mind really, but she felt bad when Ella reminded her that she was deceiving her mother.

'Mr Luverman? I call him that 'cos he can take you places that nobody else can.'

'Ella, give it a rest.'

'OK, but I'm just jealous. Being a boring old student with no boyfriend and exams on the horizon, I have no sex life and I want to hear all about yours. I don't know how you're doing any revision at all. Are you?' Ella asked suspiciously.

'Of course,' Amber snapped.

She still hadn't told Ella that Karl had asked her to travel to America with him and the band. She didn't know why; it wasn't as if Ella would disapprove. They'd wanted to be daring, the opposite of sensible, and skipping the exams was just that. But she hadn't managed to say it yet.

It was Thursday evening, less than a week to go to Amber's eighteenth birthday, and less than three weeks to the exams. Faye paused in her driveway and looked across Summer Street to the park. There were no children running or scampering there now, but the evening dog walkers were out in force. She could see Christie Devlin in the distance, light and elegant as a ballerina, with those two cute little dogs skipping around her feet. Mr Coughlan, a very elderly gentleman who owned three pugs, was just in front, walking slowly with his nose in the air, just like his dogs with their squashed-up faces and airs of refinement. People did look like their dogs, Faye thought with a grin.

When Amber had been younger, Faye had spent many

hours in the park, overseeing five-a-side football matches or watching racing games. They'd both loved the park then, but now, well, Faye rarely went in there. There wasn't any time in her life for sitting in parks, she was always busy.

And yet now it was going to be ripped in half, she felt oddly angry.

Summer Street wouldn't be the same without the rackety old pavilion surrounded by its carpet of green. Faye knew it was crazy to mourn something she never used, but just because she didn't go into the park, didn't mean she didn't appreciate it.

If only she had the energy or the time to do something about it, to fight the council, to insist that they stop the deal. But that would involve going around the neighbours and getting names and signatures, drafting petitions, all sorts of work that Faye didn't have time for. Also, that job was for people who were good at chatting to strangers and Faye had lost that ability a long time ago. No, somebody else would be bound to start a campaign and she would add her name to the signatures. That'd be enough. Getting involved was always a mistake.

The house was quiet. Amber wasn't home yet. Probably at Ella's revising. Good, Faye thought. It gave her a chance to make a special dinner for the two of them. A pre-birthday dinner. She'd decided to give Amber the portfolio tonight instead of waiting until her birthday the following Wednesday, half hoping that the gift would have a magical effect on the coolness between them. And as an extra treat, she quickly rustled up some flapjacks. They used to be Amber's favourites years ago, and although they were such a childish food, she'd suddenly felt like making them. Feeding her daughter the love that Amber didn't seem to want any more.

Amber arrived after seven, laden down with her school books and looking, yet again, oddly alert and excited.

The portfolio lay at her place on the table, a giant package wrapped in gold paper, tied with narrow gold ribbon.

She stared at it in silence for a moment. A present? She'd planned to talk to her mother about Karl tonight, had spent ages with him to buoy herself up for this moment and now her mother had ruined it all with a gift. How could they have the conversation from hell now?

Mum, I'm not going to do my exams because my boyfriend and his band have a development deal with a New York producer and I'm going with him because he needs me and I love him. Oh yeah, and thanks for the portfolio.

'It's an early birthday present.'

Mum looked so thrilled with herself. And she'd made stupid flapjacks too. Kids' biscuits. That was what was wrong with Mum, Amber thought, guilt making her angry. She still treated Amber as if she was a kid.

Don't stay up too late: you won't be able to get up for school.

Take a scarf in case it's cold.

I don't care if everyone else in the class is going, you're not.

She meant well, but she'd never accept that Amber was an adult with adult desires and her own choices to make.

Amber knew with sudden certainty that there would be no easy way to tell her mother about Karl. The umbilical cord couldn't be stretched – only severed.

'Open it.' Faye couldn't understand why Amber hadn't launched herself on the gift and ripped it open, the way she used to do with presents.

Amber shot a tense look at her mother, then carefully opened the gift.

'Well, do you like it?'

Amber bit her lip. The portfolio was beautiful, and had cost her mother a fortune she didn't have. Worse, the treacherous thought slipped into her mind of what she and Karl could have done with that money. It would have paid Amber's ticket to America. The band's fare would be covered by the production company but she and Karl had to come up with hers.

This present was so typical of her mother: spend what she didn't have just so Amber could have the best. It was so unnecessary. And it made Amber feel guiltier than ever.

'Of course I like it.' She managed to keep the irritation out of her voice.

'Really?'

Amber felt the tension coil in her.

'Really,' she said. 'It's lovely.' Lovely but totally bloody useless, since she wasn't going to art college and wouldn't need it. Not yet, anyhow. She could study art anywhere, any time. When she and Karl were settled, she'd do it. A gift like hers couldn't be lost.

'I thought you'd prefer the cream but we can change it if you'd prefer a black one,' Mum went on fondly.

The hands holding the portfolio tightened and Amber felt as if she was holding in a scream. Would her mother ever stop?

'Thank you, it's lovely,' she said, forcing the words out of somewhere. She pecked her mother on the cheek. 'I've so much work to do.'

'But what about dinner?'

'I'm not hungry. I ate at Ella's,' improvised Amber.

'Amber, I know you're worried about the exams . . .' began Faye, desperate to get her daughter talking.

The tension in Amber finally sprang free. 'The fucking exams aren't what this is all about!' she yelled. 'You don't understand, you don't understand anything!'

Faye's face was stricken. 'Amber, please, talk to me. We've always talked about everything. What's wrong?'

'I told you,' hissed Amber, 'you wouldn't understand. You've never done anything with your life, you've never taken a single risk. I'm different from you. I need space, not you hanging over me waiting and hoping for me to live my life the way you want!'

'I never wanted that.' Faye could hardly speak with the hurt. How could Amber accuse her of this, of expecting too much from her, when all she'd ever wanted was for Amber to be safe and not to have to go through what she had. 'I only ever wanted you to be happy.'

'No,' shot back Amber, and it was fear and guilt talking, making her say hateful things because she couldn't bear her mother looking at her with those huge wounded eyes. 'You wanted me to be happy in your way. The sensible, dull and boring way. That's not what I want. I don't want to end up like you.'

'Oh, darling, please, listen to me . . .'

'No, I won't listen to you any more, Mum. I'm an adult now and I've got my own life to lead, and so do you.' Amber paused, flushed with emotion. 'I can't be responsible for being here with you, you've got to move on and not stay stuck in the past, stuck remembering Dad. Being a widow shouldn't define your life.'

There, she'd said it: told her mother to move on. It wasn't quite how she'd meant to put it but it was a start. She wouldn't be around any more, she'd be away with Karl and even if she hadn't got round to saying that, she'd said the main part. They weren't a little family unit any more. She and Karl were the unit. Her mother had to be made to understand that.

Faye said nothing at all. She watched Amber as she tucked her present under her arm and left the kitchen, anything to be away from her mother's anxious face and the weight of her expectations.

Alone, surrounded by flapjacks, Amber's favourite feta and filo-pastry pie, and torn wrapping paper, Faye felt lost and unbearably hurt. What had she done wrong?

For once, she didn't bother to tidy up the kitchen, scrubbing with her own solution of bleach and water, eau de Faye, as she used to joke. The dinner sat untouched on the table and she walked, sleepwalked almost, to her bedroom.

It was a pretty room, feminine, luxurious in its way, a boudoir that nobody at Little Island would easily identify as hers.

Her office, with its clean surfaces, tables and chairs set at precise right angles, and the pot plant whose leaves she cleaned every week, was a far cry from this haven of soft fabrics. There was a luscious velvet throw in antique rose on the bed, and Tiffany-style lampshades that cast a soft burnished light.

Not knowing quite what else to do, Faye sat on the edge of her bed. She felt powerless. It was so long since she'd had that feeling and it flooded back into every vein as if it had never been away.

'What can I do now?' she said aloud. Inner strength could get you through anything. She'd trained herself to believe that and loved to read about other women who'd gone through pain to emerge stronger, tougher, untouchable. They were proof that she was in some kind of women's club. The We Screwed Up But Hey, We're Still Here Club.

But to do it, you needed that inner strength and hers was centred around one central core, Amber. Golden, loving, talented, funny Amber. Without Amber's love, that strength crumbled. And Amber had just cast herself off like a shard of ice shearing off an iceberg.

She sat on the bed for a long time, hearing Amber moving around upstairs, then the sound of music thumping through from the attic bedroom. The Scissor Sisters were playing, and

Faye managed a half-smile because to her they sounded like a classic seventies rock band, like one of her old vinyl records. She still had some of her old LPs. And the photos.

They were hidden in the big bottom drawer of Faye's 1930s wardrobe, under a bundle of spare sheets and a couple of elderly Foxford rugs. She got up and pulled open the drawer. *Spare pillowcases*, said the label on the box. Who'd open that? Faye had reasoned. Not even Amber, who rooted around in her mother's dressing table for make-up, would bother to look in there. Perhaps if Amber had known her mother had something to hide, she might have found it. But Faye knew that she'd managed to keep her secret very well.

What had her daughter called her? Sensible, dull and boring. Seventeen years of trying to become someone she wasn't had been very successful, it appeared.

She hadn't touched the box for years, but now she carried it over to the bed and, settling herself against her pillows, took off the lid.

On top of the pile of memories inside was a grainy colour photograph of a girl with wide, laughing eyes and tawny hair rippling around her shoulders. Very like Amber, in fact. She was sitting in the middle of a group of smiling people, captured mid-laugh, frozen in time. Behind them was a wall of leatherette from a curving banquette; in front of them, a bar table spread with bottles, glasses, cigarette packs, ashtrays.

Faye didn't remember the names of everyone in the picture, but she could hear the music that had been playing when Jimi had taken it – Led Zeppelin, something dark and moody, the mahogany darkness of 'Kashmir', perhaps.

She wondered where Jimi was now. Then, he'd been a sweet guy with spiky punk hair and a lost puppy-dog expression who hung around the fringes of the gang. He was probably unrecognisable now, working in a strait-laced office job with

132

a tie, lace-up shoes and normal hair. But then, she was hardly recognisable herself.

Nobody looking at mumsy Faye Reid in her high street navy suit and her neat little earrings could imagine her as the girl in that picture, the one who'd been swaying sexily to the music moments before the photo had been taken.

When she moved the pile of photos, a faint scent of perfume rose from the box. YSL's heady Opium, she remembered. She closed her eyes, and it was as though she was there once more in her former life. She could almost smell the atmosphere of The Club. Smoke, marijuana, the full-bodied reek of Jack Daniel's, perfume and sweat. And excitement. The excitement of not knowing what might happen next.

The mixed-up girl she'd been then was no more, but Faye would never forget her.

That girl represented both the great tragedy and the triumph of her life, a former life she'd never been able to share with Amber.

Keeping it all a secret had been an obsession with Faye because if Amber knew, she'd never understand and their relationship would be destroyed. Except that somehow, her relationship with Amber was fracturing more every day anyway. Faye was beginning to wonder if things might be better if Amber actually knew the truth.

CHAPTER NINE

Hi Shona,
How are you? Is all still well on your planet? I miss
you, Paul and Ross and the fun we had.

So much, Maggie thought. How come you only realised how
great your friends were when they weren't around?

No news here at all. I am sitting in my bedroom at
my dad's ancient laptop on Friday morning and I keep
getting this weird feeling that it's a Sunday night and
I've got school in the morning. If Hart to Hart was still
on the telly, it'd be like nothing has changed.
Did I ever tell you that I wanted to be Jennifer Hart?
She was always so nice, so beautiful, had a rich husband
and never had to do housework. I honestly thought that
was an option when I was small: that one day I'd grow
up to be her and I'd have a gorgeous Mercedes-driving
husband who happened to be a multi-millionaire and my
hair would look fantastic, auburn rather than carrot, and
there'd be a Max around to do stuff. Where have all the
millionaires gone? I might sign up to a class to find one.

Ooops, can't. I couldn't keep up the act: the long nails, the long blonde hair or the giggling at my chosen million-aire's stupid jokes – which is what all the magazines say is vital. I am also at a loss in the boob department. Millionaires seem to like women with tiny waists and big boobs who simper that they only eat grilled fish and nothing but nuts after six o'clock. My chest and my waist are the same size and I like a proper dinner, plus dessert and maybe a bar of chocolate or two after six. I would not fit in.

Anyway, I hate men. Except for Ross and Paul, and they don't count. And Dad. Nice men who don't hit on me don't count, either. Not that any men are hitting on me, Shona. So no mad phone calls about how I should put mascara on and wear flat shoes so I'm shorter than them because men like short women, OK? Summer Street is a date-free zone, like wildlife preserves where hunters can't go after ducks. Men around here are like my parents' friends, the nice dad sort who worry about when they're going to cut the hedge.

And when did men fling themselves at me anyway? Like, never.

Elisabeth had been on the phone a lot from Seattle telling her to get out and get a life.

'Please don't say that the only way to get over a guy is to get under another one,' warned Maggie, which was what Ross had said to her on the phone, adding that if he left it too long between dates, both he and Nureyev got depressed.

Maggie got depressed just thinking about having sex with another man. That electric attraction she'd felt for Grey could hardly be found twice in a lifetime. All she wanted was him and she couldn't have him, mustn't have him.

'That's old-fashioned drivel about getting another man,'

Elisabeth said, 'and I'd never give advice like that. A man's the last thing you need. I mean go out with co-workers, friends. Go to galleries, take up charity work, try a new sport, have fun.'

Maggie didn't think she knew how to have fun any more.

Don't know if the boss told you but they've let me extend my unpaid leave. After that, I have to put up or shut up. Get another job or come back. Don't know if I can face the college again.

Mum's librarian friend who gave me my first job years ago has asked me to do a few shifts in the local library as a huge favour. One of her people is pregnant and has had to go off early because of back pain. So I'm filling in and it's great, actually. Almost a relief, which sounds unkind to Mum and Dad, but you know what I mean.

She hadn't worked in a public library for years and it was quite nice to get out of the house for a few hours, to escape from the claustrophobia of home.

I'm in the children's department and I really like it, actually. The kids are gorgeous and no, I'm not broody, so don't even go there. Kids say the funniest things. They're so blunt, it's hilarious. Plus, I get to flick through the books I loved as a kid. I'm rereading the Narnia series. I can't believe I haven't read them for years.

Have you seen Grey? No, don't answer that. Yes, do. And as for that blonde piece, put a note on her file. 'Slept with librarian's long-term boyfriend' should do it. 'Known for ripping pages out of books' might be even better.

I don't know what her name is. Probably something

*like Flower or Petal or Butterfly, stupid bitch. He must
still be with her. It's been two weeks and I haven't heard
anything from him since the first day. Some boyfriend
he turned out to be.*

Not that I'm bitter. I am better off without him.
Love Maggie.

She logged off. The last bit was untrue. She was bitter and
right now, no, she didn't feel better off without Grey.

Since she'd been home, her mother had perked up no end
having her daughter around, while Maggie herself felt
strangely adrift. She was living in the house she'd grown up
in with her parents – whom she loved, even if they did occasionally drive her mad – and yet the sense of belonging had
gone.

All the remaining remnants of her younger self – the furry
cushions on her bed, the Holly Hobbie dolls on the shelves
– only made her feel more alone, more isolated.

In this bedroom, she'd cried with misery over the hell of
school and dreamed of a wonderful future, where she would
be wise and successful. Now she was back, futureless and
feeling not a lot wiser.

'Bean!' her father yelled. 'We're going to the café for lattes
and paninis. It's the Friday-morning special. Want to come?'

Sense of belonging wasn't the only thing to change. When
had her parents started having lattes and paninis? What was
wrong with a coffee and a bun, which was what they used
to sell there. Home had moved on without her, Maggie
thought, almost childishly. It wasn't supposed to change. It
was supposed to stay exactly the same so she could come
back and refresh. Still, latte and panini was better than sitting
in her bedroom.

'OK, coming.' At least in the café, there couldn't be too
many probing questions about Grey.

137

Breakfast in the café ended in a cholesterol-inducing flurry at eleven when eggs done every which way came off the menu, and wraps, paninis and ciabatta bread sandwiches went on. Henry was painstakingly writing the day's lunch specials on the blackboard outside the café when the Maguires arrived, first Una, regal with her crutches, and then her people-in-waiting, Maggie and Dennis, bringing up the rear, carrying Una's handbag and a cushion so she could rest her leg on a hard chair.

'Henry, love, how are you?' asked Una.

Henry, a fatherly balding man in cords and a checked shirt, stopped writing to greet Una, who was one of his favourite customers.

'How's the poor leg?' he asked solicitously.

'Sore but what's the point of complaining?' said Una. 'If that's the worst thing that happens to me, won't I be fine?'

They went in and arranged themselves at a table by the window, Una swivelling herself until she was comfortable before handing her crutches to Maggie. Xu, the petite Chinese waitress, appeared with a silent smile and gave them menus. Maggie smiled hello back at her. There was something that fascinated her about Xu. Imagine coming all that way to a country where you knew nobody. Yet Xu didn't appear lonely or sad, just grateful for this chance of a new life in Ireland. Her life must have been hard before, Maggie surmised, but she didn't want to offend Xu by asking intrusive questions, so she settled, Maggie-style, for smiling a lot at her.

Henry finished working on the blackboard and came inside.

'Tell me, Henry, what's good today? We're trying to feed poor Maggie up or she'll go home to Galway and Grey will think we starved her here. Grey's her partner,' Una added in her version of sotto voce, which meant only half the street heard.

Maggie managed the required polite smile at this. Had her

138

mother always mentioned Grey this often or was it notice-able only now that he was gone?

'Great soup, wild mushroom,' said Henry, who had come in after them. 'Jane's trying out this new cookbook and herself and Xu were slaving away all morning at it.'

'Let's have that, then,' said Una. 'We love trying new things, don't we?'

She beamed at Maggie who was trying to make herself think cheerful thoughts so she could join in this happy family lunch instead of looking like a shrivelled old misery guts. But what was a cheerful thought?

Let's face it, she decided, she had better take the bull by the horns. It would be easier to tell the truth than to suffer endless public comments about how wonderful Grey was.

'Grey and I have split up,' she blurted out.

Her father immediately looked concerned and laid a hand on hers, while her mother bit her lip.

'Oh, Maggie, love,' Una sighed. 'I wish you'd told us before, you poor pet, instead of bottling it up. We love you.'

There it was: the most simple and most poignant thing any parent could say. They loved her and it didn't matter if she was single or about to be married to the planet's most eligible bachelor, they loved her.

'I didn't mean to cry,' she said, crying. Honestly, what was wrong with her? It was like being sixteen again, tearful at the drop of a hat. 'We broke up just before you had the acci-dent and I thought you had enough to deal with without my worries as well. I – well, he – it wasn't working.' She couldn't tell them about the blonde. It would be too humiliating.

'He wasn't good enough for you,' snapped her father, angry wolf circling his precious cub. 'Should have asked to marry you. I said that all along, didn't I, Una? What sort of a man goes out with a girl for five years and never wants to make an honest woman out of her?'

139

'Dennis,' warned his wife. 'This is not the time for recriminations.'

'Well, he never asked, did he? Marriage isn't that unfashionable now, lots of people are doing it, but it wasn't good enough for me bucko, no sirree . . .'

'Dennis!'

'Dad, Mum, it's OK. I'm OK about it all,' Maggie lied. 'Really, we both knew it wasn't working.' She was glad she hadn't mentioned Petal, or whatever her name was. Her normally mild-mannered father might run off to purchase a gun and remould Grey's intestinal tract with a bullet. Who could tell?

'You'd had enough of him?' asked Dad, suddenly concerned with getting a speck of dust from his eye. 'That's my girl. Dump him and move on, that's the ticket. You always knew how to take care of yourself.'

It was almost too much for Maggie. She'd never known how to take care of herself. She'd spent four years of hell in school for that very reason. But inexplicably her dad believed otherwise. She wasn't sure whether to laugh or sob. Did he and Mum not understand what sort of a mess of a person she really was?

The next morning, Maggie was on her knees in the library playhouse tidying up books when she heard her name called.

'Maggie!' Tina, the other librarian in the children's section, hissed urgently. 'You've got a visitor.'

It was hard for a tall person to squash down enough to get even half of themselves inside the library's red wooden kiddie zone, so Maggie figured that unless Bill Clinton was outside exuding charisma and charm, whoever it was could wait until she'd finished tidying up the picture books that small kids loved to take into the house.

'Maggie!' hissed Tina again.

'Keep your knickers on!' Maggie hissed back as she grabbed *The Very Hungry Caterpillar*, and instantly wished she'd said nothing. It had only taken one day of being under the watchful gaze of wide-eyed primary school kids for her to realise that children loved saying things to their parents like: 'The lady behind the desk said "crap", Mummy. That's a bad word. Is she going to get into trouble?'

Books still in her arms, she wriggled out of the small space and sat back on her knees. There were no kids in hearing range, thankfully. But standing beside Tina, who looked intrigued, was Grey, particularly drop-dead gorgeous in his serious business outfit of dark brown jacket, collar and tie. It was his meeting-with-the-boss outfit, and today, it seemed, Maggie merited boss treatment.

It was strange how easily she'd managed to forget the effect Grey's physical presence had on her. Away from him, it was simple to think him ordinary, a man who left beard scum in the bathroom sink, upturned his cereal bowl to drink the milk, and snored like an asthmatic pig in bed. Now that he was here, arrestingly handsome, her stomach flipped, remembering.

'Hello, Grey.'

'Hi, Maggie.'

They stared at each other. Maggie's instinct was to move to hug him until the picture flashed into her mind again: Grey and his blonde in their bed. Immediately, her stomach did the other sort of flip, the betrayed and devastated flip that completely neutralised the effect of his charisma.

'How are you?' he said. 'I've really missed you.'

For an instant, she forgot where they were: all she could think was that Grey was here to tell her that he loved her and that they should forget the past, she was the one for him. Then, reality reasserted itself. She was at work. Grey was saying these things in front of Tina, whose eyes were protruding so far it looked as if she was a rabbit with myxomatosis.

She imagined his face if the positions had been reversed and she'd accosted him in a tutorial. He'd have been furious.

This was not a game, Maggie thought darkly. It was her life and she wasn't going to be played with.

'Long time no see. What are you doing in Dublin?' Maggie asked evenly.

'I came to see you,' he replied. 'To bring you home.'

He hadn't spoken to her in two weeks and now he'd just turned up at her place of work and thought he could fix everything. How dare he?

Anger and heartache fought in Maggie's head and anger won.

'How did you know I was working here?' she asked.

'Paul told me. By mistake,' Grey added. 'He said Shona would kill him. And me,' Grey added, as if the possibility was ludicrous. Women never stayed angry with him for long, he was too charming. Able to charm them into bed, Maggie thought.

'I'm at work, Grey,' she said with a coolness she didn't know she possessed. 'I can't talk.'

'Later then?' he asked. 'Lunchtime?'

Maggie managed to keep her game face on. 'I'm busy at lunchtime,' she said with the air of someone with so many appointments she needed an assistant to keep her diary straight. The keep-'em-keen angel that was Shona hovered in her head, shrieking, *make him suffer, make him wait for you!*

She remembered Shona's advice when she had told her what had happened.

If you go back to him, I'll never speak to you again! Don't ditch your principles just because you're crazy about him. You deserve better.

Grey leaned against the end of the J–K shelf, graceful as

ever, long legs crossing at the ankles. Maggie could almost sense Tina sighing in appreciation, and she felt irritated again. Not for jealousy's sake but because Tina – who was twenty years older than Maggie and should know better – was falling into the same trap Maggie herself had tumbled into: believing that a stunning-looking man was a prize beyond rubies.

Only if he was faithful.

'When then?' And Grey looked straight into her eyes as if they were in a private room and he was able to caress her into agreeing to anything.

'After work. Half five.' Maggie felt jolted by how much she suddenly wanted him to hold her, despite it all.

'The Summer Street Café.' It was the only place she could think of and instantly regretted it. Just up the road from home and her parents might drop in, you never knew. Maggie couldn't cope with a scene, not now.

'That pretty little blue and white place on the corner?' Grey asked.

She remembered she'd taken him there once before when he'd visited her parents. It had felt like a royal tour, showing him where she'd grown up, wanting him to love it all and approve of it, and Grey had said he did, but she'd imagined he felt it all a bit provincial really. A street where everyone knew everyone else. The only street where Grey would like to know everyone was probably in a toney neighbourhood in Washington DC where world policies were discussed with under-secretaries at dinner parties, not gossip over muffins in a little café.

On that occasion, Maggie had lost count of the people who'd come up to them in the café and said, 'I haven't seen you for ages, Maggie,' and then, with unconcealed fascination: 'And who's this gentleman?'

'Yes. We'll only have half an hour but I'm sure that'll be long enough,' she said coolly.

143

He didn't respond to the barb.

'See you then.' He touched her arm gently as he left and Maggie closed her eyes in pain.

Tina took the books from Maggie's arms. She was at least a foot shorter than Maggie and favoured pale blue above all other clothes colours.

With books in her arms and a glint of pearl earrings peeking out behind a grey bob, she looked like the archetypal librarian. But Maggie knew she had a wicked sense of humour and could make the library staff room rock with laughter.

'There's a new hair salon up the road,' she said, eyeing Maggie's unwashed, tangled locks. 'You could take early lunch today. It's my turn, but I don't mind. I wasn't going anywhere.'

Maggie felt herself come back to earth and smiled at Tina.

'I need a hairdo?' she asked in mock surprise.

'It wouldn't hurt,' Tina said. 'Might make him wonder what you were doing for lunch and with whom.'

'I don't want him to think I got my hair done for him, though.'

'When did a man ever notice your hair?' Tina demanded. 'He'll think you're looking amazing without him, and you'll feel better if you're going to dump him and you look marvellous.'

'True,' sighed Maggie without much enthusiasm.

Tina shot her a gimlet-eyed look. 'You are going to dump him?'

Maggie nodded, and found herself confessing. 'I caught him with someone else. Younger, sexy, big boobs: your basic nightmare.'

'Well, you're hardly the hunchback of Notre Dame yourself,' Tina responded.

'Oh, I'm just thin,' Maggie said, exasperated. People who weren't thin always thought it was the be-all and end-all of looks. It wasn't. Sexy and curvy, and with skin that could be tanned and hair that could be tamed: *that* was something.

'Just thin, huh?' Tina came closer. 'Do yourself a favour, Maggie. I don't know where they've put the mirrors in your house, but there's a lot more to you than just thin. And if Romeo hasn't told you so, then you've got to dump him because he's a vampire sort of guy – sucks the life force right out of you and convinces you that you're ugly and useless.'

Maggie stared at her. She wanted to say that Tina was wrong, that Grey was the only one who'd made her feel sexy and gorgeous, and that his leaving her had taken it all away from her. But it would sound so silly.

All afternoon, after she got back from the hairdressers with tumbling glossy curls that made a gang of workmen on the road whoop and whistle at her, she thought about what Tina had said. And Shona. And Elisabeth.

You're worth more, they'd said. Grey didn't deserve you, they'd said. And she'd dismissed their advice because it was well-meaning girlfriend talk where people said the right thing to buoy up your spirits. It didn't have to be true. It was just verbal hugging. *We love you even if he doesn't.*

But for once, she tried to step outside herself and imagine if she was wrong. What if Grey wasn't good enough for her?

He'd never asked her to marry him, though they'd been going out for five years and it seemed like the next logical step. Even at Shona and Paul's wedding, where Maggie had been a bridesmaid and had caught the bouquet – well, Shona had flung it directly at her, so catching wasn't the operative word – even then, Grey hadn't held her hand tightly or looked at her in a manner that suggested it could be them next.

'Hasn't today been romantic?' she'd said that evening as they sat in the sunset on the hotel terrace, Grey handsome in his pale linen suit, Maggie like a wood nymph in hand-dyed green silk, with tiny creamy flowers woven into her hair.

145

'Must be costing them a small fortune,' Grey had remarked, sucking on his cigar. Shona's dad had passed round cigars after the toasts and Grey had insisted on going out to smoke it instantly. He looked like a character in a Scott Fitzgerald novel, Maggie thought, with love. His hair suited him swept back and he twirled the fat cigar expertly, savouring it. 'You could put a down payment on a fine house for what today's costing. Is it typically Irish, I wonder,' he added thoughtfully, 'this business of a huge, costly ceremony with everyone you know there? It's like our obsession with owning land. We can't just rent, we have to own. It's always the grand gesture. I could write a paper on it, what do you think?'

In the library, an entire year after the event, Maggie felt suddenly aflame with anger at what Grey had said. She'd been annoyed then, too, but hadn't said it, assuming Grey was just bored because he wasn't Shona's biggest fan – it was mutual – and wasn't as fired up with enthusiasm over the whole event as Maggie had been.

'It's nice to have everyone you care about watch you marry the person you love,' she'd said hopefully. Her mother would be in seventh heaven organising Maggie's wedding, and her father would probably spend months working on his speech, a speech that would be loving, respectful and would prob-ably halt halfway through for Dad to wipe his eyes behind his glasses.

That's what she'd been thinking of at Shona and Paul's wedding, and bloody Grey had been thinking of another bloody paper. It wasn't that he wasn't clever enough to understand what Maggie had been getting at: he wasn't one of those academics who understood chaos theory but couldn't change a light bulb. Grey was savvy. He'd simply avoided a discussion about marriage because he wasn't interested in marrying her.

And she'd been so besotted, so terrified of frightening him

off, she'd let him get away with it. She'd shut up like a good girl.

Maggie wasn't sure which of them she was most angry with: herself or Grey.

She'd never seen Summer Street quite so busy as today, when at 5.28 she walked up to meet Grey at the café. Just when she wanted no one to notice them. 'Hello, Maggie!' Somebody waved across the road at her. Maggie felt cornered. A woman with grey-blonde hair, vaguely familiar. Maggie had no idea who it was.

'Hello,' she said brightly. 'How are you and . . . er, everyone?' Everyone was the fail-safe for when she couldn't remember if the person in question had a husband or children or a budgie menagerie.

'Oh, they're all fine,' said the woman. 'Fine. How are you? Your poor mother, I heard about her leg. I haven't dropped in to see her because I'm just so busy with the Guides.'

The Girl Guides! That was it, thought Maggie, delighted. Now she knew. Mrs Cooke, lived at the bottom of the road and was an outrageous busybody. It was a complete miracle that she hadn't been to the house already to see Mum's leg, pass comment on the furniture and circulate details of her visit.

'I'll call in now, though,' said Mrs Cooke with horrible intent.

'Well, she's not really having visitors today,' Maggie said hurriedly. 'She's tired, needs to sleep a lot really. It takes it out of a person when they break their leg.'

'Of course, I completely understand,' said Mrs Cooke. 'I'll drop in next week instead. She'll be feeling better then.' And she was gone.

By the time Maggie made it to the café, she had nodded, waved, smiled and recounted the story of her mother's leg

147

to two more people. So much for trying to meet Grey in a quiet place.

The café was the centre of the local universe and entirely the wrong place to meet a man whom your parents were hatching a plan to stab.

Not that the lovely Henry and Jane would breathe a word to Dennis and Una if Maggie had met King Kong himself and sat at one of the back tables, stroking his furry arms and discussing big buildings to climb. But someone else might blab.

It was in this frame of mind that Maggie shoved open the door of the café and looked around suspiciously. It came as a great relief to see that, apart from Grey, it was empty.

Grey had naturally got the best seat, at a slightly larger than normal table in the window. There he sat, looking gorgeous and relaxed, a black coffee in front of him along with a croissant that he had half nibbled and pushed away. How typically man-like, Maggie thought, irritably. He'd only eaten half the croissant and realised he didn't need the rest. A woman would have eaten it no matter what: she'd bought it – she'd eat it.

'Hello,' Maggie said, and plonked herself down in the seat opposite him. She was angry and nothing Grey could say would change it.

'Maggie,' said Henry, coming up before Grey could open his mouth. 'Can I get you anything?'

'Erm, ah, coffee, black,' she said stupidly, because she took milk and sugar.

'Anything to eat?'

'Muffin, erm, sugar-free.'

'Carrot or lemon or chocolate?' Henry asked politely.

It was as if her ability to speak had disappeared.

'Lemon,' she said finally.

So much for getting her hair blow-dried into tousled, artful curls at lunchtime. What use was looking glamorous and untouchable when she couldn't string two sentences together? Henry vanished and Grey and Maggie stared at each other.

'So,' she said.

'I'm really glad you came to meet me,' Grey said, looking the picture of penitence. 'I've missed you. You've no idea how much.' He reached across the table and grabbed her hand. Maggie pulled it away.

'Sorry. I shouldn't rush it,' he said.

'No,' she agreed.

They sat in silence.

'How have you been?' he asked.

'Fine.'

'You don't look fine.'

'Thanks for that vote of confidence,' she said sarcastically.

'I didn't mean it that way. You look beautiful.' He reached out again for her hand but thought better of it. 'You always look beautiful.'

'I thought you preferred blondes with big tits,' Maggie said, aiming for flippant and sounding desperately hurt instead.

Henry put a coffee in front of her and pretended he hadn't heard.

'You know, Henry, maybe you could put a bit of frothy stuff on the top of it, I changed my mind.'

'No problem.' Henry whisked it away. Thirty-five years in the café business meant he knew better than to question a woman's change of mind.

'I don't prefer blondes,' Grey said earnestly. 'I prefer women with wild red hair, and liquid blue eyes I can't stop thinking about . . .'

'Oh, Grey, stop it,' she said. 'That's crap. You were in bed with her. Nothing you can say can change that.'

'I know.'

'Let's talk about the apartment and what we're going to do with it,' she added. That was good, she was firm, in control. She would not turn into the old Maggie, desperate for approval.

'I'm not here to talk about the apartment. I'm here to make you come home.'

'I left two weeks ago, so it's taken you quite a long time to get here,' she said sharply.

'I was giving you time to think, time to get over being mad at me,' he said with such simple sincerity that she felt herself being pulled back in.

'I'm not mad, I'm hurt. Betrayed. Devastated,' she emphasised. 'Mad is what you get when you stub your toe. I loved you with all my heart for five years and you threw it back at me by taking another woman to bed in our apartment, so no, mad doesn't quite do that justice.'

'It was just a figure of speech,' he said, giving her that wry grin she adored.

Maggie felt herself being reeled in again, despite her plans to tell him it was all over. Because that's what she'd told herself she'd do, wasn't it?

Henry put the coffee down a second time.

'Is that all right for you, Maggie?' he asked.

'Yes, thank you, perfect,' she said.

Henry looked shrewdly from one to the other, smiled and walked back into the kitchen.

'You've every right to be angry with me,' Grey went on, as if they hadn't been interrupted. 'I didn't know what to do to make it better, that's the truth. I . . .' He hesitated. 'I know what you think, but nothing like this has ever happened before, I want you to believe that, Maggie. It was a stupid one-off thing and I can't forgive myself – that's why I haven't been in touch. I didn't think you'd even want to see me. I can understand how hard it is for you to forgive me but

150

please, we've got so much going for us. We can't throw it all away.'

'I didn't throw it all away – you did!' she breathed. 'You did.'

They both sat back in their chairs, a pair of gladiators wondering how to attack next.

Again, the moment on the terrace at Shona and Paul's wedding flashed through Maggie's mind. She hadn't been a strong modern woman and asked her boyfriend if he thought they should get married. She'd wittered on about how romantic the wedding was, waiting for him to say something, and then when he'd dodged the subject, she'd never mentioned it again. What a wimp.

'Why did you never want to get married?' she demanded suddenly. 'You knew I did. I hinted that I did. But you avoided the subject.'

'Well . . . I . . .' For once, Dr Grey Stanley was nonplussed.

Maggie watched him think. She could read his face like a book, or so she'd once believed – now she realised she was wrong. She hadn't read signs of his infidelity. Another certainty crumbled.

'You didn't want to get married, did you?' she said, looking down at her coffee.

'No,' he said. 'Truthfully, no. I thought we had everything already and that marriage would spoil it. Why fix what's not broken, right?'

'You're the one who broke it.'

He bowed his head, as if the weight of the pain was too much to bear. 'I can't tell you how sorry I am, Maggie. I miss you so much, I want you back, I should never have let you leave that morning. Everyone says I must be mad to have let you go, you're so stunning, beautiful, too good for me, they tell me.' And he laughed, but it was clear that somebody had indeed said that to him. And Maggie felt a surge

151

of pleasure that at least someone on campus had thought good of her.

'Is that why you're here? Because your colleagues think you should be with me instead of some beautiful little blonde?'

Grey looked up and stared at her with mystification. 'Beautiful? She's nothing compared to you. You've never had a clue how beautiful you are, Maggie. It's one of the most beguiling things about you. Most beautiful women are like stockbrokers, always bartering. Their presence costs. Presents, dinner, compliments. But not you. Even when you're sitting on the couch in your old jeans and that horrible cardigan you love, with your knees scrunched up, biting your cuticles watching a movie, you look like someone should be photographing you,' he added. 'I suppose I'm more used to the stockbroker beauties, they've got hard shells. They know their worth. But you don't.'

He reached out and took her hand now. 'Please come back to me. I do love you. Don't you believe me?'

'I believe you,' she said in a small voice, loving the feeling of his hand on hers. Her resolve to tell him it was over between them crumbled some more. 'But what does that mean, Grey? What does your loving me mean? I only want the sort of love that's not shared. I can't share you. That would kill me.'

'Let's get engaged,' he said eagerly. 'We'll set a date. Soon, let's get married soon. Please, can't you see that I'm serious?'

It sounded so seductive the way he put it. How easy it would be to go back to him. Familiarity lured her in. And marriage. Was this a proposal? If so, she would never have the face to tell people how she'd got engaged. Because her fiancé had had an affair . . .

'Now's not the time to talk about getting engaged,' she said firmly, taking her hand back.

But marriage. It was what she'd wanted ever since that day watching Shona and Paul make their vows.

There was one question she still had to ask.

'I know what you said, but I need to be certain: were there others?' She was sure she'd seen it in his eyes that night. A flash of guilt when she'd asked him if he'd slept with other women. Yet now, there was no guilt in his face, no sign that he had ever cheated before.

'I swear to you,' he said fervently, 'there has never been anyone else, Maggie. She came into my office and she was coming on to me and . . . I don't know, I felt flattered.' He hung his head, paused for a moment before looking up at her again, pleading. 'It's stupid, isn't it, stupid to be flattered by a student? She's just a kid and not even very bright. And I had you and you're so clever and brilliant and wonderful and a grown-up. Oh, I can't articulate all the things that you are, all the amazing things you are to me.'

In her head, Maggie computed that he was saying all the right things. But in her heart, she didn't care whether he was or not. He loved her, wanted her. That was what mattered. She needed him in her life.

'There was nobody else, ever?' she asked.

'No, never,' he said. 'I'll be honest, I was tempted. Sometimes kids get a crush on lecturers. You know that, we've talked about how flattering it is. Come on, I'm nearly thirty-seven, I'm over the hill as far as these kids are concerned and it's hard to resist their attention. Who wouldn't be flattered? You know what I mean,' he pleaded, 'you've had the guys come into the library, smile at you and flirt. It turns you on a little bit and you feel good. But it doesn't mean anything. None of that takes away from the love that you feel for one person, and that one person is you, Maggie, I love you. I don't love some kid. She's nobody.'

'Which is worse,' Maggie said, all the hurt of seeing him in bed with that blonde nobody flooding back, crashing into her hopes of them being a couple again, 'that you think she is a nobody or that you could have sex with someone you think is a nobody?'

He leaned back in his chair and his eyes glittered, the way they did when he was thinking. He was so clever. His mind could work on so many different levels and today Maggie could almost hear the cogs whirring.

'I didn't mean it like that,' he said. 'I don't think of women in that way.'

'Oh, for heaven's sake,' she interrupted, 'this is not a party political broadcast. I'm not a feminist voter you have to convince to come over to your side. I'm not worried about being politically correct when it comes to the person you fucked on our bed. I'm making the point that it says a lot about you when you can have sex with someone and then say they're nothing. I'd prefer it if you told me the truth.'

But she didn't really want to know the truth.

'You know what, this is a mistake,' she said wearily. She couldn't go back to him, not yet anyway. She needed more time to think about everything that had happened. 'You coming here. I was wrong. It's too soon. Maybe we should just talk on the phone or something. I'm not ready to see you and Mum's sick and . . . it's difficult.'

She had mused that afternoon in the library that two weeks was plenty of time to get over the fierce pain of his betrayal and talk sensibly but two weeks had turned out to be just a heartbeat after all. The agony was just as intense as it had been. She felt angry, hurt, stupid, so many conflicting emotions. She couldn't make a decision now.

'Let's talk about everything later. I'll come back to Galway soon and we can talk then.'

'No,' Grey said firmly. 'I want to talk to you now. I want to get it sorted out now. I can't go on living like this, with this uncertainty, wondering what's going to happen, wondering if you're going to come back to me.'

'Oh, so it's about you now, is it?' retorted Maggie furiously. 'You sleep around, wait two weeks to come to see me, then you have the audacity to say you were waiting for me to phone and you want to get it all sorted out and back to normal. Well, no thank you very much, Dr Stanley.'

'Please.' He grabbed one of her hands between both of his and his touch was electric.

'You shouldn't do that,' she said weakly, but she didn't mean it.

'I love you, Maggie,' he said. 'I'm going to go in a minute because I think that's what you want me to do, but I just want you to remember that I love you so, so much. Please remember that. I made a mistake, *one* mistake, don't crucify me for it, please. We're stronger than that. We're worth more than that.'

He stood up and leaned over the table and kissed her very gently on the lips. Almost against her will, Maggie found her head tilting up to get closer to him.

Then he moved away and stroked her cheek with exquisite gentleness.

'I love you,' he said. 'Please believe that.' And then he left.

Maggie stared back down into her coffee and stirred it. She added a couple more little packets of sugar and drank slowly, thinking. What on earth should she do?

Part of her desperately wanted to run out on to the street and call him back, to say that she couldn't live without him. But part of her was still too hurt to do that. His betrayal had broken something precious inside her and it could never be fixed.

No matter what, their relationship would never quite be the same. And, inside her, a voice relentlessly whispered: if they got back together, would Grey cheat on her again?

155

CHAPTER TEN

The brass knocker shone, the doorstep was spotless and delicious scents of beeswax polish and home baking wafted from the hallway.

Faye loved the home she'd grown up in but there was something about walking back through the door that made her feel she'd failed her mother in some way. From this tiny council house, with a combination of her widow's pension and what she earned in her part-time job, her mother had put Faye and her brother, Miles, through college at a time when there weren't many kids on their street in third-level education.

The maze of houses in the vast Linden Estate had been a tough place to bring up children, riddled as it was with petty crime and the scourge of drugs.

But Josie Heffernan had managed to keep her children on the straight and narrow so that Faye could win a place at art college and Miles could achieve the school exam results he needed to study economics at Trinity.

Now Miles was a high-flyer in corporate banking, making good use of his mother's hard work. Although Faye regretted that they didn't make enough time to see each other very often, she knew he was a loving husband and father as well as a hard worker. He'd never gone off the rails in his life. But Faye still felt a twinge of guilt that she had wasted her early promise.

It was late on Sunday morning and the house was full of Josie's friends from St Michael's Church. Josie was what people called 'a pillar of the community' in the best sense of the phrase. She got involved with kindness and capability and really made a difference.

Today, as usual, her mother was holding court in the kitchen, with every seat in the place taken, the big stainless-steel teapot on the oilcloth, and the remains of some home-made scones on jammy plates.

'Hello, Faye,' said her mother, jumping up lithely. Josie was light on her feet. A small woman, like her daughter and her granddaughter, she didn't carry an ounce of spare fat because, as Amber accurately put it, 'Gran never sits down for long.'

Whether it was cleaning St Michael's, taking care of meals on wheels or working in a local daycare centre for disabled children, Josie gave it her all.

Stan Stack, Faye's stepfather, was reading the newspapers in the quiet of the tiny living room, although how he could concentrate with the laughs coming from the kitchen, Faye didn't know.

'When Father Sean said she could feed the baby in the church and she says "fair enough" and whips out a boob, I swear, I thought I'd laugh up a lung!' shrieked one woman, church perfect in a navy suit.

'Ah, Father Sean wouldn't mind, he's been on the missions and he's seen it all,' grinned Josie. 'He'd take that in his stride.' She loved Father Sean and called him the Under Boss, in that he answered to the Man Above.

'It wasn't the boob so much as the tattoo,' insisted the

navy-clad woman. '*Robbie 4Ever* in a heart. And the husband's called Tom. That's what got me.'

'Robbie Williams,' suggested one of the ladies thoughtfully over her scone. 'I do like him.'

'They can get them off with lasers nowadays.'

'Robbie Williams?'

'No, tattoos.'

More howling ensued.

Eventually, the visitors had had enough scones and tea, and took their leave. Mother and daughter were left alone in the kitchen. Without Josie's chatty, lively crew of friends, it seemed very quiet indeed.

'How's Amber?' asked Josie, making quick work of tidying up her kitchen.

'Fine,' Faye said.

Her mother said nothing but looked at Faye inquisitively.

'All right, she's not fine,' Faye gave in. Her mother would get the information out of her anyway. She might as well explain that Amber had been avoiding her since Thursday, using the excuse of studying to rush upstairs any time Faye tried to talk to her. 'She's moody and she wants to eat her dinner on her own instead of with me.'

Josie nodded.

'She shouted at me for going into her room the other night too, because I thought she was having a nightmare.' Faye could barely cope with how much it had hurt when Amber had sat up in bed and shouted at her, hissing that she needed some privacy. Faye was used to wandering into Amber's room any time, to chat to her daughter. Now she felt that she couldn't do that, either. 'She's cutting me off.'

'And you can see how it hurts,' finished Josie softly.

Shocked, Faye looked into her mother's face and saw remembered pain there. Nearly two decades ago, she'd caused Josie exactly the same hurt Amber was causing her, she realised. Yet her mother had never for a second betrayed how wounded she'd been. There had been no recriminations. Nothing but help when she'd needed it. Her mother was extraordinary, Faye realised, not for the first time.

'Is it a man?'

'She's not that into boys,' Faye said. 'You know what she and Ella are like: they run rings around Ella's brothers and they're dead set on getting into college. Modern girls are different, they're sorted, they know what they want and they won't let anyone or any man stop them.'

'If you're sure . . .' The rest of the sentence hung in the air.

'I'm sure,' Faye said. She'd know, wouldn't she?

'Where is she today?'

'Off at Ella's, studying. It's these bloody exams,' Faye went on. 'That's the problem. When they're over, everything will be fine again.'

'For sure,' said Josie. 'Myself and Stan were going to take the train out to Howth for a bit of lunch. Would you like to come?'

Faye smiled. 'I'd love to,' she said. After all, it wasn't as if she had anything else to do without Amber.

Sunshine, beautiful food and all the people she loved most in the world together – what could be better than that? thought Christie.

It was the Sunday of the celebration, the day the Devlin family celebrated the new life they'd nearly lost. Christie stood in her kitchen and thought of dear Lenkya's pronouncement on how you could kill or cure in the kitchen as she got ready to carry trays of food outside to the garden where her family sat, some in the full sun, some in the shade of the terrace. Dear Lenkya. She'd left Ireland many years ago and although they'd kept in touch for a long time, there came a

159

point when her letters stopped and Christie's ones were never replied to. Christie hoped she was happy wherever she was.

Today, in the same way Lenkya had woven comfort and friendship in her stews, Christie had put all her wisdom and love into her cooking to nourish her family every way she could. She wished and prayed happiness into every recipe, hoping that the ferocity of her love would provide a talisman for her sons, their wives and her born and unborn grand-children.

And hoping that this love could keep the feelings of danger away.

But no, Christie refused to think about Carey Wolensky. That man would not ruin today. This Sunday was for her family, a day of love, celebration and food.

There were tender chicken kebabs and bowls of chilled salad heaving with avocado, cherry tomatoes and honeydew melon. Baked potatoes laced with sour cream and chives sat with a dish of grilled rosemary-scented slivers of lamb, and Christie's own sliced tomato and fennel bread nestled in a basket with crusty white rolls.

'Are you cooking for the apocalypse?' James had teased the evening before when Christie missed her favourite TV show because she was up to her eyes in flour, baking, measuring and peering into the oven to see if the honey and poppy-seed cake had risen. 'I haven't ordered the nuclear shelter for the garden yet, but I can if you want. Although most people take cans of food with them . . .'

'I cook therefore I am,' Christie said serenely, spooning mixture into muffin cases.

Which was true. Cooking was therapy for her as well as an expression of love for her family and right now, she needed that spiritual nourishment.

James's hand snaked out towards the mixing bowl.

Christie laughed and let him take one finger's worth of dough, before slapping his hand away.

'People who tease me don't get fed,' she said.

'Are you making guacamole for me?' he asked, eyeing the avocados. James loved food and would eat most things, but his love for guacamole was legend in the Devlin family annals.

'Have I ever forgotten to make it for you?' Christie patted his cheek with a floury hand and went on with her spooning.

'No,' said James and put his arms around his wife for a kiss.

Who'd have thought guacamole would be the secret to love, Christie thought, closing her eyes and leaning back into his arms: on such strange things were marriages made.

'Mum, this is delicious,' sighed Ethan, sitting back in a striped deckchair, the dogs at his feet and a plate piled high on his lap.

'Yes,' murmured Janet, who was paler than usual, but had a light in her eyes that Christie had never seen there before. 'I like this eating for two thing.'

'It really kicks in at dessert,' Ethan's wife, Shelly, informed her sister-in-law. 'You don't think you can eat two entire pieces of cheesecake or two wedges of chocolate cake, but you can.'

Ethan and Shane, well trained by their mother, helped her tidy up so she could bring the desserts out.

'Thanks,' Shane said, kissing her affectionately on the cheek. 'This is a lovely party.'

It was getting so hot that the dogs came in to lie on the kitchen floor, panting in the heat.

James carried in the last of the buffet plates and stacked them in the dishwasher.

'I don't know if it's the wine talking, but today has made me think. We're very lucky, Christie, aren't we?' he said as he straightened up. 'We've got everything, a healthy family, each other, a few quid in the bank.'

161

'Hey, don't you think I know it?' replied Christie, smiling at her husband. She'd had a glass of wine too and finally felt the tension leave her. She must stop thinking about Carey Wolensky. After all, how could something from so long ago touch her now? 'I thank God every day for what we've got.'

From outside in the garden came the sounds of their family enjoying themselves. Sasha was shrieking as she chased around after balloons that Christie really hoped wouldn't get caught on the spiky thorns of her Madame Pompadour rose. Children always got so upset about balloons popping.

Christie didn't have to look out to know that Shane would be beaming from ear to ear, the proud look of the daddy to be. He'd had that look on his face all day and Christie could remember when James looked exactly the same. The pride of the family man.

'I say thanks every day too,' said James. 'But, you know,' he paused, 'do you ever worry that something will happen? That one of us will become ill, something random, something we can't do anything about.'

Christie stared at him. James was never maudlin, not even after a glass of wine. Instantly, she wondered what he knew, how he'd found out. Yet he couldn't know anything, could he?

'What do you mean?' she asked tightly.

'No, no, it's nothing,' James said. 'It's just . . . I don't know. It all seems so good. Sometimes I worry that it could all go horribly wrong and we could end up bitter and twisted.'

Christie's anxious eyes looked for some sign that he knew, but there was none. Perhaps it was just that her feeling spooked had transmitted itself to him.

'Is that all?' she said with relief. 'You're the least bitter and twisted person I know. Just because we're happy doesn't mean something has to come along and ruin it all.'

'Ah, it's nothing.' James brushed his melancholy thoughts

162

away. 'I'm just being stupid. It's probably the male menopause.'

'You're too old for the male menopause,' Christie teased. 'That was supposed to happen ages ago, when I went through mine. I didn't do too badly, I didn't run off with some handsome young stud.'

'If you had, I'd have bloody killed them,' James said, suddenly serious.

'Lucky no one fitted the job description at the time,' she teased, but felt sick inside. Why had she said that? How stupid. 'Seriously, you're safe enough, my love. What would I want with a young stud, when I have you?' Christie put her arms around James, and they kissed, sinking into an embrace that was familiar and reassuring, except that today Christie didn't feel reassured.

'OK, back to basics,' she said, leaning against him. 'What are we going to do, financially, for Shane and Janet? We've got to do something. They're totally broke and they have no idea how expensive babies are.'

'I was thinking about that too,' James said. 'We've got some savings. What are we keeping them for?'

Christie kissed him. 'You're a great father,' she said, thinking of how hard it had been to save that money.

'What are you two looking so thoughtful about?' said a voice. It was Ana wandering in with another empty wine bottle. 'This is a celebratory day,' she added a touch too merrily. 'We should be happy, celebrating.'

'We're just having a chat,' Christie said lightly. 'James, will you get another bottle out of the fridge and I'll sort out the cake? Ana, you could take out these little fairy cakes I've made for the children.' She'd spent ages doing them the night before: pretty-coloured iced cakes with little animal faces to tempt the toddlers' appetites.

'Delighted to help,' said Ana, slurring her words slightly.

Over her head, James and Christie exchanged a glance. Ana had never been used to drinking and after two glasses really needed to lie down in a darkened corner.

'Come on, Ana,' James said, putting his arm around his sister-in-law affectionately. 'I'll take the plate.'

Christie was left alone in the kitchen to sort out the cake. Looking out the window, she could see Ethan cuddling little Sasha. Shelly and Janet were engrossed in baby talk, while Janet's mother, Margery, threw a balloon up into the air for Fifi. James was smiling as he helped a giggling Ana to a comfy chair.

Christie watched her family and wished she could see the future when it mattered.

James was right, they had been lucky. But it was more than luck that had made their marriage so strong over the years. You didn't spend thirty-five years with somebody without wanting to kill them occasionally. Or even leave them.

There had been that time when the children were very young and she and James had drifted far apart, when work had taken over his life and Christie had been low on his list of priorities, but they'd got over that. Eventually.

They'd worked hard to get over their differences. There hadn't been many big rows in the Devlin family household. Having grown up with nervous tension as a constant backdrop, Christie hated rows. Her father's rantings had been enough to put her off arguments for life. James was easygoing and affectionate and had brought their children up to be the same. So yes, there had been hard work involved. All the same, they were lucky. Why was James suddenly worried that their luck was about to turn? Christie shivered despite the heat.

CHAPTER ELEVEN

It was Sunday evening, one of the most important evenings ever for Karl and the band. Amber had escaped from Summer Street by telling her mother she was going to be studying late and not to bother her.

She'd left the radio on low in her room, closed the door, and hoped her mother had listened the night Amber had made her point about deserving a little privacy. That privacy meant keeping her mother away from her room so she could escape out to Karl. It also meant huge guilt over the deception.

Now, despite the two giant Southern Comforts Karl had bought her, Amber's mouth was dry and her heart was thudding. She prickled with nerves. She'd found the perfect position at the right side of the SnakePit stage, behind a giant light where there was a small box she could sit on and see perfectly, yet remain out of sight.

Huge cables trailed around her feet. The stage and backstage were both hives of activity as muscle-bound guys with tattooed biceps shifted amps and equipment, shouting to each other as they worked. Two men with radio headsets directed the backstage dance, snapping out directions, ticking off on clipboard lists. Everyone backstage at the venue appeared to have a role, from the various promoters' staff rushing round with laminates rattling off their chests to the bands themselves, cocooned in their dressing rooms to get ready.

'Give us a moment, kid?' Karl's newly appointed manager, Stevie, had said to Amber in the band's poky little room fifteen minutes previously. Before she'd been able to throw a questioning look at Karl to say how dare the man dismiss her like that, Stevie had hustled her out into the dimly lit corridor right behind the stage. Here, nobody seemed to know or care that she was Karl Evans's girlfriend and muse. Here, she was a blonde in jeans in a place that had seen a lot of blondes in jeans who were *with the band*. Amber had felt she might cry. This Sunday evening event was so important for Karl and, therefore, for her. A big showcase gig that horrible Stevie had got for them. Producers, heads of record companies, everyone who was anyone was going to be there to see the hot new bands. It was huge, but Amber, who felt she was irrevocably tied up with Karl and his future, had been sidelined.

Anxiously, she fiddled with the tiger's-eye pendant she'd found in her mother's drawer and which she wore on many of her trips with Karl. It had always comforted her before, making her think of Mum and home, where she was safe, treasured, much more than a hanger-on.

But since the terrible row on Thursday evening, when Mum had given her that stupid present, nothing had given her much comfort.

They'd had rows before, but never like that. Never with such words of bitterness and anger. Amber could hardly bear to think of what she'd said, but she couldn't back down and say sorry, because there was so much more to be said.

Mum, I'm leaving with Karl and I won't be sitting my exams, won't be going to college.

She'd done her best to avoid her mother all weekend,

muttering about having to study and not meeting Faye's eyes. She couldn't face it. The tension was killing her.

She hadn't told Karl about the row, either. He had been worrying so much about tonight he hadn't noticed how upset she was. And now he'd let Stevie throw her out of the dressing room, hadn't fought for her, hadn't sneaked out to see whether she was all right.

She hugged her knees up close to her chest, and laid her cheek on one knee. Hidden away here, safe and unseen, she'd be fine.

There were three bands before Karl's, and Amber listened, her eyes half closed in concentration, jealous of any sign of anyone better than him. And then they were on stage and her nerves returned in force.

Please let them be brilliant. Please let there be no bum notes. Don't let Karl fall apart from stage fright.

There were four of them in the band, Ceres: three other guys who were good-looking and good musicians, too, but Karl had been right when he'd told her that first night that he was the band. It was the simple truth. The magnetism he had offstage was magnified tenfold on it. Brooding and Byronic, he held the mike to his mouth with two hands, like a man might hold his lover's face cupped close to his own before kissing her lips.

Now I've found you, I can't let you go
You're in my blood
In my dreams
Like a sleepwalker, I'll come back to you
My love

It was the song he'd written for her.

'You inspired me,' he said softly after he'd played it to her one afternoon in the quiet of her bedroom when she should

167

have been at double history. Amber had listened with her heart singing along, because this was pure, true love: to be immortalised in song as the beloved of a man as gifted as Karl.

And it was all worth it, even putting up with nasty Stevie, who looked at her with appraising eyes as if she was a piece of meat he was bidding for at a market. He'd only known Karl for a week. Wait till he realised that Amber wasn't some bit of fluff, that she was part of Karl, then Stevie would change his attitude.

The last note of their three-song set finished, and Karl raised his hands in triumph at the crowd, who cheered wild approval.

They'd loved him and his band.

A huge grin split Amber's face as her lover turned to where she sat hidden and smiled that private, sexy smile he kept for her alone. He'd seen her! But just as quickly, he turned to his audience, still with her smile on his face, a smile of such languorous heat that people screamed. Then, applause ringing in his ears, he dragged himself away from the drug of the crowd's approval and stalked offstage, long-limbed, panther-like, utterly fuckable. He passed feet away from Amber's hiding place and never glanced her way. He hadn't seen her at all, she realised with a jolt. That private smile had not been for her, but for the thousand-strong crowd he'd held in the palm of his hand. It wasn't her smile any more: it was everybody's.

Amber snatched at her tiger's-eye pendant for comfort but there was none there.

An hour later in a small, late-night restaurant, Amber went to slide into the curved banquette seat beside Karl, but Stevie – stocky, slicked-back hair Stevie in his heavy leather jacket and chunky Tag Heuer watch – muscled in past her so subtly that only Amber felt the nastiness of the gesture.

'How's my best lead singer?' he said, grabbing Karl's shoulders in a matey manner.

'Walking on air,' replied Karl. 'That was some buzz in the SnakePit, wasn't it?'

'In two words, in-credible,' said Lew, the drummer, moving in to sit the other side of Karl, pulling his girlfriend, a shy girl called Katie, in after him.

'Amazing,' Kenny T, the keyboards man, pronounced, squashing up beside Katie.

'Total blast,' sighed Sydney, bass guitar. Sydney's girlfriend was away, so had missed their night of triumph. Syd had spent ages on the phone trying to describe how wonderful it had all been, and was now drinking himself into oblivion to make up for her absence. Syd settled in beside Stevie and then looked up at Amber, still standing beside the table, waiting for Karl to notice her and make space for her beside him.

But Karl didn't notice. He was wrapped up in Stevie and the flannel that spewed effortlessly from the manager's mouth.

Everyone wanted to sign the band.

They were the hottest ticket there. Stevie was so shallow, so fake, Amber thought.

Could nobody see it except for her? They were all in thrall to Stevie, laughing at his hopeless jokes. What do you call a drummer with no girlfriend? Homeless.

Lew, the drummer, laughed himself sick at that one, seeming not to realise that it was totally true in his case because Katie's teacher's salary supported him.

It was a horrible evening and Amber had never been so glad as when it ended and she and Karl were alone in the taxi.

'Will you stay the night? Please, this was so special. I want you here beside me when I wake up so I know it hasn't all been a dream.'

Karl's head was resting on her shoulder in the taxi, his breath still sweet with the orangey tang of the final glass of Cointreau. There had been endless drinks, champagne even. 'You better get used to it because it'll be premier cru all the way from now on,' Stevie had said, summoning waiters with a rude click of his fingers.

At least the waiters could see what he was like, filling his glass more slowly than anyone else's, glaring at him. She hoped they'd spat in his coffee.

'Stay,' repeated Karl sleepily.

Amber never stayed. Staying might mean her mother finding out that her bed wasn't slept in, that she hadn't been burning the midnight oil in her bedroom, studying diligently like the sensible schoolgirl she was supposed to be.

And then Karl's hands unbuttoned her jacket and reached into the cavern of her cleavage, expertly finding the exact place where the lacy strap of her bra gave a finger's-width access to the bare skin beneath.

She felt the liquid rush of desire hit her groin and moaned softly, moving closer. 'I want to be with you tonight, Amber. Please.' Suddenly, the words of the song he'd written for her came into her mind.

To hell with not wanting her mother to know. She'd have to know sometime. Karl was a part of Amber's life now, for ever.

'I'll stay,' she murmured back. 'Just try and stop me.'

Faye woke early the next morning. It was Monday and she hoped that a new week would bring peace between her and Amber. Her daughter was definitely avoiding her and, yesterday evening, had gone upstairs to study at six, saying she'd see her mother in the morning.

Faye had stood at the door before she went to bed, but she could still hear the low sound of the radio Amber always

170

listened to when she worked, and she decided that inter-
rupting the study might result in another argument.

Faye normally liked waking early and would get a cup of
coffee and sit up in bed reading and thinking. But today, she
was too restless to sit. She brewed coffee and decided to take
a cup in to Amber both to wake her up and as a peace
offering. Not that Faye felt she was the one who had to say
sorry because Amber had been the one to fight.

But being a parent had taught her that getting over an
argument was what mattered: not how you did it or who
felt they'd won. You could be victorious or be happy was
the child/parent mantra.

She knocked on Amber's door and then walked in,
expecting to see the gloom of shut curtains and Amber, a
sleepy lump, huddled in her bed.

But the curtains were open, so was the sash window and
Amber's bed was patently unslept in. The radio hummed low
in the background, set to Amber's favourite station. The room
was cool from the window being open a long time and Faye
realised that her daughter hadn't slept at home the night before.

Faye dropped the cup of coffee, didn't care that it spilled
all over the floor.

'Oh Lord, what's happened?' she cried. 'Amber, where are
you?'

She ran for her phone and dialled Amber's mobile but got
nothing but the automated message asking her to leave a
message.

'Amber, wherever you are, please phone me back, love,
please. It was only an argument, that's all. I understand how
stressed you are, just call. It's all OK.'

Faye had no idea what she should do next. She certainly
couldn't go into work as normal with Amber missing. Panic
had robbed her of her senses. Finally, she sank to her knees
on the landing floor and prayed. Dear God, I know I haven't

been around much lately after all I prayed to you when she was a baby, but find her for me, please, please, I beg you.

Ella's phone was off too. They could be together. That might be something, at least together they'd have each other. But if Amber was alone and unhappy, out there somewhere thinking her mother was furious with her . . .

Faye scrolled through her mobile directory, found the number for Ella's house and phoned. The fact that it was six forty-five in the morning was immaterial.

A male voice answered.

'Marco, it's Faye Reid. Is your mother or Ella there?'

'Hang on,' Marco said, catching the urgency in her clipped tone.

She heard muffled conversation and then Trina, Ella's mother, came on the line.

'Faye, it's Trina. What's wrong?'

'It's Amber, she's not here and her bed's not been slept in,' Faye said shakily. 'I can't get her on her phone. We had a row on Thursday, it was over nothing, you know how it is. But she's been avoiding me since then, barely said two words to me, and now, when I went in to wake her, she's gone. I'm sure she hasn't been home all night. Trina, is Ella there? Amber might have stayed with you, or Ella might know where Amber is.'

'Ella's here but I know that Amber isn't,' Trina said, doing her best to hide the instinctive relief that at least she knew where her daughter was. 'I had to wake Ella for school and Amber's not there. Hold on, I'll get Ella now.'

'Ask her,' Faye begged, 'ask her if she knows where Amber is, if they talked about the argument.'

It was several long minutes before a reluctant-sounding Ella said 'hello' into the phone.

'Ella, I know she'd talk to you if she was upset,' began Faye, her voice shaky. 'Just tell me where she's gone.'

'I can't, Mrs Reid,' Ella said slowly. 'I think I know who she's with but I don't know where exactly. I'm sorry – I shouldn't be telling you this, Amber should.'

'Tell her what?' demanded Trina's voice in the background. 'If you know anything about where Amber is, you better spill the beans now. Her poor mother is sick with worry.'

'She'll kill me if I do,' Ella hissed at her mother.

'I'll kill you if you don't,' Trina hissed back.

'Where is she?' demanded an anguished Faye.

Ella sighed. 'His name is Karl and he's in a band called Ceres. We met him in a club in town and they've been going out for a few weeks. She's probably at his flat. I don't know where it is, though, sorry.'

Two mothers made involuntary gasps of shock.

The phone rattled as it changed hands and Trina came back on the line.

'Faye, I'm so sorry. I had no idea,' she said. 'Is there anything I can do?'

'No, thanks,' said Faye, sure that Ella had already fled the scene to text the grisly news to Amber. *Your mother knows and you're up to your neck in it.* 'I'll leave a message on her phone and then, I'll have to wait until she decides to come home.'

Faye rang in sick. She couldn't cope with work with this huge issue unresolved. She was tidying the kitchen when Amber finally made it home at half eleven that morning, still in her going-out clothes, her eyes wary, her pale skin evidence of lack of sleep. And sex, Faye thought, horrified. Her baby had been out with some man having sex when she'd thought Amber was tucked up in bed.

'Tell me about this Karl,' said Faye grimly.

'I love him. I'm going to New York with him.' Amber snapped the words out in a voice that brooked no opposition. On the journey home, with both Ella's text and a phone message from her mother telling her that she knew about

173

Karl, she'd been caught between fear and fury. Her mother would not stop her seeing Karl. No way.

'You're what?' said Faye, disbelieving. 'Don't be ridiculous. You don't even know him, how can you love him and leave the country with him?'

'I know enough to know he's the man I love.' Amber spat it out.

'When did this happen?' This had to be a sick joke, a game that Ella and Amber had dreamed up.

'Last month. He's a musician, he's in a band. He's a song-writer, he's brilliant,' Amber said fiercely. 'I love him.'

'You love him? You can hardly know him. And what do you mean about going to New York with him?'

'I do love him and I do know him. Where do you think I've been every night for the past month?' hissed Amber. 'Not in my room, that's for sure.'

The kitchen suddenly seemed cold to Faye, even though it was sunny outside, as the enormity of what Amber had kept from her struck home. Nothing or no one in her past had ever made her feel so betrayed before, simply because she'd never loved anyone the way she loved her daughter.

'I can't believe you lied to me,' she said, then tried a different tack. 'Amber, you know this is crazy. You can't head off with a strange guy. You've got exams. You can't have been studying and you'll never pass . . .'

'I'm not doing the exams, didn't you hear me?' shouted her daughter. 'Don't you ever listen? I'm not going to college, I'm going away with Karl. You can't stop me, you know.' Amber realised her mother looked as if she'd been struck in the face. Well, it was her mother's fault – she never listened.

'You can't stop me,' she yelled again. 'I'm an adult. I don't want to go to college. You've always said an education was the most important thing in the world, well, you dropped out of college and you've done fine. I can paint any time I

174

want to, Mum. This is about living life now, something you've never understood.'

Faye thought of how she'd lived her life and the pain it had brought her and how the only good decent thing she'd felt she'd ever had was her life with Amber. Now it was disappearing in front of her eyes.

'Running away with some guy in a band isn't a life,' she said softly. 'You think it is but it isn't.' She took a deep breath. 'I know.'

'You don't know a thing about it,' yelled Amber.

'I've been there,' insisted Faye.

'Yeah right!'

Amber's gorgeous face was angry and bitter. She'd never looked at Faye like that before and it was crueller than all the words to see the fury and resentment in her eyes.

'How did all this happen?' Faye asked helplessly, knowing the question sounded stupid but not knowing how else to put it.

'It happened while you were trying to make me live the life you want me to live,' Amber said. 'I'm not that sort of person, Mum. You can't make me just like you.'

Faye choked back a bitter laugh. There were so many things she should have taught Amber. Things *she'd* had to learn the hard way, lessons she'd sworn her daughter would never need to learn.

Instead, she'd hoped she could keep Amber cocooned from the crazy wild world and wrap her up in mother love and domesticity. A good school, nice friends, cosy happy families – that would keep her safe. And she'd still failed.

'I'm going,' Amber said briskly, wanting to be out of there. 'I'm sorry. I don't mean to hurt you but I've got to live my own life and you've got to too. You can't live through me.'

'Is that what you think I've been doing?' asked her mother quietly.

'Isn't it?' Amber's face was the impetuous mask of youth. She knew everything and her mother knew nothing, right?

'I'll be in touch.'

'You can't go now.' Faye came to life and dragged herself to her feet. 'Don't be silly, I've got to meet this guy. And your exams are only a couple of weeks away, Amber. Think about what you're doing.'

'I have thought about it,' Amber said simply. 'And I'm going. There's nothing you can do about it. I'll be eighteen in two days. Old enough to vote, old enough for anything.'

'You can't leave now.' Her mother looked crazy, fluttery, uncertain, which was scary because that wasn't Mum.

'I'm sorry, I can't hang around. We'd just fight and you'd stop me seeing Karl.'

'Karl,' repeated her mother bitterly. 'Why can't I meet this Karl, then, if he's so fabulous? Or is he a down-and-out in a band of no-hopers?'

'He's amazing and I love him. He makes me feel alive.'

She couldn't bear anyone to criticise Karl, not even her mum. Especially not her mum. Her mum didn't understand, nobody did, not even Ella.

'I'm going to pack,' Amber said coldly. 'Don't bother running after me. I want to live my own life now and you can't stop me.'

Faye was silent, thinking of the many things she needed to tell Amber but couldn't. Because then she'd have to give up her secret and that was the one thing she could never, never do. Amber would hate her for it. Faye hated herself.

Amber ran upstairs to pack, trying to quickly work out what she needed in her new life: not the knick-knacks on the white chest of drawers, which she'd lovingly painted with butterflies one weekend, Mum varnishing the artwork afterwards, saying how beautiful it was. Not all the good-girl clothes. But she'd take a lot of her stuff. She was moving out, after all. This wasn't just a holiday.

And she'd take the pendant. She'd take it because it was beautiful and it was a reminder of home. Not that she needed it but something of the past was good. God knows where her mother had got it in the first place. She couldn't imagine her mother wearing it, looking cool. What had she said: *I've been there*. Oh yeah, right.

As if her mother had ever done anything wild in her life.

Maggie was walking briskly past the railway cottages when she saw the woman standing at the gate of the first cottage, staring wild-eyed up the road, her face wet with tears. She was dressed in a plain navy suit with her hair tied neatly back, but there all vestiges of normality ended. Her face was distraught, as if she'd had the worst news ever and her world was crashing around her.

Maggie didn't know the woman's name, although she sort of recognised her, and for a nano-second, she wondered what the etiquette was for this situation.

'Are you all right?' she asked, stopping. To hell with etiquette. If the woman wanted to tell her to get lost, then that was fine too. But she just couldn't walk on by in the face of such human pain.

'No,' said the woman in a low moan, not even looking at Maggie. 'She's gone and I didn't try to stop her. I knew I couldn't and now she's gone and I don't know where. What am I going to do? I should have locked her in the house, made her stay, but I didn't.' She began to cry again, a low keening noise.

This was bad. Maggie looked around and saw the familiar figure of Christie Devlin on the other side of Summer Street walking her two small dogs back from the park. Christie might know this woman and what to do, because Maggie sure as hell didn't.

'Mrs Devlin?' called Maggie. 'Mrs Devlin? Can you help? *Please.*'

Together, Maggie and Christie helped Faye into Christie's house where they sat her on an old soft armchair in the living room. Once Christie had established what had happened, she thought that Faye might be better off away from her own home and the scene of the row, where Amber's presence was everywhere. Maggie had located house keys and Faye's handbag in the Reids' kitchen, closed the door, and then the trio had walked to the Devlins' house, with the dogs following quietly, anxious at all the crying.

'I'm sorry, I'm sorry, but Amber, she's a good girl. You know,' Faye kept muttering over and over. 'She's run off, you see. With a man, someone I've never heard of before and have never met, and I didn't try to stop her. I let her go and I don't know where she's gone.'

'It's hard to stop someone when they've made their mind up,' Christie said gently. 'Amber certainly has a mind of her own, Faye, and she's an adult now. She's nearly eighteen, right? So legally, she's an adult, whether or not she is emotionally.'

'She's still a baby,' wailed Faye. 'She's nearly eighteen on the outside but she's so vulnerable on the inside and I've let her down because I never told her the truth. I thought she'd be better off not knowing and now she thinks I want her to be boring and have no fun, except it wasn't that. I wanted to protect her from what I went through.'

It was like watching a rock crumble, Christie thought compassionately. She hardly knew Faye Reid and, from the outside, nobody would have guessed that this outwardly together woman would ever react with such wild grief.

Christie knew that Amber was Faye's life and that the two were very close. But a man had come into the mix – that's what Amber must have been up to the day Christie had spotted her skipping school, Christie remembered, and shook her head grimly. The result was the sort of relationship triangle that could never work and Christie felt sorry for the loser – Faye.

In spite of her exasperation at Amber for leaving her mother in such a way, Christie could see that running away from the scene of the emotional crime often seemed like the only option. It was what she herself had done, wasn't it?

'You stay with Faye,' she told Maggie now. 'I'll make tea, hot and sweet to give her energy.'

A faint grin lit up Maggie's face. 'Now I know why you and my mother are such friends, Mrs Devlin,' she said. 'She thinks tea is the answer to all life's problems too.'

'And shortbread biscuits,' Christie added wryly. 'Don't forget the biscuits. They might not be the answer but they help you back on your feet so you can deal with the pain. And don't call me Mrs Devlin. It makes me feel about a hundred when I'm not at school. I'm Christie.'

It wasn't like talking to someone of her mother's generation, Maggie thought when Christie had gone.

She could also see why her mother said Christie Devlin was sought by all in times of crisis: Una Maguire would have made the tea, all right, and then talked rapidly about anything to fill the air in case anyone started talking about what was really wrong. But Christie said little, and waited calmly and serenely in case Faye needed to talk. And she'd know when there was a deep, dark subject waiting to be brought up, Maggie thought with a flash of pain. She was thinking of herself as a teenager when the painful subjects had never been touched upon. If Christie had been her mother, she'd have seen the trouble Maggie was going through from the very first day she came home from school, shell-shocked at the naked hatred she'd encountered from the gang of bullies.

179

And she'd have sorted it all out, too. And Maggie might have become a different person, not anxious and insecure. She might have become the person she'd like to be.

'Are you all right, Maggie?' whispered Christie, coming back with the tea and laying a cool hand on the young woman's wrist.

Maggie nodded, flashing a smile. Christie thought that, with her flaming hair and wistful eyes, she looked more beautiful than Una had been when Christie met her thirty years ago. But Maggie was different from her mother in other ways, Christie realised. Una was a whirling free spirit, happy wherever she was, content in herself and her world. While Maggie was like a nervous deer, easily startled, unsure of herself, hopelessly unconfident.

Faye was not the only one here today with some secret past, Christie decided.

The hot, sweet tea did as hoped and stopped Faye crying, but she still looked bereft.

'I suppose you think I'm a hopeless mother,' she muttered to Christie. 'I didn't know what was going on under my own nose. Teachers always say they hear the real story from kids when the kids can't talk to their parents at home, but Amber did talk to me, she did.'

'I don't think you're a hopeless mother at all,' Christie said. 'I think you're a wonderful mum, and it's not an easy job, I know.' She gave a rueful laugh. 'You should try having two boys. They can challenge you, that's for sure. And there were lots of times – are lots of times still,' she corrected herself, thinking of Shane and news of the precious third grandchild on the way, 'when you think you know what's going on and really you haven't a clue. Any teacher who says otherwise doesn't know much about human nature.'

Faye nodded, sniffing.

'We were so close, you see, that's what's hard.' She turned

180

to Maggie. 'I know you don't really know me, but I know your parents and they'd tell you, Amber is a good girl.'

'Mum's said,' Maggie interrupted. 'She's a wonderful artist, right?'

'Right.' Faye looked so pleased and proud for a moment, before the realisation hit her again – Amber wasn't going to college to work on her great artistic ability. She was going off with that horrible man.

'Could we phone the police?' she asked suddenly.

Christie looked at Maggie, a look shot through with pity, before replying: 'They can't help much when the person is of age, you know. She can go where she wants, really. When's she eighteen?'

'On Wednesday,' said Faye.

'And she's taken her passport, I suppose. Has she got one?'

'Yes, but I didn't look. But how can she go to America without a visa or anything ... Maybe she won't go if she can't get into the country?' Faye was hopeful.

'If he's in a band and they're going there for work, they might organise visas through the record company, with one for her too,' Maggie said, shrugging. 'With travel security so tight, they might get round it that way.'

There was a silence as Faye digested that bit of information. 'So she's really gone. After eighteen years, she's gone.' And she began to cry again, only this time they were the silent, body-wrenching sobs that were somehow more painful to hear than any noisy ones.

'Oh, Faye,' Maggie said in anguish, grabbing Faye's hand. 'She's a clever girl, everyone says so. She'll be able to look after herself and growing up with just the two of you, she'll have learned so much about taking care of herself. She'll be fine. This guy could be a wonderful guy after all. Think of all you've taught her and trust her.'

Faye's eyes, when she looked up, were hollow with pain.

'That's it, you see,' she said bleakly. 'I could have taught her so much but I didn't. I wanted to protect her. There's so much badness in the world, men who treat you like dirt and really don't care. I've been there, I've been down there. I'll never forget it. I never wanted my daughter to go through what I went through.'

'But you never told her what you saw and experienced, did you?' Christie asked intuitively.

'No,' Faye said. 'I never told her. I was ashamed of what I'd been and done, and thought if I could just keep her in this cosy world, then she'd never go down the same path as me.'

Christie could suddenly see everything. The old Faye Reid had gone, her façade was shed like an old skin and the real Faye sat there, a woman without all the answers for the first time in years.

'And that's just what she's done,' Faye finished. 'I've sent her off into the world not knowing the truth about anything that mattered because I wanted to protect her, and it turns out, I haven't protected her at all: I've left her completely unarmed.'

'Music,' Faye said, as she began to tell her story. 'That was my passion when I was a teenager. Music and stories about love. I spent every penny on records, and myself and Charlotte, my friend from school, read romance novels and dreamed. I loved the books with the clinches on the cover. You know the ones: there was a woman and a gorgeous man holding her to him, as if he'd never let her go.' Her eyes were misty, dreaming of that time.

'That's what I wanted. I wanted to be beautiful and adored. I wanted to be the woman in that picture with the man telling me I was too beautiful, too incredible for him to live without me. I grew up in a place called the Linden Estate, it's a council estate and not many dreams came true there. But there were ways of escape and I chose mine: I remember the first time Charlotte and I went out like grown-ups. I was in college then, and there were all these cool places to hang out. One in particular was on the quays. They had late-night live music. It was all red inside, dark red with smeared mirrors and shiny seats where you could sit for hours making your drink last,' she said. 'It wasn't like I'd thought it would be at first. There weren't people fighting over us, we were on the edges. Charlotte didn't like it much, but I did. And I wanted to fit in. I figured out that if you hung around long enough you'd become part of the scene and somehow I did. I was supposed to be working on my degree but I wasn't doing any work. I loved sitting and watching, learning about life but not out of a book.'

Faye's eyes were dreamy. They were the same as her daughter's: a luminous and magnetic pewter grey with that startling ring of amber around the inky black of the pupils, Christie realised. She could suddenly see the beauty of the young Faye, the girl who'd cared how she looked, with long streaked hair like her daughter's, a grown-up woman's body, and the heart of an eager young girl who'd wanted to be loved, to be part of something.

Christie reached out and took Faye's hand, but Faye didn't appear to notice. She was lost in remembering the past . . .

There was TJ, there was always TJ. In the outside world, there were no jobs then, people were leaving the country for London and New York looking for work, wearing their best suits and fine-tuning their résumés. But not TJ. He wasn't cutting his long, dark hair to get a boring job. He wore his in a ponytail and it suited his long, lean face with its soulful hollows. He wasn't a man from a romance novel, he wore a leather jacket instead of a white shirt, but his body was the same sinewy combination of muscle and energy, and there was passion in his soul and in his eyes. Faye had seen it, seen the way he looked at her, knew he wanted her.

There were a lot of them from her college hanging around The Club, and they all looked up to the older guys, the regulars like TJ, who'd seen it all and bought the ripped T-shirt. And she was a regular now, too, as much part of the place as the scent of stale smoke – cigarette and other kinds – in the air. The Club was like a second home to her.

'Silver, baby,' TJ said that night, 'they oughta have a picture of you over the door.'

He called her Silver, even though it wasn't her name. It was her new name, her club name, so it was what she was called now. She loved it. Her hair had long strands of platinum through the tawny golds and browns. Silver strands.

The music was low with an insistent bass. No matter what music was in fashion, The Club played rock – tonight, TJ's favourite, the Stones. Faye loved their music. Song after song, reaching into her heart and tearing it out. Every emotion was there: pain, love, sexual ecstasy, heartbreak, Mick's voice speaking directly to her.

TJ passed her the joint.

'Try this, Silver, you'll like it.'

His hand was around her shoulder, touching her breast through her thin T-shirt, a gesture of possession to all the other men around the booth. Telling them she was his, Faye thought with pride.

There was a moment before she took the first drag of the joint when she thought how odd it was – her, goody-two-shoes honours student, here in a smoky bar about to smoke hash. This was unlike anything she had envisaged before. And then, the moment passed, for the heady numbness soaked into her limbs.

TJ smiled, sipped more of his Jack Daniel's and smiled some more as he watched her get happy. When she was happy, Faye got up and danced on her own, with TJ looking on from the back booth, his eyes hooded, watching her body undulate to the music.

That night, he sent Faye up to the bar to order drinks.

'Hi, Maria,' she said to the barmaid. 'Can I have four JDs, one Coke, and three double vodkas, no ice.'

Maria was forty, maybe older. She had dyed red hair, big brown eyes and a smoker's mouth with lots of lines. In her black jeans and teeny T-shirt, with the tattooed butterfly on her biceps, she didn't look like Faye's mother, but she spoke to her like a mother now.

'Honey, you shouldn't be here,' Maria said, expertly filling the drinks order. 'You're just a nice kid. What are you, nineteen, twenty? This place isn't for you.'

'Why not?' Faye asked, confused.

''Cos that man is using you, can't you see? They're laughing at you, honey.' Maria paused at the disbelieving look in Faye's eyes. 'I'm only trying to help. I hate to see you get tangled up in this world. Get out, while you can.'

'You're wrong,' Faye said. 'Nobody's using me.'

Maria moved closer to her. 'Honey, you know what they call you? Silver.'

'It's because of my hair,' Faye said, smiling, shaking her mane.

'No,' said Maria flatly. 'It's because TJ's the Lone Ranger. His horse was called Silver. It's because he rides you.'

'What's up, Silver?' TJ asked when she came back with the drinks. 'You don't look happy to see me.' He didn't like people's minds moving from him. Except when they were wasted, and even then, he'd keep his hand on her thigh possessively, reminding her of his presence.

'Nothing,' she said. She drank half of her vodka and leaned in against him to take the joint.

This was it, right? What else was there?

The next morning, there were so many of them lying around TJ's tiny flat, the usual assortment of bodies on the floor, the smell of dirty feet, sweat, cigarette smoke, who knew what else. Faye sat up in the bed. She was wearing her T-shirt and knickers but no jeans, and she couldn't really remember getting here. She hugged her knees up to herself in an attempt to get comfort. From somewhere she could hear 'Gimme Shelter' playing on the stereo, another song in the soundtrack to this life. This life, the life of being TJ's Silver.

She felt her skin crawl.

Faye had never liked herself much. Other people she liked. It was herself she had no time for.

She had been grateful to lose herself in this numbing new life with TJ and The Club. But now she saw it all with stunning clarity and she loathed who she'd become.

'Hey, Silver,' said one of the guys from the floor, opening an eye. 'How's it going?'

Silver. Everybody had known what it stood for except her. That's all she was: Silver, the Lone Ranger's ride, nothing more. Not a person. A ride. All the hopes and dreams of a young human being cruelly dismissed by one word.

She found her jeans at the end of the bed, pulled them on.

She bent down to put on her socks and winced. In the mirror, she saw the reason for the pain: there were bruises down her back, angry, livid marks.

Trawling back through the mental fog of the night before, she could remember her and TJ in the kitchen having sex up against the kitchen cabinets, with people everywhere, nobody noticing, nobody caring. Even now, she could feel the ridge of formica digging into her tender back. This was the great new world she was in, this was where she'd thought she was special.

A world of being treated like dirt by people who didn't care, who were looking for victims, people to use.

Faye didn't know where she got the strength but, some-where deep inside her, she found courage. She gathered her stuff together. There wasn't much really, nothing to mark her presence there at all.

There was no sign of TJ. He was probably off with some other woman, poor cow. Faye felt sorry for her.

Nobody noticed as she slipped out and closed the door behind her.

'But I was pregnant,' she told Christie and Faye as they sat in Christie's beautiful room with the dogs at their feet. 'It must have happened that night, the night before I left. I worked it out. Him and me in the kitchen, up against the cabinets.' She wiped her eyes with a rough gesture. 'Preg-nant and alone.' She laughed, mirthlessly. 'Because I was hardly going to find TJ and say, "Hi, Daddy, what sort of cot will we buy? Are you planning to be there at the birth?" I had to leave college because I was so unwell and couldn't cope. My mother was so good to me and took care of us both. She helped through the pregnancy, then, after Amber was born, she would babysit so I could work. I did anything – bar work, McDonald's. You can eat your dinner off the floors in McDonald's,' Faye said, suddenly smiling. 'I know, because I've scrubbed them. You wouldn't believe how fussed they are. Finally, when I got a proper job we moved here, to start again on Summer Street. There's something so hopeful about this place, isn't there? I felt it from the first.' She looked beseechingly at Maggie and Christie, wanting them to under-stand. 'I could begin again here, I could be someone new, someone Amber could be proud of. And I wanted her to be proud of me. The only other person who knows the whole story is my mother,' Faye added. 'Nobody else. I was too ashamed. My mother worked so hard all her life to put me and my brother through college and I paid her back like that,

187

thinking so little of myself that I let people use me. Mistaking sex for intimacy, thinking TJ's behaviour signified love and respect and affection. How dumb could I have been?' she said hoarsely.

'You were only a kid,' Christie said, feeling nothing but compassion for Faye. 'You did what so many women do: think sex is love, when it's not. You know now, and you must forgive yourself. You can't feel guilty for ever.'

'I should have told Amber,' said Faye blankly, as if she didn't hear Christie. Or, at least, couldn't hear the words 'forgive yourself' because she'd told herself so often that she had ruined her life. 'As a parent, you want your child to look up to you, to respect you and, as I don't respect myself for what I did, how could she? How could I tell her that her father was a low-life scumbag who had never cared?'

'Did he know about her?' Maggie asked.

'I brought her to see him at The Club when she was six months old.'

Faye thought she looked pretty good by then. A lot of the baby weight was gone and she could fit into her old jeans. Men still looked at her, admiring.

Amber was so cute, fluffy hair spilling out from under her crimson fleecy hat, wrapped up against the cold. Even then, her intelligence was apparent. She was so alert, watched everything with those huge magnetic eyes. How could anybody not love her, not want to be her father?

The Club hadn't changed an iota, even the people slumped at the bar in the early evening looked the same

'You can't bring a kid in here,' yelled the barman grumpily.

'Why not?' Faye said.

He shrugged. 'Don't come moaning to me about passive smoking, OK?'

'I'm looking for TJ.'

'He's in the back booth.'

She should have known. Why even ask? The back booth: their spiritual home.

Some of the faces round the table had changed. There was no sign of Jimi. She hoped he'd got out. He was like her too, a sweet guy in over his head.

Everyone at the table was clearly out of it, and holding court in the middle was TJ, the inevitable girl on his arm, not someone Faye knew. Except he was thinner now, and his face was even more gaunt.

'Hey, darlin'.' He smiled. 'You joining us?'

He didn't recognise her, Faye realised, and she was standing there with his child in her arms.

'TJ, it's me, Faye,' she said. His eyes remained distant, the thousand-yard stare of a joint-smoker.

Then, with a shock, she saw that the long, sinewy arm thrown around the girl had needle tracks in it. That was the one thing she had never known TJ do: shoot up. He could drink or smoke anyone under the table. He smoked dope and when he could get it, he was a hound for coke, but heroin had been off limits. Heroin was playing Russian roulette with a bullet in every chamber. Thank goodness she had got away.

'It's Silver!' said someone.

It was Jackie, older than TJ, one of the leaders of the crew, a man with a face like a gravel pit.

Jackie raised a glass to her. 'Hey, sweet kid you got there. She's not yours, is she?'

'Yeah, she's mine,' said Faye, holding Amber so tightly to her that the baby, who'd been drifting off to sleep, woke up and mewled with discomfort.

'What are you bringing a kid here for, Silver? It ruins the atmosphere. How can we party with a kid around? You up for a party?'

'I was supposed to meet someone,' Faye said, realising there would be no sign of recognition from TJ. 'But I guess they're not here.'

And without looking back, she walked out of The Club. Amber, her reason for living, snuggled in closer, happy, in her mother's arms.

'I never saw him again,' Faye told her audience. 'I never even tried to look for him. I told Amber her dad was from Scotland and died in a car crash soon after she was born. I said we'd never married, but we meant to, so it was like being a widow. I changed my name to my mother's maiden name but called myself Mrs so people wouldn't label us. And I said when he'd died, I'd lost touch with his family, that his parents were dead and he was an only child. More lies. It scared the hell out of me to wonder what would happen if Amber discovered the truth and tried to find TJ. He might still be a junkie.' She shivered. 'If he hasn't died of his habit – ninety per cent of heroin addicts do, you know. So that's the story. Memoirs of a woman from The We Screwed Up But Hey, We're Still Here Club, that's what I used to think it should be called.'

Maggie burst out laughing. 'Hey, can I join up?'

Faye looked at Christie, as if expecting the older woman's disapproval but there was nothing but sympathy and warmth in Christie's kind eyes.

'You deserve to be president of that club and get a medal,' she said. 'Amber's a beautiful girl, Faye. You have nothing to be ashamed of. You should be proud of the way you've brought her up on your own and she should be proud of you. But she deserves to know the truth, doesn't she?'

Christie stopped. The truth. It was easier to say it than to live it. She wasn't telling anyone her own truth, was she?

'We've all done things we thought we should hide,' she

said carefully. 'I've hidden stuff from the people I love and I wish to God I hadn't because it eats you up from the inside out.'

'How can I tell her any of this now?' Faye groaned. 'After all the lies I've told her.'

'You've reached the point where you can't do anything but tell her,' Christie said. 'She knows what a good person you are, because that's how you've brought her up. And the truth is it wasn't completely your fault, Faye. Stop imagining what other people will think and realise you were a scared, vulnerable young woman. Forgive yourself. Stop thinking of how everyone else would live your life in your shoes. You have to live it. You had to live it and you did your best. Tell her, face that truth.' Christie knew now she wasn't just talking to Faye, but also to herself.

Maggie, hanging on to every word, stared at Christie. Her hand unconsciously stroked the top of her thigh through her jeans, touching the scars that lay underneath, scars that would never go away.

So facing the truth made you stronger? She hadn't thought of that before. She'd certainly never faced any of the truths in her own life, she'd buried them instead, kept them from her family and friends, from everyone. But perhaps she had been wrong to do that.

'But what if Amber doesn't come back?' Faye asked.

Christie tried to push her mind into the future. It never worked that way, not usually. The future came to her, rather than the other way round. But now, in the face of Faye's raw, naked pain, she tried. And when the answer came to her in a flash, it was a mother's intuition rather than anything other-worldly.

'You've got to go and find her.'

191

CHAPTER TWELVE

Amber had expected flowers and wine, well, even a few beers. After all, it was a horrible Monday morning and she'd just had the row from hell with her mother and had left home. It was like something out of one of those sweeping romantic epics on Saturday afternoon television.

Despite her misery, Amber's sense of the dramatic meant she could see herself in the role of tear-stained heroine fleeing from a tyrannical home to the arms of her lover.

Except that Karl clearly hadn't seen the same movies.

When he'd met her off the bus, he'd hugged her, taken the big suitcase from her and pulled it along, chatting all the while. There was no wild passion at what she'd given up for him, how he'd never forget her leaving her home to be by his side.

'What is it with women and all this stuff?' Karl grimaced, pretending he had put his back out hauling her case. 'How can one small woman own so much? Or is this just the make-up?'

Amber, still torn between tears and defiance, was not in the mood for jokes. She wanted passionate declarations of how he loved her and would take care of her.

But perhaps she mustn't be too clingy or needy.

'It's all my stuff from home,' she said shortly. 'Nearly eighteen years of belongings.' Including her four cuddly toys, although she'd stashed them in a pillowcase.

'Only slagging you, babe,' Karl said. 'Dunno where you'll put it all, though. The flat's a bit cramped.'

They reached Karl's front door. He manfully hauled her case into the rather smelly hallway and up two flights of stairs to a scuffed blue door that stood ajar.

'We're having a band meeting,' Karl said, as he kicked the door of the flat open with his foot.

He left her case in the hall, and pulled her into the cluttered living room that was testimony to a cleaning rota gone very wrong. Old papers and magazines, dirty dishes, empty take-away containers, ashtrays, items of clothing and dust covered every surface. Kenny T, Lew and Syd were sprawled on the room's couch and single armchair that were grouped around a coffee table that Amber had never seen without its coat of detritus. In turn, they all got up to hug and welcome her. To her shame, Amber burst into tears. After the huge row with her mother, it was so lovely to feel welcomed again and not a wayward child.

'There's no need to cry,' Karl said, hugging her.

'It's just I've never had a real row with my mother before,' she sobbed into his shoulder. 'We've been there for each other always. Her and me. But she's so square, she can't understand this and she never will. You didn't hear her, Karl: she hates me for this, hates me!'

'Your ma will get over it. My ma was the same,' Syd said easily. 'She never copped on that there's more to life than exams, you know. Saw me as a lawyer, she did. Jaysus, can you see me in court?'

'Only in the defence box,' cracked Lew.

'You'll be fine with us, Amber,' Kenny T added. 'You can

teach Karl how to wash his underpants. I've seen him using the cleanest ones off the floor.'

'No, I've seen you taking my cleanest ones off the floor, you skanger,' joked Karl in return.

Amber wiped her eyes and tried to join in the joking. She felt absurdly pleased to be welcomed in like one of the boys. Never mind that the place was a pit. She'd show them how to be tidy. It might be nice to be the mother figure for a change.

She'd show her mother that she could survive and be happy. There wasn't just one way to live your life, by the bloody boring book.

'Lew was just going to phone out for pizza,' Karl said to her. 'But now you're here, could you cook? We're mad for some lunch.'

'We've got chicken,' Lew said hopefully.

'It smells a bit,' Syd warned.

'Nuke it,' advised Karl. 'It'll be fine then, won't it?'

All eyes turned to Amber, who was a girl and, therefore, would know all about cooking chicken.

Cooking was her mother's department, Amber realised with a jolt. Hers was reheating or writing things on the list on the fridge, like *Out of muesli* or *Can you get me shampoo?*

'Sure, it'll be fine,' she said confidently. How hard could cooking be?

The fridge stank. Syd had been right about the chicken, although he should have just binned it, which was what Amber did.

Nothing else in there would have stretched to a meal for five without a bad dose of salmonella ensuing. There were lots of packets and cartons, but they were mostly empty, with the exception of a half-full orange juice carton which was curdled with age. The freezer box was jammed icily shut and

Amber couldn't prise it open. And the cupboards, stocked with crisps, cereal and lots of nearly empty bottles of booze, yielded nothing but a few stray bits of pasta and rice.

She marched into the band meeting.

'The chicken is an ex-chicken,' she announced. 'I'll go to the shops and get something for lunch but I need money.'

'Yes, ma'am,' said Karl and made a collection.

Amber smiled. She was in charge, what a nice feeling. Last week, she'd been a schoolgirl with a uniform and a childhood bedroom. Now she lived with a man, shared his bed, cooked his meals. How was that for progress?

But later that afternoon, she started to feel tearful again.

'I might call Gran,' sniffed Amber on the phone to Ella.

'Why?' Ella couldn't see the point in this. Any grandmother worth her salt would surely side with Faye's mother. There would be tears and shouting. 'Why don't you call your mother?' Ella said. 'She's the one you should be talking to, not your gran.'

'My mother will only go on about the bloody exams,' said Amber bitterly. 'There's more to life than exams. It's a stupid system to put people in little boxes based on how well they do on one particular day when asked one particular set of questions. How does that work out what sort of person you are and what you're capable of doing?'

For someone who'd been the poster girl for education for all her school life, Amber had honed her arguments against it pretty quickly. She didn't know how any of her new flatmates had got on in their final-year state exams, but Karl, who had passed his, was always saying that life was the real educator, not school books. She said this, not mentioning that it was Karl-speak.

Ella's lip curled. 'The hottest band on the planet all failed their exams, right?' she said succinctly.

195

'Karl is brilliant,' Amber snapped back.

'Yeah, well, did he stay in school to finish the year and his exams?'

Amber knew he had. After school, he'd gone to university for two years but had dropped out of his arts degree.

'But that's not important,' she said.

'Course it is. So he did pass them and now he's forcing you to skip your exams so you can be with him. Your mother's right, Amber. Why don't you finish school properly? It's only a few weeks away and you'd be wasting years of study for no reason. If Karl doesn't want to wait for you until the exams are over, then he doesn't deserve you.'

'He loves me,' said Amber, hurt and angry. 'I thought you were on my side.'

'I am. I'm only saying what I think.'

'Karl would love to wait for me but they've got to travel now.'

'And you can't stay here, do your exams and join him later?' Ella demanded. 'Or are you scared that if you're not with him, he'll find someone else to be his muse and keep his bed warm?'

The barb hit home. Amber was glad Ella wasn't there to see her blush. She knew it was stupid to feel so unsure of Karl after all he'd said to her, but doubt was a sneaky bedfellow and crept into her mind when she least wanted it. She could stay and make up with her mother, but what if Karl left and she never saw him again?

'We love each other,' she said coldly to her best friend. 'You wouldn't understand.'

'I understand plenty. I understand that you used to listen to me. We shared everything and now Karl's on the scene, I'm not important any more. That's a nice way to treat your closest friend, Amber.'

'Oh, grow up, Ella,' snapped Amber. 'You make it sound

like we're kids again, with nothing to worry about except which My Little Pony is our favourite.'

Ella had had enough. 'I liked you better then,' she said. 'You were still Amber Reid, my best friend ever, and not Amber the dizzy groupie who's forgotten everything she ever stood for. You were the clever one in school with the future and you're risking it all to behave like a *Ricki Lake Show* guest and cling to a loser guy. He'll dump you, you know. And you'll ask me why I didn't stop you. Just so you remember, I did my best. Bye, Amber, have a nice life.'

Amber hung up feeling lonelier than ever. Why didn't anyone understand?

Love changed you and made you a different person. What was wrong with that?

Why did everyone think she had to choose: them or Karl? Couldn't she have both?

CHAPTER THIRTEEN

The card was nothing but a rectangle of fine cream paper, folded over, with a heart hand-drawn on the front, and on the inside written in Grey's unmistakable copperplate hand-writing: *I love you. I miss you, please come home.*

Maggie reread the card yet again, then traced her fingers over the writing reverentially. A shop-bought one wouldn't have touched her but this, this gesture of love, made her ache with wanting to go back to Grey.

She'd been thinking about what Christie Devlin had said earlier, and then she'd come home from work to find this on the bundle of post on the hall table, a card from Grey wanting her back.

Stop thinking of how everyone else would live your life in your shoes. You have to live it, Christie had said to both her and Faye.

And she'd been right. Maggie hadn't been able to get the words out of her head.

She wanted to go back to Grey, that was all that mattered. Not what anyone else said. Not her pride or fear or lack of trust. It could all be worked through. What had happened had changed her, so their relationship wouldn't go back to the way it had been before: it would be better, stronger. Like her.

It was half seven in the evening and Grey would certainly be home from work. She desperately wanted to speak to him now.

She dialled the apartment but got their answering machine, still with its message saying that neither Grey nor Maggie could come to the phone right now. She hung up without leaving a message. This conversation had to be in person. Next, she dialled his mobile but it was switched off.

Damn. She felt so wound up. She wanted to talk to someone . . .

'Hi, how are you?' she said, when Shona answered the phone.

'Great,' said Shona breezily.

There was a lot of noise going on in Shona and Paul's flat. The noise of two people who knew how to enjoy themselves and weren't worried about bothering the neighbours by having the stereo turned up to This May Damage Your Hearing level.

'I just wanted to talk,' Maggie said.

'Serious talk?' asked Shona.

'No, not really.' She paused. 'Yeah, serious talk.'

'Turn the music down,' Shona yelled.

'So what happened?' demanded Shona, when the noise level dropped slightly. 'He turned up on your doorstep, confessed undying love and promised never to be a naughty boy again.'

'How did you know?' Maggie asked. She hadn't spoken to Shona since Grey had turned up to see her.

'You mean he did?' said Shona. 'Talk about Cliché City.'

'I didn't know he'd come,' Maggie said.

'Well,' said Shona, 'it's just the sort of thing a man like Grey would do. Bonk somebody else on your bed, not know how to say sorry properly, let you run away while he thought

199

about it and then rush into your arms and bleat, "I'm sorry darling, it will never happen again", because he realises it's very boring doing your own washing and cleaning. And besides which, it's against faculty rules to screw your students and his college career would be finito if word leaked out. Not that myself or anyone in the library would say anything, no.' Shona sounded gleeful. 'Silent as the grave we are. Gossip never touches our lips – we spit it out so fast, it never gets to touch our lips.'

Maggie had felt cheerful a moment before but Shona's analysis of Grey's behaviour made it all sound so sordid and miserable. Not so much a great passion as a tawdry fling.

But Shona hadn't heard him speak, hadn't heard the tenderness in his voice.

'He said he missed me,' she protested, 'in public. And that he loves me. He means it, Shona. I know you think he doesn't, but if you'd seen him . . .'

'Oh, that's so Grey,' Shona said critically. 'He loves a scene, that boy, just loves it. I don't know why he's pretending he won't go into politics. If ever a man wanted to stand on a podium and have the party faithful worship at his feet, it's your ex. He's addicted to the applause, darling. That's why he likes bonking girl students.'

There was a sudden pause.

'What do you mean he likes bonking girl students?' Maggie asked fiercely. 'I knew he liked bonking one particular girl student but students plural . . . ? What have you heard?'

She could almost hear Shona running through escape scenarios in her head.

'The truth, Shona,' she insisted. 'Tell me the truth. I wish somebody had told me the truth a long time ago.'

'Oh sweetie,' sighed Shona, and Maggie knew it was bad news. 'Don't worry, I was going to tell you. You know me, tell all. I don't believe in that shoot the messenger crap. Well, like a good pal, I've been asking around ever since you caught Dr Grey Stanley sticking it to his cutesy, blonde student and it seems that she wasn't the only one getting some private tuition. Turns out, he's got quite a name for it.'

'Oh.' Maggie couldn't manage to say anything else. It was like thinking the world was round, and then finding out it was flat after all.

'Sorry, darling, but you had to know.'

If anybody else but Shona had told her this, Maggie realised, she would've wanted to shoot the messenger. But Shona was a true friend. She loved Maggie. It was comforting to think that somebody still did.

'I want to hear everything,' she said.

'Are you sure?'

'Yes,' she said firmly. 'Everything.'

'Paul,' called Shona. 'Turn off the music and make me a cocktail. This is going to be a long conversation.'

She could hear Paul reply: 'You're not telling her everything about that bastard, are you?'

'Somebody has to. The girl needs to see sense.'

There had been four women that Shona had been able to find out about, including the latest blonde. All students of Grey's, which was probably the worst thing about it. He was always such a stickler for ethics and doing the right thing, Maggie recalled.

Having sex with people whose papers he marked was breaking every rule of teaching.

'The good news is that none of them was long term,' Shona finished up. 'So you can console yourself with that, darling. I mean, he did love you in his own screw-around way. I had to dig deep to find it all out, so I honestly don't think he meant to humiliate you.'

'Doing it in our bed wasn't supposed to humiliate me?' Maggie shouted.

'Don't scream,' Shona screamed back. 'I'm clutching at straws here, trying to make you feel better. Yes, he's a class A shit but it's obvious that his brain is not his primary organ and he's clearly not as cerebral as he'd like us all to think.'

'Meaning he thinks with his dick,' Paul yelled in the background.

'He still didn't have to do it in our bed,' Maggie said, still reeling. 'Doesn't that say he wanted to be found out?'

'Oh I don't think he wanted to be found out,' said Shona. 'Come on, why would he? I think there was nowhere else to go, you were off at work, then you were doing your Pilates or whatever, the coast was clear.'

'He asked me to come back to him,' Maggie said, with a little laugh that held no humour.

Only minutes ago, she'd felt a little bit of hope warming her at the idea that it might all work out, she could have it all, again, only better this time. 'He wants us to be together. He said we should get married.' Her voice broke. 'And you tell me he's had four girlfriends in the past ... how many years, five? Why marry someone if all you want to do is sleep around?'

'It's the eternal question of life,' Shona sighed in a world-weary way.

She could hear Paul wanting to know what the eternal question of life was. Shona told him.

'I thought it was, was there life on other planets?' Paul could be heard saying, plaintively.

'No, that's the third eternal question, after why all the good ones already have boyfriends.'

Despite herself, Maggie managed a hoarse laugh.

'What a lovely sound.' Shona was pleased. 'Don't let Dr Dick ruin your life, Maggie,' she pleaded. 'You're an old romantic despite your best attempts to hide it. You want the fairytale, darling, and you're not going to get it with him, are you?'

'They say serial monogamy is the way forward,' Maggie said, not wanting to answer Shona's question. 'I wanted something longer and Grey obviously doesn't. Am I the old-fashioned one? Is everyone at it? Should I have been having an affair too?'

'No,' said Shona, 'joking aside, you shouldn't have been having an affair. You're too straight, it would kill you. When you love, it's with all your heart. He's different. If he'd gone to you and admitted about the other women, said he'd never do it again, well, there'd be some hope. But he didn't, did he? He just said sorry for Miss Bimbo. And by the way, her book-borrowing days are over. I'll have the word out in the library and that girl will never get another book out. She can try, but no matter what book she wants, it'll be unavailable or her card will be out of date. The library looks after its own!'

Maggie smiled.

'What am I going to do now, Shona?' she sighed. 'I was going to go back to him. I can't stay with Mum and Dad for ever, it's lovely and everything but . . .' She paused.

The shock hit her again. Damn Grey, damn him. Just when she'd begun to think there might be a future for them, his past had ruined it all again.

She'd begun to feel a little better the past day or so. Insulated in Summer Street. She'd even got used to her old bedroom again and the reassurance of looking at the same wallpaper she'd grown up with. It was easy to block out the pain of finding Grey in bed with another woman. The pain of feeling so stupid, so betrayed. And she liked the local library, it was a nice place to work. Maggie knew she was hiding, just a tiny bit, from the past and its power. But she didn't care. She wanted a little peace after everything that had happened.

And now Grey had knocked her right back to square one.

203

He'd reminded her why she was here, alone. What's more, he hadn't betrayed her with one woman, he'd betrayed her with four.

'Are you still there?' asked Shona gently.

'Yes,' Maggie said. 'Sorry. I don't know whether to stay here or go back to Galway. I don't know what to do about anything. I'm a mess.'

'Join the club, darling,' Shona said lightly. 'My roots need doing, my nails are like hooves and I haven't had a moment since you left, you know. The relief librarian they sent thinks the rota is set in stone and I'm having terrible trouble trying to swap shifts with her. Anyway, listen, sweetie, take your time, you don't need to make a decision quickly, you've got another week. You could come back and have nothing to do with Dr Grey or his nymphets. He's not in your life any more, you don't need him.'

Shona would say that, Maggie thought ruefully. Shona was strong and knew her own worth. She hadn't needed Paul to make her feel fulfilled. But Maggie wasn't so strong, she didn't know if she could go back and start again with all the memories of her and Grey everywhere she went.

But then, there were painful memories everywhere, even here, on Summer Street.

She wished she had told Shona about her school years, then maybe she'd understand why Maggie was so anxious about staying in Summer Street. But there had never been a right time to tell her. Shona knew the reinvented Maggie, the feisty person with a kooky personality, a soft heart and a clever word for every situation. It would be strange to tell her now. Talking about the bullying would make it all real and she would only have to confront it. Despite what Christie had said about facing the truth, it was far easier to keep the memories buried.

CHAPTER FOURTEEN

If wishing could make a phone ring, Faye's mobile would have been blistering loudly all Tuesday morning. Her office phone rang every few minutes but her mobile, the number Amber always called her on, just sat there on the desk, silent. And despite being surrounded by all the other people in the office, Faye had never felt more alone.

It was a little over twenty-four hours since Amber had run off and changed Faye's world. There had been no phone call from her, nothing, just the blank emptiness of the house without Amber in it and Faye reliving her mistakes over and over again in her mind.

She'd spent hours the evening before with Ella and her mother, trying to work out where Amber might be, but Ella honestly didn't know.

'If I did, Mrs Reid, I'd tell you,' she said. 'I think she's crazy and you know she's my best friend. And I've told her I think she's crazy too,' she added, just in case anyone doubted her determination to make Amber see sense.

'I just don't understand,' said Trina, Ella's mother. 'She's always been such a good girl.'

Both mothers had talked before of how lucky they were

with their daughters. Amber and Ella had never given any trouble before, and their parents agreed that having tough rules about what was and wasn't allowed was certainly a factor.

'When she gets home, you should ground her for a month!' Trina insisted.

Ella and Faye looked at each other. They both knew it had gone far beyond that.

When Faye had left Ella's house that evening and returned home to Summer Street, she entered a house that felt like an empty shell. With Amber there, it had been a lively home; now it was cold and hard, all the life and the warmth gone. This was the rest of her life, Faye realised bleakly: being alone without the one person she loved most in the whole world. It was like the end of a love affair, except Faye knew she'd never have felt the loss of any man the way she felt the loss of her daughter.

Christie had phoned on Tuesday morning before Faye went to work.

'I wanted to see how you were,' she said, in her soothing way. 'To remind you that you're not on your own, that you've got people to talk to in this.'

'Thank you,' said Faye.

'Did you sleep?'

'If you call lying in bed crying, yes, I slept really well.'

'I'll bring you over some wonderful herbal tea later this evening,' Christie promised. 'I got it in a little shop in Camden Street and it's called Sleep Tea. It's very relaxing.'

'Do you have Instant Happiness Tea or Make Everything Better Tea?' Faye inquired.

'No,' sighed Christie. 'I wish I did. In fact, I'd also love a packet of the Make All the Old Secrets Disappear Tea but they were out of stock. Are you going into work?'

'Of course.'

The idea of doing anything else was ridiculous to Faye.

Work had been her saviour for many years. Work made you forget about humiliation and pain, and people who treated you like dirt. Work gave you confidence and courage and a tiny glimmer of self-respect.

Except not today. No matter what she tried, she couldn't concentrate.

She sat at her desk miserably. She had no idea how to get Amber back and all she could do was see the mistakes she had made and regret them. Faye had been so sure that she had brought Amber up in the right way, in a lovely cosy world, where education and faith in your own power were the most important things. She had been so sure that was right, and now it seemed, like mother, like daughter. Amber was merely repeating her mistakes. And Faye, who, she could see now, should have told Amber the truth, had let Amber grow up thinking her mother was a plaster saint.

She didn't tell anyone at work about Amber going. She couldn't. Keeping people at a distance was too firmly engrained in her. Yesterday, she'd let Christie and Maggie get closer to her than anyone had in years – she was still getting used to having done that.

Grace popped her head round the door at eleven. She didn't come in because she always felt it was really only a quick chat if she didn't stand entirely in a room.

'I've someone you've just got to meet, Faye. She's an image consultant and a life coach. You know, that's not even describing her properly, she changes people's lives. She has degrees coming out of her armpits and I thought it would be a brilliant idea to bring her into the business as part of our getting women back to work campaign.'

Faye had come up with the idea of a drive to recruit women coming back into the workplace after a few years of being at home taking care of their children and the campaign had become Grace's special project. Grace set up the interviews and had organised a whole retraining programme for mothers wanting to brush up on interview techniques and computer skills. It had been a huge success, with scores of brilliantly qualified women signing up, but the only problem, Grace said, was that some of the women coming back to work were terribly anxious about it all.

'No matter what top job they had before, they keep saying everyone's moved on and they've become mumsy and out of touch. You wouldn't credit the sort of superwomen who say they don't know what to wear or what to say because they've lost the knack. I tell them you never forget,' Grace added, 'but honestly, women's anxiety is terrible. Why do we do this to ourselves? I bet men don't obsess that they won't fit back in if they haven't been in the workplace for a few years? I mean, can you imagine Neil feeling like that?' she asked Faye.

As Faye felt that Neil didn't really work in the first place, she couldn't answer this accurately. But she nodded and said yes, she knew what Grace was getting at: the age-old problem of confidence had undermined many a woman.

'So your plan is to help people dress properly and do their hair and be full of enthusiasm?' Faye asked now.

'That's part of it.' Grace inserted her whole body into the room. 'It's giving women back their confidence more than anything. This life coach is just totally amazing. Her name's Ellen. You'll love her. She's in my office now and if you've some free time, come on in. She's going to do a consultation on me.'

A few days ago, Faye would have loved to meet this woman, but not today. She couldn't summon up the enthusiasm for life coaches or even her beloved business.

'Grace, you don't need a consultation. Nobody has more confidence than you and they don't do any better ball-busting office suits than the sort of things you wear. What help can she give you?'

'Well, I'd love to know if longer hair would suit me,' Grace said, thoughtfully, fingering her short, expertly high-lighted blonde hair. 'And Ellen has such an eye. You know, my hairdresser says he likes the way my hair is, but he would say that, wouldn't he? He cuts it. Come on, meet her.'

'Just for ten minutes,' countered Faye. 'I'll follow you down to your office.' She shouldn't have come into work at all – she should have phoned in sick. How could she make polite conversation in the midst of her grief?

She delayed following Grace, hoping that by the time she arrived in Grace's office, Ellen might have gone. No such luck.

'Hello,' Faye said. 'I've really only got a minute, Grace, because I've got to . . .'

'Hey, sit down,' interrupted Grace, in a voice that brooked no opposition.

Faye knew when she was beaten. Still, she could say hello, be charming and leave in five minutes.

'Meet Ellen.' Ellen was not the tall and exquisite creature that Faye expected. All the life coaches and stylists she had ever seen had exuded as much glamour as confidence. Ellen was remarkably normal-looking, around Faye's age and was simply but elegantly made up. She was beautifully dressed in a fitted skirt suit in a lovely pale grey that Faye wouldn't have looked at in a million years. Her eyes shone with a wealth of experience and innate self-confidence.

'Hello,' said Ellen. 'Nice to meet you, Faye.' Even her voice was elegant.

They talked about the business for a few moments, with Faye eager to be gone. This was Grace's area of expertise.

Grace liked nice clothes and high heels because she liked attracting attention, sexual allure was part of what made Grace tick. It was a part of Faye that she'd ruthlessly ripped out. She never wanted a man to fancy her again.

No man would ever call her honey or Silver or touch her again. Men were not on her agenda, ever.

'I've got to go,' she said finally, when she judged she could leave.

'It was nice to meet you,' said Ellen, and Faye could see the other woman's eyes on her, perhaps itching to do a makeover on her.

It was all so superficial – *style your hair, wear better suits, have a make-up lesson* – who cared? Faye thought, rage from somewhere deep inside her bubbling up. Who really cared what people looked like? The outside didn't matter. It was the inside that counted – didn't anybody understand that? Never mind that Faye's inside was a mess.

Five miles away, in the comfort of Karl's admittedly rather fusty-smelling bed, Amber stretched and luxuriated. It was eleven o'clock in the morning and she wasn't sitting in crappy old Irish class, bored out of her brain, thinking of the exams and what she was going to do for the summer. No, she was lying beside the man she loved, the man who was soon going to wake up and start kissing her gently, nibbling her neck and making love to her.

Then, maybe they'd get up and have a late, luxurious breakfast, padding around the flat together in their bare feet. She might wear one of his shirts: people did that in films, it was sort of cute. Then they could curl up on the couch and watch old movies and it would be blissful.

She and Mum used to love the afternoon movies when she was growing up, all those black-and-white classics. It was especially nice on winter weekends when the rain pelted down outside and they'd sit, cosy in their home, and . . .

Amber didn't want to think about Mum, because then she'd feel guilty. But it was all her mother's fault really. Her obsession with never upsetting the neighbours and having to always be whiter than white because 'you've got no dad and we don't want anyone looking down on the Reid family, making assumptions and remarks'.

What sort of assumptions would they make? It used to drive Amber mad.

If only Mum hadn't been so obsessed with all that crap she might have noticed Amber changing, or she might have understood why Amber had wanted to change.

None of it mattered any more anyway. She was with Karl and that was what mattered, as she'd told Mum. It had been horrible but it was over.

Amber had kept her mobile phone off since, afraid her mother would ring, demanding that she come home. Or worse, crying and looking devastated, as she'd been yesterday. It had been weird to see her like that, all sad and pleading. Not like the strong mother she knew.

'Hiya, baby,' murmured Karl, half awake. He rolled over in the bed, closed his eyes and appeared to sink back into sleep.

Amber stroked the back of his neck hopefully. She didn't want to lie here with her feelings for company: she wanted Karl to take her mind off them.

But Karl was asleep again.

Maybe she'd ring Gran, just to tell her to keep an eye on Mum, because knowing Mum she wouldn't tell anybody that Amber had left. That would be so her.

She'd ring Gran and explain, then Gran could explain to Mum, who'd get over it and perhaps, even fly out to New York to meet them when she and Karl were settled. Amber hoped the record company could sort out an apartment for them to stay in, something with a balcony, perhaps.

Or maybe a modern house, with huge glass windows that looked out on to the sea in the Hamptons. Now that would be major league. Ella could come and stay too, when they were back talking to each other again.

211

Time, Amber decided, was all it would take and everyone would get used to the idea. Stan answered the phone at Gran's house and he sounded as he always did, relaxed and laid-back, as if every day was a joy to be savoured, which indeed it was, according to Stan.

Ella and Amber thought Stan was a howl. The complete opposite to Gran, who fired on all cylinders and never stopped moving or talking. Stan could sit in his chair and listen, without saying anything for ages. He was a good step-granddad, Ella used to say, seeing as Amber couldn't really remember her real granddad.

'You don't have much luck with male relatives, do you?' Ella had said one day. 'I mean, your dad's dead, your granddad's dead, you don't know your dad's family, what's all that about?'

'Dad was Scottish and he was only working in Ireland, I told you that,' Amber said, annoyed at her friend's thoughtlessness. 'Oh, it's complicated.'

Ella was such a pain sometimes. Just because she had all her family around her with relatives coming out her ears, she thought everyone else should be the same.

'But it's romantic, isn't it?' said Ella, wistful now.

'Make up your mind,' Amber said crossly. 'One minute it's weird and strange, the next minute it's romantic, which is it?'

She'd often wondered about her dad, and what sort of father he'd be: strict and tough, or pretending to be strict, a bit like Ella's dad, who was a total softie under all that cross-patch, 'I'm your father and listen to me' stuff. Amber's mum didn't talk enough about Dad, she felt. She knew so little about him. Even Gran said practically nothing about him. She just knew he'd loved her. They hadn't known each other long when Mum got pregnant.

'We wanted to bring you up properly, together,' Mum had

said. And then Dad was killed in a car accident, and he'd only a few relatives left and they'd moved, so Amber and her mum had lost touch with them. She'd like to search for them sometime.

'Your gran's in the kitchen baking,' said Stan now to Amber. 'Yet another church event she's been asked to make cakes for.'

Just like Mum, thought Amber, another tinge of irritation hitting her. What was it with her mother and grandmother and all this church baking, holier than thou stuff?

'I'll get her for you,' said Stan.

'Hello, love,' said Gran cheerily after a long period when Amber could imagine her dusting off her floury hands and sitting down on the tapestry stool in the hall where the old-fashioned round-dial phone sat. 'I can't talk for long. I'm about to put my cakes in the oven and you know how cakes can flop if you hesitate. How are you, love? And why are you ringing me now? You should be at school – is something wrong?'

'No, I'm fine. The thing is, Gran,' said Amber, and suddenly it seemed quite hard to say this, 'I'm not at school because I've left home and ...'

'You've left home?' The tone of her grandmother's voice didn't change, but something steely came into it.

'Yes,' said Amber. This was definitely more difficult than she'd thought. 'I've left home because I've fallen in love with somebody and Mum doesn't understand. I want to go to America with him. I just thought I'd tell you so that you'd keep an eye on Mum, because she's really upset.'

'Really upset, was she?' asked her grandmother, still steely, and Amber winced. 'That's not surprising if you told her you were leaving school to go to America with a man. When did all this happen?'

'Yesterday.'

213

'I meant,' Gran said, 'when did you fall in love with this man?'

'Over a month ago.' It seemed such a short length of time and yet, Amber felt as if she'd been with Karl for ever. Like Romeo and Juliet. Héloïse and Abelard. Kate Winslet and Leonardo DiCaprio in *Titanic*.

'His name is Karl. He's a musician, Gran, he's so talented. You'd love him, really you would. And he loves me. Oh, Gran, say you'll be on my side? Mum doesn't get it, you know what she's like. I told her yesterday and, well, we had a row.'

'Hold on and start from the beginning,' her grandmother instructed.

So Amber did, leaving out the bit about how she and Ella had got into the club illegally and leaving out the sex stuff, obviously, because she couldn't tell her grandmother that, but giving her the basics. How she and Karl were each other's futures, how he really wanted her to come to America with him because he wrote better songs when she was with him. It made so much sense. She could study art any time, that was a gift you never lost, wasn't it? She could paint in America just as well as she could paint in Ireland and, as for the exams, she didn't need a bit of paper to prove that she was going to be a doctor or a scientist or a teacher. She wanted to paint, it was simple, and she could do that anywhere.

Education was a fine thing in principle, but really what was the point of putting people in little boxes, so that you could decide what they were going to do for the rest of their lives, when you knew already what you wanted to do?

Amber finished this explanation in a rush and there was a pause. A long pause, that she found a bit uncomfortable.

'Are you still there, Gran?' she said, anxiously. 'You haven't gone off to put your cakes in the oven?'

'I'm still here,' her grandmother said with a certain coolness in her voice. 'The cakes have shifted down my list of priorities, Amber. I'm trying to work out why you can't be in love and be somebody's muse without finishing your exams first, or perhaps without telling your mother in such a way that the two of you ended up in a big fight.'

Amber flinched at the way Gran said 'muse', much the way people said 'door-to-door double-glazing salesmen'.

'That doesn't sound like you, Amber, and it certainly doesn't sound fair to your mother. You know how much she loves you.'

Amber did and this wasn't what she wanted to hear.

'Look, Gran, I'm not telling you this so that you can change my mind, I'm telling you so that you can keep an eye out for Mum. Obviously she doesn't want to talk to me right now.'

'I think that's highly unlikely. I'm quite sure she has been ringing you on the hour, every hour,' snapped her grandmother.

Amber flushed. She knew there were probably millions of messages on her phone but she didn't want to listen to them, didn't want to hear her mother's anxious, pleading voice. Everybody was blowing this whole thing out of all proportion: it was getting bigger and bigger, and it was going to be harder to sort out.

'Look, all I'm saying is that you can be a grown-up, live your own life and do what you want with the love of your life, but you can do it gently, in such a way that it doesn't break your mother's heart, Amber. And you can do your exams while you're at it. You've spent your whole school life working towards this moment. What's another month?'

'That's what everyone says,' Amber said furiously. 'It's my life, I can make the decision. Isn't that what you and Mum have always told me? *To be in charge, to make my own decisions, not to follow the crowd.*'

She knew that they hadn't wanted those same words and ideas turned against them.

Gran sighed.

'Without your father,' she said delicately, 'it was a very hard time for your mother.'

'Yeah, well, I didn't ask her to bury herself for me,' Amber insisted. 'That was her choice, Gran. She built her life around me, but I can't be responsible for that, so don't try to make me feel guilty, because I'm not.'

That was what Karl had said when he told her she shouldn't feel guilty. 'You're going off to have your life and she's got to get it together on her own.'

Except that she did feel guilty and nervous: everyone was furious with her. What had she started?

'Amber, why don't you come here and I'll ring Faye and get her to come here and we can all talk and get over this and maybe move on and . . .'

'No,' said Amber, thinking of Karl and how she couldn't risk not being with him. If she contacted her mother, Mum would stop her and she had to be with Karl, she had to. 'It was a mistake ringing you, Gran. I just wanted you to check up on Mum. I wanted you to know what had happened, that we'd had a row, but that's it. I'm going, OK?'

'Call your mother, please,' Gran begged. 'Does she even know where you are? If you give her a chance to talk to you, you might understand. You've got to see her side of the story, Amber, promise me you'll phone her.'

'Gran, I can't,' Amber blurted. She couldn't face her mother.

'Please, Amber. She tried so hard to give you everything because you didn't have a father, you owe her the chance to explain it all to you, why she was so protective . . .'

'Bye, Gran,' said Amber and pressed the end call button. She felt shaken. What was Gran harping on and on about? Get your mother to tell her, tell her what? Tell her how to make the perfect muffin, the perfect flapjack? What could Mum possibly teach her? If it was anything important she needed to tell Amber, she'd have told her by now, wouldn't she?

It was all just a ploy to get Amber to stay, but she wasn't going to stay, she was going on to her new life with Karl. Older people were so obsessed trying to tell you about the mistakes they'd made. You had to make all the mistakes yourself, didn't you? Besides, Mum had probably never made any bloody mistakes apart from being the over-protective mother from hell. She was always Mrs Perfect, wasn't she?

'Hey, baby, where are you?' called Karl.

'In here,' said Amber, trying to calm herself down.

Karl padded into the kitchen, sleep-fogged and beautiful.

'I was going to make some breakfast,' said Amber, trying to recover from the horrible conversation she'd just had.

'Breakfast, I could kill some breakfast,' said Karl. 'What are you going to make?' He sat down on one of the stools and looked at her patiently.

'I don't know,' said Amber. Cereal or toast was her limit. Her mother was the scrambled eggs expert. Amber gritted her teeth.

'Scrambled egg?' she said confidently.

'Yeah, sure,' he replied with a sleepy stretch.

Amber opened the fridge where one egg sat in glory in the box. She was sure there had been a few more last night.

'No eggs,' she informed him.

'Hey,' Karl said, 'maybe we'll go out.'

He reached and pulled Amber up against him, until she was resting between his legs, his arms around her waist. 'Or we can go back to bed and go out in another hour?'

Amber leaned into him, loving the feel of his skin against hers, this was so much better than Irish class.

'That sounds like a fabulous idea,' she said.

*   *   *

After saying a polite goodbye to Ellen, Faye stuck it out at her desk for another half an hour. Her head throbbed. Her daughter had run away and not bothered to so much as phone to tell Faye where she was. It hurt so much.

She left her desk and went into the women's room. The women's room in Little Island was big, airy and full of light so that you could see to put your make-up on. It also boasted a small bench seat so that people could sit down during important searches of handbags or for tights-changing exercises.

'I've worked in far too many offices with appalling loos,' Grace had said when they were checking over the premises originally. 'This is a woman-oriented company, so let's have a woman-oriented loo!'

One of the stall doors was shut when Faye came in. She went over to the sink and splashed water on her face. She had painkillers in her bag, she'd take them too. Although the real ache wouldn't be lessened with aspirin.

Despite Grace's beautiful lighting, the face that stared back at Faye was grey and tired, with violet bags under the eyes. Even her skin looked grey.

The stall door banged. 'Hello again.'

Hell, it was Ellen, the super-duper life coach and life revamper looking appallingly marvellous beside her. Ellen washed her hands, but surprisingly she didn't have a bag of tricks to apply half a stone of lipstick or glue her hair into place. In fact, Ellen looked remarkably good without doing any of that. Her hair was dark, shoulder length and glossy. Simple but it suited her. She looked confident, happy, businesslike.

Beside her, Faye felt like a lost soul who kept all her belongings in a shopping trolley.

'Hello,' Faye answered automatically, as she searched her handbag for the aspirin.

Ellen didn't say anything for a minute. She appeared to be watching Faye in the mirror, thinking.

218

'How are you?'

'Fine,' snapped Faye, finding the elusive painkillers. 'Just a headache.'

'You don't look fine,' Ellen said candidly.

Faye was stunned by this honesty.

She thought that faking sincerity was top of the list for stylists and life coaches.

'Listen, I'm fine. I'm going through a bit of a personal crisis at the moment,' she said, 'that's all.'

Her eyes saw in the mirror what Ellen could see – her hair looked as if she'd slept on it badly instead of being smoothly under control as usual. She pulled the scrunchie from her ponytail, raked her fingers through it like a comb, then corralled it all back into the band again.

'I used to be just like you, Faye,' Ellen said suddenly. 'Invisible. I dressed down, wore no make-up, hid behind boring clothes and banished any vestige of attractiveness I had. It kept people at bay, you see. I used to think that if nobody saw me, it was safer.'

Faye's hands stilled on her ponytail.

'I'm not asking you what's going on in your life,' Ellen went on. 'I'm just saying I can recognise the signs, because that was me. Invisible and in pain. You're not doing yourself any favours by living like that.'

'Grace put you up to this, didn't she?' Faye said furiously.

'She didn't set me up to do anything,' Ellen said bluntly. 'I just recognise something in you that used to be in me. The same utter hopelessness. Someone helped me to move on and I did. I'd like to help you do the same, but you have to come to terms with it yourself.'

'So what if I don't care about clothes or having my hair done in a fancy place,' Faye said sharply. 'Big bloody deal. Those things don't matter.'

'It's not your clothes or your hair that tell me you think

219

you're invisible. It's in your eyes. Most people don't see it, only a woman who's been in that place too. You might as well have a sign around your neck saying keep away.'

Faye stared at her silently, her heart thumping as hard as her head.

'You know, I think you've got the wrong idea about what I do,' Ellen went on. 'I'm not here to make a fortune on the back of telling women to change their hair, wear red lipstick and high-heeled shoes and, wow, life will be suddenly better. That's not what it's about. It's about looking at your life, trying to change it and change it for the better. Taking back some power. You might be running the company here with Grace, but somewhere along the way you've lost some of your power. I did the same thing too, thanks to a bad marriage, and one day, I copped on and took my power back. Anyway,' she said brusquely, 'I didn't mean to insult you, just wanted to say I was like that too and I found out how to change. Right now, despite all the bad things that have happened in my life, and, trust me, there have been a few, I'm happier than I have ever been. And it doesn't involve a man, by the way, Faye, that's not what this is about. So if you ever want to talk, you know where to find me. Otherwise, I'll see you around. Bye.'

She swept out the door, leaving only a scent of jasmine and vanilla perfume behind. Faye slumped down on to the bench seat, stunned and angry. How dare she?

And yet, her words drifted back. Invisible, yes – Ellen hadn't got that one wrong.

Faye had tried very hard to be invisible, for a good reason, and she'd succeeded. People didn't notice her. They saw a business person, not even a woman.

And who had she done that for? She had believed she was doing it for Amber, but Amber was gone now, and, suddenly, she knew.

Standing in the bathroom, Faye faced one of her uncomfortable truths. Although Ellen had said that a man was not responsible for her becoming strong again, Faye realised that fear of being involved with a man again was the reason she, Faye, had made herself invisible. She'd spent years telling herself that men were not part of her plan for her and Amber's lives, that men only complicated things, that it wasn't fair on a child to bring boyfriends into the fold because they would inevitably leave. And how could she face Amber's hurt little face, wondering where the latest father figure she had come to trust had gone?

But that wasn't why she'd kept away from men, Faye knew.

She'd simply never wanted to go through the pain of being with a man again.

As Faye sat on the little bench in the women's room, thinking over the past, a sense of longing suddenly came over her. Amber might not need her mother at the moment, but Faye certainly needed hers.

She picked up her bag and hurried back to her office. She grabbed her jacket and her phone and ran downstairs, shouting over her shoulder to Jane on reception: 'Jane, I have to go. Family emergency. Tell Philippa to handle my calls.'

'Can I do anything to help?' asked Jane to Faye's retreating back.

'No, nothing, but thanks.'

Her mother's front door opened as soon as Faye rang the bell and before Faye could say anything, her mother put her arms round her.

'I know,' Josie said.

'You do?'

'She phoned a while ago.'

'And what's happening?' Faye almost wailed. 'Is she safe, is she coming home . . . ?'

221

'She's still going away with him,' said her mother. 'Come on in, we'll talk.'

When they'd shared all they knew, mother and daughter sat quietly at the kitchen table.

'Not hearing from her is the hardest thing,' Faye said.

'I think she's realised what she's done and she's scared to get in touch with us right now,' Josie said. 'But she'll change her mind. She'll miss you, you pair are so close. Don't worry, it'll work out.'

'What if it doesn't?' Faye demanded. 'I've got to do something.'

'Like what?'

'I'm going to go after her,' Faye said simply. 'Find her, tell her the truth and then, it's up to her.'

'You should have told her the truth a long time ago,' her mother said, although there was no criticism in her voice. It was just a statement of fact. Josie had always told Faye that she should tell the truth to Amber. She'd never wanted to lie to her granddaughter although she had, for Faye's sake.

'How did you feel, back then, when I was ruining my life and dropping out of college?' Faye asked. They hadn't had a conversation about this for so many years that she couldn't precisely remember it all. She knew her mother had tried her best to tell Faye that she was hanging around with people who'd hurt her. But Faye had refused to listen, just like Amber was doing now.

'I felt as if I'd failed as a mother,' Josie said. 'My friends said I couldn't live your life for you, but I kept thinking that if I'd been a good mother, you'd have been able to see that those people were bad for you and that you'd only get hurt.'

'You didn't fail,' Faye insisted, getting up to sit beside her mother. 'It wasn't you. I wanted excitement and thrills and romance, you couldn't have stopped me.'

'And you couldn't have stopped Amber,' Josie added.

The comparison was neatly done.

But in her guilt and self-contempt, Faye still refused to see it that way.

'It's different. You had always been truthful with me, had warned me about things. But I knew things I didn't tell Amber and I lied to her. If I had been more open with her, then she'd have known that men like this Karl are all smoke and mirrors . . .' Ella had not held back in her unflattering portrayal of Karl. He sounded like the worst sort of man – beautiful on the outside, vain and selfish on the inside. Men like him never thought of others.

'It's not different at all,' Josie interrupted. 'It just seems worse because you're so close.'

Faye nodded, tears in her eyes now. That was the awful thing, how she and Amber could share so much and that Amber could still leave. Christie had said something similar: that it was because of their very closeness that Amber had made the break this way.

You have huge love and closeness, leaving you was like leaving a lover: to be done quickly, ripping the ties, before she'd have a chance to change her mind. She's only just eighteen after all. It's a time of passion, isn't it?

As Faye sat in her mother's kitchen, she felt heartfelt gratitude to Christie again. It was comforting to interpret Amber's leaving that way, though it didn't make it hurt less.

'You know it wasn't your fault, don't you?' she asked her mother. 'About me.'

'I do now. I blamed myself for a long time. But blaming doesn't work. You can't beat yourself up about everything for evermore. I realised that you can't lay every problem at someone else's door, either. Your parents might do their worst, but then you're on your own and you can shape yourself the way you want and learn from what they did

223

wrong. Stan taught me that,' she added, smiling. 'He says learn from the past and move on. I'm not saying your father wasn't a wonderful man, but he didn't think the way Stan did. Stan doesn't say much but when he talks, he makes sense. You can change up until your dying day, he says, so there's no point blaming the people who only had the moulding of you until you left home.'

'He's right,' Faye said, 'except he isn't accounting for parents who try to mould you too much. I didn't want Amber to have my past as a template. I wanted to give her a clean slate, not to have to learn from my poor example. I don't know why I never thought she'd rebel against that. Stupid really. She's my daughter, after all.'

'If you'd told her, she might have run off all the same.' Josie shrugged. 'You'll never know. But if you can sleep better at night having told her, then do. I don't worry about Amber so much as you do, love. I have great faith in her. You've brought her up well and she's a clever girl. She won't do anything really stupid, you'll see.'

But Faye, who thought of drink and drugs and what damage they could do to a clever girl's common sense, and of the people who take pleasure in destroying innocence and girlish dreams, did worry.

'Look at what happened to me,' she said.

Her mother laid a hand on Faye's and her eyes were shining with pride. 'Yes,' she said, 'look at you.'

CHAPTER FIFTEEN

People's concepts of time were strange, Christie reflected. When you were six, a child of twelve was like a being from another planet. And when you were sixty, those six years meant nothing.

The six years between herself and her younger sister Ana had shortened over their lives so that they now spoke of 'people our age'.

But the maternal feeling Christie had for Ana had never quite gone away and she'd always looked out for her sister, trying to take care of her the way she had all those decades ago in Kilshandra, when their father raged and their mother tried to ignore it all.

Which was another reason why the thought of Carey Wolensky hurt so much. For when he'd come into their lives, Christie hadn't taken care of her darling little sister. And she simply couldn't forgive herself for that.

Ever since she'd seen his name in the paper, she had thought of little but Carey and the past, which was why she felt so jumpy and guilty when Ana phoned later that week and asked to meet her one afternoon.

'I want to talk about Rick's birthday surprise.'

Ana sounded breathless, as if she had a huge secret to impart.

'In the Summer Street Café at three?' Christie suggested.

By ten past, the two sisters were sitting at a window table with coffee and cake in front of them. At a table outside sat a group of girls from St Ursula's sixth year and they'd smiled at Christie. She grinned back, imagining them cursing her under their breath because they'd undoubtedly chosen that table so they could enjoy forbidden cigarettes – smoking while in uniform was supposed to be off limits. They were like glossy birds of paradise in the royal-blue uniform, with long colourful scarves wound round youthful necks and gorgeous long hair whipping around in the breeze, all looking far older than their years. Ella was there, and she looked diminished without Amber, her partner in crime. Where was Amber now? And how was poor Faye coping?

It was four days since Amber had gone and Christie and Maggie had dropped round to Faye's each evening, just for a chat and a cup of tea. Faye was travelling to the States the following morning even though she didn't know exactly where Amber was. Ella's information had been patchy. All she knew was that the band had talked about being produced by some company based in New York.

'That's not much to go on,' Maggie commented.

'If I'm in the same city, I'll find them,' Faye said firmly.

She'd spent the past few days sorting out things at work so she could take extended leave. She was being outwardly businesslike and calm, but inside, she was still broken-hearted. Each day, she sat on the bed in Amber's room, looked around, and wondered at how she'd managed to get it so badly wrong. Amber had left one message on the house phone:

'I'm fine, Mum. We're going to the US. I'll talk to you. I'm fine, really. Bye.'

If only she'd phoned on the mobile, Faye thought. But

Amber had undoubtedly not phoned Faye's mobile on purpose, and at least she knew Amber was all right.

'You'll get through it,' Christie had told her.

It was good to see Faye getting to grips with her situation, but Christie was beginning to feel like a fraud giving any advice. She had her own dark cloud hanging over her and she'd done nothing to address it. She didn't dare. She just longed for some peace in her head. Perhaps she'd never have peace again, or at least not until Carey Wolensky packed up his exhibition and left the country.

'I love it here,' sighed Ana, stirring her cappuccino happily and licking the spoon. 'It's so homey. You can just imagine this sort of place in Kilshandra when we were growing up, everyone knowing everyone else. Summer Street's great for that sense of community, it does remind me of home.'

Christie didn't agree but said nothing.

The difference was that she'd have hated people in a small café knowing her business in the home town of their youth because everyone would have looked at Christie and Ana MacKenzie with pity. Their father didn't confine his bullying and bad temper to his own home but spread it around liberally, so people knew what the MacKenzie children and poor Maura MacKenzie had to put up with.

'He's not an easy man, your father,' was about the kindest thing anybody had ever said of him.

The idea of drinking your tea in a public room where everybody pitied you was not Christie's idea of fun. The Summer Street Café was a haven for many reasons and the fact that she was happy with her own life meant she could appreciate it. Nobody had reason to feel sorry for Christie Devlin here.

'Actually, I don't want to talk about Rick's birthday,' said Ana. 'I've something to tell you. A secret. If I don't tell somebody I'll go mad.'

227

Christie felt herself go icy cold in spite of the warmth of the sun beating down on the window.

'You won't tell anyone, not even James? I know you tell him everything, so promise.'

'I promise,' said Christie, dread in her heart.

'It's Carey Wolensky. He's going to be here in Ireland for an exhibition, so I contacted his hotel and left a message for him. It's so strange,' Ana went on, looking flushed, 'an old boyfriend coming into your life. I haven't told Rick. Not that Rick would really mind. He knows it's all in the past and it was before I met him, so it's not as if he and Carey were rivals or anything.'

'No,' agreed Christie automatically. 'That might be hard for him.'

'Well, it could be, so I haven't told him and I feel awful about it. Not that I still have feelings for Carey or anything like that.'

Christie sat immobile and felt sick. This was the meaning of the great dark wing of fear in whose shadow she'd been ever since that morning at the end of April. This was the disaster she'd seen in the future, in *her* future.

'Besides, Carey's had women to beat the band since. I've followed his career; I know it's wrong,' Ana went on guiltily. 'But only out of interest, honestly. I love Rick. Me and Carey would never have made it as a couple. We were wrong together, I know that. He was too old for me, too sophisticated, too mad about art. He was much more your type, really. At least you and he could talk about art together. I didn't know a Picasso from a can of soup.

'But it's interesting when someone you were once in love with is famous and you can watch them. Of course, he's gone out with all these younger women. How is it men can do that? Imagine me with a thirty-year-old? Everyone would fall about laughing, but men can do it.'

Ana held up her knife to look closely at her reflection, squinting so that the lines around her eyes became more pronounced. She favoured their father's side of the family, with fair hair, pale eyes and sun-shy skin. Christie looked more like their mother and was the picture of her maternal grandmother, who'd died before she was born, a woman with the fine bones of Breton heritage, and slanting dark eyes like Christie's.

'Would Botox help?' sighed Ana. 'I have furrows like trenches everywhere and I don't care what they say about rubbing creams and serums in. I've done everything I was supposed to. I've cleansed, toned, moisturised and dabbed eye cream on with my ring finger. I haven't gone to bed once in my whole life with my make-up on and look at me: I'm a human Shar-Pei.'

In spite of the knot in her stomach, Christie laughed. 'You don't look a bit like a Shar-Pei,' she said. 'They are adorable, though. I wouldn't mind one, although the girls would go mental.'

The velvety Chinese emperor dogs with their heavily wrinkled skin were exquisite, but Christie knew that Tilly and Rocket would be devastated if another dog invaded their kingdom. Dogs were like children: fiercely territorial.

'You're still lovely, you big muppet,' Christie said, forgetting her shock to berate her sister in the way she'd been berating her for decades. Ana had gone through life thinking she was too fat, too fair, had bad ankles, and Christie had been the one who'd buoyed her up, told her they were needless worries.

'Was I wrong to phone his hotel?' Ana went on anxiously.

The thought that she was the biggest hypocrite ever danced in Christie's head.

'He might never get back to you,' she said, hoping. Please, please let Carey have forgotten the MacKenzie sisters.

'That's it, you see.' Ana bit her lip. 'I got a call from his assistant to say he'd love to meet up and talk about old times except that his schedule hasn't been finalised yet and she'd get back to me. But imagine, he'd love to meet up. He hasn't forgotten after all.'

When Ana had gone home, Christie sat in the garden and sipped a large glass of wine. James would be astonished to see her drinking at this hour of the afternoon. She'd tell him she just felt like a moment of hedonistic pleasure, sitting in the sun-drenched garden with chilled Chablis. Which was all complete rubbish. She'd simply wanted something to dull the spike of fear inside her. Carey Wolensky was back in her life. All those years of trying to forget it and her guilty secret had sneaked back into her life as easily as if it had all happened yesterday.

The months leading up to Christie's thirty-fifth birthday were endlessly busy. She'd started working part time at St Ursula's and in an attempt to make some extra money, was painting botanical watercolours which a dealer friend sold in markets at the weekend. James was working all the hours too, on a massive environmental study that meant late nights at the office and monosyllabic conversations when he did come home.

Christie could have coped with him working hard, but not with his withdrawal from the human race. It was as if he wasn't interested in her any more and the only bit of affection left in him was given to their sons.

'How was your day?' Christie would ask when he came home, trying to keep the lines of communication open.

'Fine,' he'd mutter, hugging the boys.

Once the children were in bed, James worked silently at the dining-room table.

Christie started to go to bed early to read, and was often

asleep when he came upstairs. If it hadn't been for Ethan and Shane, she'd have packed her bags and left.

She adored her sons, loved every moment of their hectic days, and sometimes felt overwhelmed by love for them: two small boys who did everything passionately, whether it was cycling tricycles hell bent around the garden or fighting to the death with toy soldiers.

'It's scary, loving them so much,' she told Ana on the phone one day. She hadn't talked about the crisis in her marriage with Ana: doing so would make it more real, more raw. Part of Christie hoped that eventually, when James's study was done, he'd come back to her. 'When I read about a disaster or an accident in the paper, I think what would I do if anything happened to the boys?' she told her sister. 'It's like a physical pain thinking about it.'

Ana, working in administration in a hospital and enjoying a series of relationships with hardworking doctors who didn't have the time to find girlfriends anywhere else, said she wished she knew what Christie meant.

'I'm never going to find a man to settle down with and have babies,' she said morosely. 'I worked it out the other night: in the past two years, I haven't gone out with anyone for longer than three months. I must have a "ninety-day limit" sticker on my forehead. Three months and zip, they're gone. I am so fed up of hearing "you're a wonderful woman, but . . ." I'm going to shoot the next man who says "but" to me. And I've had it with doctors. They're all obsessed with work. Girlfriends are just a mild diversion between shifts. Never again. I need to get out and meet different types of people.'

Christie felt guilty for being so insensitive and reminding Ana, who was wildly maternal, that she was still childless with no hope of a daddy for her children in sight. It was James's fault, she thought crossly. If he wasn't so tied up with his work, so oblivious to her, she could have talked about her love for the boys with him, instead of upsetting poor Ana with it. What was the point of being married if the extent of your conversation was competitive exhaustion?

'I'm tired.'

'No, I'm tireder.'

'Of course you'll meet someone,' she said quickly to her sister. 'You're gorgeous, Ana, your time will come, I promise. You've been going out with the wrong sort of men, that's all. Get out and meet other people, go to museums, lectures, parties. Enjoy yourself and don't look for a man. When you're least expecting it, one will come along.'

How she was to regret that advice.

The day before Christie's birthday, she told James that they were going to a gallery to meet Ana's latest boyfriend – a Polish artist who was years older than her and sounded like he'd be another guy for the 'you're a wonderful woman *but* . . .' speech – and then on to dinner for a birthday celebration.

'I'm sorry, I forgot to organise anything for you, Christie,' James said matter-of-factly.

He wasn't even apologetic, Christie realised in fury. It was as if what he was doing was so important that everything else came a poor second, including her.

'What do you want?' he asked.

'A husband?' she said bitterly.

'Christie, don't be such a nag,' he snapped back. 'You know how busy I am.'

'I'm not nagging. I'm being honest. The boys and I never see you any more, James. You're obsessed with that bloody study. I cook, clean, work and take care of our sons, and the least I can expect is you to remember to buy me a birthday present. It's not rocket science. Even a card would be nice. I bet you haven't got a card for me for tomorrow either.'

He grimaced and said nothing.

Which meant no. 'Thank you, James. I'm touched by your thoughtfulness,' she said, hurt beyond belief. Not even a card. It was like her parents' marriage all over again. She must have been mad to get married. She should have just had kids and lived on her own. Men and women were utterly unsuited to being together for ever. It was the hunter-gatherer thing: men were warriors at heart, more suited to roaming, while women were better at taking care of their children and fighting their own battles.

They were on the bus from Summer Street into the city and they sat in silence for the next ten minutes.

'So,' said James, keen to end the cold war, 'tell me about this new bloke of Ana's.'

Christie, who had many friends in the art world, had heard that Carey Wolensky was a charming and wildly sexy genius with a brilliant future ahead of him and many dumped besotted women in his wake.

'He sounds like a nightmare,' she said to James. 'The more brilliant they are, the madder they are.'

'You're an artist and you're not mad,' said James equably.

He was obviously trying to make up to her for not remembering her birthday.

'I'm one of the practical ones and we're a rare breed in the art world,' she said. 'Besides, I haven't been able to earn much of a living painting, have I? I'm missing the mad gene. Thank God for teaching.'

'He might be as normal as you and me and turn out to be just the man for Ana.'

'I doubt it. If he messes with Ana, I'll throw turpentine on all his canvases, I swear,' she added grimly. She'd been protecting Ana all her life and she'd protect her from this maniac if it was the last thing she did. Then again, who was she to say what sort of man was right for Ana? She'd picked

James and he'd recently transformed himself into a grumpy chauvinist.

Word of Carey Wolensky's fame had certainly spread because there were bodies crushed all around the entrance to the Bamboo Gallery when they arrived, and people clutching catalogues emerged from the gallery itself, crying 'fabulous', 'marvellous', and 'such talent!'

They joined the crush and squashed their way inside, where walls of dark and brooding Wolenskys glared down at them. Christie loved art in all its forms, but she'd never been a fan of dark abstract work like this. Oils painted with masterly knife strokes, these pictures were like tornadoes caught on canvas, full of energy and power, and infinitely startling.

There were a few portraits in the collection, but the people in them were cold, harsh and angular, not warm and curved like the Gauguin women Christie loved.

But clearly she was the only one who didn't approve. There were lots of little red sold stickers stuck on the frames and it was clear that Wolensky would not need to teach at St Ursula's to pay the rent.

This was all wrong, Christie felt. This man with his dark sinister paintings was not the right sort of man to court her sister. Ana didn't know a sausage about art and didn't have a pretentious bone in her body.

The man who'd painted these pictures was fierce and utterly in control. She'd have to warn Ana off him. Christie didn't want another controlling man like their father to take her over.

'You got here! And you look wonderful, almost Birthday Girl!' Ana proclaimed, admiring her sister.

In honour of her birthday dinner, Christie had left her hair down and had stuck heated rollers in it, so it now tumbled darkly around shoulders gleaming in a plum velvet halter-neck dress that clung to her tall, womanly body.

234

'Really, you don't look like fifty at all,' Ana teased, and Christie threw back her head and laughed her rich, deep laugh. It felt lovely to be with her sister, someone who appreciated and loved her.

When she looked back at Ana, a man was standing beside her, and Christie felt something she didn't think she'd ever experienced before: a spark of tinder and a sensation that this was a person she'd known all her life.

Carey Wolensky wasn't any oil painting himself, Christie thought drily, but the same passion and vivacity that inhabited his work inhabited his person too. She was tall but he was at least six inches taller and lean, with rather wild dark hair and deep-set eyes that stared bird-of-prey-like at her over a broken boxer's nose, taking in every detail. He was around her age, maybe older, and looked as if he wanted to taste every emotion, touch every second of life, in case he missed anything. There were many people crowded around and yet Carey Wolensky had that rare ability to be the person every eye was drawn towards.

'Pleased to meet you,' said James, who seemed to be enjoying himself now he had relaxed with a couple of drinks.

Carey nodded and smiled, and the bleakness left his face.

More people gathered round him to say how much they admired his paintings, and Ana's friend Chloe announced that the gallery owner was having a huge party in his house, 'a mansion on Haddington Road, with a swimming pool in the basement!' and they were all invited.

'We're going out to dinner,' said Christie loudly. 'We can't come.' She didn't know why but she knew that staying here was a mistake.

'A party's exactly what we need,' James said, 'a wild, music-filled night to get you over the misery of being thirty-five.'

'I'm not miserable,' insisted Christie. 'I just don't want to go.'

'If Christie does not want to go, she does not have to go,' said a voice. It was the first time Carey had spoken and she thought his accent was like Lenkya's, the deep purr of drawn-out syllables. It was a voice used to the harsh rasp of Polish consonants and it growled over the softness of her language, making it a language of love.

They stared at each other, oblivious to everyone else. Christie could have drawn his face instantly, she knew it so well. He watched her as if he would touch the contours of her face, then move down to her body, unhooking the halter-neck dress to caress the skin beneath . . .

'Isn't he wonderful?' sighed Ana, taking Christie's arm. 'I think he's the one,' she whispered for Christie alone. 'Well, I hope he is. He says he's too old for me and that's sexy, isn't it? Reverse psychology. It makes me want him even more now.'

Carey still locked gazes with Christie and she knew she'd have to look away or it would be obvious to everyone around them, obvious that Carey Wolensky and Christie Devlin were experiencing a physical attraction hot enough to send the whole room up in flames.

'Wolensky, marvellous show.' A well-dressed and well-padded man with a cigar broke the spell by standing between them.

A rich collector, Christie surmised, exactly the sort of person to take Wolensky's attention. Only the greenest artist didn't know that the official language of art was hard currency.

Christie stood back and breathed deeply. She was married. This was her sister's boyfriend, her beloved Ana's man. There would be, could be, no electricity between them.

'Shall I take you round the exhibition?' asked Ana.

'Yes, take me round,' Christie said.

With James at one side and Ana at the other, they toured

the pictures, Ana explaining what each canvas was called and James standing back and raising his eyebrows occasionally. Normally, Christie would have teased him every time he did this, whispering that he was a philistine and the only picture he'd really adored was the one of the tennis player scratching her knickerless bum. Which would make James grin and say no, he liked the poster of the dogs playing poker best.

This time, James's lack of comprehension irritated Christie. Couldn't he see how amazing these paintings were, the energy and fire that burned out at the audience?

By the time Lenkya arrived at the gallery, Christie and James weren't talking to each other.

'Argument?' asked Lenkya, kissing Christie twice, European-style.

'Yes,' sighed Christie. 'What's new?'

Lenkya was with her partner, a sculptor, and they toured the exhibition quickly.

'We're going to dinner,' Lenkya said, putting an arm round her friend. 'You are sad, you should come with us. You and James will never make up your differences here in this noisy place.'

'No,' said Christie firmly, 'we're staying a little longer.' Another thing she regretted. For if she and James had left then, it might never have happened.

As the crowds milled around, Christie could feel Wolensky watching her, feel the intensity of his mind turned towards hers. She did all those things you did when you were being watched: stood up straighter, held herself even more gracefully, smiled more, wanting to look more beautiful in his eyes even though, as she did it, she knew it was wrong.

They went to the party on Haddington Road.

'It'll be a bit of craic,' James said. 'We said we'd be home by twelve and it's only half nine now. We can phone Fiona on the way to say we won't be in the restaurant but we won't be late, either.'

Fiona, who was babysitting, was a college student who lived on Summer Street with her parents. Her mother was a nurse, which gave Christie peace of mind that if anything did happen – please God it wouldn't – Fiona's mother would be at number 34 in a flash with the full breadth of her medical training.

'I don't know . . .' Christie began, feeling strangely edgy.

'Stop being a martyr!' exploded James. 'You're furious I didn't arrange a big birthday evening for you, and now we have a chance of a party where we'll have some fun, and you don't know if you want to do that either! You don't know what you want to do.'

Perhaps if they hadn't had the argument, perhaps if Christie hadn't felt so lonely and neglected for so long, perhaps if Ana hadn't started flirting with a young man with merry eyes, and perhaps if Christie hadn't felt pure admiration at Wolensky's stunning paintings, then none of it might have happened.

The house on Haddington Road was a large Victorian mansion with pale floorboards and walls, perfect for displaying art, and utterly unsuitable for a wildly boozy party. Christie felt old surrounded by Ana's friends, who'd soon located a stereo and a stack of records to organise an impromptu disco. Ana and a group of her girlfriends began to dance. The young man with the merry eyes joined in, and Christie watched as Ana laughingly held his hands, clearly not caring whether her supposed artist boyfriend saw them or not. He was nothing compared to Wolensky, Christie thought, mystified.

James was still barely talking to her and was ensconced on a deep window seat with a man who turned out to be one of his brother's old friends.

Christie felt alone and miserable, until a hand took hers and led her out of the kitchen, into a small hallway and up three flights of stairs to a huge attic room hung with paintings.

'This is where he keeps the good stuff,' Carey said, not letting go of her hand. 'The paintings that are valuable. He has two of mine, see.'

They were alone, standing hip to hip, and even though her head told her it was wrong, her heart screamed that it was right.

She adored Ana, and she adored James. This should not be happening, she had to get out of there. Yet she felt as if she'd die if Carey didn't swing round and haul her into his arms, sinking into her soul and her body.

'You feel it too,' Carey said softly. He was looking down at her hand now, examining it, touching the palm as if he could see her whole life through the lines on her hand. 'What is between us. You feel it, I know.'

'No, I don't,' she lied. 'I'm married.' As if that was a talisman she could hold up like a crucifix to Dracula.

'So,' he said, still looking down at where her hand was trapped by both of his. 'Marriage severs the mind from the body, yes?'

'It does for Catholics,' Christie replied in an attempt at levity. 'It's in the ceremony. Forsaking all others.' She couldn't remember the rest of the vows, to her shame.

'Men who are not allowed to have women make up those rules,' Carey murmured. 'They cannot be expected to understand that such rules cannot always be followed.'

'I believe in those rules,' Christie said. 'And I love my husband.' This was true, utterly true. But she felt shaken still. For if she absolutely loved James, how could she feel so wildly attracted to this man? If he made just one move towards her, she'd offer herself to him, here on the floor with scores of people beneath them.

'Ah.'

He let go of her hand and Christie felt bereft. She hadn't been teasing. She'd meant every word she said, but having him touch her had been so tender.

'I will let you go,' he added, 'but can I touch your face, first, to remember?'

Her eyes, shining with excitement, must have said yes, because Carey stood inches away from her and with both hands cradled her face, rubbing his thumbs over the high planes of her cheekbones, down to the sweep of her jaw, and over the softness of her mouth.

When his thumb massaged her lower lip, slipping into the cavern of her mouth, she couldn't stop herself biting gently.

Watch out, said every instinct inside her. *This is not a game.*

'Not a unicorn after all but a lioness,' he said as her bite eased.

She made herself pull back from his touch.

'Married lioness,' she reminded him. 'And you're supposed to be going out with my sister.'

He shrugged. 'She is happy tonight,' he remarked. 'She has found the sort of young man she should be with. I told her so. I prefer' – he paused, looking at her – 'more complicated women.'

'I've got to go,' Christie said. 'Nice meeting you, Mr Wolensky.'

'Is that it?' he called as she almost ran down the stairs.

'That's it,' she replied over her shoulder.

In the kitchen, she filled a glass of cool water and drained it quickly, hoping it might douse the heat on her face and neck.

Back in the main part of the house, she searched for James. They had to go. He was still sitting on the window ledge laughing. Christie watched the man she curled up beside in bed, the man who'd held her hand through the births of two

240

children, the man she loved. Despite his current obsession with work, James was a good man. He was being blind, not seeing how he was hurting her, that was all. If she told him, sat down and said she was on the verge of walking out because of his behaviour, he'd be shocked and she knew he'd change in an instant.

And yet the image of James in her head was being crowded out by the dark brooding face of Carey Wolensky, who was all the things she'd ever dreamed of when she was young, and who'd come into her life when it was already full. Too late.

In the taxi on the way home, she held James's hand tightly. She would force Carey Wolensky out of her head. This was the man she loved, the father of her children.

James was exhausted and went to bed after politely walking Fiona, the babysitter, home. Christie stayed up and scrubbed the kitchen tiles with the small scrubbing brush. She made James's favourite apple cake, diligently and carefully, where normally, she flung ingredients in at high speed. She would push Carey out of her mind.

Ethan and Shane's little trousers hung on the clothes horse and she ironed them. Normally, she folded carefully, not bothering ironing garments that would be on and off within an hour.

She couldn't stop it: more than anything, she yearned to have Carey holding her in his arms, taking off her clothes, touching her breasts, lowering his head to kiss them, to feel his body covering hers, against hers, in hers.

Like the magic that came into her head unbidden and told her of the future, this longing was too powerful to push away.

Christie could no more resist Carey Wolensky than she could stop her mind from seeing what might happen.

CHAPTER SIXTEEN

Faye and Maggie sat in Faye's garden listening to the exquisite tones of Julie London on full blast telling everyone about how she'd cried a river and now it was his turn.

They had a bottle of rosé between them and a giant box of Ferrero Rocher half gone, with scrunched-up gold foil wrappers littering the table. Christie had said she'd drop in but hadn't turned up.

It was four days since Amber had left and, the following day, Faye was going to the States to find Amber and she couldn't wait to be off.

At least if she was travelling, trying to find Amber, she'd be doing *something*. And that was preferable to being at home in the silent misery of number 18. Without Amber, the house was grave-like. Faye jumped every time the phone rang in case it was Amber; she checked her answering machine by remote access ten times a day, and in the morning, she ran to the letterbox when the postman came just in case there was a card, a letter, *anything* saying that Amber was all right.

'Should I turn the music down,' asked Maggie, 'in case the neighbours go mad?'

Faye's next-door neighbour was an irascible man who had

no animals, no wife, no children and no sense of humour – or at least, that's what Amber had always said. Faye used to hush her when she said this. 'He might hear!'

'Screw the neighbours,' Faye muttered. 'If Mr Dork next door has a problem, he can come in here and tell me face to face.'

'Fine by me,' said Maggie, who knew a woman gunning for a fight when she saw one.

Since Amber had gone, Faye had appeared defeated and sad. Today, something had clearly changed inside her and she was filled with fierce energy and rage.

Maggie suspected she was going through the phases of grief: she'd done disbelief, and hopelessness, and now was on to anger.

Maggie had been through that herself.

'Exercise helps me,' she volunteered. 'I do Pilates when . . . sorry,' she added. 'It's very boring to have people giving you advice all the time, isn't it?' She wished Christie were here. She felt singularly incapable of saying anything useful. Her boyfriend had been cheating on her for years and she hadn't had a clue about it, so both her skills of observation and her credentials as agony aunt were questionable.

Faye shot her a genuine, warm smile. 'Thanks,' she said. 'I appreciate that. Everyone else wants to tell me what to do.' Everyone else was Grace, whom she'd told about Amber's disappearance, and who was full of suggestions about what action Faye should take next.

'Grace at work has my head wrecked saying she's there if I need her and after all, Amber was going to leave eventually and all families fight, don't they? She's trying to help but she doesn't understand. She doesn't have kids . . . Well, perhaps that's not fair,' Faye amended. 'You don't need to have children to understand and I've only told her half the story. Me and my secrets. Perhaps I should have brazened it

243

out and told her the truth years ago. We've been through a lot together professionally, so in many ways we know each other well. But at first I was too ashamed, I thought she'd look down on me. Grace is so together, I couldn't imagine her doing anything she was ashamed of. And then, too much time had passed for me to suddenly say: hey, Grace, I'm not really a widow after all. I just say I am.'

'When you're ashamed, it's easy to build it up into a huge secret you dare not trust anyone with,' Maggie reflected, thinking of her own past.

Faye looked interested now, so Maggie had to go on.

'My problem was that when things went wrong for me, I felt I couldn't confide in my parents,' she said, amazed at her courage now. She'd never said that to anyone before.

'About Grey?' Faye was puzzled. Maggie had said her parents knew about her break-up, though not about Grey cheating on her.

'No, before that.'

'What . . . ?' began Faye, and stopped.

Maggie's eyes had filled with tears. Whatever her big secret was, it was too painful to touch.

'So, back to this cheating man of yours,' Faye said firmly, switching subjects. 'What has your dad threatened to do to him lately?'

Despite herself, Maggie laughed. 'They don't have a surgical name for it yet.'

'But it's performed without an anaesthetic?'

'With two bricks and a rusty razor blade,' said Maggie. Then sighed. 'Poor Dad has got it into his head that I left Grey because there was no sign of us getting married. He calls Grey "that bastard who felt he was too good to put a ring on my daughter's finger after five years".'

'That is a very dad thing to say,' Faye agreed. 'Luckily for Amber's father my poor old dad wasn't around by the time

244

I started getting into trouble with men. But what happened to you was pretty rough.'

'You don't seem that shocked actually,' Maggie said, surprised. 'Not that I've been broadcasting the information but so far, everyone I've told about what Grey did has been stunned.'

'They all live sheltered lives, I guess.' Faye grinned. 'I've heard of guys doing much worse and he did say sorry afterwards, although I know that's not the point. You were living together, he was your partner and it was way out of line. You're not taking him back, I hope.'

'I wanted to,' Maggie said. 'Isn't that pathetic? I thought he was right for me. I loved him and our life together.'

Faye interrupted: 'You just don't love coming home and seeing him bonking some blonde babe on your bed.'

'No,' agreed Maggie, 'that does sort of ruin things.'

'So you've got to dump him and start again.'

'I'm going to dump him all right.' Since Shona had told her about Grey's other women, she'd thought of practically nothing else. She felt so humiliated by the news. To think how he'd looked her straight in the eye and lied to her.

It's never happened before.

I love you.

To think of him offering to marry her while hiding the fact that he'd betrayed her in the past.

Grey had tried to phone her every day but she never answered when she saw his number appear on her phone screen. She wasn't ready for him yet. She'd cry if she spoke to him and she didn't want to do that: she wanted to build herself up to be strong and angry for that conversation.

'I'm not starting again with anybody ever,' Maggie said decisively. 'I can't go through all that dating, smiling and trying to be something you're not. Hoping they'll like you.' She shuddered, partly with remembered shame. She'd tried

245

so hard to be what Grey wanted and, in the process, had lost sight of who she was. The past had scared her and Grey had made her feel safe, so she'd never tried to work out who Maggie Maguire actually was and what she wanted from life.

'Hoping they'll like you sounds like me once,' reflected Faye. 'Trying to be something I wasn't instead of having the courage to be what I really was.'

There was silence. The CD had stopped playing and there was no noise at all, apart from the sound of somebody's lawn mower and a dog barking, far away in the distance.

'You have to tell Amber about the past when you see her,' Maggie said. 'All of it.'

Faye nodded. She had been thinking a lot about everything over the previous few days.

Ellen, the makeover lady, had been right when she said Faye tried to be invisible. Faye had tried to blend into the background, to make herself as asexual as possible, so nobody could connect her with the wild child she'd been. And she'd protected Amber like a crown princess, stifling her out of love, never telling her the truth. It kept coming back to secrets and lies.

'I'm going to tell Amber everything when I see her,' she told Maggie. 'It's just that I thought I was doing the right thing by inventing this person: Faye Reid, mum extraordinaire, conservative, decent, long-skirt-wearing person, pillar of the community, the sort of woman no one would ever imagine hanging out with dodgy men, having no respect for herself. I thought if I insulated Amber from the world, bad things would never touch her and she would grow up strong and confident. And if she ever met a man like her father, I thought by then that she would know better, that she would be stronger than I was. But I was fooling myself.'

'Me too,' said Maggie, thinking that she wasn't much

246

different from Faye after all. At least Faye had changed her life and begun to respect herself once she'd given birth to Amber.

While Maggie had always felt as if she wasn't worthy of Grey, that it was surprising someone like him loved her. She'd had to pretend to be the confident person to hide her insecurities. If that wasn't living a lie, what was?

'And the more you lie, the more you have to lie. The lies become bigger until there's no way out, apart from admitting that you're fabulous at being deceitful. What mother wants to say that to her daughter?' Faye asked.

'You thought you were protecting her,' Maggie said. 'She'll understand that, when you tell her.'

'But it's gone on for so long,' sighed Faye. 'Imagine if you have an adopted child and you never find the right time to tell them. Maybe, you miss that window of opportunity when they're two or three, when it should become part and parcel of their life – *You're adopted. Mummy and Daddy love you and picked you to be our baby, so our love is special* – and time moves on and you haven't told them. So you wait a bit longer and then you have to turn around when they're an adult and go, *Well, actually, by the way, we're not your parents, we adopted you.* It's like that with me and Amber. I should have told her in the beginning, but I didn't know how. It's gone on so long that telling her will destroy her and she'll hate me and I . . .' Faye paused. 'I don't know if I can face that. I love her so much, Maggie. Everything that I've achieved in my life this past eighteen years, has been for her. I couldn't bear for her to hate me.' Maggie got up and put her arms around Faye, holding her tightly.

And Faye, who longed for the comfort of another human being since Amber had stormed off, leaned against Maggie and began to sob.

'I just wish she'd come home, I wish she'd make contact,

anything. Just so I could tell her I love her and explain it all to her, that's all I want,' she said, as she sobbed. 'I'm sorry, Maggie, I'm sorry. You don't need this.'

'Don't be silly,' said Maggie, still holding Faye tightly, as the other woman's sobs subsided. 'Hey, you'll be doing this for me in a minute, when I tell you all my deep, dark secrets.'

'You mean you have deep, dark secrets too?' hiccupped Faye. 'Oh please, tell me, I don't want to feel like the only screw-up on Summer Street.'

Maggie laughed. 'There are lots of screw-ups on Summer Street,' she said. 'It's just we don't know about them, that's all. Do you think everyone hiding inside the pretty houses, with the coloured doors and the beautiful maple trees, lives a perfect life? Of course they don't. If you knew my mother, then you wouldn't think that. She knows everything that goes on around here.'

'Really?' asked Faye.

'Oh yes,' said Maggie, seeing that Faye looked cheered by this line of conversation. 'Mum is a fount of knowledge about everyone on Summer Street. It's the café, you see. She and dad go into the Summer Street Café at least once a day and Mum learns things, all the time. Not in a bad way: she's not a gossip, but she's interested in people's lives and she knows what goes on. Christie's the same, really,' she added thoughtfully. 'Christie seems to know about everyone.'

'She's a wise woman,' agreed Faye. 'I wish I'd known her properly before, instead of just nodding a distant hello in the street. That was another one of my obsessions,' she added. 'I thought if we kept ourselves to ourselves, nobody would get close enough to ask what exactly happened to Amber's father. But someone like Christie, she'd never ask you those sort of questions, would she? If I'd known her then, she might have been able to help me, stop me screwing everything up.'

'No,' insisted Maggie, 'we've got to help ourselves. I've got to fall out of love with my cheating boyfriend, a man who must think I'm the dumbest woman on the planet if I agree to marry him when he's had other women all the time we were going out.'

'You can't be the dumbest woman on the planet,' Faye joked. 'That's me.'

'No,' argued Maggie. 'It's me, I'm afraid.'

'Did you cut the arms off his suits and throw paint all over his car before you left?' Faye inquired.

'Don't be daft,' said Maggie. 'I'm a wimp. I went back to the apartment that night, talked to him like an adult and even considered – in my own head of course, I didn't say this out loud – letting him sleep in the bed with me because then he'd hug me and cuddle me and it'd all be all right.'

'Ouch,' said Faye.

'I know,' Maggie agreed, 'not just the world's dumbest woman, but the wimpiest too. But fortunately I stood firm and made him sleep on the couch. Then, the next morning, I packed and flew home to Summer Street. Cutting the arms off all his clothes might be fun though. He doesn't really wear suits, he's more of a casual jacket type of guy.'

'You could tell people he had some appalling venereal disease?'

'My friend, Shona, thought of that one too,' laughed Maggie. 'She works in the library with me and was all set to spread the rumours, but I said that sort of revenge would be beneath me.'

Faye grinned. 'It wouldn't be beneath me. Fight fire with fire. He slept with a student, so why don't you let that be known? He'd be sacked. The ultimate revenge.'

'True,' said Maggie, 'but I'm trying to put myself in that happy, Zen state where the only true revenge is living my own life well.'

'You're right,' Faye said gravely, 'that's exactly the right thing to do. Modern and very politically correct.' But she added wickedly, 'It would be great fun, wouldn't it?'

'Not as much fun as telling him I don't need him,' said Maggie firmly.

'Good for you. When are you going to do it?'

Maggie took the last chocolate. 'Tonight,' she said. 'I'll tell him tonight.'

'I've got some chocolate-covered biscuits in the kitchen,' Faye said. 'I quite fancy one of them. What do you think?'

'Good plan,' said Maggie. 'Men are nothing but trouble. We should stick to chocolate. It's safer.'

When she left Faye's house, Maggie walked across Summer Street to the park. Its cast-iron gates would close in half an hour but there were still plenty of people enjoying the summer evening. She headed for the pavilion and climbed the old wooden steps to sit on one of the built-in benches that overlooked the tiny fountain.

Birds sang to one another in the trees overhead, and there were giggles coming from the group of girls huddled on the benches beside the playground. Normal life went on no matter what personal disaster you were living through, she thought, taking out her mobile.

Grey answered the apartment phone quickly.

'Maggie, hello,' he said warmly.

'Hi, Grey,' she said, her voice flat. She still didn't feel angry. Her anger seemed to have deserted her and her main emotion was sadness at seeing how hollow her life with Grey had turned out to be. 'I don't want us to get back together, I'm afraid. It wouldn't work.'

'What?'

'It's over. I can't go back.'

'But Maggie, you want to, you know that. I love you and you love me. That's all that matters. We can get over what happened. We could have couples' therapy,' he volunteered, which made her smile wryly. Grey was proud of the workings of his own mind but would hate to have a third party probe it and question his beliefs.

'I don't want therapy,' Maggie stated. 'I want to sell the apartment and move on. You could buy me out, if you'd like. It's a good apartment and I don't want it. I'm not sure if I want to move back to Galway at all.'

She had friends there but a total break would help her more. The whole city was filled with memories of the past five years.

'We can start again, Maggie. We can move apartments, get married, do all the things I said.' He sounded earnest and Maggie's feeling of sadness grew. How easily he lied. And how easily she'd believed it all.

'I want to be with someone I can trust, Grey,' she said, 'and you're not that person. It's not easy doing this. I feel like I'm wasting five years of my life . . .'

'You are!' he cried. 'You can't give up on us that easily.'

'I'm not the one giving up,' Maggie replied. 'You are. Because you lied to me about how you'd never cheated before and now I know that's not true. There have been other women. Don't try to deny it. Shona told me. It's no secret apparently, except to me, that you've had other women.'

'Why does she have to interfere?' he growled.

'That's not interfering, that's telling a friend the truth,' Maggie said. 'I can't live that way any more, Grey. You've cheated on me, not with one woman, but with at least four – who knows how many? So you're the one who's ending our relationship. You made the choice to sleep with other women. Not me.'

There was silence on the other end of the phone. She wondered if he'd lie again or confess. What would the politician in him do?

251

'It was stupid,' he said finally. 'I have no excuse, Maggie. None whatsoever. But it will never happen again, I promise. Please come home. I love you.'

Maggie wiped her eyes but once the tears started to flow, she couldn't stop them running down her cheeks.

'You just don't love me enough, Grey,' she said. 'I won't accept second best. I'm sorry. I'll call again about the apartment but don't call me. It's over. Believe me. I won't change my mind.'

And without giving him a chance to beg, she hung up.

The birds singing in the trees didn't take any notice of the woman sobbing silently on the pavilion. Neither did the teenage girls chattering and texting furiously on the opposite side of the park.

They probably still believe in true love, Maggie reflected, watching them through blurry eyes.

She wished she could warn them, but there were some things you had to experience yourself.

Mum and Dad were in the kitchen watching a film when she got home. It was *National Lampoon's European Vacation* and the Griswold family were touring Europe, leaving mayhem and bewilderment in their wake.

'Sit down, Bean,' said Dad, wiping the tears from his eyes. 'This is hilarious. You used to love it.'

Maggie pulled up a chair, settled the cushion on it, and sat down.

'Did you have any dinner?' asked her mother.

'Yes,' fibbed Maggie. She'd had chocolate biscuits after all. She didn't feel up to eating anything else now and her mother would be bound to start fussing if Maggie had said no.

'I'll make us a pot of tea,' Dad said, patting her knee. 'Isn't this nice? It's like old times, isn't it, Una?'

252

'Yes,' sighed Mum happily.

Maggie looked at her parents with love. It wasn't what she'd planned to be doing when she was thirty – back living with her mum and dad, boyfriendless, and with her confidence shot to pieces. But it must have all happened for a reason. Faye wasn't letting circumstances stop her in her tracks: she was going to find Amber and try to make sense of the past. And that's what Maggie had to do too. If this was what a new life was all about, then she was going to give it her best shot.

CHAPTER SEVENTEEN

On the plane, Faye sat in an aisle seat and watched her fellow passengers board. She had a fat magazine on her lap, but the scenes playing out in front of her were far more intriguing than anything else.

An older couple walked down the aisle slowly, resigned expressions on their faces at such a long flight ahead. A large group of teenage schoolgirls in some kind of sports strip arrived in a frenzy of excitement, already discussing swapping seats for maximum fun.

'Girls, you're supposed to sit in your correct seat,' said one of the harassed adults with them, either a teacher or a parent, already, Faye reckoned, realising that they'd bitten off more than they could chew.

'Oh, a baby, how cute!' one of the girls said, and the woman in the opposite row with an infant on her lap smiled weakly because at least she'd be surrounded by people who wouldn't object to the poor child's crying.

It had been years since Faye had been on a plane on her own. It was nice, she decided. Freeing. There was nobody to worry about but herself. Nobody could reach her on her mobile phone with bad news; nobody needed her.

For the first time since Amber had left, Faye felt a strange sense of acceptance at being alone. Amber would have left home inevitably and Faye would never have been ready for it. She could see that now. Her world was too tied up with her daughter, which hadn't, it turned out, been the right thing for either of them.

Faye ate the airline meal, watched the movie, then stuck in earplugs, pulled on a home-made lavender-filled eyemask Christie had given her for exactly that purpose and went to sleep.

The midtown hotel where her taxi pulled up was part of a budget chain and looked nothing like the adorable boutique hotels that the airline magazine had mentioned glowingly as places to stay in New York. Here, she reckoned the concierge wouldn't be able to whisk tickets for a Broadway show out of thin air. However, the marble lobby was clean and the whole place felt safe to Faye. Her room was a tiny twin on the seventh floor, with a microscopic bathroom and a mini kitchen that consisted of a kettle, toaster, microwave and sink, all cunningly concealed behind one cupboard.

Faye double-locked the door, stripped off and climbed into bed for another hour's rest.

It was mid-afternoon when she woke up and she stood at the window looking out over the city. She couldn't see much but other buildings, and directly below, she was staring at a grimy rooftop where somebody had once put a few wooden deckchairs, then forgotten about them.

But never mind the view, this was New York. She wasn't the victim any more, she was doing something, taking her power back, as Ellen, the makeover lady, had said. Ellen had a point, Faye realised. Somewhere along the way, she'd lost her power. Not any more.

In the lobby, she sat at a public phone and fed in her credit card. She couldn't afford the hotel-room charges, but down here, the price was pretty standard. It took seven calls to track down the production company who were supposed to be working on Karl's album with the band, Ceres. Then an interminable wait followed as a bored young guy searched for details of the band's schedule, saying all the time: 'I can't give you inside information, lady, this is only public domain stuff. If you're a stalker, I'm not taking the rap.'

'Do many unsigned bands have stalkers?' Faye demanded. 'I wouldn't have thought so. I told you, I'm Amber Reid's mother, she's Karl Evans's partner, and I have an urgent message for her.'

He didn't reply for a minute, then said: 'They did a gig at the O'Reilly Tavern recently, and that's all I have written down here because Sly was supposed to go to it. That's all I can help you with.'

'But they're recording an album and your company are producing it. I can leave a message for them, surely?' said Faye, who planned on just turning up and surprising them but wasn't going to tell this guy so.

'They were,' the guy said, and she could hear him flipping pages, 'but they're not down in the log any more. Doesn't say why.' More pages flipped. 'Not down for next month neither.'

'How could that be?' asked Faye, confused.

'Hey lady, it's all about dollars. If you can't pay, you can't stay. Guess whatever deal they had fell through. If they're good enough, Sly and Maxi will produce your album for a percentage deal. If you're not and nobody else is paying, it's *hasta la vista*.'

'Oh,' she said in horror, her only lead gone.

Her anxiety finally transmitted itself to the guy on the other end of the phone.

'All right. They were staying in the Arizona Fish Hotel

over beside the Port Authority,' he said. 'You didn't hear it from me, OK?'

'Bless you,' said Faye with gratitude.

It was the sight of the Arizona Fish Hotel that made Faye begin to feel really worried. Her own hotel was hardly a palace, but it was Trump Tower compared to this run-down place with its tawdry cloak of hip.

It might have boasted a lobby full of retro chic furniture and framed yellowing sheet music of hit songs allegedly penned in the penthouse suite, but Faye could see the seediness seeping from the walls.

No amount of trendy furniture or psychedelic prints on the walls, or even the neon sign for the hotel's own night-club, A Fish, could hide the dirt.

It reminded her of The Club in her previous life: a dump dressed up as a cool hang-out by virtue of the fact that some band or other played there once, partying till the LSD or the heroin was gone. Not that she'd ever travelled anywhere with TJ, but she knew that if she had, she'd have loved the decayed glamour of the Arizona Fish. To a girl like Amber, raised in the quiet of Summer Street, hearing of the songs allegedly written in room seven, or the bed that had probably fallen through the roof in room eleven during an unbelievable party after a rock festival, would have made her feel a part of it all. This was excitement, this was life. And she was in the middle of it.

Faye knew exactly how excited Amber would be to be living this life, because she'd been just as excited twenty years ago to find herself in the world of The Club. But that life was like being in the eye of the storm. You thought you were safe, untouchable, when the storm was actually raging inches away. Then, nobody could have told Faye Reid that. She'd had to find it out for herself.

Faye wanted to get her daughter out of that storm before it hurt her. She wouldn't stop searching for Amber until she found her. And if she had to stay in New York for ever, she would. She'd get Amber back.

Amber looked at the cockroach and the cockroach looked back calmly. It wasn't as big as a rat, as some people claimed they were in this part of Utah, but she wouldn't have minded a rat. Furry was infinitely preferable to scuttling, crackly insects.

Breathing deeply, she backed out of the room, past Karl and the man with the dirty T-shirt, and stood in the hallway, feeling her skin crawl.

'I am not sleeping in there,' she said.

The man moved into the room, banged about a bit, and emerged smiling.

'He is gone, you can go in now.'

'Where is he gone?' demanded Amber, looking around the floor in the hallway with distaste. 'Into the corner he hides in with his eight million relatives until we're in bed asleep and he comes out to dance the Macarena?'

'No Macarena. He is gone,' the man repeated.

'It's all we can afford,' said Karl, sighing and hauling his stuff into the room. He'd stopped hauling Amber's stuff days ago.

It was hard to imagine that she'd once felt that the Arizona Fish Hotel was a bit on the grubby side, Amber thought wryly. The Arizona's dust balls and smeary windows were nothing to the squalor of this joint, a place where health inspectors clearly feared to tread.

Karl was right: it was all they could afford. The band were travelling across the country in a rent-a-wreck van, which was the cheapest way to get them all to LA, and staying in the most inexpensive motels around. This way, Karl had

258

worked out, they'd have enough money to survive in LA for a few months in order to set up another production deal with somebody hot.

'Screw Stevie,' Syd muttered every day they climbed into the van and set off on the interstate. The suspension was not what it might have been and it took a while each day to get used to the bumpiness of the ride.

'Like a roller coaster,' said Lew the drummer happily.

'You must have a stomach of steel,' Syd replied in disgust.

When Demon had decided against producing the band's album, Stevie's big talk had dried up along with the meals out and the free-flowing booze.

Citing problems at home, Stevie had hopped on a plane back to Ireland, saying he'd work on a new deal for them and they'd talk when they were all back in Dublin.

'Crap,' said Syd succinctly. 'We'll never see him again.'

Stevie hadn't bothered with the last outstanding two days of their hotel bill, either, so when he left for JFK, reception were on the phone asking if the band were moving out or not, because with Stevie's credit card gone, they had to pay up or pack up.

Everyone had return flights home, a precondition of their entry visas, so following Stevie's yellow belly seemed like a sensible option.

'We can't go home with our tails between our legs,' Karl said furiously. 'I'm not anyway, I don't care what you guys want to do. This is my dream. I don't need guys like Stevie. I'll do it in spite of him.'

Amber waited for him to put his arms round her and say that the two of them would make it one way or the other, but he didn't. This was a band discussion, it seemed.

'I think I'll go for a walk,' Amber said abruptly. She grabbed the room card and was halfway to the lift when Karl caught up with her.

'Baby, don't go,' he said.

'You were talking as if I wasn't there,' she accused, tears stinging her eyes. She brushed them away with her sleeve. She would not cry.

'That was band stuff,' Karl said, pulling her into his arms. 'Course you're staying with me. Aren't you?'

And he'd looked worried, as if there really was any chance of her leaving him.

'I'm staying,' she said, leaning against him with relief. For one awful moment there, she'd thought she didn't mean anything to him. She'd given up so much too: home, Mum, Ella . . . so many things, really. If Karl went off without her, she'd have done it all for nothing.

'Let's go out on our own, to dinner and a club,' he murmured against her ear.

'Can we afford it?' asked Amber, ever practical.

'Anything for you, baby.'

That evening had been the last romantic moment they'd shared, Amber reflected now as she pulled her case into the now allegedly cockroach-free motel room in some truck-stop off the Utah interstate. They'd rented the van, left New York and were now driving hundreds of miles every day through the vastness of America. It should have been a dream trip, like the kooky road trips of teenage movies, but those movie-star kids had dollars to spare, while the band had none.

Their mobile phones didn't work here, even Syd's, which was a super-duper thing his girlfriend had bought him. He'd spent so long messing with it that it had locked itself and was now useless.

Karl was relentless in his quest to reach Los Angeles with the minimum number of nights spent in motels ('every night on the road is another few days in LA renting,' he insisted), so they couldn't dawdle in pretty towns off the interstates or take trips to places that caught their eye.

Karl was a man with a mission, and Amber and the band were following in his wake.

'I'm beat,' he said now, lying down on the bed cover. 'Three hundred and fifty miles today, it's got to be a record.'

Amber didn't reply. She was looking at the stains on the carpet and wondering what had made them. If only she had a vacuum cleaner and maybe some carpet stain remover, and cream cleaner . . . It could have been her mother talking.

Look at the state of this place! Amber, get the antiseptic wipes out of my bag.

They hadn't gone on many holidays: the money hadn't been there. But Mum had always packed cleaning materials so that if the place they stayed didn't come up to her standards, she'd clean it herself.

Amber felt a lump in her throat at the memory of the laughs they'd had in the places they'd stayed.

Turning to the bathroom, she went inside and shut the door. There was no tub, just a lived-in shower with a curtain beaded with other people's dirt. Amber sat down on the toilet seat and buried her face in her hands.

This was so not what she'd expected when she'd left home.

She'd thought she was running off to experience life and become a woman: instead, she was enduring life on the road with an obsessed boyfriend and staying in a series of dumps. She mightn't have minded if only Karl was obsessed with her but he wasn't.

He hadn't called her his muse in a very long time. We are not amused, she thought. And then she did cry.

CHAPTER EIGHTEEN

The Monday after Faye had left the country, Christie came home from school to find a disturbing message on her answering machine.

'Hello, my name is Heidi Manton and I'm phoning on behalf of Carey Wolensky. He's trying to locate a Mrs Christie Devlin to invite her to the private viewing of his exhibition in Dublin in two weeks' time except he's not sure if she still lives at this address. If Mrs Devlin could phone me, I'd be most grateful. And if she's moved, any information on her whereabouts would be marvellous.'

The clipped tones of the woman recited a number in London and Christie allowed herself to take a deep breath. At least Carey wasn't in the country yet.

'From next week, you can contact myself or Mr Wolensky in Dublin at this number.'

The voice reeled off another number and Christie's relief evaporated.

He was coming here and he wanted to see her. It couldn't get any worse. What on earth was she going to do?

* * *

While the maelstrom of Summer Street relationships whirled unnoticed around her, Una Maguire had taken it upon herself to set up the 'Save Our Pavilion' campaign.

'We can't let our lovely park be destroyed by those developers,' she said to Dennis and Maggie. 'Evil, that's what they are,' she added, as though the developers were in league with the devil and were ripping down the pavilion as part of some satanic bargain for making loads of money out of big ugly apartments.

'You don't want to overdo it,' said Dennis, attempting to be the voice of reason. 'Don't forget, darling, your leg is still broken and . . .'

'Oh fiddle faddle, my leg is fine,' said Una. 'Isn't it better to be doing something to help our community than sitting at home worrying about my old leg and thinking that I'll be ending up in a wheelchair before long?'

Maggie glanced over at her mother, but Una went on regardless.

'Somebody needs to stand up to those developers and I'm going to call a meeting of the residents of Summer Street and the streets all around. We don't want to use some hopeless new park three miles down the road when we have this lovely little jewel right here beside us. We will fight the council all the way!' and she waved her crutch menacingly in the air.

'Right, Mum,' said Maggie, alarmed her mother might take someone's eye out. It was easiest to humour her when she was in this mood. 'What do you want me to do?'

A printing firm would run off a hundred flyers for next to nothing if Maggie dropped by with details of the meeting. The only problem was that the firm's office wasn't on a direct bus route. The task would require the car.

'Your dad can drive,' Una said, then added, 'You won't be long, will you?'

She didn't like being left on her own these days, Maggie

had noticed, sure it was fear of falling and hurting herself again.

'Dad can stay with you. I'm sure I can remember how to drive,' Maggie said a little wearily. If she was going to become a stronger person, she had told herself, she would need to accept life's challenges, and trying to drive again would be the first. At least the fear of driving might take her mind off her own personal misery, the misery that kept her awake late at night, thinking about her and Grey.

'There's nothing to it, Bean,' said Dad, delighted.

'Of course there isn't,' she said cheerily. 'It's a long time since I've driven, that's all.'

'Any eejit can drive,' said her father. 'And you're so clever, it'll be nothing to you.'

With both parents smiling at her proudly, clearly believing that their only child was a cross between Stephen Hawking and Condoleezza Rice, Maggie had to smile back. They didn't have anything particularly to be proud of, but what was the point of telling them that? She'd managed to hide her misery pretty well. So well, in fact, that nobody at home appeared to see how sad she was underneath the smiling exterior.

The family car was a Volvo, like all the Maguire cars had been. Her father felt that Volvos could tackle the world head on and still win.

'Reliable,' her father insisted.

'You could hit a moose with one and there wouldn't even be a dent,' her mother would add. 'Extra hard side bars or something.'

Maggie sat in the driver's seat, looked at all the pedals, buttons and dials and hoped that the local moose population was safely off the road today.

The car started first thing and despite its general air of decrepitude because it was almost an antique, it moved forward smoothly when she let off the handbrake.

Indicator, check the road, off in first gear, smoothly into second. It was like riding a bike, Maggie thought triumphantly. She was driving. Nothing to it. Pity Grey couldn't see her now, the lying, cheating pig.

At a sedate twenty-five miles an hour, she made it to the printer's where they ran off her leaflets at high speed and she was back in the car within half an hour. Next, she stopped off at the supermarket and loaded up a trolley. The petrol tank was almost empty, she noticed as she pulled out of the supermarket car park on to the road.

Emboldened by her success at driving, she decided that a trip to the garage would round off her maiden voyage nicely.

A confident woman driver with a brave new life ahead of her would know how to pump her own petrol. Why had she never had a car before? The sense of freedom was heady.

She had to jiggle the pump nozzle a bit to fit it into the tank, and even then it leaked, but then the numbers clicked up on the pump counter in a most satisfying fashion, and when she reached twenty euros, Maggie pulled the pump out. She'd been thinking she'd make a gorgeous dinner for the three of them, nutritious, something out of a book perhaps, looking after her family and . . .

The little sticker on the petrol tank flap winked up at her. Diesel. Diesel.

With whiplash speed, she turned to the pump. Unleaded petrol. She'd just put unleaded petrol in a diesel car.

She stared at the car in shock. Trust her parents to have a diesel car and not tell her. No. Trust her not to notice. Shit.

She ran into the shop and stood at the back of the queue, thinking she might cry or maybe even laugh. She could feel her paper-thin happy face beginning to crack.

Anyone could do it, right? Someone could suck it out, couldn't they? Or something.

The man in front of her swivelled round and Maggie realised she'd spoken out loud.

'Anyone could put petrol in by mistake when it's a diesel,' she said, trying to put the whole 'they could suck it out' remark into context. 'It's my parents' car and I was doing them a favour and I didn't look at the tank. Thought it was petrol, not diesel. Could happen to a bishop.'

There, it was better to say it and surely he'd laugh. It had to happen all the time. There was probably a special queue for people who did it.

But the man gave her a glare that she instantly translated as All Women Are Idiots with a hint of We Should Never Have Given Them the Vote added in for good measure. 'Of all the thick things to do,' he grunted and turned his back on her.

'But the nozzle isn't supposed to be able to fit in,' pointed out the woman who'd just joined the queue behind her.

'Yeah, they're different, the diesel and the petrol ones,' someone else said unhelpfully.

'I thought I was doing it wrong, so I made it fit,' said Maggie forlornly, thinking of all the petrol she'd spilled on the ground. She hoped nobody lit a match out there or the whole place would go up.

Mr Stupid Woman Glare gave her another withering blast of it on his way past.

Maggie tried to ignore his contempt.

'You'll never believe what I've done,' she said to the impassive woman behind the counter, pleading with her eyes to be given a bit of female bonding.

The woman blinked slowly during the story, then jerked with her thumb.

'Out back. Ask for Ivan. Ivan Gregory. He owns the place. He's busy but he might help you.'

There was a queue waiting for the pump where the Volvo

266

was parked but Maggie ran past it to the back of the garage. Away from the shiny forecourt, she found a small workshop.

There were several cars in various states of disrepair suspended over pits or parked in small bays, and a radio tuned to a local station provided a backdrop to the noises of banging and welding.

The only person not working on a vehicle was a fresh-faced young man who was leaning against a desk with a mug in his hand.

'I'm looking for Ivan, the owner?' Maggie said.

'He's under there.'

She followed his gaze. A pair of overalled legs stuck out from under a large green Jeep, legs with big round-toed boots that a clown might wear. Were they hobnailed boots? she wondered irrelevantly.

'Hello,' she said, leaning down, 'are you Ivan? I was told you could help me. I've . . .' God, she felt stupid. 'I've just put unleaded in my parents' car and it turns out, it runs on diesel. Wouldn't you know. I hoped there might be some gizmo to suck it out. Like a vacuum cleaner. Can you vacuum out all the unleaded?'

The legs seemed to shake a bit.

'Or drain it?' Maggie went on.

Yes, draining, that sounded like the business. They were always draining things in garages and doing stuff with stop-cocks, or was that cisterns? Whatever.

'I'm sure you're busy but I'd be really grateful if you could help me. My mother's sick and I've got all her shopping in the car and there's a big queue behind me . . .' Maggie didn't say she thought she'd cry if anyone in the queue shouted at her for blocking the petrol pump. 'They're probably all going mental, saying they bet it's some stupid woman who's left her car there.'

One enormous oil-stained hand appeared from under the

Jeep, gripped the edge of the car and pulled. Maggie found herself staring down at a giant of a man who was looking up at her with undisguised mirth. He was filthy with dirt on his overalls, in his face, even in his hair, which was dark except for a few streaks of grey near his temples, and cut as close to his head as any marine's.

She was relieved to see that his face was nice, a bit square with a nose that looked as if he'd taken a few punches in the ring, and that his smile, because he was smiling broadly, was friendly.

He got to his feet lightly for such a huge man and stood towering over her. Good-looking, in an outdoorsy way, she thought absently, and probably Grey's age or thereabouts.

'You want to use the petrol-sucking vacuum?' he said evenly in a low gravelly voice. He wiped sweat off his brow with the back of his hand.

'If that's all right?' said Maggie. With any luck, she'd be home in no time and nobody would be any the wiser.

'Jack,' he called to the young guy. 'Where's the petrol-sucking machine?'

Jack had to bend over with a sudden spasm.

'You're telling me you don't know where it is?' inquired Ivan. 'What do I pay you guys for? Mick?'

A face appeared from under the bonnet of a Citroën. 'Yeah?'

'The petrol-sucking machine. You got it?'

Mick's gaze flickered over Maggie and knowledge began to dawn.

'Right,' she said, in a shaky voice. 'The joke's on me. There is no petrol-sucking machine.'

'Whaddya think this is? A milking parlour?' asked Mick, before succumbing to the same spasms as Jack and doubling up with laughter.

Ivan, the giant, looked at her with mischief in his face.

He had the deepest brown eyes she'd ever seen, and they positively glittered with humour. His mouth quivered at the edges, as he tried to stop himself grinning and failed.

It had been a horrible few days, in which her world had turned upside down, and Maggie felt that if one more person made her feel she was stupid, she was going to hit them, so help her. Her composure shattered.

'It's not funny!' she shrieked, reaching out and thumping the bonnet of the Jeep he'd been working on.

This was it, the last straw. All the pent-up fury at seeing Grey in bed with someone else, at running home to find her mother injured and herself appointed in charge, at discovering that Grey had a bloody harem and it had been happening under her nose, it all came flooding out. Thump, thump went her curled-up fist on the bonnet.

'I just wanted some help and nobody appreciates it. You jackasses think it's the biggest laugh ever to snigger at someone in trouble.' Thump, thump.

Ivan clamped her wrists in his steely hands and gently lowered them to her side.

'You'll hurt yourself and it was only a joke,' he said tenderly. 'I'm sorry, I thought you sounded so funny.'

'You thought you'd take the mickey out of me, well, I've had that done enough lately, thank you very much,' Maggie said, dry sobbing. She ran out of the workshop to the car, sat in the driver's seat and started it up. The engine turned over instantly, allowed her to drive a few yards then suddenly belched loudly and died like an elephant in great pain.

'Horrible, horrible car!' she said, crying on the steering wheel. She banged it hard, succeeding only in making her aware of how much she'd hurt her hand from bashing the Jeep in the garage. 'Ow!'

The driver's door was opened and Ivan squatted down beside her seat, apology written all over his face.

'It's better not to drive it,' he said. As kindly as if he was taking care of a tiny baby, he helped her out of the car and took the keys. 'I'll drive you and your shopping home, and I'll look after the car.'

'You will do no such thing, you jumped-up pump jockey,' she hissed. 'I'll bring my own bloody shopping home, thank you very much.'

Ivan looked into the back of the car which was piled with grocery bags.

'You sure?'

'I'm sure.'

She pulled every single bag out and dragged them to the kerb. 'I'll be back for the car tomorrow,' she said. 'Just bloody fix it, will you?'

Ivan nodded and went back into his workshop, whereupon Maggie got out her phone and dialled a taxi. So much for self-confidence.

Una was thrilled with the leaflet, which advertised a meeting at the park at eight o'clock in the evening in two days' time. And to Maggie's relief neither of her parents laughed or were angry when she explained, rather bashfully, what had happened to the car. 'I can't face going there to fetch it, I'm so embarrassed,' she said, 'but I suppose I must. Except I've got to work.'

'Don't worry, darling,' said her father, giving her a hug. 'The garage isn't far from the doctor's surgery and I must fetch a new prescription for your mother. It won't take me long to walk up there and I'll kill the two birds with the one stone.'

'Are you sure?' said Maggie, remembering that she was supposed to be strong and confident now, facing up to her mistakes. Except she just couldn't face those men in the garage again, especially the big one, Ivan. 'I could go after work,' she said.

'It'll do your dad good to get out,' said Una sternly, and so the burden was lifted.

In return, Maggie wasn't surprised to find that she was expected to be postie for the leaflets. She spent several hours late the following afternoon braving yappy dogs and pushing the leaflets through doors of the neighbouring streets and asking local shops to site them in their windows. One of the last places Maggie visited was the Summer Street Café, where Henry and Jane were thrilled to hear about Una's call to arms.

'That's fabulous, and so professional,' said Jane, reading the leaflet Maggie showed her and passing it to Xu, the shy Chinese waitress.

Xu smiled but said nothing. In all the time Maggie had spent in the café recently, she'd never heard Xu speak a word. But she smiled a lot, like she was doing now.

'Well done to your mother,' said Henry. 'She's a great woman. I can see where you got it from.'

'Oh,' said Maggie, pleased, and she flushed.

'It's very good of you to come home and look after her,' Henry went on. 'I know it has been difficult for you, but she's a good woman. Now, since you're doing so much for the community, would you like a latte on the house, or is it cappuccino you drink?'

'Plain old white coffee for me,' said Maggie, 'and thank you, that would be nice. It's weary work delivering all these.'

'That looks lovely,' said Maggie politely, when Xu brought her the coffee.

Xu bobbed her head in reply. She must be lonely, Maggie thought suddenly. The girl was young, probably only in her mid-twenties, half a world away from home. Maggie wondered whether she had any friends. Jane and Henry were sweet people but probably not sparkling company for a young girl.

*   *   *

271

Word of the onslaught against the council quickly spread and the following night, at eight o'clock, the park was jammed with people from Summer Street and the surrounding streets all wanting to know what they could do to save it.

Maggie had been at work all day and so wasn't entirely sure what her mother's plan was. She was a bit disappointed to find out that all Una had thought of was a petition, signed by everybody and their granny, saying the evil developers shouldn't get their way and the council owed it to the people of Summer Street and the whole area to save their park. 'We need our voices to be heard!' said Una Maguire, standing at the front of the crowd, brandishing a crutch.

Maggie thought her mother had turned out to be surprisingly good at this rabble-rousing. Who'd have thought it?

'A petition is going to be no good,' a man down the back shouted dismissively, and privately Maggie had to agree with him. 'They don't take notice of petitions. We'll have to do something else, something more forceful.'

'Like what?' demanded Una. 'Come on, suggestions, please. If you're not part of the solution, you're part of the problem.'

This started a row with people shouting at the man down the back for trying to rain on their parade, while his supporters shouted that a petition was going to be no good whatsoever. What was needed was legal action or political involvement.

It was descending into chaos and even Una seemed to have run out of energy.

The man at the back got fed up and shouted, 'Who else can help? Anyone with friends on the council?'

Maggie looked around to see if there was somebody there who was up to leading the charge. Ideally somebody who knew how councils and businesses worked, she thought, and who could go through the proper channels. But she realised there were no volunteers. Everyone wanted the park saved, but, apart from Una, there wasn't anyone ready to stand up and do it.

It was the curse of the modern age, her mother often said, when it came to getting people to help out with charities and meals on wheels: everybody was too busy with their own lives to do much for anyone else.

'Well,' Maggie said, reluctantly, feeling she ought to help her mother out. 'I do work in the library and I suppose I would be able to research how we could go about this.'

She'd hardly got the words out of her mouth before people were saying, *Yes, good woman, fair play to you, brilliant idea.* Then the man who had heckled Una smiled broadly at the tall, slender redhead and called out, 'Chairwoman, let's have her for chairwoman.' And, without realising it, Maggie Maguire – who'd never so much as captained a friendly netball game in school – was elected chairwoman of the rapidly formed Save Our Pavilion committee.

'I'm so proud of you,' said her mother as they headed home, after several other people had been elected on to the committee, buoyed up by Maggie's supreme sacrifice and the hope that she'd do all the work. 'I knew you'd know what to do. I thought, if I started you off on the right path, you'd follow through. Didn't I say that, Dennis, didn't I?'

'Yes,' said Maggie's father happily. 'Your mother always says you're well able to run things. You can do anything, our Maggie can do anything.'

'And,' her mother went on, 'we should have a big party, in the park, when we get it all settled.'

'Hold on a minute,' said Maggie, 'nothing's settled yet. We might not win. Mum, be realistic.' Maggie was still shocked at how quickly it had all happened – shocked and horrified. *She* was chairwoman of the committee. Chairwomen were tough, no-nonsense women like Shona, not wimpy people who had cheating ex-boyfriends and put petrol in diesel vehicles. If only there was a way out of it, but she knew there wasn't. What if she made a complete mess of the whole project?

'Ah now,' said her mother, confidence written all over her face. 'You'll have worked it out, I know well you will. There's nothing you can't do.'

'She's mad. Breaking her leg has affected her brain,' Maggie said on the phone to Elisabeth. She'd needed to get out of the house and had taken her mobile and walked slowly along Summer Street, thinking that Elisabeth might understand.

'Your mother was always mad,' said Elisabeth absently. Her office sounded noisy and busy.

'Not normal mad: thinking-I-can-do-everything mad. It's different,' Maggie went on.

'She always thought you could do everything,' Elisabeth said, surprised. 'It used to drive me nuts. Your mother never stopped talking about how clever you were and how marvellous your report cards were, which made my mother obsessed with my report cards being as good. The pressure.'

'Really?' Maggie couldn't quite remember that. All she could recall from school was the misery and how she'd never been able to tell anyone, apart from Elisabeth. 'If only I could do everything,' she added gloomily.

'Maggie, listen to me.' Elisabeth sounded stern, the way she spoke to teenage models on the phone, Maggie guessed. 'I'm up to my tonsils with work here and I'm irritable, which means I'm going to say something I've wanted to say for a long time, something I'll probably regret saying because you'll be hurt but I've got to do it: stop feeling sorry for yourself about what happened at school and get on with your life.'

Maggie gasped.

'I know you're going to hate me for saying this, but I've got to. You *are* clever and funny, you *can* do anything, and you should stop thinking otherwise. Now you've dumped that loser boyfriend of yours for good, go out and get a life. Auntie Una's right: you can do anything. You're the only person who doesn't believe it. Gotta go, bye.'

It took Maggie a full thirty seconds to take the phone away from her ear. Elisabeth had never spoken to her like that in her life. She was shocked. Elisabeth was the only one who'd known what had gone on in school, her only ally and now she had turned against her.

Maggie walked along in stunned silence, oblivious to where she was going. But finally something odd happened. In the midst of the shock and the self-pity, she began to feel a glimmer of self-worth. Everyone seemed to think she was capable of so much. They couldn't all be lying, could they?

Later that night, the gloom settled once more. It was sinking in that she'd somehow been elected as chairwoman of a committee with a tough job to do.

'I don't even know how to run a committee,' she moaned to Shona on the phone. 'I was never even on the debating team in college!'

'Oh, babes,' said Shona easily, 'it'll be no bother to you. You've seen plenty of university committees at work, you know how it goes. People sit around in rooms, have arguments, discuss things, discuss them even more, break for tea and biscuits and finally agree to disagree. At the end, they make arrangements to meet up at the same time next week where they'll go over all the same stuff again. Simple.'

'I know,' groaned Maggie. 'That's what I don't want. I want this committee to actually save the park, not talk about it until the cows come home – or until the developers whip a JCB in one night and pull the pavilion down, making the whole thing a fait accompli.'

'Right,' said Shona, thoughtfully. 'You mean this is a committee where you actually want to achieve something.

Mmm. University life doesn't prepare you for that. Paul,' she shouted, 'Maggie's chairwoman of a committee and they actually want to get something done. What should she do?'

Paul was one of the top research and development men in a computer software firm with dozens of people under him.

Maggie heard a rustling noise like the sound of a paper being folded. It was late and she could imagine Paul sitting on the cosy couch in his and Shona's apartment, the newspapers around him, with his feet up on the coffee table and the remote control on his lap.

'Hello, Maggie,' he said, taking over the phone. 'My advice is to write out what the aim of the committee is on a big sheet of paper, take it to your first meeting and stick it up on the wall. Explain that nobody is on the committee to make themselves popular or to give themselves something to brag about. They're there simply to achieve the aim you've written on the paper. What's the committee for, exactly?'

'We want to stop the council selling half of our park to a developer who's going to build apartments there.'

'Well, I guess you need to lodge a formal planning objection with the council, then talk to local politicians . . .'

'Talk to the newspapers,' said Shona in the background.

'Yes,' said Maggie excitedly, writing this down. She had an inspiration. 'What about finding out more about the park? They want to pull down this beautiful old pavilion. It's Victorian at least and it could be a meaningful historical site.'

'Exactly,' said Paul with satisfaction. 'Tie them up with surveys and formal objections and politicians complaining so that the whole thing's not worth their while. Or so that the bad press they'll get for it will scare the developers away. The key to committees, Maggie,' he said, 'is like amateur dramatics. Never let them see you're afraid.'

* * *

The following night at eight, Summer Street Café was closed to everyone except the Save Our Pavilion committee. There were ten of them sitting around two tables pushed together, with Maggie seated at one end.

She'd gone out and purchased a businesslike navy jacket which she wore over her best dark denim jeans and a turquoise camisole. She'd tied her hair up into a chic knot, had a writing pad and pens in front of her, and was keeping all her anxiety firmly locked on the inside. The other committee members were all older than her and probably had miles more experience than she did, but she was still chairwoman and she was going to make this a success.

'The most important thing tonight,' she said, 'is our aims. None of us are here so we can boast that we're on a committee, or to have something to talk about or because we like arguments.'

One man opened and closed his mouth like a goldfish at this.

Paul had said there was always one person who joined up because they liked both the sound of their own voice and a good fight.

Maggie felt a wave of confidence hit her. Forewarned was forearmed.

She was ready for Mr Goldfish Face. 'We're here to save something very important to Summer Street. So this is not going to be one of those committees where everyone argues or grandstands or tries to get the better of anyone else. We're here to save the pavilion, that's it.'

The nine people facing her stared back, nodding, and Maggie thought how unbelievable it was that she was able to confront them and talk in such calm, measured tones, when inside, she really was quivering.

Luckily, nobody could see the inside.

'I've made up a list of what I think we should do and I'll

go through it. Then everyone else can come in with their suggestions until we've come up with a blueprint for what we're going to achieve over the next few days, right? I'm new to this and would appreciate ideas but we've got to work as a team, or we're going to go nowhere fast.'

The next hour and a half passed in a flash, but when Maggie wound up the meeting everyone had been allocated a useful task to perform before they reconvened. Maggie herself was to try to interest several politicians in their cause.

When everyone was gone, Maggie and Xu, who'd stayed behind to help and make coffee, tidied up.

'I hope you weren't bored out of your mind listening to that,' Maggie said to Xu.

Now that they were alone, she hoped Xu might talk to her.

'It was interesting,' Xu said. She had a low sweet voice and perfect English. 'We do not do this in my country. If the authorities want to pull down a building, they pull it down. It's very different.'

Maggie stopped collecting cups and sat down. 'Tell me,' she said. 'Tell me how you came here and what you'd like to do and what your country's like. I'd love to hear.'

She'd never seen Xu give anything other than a shy smile that was more defence mechanism than emotion, but now Xu really beamed at her.

'I never asked before because I was afraid I'd insult you or something,' Maggie admitted. 'You're very brave to come here on your own.'

'Brave is the only way in China,' Xu shrugged. 'My mother is much braver than me. This is nothing compared to what she suffered during the Cultural Revolution. I only had to get on an aeroplane and learn another language so I could go to college here. I can make choices in my life – she could make none.'

278

'Will your mother come here too?' asked Maggie, not wanting to upset Xu now she'd got her talking.

'Maybe. She loves China, it's her home. I'd like her to visit. But she doesn't speak English.'

'And will you go back?' asked Maggie.

'I don't know. I love China but I feel at home here. We are very alike, the Chinese and the Irish. We love our families.'

'Your English is fantastic. When did you start learning?'

'Nine months ago,' Xu said casually.

'Nine months ago! You're so fluent. I can't imagine being that good in such a short length of time.'

Xu laughed so loudly that her curtain of thick dark hair shimmered. 'Chinese people know how to work.' She grinned.

They sat talking for an hour, whereupon Xu said she ought to go home and Maggie said the same, because she knew her mother would be sitting up waiting for her to hear how the meeting went.

'Perhaps you'll come out with me sometimes?' Maggie asked Xu. 'To see a film or something?'

'I would like that very much indeed,' Xu replied.

On the way down Summer Street, Maggie reflected that if a girl from a small town in China could travel thousands of miles to a strange land where she knew nobody to start a new life, then she wasn't going to spend the rest of her life being afraid of what happened to her when she was a schoolgirl.

'Well, how did it go?' demanded Una, when Maggie got home. Her mother had been mad to go to the meeting, but since she wasn't on the committee, she couldn't.

'Marvellously,' said Maggie, still astonished at how she'd stood up in front of a room of strangers and handled it well. 'Everyone had loads of ideas and we've all got various jobs and I think we have a really good chance.'

'I'd like to be involved though,' said Una.

'Of course you're involved,' Maggie placated her. 'It was your idea in the first place, don't forget that. But you do need to rest.'

'Ah, rest, schmest,' muttered Una. 'I'm sick of resting. I want to do something.'

'Well, I need to make appointments to see three local politicians and you could come with me to see them,' Maggie said, thinking that she'd be braver with company.

'Marvellous,' Una said, satisfied. 'I better get my best suit out. Don't want to go stalking the corridors of power looking like some mad old dear in a bobbly cardigan, do I?'

CHAPTER NINETEEN

The following morning, Christie phoned Maggie to ask her round for coffee.

'You can fill me in on the meeting,' Christie said. 'I couldn't make it, although the Summer Street grapevine has already broadcast the fact that you're in charge.'

Maggie laughed. 'The lunatics have taken over the asylum,' she said. 'But yes, I'm in charge. I'd love a coffee.'

When she arrived, Christie hugged her and rushed back into the kitchen to take scones out of the oven.

Maggie took the chance to stop and admire the paintings in Christie's hall, marvelling at the intricate watercolour strokes that brought delicate plants to life.

One wall was covered with lily paintings, interspersed with tiny Klimt prints in antique gold frames and black-and-white family photographs. On the other were displayed exquisite paintings of herbs, from the lacy froth of sweet cicely to the fire-red flowers of bergamot. There were herbs Maggie had never heard of, like comfrey, lovage and feverfew, alongside the soft purple of French lavender and sleek, slender chives, so well drawn she could almost smell their tangy scent.

'These are beautiful,' Maggie called into the kitchen where Christie was brewing coffee. 'You're so talented.'

'I love herbs and foliage,' Christie said. 'So many artists only want to paint flowers, but plants and the history behind them are fascinating. They have incredible medicinal uses and we've lost that, sadly. I try to put herbs from my own garden into my cooking. And if you haven't tasted proper fennel and lemon balm tea, you haven't lived.'

A lovely sense of warmth and comfort emanated from the Devlins' house. It was partly due to the scent of Christie's white tea roses with their tightly furled buds, and a burning candle that filled the downstairs with a citrus scent. But there was something more, more than the sum of its parts. It was a house of peace and security. Maggie felt as if nothing truly bad could ever happen as long as there were people like Christie in the world to make sense of everything and to offer her home as a refuge.

Finally, with the dogs scampering ahead, she wandered into the kitchen. Christie had laid coffee cups and the scones on a tray.

'You carry this into the garden,' Christie said, 'and I'll be out in a moment with the coffee.'

Christie had been thinking so much about Maggie and Faye lately that it was no surprise to wake up that morning with Maggie again in her mind. Only today, as Maggie stood there, holding out her arms for the tray, Christie had a moment of seeing exactly what had hurt the younger woman so much.

Sweet, tall, kind Maggie, who should have had lots of confidence, but didn't. Lovely Maggie, who'd been bullied when she was at school.

Lying in bed, listening to the birdsong and the rising and falling of James's breath the past came flooding back. Hers and Maggie's. It was easier to think about other people's problems than focus on her own. She'd tried to put Carey Wolensky out of her mind, but hadn't managed it. He loomed large in her fears.

So she made herself remember Maggie starting at St Ursula's almost twenty years before: shy and lanky, falling over her own feet all of the time. She was clever and good fun, so it was hard to work out why bullies had picked on her. Sister Aquinas, who had been headmistress at the time, had talked in the staff room one day about bullying in general and the fact that young Maggie Maguire appeared to have been targeted by a particular coterie of little madams in her year, led by a really nasty piece of work called Sandra Brody.

'We'll just keep an eye on it for the moment,' said Sister Aquinas, who was a great believer in not rushing into things. Girls needed more backbone, she felt. Sister Aquinas had spent twenty years in the field in Africa and was of the opinion that Irish girls could do with a little hardship because, compared to the children in the townships, they hadn't a clue about life.

Christie hadn't thought too much about it because Maggie hadn't been in one of her art classes, but she'd seen her sometimes at lunch. Maggie was so often on her own, reading, when everyone else was out playing tag or netball, or sitting in little groups discussing boys and the unfairness of life.

When Maggie went into the fifth year, the leader of the gang of bullies, Sandra Brody, left, although Christie couldn't recall why, and her gang fell apart without their natural leader.

But it seemed obvious now that the damage had already been done where Maggie Maguire was concerned. There were lots of naturally quiet, shy people in the world, but Christie now felt that Maggie hadn't been one of them when she'd arrived. It was as though she had found that keeping her mouth shut and blending into the background was the easiest way of survival.

Having taken the jug into the garden, Christie poured coffee into the cups and proffered scones.

'This is lovely here, a little oasis,' sighed Maggie, sitting back and looking around her. She wondered what Christie wanted to talk to her about. Perhaps she was going to help with the Save Our Pavilion campaign, which would be wonderful. Christie would be great at getting people to return her phone calls.

So it came as a total shock when Christie asked: 'Were you bullied at St Ursula's?'

Maggie's head shot up and the colour drained away from her face.

'What? How ...?'

'I didn't know at the time,' Christie said apologetically. 'You weren't in any of my classes and I hardly knew more than your name then, but it suddenly made sense to me. It's your secret, isn't it? The thing that holds you back.'

Maggie could only nod silently.

'I'm so sorry. I was there and if I'd really been aware ...' Christie said. 'Your mum doesn't know, does she?'

This time, Maggie shook her head, biting her lip to make sure she didn't cry. This was so unexpected, like the ground being pulled away from her feet.

'I couldn't talk about it because –'

'– Because you thought she should know without you having to say it?'

'Yes, I suppose so.'

Tilly leaped up on to Maggie's lap, circling slowly on delicate paws, before lying against her. Maggie clung to this soft comfort, stroking the pansy-soft fur, grateful for a creature to hold. And she felt her shock subside slowly.

Christie leaned across the table and touched Maggie's hand gently, a touch that helped even more, filling her with peace.

'It's all right to talk about it,' Christie said. 'The people

284

we love often don't see our pain, and that's one of the hardest things in the world to cope with. We think they should see, they should *know*. If they don't, we feel as if they've failed us somehow and we have to deal with it all on our own.'

Maggie nodded. Mum hadn't seen what was going on and that had made Maggie lonelier than ever. Home hadn't been her refuge: it became a place where nobody understood her and what she was going through. Her parents' lovable idiosyncrasies had become irritating, their cheerful innocence annoying. If only they'd been more observant, they'd have *understood*.

'It's not their fault,' Christie said. 'It was St Ursula's fault. Bullying shouldn't have been tolerated. And it was Sandra's fault.' She noticed how Maggie winced at the mention of her tormentor's name. 'You were not to blame.'

'I thought I was,' blurted out Maggie. 'Something about me that was weak or odd.'

'Nothing I could see, though we all have weaknesses. But that's no excuse for their behaviour. You were just someone to pick on, nothing more.' Christie paused. 'Have you ever seen Sandra since?'

'No, although . . . I've been thinking about it a lot,' Maggie admitted. 'Since I met Faye and you, and Faye has had to face her own demons, I keep thinking I should face her. Stupid, I know. I haven't seen her for years.'

'Not stupid at all. You last saw her as a child. As an adult, you could put it all behind you, lay the secrets to rest.'

'Yeah, but who knows where she is.' Maggie couldn't even bring herself to say Sandra's name. 'What are the odds on her walking back into my life now?'

'You'd be surprised,' said Christie thoughtfully. 'You're thinking about her and talking about her. You're ready to meet her again. That's happened for a reason. Life is never random: I always find that, don't you?'

Maggie was on a late shift at work which meant she started at noon. As she walked towards the library, she went over what Christie had said to her.

Christie seemed to think that seeing Sandra Brody would allow the past to settle into the past, but it wasn't that easy, was it?

And Maggie had quite enough on her plate right now, anyway, what with being chairwoman of the campaign, getting over Grey and trying to get her life back on track.

She could face most things, but not Sandra Brody.

CHAPTER TWENTY

That afternoon, Christie went into St Ursula's and found that overnight, almost the entire teaching population had plunged headfirst into exam anxiety. June was fast approaching and on the third of the month, the state exams would begin, the culmination of years of hard work distilled into a dozen two-and-a-half-hour exams spread out over three tortured weeks.

'It's like an incessant headache pounding away,' said Mr Sweetman, thinking of the third years' still-limited interest in *As You Like It* and how a small section of the English sixth-year class had still only half read *Pride and Prejudice* and were using one of the movie versions as their guide instead of the actual novel.

'*C'est vrai*,' sighed Mademoiselle Lennox, who was reciting Guy de Maupassant in her sleep because of how many times she'd read out passages to her beloved girls in 6 and 6A.

'We must be positive, for the girls' sake,' boomed Ms Ni Rathallaigh, the sports teacher, who didn't care much because the fifth-year netball team had won the league.

Everyone in the staff room glared at her.

Everyone except Christie, who was finding it hard to concentrate on worrying about the exams because of how much she was worrying over Carey Wolensky and his trying to track her down. She hadn't returned the strange phone call asking her to get in touch, and during the day, she left the answering machine off in case James came home early and heard another message on it. Nobody, she hoped, would phone in the evenings, would they?

In the meantime, mentions of Carey were everywhere. The arts section in one of the Saturday papers had carried a review of his work, accompanied by photographs of three of his paintings. Thank heavens there wasn't a picture of him, Christie thought with relief. She couldn't have coped with seeing his brooding eyes gazing out at her from a photograph.

Instead she had to look at one of his trademark wildly furious landscapes, and two of his rare – and infinitely more valuable – paintings of a dark-haired woman. In one, she was lying between the paws of a predatory stone tiger in a crumbling Greek temple, and in the other, she stood in the centre of a Turkish bath, where other women chattered and bathed, and she was alone, staring out, hair partly covering a face that was never completely shown in any painting.

'It is his uncanny ability to bring new meaning to traditional themes that makes Wolensky a master,' raved the article. 'His moody landscapes are imbued with energy, but it's his Dark Lady paintings that elevate him to another level. They are his masterpieces, but the identity of the lovely Dark Lady remains one of modern art's most fascinating secrets.'

Those words made Christie break out in a sweat. She'd spent long enough studying symbolism in art to understand that the dark-haired woman in Wolensky's paintings was always slightly beyond his reach, and by obscuring her face, he wanted her to be beyond everyone's reach. If he couldn't have her, nobody else could, either.

Her naked body was womanly, complete with the not-so-pert breasts and stretchmarks of childbirth. He'd painted his first Dark Lady some twenty-five years before and she was no figment of the imagination, the art critics reckoned.

Wolensky had lived in Ireland round about then, the article went on, and this was his first trip back with this triumphant exhibition. Christie thought of Carey Wolensky back in her city, living, breathing only miles away in some classy city centre hotel, and felt sick.

If only she could really see the future and know what was happening, then she could deal with it all. Tell James, if that's what it took. Face his pain. Whatever was required.

But the waiting and not knowing was killing her.

Ana hadn't mentioned Carey again, which was something, but still Christie couldn't think of anything else. How she'd betrayed James and Ana in one fell swoop.

Suddenly fed up with the stuffy staff room and everyone's moaning, she left early for her next class. At least she'd have a few moments of peace before the lesson started.

In the blue-painted corridor that led to the art room, a pile of papers lay scattered on the floor. Bending, she slowly gathered them up and as she did so a white feather fluttered out from underneath, lifting in the gentle draught, drifting away.

White feathers were a sign of angels passing by, her mother used to say.

Christie looked down at the papers. They were exam notes, several scrawled sheets of foolscap with a small bit of paper sandwiched in the middle. She pulled this out. It was a flyer for a market where stalls promised second-hand books, antiques at prices nobody would believe, plants, home-knitted sweaters, a coffee shop and there, at the bottom, almost as an afterthought, were the words, fortune-telling.

Things happened for a reason – wasn't that what she'd told Maggie only the other day? This flyer and the white feather had come to her for a reason. She folded the flyer up and put it in her pocket. She'd think about it later.

That evening, she and James were supposed to go to a party at the house of some neighbours. The Hendersons had lived on Summer Street for fifteen years and they had been good friends with James and Christie for most of that time. Tommy Henderson, the husband, was a motorbike aficionado and while James had never had the funds for a bike, he loved standing in Tommy's garage watching him take apart the latest model, discussing the merits of the new BMW versus the classic Norton.

While James got on with Tommy, Christie found that she got on pretty well with Laurie Henderson. Tom and Laurie had three sons around Shane and Ethan's ages, and Laurie had worked outside the home for most of her life too, so she and Christie had reached the same stages in their lives together. Therefore, when Tommy Henderson hit sixty and a big party was to be held in the Hendersons' back garden, it was natural that the Devlins should be the first on the list.

'I'm not really in the mood to go,' said Christie as they pottered about their bedroom getting ready.

'You'll change your mind when you get there,' said James soothingly. 'It'll be fun. There'll be loads of people you'll know.'

'That's the problem,' said Christie, with irritation. 'I'm not in the mood to talk to the same old people.'

James stopped putting in his cuff links and began to massage her neck tenderly. For once, it didn't instantly relax her. 'You are tense, Christie,' he said. 'Is everything OK, darling? Do you have a headache?'

'No,' said Christie, slightly crossly. 'I don't, I'm just tired, that's all.'

Being tired was the ultimate excuse for everything, wasn't it? Any bad behaviour could be excused with 'I'm sorry, I was just tired.' *I'm sorry, your honour, I didn't mean to steal*

a million pounds, I was just tired. I'm sorry, darling, I didn't
mean to cheat on you with another man, I was just tired.

She turned to face James. 'I am sorry for moaning. I'll be fine.'

'Good,' said James, pleased. 'It'll be fun. You got flowers, didn't you?'

'Yes,' said Christie.

'I'll find a bottle of wine and we're all set.'

James finished getting ready, a job that took perhaps seven or eight minutes, and he was gone, leaving Christie sitting at her dressing table, staring at herself in the mirror, wondering if guilt was written all across her face.

They got there a bit late and the fun had obviously started.

'So you decided to grace us with your presence?' beamed Tommy Henderson, at the front door.

He threw an arm around James and Christie and pulled them together in a giant bear hug.

'So glad you could come,' he said.

'We only came for the free drink and the free food,' joked James.

'Free drink? You mean you didn't bring your own?' demanded Tommy. 'You lousers, I never had you down as mean, James Devlin.'

And the two men were off, joking, teasing, laughing, James asking what fabulous motorbike Tommy had got for his birthday from the family and Tommy jovially explaining that they hadn't got him a bike at all, but a girlfriend in a flat. 'That's what every man needs when he hits sixty,' he said. 'The wife thinks it's a brilliant idea too. No more messing about giving me my conjugals!'

The two men roared with laughter and Christie tried to join in, half-heartedly. She was so fond of Tommy and normally loved his palace jester persona, but not tonight.

The party was set up in the garden and it seemed as if half of Summer Street were there, talking, chattering animatedly, laughing, drinking, spearing bits of chicken into dip, discussing house prices, what their children were up to, what their children weren't up to and, of course, what the developers planned to do to the Summer Street park.

'I was at the meeting you know,' said one woman, 'and Una Maguire suggested a petition, but really a petition isn't the way to go. No council are going to be moved by a load of names on a list. Her daughter, Maggie, is taking it over, she's chairwoman. Clever girl, I always say, quiet though. I think there was some problem with her and the boyfriend, you know.'

Christie moved on, irritated by this gossipy attitude to Maggie. She must be growing old, she thought. So many things irritated her now. Some stranger, who barely knew Maggie, talking about her life and her pain, as if it didn't matter a bit. There was probably lots of gossip about Faye and Amber too. How the ultra-private and conservative Faye Reid hadn't a clue what was really going on in her house and what a wild one that Amber had turned out to be, for all her nice manners and the way her mother had tried to bring her up.

Christie moved over to where Laurie was holding court, wondering if in a few weeks the neighbours would be able to talk about her.

Did you hear about Christie Devlin, the most incredible news ever. Split up with that lovely husband of hers, I always said he was too good for her. She was a bit wild and arty really, despite her airs and graces and reputation for wisdom. Hem, if she was that wise she might have seen this one coming. Imagine, some story about a Polish artist who painted her in the nude. He's filthy rich apparently. Disgraceful. Goes to show you don't know people, do you? You can live beside

*them for thirty years and you haven't a clue what's going on
in their lives.*

'Christie, how lovely to see you.' Laurie moved away from
the group of people she was talking to, reached out, and
gave Christie a genuine, welcoming hug. There was nothing
two-faced about Laurie. She wouldn't gossip about Christie,
no matter what happened.

'Sorry we're late,' said Christie. 'I'm a bit tired and I
couldn't get ready, to be truthful.'

'That's fine,' soothed Laurie. One of the many nice things
about Laurie was that she wasn't the sort of person with
whom you had to pretend. 'Come and let me introduce you
to my sister-in-law, Beth. You met before I think? She's a
teacher too, and a gardener, you'll have a lot to talk about.'

Christie smiled gratefully at Laurie.

Mercifully, Laurie's sister-in-law wasn't an art teacher, so
there was no conversation about new, exciting exhibitions
by enigmatic Polish artists who painted nude, dark-haired
women over the past twenty-five years. She was an English
teacher and they enjoyed a highly pleasurable hour talking
about the difficulties of teaching, how hard the exams were
on the students and how schools had changed so much over
the past few decades.

'Oh, look,' said Beth.

Laurie had wheeled in a hostess trolley with an enormous
cake on top. For pure fun, she hadn't gone for the one big
candle saying happy sixtieth: she'd gone the whole hog with
sixty single candles blazing with heat and possibly visible
from space.

'There's a lot of candles there. Is it your ninetieth, did you
say, Tommy?' said one wag.

'Call an ambulance, please,' said another. 'He'll need it by
the time he's blown all them out.'

'Come on everybody,' insisted a third voice. 'We'll have

to help him. Poor Tommy doesn't have the energy for anything physical any more, apart from the mistress in the apartment that they're setting him up with.'

'Tommy!' came Laurie's voice furiously. 'That was a family joke, you didn't have to tell everyone! What will people think?'

'Ah, Laurie,' grinned Tommy happily, putting his arm around his wife and standing as close to his cake as the furnace of candles allowed. 'People know I adore you. You keep me busy enough, how would I have time for a mistress, tell me?'

Everyone laughed. From the other side of the garden, James smiled over at Christie. He motioned that she should come over and stand with him. But Christie shook her head, as if to imply that it was all too squashed to get there. She blew him a kiss, feeling like an absolute traitor. For the truth was that she didn't want to stand beside her darling husband and shriek happy birthday to one half of a happily married couple. Proximity to such a loyal marriage made her feel even more disloyal than ever. When Tommy closed his eyes to blow out his candles and wish, Christie Devlin closed her eyes too and wished with all her heart that she had never met Carey Wolensky. She knew that everyone did silly things in their youth, in their middle and old age too. But they moved on, made their peace and got on with life. Except, this was one thing she had never made her peace with and it had hung over her for years: Carey Wolensky and how he'd changed her life. It was the one big secret in her life and she was terrified, petrified, it was going to come out now and ruin everything.

A few days later Christie made a trip to the market advertised in the flyer she'd found on the floor of the corridor. The market itself was based in a big covered-in former flower market which had been taken over by stallholders who sold everything from dodgy antiques to velvet scarves, old leather-bound books and health food.

Christie walked through the market with a shopping bag slung over her shoulder. It was a perfectly reasonable place for her to be, she thought. She could buy some vitamins and perhaps some nice organic vegetables. Maybe think ahead and pick out some things for Christmas.

The reason she was trying to convince herself that this was a normal shopping jaunt was in case she met anyone she knew. In fact, the only excuse she needed was for her own conscience. For someone with a traditional Catholic upbringing like herself, going to see a fortune-teller was a big, slightly frightening step. Her gift of foresight was just that, a gift she had been born with. But deliberately consulting someone else who had that gift might well be frowned on by the Church, even in these more flexible times.

She circled the market once, purchasing some organic mushrooms, still fluffed with the earth they were pulled from, and some tea brack, darkly wet and honeyed-looking. James would love that for his tea. And then, she saw the fortune-telling stall. It wasn't the exotic spot she had been expecting. There were no velvet curtains or gold-sequined chiffon trailing all over the place. Just this small stall with a seating area of two chairs in front of a wall covered with old French posters, obviously from the stall next door. There was a little door, made of the same thin board as the wall, and presumably behind that lurked the fortune-teller. She looked about in case someone recognised her. There was no one. It was now or never.

She sat down in one of the chairs and waited. A few minutes passed and she was just about to get up and go, thinking that there was clearly nobody behind the door, when it creaked open and a woman appeared.

She was remarkably young, Christie thought, cross with

herself for expecting some wizened little old Romany woman, but this woman couldn't have been more than thirty. Pale and small with long dark-blonde hair tied back, the woman wore a decidedly plain blue blouse and dark trousers. Neatly put together, she could have been working behind the counter in any bank. Christie berated herself for stereotyping.

'Would you like to come in?' the woman said to Christie, her accent putting her from somewhere in the midland of the country.

'Yes, of course,' said Christie.

The little room boasted a table covered with a black velvet cloth, two chairs and was lined with heavy curtains.

'Sound-proofing,' the girl said matter-of-factly.

She tilted her head slightly. 'Why are you here?'

'What do you mean?' asked Christie, wrong-footed.

'Why do you want me to tell you things?' the girl said, sitting down and gesturing for Christie to do the same.

'Well, you're a fortune-teller,' Christie said.

'Yes,' said the girl, 'but so are you.'

Christie sat down, dropped her shopping and her handbag and leaned on the table. 'Sorry, what?' she asked.

'You can See, can't you?' the woman said, saying the word with a gravity that gave it capital letters. 'I can always tell.'

Whatever Christie had been expecting, it wasn't this. 'I'm Christie,' she said.

'I'm Rosalind,' said the girl. 'Nice to meet you.'

They shook hands across the table and it felt odd, this formality in such strange circumstances. Christie only hesitated a moment, she had come here not knowing what to expect, yet faced with Rosalind, who clearly could see that Christie had some sort of gift, she felt there was no point in hiding or prevaricating.

'You're right,' she said. 'I can see, I've always been able to see, but it's a strange gift. I've never been able to control it, it just comes to me sometimes. And I can never see anything for me.'

Rosalind nodded. 'That's often the way it is,' she said. 'There are plenty of people in my mother's family like you, they have a great gift, but they have never developed it. Not being able to see for yourself is common enough. Lots of people with the gift don't see for themselves or deliberately blank it out because they don't want to know. I try not to look into my children's lives,' she said with a shudder. 'I'd be afraid of what I would see.'

'So, what is your gift and how did you know about it?' asked Christie.

'I can see into the future, the probable future,' Rosalind said slowly. 'I'm a medium too, although I don't work as a medium very often because it drains me. It's exhausting.'

Christie shivered. 'I don't want to see a medium, I don't want to see people there beside me.'

'That's fine,' agreed Rosalind. 'A lot of people don't want that. Even as a child, I knew I had the gift. My mother has it too. It's a gift and a curse because there is no escaping it.'

'I know what you mean,' said Christie with feeling, thinking of the last month and the fear she'd felt. 'It comes when you don't want it to.'

'And you came here to me because you saw something you didn't want to?' Rosalind asked suddenly.

Christie nodded.

'I can never see for myself, I wouldn't want to, but I've just had these feelings of fear, of anxiety. Somebody has come into my life from the past and . . .'

'A man,' said Rosalind. She sounded a bit different now, more professional. 'A man once came into your life and you felt something for him but you were married and he went and you thought it was safe and now, a long time later, he's back making contact.'

'How did you know?' sighed Christie. It was a relief to hear somebody speak her fears aloud.

'The same way you've seen things before,' Rosalind said. 'I've learned how to develop my gift. You never did?'

'I wasn't brought up in that sort of home,' Christie explained. 'My father was religious and he would have gone mad. He didn't believe in seeing anything unless it was there in front of him or unless Father Flynn talked about it. I couldn't have told Dad.'

'But you know it must have come from somewhere?' Rosalind said. 'Would you like me to see where?'

Christie Devlin, possessor of a gift she had never understood, felt like crying. For the first time in her life she was able to talk about it to someone who understood. Why hadn't she done this years ago?

'You didn't know your grandmother, did you?' Rosalind asked and her voice was slower now, as if she was concentrating hard. 'Your mother's mother, I mean. I can feel that you didn't.'

Christie nodded. 'I never met her. She was a quarter French –'

'– And she died before you were born. She was from a large family and was the seventh daughter, and so was your mother. And you're the seventh child too, aren't you?'

Rosalind looked straight at Christie, who nodded again. She wasn't feeling shock or astonishment any more.

'Your grandmother had the gift,' Rosalind said. 'She could see things and if she'd been around she'd have told you what to do with it. She's here, you know. She's with us in the room.'

Christie gasped. 'I don't want to know that type of thing,' she said.

'Fine,' said Rosalind calmly. 'She's the one who had the gift and she's sorry that you had to grow up not knowing anything about it, but your father wasn't the sort of man to

298

let you know. Your mother had the gift but when she married your father, he hated it so much, he forbade her to use it. She would have liked you to know that you might have it too, but your father told her never to talk about it, ever. She was very nervous of him, I think, he overpowered her.'

Christie smiled sadly, that was right for sure.

'There's nothing wrong with being able to see. Your grandmother was a good woman, she helped lots of people, she was kind, Christian, good. She said there was a lot of fear in her day. People thought that if you could see, you couldn't possibly be a good, true religious person. She says to tell you it's just another type of seeing, another type of wisdom, that's all. She'd have told you that, if she'd been alive.'

'I never wanted to see too much,' Christie said. 'It allowed me to be wise and I could help people and that was lovely, but I never wanted to be able to see for myself or see bad things coming or . . . I suppose that's why I was frightened of coming to you, that you could see all the bad things.'

'Bad things happen whether you see them or not,' said Rosalind firmly, 'and anything I see for you in the future is the probable future. Nothing is set in stone, we can all affect our own destiny. If you read the cards and they tell you there is danger ahead, you will change your life: change what you do so that the danger doesn't affect you. Destiny is in our own hands. We all have choice and free will. Seeing the future is merely another type of wisdom.'

'Well, why are we so frightened of it?' Christie asked, thinking of her father. It all made sense now, how he hated the Gypsy fortune-tellers that used to come through Kilshandra occasionally. He hated them because he'd known that his wife's mother could have been one of them, and it frightened him. Maybe her grandmother had seen that her son-in-law was a bully and had warned her daughter against him.

'People don't like what they can't understand,' said Rosalind, shrugging. 'The reality is that there are people like you and me, who can see, for whatever reason. We'd be stupid to turn our back on it, because it's a gift, like any other gift, like being musical or having a lovely voice. As long as you are not seeing things to hurt people, as long as you're trying to help, well then, what's wrong with being a wise woman?'

'Yes, that's it,' said Christie, feeling a little peace enter her soul, 'a wise woman. People often say I'm a wise woman.'

'And you are.' Rosalind smiled. 'But even wise women need a little help sometimes. This man ...' She reached out and touched Christie's hand. 'Why are you frightened of him coming back into your life?'

'Because if he came back and he told about what he meant to me, it would hurt the people I love most in the world. I don't want that to happen. I feel so powerless, that he's coming and I can't stop him and I've had this sense of fear for so long now that it never goes away.'

Rosalind nodded. 'I could read the cards for you,' she said, 'but I don't think I need to. I think you understand what you need to do. You're just afraid of doing it.'

'I don't understand at all,' said Christie.

'Yes, you do,' insisted Rosalind. 'Look in your heart. Close your eyes and think.'

For a moment, Christie thought of herself and Liz in the staff room in St Ursula's, when Liz had been worried about the man she loved and how he wanted to run out on her because it was all getting too serious. Christie had told her to close her eyes and think about what was in her heart. It was funny, she realised, she'd been using her gift just the way Rosalind did without any training or help. Perhaps she was a wise woman after all.

Closing her eyes now, she thought of Carey Wolensky and what he had meant to her. How his coming back could hurt so many people: Ana, Ethan and Shane, and James, most of all James. Because it really hadn't been his fault, it had been a series of coincidences and happenings that had led Carey to her.

She opened her eyes. The answer had come. 'I need to see him and tell him to leave my life, that he's not a part of it, that if he's kept a torch burning for me all these years he should let it go out. I've got to talk to James about it and tell him. Let him know, whatever the consequences.'

She shivered because she didn't know what those consequences would be, but she knew that's what she had to do.

Rosalind didn't comment on this. 'Maybe you'll come back and see me again some other time,' she said. 'I could read your cards.'

Christie smiled. She wasn't sure if she was ready for that. Better to get used to the information that the gift did run in her family and see where telling James about Carey Wolensky would lead her and then . . .

'Thank you,' she said. She opened her purse. 'How much do I owe you?'

'No.' Rosalind stilled her with the word. 'There's no fee. People who share the gift never charge other people who share it,' she said.

'You're sure?' asked Christie.

'I'm sure,' said Rosalind, 'and please, come and see me again.'

It was odd, Christie thought, as she walked back through the market, she felt a lightness in her heart that she hadn't felt in a long time, ever since the gloom had first appeared. She'd been so stupid really. For the past month, she'd let the memory of Carey Wolensky overshadow everything else in her life, all the wonderful things: James, her family, Janet's

301

pregnancy, the good things she had. She'd let Carey over-shadow them all, because she'd allowed herself to be a victim.

She'd done something she'd been ashamed of and, instead of facing up to it, she'd been scared it would destroy her family. In doing so, she'd almost allowed it to destroy her family. Ironic that, she thought wryly. But she wouldn't be scared any more. Rosalind had just helped her to see what was in her heart and what she had to do.

She sat down on a bench near the market and made the call to Carey's hotel from her mobile phone. She was put on to Heidi, Carey's assistant, instantly.

'This is Mrs Christie Devlin,' she said coolly, although she was quivering with nerves. 'You've been trying to contact me with regard to Mr Wolensky's exhibition.'

'Yes, he'll be so thrilled you've got in touch,' said Heidi with obvious enthusiasm.

'I don't want to go to the private viewing. I'll be away,' Christie said, lying. 'But I'd like to meet with Mr Wolensky, if that's possible.'

'I'm sure it is. He was most keen to see you.'

Christie nearly hung up there and then, but she had to be strong. She had to do this.

'He's here next week from Wednesday on for ten days.'

'I can see him on the Monday morning,' Christie said, shocked that she'd have to wait that long to get this all over with. 'No other time, I'm afraid.'

'He's busy then but I can rearrange his appointments,' Heidi replied quickly. 'Eleven, here in the hotel?'

'Eleven would be fine. Thank you.'

Christie pushed the 'end call' button. She'd done it. She'd stopped running from the past. But she didn't feel any sense of relief – only pure panic. She could have just made the biggest mistake of her life.

CHAPTER TWENTY-ONE

Thousands of miles away, sitting in the back of a beaten-up van with the band, Amber was wondering the same thing. Was this whole trip the biggest mistake of her life?

They hadn't expected a traffic jam in LA. Gridlock, a freeway nightmare. Cars jammed end to end, creeping along. That sort of stuff happened at home, not here, not in fabulous LA. But they still got stuck in it until finally, after three quarters of an hour in the heat – the air con didn't work very well in the rent-a-wreck – Syd took an off ramp and they ended up in a small, beat-up neighbourhood, with a couple of pool halls and what looked like a pub.

They all piled in. None of them really had enough cash to spend on drinks, but they were dying for something cool: cool beer, cool lemonade, cool anything. The bar was half full, but nobody even glanced at Amber, which made her feel even more miserable, although she knew she looked a sight. How was it that men ignoring her could be so depressing, when she and Ella had so often been dismissive of men who did notice them? Her skin was greasy and she'd got spots. She hadn't washed her hair for the last couple of days, she'd been so tired. How could you be tired getting up in the morning when you hadn't done anything all day except sit in the back of a van, bumping along?

They ambled over to the bar and ordered some drinks.

'You can drive from now on,' Syd said to Karl. 'I'm having some real liquor.'

'Hey, you're turning into an American,' laughed Lew.

'Yeah, right,' said Syd glumly.

The night before he'd confided in Amber that he was missing his girlfriend, Lola, so much. She was a make-up artist who worked for herself, often travelling around Ireland for jobs. There was no way she could have come on this crazy trek across America.

'It's impossible to get hold of her without my mobile,' he had grumbled to Amber, as they sat on the fire escape of last night's crummy hotel, Amber sipping a Coke, Syd chain-smoking.

'She wasn't worried that you were going away without her, was she?' asked Amber doubtfully, thinking that she'd been too nervous to let Karl go off on his own.

'No,' said Syd, with a laugh. 'We're too close for that.'

And then, she could see him realise what he had said, realise he knew exactly why she'd tagged along with the band to New York and now on the trek to LA: because she didn't trust Karl.

'But you know,' Syd said rapidly, 'people are different and she's busy. Plus, she's been to America a few times and she'll come out when we're settled. It's different for you and Karl, right?'

'Yeah, different,' said Amber, thinking of the exams her friends at St Ursula's were sitting now. Thinking of her seat in the big exam hall, near to Ella, and the grins and the glances and the anguished stares they'd have exchanged, had exchanged for every exam they'd sat through together since they'd met. Ella always had a supply of sweets and crunched them noisily. Amber was more a chewing gum sort of girl. She wondered who was sitting in her place now, what dreams and hopes they had.

Thinking of Ella made her think of Mum. The guilt about Mum was always there in the pit of her stomach. Mum had done nothing wrong except stifle Amber in an attempt to protect her, and look how Amber had repaid her.

She was a horrible daughter and her mother must hate her. Every time Amber thought longingly of home and of hearing her mother's voice, she reminded herself of her mother's hurt face that last day. She, Amber, had done that – hurt her mother as much as if she'd stabbed her. She didn't know how she'd ever say sorry for that. It was such a huge weight to carry that she didn't know how to try.

'It'll work out,' Syd said.

'What?' said Amber, half lost, not quite knowing what he was talking about. 'The band, you mean? You're all very talented, I'm sure it will work out.'

Syd looked at her silently, for a moment. 'Yeah,' he said, 'that's what I meant: the band. It'll work out, I'm sure of it.'

Now in the seedy bar in LA, Karl sloped off to phone Stevie in Dublin, just in case there was any news. Syd looked at Amber.

'What'll you have?' he said, gently.

Normally, Amber stuck to a couple of light beers, since she still wasn't the drinking sort of girl. Ella would laugh at that: to think they'd both been keen to have grown-up drinks in grown-up bars and now that she could, Amber had discovered she didn't like them that much.

'I don't know, Syd,' she said now. 'Something to cheer me up.'

Syd grinned. 'I know just what you need!'

By the third tequila shot, Amber was feeling no pain.

'It's great this stuff. Why did I never try it before?' She

was smiling happily, arranging and rearranging her shot glasses in different patterns.

'We never could afford it before,' Kenny T laughed.

'We can't now,' added Lew. 'Karl will go stark, staring mad when he comes back and finds that we've been spending the savings on tequila.'

'Well, Karl's not the boss, is he?' snapped Syd. 'Amber can have Cuevo Gold if she fucking well wants to. In fact, she'll have another one and so will I.'

When Karl came back from the phone a few moments later, Amber looked at him with eyes of love. She felt warm and hazy inside. It was all going to be wonderful. LA was a fabulous place, they'd live in a gorgeous house and go to amazing celebrity parties. Karl would be a world-famous musician, they'd have loads of money and people would look at her, envy her and think she had a fabulous life . . .

'Tequila?' said Karl, looking down at the empty shot glasses on the table.

'Hey, we felt like cheering ourselves up,' Syd said defensively.

Karl didn't look upset, though.

'You're not going to believe it,' he said, 'but Stevie came through.'

'Came through how?' asked Lew.

'Came through in that he's got us a meeting with a production company out here. It's a guy called Michael Levin and he's hot, Stevie says. He's one of the best producers around and he liked the stuff Stevie sent him. We're to meet him in his office tomorrow. Guys, it's going to be OK.'

The tequila-drinkers erupted in a cheer.

'That's incredible,' said Amber, getting up to throw her arms lazily around Karl's neck. 'You're incredible. Oh, I love you, I love you so much, that's wonderful. You're so talented and clever and . . .'

'Right,' he said, moving his face away from her boozy breath. 'You shouldn't drink tequila, Amber, it smells horrible.'

'We needed cheering up, you see,' she whispered. What he'd said hurt, but she was still insulated by the cosy fire of the alcohol.

'Yeah, yeah, whatever.' Karl settled her back in her seat. He sat down beside the band and began to plan with them. What they'd say to this producer, what they'd play for him, how they weren't going to be taken for some load of green young guys because now they'd been around.

Amber sat on the edge, sidelined again, but she didn't care. It was all working out, it was all going to be great. She knew it.

That night they stayed in another fleapit motel, the sort of place that was quite safe, mainly because there were two police cars parked outside the door most of the night. Sirens blared, people screamed and laughed and Amber barely slept a wink, partly because of the tequila hangover that had kicked in at about ten, and partly because of anxiety. She didn't like this town: it was scary. These constantly bright and busy streets weren't the palm-treed oases she'd imagined. There were no haciendas in this part of town, no nice cafés with movie stars sitting outside, no sense of Hollywood glamour: just dangerous guys driving big cars with music vibrating out from everywhere, and skinny girls in hotpants on the street corner opposite the hotel, watching every car that slowed down. Nobody smiled at anyone, nobody looked at anyone, as though eye contact was a threat.

However, in the California sunshine of the next morning, the streets didn't look menacing any more: just edgy and hip, like a scene from a video on MTV.

'Come back to bed,' murmured Karl, sitting up against the pillows, watching her looking out the window and admiring her body in the pink spotted G-string she'd slept in.

'Bed?' she said, doing her best call-girl voice. 'Can you afford me?'

She climbed on to the bed and began to crawl towards him, swinging her hair provocatively.

'I don't know,' Karl said, pulling her closer. 'I'm pretty broke now but I think there might be some money coming my way soon. Will you take an IOU?'

Amber straddled him. 'Only for you, my love,' she crooned before kissing him.

Within hours, their fortunes had changed. It took one trip to the producer's office. Michael Levin was a small, slim, dark-eyed guy who clearly liked the band's work. He said he'd work with them and that they needed to sort out some paperwork, as well as a lawyer to go over the small print. He recommended someone.

Amber raised her eyebrows at this: surely if the producer recommended a lawyer he knew, this was a conflict of interest? They should find their own lawyer to work out the percentages, etc, but nobody else looked askance at the suggestion.

Michael Levin was offering some money upfront and got them a deal in a lovely hotel near his office until they could sort out a house to rent.

Two hours after meeting him, they had four beautiful suites in the Santa Angelina Hotel, a hip little place with the requisite palm trees outside. Amber felt the bellboy looking at the five of them in faint disgust as he showed them up to their rooms. She was sure that they smelt of poverty, of life on the road in crappy motels where the toiletries ran to thin bars of soap and even thinner towels. She couldn't wait to get into that vast bath tub in the huge pale marble and mirrored bathroom and sink into all the bubbles that would be sure to emerge from the beautiful aquamarine glass jars.

'Wow, this is some place,' said Syd, admiring Karl and Amber's suite.

'I've never seen anything like it,' gasped Lew.

'Hey, relax, guys,' said Karl, trying to be cool. 'You've gotta get used to this.'

Amber felt a flash of impatience with him. Who did he think he was? They had just spent ten days on the road in cockroach-infested fleapits with no money, eating endless fast food until they were all spotty and lank-haired, and it seemed like sheer fluke that had brought them to this beautiful place. Now was not the time to be doing the 'we're so cool, we deserve this' act.

'Cop on, Karl,' she said sharply. 'We're lucky it's working out, let's not count our chickens. We did that the last time, remember? And then Stevie left and we were up shit creek without a paddle.'

Karl glared at her. 'I knew it would work, even if you didn't.'

He marched into their suite's second bathroom and slammed the door.

'Hey,' said Lew, grinning at Amber. 'Just as well you've got two bathrooms.'

Karl and Amber didn't talk to each other for the rest of the afternoon, although Amber didn't care. She was perfectly happy being in her own bathroom, lolling in a bubble-filled bath, scrubbing herself clean, rubbing scented body lotion into every inch of her body, washing her hair till it squeaked, feeling good about herself again.

They were being taken out to dinner tonight by Michael Levin, and as she rooted through her dirty, faded wardrobe, she realised she actually had nothing to wear and no money to buy anything. It was different for the guys, they could wear jeans and a T-shirt and still look fantastic, but girls needed something a bit more special.

She could have gone and asked Karl if there was any money to spare to buy something new but she didn't want to. Instead, she went over to Syd's suite.

'What's happenin', baby?' he said, opening the door, a fat cigar in one hand, the TV remote in the other and himself wrapped in a big, fat towelling robe. The huge TV blared a pay-per-view movie and a room service cart lay pushed to one side with the remains of a club sandwich and a bottle of champagne.

'You're fitting in around here very well, Syd,' Amber grinned.

It was funny, she got on better with Syd these days than she did with Karl.

'Yeah, I think I like this lifestyle, Amber. Better not get used to it, though, as you pointed out.'

'Sorry,' Amber apologised. 'I didn't mean that, I didn't mean that the band wouldn't make it. I was only trying to be realistic. We, sorry, *you* shouldn't count your chickens.'

'I know that,' Syd said, drawing her into the suite. 'You look all lovely and shiny.'

'I feel great,' said Amber. 'And clean! I thought I'd never feel clean again. There's only one problem, I have nothing to wear.'

Syd laughed. 'It must be a chromosome thing: women and shopping. Lola's just the same. Shop or die. I've got a few quid left.' He handed her over a hundred dollars. 'Sorry, it's not much, but it's all I can afford until we get some of the upfront signing money.'

'Oh, you're a star!' Amber said and threw her arms around him and gave him a big hug.

'Steady on,' laughed Syd, 'or you'll have Lola on the phone soon, giving out that I found me another woman.'

'Oh, sure,' teased Amber. She knew he was only kidding, he loved Lola to bits. 'Thanks, and don't mention this to Karl?'

'I won't,' said Syd. 'I understand.'

As Amber went downstairs in the lift, she pondered those last words. What did Syd understand? That she and Karl were breaking up in front of his eyes and that she couldn't go to Karl and ask him for a few dollars to buy a new outfit? Or that he wouldn't understand why she needed to in the first place?

Far away in New York, Faye Reid wondered if she should just go home and give up. She'd been in New York for two weeks now and she felt she was dying of loneliness. She missed Amber so much. And since that first phone call just after she'd left, Amber hadn't even phoned home again. Faye checked her Summer Street answering machine with a frequency that was verging on the obsessional.

Above all, she felt as if she'd failed her daughter spectacularly if Amber could run away and never contact home. What sort of a mother did that make her?

When her own mother phoned her to see how she was doing, Faye could barely speak from misery.

'I don't suppose Amber's been in touch with you, Mum?' she asked, ever hopeful.

'No,' said Josie. 'I suspect she feels so guilty and anxious that she's deliberately not phoning now. She knows I'd give her a piece of my mind for running off like that.'

'You're not to say a thing to her if she phones!' shrieked Faye. It might frighten Amber off and . . .

'Faye, listen to me!' said Josie calmly but firmly. 'If Amber phones, I will give her a piece of my mind because what she's done is unforgivable. I know she's only eighteen, she's in love and she's all upset, but that's no reason to treat your

311

family this way. Yes, I'm sure she's afraid we'll be furious with her for what she's done, but that's no reason not to call again. I am furious with her and when you get over your fit of the guilts, you should be too. Yes, you lied to her.'

Faye winced.

'Yes, you made up a nice little fairytale about her father and you know I disagreed with you about that, but it was your choice. The bottom line, Faye, is that you've done everything you could for that girl, everything. You've given up your life for her. The Lord only knows I love her, but I am angry with her.'

'Oh, Mum . . .'

'Don't "Oh, Mum" me,' said Josie fiercely. 'If you don't make some progress in the next few days, then you've got to come home. Amber is a clever girl. She'll survive. She's got our blood running through her veins and we've survived, haven't we? So have some faith in her.'

'You really think she'll be all right?' Faye said, starting to cry.

'She might be wrapped up in young passion, but she's not stupid,' Josie said with a touch of pride. 'She's a strong girl. You've done a great job with her. Remember that.'

'I will,' sobbed Faye. 'I will.' But it was easier said than done.

Her mother was right: she'd have to go home soon. What was the point waiting here? Amber could have left New York days ago. She could be anywhere by now, and at least when she phoned home again – and she would, Faye was sure she would – Faye would be there to talk to her.

The fashion magazines were wrong, Amber thought crossly, after an hour and a half. They were always implying that Los Angeles thrift shops were full of exquisite vintage

312

clothes: barely worn Schiaparelli gowns, original Dior suits, everything for next to nothing. In fact, she was finding an awful lot of very dull clothes and lots of jeans in teeny, tiny sizes. She *had* jeans. But jeans were not going to cut it in a town where people only wore jeans with half a million's worth of Harry Winston diamonds, accessorised with Manolo Blahnik shoes and a Judith Leiber clutch.

Then, finally, in a tiny little shop off Melrose, with rails so crammed full of clothes it hurt her arms to rifle through them, she found it. It looked like a 1930s nightie, which in fact it probably was: an emerald-green bias-cut silk-satin dress with spaghetti straps and a scalloped hem. It clung to her curves in all the right places and highlighted her creamy skin and her tawny mane. It was fabulous and, better still, only sixty dollars. With the rest of the money she bought an embroidered shawl with fringing, to throw over her shoulders, and a shiny lip gloss. There, she'd do.

Karl was sitting on the superking-sized bed putting on his watch when Amber emerged from her bathroom, all ready to go, a vision in shimmering green, her tiger's-eye pendant highlighting the silkiness of her slender throat.

'Wow, you look amazing,' he said in admiration. 'Come here.'

It was as if the row had never happened, as if there had never been any coolness between them on the road. He began to kiss her and suddenly Amber wasn't in such a rush for the dinner party after all. Karl's hands caressed her body and gently pulled the straps of her beautiful dress over her shoulders so it slithered like a skin to the floor.

'You're so beautiful,' he said, 'my muse. I couldn't have done this without you.'

As they made love, Amber thought that these were just

the words she wanted to hear. Karl loved her, adored her. That was what mattered, wasn't it?

They were late getting downstairs but the limo driver didn't seem to mind.

'What the hell were you pair doing?' grumbled Kenny T, who had been sitting in the back of the limo with Syd and Lew for ten minutes and was agitated, as if he wanted to get to this fabulous party soon.

'Nothing,' said Karl, with a grin that said quite plainly that he had just had mind-altering sex.

Syd said nothing, he just looked at Amber and smiled a small, knowing smile. She grinned back, feeling slightly treacherous for telling Syd she couldn't ask Karl for the money for the new dress. This was Syd's money she was wearing and she couldn't tell Karl. But couples had rows and arguments all the time, Syd must know that.

Los Angeles was a strange mix of dress up and dress down. The restaurant they went to looked as if half the clientele had come straight from the Oscars and the other half straight from doing their grocery shopping. There were willowy girls in jeans and socialites in Versace. Jewels gleamed on both men and women and everyone looked fabulously tanned and healthy.

In her second-hand finery, Amber felt she fitted in pretty well and she was with the most handsome man in the room, the superbly talented Karl Evans. Michael, the producer, thought so too, he spent the night talking about the band with Karl. They discussed different songs, what they'd rearrange, how they might bring in some other songwriters – people Michael worked with all the time – just to tweak, and perhaps to write a couple of new songs. Karl, who normally maintained that his work was not to be touched, and wouldn't even dream of singing anyone else's music, nodded vigorously to all this. He seemed fascinated by the talk of business.

There were ten people at the dinner table but Amber felt bored. Nobody was talking to her. It was as if, she realised sadly, she didn't quite exist.

She felt just the same as she had at the SnakePit that night when she'd had to hide at the side of the stage to watch the band play – a hanger-on. That's what Stevie had wanted her to feel, she was sure: that she was nothing but the girlfriend, and of course, the role of the girlfriend was to keep the lead singer/songwriter happy, as well as being attractive and sexually available. So much for feminism, Amber thought grimly and took another sip of wine.

The waiters, all staggeringly handsome out-of-work actors with cheekbones like cliff edges and bodies sculpted by hours in the gym, kept filling the wineglasses so stealthily and discreetly that it was hard for Amber to know how much she'd drunk. At first, as she toyed with her Caesar salad, she tried to keep a tab, but after a while she gave up. Karl was at the end of the table, separated from her by Michael and one of his assistants, who were talking to Karl at length about musicians they all admired and where Karl's inspiration had come from.

'It's got to be Robert Johnson, hasn't it?' Karl was saying intently. 'Oh, and Hendrix, naturally.'

'Well, you've got his gift too,' said the assistant, smiling, flattering.

Amber thought she was going to puke. Michael had seemed upfront and honest when they'd first met him, but tonight, he had changed: he was fawning on Karl, hyping up the band and their brilliance. What a fabulous team they'd all make. How they'd change the world. And Karl didn't seem to see.

Amber pushed her plate away, her appetite quite gone. She loved the climate in LA, adored the sense of freedom. But the insincerity was something else. Everything she saw or heard in this town was wrapped in a fleecy parcel of bullshit. She almost longed for the straightforwardness of the places they'd stayed on the road: ordinary towns where people said what they meant. Or even miserable old Gretchen in the mini-market back home, who'd glare at you rudely if she was in the mood.

Or her mum. The mini-market made her think of Summer Street and of home. Could Mum ever forgive her? At that moment, Amber didn't feel as if she deserved forgiveness.

Karl didn't seem to notice her unhappiness. He didn't smile or even give her one of those 'are you OK, honey?' looks across the table. On her other side was a female producer. A slim, beautiful woman with olive skin, dressed in an exquisite coral wrap dress, she was talking intently to Syd and Kenny T.

Even Lew, who was never going to be a contestant on *Mastermind*, was busily being chatted up by yet another member of Michael's team on the other side of the table. But nobody was bothering with Amber. And she didn't like it. She was clever, she wasn't some bimbo girlfriend.

She lifted her wineglass and took another big sip and thought of her mum. Mum always said that beauty could only take you so far in life, while intelligence and self-belief could take you a lot further. Amber didn't allow herself to think about her mum much, although she fingered her tiger's-eye pendant thoughtfully. She wore it all the time and she did think of Mum when she put it on. It was her talisman of home. She hadn't rung since that first phone call, she knew she should have but the argument was all too raw, too painful. She'd been horrible, she knew that now. Not that she'd made a mistake, no, she'd done the right thing to go away with Karl.

But she still felt guilty when she thought of Mum's hurt face and what was it that Gran had said?

You should let your mother tell you.

316

She sometimes wondered exactly what her mother did have to tell her. Gran wouldn't have said it if she hadn't meant it, if there hadn't been some intelligent reason behind it. So what could her mum have to tell Amber that could possibly change the way she had decided to live her life?

'Was your salad OK for you?' asked the waiter.

'Yes, it was delicious,' said Amber, pathetically happy that at least someone was talking to her. 'It's just I wasn't hungry.'

The evening might have been endured if another party of people hadn't arrived when their table was drinking coffee. There was no dessert of course. God forbid that anyone in LA would actually eat dessert, apart from toying with some fresh fruit. Amber was cross because she felt like something sugary.

The party included a very beautiful woman with skin like ebony, the body of a supermodel and a face that Tyra Banks would envy. She came over to the table and kissed Michael Levin on both cheeks, a proper kiss, not just air kissing.

She was, Amber heard her neighbour whisper, the latest hot singing sensation with her first album just out, produced by Michael.

'She can sing too?' said Amber, staring at this vision of a woman. She was like an exquisite Somalian empress.

Wow, Amber thought, she'd be beautiful to paint: that face, that figure, that elegance.

'Yeah, she's going to make it really big,' said Amber's neighbour again. 'Everyone will know about Venetia, I promise you that. She's gonna be hotter than Beyoncé.'

Venetia. Even her name was beautiful, thought Amber mistily. And then, suddenly, she stopped feeling so friendly towards Venetia because Michael introduced her to Karl, not any of the other band members, just to Karl. A few more chairs were brought up and the exquisite Venetia snuggled in close between Karl and Michael, though slightly closer to

Karl than to anyone else. They were talking and laughing, and Amber couldn't hear what they were saying but she could see Venetia touching Karl on the shoulder and on the knee, as if she had known him for ever.

'She needs somebody to write some new songs for her,' said Amber's neighbour, catching Amber's fierce glare. 'Fabulous voice and she's written a few good tracks herself, but basically she needs songwriters and Michael thinks Karl has a few songs that just might suit her. He's a very talented songwriter.'

'Well, Karl doesn't write songs for anyone else,' Amber said heatedly. 'He doesn't believe in that type of thing, he only writes for himself.'

Her neighbour gave her a long, steady gaze.

'Karl seems like a pretty bright guy and if you want to get ahead in this business, you make your own music, you make music for other people, hey, whatever it takes. Venetia is going to go a long way, it mightn't be bad for him to be attached to her coat-tails.'

Amber was sick at the thought of Karl being attached to any part of Venetia.

She finished her wine with a flourish. She'd had enough of this. She was going back to the hotel and Karl was coming with her. They had been nice, charming, they had partied, you name it, but now they were going home to bed together and bloody Venetia had better get her hand off Karl's knee damn quick.

Amber got to her feet unsteadily. Her handbag was under the table, so she had to bend to pick it up and she banged her forehead on the table.

'Ouch.'

'You OK?' said Syd.

'Fine, fine,' said Amber with the unconcern of the very drunk. She swayed a little where she stood. 'I am perfectly fine, just think I'll go. Me and Karl, we're tired.'

'I'll take you home,' said Syd, pushing his chair back.

'No,' insisted Amber. 'There's no need. Karl will bring me home. I came with Karl, I'm going to go with Karl. He is my boyfriend, I am his muse,' she said loudly, so loudly that nobody at the table could have missed it. But Venetia, Karl and the producer didn't appear to have heard because they were all talking and laughing happily together.

Amber shoved her chair back and made it rather erratically around the table to Karl's side. She laid a hand on his shoulder. 'I want to go home, darling,' she said. 'Are you ready?'

Karl looked up at her. 'No, no, you go,' he said. 'I'm fine, baby. Don't wait up, whatever.'

Michael raised a hand and suddenly one of his team was escorting Amber outside.

'But I'm waiting for my boyfriend, for Karl,' she said. She could see Karl, but he wasn't watching her, although Venetia was looking at her with those exquisite cat-like eyes, her expression one of pity – not malice or jealousy or triumph, but plain, old-fashioned pity. It was the last thing Amber remembered as she was put in the back of the beautiful limo and whisked away to her exquisite, empty, hotel suite.

The next thing she knew there was so much daylight she could hardly open her eyes. She lay there, wondering where she was and then everything that had happened the night before flooded back. Karl. He hadn't come home with her. How dare he do that to her? She was going to give him a piece of her mind. She sat up in the bed, ignoring the murderous throbbing of her head, and turned to where he should have been, but she was alone. The bed was so big she'd only taken up a quarter of it. The other three quarters were pristine, unslept in. She threw back the covers and ran through the suite, but there was no sign of Karl.

Next, she phoned Syd and Lew in their respective suites.

'Gee, Amber, why are you ringing me at this hour?' groaned Lew.

'It's half eleven,' she snapped, 'hardly dawn.'

'We were out late, must have been six when we got in. Those people know how to party, one club after another.'

'You went clubbing?' she asked.

'Well, yeah, eventually. What a blast. You shouldn't have gone home so early, Amber. What was up with you anyway? Karl hates that sort of jealous stuff, you know.'

'I wasn't jealous,' said Amber, feeling wildly embarrassed that even Lew, who wasn't intuitive, had noticed.

'You were nearly spitting when you were going. I thought there might be a cat fight between you and Venetia. She's some babe. I'd pay to see that.'

'Thank you, Lew, you've been a great help,' hissed Amber and hung up.

Syd was more on the ball, but sounded just as hung-over.

'No, I do not know where Karl is,' he said and, to Amber's ears, his words sounded like a statement he'd been practising just in case she should call.

'Well, did he go off or did he come back with the rest of you? I mean he could have got another room here so he wouldn't wake me,' she said dubiously, knowing this was highly unlikely.

'Look, Amber, this is between you and Karl,' said Syd. 'OK? Just leave me out of it. You know what I feel.'

Amber didn't know what he felt, but she said thanks and bye and hung up anyway. Was Syd telling her that Karl had a thing going with Venetia, or that Karl was the sort of man that always had a thing going with some woman? Or was it something else? Syd was deep.

She went into her lovely bathroom and blasted herself under the shower, anything to get rid of this horrible old groggy dead feeling.

Next, she ordered breakfast. Not because she was hungry, more that she thought strong coffee and maybe fruit would jerk her out of her hangover. Afterwards, she sat outside on the balcony, which overlooked the pool and watched beautiful people having business meetings around the glistening water. There were also plenty of people sunbathing, women with beautiful bodies, tanned and oiled, in white bikinis or exotic designer ones in Pucci prints. There was so much money here. In their trip across the States they had seen the richest and the poorest. They had certainly stayed in the poorest places, and now they were in one of the wealthiest towns on the planet but Amber didn't feel happy or thrilled, the way she thought she'd feel.

Her dreams of it had been about her and Karl being happy together. The problem was, there was no togetherness. Here, Amber was even more alone than she had been before she met Karl, when she'd only been dreaming about what love might be. And now she had the guilt to carry for hurting her mother too.

Finally, she went out to the pool herself and lay there with a book, peeping over the corners of it, watching what was going on.

Eventually, the heat of the sun got to her and she fell into a dreamless sleep.

'So this is where you are,' said a voice. 'I've been looking everywhere for you.'

It was Karl, except he didn't look as if he'd had a wild night out in clubs. He looked like he'd had a very good night's sleep. There was that faint hint of stubble on his jaw, his hair was tousled. The look in his eyes gave it away though. It was a look Amber had come to recognise when he walked offstage: a look of triumph, of sheer, almost sexual, pleasure. The look said: *I've just stood in front of all these people and they all wanted me.*

'You can't have been looking too hard for me,' she said sarcastically. 'I've been here all day and all last night,' she added pointedly. 'Where were you?'

'Out,' he said, his gaze raking over her, as if he didn't like what he saw.

'Out?' demanded Amber, feeling her temper rise. 'Out with whom?' she added for effect.

'With Michael, doing what we came to LA to do, Amber, remember? Hook up with a big producer, make our names, you know. We're here to do more than just lie around the pool all day and work on our tans.'

'I'm only working on my tan because I have no money and I can't go anywhere and because I was waiting for you to come home,' she snapped back, stung. 'And I was worried, anything could have happened to you, anything.'

She could see his face soften at the thought that she'd been worried about him, and he smiled at her, became the old Karl again.

'Oh, baby, you shouldn't worry about me. Last night was so amazing, such a blast, talking about music all night long with someone like Michael.'

He sat down on the sun lounger beside her, leaned forward, his face boyishly excited.

'You wouldn't believe the people he's worked with, the bands, the names, people whose albums I have and he knows them, he's worked with them. Jesus, it's incredible. I can't believe we're here.'

'So that was it?' Amber asked hesitantly.

'That was it. Sorry, you're right, I should have called. I stayed over with Michael, he's got the most amazing house in the hills, you should see it, all glass and beautiful. Rebuilt after the mud slides, totally incredible. He said it was an amazing house before but now it's doubly amazing.'

322

'Somebody said he had lots of art as well, didn't they?' Amber asked. 'He's a collector.'

'Yeah, yeah,' said Karl. 'There were paintings and stuff, you know me, I'm not into that, I didn't really notice, but yeah, sure, lots of fantastic stuff. You'll see it. Listen, why don't you and me go out to dinner, just on our own, not the gang, somewhere nice?'

'How can we afford it?'

'It's OK, Michael's given us an advance against the advance, if you know what I mean.' Karl grinned. 'Money, we've got money, baby.'

'Somewhere casual,' said Amber hopefully, 'because I still don't really have anything to wear, except what I was wearing last night.'

'What was that you were wearing?' Karl said, furrowing his brow.

'The green dress?' Amber said. 'Remember, you took it off because you thought it looked so nice.'

'Oh, yeah, yeah. Wear that, it'll be cool.'

The concierge recommended a little crab restaurant out in Venice, and they got a cab, sitting in the back, holding hands like teenagers, pointing out the sights and looking at people, admiring this place that was so different from home. The cute little restaurant looked like a shack but with non-shack prices, Amber realised. That was the problem with staying in really cool hotels. When you told the concierge you wanted to go somewhere cheap and nice, he sent you to the cheapest place rich people went.

'This is so expensive, we better not have starters,' Amber whispered, scanning the menu.

'Hey, no problem, baby,' said Karl. 'I've got money, remember?'

It was lovely, Amber thought, to have some cash finally. At last she could buy some more clothes because her stuff from home wasn't suitable. Her flowery chain-store bikini, which looked really nice at home, looked sort of ordinary among all the little designer pieces the girls wore here.

'You'll have to give me some cash too,' she said, thinking of what she'd buy. 'For clothes and things.'

'Sure, should have thought of it before. Sorry.'

He took out his wallet, a new wallet, Amber realised, made of very soft suede leather. When had he been shopping? There was a nice fat wad of green notes in it, and Karl pulled out a few and handed them across to her at the precise moment that their waiter reappeared to take their order.

Amber grabbed the money and stuffed it into her purse, feeling hideously embarrassed. It was like she was a hooker and being paid in a restaurant. But neither Karl, nor the charming waiter, appeared to have thought so. The only person dying with embarrassment was Amber. Despite her happiness that things were working out for the band and that running away from home hadn't been in vain, and despite her joy that her relationship with Karl seemed to be back on track – even though he was a little different, and LA was working some magic on him – despite all the things she should have been grateful for, Amber was suddenly aware that something was wrong. She, Amber Reid, raised by her mother to believe in personal power and a woman's right to independence, had no job, no qualifications and was being handed 'pin money' by her boyfriend. That's what was wrong.

CHAPTER TWENTY-TWO

Maggie always laughed when people imagined there was any faint glamour to the world of academia.

Nobody in academia ever had any money and the only glamour resided in the feverish dreams of brilliant students who longed to star on *University Challenge*.

However, she got caught in precisely the same trap when it came to politics, assuming that politicians worked in a corporate world of money and style. It took just one visit to a city councillor to realise that politics was as much a glamour-free zone as college.

The knowledge hit her as she and her mother waited in the office of Liz Glebe, their local councillor, who was having her afternoon surgery. The only person there before them, an elderly man who kept anxiously scanning a well-thumbed piece of paper, had gone in to see Ms Glebe, so they were alone. The waiting room and the office reminded Maggie of an old shop where someone had ripped out the shelf units, painted the walls a sickly yellow and stuffed political pamphlets and posters everywhere, claiming better futures, better Irelands, better everything.

'Pity they don't have better chairs,' muttered Una, as she shifted to get comfortable on the plastic chair.

Liz Glebe was the first politician Maggie had contacted and when they finally got in to see her, she looked nothing like the glamorous, heavily made-up woman in the election posters that hung in her waiting room.

She still had short blonde hair and a wide smile but there were dark bags under her eyes, and her very conservative jacket and shirt looked as if they'd been to the dry-cleaner's too many times.

'Now, what's the problem?' she said, barely looking up at them while she shifted through sheets of paper on her desk. 'Summer Street pavilion, right? I know the background, shouldn't have happened, I voted against it. I have young kids myself and I hate to see the community being ripped apart, but I was in the minority, I'm afraid. It's pretty straight-forward – the pavilion was never a part of the park proper. It's officially council property. I'm not sure what you can do at this point.'

'Don't the people who actually use the park get any choice in the matter?' demanded Una irritably.

'Well, the concept of politics is that you elect us in, and we make the decisions,' Liz said, the mask of politeness slipping.

'Ridiculous idea,' Una snapped.

Maggie shot her mother a warning look.

'I'm on your side about the park,' Liz said.

'That's what everybody says come election time,' Una said, eyes narrowed.

'If you're on our side,' Maggie interrupted gently, 'perhaps you'd give us some advice on what we should do.'

Liz Glebe looked from mother to daughter and sighed.

'Go to see Harrison Mitchell. He's the Green Party coun-cillor for the area and he's made his name preserving old buildings. If there's any history at all to your pavilion, he's your man. And he likes hopeless cases – he loves appearing in the papers as the champion of the underdog.'

'Meaning he loves appearing in the papers or meaning he likes being the champion of the underdog?' Maggie inquired sharply.

'Think media whore and you won't go far wrong,' Liz said. 'Good luck.'

Harrison Mitchell wasn't keen on meeting the members of the Save Our Pavilion campaign because he was busy fighting for a medieval castle that the government were trying to build a motorway over. In terms of column inches, fighting the government and the motorway was a much more interesting story than fighting over the fate of a little park on Summer Street.

'He's very busy at the moment,' said his constituency secretary on the third occasion Maggie phoned. 'I have put your proposal to him but I just don't think he has the time.'

Something in Maggie snapped. The night before, she and her dad had walked around Summer Street park, talking about life, the universe and everything, admiring the flowers and ruefully thinking that if the campaign wasn't successful it might all look so different in a few months. Maggie had decided there and then that she was not going to lose this fight. She had lost so many fights in her life. Things were going to change.

She'd got a book from the library on self-confidence and had read it twice. Practising affirmations in front of the mirror in the morning felt a bit silly at first, but it seemed to work. After all, if you said, 'I feel useless', it had an effect, so surely the opposite was also true.

Start believing in yourself and stop knocking yourself, the book said. So simple and so true. And it was working.

327

'Fine,' Maggie said to the constituency secretary in pleasant tones. She knew exactly what to say, having practised this argument in front of the mirror earlier. 'You can tell Mr Mitchell that I'm giving a newspaper interview tomorrow and one of the main points I will be bringing up is his complete lack of interest in our pavilion. I'm going to point out that Mr Mitchell is obviously only interested in projects that get his name in the paper and that he has refused to see us on three separate occasions.'

'Now there's no need to be like this,' interrupted the secretary.

'Oh, there's every need,' said Maggie. 'Watch me.' She hung up.

Within fifteen minutes, she had an appointment to see Mr Mitchell the next afternoon.

'I can't go with you,' wailed Una. 'I've a doctor's appointment. You really need someone to go with you. You can't go and see someone like that on your own.'

'Nonsense,' said Maggie, feeling a certain amount of renewed vigour. 'I'll be fine.'

Harrison Mitchell's office was much grander than Liz Glebe's and was in the basement of his imposing Georgian three-storey terraced house. Handy to be a councillor when you were independently rich, thought Maggie, as she went down the steps into the basement, admiring topiary box trees sitting in giant stone troughs with just the correct amount of lichen on them. The effect was very beautiful and very grand.

She doubted that Mr Mitchell's waiting room would be covered with awful, sick yellow paint. She was right. It was a tasteful light blue with white cornices and a flower arrangement on a stand in an alcove.

'Sorry about the delay in seeing you,' said a man opening the door to her. It was Councillor Mitchell himself. Maggie recognised him from the newspapers. He was tall, good-looking, charming, and the product of an expensive education that gave in-built confidence. Maggie drew herself up to her full height and gave him a half-smile.

'I'm sorry it's taken us so long too,' she said coolly. Start as you mean to go on.

Politely, charmingly, Harrison Mitchell did his best to get out of helping with the Summer Street park campaign.

'I think that local people working together on something they really believe in is very powerful,' he said finally, after half an hour of discussing vague plans for what the protesters could do for their cause.

Maggie had had enough.

'You're a bit of a snob when it comes to conservation, aren't you?' she said. 'You like projects with historical connections or fabulous architectural proportions and to hell with anything that's of use to the community but doesn't fit your criteria.'

'That's not true,' he snapped.

'Yes it is,' said Maggie, listing the last five projects he'd been involved in. Every one of them was a historical site, despite his political literature claiming he was interested in saving community landmarks irrespective of their age or architectural beauty. 'I work in the library,' Maggie went on. 'And research is my specialist subject. We need your help. We've a lot of press planned,' she said, which was more or less true. Lots of newspapers and radio stations had been contacted but nobody was very interested yet. 'This could be a wonderful campaign for you. At least it would stop critics from saying you're only interested in getting your name in the papers,' she added, thinking that a month ago she'd never have had the courage to say something that ballsy.

Mitchell narrowed his eyes and looked at the telegenic

redhead before him. She'd be stunning in front of any sort of camera and she had chutzpah too.

'All right,' he said. 'But let me deal with the press.'

'Sorry,' said Maggie calmly, 'we'll deal with it together. This is our campaign, remember.'

She saw a flicker of respect in his eyes.

'OK,' he said. 'It's your campaign, Ms Maguire. You're the boss.'

Yes, thought Maggie proudly, I'm the boss.

It was nearly half past seven when she walked up Summer Street from the park end, still running over the meeting in her mind. She was so engrossed in her triumph that she almost didn't notice the man getting out of a car outside her house.

'Coming home from your car maintenance class?' said a low, deep voice behind her. Maggie knew it instantly. Big bear of a man with absolutely no social skills, greasy overalls and dirt under his fingernails. The man with the petrol sucker-outer.

She turned and stared at him. She might have walked in her gate without recognising him if it hadn't been for that voice. The overalls were gone and he was dressed casually in jeans and a cotton jumper that stretched slightly across his huge shoulders.

He cleaned up well, she conceded. Without the patina of garage grease, he was really rather attractive with those sparkling dark eyes. Not her type obviously; she didn't go in for those big men who looked like they never went to the gym, just heaved trucks around the garage to keep their muscles in shape.

'No, I've given up car maintenance. I'm in training for the space programme,' she said gravely. 'We're working on a plan to ship mankind off Earth and leave womankind behind.'

'All men? Or just ones who work in garages and make stupid jokes?'

'All men,' she said firmly.

'Where are we being sent?' he asked. He really was tall. Beside him, she felt positively fragile, which was something Maggie wasn't used to feeling.

'Somewhere with no oxygen.'

She tried to glare at him, but it was hard, because he was smiling at her, a relaxed smile as if he felt utterly comfortable.

'I don't suppose you can tell me when we're being shipped off: mankind, I mean,' he said, and it even *sounded* as if he was smiling. Honestly, what was the point of trying to be clever with someone who glinted sexy eyes back at you and looked wildly amused. 'Except I came to apologise. Sorry, I should have done it the day afterwards but I thought you might be too angry to listen to me. I wanted to invite you out to say sorry. By the way, how much time has mankind left before being shipped off to this unoxygenated planet?'

'You came to apologise and ask me out?' Maggie repeated, wondering if this was another joke.

'Unless NASA has a non-fraternisation policy,' he added, 'and you can't. For reasons of international security.'

He *was* teasing her, but it was gentle and Maggie found she quite liked it.

'Only intelligent life forms are considered a threat to national security,' she pointed out with a hint of sarcasm, leaving him in no doubt that she figured he was in the non-intelligent life-form quotient.

'Well, then it'll be fine for you to go out with me,' he said evenly. 'Next Saturday at two. It's my cousin's wedding.'

'A wedding? You don't ask someone you've just met to a wedding,' she said suspiciously. 'I barely know you. I can't remember your name.'

331

'Ivan Gregory,' he said. 'We met at my garage.'

'I know where we met,' she said hastily. 'So, why are you here asking me out? Did your girlfriend dump you because of your awful practical jokes?' Even as she said it, she knew it was bitchy and not worthy of either her or poor Ivan. But he took it well.

'No,' he said, 'she dumped me because of the body odour. Every Christmas I got deodorant, aftershave, washing powder. I think finally she realised the message wasn't getting through.'

'All right,' said Maggie, grinning in spite of herself. 'Go on, what's the real reason? You don't turn up at your cousin's wedding with a woman no one in your family knows and nobody has ever heard of.'

'They're a bit mad in my family,' Ivan said, with a glint in his eyes. 'They won't mind. They'll be astonished that a jumped-up pump jockey has a date at all.'

Maggie flushed at that, remembering what she'd called him before. She'd better rethink her original evaluation. He was anything but stupid.

'Are we going to the whole wedding?' Maggie asked. 'The church, the dinner, the whole thing? Because if we are and it's fancy, I have to tell you, I don't do fancy. I'm more of a jeans woman.'

'I don't do fancy very well myself,' Ivan said gravely. 'Although I was going to make an exception in this case. Maybe buy a new pair of overalls. But the rock chick look would be fine.' He flicked an appreciative eye over her outfit, which was Maggie's standard look of jeans, cowboy boots and a peach-coloured T-shirt that clung to her slim body and showed off the rich russet of her trailing curls. Her new business jacket was slung over one shoulder. 'Be yourself,' he said.

Now Maggie really did laugh. 'Be yourself is one of those things people say when they don't really mean it and they don't know what else to say.'

'No,' said Ivan, with all seriousness. 'I mean it: be yourself. What else would you be?'

Maggie thought of all the different people she tried to be in her life. At school, she'd tried to blend in so nobody would notice her. Eventually, she tried to be tough, because invisible hadn't worked. Tough had been a good compromise. People left you alone if you were a bit tough.

She'd been working that whole 'don't mess with me' phase when she'd met Grey. She toned it down, then, becoming softer, letting her hair grow the way Grey loved. In other words, she'd been what she thought everyone wanted. And here was a man who wanted her to be herself.

Well, she might as well give it a try. After all, she had nothing very pressing to do.

'OK,' she said. 'I'll come with you. Not as a date, right?' The new improved Maggie, chairwoman of an important committee and worthy foil of politicians, said what she meant these days.

'No,' agreed Ivan easily, 'not as a date.'

Maggie didn't pursue why he needed somebody at such short notice. There was bound to be a story in it, but she'd find out later. 'You'll pick me up then on Saturday?'

'Your house at two?' he said.

'Done,' Maggie said, 'and I won't be wearing a hat.'

'A hat's not required.'

For a wedding she didn't want to go to, where she was going to meet lots of people she didn't know, Maggie found herself remarkably involved in trying to work out what to wear. On Friday evening, her mother sat on the bed and they went through all the various options.

'A little dress always works,' said Shona on the phone earlier when asked for advice, 'but then you don't have any little dresses, do you?'

'Shona, you know my wardrobe,' Maggie said. 'The last time there was a little dress in it, I was four. Although Mum probably still has the item in question stuffed up in the attic, I am unlikely to fit into it.'

'What about the bridesmaid's dress you wore to my wedding?'

'There is that,' Maggie conceded, 'but it's very glamorous and over the top for a man I don't know. I can't wear that.'

'Oh God, I don't know,' groaned Shona. 'Ring me when you're sorting through the clothes and I'll give advice.'

'Trinny and Susannah by phone?'

'Maybe not,' agreed Shona. 'Wear lots of lipstick, then. It'll detract from the jeans.'

'I have more than jeans, you know. I have other trousers too.'

'I know, but unless the trousers are part of a chic trouser suit with a matching jacket, then you're not going to be very weddingy, are you?'

'What do you think of this?' Maggie asked her mother, holding up a midnight-blue silk camisole, with sparkly, fake jewels sewn on the front. A thrift-shop purchase, it was a little worn around the edges but Maggie liked it.

'That's lovely,' sighed her mother. 'It's pretty. Now, what will you wear with it?'

There followed a big search through the piles of jeans, smaller pile of black trousers and Maggie's two skirts. One was a distressed velvet affair that had possibly once been brown and was now mottled and faded, in a way that was either fabulously beautiful or totally shabby, Maggie wasn't sure which.

'I don't know about that now,' said Una doubtfully. 'If it was fancy dress, that would be great but . . . Well, try it on anyway and we'll see.'

'Cinderella, before the transformation by the fairy godmother,' Maggie decided, when she'd pulled on the skirt.

'Oh, now, don't say that,' chided her mother. 'With a bit of make-up and if you curl your hair up, you'll be the belle of the ball.'

'Mum, I think that fall affected your brain,' teased Maggie, stripping off.

Her mother laughed. 'That's what your father says. How would he know, that's what I say! Now look at that lovely skirt.'

She pulled out Maggie's only other skirt, which Grey had once urged her to buy. A fitted pencil skirt that showed off her long, slim legs, she had worn it only once, for the purpose of Grey removing it.

'That'd look beautiful on you, Maggie. You never show off your legs.'

'I don't know,' said Maggie reluctantly, because there was a very good reason why she didn't show off her legs, which was that people would look at them. 'Anyway, I've no tights.' What would you need tights for if you didn't wear skirts?

'I'll get you some of mine,' volunteered her mother, hobbling off on her crutches at speed.

Finally, there were the beginnings of an outfit.

Maggie barely recognised this slim girl in the mirror with the long, long legs encased in sheer nylons and the sleek skirt clinging to her hips.

A memory came to her, a harsh, bullying voice telling her she was ugly, *a long streak of misery*, *like a boy*. Those taunts had had their effect: for years, Maggie had believed them. And yet now, she looked all right, didn't she?

'I suppose a white blouse maybe?' she said, unsure.

'You'll look like a waitress,' said her mother. 'No, it has to be colour. What's wrong with the midnight-blue camisole?'

'No,' said Maggie, thinking that she'd look totally unlike herself then with shoulders and throat on show as well as her legs. 'I wish I had someone to borrow something off.'

335

'Pity Elisabeth's in Seattle,' said her mother. 'She always has amazing clothes, all designer stuff too, you know. And if you had kept in touch with some of the girls from school, you'd be able to ring them up and borrow clothes off them too.'

'Yeah,' said Maggie shortly. She put the camisole back on.

'You look beautiful,' sighed her mother. 'I'll get out my marcasite earrings and necklace for you and Ivan won't be able to take his eyes off you.'

'He's only asking me because his date did a runner,' Maggie pointed out, not entirely correctly. It was what she'd said to her parents to explain how she'd happened to be invited to a wedding by a man none of them knew.

'Well, it'll get you out of the house and over that horrible old Grey,' said her mother, firmly. 'The louser. If your father ever gets his hands on Grey Stanley, well, let me tell you: we'll need bail money, that's all I'm saying.'

Saturday morning in the library flew by. They were incredibly busy and Maggie didn't have a moment to mull over her pleasure that she had a date for the rest of the afternoon. Still, it was nice to be able to answer, 'Yes, I'm going out to a wedding,' when people asked her what she was doing with her half-day off.

Better than saying, 'No, I'm going to sit at home and mope about my ex-boyfriend who bonked someone else.' Definitely, a social life made you feel more positive. She'd got up early and washed her hair and even put some of that curl separator stuff in, so that it was now lots of rippling, glossy waves, instead of the usual faintly frizzy curls.

'You look lovely,' said Tina as they rushed about behind the desk. 'Is your man from Galway coming back?'

'No, actually,' murmured Maggie. 'It's a different guy altogether.'

Tina looked impressed. 'I'm pleased for you. I mean he seemed lovely, your man, and everything, but . . .' she stopped.

'But what?' asked Maggie, fascinated.

'He was a bit too pleased with himself, wasn't he? Those gorgeous fellas always are. No one will ever love him quite as much as he loves himself.'

Maggie grinned. 'I think you hit the nail on the head there, Tina,' she said. 'It's one thing competing with other women, but you can't compete with the guy himself, can you?'

'You said it,' replied Tina, in a voice that said she knew what she was talking about.

Funny, thought Maggie, turning back to the desk, who would have thought that sedate Tina had a big history of men behind her? But you never knew. Everybody had secrets and dramas in their lives, they just didn't wear them on their faces.

Maggie had just come back from her coffee break and was making her way back to the library desk, when she realised with a shock that she recognised a woman who had just walked in. Billie Deegan, one of the bullying gang of girls who'd made Maggie's life hell.

Billie had never been as bad as the gang leader, Sandra Brody. But just seeing her made fifteen years drop away. Maggie felt the way she always had: her intestines literally churning with fear, her heart thumping, her hands clammy.

Billie was holding a small boy's hand and seemed totally and utterly oblivious of Maggie. Her hairstyle, her expression, were exactly the same as they'd been all those years ago when she'd swiped Maggie's school bag and tossed it to Sandra, laughing like a hyena as Sandra tipped the contents over the playground.

Unable to stop herself, Maggie ducked in behind a shelf, heart pounding, and listened.

'Now, love,' Billie said to the boy, 'we've got to be out of

337

the library in five minutes. Come on, pick a book, will you? We can't be here all day, we're going to meet Daddy. He'll go mad if we're late, you know what he's like.' The boy stood looking lost. 'Oh, come on now! Hurry up!'

Leaning against a shelf, knowing it was ridiculous to feel the fear still, Maggie lived again those four years of hell. Even now, she couldn't quite explain how it made her feel, how frightened, how despairing. There was a brief time when Sandra's game was stealing and vandalising her possessions, when she'd wondered if killing herself was an option.

At least then she wouldn't be picked on. At least then she wouldn't wake up on a Monday morning with sheer dread in every atom of her being.

Sometimes now she read articles in the newspaper about bullying. The reporters who had written them had never been victims themselves, she could tell. They wrote about it as if it were a minor blip, something that occurred a couple of hours every day and then you'd move on to another part of your life. Those writers never realised that the bullying *became* your life, took hold of it, destroyed you.

'Maggie,' said Tina loudly, indicating the queue. 'We need you over here, sorry. I'm on the phone.'

Maggie took a deep breath and almost ran to the safety of the desk. Automatically, she stamped books, smiling at the children and their parents, saying things like 'The Narnia books are fabulous. I loved them when I was little, still reread them.'

And the children would grin and their parents would grin even more, glad to see their kids reading.

Tina was on the phone again, trying to tell some woman that the Jacqueline Wilson still hadn't come in. The queue was getting shorter, bringing Billie closer to Maggie.

Get off the phone, please, Tina, Maggie thought in anguish. Please get off the phone and deal with this woman. There were two more to go before Billie and her son now.

Peering up surreptitiously, Maggie watched her. Yes, Billie looked exactly the same, still hard and still with that dead-straight platinum-blonde haircut, probably not dyed at home any more, and the heavy eyeliner ringing her eyes into two cold slits of muddy blue. She and Sandra had been the eyeliner queens of St Ursula's, even when make-up was forbidden. They hadn't paid attention to the rules, naturally: rules were for other people.

Her clothes were remarkably normal: a long-sleeved top and pale trousers, none of them ripped or bearing a rude logo. That had been another of Billie and Sandra's idiosyncrasies. Outside school, they'd favoured tiny T-shirts, ripped leather jackets, tight pale-blue jeans and high-heeled boots. The punk slut look, Maggie's friend, Kitty, called it.

She and Maggie loved that name: being able to call the bullies something rude. It gave them a tiny, welcome sense of power. It was a shame when Kitty's family had moved away.

'Now, Jimmy, give the woman your book and we'll get out of here,' said Billie.

Maggie had no option. Keeping her eyes down, she scanned the book number, stamped it and handed it to the child, not saying one word.

'Thank you,' the woman said. 'Jimmy, say thank you.'

Maggie was gobsmacked. Thank you hadn't been in Billie's vocabulary when Maggie knew her.

'Thank you,' said Jimmy obediently.

He was eight or nine, Maggie reckoned, so Billie must have got pregnant soon enough after they'd left school. For a flicker of a moment, she wondered if Billie's life had been hard at that time, then dismissed it: Billie Deegan didn't need her pity.

'Come on, Jimmy, we'd better go,' and without exchanging one single glance with Maggie, Billie marched him out of the library.

There was a small stool behind the counter and Maggie sank on to it. Only days before, she'd spoken to Christie Devlin about laying her demons to rest and now, here was one of the bullies in her life. That bitch. Maggie hated her with a venom time hadn't diminished and, yet, Billie had strolled in happily, smiling, lively, as if she had no idea what she'd done, what she and her mocking pals had done to Maggie's life. How could she not know?

'Tina,' Maggie said urgently, 'I just feel sick, can I run to the loo for one minute?'

Tina, who had just replaced the phone, nodded. Maggie fled to the staff toilets where she locked herself in a cubicle, sat down on a seat and held her face in her hands. She could feel her cheeks burning and still, that familiar ache in her intestines. Sandra and her cronies had always been a cure for constipation. Rage, anger, impotence and fury flooded through Maggie. Laying your demons to rest was one thing but why now, why today?

Maggie had cleaned up the mascara that she had cried down her cheeks and reapplied more by the time Ivan arrived at the house to pick her up.

'Hello, Maggie,' he said, admiring her outfit. 'You look great.'

He looked pretty good too, all spruced up in a suit and tie.

'Thanks,' said Maggie shortly. She had read a book once about accepting compliments and apparently you had to say, 'Thank you, that's lovely,' instead of 'Oh, this old thing, I've had it for a hundred years,' or 'My boyfriend gave me this skirt and I never normally wear it.'

They got into Ivan's car, which was suitably Ivan, being a classic something or other. Maggie knew nothing about cars but it had to be old, what with the ancient dashboard and seats that looked like they came from a 1960s art installation.

He was playing classical music, Dvořák, if Maggie could remember anything from her music classes, a million years ago.

'That isn't the music I pictured you listening to,' she said.

'No?' he said good humouredly. 'What did you think? I'd be a Guns N' Roses sort of guy, one of those dudes who plays air guitar and dances with his legs spread apart, shaking his head.'

As this was an accurate assessment of what she'd thought of Ivan the first time she'd met him, she didn't reply to that but said: 'Lots of people aren't into classical music any more.'

'My mother taught piano,' he said. 'I grew up with music. It lifts me.'

'My dad's the same,' she replied. 'He went through a classical music phase. There were phases for everything. Phases for learning about stars and phases for learning about classical music. He's into opera too. I quite like it as well, but not played full blast, which is how Dad says you have to play it. His current phase is model-making. Planes and boats.'

'That sounds nice,' said Ivan. 'I like the idea of being a model-maker myself.'

He was easy company, Maggie thought. She didn't have to make an effort to be scintillating or funny. She just had to be. Sit there in the car and let the conversation roll on, or not, as the case may be. Ivan was quite happy to let the strains of Dvořák glide over them. Undemanding, that was it. Grey had been demanding, she realised suddenly.

She'd never had anything to compare him to but Ivan was so relaxed, the contrast showed Grey up.

'You're not quite yourself today,' Ivan said abruptly, putting the kibosh on the judgement.

'What do you mean?' she asked defensively.

'You've been crying.'

She flipped down the passenger visor and looked into the mirror. She'd cleaned away all the mascara, but her eyes were a teeny bit red.

'Most guys wouldn't have noticed,' she said.

'I'm not most guys,' he replied. 'Do you want to talk?'

'No,' she said firmly. 'I don't.'

But she couldn't stop thinking about her shock that morning. The worst thing about it was that she had been made to realise that she hadn't got over being bullied, not one little bit. And that made her conscious that the past would always imprison her unless she did something about it. But what?

It was a very modern wedding, although nobody seemed to have told the majority of the guests. The women, decked out in floral frocks, hats like galleons perched on their heads, with fluffy feather boas, dainty jewelled handbags and shoes in summery colours, all stared aghast at the bridal party who might have come straight out of Italian *Vogue* in their shades of cream and slate grey.

The bride wore a cream shift, so simple it looked as though Maggie herself could have run it up on her mother's old Singer machine, although it was so stylish the label undoubtedly proclaimed it as a piece of designer art from a Milanese atelier.

The groom wore a Nehru-collared suit in slate with his groomsmen similarly attired and the bridesmaids wore slate-grey shift dresses, with tiny posies of cream roses.

'Very hip and trendy,' Maggie said, trying to find the right thing to say.

'Where are the frills?' a woman in the pew beside her was wailing. 'What's the point in getting married if you can't have frills and flowers and ... look at that for a bouquet, one hopeless flower. Desperate, that's what it is.'

The bride indeed carried only one flower, although Maggie wouldn't have called it hopeless, but she had never been a fan of those birds of paradise blooms. It looked like a plant that had somehow eaten a passing bird.

'Well, it's what they wanted, obviously,' she said to the woman beside her.

'You're very diplomatic,' said Ivan. 'I hate it.'

'I didn't think you had any interest in high fashion at all,' she teased him. 'I thought your only cosmetic interest would be in whatever miracle product you use to get the grease out of your hands after a day in the garage.'

'You mean after a day of honest, hard labour?' he said, holding up hands that were spotlessly clean.

Without thinking, Maggie took one of them to examine it. 'How do you manage that? If I do any painting or anything in the apartment, I'm filthy for days. You can't get stuff like that off your hands. What do you use?'

'Trade secret,' he murmured, 'but I might be prepared to reveal it to the right person.'

She dropped his hand quickly.

At the reception, they were at a table made up of various cousins, which included Ivan's brother, Leon, who looked a lot like Ivan, although Leon had more of a wolfish look to his face, as if he might pounce at any moment.

'Where has my big bro been hiding you?' he said to Maggie.

'Leave her alone,' said Ivan, good-naturedly. 'Leon's always wanted everything of mine,' he added to Maggie. 'Trains, toy soldiers, whatever.'

She was about to say, sharply, that she didn't belong to Ivan, therefore it was immaterial whether Leon wanted her or not, but for some reason she didn't. Instead, she talked to the cousin on the other side, a seventeen-year-old boy who'd brought along his girlfriend but who was clearly desperately shy, amidst all these idolised big cousins.

343

It was a wonderful day. Maggie normally enjoyed weddings about as much as she enjoyed twenty-four-hour migraines, but this one was different. Despite the bridal party stylefest, everyone else at the wedding was comfortingly ordinary. Most people were out to have fun – a few mad uncles throwing shapes on the dance floor, somebody grabbing the mike from the DJ to belt out 'Fever' off key and a gaggle of wildly sophisticated young girls, dancing together, looking horrified at the carryings-on of the older generation.

'Appalling!' Maggie heard one of them mutter. 'What will people think?'

'Were you like that once?' Ivan asked Maggie, watching her watching the girls dancing.

She was startled: she hadn't realised he was so close to her. People had moved seats after the meal and she'd turned hers so that she could look at the dance floor, which meant that she didn't really have to talk to anybody.

'No,' she said, caught off her guard. 'I was the ultimate uncool girl.'

'Really?' he said.

'Yeah, really,' she said.

'What about you?' she asked, just to shift the subject slightly.

'It seems so long ago, I can't remember,' he said thoughtfully, and Maggie figured out it had probably been great for him. People who didn't remember generally had enjoyed good school days. The awful stuff you didn't forget.

He added, 'I'm a few years older than you, thirty-seven next birthday.'

'Is your biological clock ticking then?' Maggie asked wickedly. 'Well, that's what thirty-six-year-old women get asked, it seems only fair to return the compliment.'

'I'm a mechanic,' Ivan said gravely. 'If anything starts ticking, I fix it, you know that.'

He persuaded her up to dance, but she only said yes because it was a fast dance, one where they could move without touching.

Not that there was something wrong with Ivan. In fact, there was absolutely nothing wrong with him from the top of his cropped dark head to his surprisingly elegant leather shoes. She was sure plenty of women longed to be in her place and she'd seen a few eyes cast enviously in their direction during the day. Well, they could have him, no matter how gorgeous he was. He wasn't for her. She didn't want any man.

'I hope you enjoyed yourself,' he said that night as he dropped her home.

They sat in the car outside her house, the engine growling while Maggie picked up her small handbag from the floor. 'Yes, I did. Thank you for asking me.'

'I wondered because you seemed to be in another place a lot of the time,' Ivan said gently. 'I hope everything's all right. If there is anything I can do to help . . .' His voice trailed off.

Maggie felt embarrassed that he'd noticed.

'I'm fine,' she said. 'Sorry, I didn't mean to spoil the party.'

'You didn't spoil it,' he said, smiling at her, those dark eyes glinting under the streetlights. 'You were lovely, they all liked you.'

'Who are they?' she asked.

The smile turned wolfish, like Leon's had been, and she could certainly see why the envious looks had been cast in their direction all day. When he smiled like that, sexily, Ivan was pretty irresistible.

'All my relatives. They were watching you surreptitiously. You didn't happen to see the big notice board in the hall with people giving you marks out of ten on performance, deportment, dressage –'

345

'Stop it,' she said, laughing. 'OK then, how did I score?'

He appeared to think about this. 'Pretty good from all I hear, although there was some talk about the fact that you didn't throw your arms around me or kiss me enough. Or that we didn't dance any slow dances together.'

Maggie felt embarrassed again, this time for a different reason. 'We weren't going as a couple,' she reminded him, although she felt strangely pleased that he might have wanted this.

'I know that,' he agreed, 'but you can't stop the relatives talking, can you? Any woman who appears on the horizon, they're hoping I'll slip a wedding ring on her finger. And don't forget, as you've pointed out yourself, my biological clock is ticking.'

'Oh, shut up, Ivan,' laughed Maggie and she leaned over and kissed him on the cheek, her lips brushing the faintest hint of stubble. 'I'll talk to you soon,' she said, and got out of the car.

He didn't drive off until she'd opened the door, stepped inside and waved at him from the lit hallway. He was a gentleman, he hadn't tried to pounce on her, he behaved exactly as he said he would behave, she thought. She liked Ivan and, as Faye said, she could do with a friend. But for the moment, she told herself firmly, as she got ready for bed, that was all.

CHAPTER TWENTY-THREE

The night before she went to see Carey Wolensky, Christie cooked the most beautiful dinner for her husband she had ever cooked in her life. She put everything into it that he loved, along with herbs, carefully tended from her own garden, and thirty-five years of love, affection, kindness and gratefulness. As she cooked, Tilly wound herself around Christie's ankles, clearly in one of her 'pet me, pet me' moods, making little whimpering noises occasionally. Christie bent and stroked the dog's pansy-soft head many times. She adored Rocket but had to admit that Tilly was, ever so slightly, her favourite. Tilly loved Christie above everyone else in the world and there was something so very wonderful about any creature who loved you with that unconditional love.

She felt a little like a white witch cooking up a spell of love in her kitchen with her familiar, gorgeous Tilly, weaving in and out of her ankles, and her modern cooker in place of the kind white witch's fireplace. Was she cooking up a meal to ask forgiveness for what would happen afterwards or to ward off anything bad happening at all? Christie didn't know which.

'Wow, that all smells amazing,' said James, coming downstairs and dropping his report on the kitchen table. Going over to the cooker, he put his hands around Christie's waist and leaned over her shoulder, giving her a gentle kiss on the cheek, before peering down to see exactly what she was making.

'Is that roast vegetable soup?' he said. 'I love that, but you said it's such a pain to make.'

'No, I didn't,' said Christie, 'it's just a little time-consuming, that's all. I felt like making soup today.'

'Absolutely,' agreed James, leaning over a bit further so he could inhale the rich scent, 'and why not. It's a gloriously hot, sunny day and roasted vegetable soup is exactly the sort of thing I had on my mind tonight.'

'Brat,' she said, laughing. 'I cook you one of your favourite things and you don't appreciate it.'

'I'm teasing,' he said. He moved away, stifling a large yawn. 'I'm wrecked. If we don't get this report finished soon, I'll retire early, I'm telling you.'

He sat down in his usual seat at the kitchen table and picked up the newspaper which was folded at the crossword.

'I got most of it done earlier but I'm stuck on eleven down,' he said. 'I'm having a mental block – it's the name of that Nathaniel Hawthorne novel: Hawthorne's red message, the clue is . . .'

'*The Scarlet Letter*,' said Christie faintly, thinking of Hester Prynne forced to wear a big red A on her chest as a sign of her adultery.

'Ah, that's it!' James said. 'Thank God I married a clever wife.'

'Yes,' she said. How did people do it – conduct full-blown affairs without dying of pain and guilt and shame? It was beyond her.

She had set up a table outside in the garden and they ate on the terrace with the dogs at their feet, the scent of Christie's flowers mingling with the scent of the food. After the roasted vegetable soup came dressed crab, another of James's favourites and a rarity in the Devlin house because crab was expensive and Christie didn't like to buy it dressed, preferring to do it herself. It was cheaper but there was still a lot of palaver about it.

'You're not leaving me are you?' joked James, when pudding arrived and it turned out to be crème brûlé, his absolute, all-time favourite.

'No,' said Christie, managing a smile. She'd recovered her equilibrium somewhat thanks to two glasses of lovely wine. 'I just can't wait for the exams to be over and life can go back to normal.'

'So this is the almost-the-end-of-exams party?' James teased.

'Yes,' Christie replied, as if it had all been perfectly obvious. 'And can I not cook you a beautiful meal without there having to be a reason?' she demanded. 'Are you implying I am such a slatternly housekeeper that you have beans on toast every night, unless I'm running off with the milkman?' There, she'd made a joke about it.

'No darling, sorry,' James said. 'I didn't mean that at all. You're amazing, you know that? I always think you're an amazing woman, Christie, and I hope I say it often enough – after thirty-five years it's easy enough to forget to say it, but you are. It was a lucky day, the day I met you.'

'Oh, stop,' she said, afraid she might burst into tears.

'No, I mean it,' James said gravely.

When dinner was over, they sat in the garden for a while, talking, finishing the bottle of wine, watching dusk darken into night. Then they cleared up and went up to bed. Christie loved their bedroom. As a child, she and Ana had shared a cold hard little room with bare walls because their father hated nails knocked into the walls in case they damaged the plaster. So nothing could ever be hung to offset the pale-blue gloom. There had never been any money for furbelows, either, so the curtains were basic bits of cloth to keep the light out, and the furniture did nothing more than hold clothes. There was no beauty, no piece of art just for the sake of it, like a pretty vase or a picture.

By contrast, this room was a comfortable, beautiful room full of lovely pieces with no use whatsoever except to be looked at, like the driftwood Christie and James had found on a beach in Connemara thirty years ago and hung on one wall, or the vintage fan that dangled from the mantelpiece as if just left there by some elegant lady of the past.

Dominating this bower of lovely comforting things was a huge bed, where Christie had sat with her sons and James, all cuddled up in the mornings. It was where she'd lain with baby Shane and breast-fed him, Ethan sitting on the bed, playing with his toys, grumbling about not getting enough attention sometimes. Other times, he'd tried to cuddle up on top of Shane and Christie, making her laugh and making baby Shane squeal in outrage. And in this bed, she and James had made love countless times over the years.

James was very laid-back about decor and had always left it up to Christie, saying he hadn't minded whatever she did. Now, the room was full of rich autumnal colours, with a huge patchwork spread in rust, copper and old gold made up in satins and velvets swathing the bed. Tonight, they pulled back the covers, sank into the sheets and James pulled her into his arms. Christie had never, or rarely, felt like crying when she made love. Sometimes the intensity of the moment would make her eyes well up afterwards as they lay there and she thought of how wonderful it was, that perfect close-ness from being with someone you loved. But tonight, every caress, every kiss, every erotic touch, made her long to cry with the meaning of it all. Because this might be the last time she and James ever made love.

When he traced a line down from her neck to the softness of her breasts – once so full and high and now, a lifetime and children later, lower, less firm, but just as beautiful in his eyes, or so he always said – she felt as if she would start to weep and not stop. As he kissed her, she felt the unbearable poignancy of doing something she loved and might lose. The last kiss, the last caress, the last time his familiar body entered hers. She knew the noises James made when he climaxed, the same way she knew her own face in the mirror, the same way she was sure he knew the small sounds she made in passion.

And then they held each other, and the tears came. She couldn't help herself, she couldn't hold them back. She'd been holding everything back all evening, thinking everything was the last time.

'Darling, are you all right?' asked James.

'I'm fine,' Christie said, her face against his shoulder, their bodies still joined. 'I'm fine, just, that was so beautiful.' And they lay there, holding each other until eventually she could hear her husband's breathing getting heavier and she knew he had fallen asleep.

She slipped away from him gently, so as not to wake him, and went into the bathroom to clean her face and wipe away the ravages of the tears. Looking in the mirror, she saw a woman who had everything and didn't deserve it. In that moment she hated herself.

Sometimes, the ordinary and the everyday was boring. When she was younger, Christie used to long for the extraordinary, something different to happen in Kilshandra, something to shake them all up and make life thrilling.

Yearning for excitement was definitely for young people, she decided, as she closed her door the next morning and looked out across Summer Street to the park. Once you had tasted extraordinary and the dangers it brought, you longed for the familiar and you thought how precious that was.

Today, she yearned for the mundane because today, she was going to see Carey Wolensky.

She walked more slowly up Summer Street than usual because she was wearing high heels. Against all her better judgement, she had decided to show off her still-good legs in high shoes and her figure in a wrap dress that clung in all the right places, with a necklace of larger-than-life pearls that hid the creeping at her throat. She wondered if he'd think her beautiful still or would he think that time had been very cruel.

'Hello, Christie, how are you?' yelled Una Maguire from her front garden where she was directing operations, with Dennis on his knees, weeding. Poor Dennis hadn't a clue about the garden, Christie knew. It was only sheer love of his wife that had him out there at all, poking around in the earth with all the vision of a mole.

'Where are you off to? Into town shopping?'

'Yes, shopping,' said Christie, because after all she was dressed very grandly for such an hour on a Monday. If it wasn't for the height of her heels and the silky sheerness of her stockings, a person might have thought she was on her way to see her bank manager, but no bank manager merited such a slinky outfit.

'How's your leg?' Christie paused outside Una's gate, not having the time to go in, but wanting to be sociable.

'Not so bad now. Before you know it, the cast will be off and I'll be a new woman.'

Would she? Christie wondered, getting that sense she had before of Una's bones as fragile and lacy, instead of strong and firm.

'You should take care of yourself, Una,' she said, sternly.

'Oh, I have Dennis to take care of me,' Una said happily. 'Don't I, love?'

Dennis nodded enthusiastically.

'How's Maggie?' asked Christie, because she knew that

352

Maggie was the person who did the real taking care of in that house.

'She's in good form, you know,' Una said. 'Very busy with the committee. You wouldn't believe all she's organised – publicity, an official complaint to the council and they're getting legal advice too. It's all go.'

Christie waved goodbye to the Maguires and headed past the café, which seemed unbearably comforting and homely this morning. Wouldn't it have been nice if it was a normal day, before all this had happened, when she could sit there, eating a scone, chatting with people, thinking about her nice, safe simple life ahead of her? Life before Carey had come back.

Christie did not frequent many of the city's grand hotels, but her very presence was commanding enough, so that when she walked into Carey's hotel, a stately block that overlooked the best square in Dublin, people looked up.

'May I help you, madam?' The young woman at the desk inclined her head graciously, like minor royalty greeting somebody.

'Yes, I have a meeting with Mr Wolensky,' Christie said coolly, hoping she looked like some important art dealer, rather than a woman with a past. 'Mrs Devlin,' she added, with a regal nod of her own. Christie didn't play games but she didn't suffer snubs either.

'Oh, yes, Mr Wolensky's waiting for you in the Maharajah Suite. Shall I get somebody to show you up?'

The receptionist's attitude had changed at the mention of Carey's name. Clearly he was just as good as he'd ever been at knocking pretension out of those around him, although he probably did it with money and power now, when once he'd done it with charisma and sheer animal presence.

'That would be good, thank you,' Christie said, as if every morning of her life involved being shown into the Maharajah Suite.

A young uniformed man escorted her up five floors in the lift and into an ornate corridor where they passed several doors bearing the names of long-dead dukes and countesses before arriving at the Maharajah Suite. A second young man opened the door and brought Christie into a huge drawing room, decorated in the eastern style.

'Tea, coffee or would you prefer something else?' he asked.

'Coffee please,' Christie said, thinking that this was getting even more bizarre.

She sat on the edge of a fat, bronze-coloured armchair with her coffee in her hand and looked around. It was an opulent room full of plump brocade cushions, rich dark splashes of fabric and vast creamy candles that had never been burned. It all screamed money, good taste and phenomenal success. What a different life Carey had led to hers.

And then, a door to the right opened and he was there in front of her.

'Hello, Christie,' he said and his voice was just the same, with the same power to thrill her, but his face was different.

He'd aged too. There was no Dorian Gray portrait in his attic. He was still tall and vibrantly alive, but now the dark hair was streaked like a magpie's with brilliant white and his face was craggy, with heavy lines where there had been smooth skin, and he had a sadness about him that spoke volumes.

'Hello, Carey,' said Christie, thinking how stupid it sounded. Twenty-five years of waiting and at least six weeks of having panic attacks about this very moment, and the best she could manage was 'Hello, Carey.'

'It's a beautiful room.' She got up and walked over to the window, to give herself something to do. She didn't really see the streets below her.

'You haven't changed,' he said. His accent was still the same: deep and dark, the Polish edge as strong and caressing as ever.

Christie turned around when she judged it was safe to do

so. 'Of course I've changed, Carey. I'm older and wiser and so are you, I hope. So tell me, tell me about your life.'

She sat down on one of the Louis XIV chairs as if they were ordinary old friends meeting up after many years to chat happily about acquaintances, times past and the fun they used to have. If she kept it at that level, then the conversation might stay there, might never stray into the terrifying territory of love, lust and passion.

'You're talking to me strangely,' he said, sitting down opposite her. 'What is this chatter? *How are you?*' he said, 'like we were strangers.'

'You know that was always one of the annoying things about you, Carey,' she said, 'you always refused to play the games, the games other people played.'

'You mean like pretending that we are just old friends, who mean nothing to one another?' he asked. 'You're right, I never played the games, and I still made it.'

'You made it because of your talent,' she retorted. 'It was nothing to do with your rudeness.'

'If speaking the truth is rude,' he said calmly, 'I'd prefer to live my life that way, not to lie, not to push the past away, like you're doing.'

'Well, that didn't take long,' Christie said and realised she'd spoken out loud. 'We're four minutes in each other's company and already all the façade is gone.' And she smiled at him, because it was impossible not to.

'That is one of the things I liked about you, Christie,' he said. 'You were not good at pretending either. You tried to be, but you were not good.'

'No,' she said quickly, 'I wasn't good at the pretence. Carey, why did you come back?' she said abruptly, and that was the right thing to say because it was what she'd wanted to know.

'I came to have an exhibition here, you know that.'

She searched his eyes for answers. Years ago, he'd been

355

good at hiding what he was feeling, but now Christie was older and wiser, she felt she'd be able to discern what he was really thinking.

'No, you didn't,' she said suddenly. 'Tell me the truth, why did you come?'

'I came to see you,' he said.

She'd known that was what he was going to say. She had never forgotten him and it seemed that he'd never forgotten her either.

'Oh, Carey, Carey,' she sighed, 'I told you a long time ago that you had to go away, for my sake, for both our sakes.'

'I just wanted to see you,' he said gently, 'to see what you looked like now, to see if you still had the power you had over me. And you do, it seems. You've seen the paintings?'

It was a question and she nodded.

'They're you, you know, all those paintings, my dark lady.'

'I'd worked that out,' Christie said carefully, 'and it frightened me, because I was afraid everyone would know and would guess it was me.'

'I never showed your face,' he said.

'I know, thank you. I was always grateful for that.'

'I could have, you know. I could have shown your face and broken up your marriage and you would have come to me.' There was real pain in his voice for the first time and Christie wanted to hold him and comfort him, but she knew she couldn't. She had never been able to touch him without feeling that flood of wild passion surge through her. It was a thing apart, a feeling she'd never been able to control. He was that other part of her, the fierce, wild side. And she'd had to give him up.

Now she picked up her coffee cup again. 'It would never have worked, you knew that. You didn't want a wife and two children tagging around behind you. That's not the life of an artist. And I had to think of my children first. I wanted my sons to know their father. If you and I had been together, they wouldn't have known James, not properly, and they wouldn't have had you either. Quiet family life was never your destiny. Your only mistress is your art.'

Sadness flitted across his face.

'That was true once,' he admitted, 'but it wouldn't have been the case if I'd had you. I loved you more than art, I could have given it up for you.'

'And made yourself unhappy not doing the thing you loved just so you could be with me? How would that have felt after a few years? You'd have resented me for ever,' Christie said. 'There was only one solution, Carey, you must see that,' she begged.

There was a long pause, a pause filled with all the what-ifs that two people can contemplate over twenty-five years.

'Why did you come here this morning,' he said, 'if this is all you want to say to me?'

'I came,' Christie said, and it was hard to say now that she was here, but she had to bury the ghosts, 'I came because I wanted to end it fully, to say everything I never said before. I needed to make sure that you didn't have the power or the desire to hurt me or my family because of what happened a long time ago. That's why I'm here.'

'Do you want a drink?' he said, and got up to move to a sideboard behind them, where a full bar was laid out with proper crystal glass decanters.

Not your average minibar for him, Christie thought.

'No,' she said, 'thank you. I don't want anything.'

He fixed himself something dark and amber-coloured in a tumbler, then another for her and laid it in front of her without saying a word.

'You followed my career?' he asked.

'No,' she said, making a hopeless attempt at pretending she had never thought about him when there were times when he'd filled her thoughts to the exclusion of everything else.

'You're lying,' he said, sitting down opposite her again, leaning forward. 'I could always tell when you were lying. There's a faint flicker of one of your eyelids, it's a giveaway: a tell, they call it in poker. I play poker now, you know.'

'Is this your poker face?' Christie asked and it was like a fencing match, him parrying, she keeping him back.

'No, this is not my poker face, but you have followed my career, haven't you?'

'Yes, all right, I have. I teach art, you know that. I couldn't teach art, talk to my students about modern art without mentioning Carey Wolensky.'

'But,' he interrupted, 'you never talked to them about the dark lady and who she is?'

'Oh, for heaven's sake,' Christie said with irritation and, unthinkingly, picked up the glass of whiskey and downed half of it. It burned her throat as it went down. But there was something about that harsh violence hitting the back of her throat that brought her to her senses and stopped her playing a game with him. 'How do you think I'm going to tell schoolgirls I teach that I'm the dark lady, that the woman who stands there naked in every bloody picture was me? Do a lot for my teaching career, that would, not to mention what it would do for my marriage.'

'I like you better when you're angry,' he said, sitting back and smiling at her, looking relaxed for the first time. 'You're too passionate to hide it, Christie. We would have been so good together.'

'No, we wouldn't,' she said. 'I have too much and I couldn't give it up and you know that.'

'I'm sorry,' he said, and she knew he was sorry because of what might have been. 'I needed to see you again, just one last time. I wanted to talk to you, look at you, remember you. I have pictures you know, but pictures don't have warmth and their eyes don't shine. I had to rely on my memories to paint you. And you must admit, my memories were good, the pictures look like you, don't they? Did your husband ever notice?'

'He never noticed,' she replied. 'He's not interested in art and I thank God for that, because I love him, I always loved him.'

'If you loved him,' Carey asked, 'then what happened with me?'

It was a question that always haunted her – how could she love James, adore Ethan and Shane and then risk all that to be with this enigmatic man in front of her? There was no answer to that question. It was like asking why did the rain fall, why did the sun shine? It just happened, and she'd been swept along in the moment, a moment she'd been paying for ever since.

'Women aren't supposed to be able to love two men,' she said, 'but that's not true. I loved James and I loved you. You were a door into another me, a Christie who was wild and had nothing to hold her back. Except I had two little boys and it wasn't a simple choice of you or James. I had to choose my family and I don't regret that. I'm not trying to hurt you, I'm explaining.'

She was determined to explain to him how hard it had been walking away from him but that it had been the right thing to do, and that she'd been so happy with James and her sons. Because the Christie who'd loved Carey was like a person from another world and she'd had to bury that person deep inside her and carry on with normal life.

She looked at Carey, remembering all they'd shared, remembering the passion he'd brought up in her, remembering how she'd touched his face in the past and thought she'd die if she didn't have enough of him. She had to put it all behind her now and move on.

'In another world, Carey, in another life, you and I could have been together,' she said.

359

She got up and sat beside him, not feeling any danger from the closeness now. He didn't have the power to hurt her. She had made her mind up to say what had to be said. She was older and wiser so that any magnetism, any passion that there had once been between them, was now gone. And she'd paid for that bliss a million times over.

She touched his hand and she was astonished to find that his skin wasn't the warm, vibrant thing she'd remembered, but felt old and papery and thin, like he was sickening, as though he was older even than he was in years. It confused her, but she couldn't see it properly. What was hiding there?

'I'm sorry, I never meant to hurt you, Carey,' she said. 'I never meant to lead you on, to make you think we had a future, when we didn't. That's why I came to meet you, not to look back and think weren't we fabulous and wonderful, because I felt guilty every day of my life for what happened. I paid for our time together. Adultery has a price and it's too high, believe me. I want to put it behind me. Can you understand that?'

His other hand reached up to touch her face and she closed her eyes as his fingers traced the bones, stroked her cheekbones, her jaw, the hollows of her eyes, the curve of her lips, the way he'd once touched her until she thought she'd scream with desire.

'You're still beautiful,' he murmured. 'No matter what age you are, you will always be beautiful because it's in your soul and I think that's what drew me to you, Christie: your soul, your goodness and your wisdom. I missed you all this time we were apart. There have been many women and they all look like you, strange, no? But none of them was you. So that's why I came. Yes, I have an exhibition here but they ask me to have exhibitions everywhere, I can say no, I have the power. But I wanted to come here, one last time, to see you.'

'Why do you keep saying "one last time"?' she asked.

There was portent behind his words and suddenly, with a shock, she knew.

'Can't you tell?' he said, half smiling. 'You have Gypsy sight after all. I'm sick. I shouldn't be drinking.' He laughed. 'I shouldn't be doing anything. I shouldn't be flying. The doctors didn't want me to. But I can keep going on and the drugs are good. Medicine has moved on so much.'

She didn't want to ask what was killing him. 'How long do you have?' she said, evenly.

'Months, they think months. I don't know, maybe not so long, but I want to make my peace before I go. That's why I had to see you. I didn't come to destroy your world, I came to say goodbye.'

'Oh, Carey,' she sighed, taking his hand from her face and holding it tightly. 'Were you happy? Did you have a good life?'

'Yes,' he said, 'I did. I didn't have you and for a long time you were all I thought about, but an artist needs something to drive him, doesn't he? And you inspired my best work. You gave me so many things, Christie.'

'You gave me things too,' she said. 'You made me see that I could still feel passion. You made me see how much I loved my husband and my children,' she added frankly, 'and I know it probably hurts you to hear that, but that's the truth. So you gave me a huge amount and I've never forgotten you.'

'It's good then that we had this chance to say goodbye,' he said, and, suddenly, he was formal again.

Christie put her arms around him. Now she could feel the frailness of his body, hidden under the beautifully cut jacket. He was dying, she could feel it, every part of her sensed it, and it might not be long. He didn't have months at all, and he knew it, knew she'd know it too.

'Don't pity me,' he said and he laid his lips against her forehead to give her a cool, dry kiss. 'Please don't pity me, I would prefer you remembered me the way we were.'

'I understand,' she said, and she did. She got up.

'I have a small present for you,' he said. 'It may be nothing you can ever show anyone but I wanted to leave it to you. A bequest, that is the word, isn't it?' He handed her an old cardboard box, large and unwieldy. 'Someone will help you out with it. Goodbye, Christie,' he said and he turned, but not before she could see the glitter of tears in his eyes. He left the room and shut the door behind him.

In the lift down, Christie stared at the box that the bellboy held carefully. She didn't want to open it here. She waited until she got into a taxi and the bellboy had placed the box reverentially on the back seat beside her. Then she carefully removed the lid. On top was a wrapped package that contained a small artist's sketchbook, like a writer's notebook, full of pencil drawings and charcoal sketches, cartoons for paintings, ideas, thoughts that had occurred to him. It must have been the sketchbook that Carey had used when they'd met.

The first few pages were full of his trademark drawings and then the pages were pictures of a woman, who could only have been Christie, her face obscured, her body the one Christie knew well. These were the sketches for his Dark Lady paintings. The masterpieces painted by a genius whom the world would mourn when he was gone.

She turned page after page, each more beautiful, interesting, alive than the rest. Some were just pencil, others charcoal, and yet more, coloured in with subtle pastels. It was an incredible gift. The second package was a small canvas, a scaled-down version of the most beautiful of all the Dark Lady paintings. The dark lady was again lying on a divan, in a painter's studio, but in this one her face was not hidden. Her face was alive with love and it was clear she was looking at the artist. Christie gazed at it, thought of Carey and what he meant to her and what was going to happen to him now, and she cried.

CHAPTER TWENTY-FOUR

Maggie loved the silence of the library. Ever since she'd been a child, and her father had explained why libraries were special places where you had to whisper, she'd loved the fact that the only sounds to be heard were muted whispers and the gentle rustling of pages.

'It's quiet because all the books are sitting on the shelves, snoozing quietly as they wait to be picked,' Dad had said, 'because being picked by you is the start of an amazing adventure for them.'

She'd told that story to a small group of children only that morning, and they'd stared up at her, wide-eyed, just as enthralled as she'd been by the idea of silently waiting books.

'Spot was waiting for me?' asked one small girl with glasses and a mummy-cut hairdo, who sat holding one of the Spot books on her lap.

'Yes, Spot was waiting for you!' Maggie said, thrilled at being able to pass on the message to a new generation.

'Wow,' said the little girl in awe.

'Wow,' agreed the other children.

Maggie was sitting in the small staff room having her

morning coffee and talking to Shona on the phone about the children when another call came through on her mobile.

'Hold on a second, Shona,' she said. 'I'll be right back to you, OK?'

It was Ivan.

'How's it going?' he asked in his calm way.

'Not bad,' said Maggie. 'I'm at work, you know.'

'I know. You have your coffee break between half ten and a quarter to eleven, don't you?'

'I do,' she said, fascinated that he'd remembered.

'I wanted to ask if you'd come to the cinema with me tonight.'

'Tonight?'

'Yes, tonight,' Ivan repeated. 'I know that's probably bad form in the big book of women's dating techniques, and I'm supposed to give you a week's notice and you're supposed to come up with four other possible dates because you're washing your hair, having your legs waxed, going out with your girlfriends, seeing other men. But you know me, I'm simple. I thought it might be nice to go to the cinema tonight.'

Maggie had to laugh. 'You're unique, do you know that, Ivan?' she said.

'It has been said before,' he replied, 'although not always in a complimentary way. My grandmother says I speak as I find.'

'I hate that expression,' Maggie said. 'It's the sort of thing that horrible fathers in gothic novels say when they're alienating people left, right and centre. But sure, I'd love to go to the cinema tonight. I have no hair-washing or waxing plans. What will we go to?'

'I don't know,' he said. 'How about I pick you up at about seven and we'll decide then?'

'Great,' she said, pleased. 'See you then.'

'Sorry,' she said to Shona when she clicked back on to the first call. 'That was just Ivan asking me out to the cinema.'

'*Just Ivan asking you out to the cinema*?' said Shona. 'Is this the same big lug of a mechanic person with dirt under his fingernails who took the mickey out of you with the petrol-sucking machine and who made you so angry that you were keen to hire a contract killer to bury him with the fishes?'

'And who took me to the lovely wedding. That's exactly the guy,' Maggie said, laughing. 'I've cancelled the contract killer, by the way. They refused to do a two-for-the-price-of-one deal with Grey included, so I said no. Seriously, though, Ivan's nice when you get to know him. He's got a great sense of humour. It just happened to be working overtime the day I met him.'

'I'm teasing you,' Shona added. 'Go for it. Go out with this fabulous Ivan and bonk his brains out in the back of the cinema. Tell me, does he own the garage or does he work for someone else?'

'Shona, you are appalling,' Maggie said. 'I'm not interested in him that way, he's just a friend. And there's more to life than money, you know.'

'People who say that type of thing are generally not in full control of their senses,' Shona pointed out. 'Money may not be everything, but it sure helps, and if you're miserable, you can be miserable in comfort.'

'Besides,' Maggie interrupted, 'I'm not in the market for a man. And rebound relationships are always a mistake and never work out.'

'Dr Phil, right?'

'You're incorrigible,' laughed Maggie. 'No, that's Maggie Maguire advice.'

Maggie was on until half past six that evening, so she had to race home from work.

'Hi, Mum, hi, Dad,' she yelled, rushing in the door and

sprinting to her room to change out of her work clothes into her most comfortable jeans.

'Where are you going in such a tearing rush?' Dad yelled after her.

'Out to the cinema with Ivan, you don't mind do you?'

'Not at all,' said her father. 'Oh, the man arrived today with the posters about the park. Your mother has them, she's very proud of them. She keeps saying "to think I designed these myself". A very talented woman your mother.'

Maggie ran a comb through her hair and considered putting on some lip gloss, then thought better of it. There was no need, Ivan was only a friend. She spritzed on a bit of perfume and ran to the kitchen where her mother was indeed admiring the posters. Above a line drawing of the park gates, which Una had traced from a picture, were rousing words about saving Summer Street's heritage from the developers.

'It's part of your community, help save it!' ran the bottom line. They looked good. Nobody would be able to resist, Maggie thought.

Harrison Mitchell was actually being useful and had given her the contact numbers for a couple of journalists who were interested in campaigns like theirs. She was meeting one of them at lunchtime tomorrow in the park and they were bringing a photographer.

'Don't they look great?' said Una happily.

'Fantastic,' agreed Maggie. 'This will make the councillors sit up and take notice.'

'What film are you going to see?' asked Una.

'I don't know,' said Maggie, 'doesn't matter. It'll be nice to see a film. I haven't been to the movies for ages.'

'He's a nice fella, isn't he, Ivan?' said her mother idly.

'Now, Mother, don't start that,' warned Maggie. 'He's just a friend.'

366

'I know, love,' said her mother quickly. 'It's nice to see you happy.'

Ivan's stylish car drew up outside.

Maggie grinned, kissed her mother on the cheek, snagged a banana from the fruit bowl and gave her dad a hug as she ran out the door. It was true, she was happy. Odd that, when just a few weeks ago she'd felt as if her heart was breaking. Something was healing her, although she didn't know what.

'We could go to the multiplex, if you like,' said Ivan, as they stood in the foyer of the tiny local cinema where they had discovered that the three latest releases were fully booked. The only film with any seats available was a classic French film, with subtitles.

'Well, maybe we'll go to the French one, what do you think?' Maggie said, thinking that if she'd been with Grey, the French film would have been their original destination. Grey had no interest in films with popular appeal. The more populist they were, the less he'd like to see them. An old French film with subtitles would top his list.

'Whatever you like,' said Ivan easily.

That was the nice thing about having Ivan as a friend, he never tried to push her into anything. And he was so comfortable in his own skin that he didn't need to prove his intelligence by his movie choice.

'I don't have the energy to go into town. Let's try the French film,' suggested Maggie.

'If that's what Mademoiselle wants, then that's what she shall have.'

He went up to the counter to pay.

'No, let me,' insisted Maggie.

Ivan glared at her.

'Or at least let me pay half,' she pleaded.

'I asked you out, so I'm paying.'

The cinema was only half full and they found two seats right in the back row.

'I always love the back row,' whispered Maggie. 'You feel sort of naughty, as if you're going to get into trouble for sitting here when you should be down the front under the head nun's beady eye.'

'I still think you must have been a holy terror in school,' Ivan teased.

'I wish. Butter wouldn't have melted in my mouth,' said Maggie.

They were old-fashioned comfortable seats and somehow Maggie found herself leaning on the arm rest that separated her and Ivan, so that her shoulder was squashed against his. And finally, Ivan put his arm around her and pulled her closer into him, which felt absolutely natural. And Maggie, the person who kept insisting that they were just friends, found that she liked it very much.

Don't think about it, she told herself. Just enjoy it.

Then, somehow, when Ivan moved his other arm around to touch her face and turn it towards his, it seemed like kissing him was the most obvious thing to do and Maggie turned her face to his and their lips met. Suddenly they were kissing, passionately and hungrily, and who cared about the film? Who cared if anyone saw them in the darkened gloom of the cinema? They kissed wildly, Ivan's hand in her hair, sliding down to caress her neck, stroking her collarbone, reaching down to the softness of her shoulders and further, until finally, he said, 'I don't want to see this film, do you?'

'No,' she muttered, pulling her mouth away from him. 'Let's go.'

They held hands and ran to the car park. As he drove, Ivan steered with one hand and left the other big hand on Maggie's jean-clad leg, stroking gently, making her feel intensely excited. It was odd: until a few moments ago, she'd seen him as a friend, and now, in a flash, it was like a curtain being pulled down to reveal a totally different picture and he wasn't a friend any more. He was a man, a sexual, charismatic man and she wanted him. The intensity of the want frightened her.

The car pulled into a lane a few streets away from home and Ivan parked outside a small mews house. He took her hand again as they went inside and she barely had time to register what the inside of the house was like, noticing a giant fireplace with open brickwork and bare floorboards, before he had pulled her upstairs to a huge bedroom that seemed to take up the whole of the upper floor, an enormous low bed dominating it.

Then they were half sitting, half lying on the bed and Ivan was tearing her clothes off as she tore his off with fervour. His mouth found hers, as if he couldn't bear not to be kissing her.

And for the first time in her life, tall Maggie Maguire felt like a small fragile creature beside this giant of a man, who touched her lovingly, as if she might break. It was that, that and the tenderness and the love in everything he did to her, that made her melt.

Afterwards, they lay coiled together in bed and Ivan gently stroked the small scars at the top of her thigh.

'We should go to French films more often,' Maggie said lightly.

'Don't.' Ivan held a finger up to the softness of her lips. 'Don't make a joke about it,' he said. 'You do that when you're unsure?'

She nodded.

'I love that you're so funny,' he added, still holding her close to him. 'You make me laugh, but I don't want you to need your defence mechanism around me, I want you to be yourself, not to joke about the things that matter.'

'I'm sorry,' she said, turning around and propping herself up on her elbow, so that she could look down on him. She ran her fingers through his close-cropped hair lovingly. She didn't think she'd ever get enough of touching him. 'I can't help it. I always think that if you make people laugh they don't see what you're really thinking or they don't see that you could really be in pain.'

'I know,' he said. 'I saw that in you the first time I met you.'

'You did?'

'And I wanted you the first time I met you,' he added and the growl in his voice made her feel faint with longing again.

'But you teased me,' she protested, and he laughed then and pulled her close to kiss her on the lips.

'I'm sorry,' he said gently, his lips against her cheek. 'Seeing you gave me such a jolt, I wasn't thinking straight. All I know is that I wanted you from the moment you came into the garage. I knew I'd have to wait though.'

'What if I hadn't wanted you?' Maggie asked.

Ivan smoothed her hair back from her forehead. 'I'd have waited,' he said. 'I'd have waited a very long time for you, for ever in fact.'

It felt odd waking up in a strange bed in the morning, but only for a moment. Beside her lay Ivan: large, muscular and warm, one arm flung over her body. Even in sleep, he was holding her close. Maggie knew you shouldn't compare, but she couldn't help it: Grey liked to sleep in his own space, on his side of the bed, and she did the same. Except last night, she and Ivan had slept curled together, drawing comfort from each other. She wriggled against him, loving the feel of his warm, hard body against hers. And it was hard, definitely: a certain part *very* hard. She wriggled closer still.

370

'I wouldn't do that, unless you like making love in the morning,' came a low, sleepy voice.

Maggie moved a sliver closer, feeling herself grow warm inside, adoring the power she had over him. Just her touch seemed to inflame him.

'I warned you,' he murmured, and then, like a great bear rousing himself from sleep, he swiftly moved till he was pinning her down on the bed, grinning at her, his face covered in dark stubble, his eyes glinting.

Maggie reached up and pulled his face down to hers, eagerly. 'I thought you had someplace to be this morning?' she teased as he rested his weight on his elbows, the lower half of him holding her to the bed, hard evidence that they weren't going to be getting up for a while.

'It can wait,' Ivan said huskily and lowered his mouth on to hers.

Ivan's bathroom was typically male with cream tiles, a bath he clearly never used because he had the last word in power showers, and a mirrored cabinet that contained nothing but shampoo, shower gel, shaving foam, toothpaste and mouthwash.

'You've got no stuff in your cabinet,' teased Maggie, rooting through, trying to find something that might remove the remains of her mascara. There wasn't even any male moisturiser. Grey had as much in the moisturising and sunblock line as she had and borrowed hers if he'd run out of Clinique for Men.

'Would you prefer if I had a ton of women's stuff in here?' Ivan demanded.

'No, but you must have had other women here,' she added, trying to sound diffident, and failing utterly. 'Go on, tell me,' she said. 'We're modern adults, we need to know everything about each other. I've told you about Grey.'

'I'd quite like to hear more about Grey, actually,' Ivan said, a muscle tautening in his jaw.

371

'Oh no, you don't.' Maggie shook her head. Grey was the past, a never to be revisited place.

'Yes, I do,' Ivan said. He'd had his shower and wore only a small towel tied round his waist as he began shaving. He looked great, tautly muscular and just as wantable as he'd been minutes before.

Maggie wished women could look as effortlessly good as men the morning after. She had panda eyes and blotchy skin from not taking off her make-up and needed a shower cap before she could shower as she didn't have her hair paraphernalia there to stop the wild auburn frizz.

'Grey was a part of your life for a long time and I want to know it's over, properly over.'

'Of course it's over,' Maggie said quickly. She didn't want to talk about this, it was too soon for her two worlds to collide. The new improved Maggie and the old, stupid one.

'But Ivan, your past is a mystery to me. When you took me to your cousin's wedding in the first place, nobody mentioned any special person you were supposed to have taken,' she said. 'Did you train them all to keep their mouths shut, because I can't believe there's really been a drought on the girlfriend front lately.'

Once she'd admitted Ivan's fierce attractiveness to herself, it was obvious that he was the sort of man who'd appeal to women. However, Ivan was a hard man to get to know. He was quiet, intense and very private. Few women would get past his outward face, to see the man underneath. The kind, gentle man who was an incredible lover.

'There have been a few women in my life,' he said, 'but very few of them got to leave their toothbrushes over.'

'You don't like sharing your bathroom?' Maggie asked lightly.

'Up till now, no,' he said. 'I think I'm changing my mind about that.'

She grinned, took his toothbrush from the holder and began to brush her teeth.

'Nobody's ever used my toothbrush before,' he said, watching her.

'So this is a first,' she teased.

'Yes,' he said, 'this is a first.'

She'd wrapped a towel around herself and stripped it off to climb into the shower.

'Show me your thigh,' he commanded abruptly.

The night before, his fingers had touched one of the pale scars on the top of her left thigh and she'd muttered about the car crash – the same story she'd given Grey when he'd seen the marks. But this time, in the bright light of his bathroom, he looked at them more carefully.

'Sit down.'

Gently, he made her sit on the edge of the bath and knelt in front of her. Maggie wished she had something to hide her thighs but she had nothing. Her wounds were laid bare. They were ragged scars, not deep, not ever having required stitches, but they'd left their mark. There were many of them, uneven marks that would never fade, like a barcode scratched into her soft skin.

'It was a car accident,' she repeated.

Ivan's fingers traced the marks.

'These scars don't look like any accident,' he said. He looked up at her, his fingers still touching the scars. 'What really happened?'

'I don't want to talk about it,' she said, anxiety blooming.

Ivan put two strong arms around her waist and locked them behind her back, pulling her closer to him. 'I want to know all about you, Maggie Maguire,' he whispered, kissing her face, 'every inch of you, every inch of your head, so tell me the truth. Tell me, where did you really get those scars?'

* * *

It had all started so innocently on her first day at St Ursula's, when she'd arrived full of excitement and enthusiasm at being in big school. She and the other first years had spent the morning being shown classrooms and meeting their new teachers. It was a busy and interesting day, learning where everything was, getting used to which lessons would be in which classrooms.

The group of girls were waiting to be told where to go next when it happened.

'Hey, lanky, what's your name?' asked a girl with fair hair, a little freckled face and eyes that made her look older than twelve.

'Maggie Maguire,' said Maggie eagerly, not seeing the word lanky as derogatory.

'Big Maggie, huh?' sneered the girl, and the small group surrounding her laughed.

Maggie had laughed too, half out of nervousness, half to show that she wasn't offended.

'Sandra, you're a panic,' laughed one of the gang. 'Big Maggie – that's classic.'

A teacher had arrived at that moment and corralled the first years into their classes.

The next morning, Maggie was in early, determined to be ready for this exciting new world.

She was sitting at the front of the class for English, her first lesson, shyly saying hello to other girls, when Sandra and her cohorts strolled in.

'Big Maggie's up the front of the class,' announced Sandra. 'You're a swot, are you, Big Maggie?'

Sandra walked past Maggie's desk and, in one swift move, shoved Maggie's neatly arranged textbooks on to the floor. 'Oops. Sorree,' she said insincerely, and the gang laughed.

Her face crimson and tears burning in the back of her eyes, Maggie bent to pick up her books, hoping somebody would stand up for her or flash her a sympathetic glance. But nobody did. Everyone was too scared.

Maggie wasn't the only one of Sandra's victims. There were several more, and as the years went on, the bullying ebbed and flowed. Maggie found if she got to class after Sandra, and ran out of the door before her, then Sandra didn't bother to follow her.

She became adept at rushing everywhere and trying to be invisible at times like lunch or break.

They even ruined netball for her. When she was alone, she loved the touch of the ball on her hand, the thought of springing it from long fingers into the hoop. But as soon as the bullies were in the background, taunting, teasing, making snide remarks, her hand–eye coordination fell apart. 'Oh yeah, look at No-Tit Maguire, screwed it up again,' Sandra would say.

Ever since she'd tried to make her flat chest look bigger, Sandra had swapped the Big Maggie name for No-Tit Maguire. Maggie pretended she didn't care and ignored her.

'You're nothing but a long streak of misery,' was another of Sandra's taunts.

In her more charitable moments, Maggie liked to think that maybe Sandra had lots of problems and that's what made her so hard and cross with the world. That was often what was wrong with people in the books Maggie read: when they were nasty, they were suffering really and they just took it out on the heroine, so that could be the answer.

But after a few years of unrelenting nastiness, she didn't want an excuse for Sandra or her gang any more, they were just bitches. Kitty, the nearest thing that Maggie had to a best friend in school, had no interest in the theory that Sandra's life was hard, which was why she took it out on other people.

'She's just a cow,' Kitty said, vehemently. Kitty was small, very clever, wore glasses and lived in the purdah of plumpness, which meant she was Sandra's ideal target.

Brains was the only obvious link between Maggie and Kitty but the two girls became united in terror. They had agreed there was no point telling anyone about it. The teachers knew what Sandra was like, they couldn't control her either, or the gang, so it wasn't as if people didn't know.

But nobody seemed able to do anything, not even that time in third year when it emerged that Sandra had been taking money from the first years. Nobody knew quite how that had been brushed under the carpet, but it had. Sandra had been off school for two days and then she was back and just as bad as ever, without even a flicker of remorse. In fact, she and her cronies seemed worse now, as if their leader had got into trouble and had walked free, so they felt they had nothing or nobody to fear.

The first and second years stayed out of their way. People in third year, Sandra's year, didn't have that option.

'Why do adults insist on that rubbish that your school days are the best days of your life?' Kitty said. 'They're not, they're horrible, I can't wait to get out of this place, away from those low-lifes.'

At least Kitty could talk about it at home. She had an older sister who was now at college and understood that being small, bespectacled and clever wasn't the route to popularity in school, and comforted her, but there was nobody Maggie could tell. Mum and Dad were so thrilled to see her fabulous reports.

'Look, five more As and an A+. You're amazing. Where did we get such a brilliant daughter, Dennis?' her mum would say delightedly, when the report cards arrived in Summer Street.

The reports always guardedly mentioned that Maggie was quite shy and needed to come out of her shell a bit too, but

376

Maggie knew that her parents couldn't quite see this because the Maggie they knew at home was funny and merry. She could see them working it out: this classroom version of their daughter was the one who worked so hard she got A+. That must be why only they saw the bright-eyed Maggie at home. In class, she was diligent, that was it.

She didn't know how to tell them that when she got home she merely felt weak with relief at having got school over for another day.

Telling them about Sandra, about how she didn't know if she could cope much longer, would have seemed such a failure. Sunday nights were the worst. From about four o'clock on, Maggie could feel her mood sink lower and lower.

Getting her bag ready for school, making sure she'd done all her homework, getting a clean uniform blouse ready, she felt like a French aristocrat climbing into the tumbrel.

She could never sleep on Sunday nights. She'd lie there in her bed, looking up at the stars on her ceiling, wondering if there was intelligent life on other planets and if there was, what did they do about bullying?

The production of *The Playboy of the Western World* in Maggie's fourth year brought matters to a head. At St Ursula's the fourth years – because they weren't doing state exams that year – put on a play in an attempt to help them understand the work of the great dramatists. There were sixty girls in Maggie's year and among the twenty-five or so with ambitions to be world-famous actresses, there was huge competition for the big parts in J.M. Synge's classic.

Maggie, who loved English and had adored the play the first time she'd read it, would rather have had an arm removed without an anaesthetic than get up on the stage and act. So she was able to stand back and watch the fights that went on in drama class. The play would be performed at Christmas with all the funds going towards a charitable concern.

'I want everyone to be involved,' insisted Miss O'Brien, the drama teacher, a woman who felt that public speaking was a great skill for any person and simply couldn't understand why everyone wasn't clamouring to be involved. 'It will be so much fun,' she said, her eyes shiny with emotion, 'the excitement, the glamour. Now, Maggie, you could be one of the people who help the actresses learn their lines, you're so good at English and you love this play. That'd be a fabulous job for you.'

'Oh, no,' said Maggie instantly, 'I couldn't.' Her school career had been spent trying to slip into the background and she'd learned that hiding was the best form of defence.

Finally, the enthusiastic Miss O'Brien persuaded Maggie and Kitty and a few of the other quieter members of their year to help with the scenery for the play. The stars of that year's art classes were going to paint the scenery, but a few more people were needed to put it together, hammer in nails and be general dogsbodies.

'Maggie, I thought you would want to be more involved,' said Miss O'Brien sadly when Maggie agreed to work on the scenery but not help anyone learn lines. 'A sense of community is vital. I'm disappointed in you.'

Maggie said nothing.

She liked Miss O'Brien. It would have been lovely to sit down and tell her the truth.

Miss O'Brien, you don't understand. I'd love to be doing something with the play, but Kitty and I have safe places we can go to at break and lunchtime to hide from Sandra. We'd be sticking our necks out working with the actresses. Some of the gang are in the play and they would make our lives miserable.

Instead she said none of this, she just looked steadily at

the teacher and Miss O'Brien studied the blank face that Maggie had perfected.

'Well, if you don't want to use your talents, that's your loss,' she said and sniffed to show her disapproval. 'You could do much more than be in the background.'

Working on the scenery proved to be quite enjoyable and there was a certain satisfaction to be had in cutting up the enormous cardboard boxes they had been given to help create the kitchen floor.

Kitty, Maggie and a few other girls had been provided with Stanley knives to do the work. As sharp as craft knives and much stronger, they ripped into the cardboard easily.

'Now, be careful,' Miss O'Brien warned. 'I don't want anyone cutting off a thumb or anything.'

'No, Miss,' said Kitty gravely. 'We'll be careful, we need our thumbs.'

The only person who hurt themselves was Maggie. She wasn't sure how she'd done it, but cutting towards herself, instead of away as they had all been taught, she'd managed to make a big swipe along her thigh. The knife cut right through her uniform skirt and made an indent, a bloody indent, into the skin of her thigh.

'Ouch,' she cried.

'Shit, what have you done?' yelped Kitty.

Maggie pulled up her ruined skirt. Her leg didn't look too bad. There was a sliver-thin stripe of red with beads of blood emerging, like a red crystal necklace, along the rip. And bizarrely, this intense physical pain was manageable. It hurt but she could see the hurt, not like the hurt inside her that nobody could see.

'I'll take you to the school nurse,' said Kitty.

'No, I'm fine, I'm fine,' said Maggie. 'It's OK, really. I'll put loo roll on it, it'll be OK.'

She ran off to the loo, still holding the Stanley knife. Sitting in a cubicle with the door locked, she hesitated before making another slice in her thigh. God, it hurt, but at the same time, it felt . . . good. She could control this pain. The fierce intensity of the physical hurt took away the pain in her head. This was centred on her leg. She was in control of it and that roar of control surging through her was like a blessed relief from all the hurt. She'd cut herself and let the hurt drip out. Who cared if she was marked or cut? Nobody cared. She'd do it again and feel the power of control over her life again.

Nobody noticed when the Stanley knife went missing. Nobody knew it was in Maggie Maguire's bedroom and that sometimes, not every night, because she couldn't do it every night, she cut small marks into her thigh. Over the months, there was a criss-cross of them: red raw and looking like she'd been flayed on one thigh. But nobody saw, she made sure of that. It was easy enough, who was going to see her with her clothes off?

Sometimes the wounds really hurt, stung her and she wondered whether they were infected. So she bought surgical spirit and doused her whole thigh in it, wanting to scream with the pain, and yet, that pain was good too, hurting her like everything else was hurting her. That knife became a symbol, the one bit of control she felt she had over her life.

The night of the dress rehearsal, Maggie and Kitty were waiting in one of the big rooms behind the stage when Sandra and her cronies came in. They were all allowed to wear ordinary clothes and Maggie was dressed in her favourite jeans and boots with a simple fleece. One of her legs was faintly bulkier than the other because it was bandaged up, though nobody else would have noticed. Her thigh throbbed all the time. There were so many cuts in it. But she didn't care, the pain made her feel stronger.

'Hello, No-Tit Maguire. Is this what you call fashion?' sneered Sandra, who was done up like a dog's dinner in the

380

best schoolgirl hooker look money could buy. Her hair was platinum blonde now and her eyes were hard blue bullets in a ring of eyeliner black as hell.

Maggie's leg throbbed. She had her knife in the pocket of her fleece. Carrying it gave her a strange courage. She clenched her fingers around it now, feeling the rage well up. Then she felt herself fall over the edge.

'Fuck off, bitch,' she howled in feral tones and stood towering over Sandra, her face suffused with anger. She ripped the knife from her pocket and flicked the blade a few notches up so it glinted its dull metallic sheen.

Sandra's eyes widened.

'Don't come near me or Kitty again or I'll make you fucking sorry,' hissed the new Maggie.

And Sandra, confronted by someone who was no longer going to lie down and be kicked, backed off.

'Yeah, whatever,' she said.

'Not *whatever*, you fucking bitch!' Everyone heard the roar and watched, open-mouthed. Maggie advanced, rage burning in her head. 'Say it. Say it or I'll make you sorry. Say you'll never come near us again, never bully anyone here again,' hissed Maggie and there was no mistaking her determination.

'I'll keep away, right? Calm down, right?' And Sandra, who had enough cunning to know how to save her own skin, backed off for ever.

'Mad fucking bitch,' she muttered from a good way away.

The bullies left and there was utter silence in the room, before Kitty went up to Maggie and took the knife from her.

'You weren't acting, were you?' she asked, putting an arm round her friend and manoeuvring her into a chair.

'No,' said Maggie, weak now.

'You'd be up for an Oscar if you were,' Kitty remarked. She neatly reversed the knife so the blade was sheathed. 'I

381

wouldn't blame you for carving Sandra up into little pieces but she's not worth the hassle. If one of you has to end up in jail, I'd prefer it to be her.'

Maggie managed to laugh. 'I can't believe I did that,' she said.

'But I'm glad you did.' Kitty laughed.

A voice from the corner of the room spoke up: 'I'm glad you did too. She's made my life hell for years.'

'And the meek shall inherit the earth, if that's all right with the rest of you,' joked Kitty.

Everyone laughed and the tension was broken.

Maggie looked up into Ivan's eyes. 'Do you think I'm a nutcase now?' she asked, anxiety flooding through her now that she'd actually told him the truth.

He smiled. 'I think you're the bravest woman ever,' he said. 'I'm so proud of you. That took huge courage.'

'Not really,' she said. 'It was more like madness, really. I just flipped.'

Ivan's hands touched her leg again. 'You don't do this any more?' he asked gently.

She shook her head. 'Without her hassling me, life was easier, better. I felt ashamed about cutting myself and I stopped it. I never told anyone, though. It seemed so stupid. I began to like school and she left at the end of that year. The relief! The gang of bitches were never the same without her. They were still nasty, but never to me or Kitty.'

'My warrior princess,' he said, hugging her. 'You vanquished your enemies.'

'I thought so,' she said, 'but the day of your cousin's wedding, one of Sandra's gang came into the library and I thought I was going to be physically sick. It all came back to me, Ivan, the fear, the terror. It was like being a kid again.' Her voice wobbled and his embrace tightened.

382

'They're the fear I haven't exorcised,' she went on. 'Like my leg, they're scars that won't go away.'

'They'll go away with time,' Ivan reassured her.

'No, I have to face them. Christie Devlin says I probably have to face Sandra to get her out of my head. She's right, you know.'

Ivan pulled her to her feet and looked stern. 'If you go near those women, I'm going to be with you,' he said. 'Let them try and bully you with me there.'

Maggie hugged him, burying her head in his chest. 'Thank you, but no. I have to do this on my own.'

Gossip central on Summer Street was the mini-market where the surly owner, Gretchen, ruled supreme. Gretchen's daughter Lorraine, the one who was married to the rich French pilot, and had been at school with Maggie, had been in Sandra Brody's gang. If anybody knew of Sandra's whereabouts, it would be Gretchen.

So that evening, for the first time ever, Maggie went to Gretchen's checkout on purpose. She might not have had the courage to do it had it not been for the afterglow of a successful meeting with the reporters.

'Hello, Maggie,' Gretchen said, with the air of a cat who had a mouse's tail trapped between her paws. 'How are you?'

'Great,' said Maggie cheerfully. She was ready for tough nuts like Gretchen now.

'How's Lorraine?' she asked idly.

'Fabulous,' said Gretchen, seeming slightly surprised that Maggie would ask after Lorraine.

'And does she still see Sandra Brody?' Maggie continued.

'Sandra McNamara, you mean? Not really, I mean you know Lorraine is living in the South of France now . . .'

'Yes,' interrupted Maggie, not wanting to hear Gretchen's

boasting all over again. 'But they were such great friends in school. Their gang did everything together, didn't they?'

Gretchen looked shifty for a moment. 'Well, Sandra was a bit wild really, wasn't she?'

'Wild?' said Maggie, acting surprised. 'In what way was she wild?'

Gretchen looked even more uncomfortable. 'Oh, you know, she was a bit of a bad influence, we were all glad when she left St Ursula's.'

'What sort of a bad influence?' went on Maggie, feeling as if the tables were turned and she was the grand inquisitor.

'You know, leading girls on, getting them into trouble. My Lorraine was always a good girl, but when she was with Sandra, well, you never knew what they'd get up to.'

Maggie looked Gretchen straight in the eye.

'Actually,' she said coldly, 'I do know what they got up to and you're right, it wasn't very nice at all. Does Sandra live around here now?'

'She comes in from time to time,' Gretchen stammered and for once it seemed as if she didn't want to talk. She began scanning Maggie's groceries with an unaccustomed speed.

'And has she changed, do you think?' Maggie asked. 'Is she still *wild*?'

'She has children of her own and she's settled down, wouldn't that change anyone?' Gretchen said, whisking through the groceries.

'So she's different?'

'You might say that.'

'What does she do?'

'I don't think she works. She's got small children and the husband has a good job, I hear. That'll be seventeen euros and eighty cents.'

Maggie counted out the money. 'Do say hello to Lorraine

for me, won't you?' she added. 'I'm sure she'll remember me.'

'Eh, yeah, yes, yes, of course,' said Gretchen.

Maggie walked down Summer Street towards her house with her shopping in two bags. She'd made progress. She'd found out that Sandra's reign of terror hadn't been a big secret, that people had known about it. Maggie had spent so many years wondering whether she had been paranoid, exaggerated the whole thing to herself, that she felt vindicated now to find out that Sandra Brody's actions hadn't gone unnoticed, that other people had seen what she was. It was just that nobody had done anything to help the people like Maggie. This knowledge didn't make her feel even more upset or betrayed, it made her feel stronger. Having horrible old Gretchen admit that Sandra had once been a vicious little bully had given Maggie the key to her own freedom. She hadn't been at fault, Sandra had been, and now, she was going to confront Sandra about it. The past was not going to keep Maggie Maguire in its stranglehold any more.

The phone book had the answer.

Tony and Sandra McNamara lived a few miles away on a new housing estate.

Maggie wondered what Sandra McNamara was like now. Could she still reduce people to quivering wrecks with one nasty look? Did she still smoke and flick her ash at other people? She'd burned Maggie a couple of times with a cigarette, always pretending that it was accidental. Once on her leg, once on her knuckle, there was still a faint mark from that. At least those scars were surface ones. The marks on her thigh were Sandra's marks, hers as if she'd made them herself, with her own penknife. Maggie would carry those scars till the day she died. But it was time to heal the scars on the inside.

'I'm going out, Mum,' Maggie called to her mother. 'If Ivan phones, say I'll be back soon.'

'Fine,' came her mother's voice from the kitchen.

Maggie hopped on the bus that would take her past the McNamaras' road. Sandra and Tony McNamara lived at number 13 and when Maggie walked up to the gate with her head held high, she noticed there were two cars parked in the driveway. One, a standard people carrier with a baby seat in the back.

Children. Imagine Sandra having children of her own! Imagine if they were there when Maggie confronted her. There was no way she wanted to hurt the kids – it wasn't their fault their mother was a cow. Maggie faltered at this proof that Sandra Brody was more than an evil presence from her past. She was a person after all.

She stood on the pavement outside, trying to summon up the courage to go to the wooden door, when it opened and a man appeared. Instantly, Maggie turned and fled up the street, her heart thumping.

She didn't want confrontation with anyone else. A husband who might have no idea what his wife had once been like. Her heart pounding, she walked home, feeling ashamed.

That night, Maggie lay in her childhood bed in the house on Summer Street and stared up at the ceiling. The events of the past couple of months ran through her head. Betrayal and misery had taunted her, yet she'd got through it. Incredibly, she hadn't been flattened by it all. If anything, she felt stronger and happier now because she'd taken back control of her life.

It seemed very obvious to her now: she'd been stuck in victim mode for so long that she'd forgotten how to take control. Being a victim was easier as you could blame everything on other people. Taking control was frightening as it meant things might go wrong and you mightn't be able to handle them. But then things went wrong anyway. So why not face the fear, and take control?

The following morning, Maggie sat in her parents' car on the road outside Sandra McNamara's house and waited until Sandra returned from the school run. She'd left twenty minutes ago with three children, and now she had just one small boy with her. Maggie walked over to where Sandra was taking the child out of his car seat.

'Hi, Sandra, remember me?' said Maggie pleasantly.

Sandra turned. She was still blonde but her hair was shorter now, and the heavy eyeliner was absent. She wore no make-up, and looked pale and plain in an unflattering sweatshirt and jeans.

'No,' she said. 'Sorry.'

It was uncanny how she sounded the same. She looked different, but she sounded just the same.

'You honestly don't remember me, do you?' Maggie said.

'Remember you, should I?'

'We were in school together, St Ursula's, until you left after fourth year.'

There was no crash of cymbals as realisation hit Sandra's face, no triumphant chorus as she stared at Maggie in dismay. Her expression was blank.

'Sorry.' She shrugged. 'I don't remember.'

And she meant it. She really had no idea who Maggie was. When the crash of cymbals hit, the noise was inside Maggie's head instead. The girl who had tormented her and made her life hell had no recollection of it. Which meant that people often did horrible things randomly and didn't remember them.

'Do you live round here?' asked Sandra politely.

'I live on Summer Street,' Maggie said. 'I've been away for a few years and I'm back now. I'm trying to catch up on old friends, and people like you. I was one of the quiet ones at school and you were the leader of the bullies.'

Maggie could see the dawning of comprehension in Sandra's eyes.

'We were all a bit crazy then, you know, teenagers,' Sandra said.

'No,' insisted Maggie. 'It wasn't just a bit crazy, it was nasty and horrible.'

'I mean we all went through phases where we weren't very nice, teenagers can be little bitches,' protested Sandra.

'I wasn't,' Maggie said. 'I wasn't a little bitch, but you were so horrible to me I hated going to school. I used to feel sick thinking about it. No, that's not right – it's not that I hated going to school, it's that I was frightened of going to school. You made my life a misery for years. Do you have any idea what that feels like?'

Sandra shut the car door, leaving the little boy in his seat.

'Listen, lady, I don't remember you, right, so go.'

'Maggie Maguire, that's who I am.'

'Oh.'

Maggie could see Sandra staring at her in horrified recognition. Maggie knew she looked so different nowadays. Everyone said she was beautiful. Today, she allowed herself to feel it and stood tall in front of this woman.

'I knew you'd remember,' she said. 'No-Tit Maguire, you called me. It's funny you not recognising me when I'll remember you for ever. You made me feel so scared of going to school, which is something so normal you're supposed to do it every day of your life without bother. But you ruined it for me. Your nastiness affected every part of my life, did you know that?'

She didn't want an answer. In a way, she wasn't even talking to Sandra any more, she was finally voicing how she felt all those years ago. Sandra just happened to be there: an ordinary, fraught woman who was the one looking trapped now.

Maggie realised that meeting your demons head-on meant you could see they weren't the huge, dark monsters of your nightmares, but just stupid, pathetic people who'd had power at the time and had used it against you.

'I'm sorry, OK?' Sandra said. 'I know I was a bit of a pain when I was in school, I had lots of problems and I took it out on other people, but please, I'm sorry, I'm sorry for whatever I did. Now, just go. I don't want anyone overhearing this.' She looked around at her neighbours' windows, clearly anxious that someone might witness this strange meeting.

Maggie smiled inside, thinking that Sandra must have calmed down if she wanted to fit in with the crowd.

'Worried what the neighbours will think? You never worried in the past. Have you reinvented yourself as a nice person now? Do you go to coffee mornings and pretend to be an ordinary mum?'

Sandra flushed.

'Guess I hit the nail on the head,' Maggie said, looking Sandra coolly in the eye. 'I've one question: how can you say sorry to me, if you don't remember what you did to me?'

Sandra remembered, Maggie was sure of it.

'What would you do now if somebody bullied your children?' she went on. 'How would you react if they came home from school and said they were terrified because someone was picking on them?'

'I wouldn't stand for it,' growled Sandra with a hint of her old menace.

'Oh, you wouldn't stand for it?' interrupted Maggie. 'You'd march into the head teacher's office to complain, would you? That'd be pretty hypocritical, given how many people you bullied in school. Would that make you realise how much you hurt me and all the other kids you bullied, if you had to watch it happen to your child? That should be the punishment for bullies, seeing their own families getting bullied.'

'Look, I can't talk now,' said Sandra, looking harassed. 'Can I make it up to you? Can we meet for a cup of coffee and talk and . . .'

'I don't think so,' said Maggie. 'I've said what I wanted to say. I guess I'm lucky enough to have the courage to stand up to you. I'm sorry I never had the courage when I was at school, except that one time.'

'I'm sorry, just go, go!' Sandra said. She wrenched open the car door and fumbled with her little boy's car seat straps.

'Bye, Sandra,' said Maggie coldly. There was no need for her to stay. She'd said what she wanted to, had given Sandra McNamara something to think about. Maybe she'd toss and turn in bed at night from now on, remembering the people she'd hurt.

Then again, maybe she didn't have the ability to see how much damage she'd done. Incredibly, her only worry was what if the neighbours overheard.

Maggie walked back to her car. She'd never been the sort of person who liked confrontation but nineteen years of bottling something up did strange things to a person. She'd faced Sandra. She'd had the courage to coolly say all the things she'd wanted to say for years. And it felt good.

Maggie drove out of the estate and headed for home. At the bottom of Summer Street, she parked and took out her mobile phone.

She dialled Ivan's number, thinking that only a few weeks ago, the person she would have wanted to ring was Grey. Except that if she was still with Grey, if her whole life hadn't come tumbling down, she'd never have reached this moment in the first place.

Besides, Grey hadn't known about her past. In five years,

she'd never been able to tell him the secret Ivan had instinctively known was there in a few weeks.

Ivan was busy, she could tell from his voice when he answered his phone. But when he realised it was her, his voice softened.

'Hello, Maggie,' he said.

He didn't call her babe or honey or any of the things Grey called her. Ivan used her name.

'What's up?'

'Just wanted to say hello,' she said. Then, 'You'll never guess who I just met.'

There was a beat.

'Not Grey?' said Ivan, strangely uptight.

'No, no,' said Maggie. 'Sandra, the girl at school, the girl I told you about.'

'And did you say anything to her?' he asked softly.

'Yes,' Maggie said and she felt proud of herself, proud for standing up for herself. 'I did.'

When she hung up, Maggie thought back to her school days. Except, today, it all felt different. Resolved. She'd faced Sandra Brody with courage and learned two lessons. First, she hadn't been the perfect victim – she'd just been in the wrong place at the wrong time. And secondly, the past could only ruin your life if you let it.

Sandra wasn't important any more. Maggie had faced her and won. The real challenge was letting the past go.

CHAPTER TWENTY-FIVE

Could you ever truly know somebody you loved? Could you ever know what went on in their minds when they lay in the dark beside you under the covers?

Those questions filled Christie's thoughts in the hours following her last, emotionally charged meeting with Carey.

As a child growing up, she'd watched her parents' marriage and known that she'd wanted exactly the opposite of what they had. There had been no real closeness between her mother and father, no knowledge of each other's inner thoughts and dreams.

Her father bullied his way through life and treated his children like bonded servants, there to do his bidding.

Christie's mother lived inside her head, not coming out for any of them. It was her survival technique and while Christie could understand it, her mother's mental retreat had made life lonely for her children.

So Christie had watched them, utterly separate and yet bolted together in marriage. She knew that she wanted something different.

That's what had made her marriage to James so special – closeness, respect, honesty. She shaved her legs and bleached her upper lip in front of James, let him know when menstrual cramps used to plague her and let him rub her knotted belly. She'd put her arms round his shoulders when he had the vomiting bugs he was prone to catch, steadying him as he threw up, wiping his face with a cool face cloth.

He'd seen her give birth to their two sons, and it hadn't diminished his desire for her, as some of the books said it might. He'd seen her cry a thousand times and knew which scenes in films and books made her upset and knew that she loved white roses above all other flowers.

Yet despite her craving for utter honesty, there were parts of her mind that she kept to herself: the parts that related to Carey Wolensky.

She'd tried so hard over the years to forget, hoping that eventually the memory would fade like writing on old parchment. If nobody could see it, it was no longer there. Except it was.

Now she could see it in full oil on canvas, hard evidence of a secret she'd tried so hard to forget.

She'd hidden Carey's gifts in Shane's old bedroom and found herself flicking through the sketchbook as a kind of punishment. There were cartoons of many of his most famous pictures here, rough sketches of paintings much prized amongst collectors. And the exquisite drawings that would become his Dark Lady series, each painting worth hundreds of thousands.

But it was the painting that revealed her secret.

She knew now what she had to do.

The day after her thirty-fifth birthday, Carey Wolensky phoned her at home, having found the number in Ana's address book.

Christie, who'd known instinctively that he'd contact her, knew what she ought to say. She'd practised it in fact. 'It

393

was lovely to meet you, but no thank you, I don't want to see you again.'

However, knowing what you should say, and saying it, were two very different things. When she heard that low, husky voice, a voice that she'd dreamed of, she found herself saying yes.

She'd just meet him, she decided, to get this crazy bug out of her system. It would all be different in the cool daylight, when she wasn't annoyed with James or when she wasn't overwhelmed by the sight of Carey's stunning paintings.

She would be able to see that the rush of fierce sexual excitement had all been in her mind, a fantasy, a little break from the real world.

It was the perfect justification for meeting him. Despite the churning guilt in her stomach, she convinced herself that agreeing to meet Carey in his studio was a wise move. There, nobody would see them.

There would be no witnesses to what would inevitably be an embarrassing moment when she apologised but explained that she was married, he was going out with her sister, and they should forget all about that inexplicable moment in the attic gallery the other night.

In the end, her meeting with Carey took little planning. She dropped the boys off to school and playgroup respectively, organising with her friend Antoinette to pick them up afterwards, in case she was delayed, in case coffee went on longer. You had to be practical, Christie reasoned.

The moment Carey opened the scuffed door that led to the huge loft studio, practicality went out the window. He was everything that she remembered, everything and more. Towering, darkly brooding, danger emanating from every pore. The electricity was still there, strong enough to power a city.

394

'I didn't know if you'd come,' he said, his eyes intense on her face.

'I said I would and I don't lie,' Christie said and then winced, thinking that she'd lied to be here.

'I want to paint you,' Carey said, which was what he'd said on the phone, but Christie knew that was just an excuse – flattering, but just an excuse.

'My studio is up the stairs,' he added, moving back to make room for her.

She climbed the wooden stairs, conscious of him close behind her, his presence at once thrilling and scary. The studio was like all the artists' studios that Christie had ever been in: devoid of glamour and warmth. It was a big barn of a place with huge windows for the light, a paint-stained floor and canvases stacked in a corner. There was a table littered with dirty crockery in a small kitchen area. None of it surprised her. She could imagine that when Carey painted, he didn't think of boring things like cleaning up.

'Do you like my work?' he asked as she walked over to look at the canvases, something she wouldn't normally have done unless she knew the artist very well. Strangely, she felt she did know him very well.

'I think it's wonderful,' she said truthfully. 'What I don't understand is why you want to paint me. I didn't think you liked painting portraits.' She was calling his bluff as there had been portraits at his exhibition.

She turned to face him and realised he'd moved to stand right in front of her. He moved so silently, like a big cat. That's what he was like: a predator, fierce, wild, taking what he wanted. Excitement rushed through her body, making her nerves stand on end with the sheer charge of sexual tension.

'I have painted portraits before,' he growled, the accent husky as his eyes roamed over her face.

He wasn't touching her, but he was standing so close she could almost feel him tracing the fine bones of her face with his long-fingered artist's hands. She had left her hair loose again today, conscious that it had been that way when she'd met him first.

'I didn't say I would pose for you,' she said, taking a step back.

'But you're here, aren't you?' he replied.

'I came to see what sort of picture you wanted to paint.'

'A nude,' he said, as if it was the most obvious thing in the world.

Christie didn't answer.

Against one wall was an old ormolu day bed, piled with cushions and swathed in a piece of crimson velvet. Artists loved velvet: painting the textured folds was a life's work in itself. To one side of the day bed was a screen over which hung a faded silk print dressing gown.

'You can change behind the screen,' Carey said, watching her.

Christie looked at the day bed and thought of herself lying naked upon it with him watching. The very thought made her feel unlike herself and enhanced the sensation that this wasn't happening to Christie Devlin, married mother of two. This was an adventure occurring to her other self. Christie wouldn't do this but the wild, fey woman she might have been would.

She went behind the screen, undressed and pulled the dressing gown on. With huge sleeves like a kimono and an oriental print, it made her feel like a geisha.

'What do you want me to do?' she asked when she emerged from behind the screen.

'Lie with your head on the pillows, one arm along your side,' he said absently.

He'd already moved an easel so he was facing the day bed and it was as if he'd forgotten all about her except as his model. Shrugging, Christie slipped off the kimono and lay down.

'No, move your hand, further, there, that's right. And your hair . . .'

He strode over to her and every inch of her flesh tensed, but Carey was not seeing her naked in front of him. He arranged a tendril of hair to brush her breast and his hand touched her nipple, making it tauten into a hard nub, yet he still didn't react.

'Better,' he said, standing back and assessing her like a horse breeder looking at a mare. 'Better.'

She lay there for three quarters of an hour until her muscles ached holding the pose. After art college, she knew that an artist absorbed in his work might selfishly want a model to pose for ever, but she couldn't hold it any longer.

She stretched, no longer feeling conscious of her nudity, got to her feet, and pulled on the kimono.

Carey grunted and went back to his canvas.

'I'll take fifteen minutes,' she said, walking stiffly into the kitchen section to make herself a hot drink.

After fifteen minutes of silence, she went back to her pose. Half an hour later, she moved again. It was time for her to leave.

'I have to go,' she said, standing. She desperately wanted to see the painting but knew better than to look. He would ask her to look if he wanted her to.

'Fine,' he said, engrossed in his work. 'Let yourself out. You can be here tomorrow, yes?'

She didn't reply but she knew that she'd be back. She couldn't help herself.

The brisk chill of autumn gave way to winter while Carey painted Christie Devlin and the studio, no doubt a beautiful place in high summer, became cold, bringing up goose pimples on Christie's naked skin. She was used to the pose now, had sat for Carey several days a week for two months and even lying on the couch at home in the evening, she unconsciously found herself sitting the way he'd positioned her that first day.

She hadn't told James or Ana that she was posing for Carey. There was no need: it was all totally innocent, she convinced herself. Carey barely spoke to her and never touched her, not after that first day. She wasn't doing anything wrong. And yet she knew that lying there naked while this incredible man took in every millimetre of her skin was not quite as straightforward as it sounded. She knew that when she lay there on the day bed, with crimson velvet caressing her body, she really wanted Carey Wolensky caressing her body. But nothing had happened, and nothing was going to happen. As November began, she knew it was time to end it. She had to because the guilt was driving her insane. The only time she didn't feel it was when she was with Carey: every other moment of her life, guilt over the people she was betraying racked her.

It was James's birthday in November and he had been talking about a long weekend away. Christie knew that if she and James were alone together, without the children, then the crystal-clear guilt of betraying him by not telling him would hit her.

Then there was Ana, little Ana whom she'd been like a mother to. She adored her sister, and even though Ana was less enamoured of Carey these days – 'He's obsessed with painting, Christie. He's not interested in going out with me. We're too different for it to work. I don't want to hurt him but remember that man from the night of the party in Haddington Road, I've seen him a few times. He's gorgeous. I know it's wrong, but . . .'

It was small comfort to Christie that Ana wasn't interested in Carey any more. It would still devastate Ana to discover her sister's involvement with him.

Finally, Christie knew she had to end it because she knew she was powerless against Carey if he raised one little finger to her. The magnetism between them was so great she would run into his arms and Christie knew if she did that, she would never forgive herself.

So, one cool November morning, she decided that this was the last day she'd pose in his studio.

Surely, he must have seen all he needed, he must have tilted his head at an angle enough times, looking at her, analysing her skin tone, her shape, the movement of her muscles and her skin. He had drunk her in for long enough and she was going to finish it.

She waited until her break, when, as usual, she went into the kitchen and made herself some tea. The weather had grown colder and the thin robe was insubstantial. She shivered, clutching the mug of tea close to her chest, with her arms wrapped around herself.

'I'm sorry, Carey, but I can't come here any more,' she said, looking out from the studio windows over the roof tops of the surrounding artisan cottages. There, she'd said it. She felt herself tremble.

'Why?' he said, and incredibly, he was behind her in an instant, his hands on her shoulders, his strong embrace filling her with warmth. She hadn't heard him approach, he moved so silently and with such animal grace.

'You know I've got to stop,' she said, determined not to relax back against him. His hands slid further down her arms, pulling her back against him, making her feel the warmth of his body. She closed her eyes and leaned back.

'Carey, you must see that?'

'I don't see that at all,' he said. 'I see that you inspire me.

I see what I feel for you and what you feel for me. Why should we stop that?'

Her eyes still closed, she sighed.

'Because it's wrong. I love my husband, my children, and Ana. I shouldn't be here. You have no idea how much I torture myself over you, Carey. I think endlessly of the people I'm betraying by coming to see you. If they knew, imagine if James and Ana knew about this.'

She knew Ana was no longer interested in Carey but that excuse wouldn't work with her husband.

'Ana is a lovely girl but she's not for me,' Carey said. 'She knows that. I told her I was wrong for her in the beginning. She's stubborn. She went out with me to prove me wrong. I have told her she should find a nice quiet man to settle down with. I am not a nice quiet man.'

'Like my husband, you mean?' Christie asked, sensing the criticism of James. 'He's a nice man and he doesn't deserve this. It's wrong, all wrong, what you and I feel for each other.'

'How can it be wrong to feel like this?' he asked, holding her even more tightly. 'I have been so cautious, Christie, I haven't touched you, even though I want to every moment you're here, every moment you're not here. But I've given you the distance you need, you deserve. I let you make all the decisions and now you say you won't come any more?'

He turned her around gently and she stared into those dark, dark eyes. She'd never felt anything like the connection between them, the feeling that she'd known him for ever, in another life.

She'd heard some say that there were people destined to meet again and again in many lives, to search each other out until some scene had been played and their spirits could rest. Was Carey Wolensky from her past? The faith she'd been brought up in didn't countenance such things but there had to be some reason for the intensity of her feelings for him, the sense that he was another part of her.

Then, he took the mug from her hands, put it down on the table, cupped her face between his long, sensitive fingers and kissed her. And Christie knew she was lost.

CHAPTER TWENTY-SIX

Her thoughts still with the distant past, Christie shut the front door quietly.

There was no noise in the house, but Christie knew James was there. She knew it because the dogs didn't come rushing frantically to greet her the way they did when she was the first person to arrive home.

James's shoes were in the hall, along with his briefcase and his jacket left on the stairpost.

Everything looked normal: except it wasn't. It was only a day since Christie had been to see Carey, and already, everything had changed.

She walked into the kitchen and the dogs bounced happily at seeing her.

James didn't say hello or get up to hug her. He was sitting at the table with Carey's sketchbook spread in front of him and the small oil painting propped up against the fruit bowl.

'I never knew,' he said, still staring fixedly at the woman in the picture.

Christie could see the real scene in her mind's eye: the artist's studio dirty, grubby and in no way romantic. The smell of turpentine and dust in the air, old paint-smeared rags thrown on the ground, and there was the divan, just as musty and dusty but with a piece of beautiful crimson velvet cloth thrown over it. Only the best painters could make velvet look beautiful with the warmth almost of living flesh. And her lying on it, naked, smiling, feeling beautiful.

'Did you sleep with him?' James asked, never taking his eyes off the painting. 'I have to know, Christie. Did you sleep with him?'

Christie hesitated, thinking. She'd thought about that for years. Which was the bigger betrayal – the act of sex, the intimacy of feeling another person's body inside yours, skin on skin, flesh to flesh? Or was it worse being close to them, talking to them, learning their most intimate thoughts, laughing to hear their voice, sharing a secret from the world? Was that a far greater crime than actually sleeping with somebody?

If their places had been reversed, if James had gone off with another woman – like dear, sweet Veronica from his office, who was shy and adored James, but would never, ever make the move on him – and shared moments of quiet time together, *that* would have broken Christie's heart. Not the fact that he'd brought Veronica to a hotel somewhere, stripped her clothes off and made love to her, the way he'd made love to Christie.

No, the intimacy, the kindness, the shared secret: that would have been the most painful thing to deal with. Not the sex.

She had to explain before she answered.

'That's not the most important thing . . .' she said.

'It is,' snapped back James. 'Did you sleep with him?'

The truth was the only answer. 'Yes,' she said quietly. 'I'm telling you because I don't want there to be any more secrets between us.' She sat down at the table beside him.

James looked haunted, aged, not the man who had left the house this morning.

403

'I'm so sorry,' she said, the words sounding useless. Sorry was too small a word to cover the huge regret for having hurt him.

'I should have told you years ago, but you know what they say, there is no point telling about an affair if the only thing you do is salve your conscience.'

'Then why did you leave this here for me to find?' he asked hoarsely. 'To salve your conscience by admitting you'd slept with another man or to hurt me by showing me his pictures of you.'

Even as she'd left the sketchbook and the painting there for him to find only hours before, Christie had agonised. But she knew she had to do it. James would be home by seven, so she'd put Carey's work on the kitchen table where he would see it, and she'd gone to sit in the Summer Street Café, staring blankly into an untouched coffee until it was time to go home and face him.

It was one of the hardest things she'd ever done but the truth had to be laid bare now. There could be no more secrets. 'I didn't want to keep this from you,' she said. 'And,' she paused, 'I was always scared you'd find out and it would destroy us. I couldn't bear that possibility.'

'You kept your dirty little secret well. I hadn't a clue,' he replied, with fingers clutching the sketchbook tightly as if at any minute he might fling it across the room, regardless of its worth. 'Ana – does she know what her beloved sister did? And why did you tell me now?'

Christie didn't know why – she only knew that she'd felt this intense compulsion to tell the truth to her husband. Beyond that, she hadn't thought rationally. Once she'd told him, he could do what he wanted with the information and she would have to take the consequences. 'It's different with Ana,' she said, thinking aloud. 'She didn't really love him. She was fed up with all those doctors, remember? They had no lives outside the hospital and they just wanted someone to date occasionally.'

'I remember,' James said grimly. 'You were the one who urged her to get a new life, to meet new people and she met him.' He snarled the word and Christie had no doubt that if Carey Wolensky had been in the room at that moment, James would have killed him.

'You said he was the wrong sort of guy for her, controlling, crazy, remember that too?' James demanded.

'I remember,' Christie replied. 'He was all of those things and he was wrong for her.'

'But not wrong for you?' James snapped.

'He was wrong for me too,' Christie said evenly.

She'd never seen James like this before, but then she had never admitted adultery to him before.

'She didn't really love him,' Christie said, and she was pretty certain of that.

When Carey had left Ireland abruptly, Ana hadn't really cared. Soon afterwards, she'd met Rick, the great love of her life.

'Are you going to tell *her* what happened?' James asked.

'No, I don't think she needs to know.' That guilt would have to live with her for ever.

'But I did?' He sounded so angry, was clearly barely holding on to his fury and pain.

'Yes, you did,' she said. 'If Ana knew, it wouldn't destroy our relationship. We'd go on. But the secret would destroy you and me. I heard he was coming back to Ireland for an exhibition and I was crucified with doubt and fear. I had to have the secret out, to tell you.'

'To tell me what?' James said. 'That he's here and you're running off with him, to the land of millionaires? Is that it?'

He looked angrier than she'd ever seen him before and

405

Christie felt humbled by his love for her, destroyed by her betrayal of this good, decent man. But she had to continue her explanation, so James could understand.

'I went to see him yesterday,' she said, 'and that's when he gave me the sketchbook and the picture. I'm not leaving you for him, there was never any question of that, James.'

'Well, that's good to know,' he said sarcastically.

This wasn't going the way Christie had planned.

'James, I wanted you to know about the past and that's all it is: the past, not the present. I've been so anxious about it and I realise that a secret like this can't be hidden, it's always going to be there and it would be better for us to get it out in the open, for me to tell you.'

'Why?' James demanded. 'To make me realise that thirty-something years of marriage have all been a sham?'

'No, they haven't,' Christie replied. 'There's nothing sham about our marriage, there never was. It was a moment of madness, stupidity.' She threw up her hands. 'I can't explain.'

It was impossible to explain that Carey had stood for the wild passion of art that she'd loved, something she'd had to suppress inside herself in order to live the life she had. Perhaps if she hadn't met James and married him and had two small children, perhaps then she could have lived happily in Carey's bohemian world. But James, Shane and Ethan meant that that path could never be for her.

'I love you, James, I've always loved you. What I had with Carey was just stupid and crazy and I knew it at the time and . . .'

'And you posed for him, naked,' James spat out, looking back at the picture. 'This is you. I looked it up on the internet just now. He's famous for these mysterious Dark Lady paintings. You knew I wouldn't know about them. Art doesn't interest me, so you were pretty safe with your secret. You knew I was never going to notice a painting by this man and

406

realise, that's my wife lying there naked, because I would have recognised you anywhere.'

'I know,' she said soberly, 'it made it easier that you weren't interested in art. It must mean something to you now that I am telling you, that I trust you enough to say all these things to you.'

'Trust?' he said. 'What's trust, Christie? I thought we had trust, but I was wrong. What was wrong with me? Was I too safe, too boring, too dependable, with my government job? Did you really want another life with someone else? Have you been waiting for bloody Wolensky to come and claim you all these years? Were there secret phone calls and trysts? Tell me!'

'No,' she shouted. 'I haven't seen or heard from him in twenty-five years. I wasn't waiting for him. If I'd wanted a life with someone else, I would have left to be with him when he asked me, but I didn't.'

'Oh, so you gave up the chance to run away with the great artist, for me and our dull life?' said James coldly. He got up abruptly, stared at her, as if she was a stranger. 'I don't know what to say to you, Christie. I've been looking at that book for what seems like hours, looking at pictures of you from every conceivable angle. Drawings by a man who looked at you in the way only I was supposed to look at you. Maybe at our age you're not supposed to care, maybe you're supposed to be beyond all that jealousy. But you know what, I do care. I care so much it hurts here.' He struck his chest fiercely. 'I don't know if I can forgive you or him. Where is he anyway?'

'No, don't go near him,' Christie said. 'That's how I have the sketchbook and the picture. He wanted to give them to me, he's dying.' She said it quickly, in case James rushed out into the city, searching for Carey Wolensky with a view to killing him.

'He's terminally ill, James. He wanted to find me and say goodbye, that's all. I knew he was coming, that's why I've been so anxious lately. Anxious that he'd come and ruin our lives. That's when I realised I had to tell you myself because I couldn't live with the fear, the fear of losing you.'

'Well, there's a pity,' said James with uncharacteristic harshness, 'because you've lost me anyway. I'll leave you with your lover's grubby little pictures. Wolensky can come here any time he wants now, because I won't be here. Isn't that what you want? Oh yes, you can talk to our sons and tell them what happened.'

'James, we don't need to bring Ethan and Shane into this,' Christie begged. 'This is not about them, this is about us. Please don't let's involve them.'

She couldn't bear it if her two sons learned of this. She couldn't bear them to look at her with disgust and anger, to think of what she'd done to their beloved father. She thought of Faye: how she'd been terrified of letting Amber know the truth about her past life, and Christie understood it completely. Could there be anything worse than having your darling children stare at you with disgust, where once they had looked at you with pride?

'Please don't say anything to them,' she begged.

'I'm not saying anything to anyone,' James snapped. 'I need some time to myself. I'll be on my mobile phone. I might go fishing.'

He hadn't gone fishing for years. She couldn't imagine where his fishing boxes and tackle were. Suddenly, she realised that that was hardly a problem and that James probably wasn't going fishing anyway. He just needed to get away, to be anywhere, except near her.

'I understand,' she said humbly, 'and I'm sorry. That's all I wanted to say, I'm sorry. It was a huge mistake and there is nothing else I can say except I love you. It was a mistake.

408

He was a mistake. But I didn't go with him when he asked me to, I stayed here with you.'

'And I'm supposed to be grateful for that fact?' James said. 'Because right now, I don't feel very grateful. I just feel very angry.'

'Will you phone me tonight so that I know wherever you're going, you got there safely?' Christie asked, not wanting to think of him driving recklessly.

'No,' he said. 'I don't want to talk to you, Christie. I can't, I have to think.'

'I don't want our marriage to be over,' she pleaded.

'I can't tell you that either,' James said.

He stormed out of the room, but for once the dogs didn't get up to follow him halfway up the stairs, torn between the humans they loved most. Instead, they lay on the floor, noses on their paws, big dark eyes looking soulfully and worriedly up at Christie.

'I know, babies,' she said. 'Daddy's upset. But it'll be OK.' She talked to them like she'd talked to her children when they were small. You always told children that things would be OK even if they weren't going to be. Christie didn't know how this would all pan out. Her gift of vision was blank. She wished she could look into a crystal ball and see James coming home, forgiving her, throwing his arms around her, saying it was all in the past and they could forget it. But that might never happen. She'd done what she thought was the right thing, because she couldn't live under the fear for ever. But now the fear that James would one day find out about her infidelity had been replaced with an entirely different type of fear. The fear that James would leave her for ever. Had she done the wrong thing after all?

CHAPTER TWENTY-SEVEN

Faye, too, felt lost and alone, waiting in New York for news of Amber. She'd meant to go home sooner: she'd been there nearly a month and it was costing her a fortune. But leaving would be like giving up on Amber and she just couldn't do it.

She rang Ella each evening, hoping that Amber might have rung her friend with details of where she was, but no such luck. It was as if Amber had fallen off the face of the earth. Now that she'd made her choice, she was going to stick with it, not talking to friends, family, anyone, she'd cut them all off. Like mother, like daughter, Faye thought endlessly, remembering how single-minded she'd been all those years ago, before she'd become pregnant with Amber. Then, she wouldn't listen to anyone. She should have known that Amber would have inherited that trait too.

Alone in New York, she had plenty of time to think. She wasn't a shopper, so she bypassed the stores that would have left Grace in paroxysms of delight. Instead, she forced herself around the sights.

She visited Ground Zero one day, and stood there silently and felt ashamed of herself. She might not know where Amber was, but she was pretty sure she was alive. She'd simply chosen not to have contact with her mother any more. Whereas the people who had died here were gone for ever. She could and would see Amber again. The Ground Zero families were not so lucky.

Faye left with a new sense of determination. There had to be something else she could do to find Amber: that was the first thing on her list. And the second was to move on. She hadn't had so much time on her own in years, time to look at herself. She found she didn't like what she saw.

Getting back to her comfortably familiar hotel room, she phoned Grace's office answering machine and left a message.

'Grace, this is Faye, I need your help. When you get this, will you ring me at the hotel? We can talk and I'll give you all the details.'

Grace phoned at eight p.m. Irish time.

'You're in late,' said Faye.

'Well, my fabulous partner and second-in-command is on leave,' retorted Grace, 'so somebody has to keep the home fires burning. But you don't want to hear my problems. How's the search going?'

'Not well,' Faye replied. 'Whatever deal the band had going is off, so God knows where they are. I imagine they'll be looking for another production company. Amber's friend, Ella, says that Karl Evans – he's the guy Amber's fallen for – is very determined to succeed, so it's unlikely they'd just give up . . . But it's a whole other world here and I can't get much information. I thought maybe you could ask around at home, see who knows of the band or their manager?'

Grace knew everybody, senior policemen, politicians, business movers and shakers. If anybody could track down Ceres and Karl, it was Grace.

'Give me all the details,' Grace insisted, businesslike. 'I'll see what I can do.'

411

Faye felt a weight lift off her shoulders; she wished she'd asked for Grace's help ages ago.

Three hours later she rang again. 'I think I've found them,' she said.

'Do you know what day it is?' Amber asked Karl.

They were sitting by the pool at a small table enjoying breakfast. The rest of the band were around them, all looking bright and energetic even though it was half past eight in the morning. There was no drinking or carousing now. Life had turned serious. They were working on their album, had been for the last three days. Amber had never doubted Karl's ability but she had never seen him so focused, so dedicated. And so happy. But she was finding it hard to see the person she loved filled with a joy that had absolutely nothing to do with her. It made her feel lost and alone.

'What day it is?' he echoed genially. He had a Californian tan now. His skin was naturally dark and even though the band had spent a lot of time in the studio, he had a fabulous glow about him. He looked different. It was as though he was moving away from her, thought Amber, with growing despondency.

'Yeah, do you know what day it is?' she repeated.

'No.' He shrugged. 'The fourth day of the rest of our lives?' Karl had said recording an album was like starting a new life, the one he'd been dreaming about since he could dream. 'I don't know, what day is it?'

'It's the day the exams end,' Amber said.

Right now, she knew Ella was probably still asleep. Back home it was late afternoon and the gang at St Ursula's would already be planning to go out partying to celebrate the end of school and the end of exams. How many times had she and Ella thought about that moment, imagining what it would

412

be like, especially in the dark days of winter when they trudged home, school bags heavy with books, their hearts weighed down with the thought of all the study.

'I know what I'm going to do when it's all over,' Ella would say dreamily, 'I'm going to go home, get into bed and lie there and turn my TV on and read magazines. And paint my nails and have a bath, oh, and do my hair and put on my make-up and dance around and go out!'

'Sounds perfect to me,' sighed Amber, although she didn't have a TV in her bedroom. Her mum disapproved of televisions in bedrooms. But she'd put on her CD player and dance around and do nothing, have absolutely nothing hanging over her.

And now, here she was thousands of miles away in beautiful sunshine surrounded by arguably some of the most beautiful people on the planet, doing nothing and it should have been wonderful. Except that it wasn't. The boys were going off into the studio soon and she'd be alone again.

She'd never been so much on her own in her whole life. She'd always been with people: Ella, girls from school, Mum, yet now here she had vast tracts of time to herself and not really anywhere to be or anything to do. It was odd. Doing nothing wasn't as much fun when there was nothing else you should be doing. The fact that she felt so out of place here added to her sense of sadness.

'Bet you're glad you missed all that exam crap,' Karl said, taking another bran and cranberry muffin from the pile. 'What's the point of all that kind of bourgeois garbage? Exams didn't get us where we are today, did they?' he said, with a touch of the smugness that was creeping into everything he said these days. The band were going to make it, they were going to be on the cover of *Billboard*. He didn't say these things quietly to Amber in the privacy of their own suite as they lay in each other's arms and shared dreams. She wouldn't

413

have minded that. But no, this unshakeable self-belief was said publicly and without a shred of embarrassment. Even Syd, who was the voice of reason, was affected by it and grinned when Karl went on about how big the band were going to be.

'I keep thinking,' Amber blurted out suddenly, 'I should have stayed at home to do the exams after all. I feel guilty now. I mean, it wouldn't have made any difference if I'd come late. I could have got on a plane tonight and been here tomorrow.'

'But you'd have missed all the fun,' said Kenny T.

'Exactly,' said Lew, who was stuffing his face with an omelette, a full egg one, a fact which had astonished the waitress.

'Not an egg white one?' she'd said, because nobody here ever ate full egg omelettes. Think of the cholesterol, the fat?

'No, the whole egg, the yellow bit and all,' said Lew happily. Lew planned on never learning how to spell cholesterol. If he couldn't spell it, it couldn't get him.

'I mean, think of the fun we had on the road, the adventures,' he said now.

Amber looked at Lew. He'd rewritten the road trip in his mind. She remembered it exactly as it had been: miserable, scary, cockroach-ridden. Being totally broke was not a nice way to travel through a foreign country where you knew nobody.

'You'd have missed being part of the adventure,' Kenny T added. 'You wouldn't have been part of our history, the history of the band.'

'You see, when they write about us in *Rolling Stone*,' Syd said, with a sly grin in Karl's direction, 'we'll be able to talk about how the five of us trekked across America with only a dream in our hearts and you'll have been a part of that.'

A part of the trip, thought Amber. But not a part of what

had happened afterwards. Having survived the travails of the road didn't make her a member of the band. Instead, she was a hanger-on, the girl with the band.

Thinking of this, she glanced at Karl, hoping he'd say the right thing and make her feel that her presence was still important to him. She wanted to hear him say that it wouldn't have been the same without her, that her presence – as his muse – had made it all work.

But he wasn't even listening and was flicking through the papers again.

A helicopter buzzed overhead, breaking up the perfect sky for an instant before disappearing. Amber looked up to see the glint of the chopper between the fronds of the palm tree shading their table. This really was a slice of paradise. Except it wasn't her paradise. She wasn't here on her dime: she was here on someone else's. Karl didn't really care whether she was here or not.

She'd been stupid to think he had. It had been fun while it lasted, but she'd given up so much for him and he neither understood nor appreciated her sacrifice. That realisation was crystal clear.

The boys sat there eating, and talking, all openly admiring an extremely attractive, very skinny blonde who sashayed past in a sliver of a dress hardly covering the most phenom-enal breasts Amber had ever seen. They were clearly not real, but the boys didn't seem to realise that, or they didn't care. They just stared anyway, watching her skinny flanks appre-ciatively, even Karl.

Amber found that she didn't mind very much, whereas, once, she'd have been outraged at Karl ogling another woman so openly. Was this her Damascene conversion, she wondered, and then grinned, thinking that at least Sister Patricia would be pleased that Amber had been paying attention at some point in religious education at St Ursula's.

She got up from the table. 'I'll see you guys later, right?'

'Yeah, sure, right,' they all said.

'Bye, babe.'

'Yeah, see ya,' said Karl absently.

Amber walked back to their suite. She shouldn't have given up her life for Karl and the realisation didn't make her feel stupid, it just made her feel sad.

She'd burned a lot of bridges for him. Even her eighteenth birthday had turned into pretty much another day with Karl.

Instead of Ella and her friends organising a night out after the exams, Amber's birthday had been celebrated in a pub in Dublin just before they left when Karl had given her a silver bangle which was now tarnished, proof of how cheap it had been. She thought of the lovely portfolio her mother had bought for her and wanted to cry.

She'd been so blind to his faults, she realised. At least she was wiser now.

That night, while she was still working out what she was going to do, Michael took them to another party. There were parties every night but nobody stayed out late. Nobody got drunk either. LA was, as Michael reminded the band, a working town. Going to parties was a public relations exercise, not an excuse for wild behaviour.

Tonight's party was in the Hollywood hills and Amber, who'd worked out in the hotel's gym and then swum lengths in the pool, felt physically tired as she got ready in her bathroom. She was wearing her green thrift shop dress and pendant again. It looked lovely and she did have a faint tan too, not Hollywood gold but certainly something she'd have considered mahogany in Dublin.

The house they were driven to in the requisite convoy of Jeep Grand Cherokees was hotel-sized, appeared to be mainly made of glass and sat perched on a hillside with an intricate terrace and a gently curving pool filled with Japanese carp. Walking in the door was like walking into an interiors magazine.

Not that it was ostentatious – quite the opposite. Painted a warm vanilla, with dark floors, creamy upholstery, and carefully placed modern lighting, the effect was of simple elegance, like the guests. The music was muted jazz, the drinks were clear cocktails, champagne and plenty of juice, and the band loved it.

Within half an hour of arriving, Karl had left Amber's side and when she saw him a few minutes later, he was talking to Venetia, who looked as exquisite as the first time Amber had seen her, white linen pants and a white silk halter top emphasising both her figure and the rich colour of her skin.

Amber didn't feel threatened by Venetia tonight, although she couldn't have explained why, if anyone had asked her. Venetia was so beautiful, she was in another dimension of beauty. Normal people like Amber could never compete with Venetia's exquisite ebony limbs, those dark, flashing eyes and lips that were full of promise.

Lew wandered up to Amber and put an arm round her.

'How's it going, babe?' he said, then, when she didn't reply, he followed her gaze and saw Karl sitting with Venetia.

'She is one amazing-looking woman,' he said with the sigh of someone who knew Venetia was way out of his league. 'No offence, Amber, I mean you look pretty good too.'

Amber smiled wryly. 'None taken, Lew.'

At first the evening was fun, seeing people who looked vaguely familiar, people from the music industry, people whose albums Amber had bought. But it wasn't always easy to join the groups of people who already knew each other and eventually, she and the band, minus Karl, ended up relaxing in a split level part of the house in front of a huge stone fireplace where vast expensive candles burned in the grate.

417

Syd was holding forth on the parties they'd been to, insisting that the people with the entourages and bodyguards were faking it, despite the bling.

'The quiet ones in jeans with those discreet watches you've never seen in any normal jewellery store, they're the multi-billionaires,' he pointed out shrewdly. 'The bling, blings aren't that bling at all. Take away the diamonds and the bulked-up bodyguards and there's nothing left.'

Amber laughed. She liked hanging around with Syd. He had a sense of humour similar to Ella's.

She'd thought about calling Ella earlier, having had one of those moments when she'd longed to hear her friend's voice, to hear someone say 'How nice to hear from you' and really mean it.

Nobody here needed her like the people back home did. Kenny T and Lew were sweet guys, while Syd was a genuinely kind, good man, terribly in love with his Lola. They liked Amber, were fond of her, probably in the same way you'd be fond of a puppy or a kitten that clambered on to your lap and wanted to be petted. Nothing more. And Karl? Karl had moved on.

She'd chickened out of ringing Ella. So much time had gone by. In their whole friendship it had never ever been weeks since they'd talked. Even when Ella's family had gone to Italy to visit relatives, they'd kept in touch, Ella facing the wrath of her mother for making so many international calls.

But it had been worth it because they were best friends, weren't they? And now, weeks had gone by without hearing Ella's laugh or hearing her joke or moan about her grand-mother. It was funny the things you missed.

She sighed and tried to stop thinking about back home in case she cried. She forced herself to observe the party and the Hollywood hierarchy. In some subliminal way people from lower down the celebrity power chain ignored each other as they tried to attach themselves to upper groups.

Amber wasn't part of any of the groups, but she didn't care. It would all make a wonderful painting, she thought suddenly, her artist's eye trying to imagine how she would sketch it out. She could see it in her head and itched to record what she'd seen. Paper and a pencil, that's what she needed.

In the kitchen, in clear contrast to the cool calm of the rest of the house, the catering staff ran around frantically. They didn't notice her in the bustle when she appropriated a pad and a pen lying on a table. She went back to the lounge, leaned against the fireplace and began to sketch. It felt great to be drawing again. Energy burned within her with each deft stroke of her pen. As she drew the room and outlines of the people in it, quickly, speedily, because they were moving all the time, she felt that buzz she'd always felt when she had a pen in her hand. That was how she saw the world: through her eyes directly into her hands and on to the page. Maybe that's why she screwed up so much with Karl. She'd seen him only with her eyes, she'd never made the connection and put him down on paper. If she had, then she might have seen that he was insubstantial, not what she'd first thought.

A tall man, dressed in a simple white shirt and khaki combats, walked over to her with a glass of wine in his hand.

'I've been watching you,' he said. 'Are you drawing us?'

He stood beside her and looked down at the picture.

'That's really good,' he said, in both shock and astonishment, 'really good.'

He looked at her again, this time with renewed respect. 'You're an artist?'

Amber turned her amazing grey eyes with their copper flecks upon him.

'Yes,' she said, feeling a surge of self. 'I'm an artist. I'm not really sure what I'm doing here, hanging out with a band and a man.'

'Which band is that?' asked the man. He was probably in his forties, way old, sort of a bit like Ella's dad actually.

'Ceres,' she said, pointing over to where Karl was sitting on a low couch with Michael and Venetia. She hadn't sketched them in her picture yet, she'd been working on the people around them.

'He's the band? Or is he your boyfriend?' asked the man.

'Both,' said Amber grimly.

The man said nothing, just assimilated the information.

'Who are you?' she asked.

'I'm Saul, this is my house, my party.'

'Pleased to meet you,' Amber said. 'Where I come from, you generally know the people whose party you're going to and, if you don't, as soon as you get there you're introduced and you say thank you so much for inviting us. It's different here.'

'You're Irish, right? Land of saints and scholars and maidens dancing at the crossroads.'

'Exactly,' said Amber, with mock sincerity, 'in the same way that Los Angeles is a glorious city where dreams come true and there are beautiful women on every corner.' She gave him a hard look.

'Touché,' he said.

'Do I look like a maiden who dances at the crossroads to you?' she asked.

'Not in that dress.'

'Good,' said Amber. 'I wouldn't want to be, any more than I'd want to be the LA version. This city does seem to suck the individuality out of people and make them different, but all in the same way.'

He laughed this time, showing beautiful dental work.

'And you have lovely teeth,' she added. 'Everyone here

420

has lovely teeth. When people smile, it's like being in a tooth-paste advert.'

'You have pretty nice teeth yourself,' he countered. 'You ought to be a writer instead of an artist. You've certainly got the bite.'

'I prefer painting,' Amber said. 'That's my first love.'

'I thought the guy from the band was your first love?' Saul motioned to where Venetia and Karl sat together.

'Touché to you,' she replied. 'The truth is I'm a total moron, following a group of guys around, watching them fulfil their dream, having dumped my own dream by the wayside.'

'A common movie theme.' Saul nodded. 'Boy meets girl, boy tells girl he loves her, boy drags girl on long trek and pretty much ignores her, boy loses girl. Boy realises what he's lost and runs after her. Cue credits. Are you at the boy loses girl part yet?'

Amber looked over to where Karl and Venetia were locked in their own world. Karl had that look on his face, the look he had all the time these days, the look of blazing triumph and excitement. The power of his talent made him sexier than ever. He was like a supernova.

'Yeah,' Amber said to Saul. 'I think we're at that stage.'

She didn't think they'd ever get to the part of the movie where Karl realised what he'd lost and ran after her. Movies and real life ran on different paths.

'And you're not going to race over to throw your drink over them?' Saul asked.

Amber smiled.

'What would be the point of that?' Amber asked. 'Apart from creating a nice little scene for everyone to laugh at. I'm with the band, you know. Girlfriends are supposed to under-stand that musicians don't have the faithful gene. Playing lead guitar removes it.'

Saul grinned. 'As long as you know your place,' he dead-panned. 'That's very important in this town. Everyone is trying to get up to a higher place, but you need to know where you are to start with.'

'Oh, I know,' Amber said. 'I know. That is to say, I didn't know when I got here, but I've worked it out.'

'You're pretty smart,' Saul reflected.

'My mother wanted me to know stuff,' Amber revealed. 'She wanted me to understand the world, my place in it, what I could do and what I couldn't do and never to follow the crowd and . . .'

'That's why you're here, with the band?' Saul said.

'Precisely. I had to do exactly the opposite of what my mother taught me.'

'I work on the belief that you've got to learn by other people's mistakes, because you never live long enough to make them all yourself,' Saul remarked.

'I'm the opposite,' said Amber. 'I have to make all the mistakes myself.'

'Will you stay in LA? It's a nice place to be an artist, the light is pretty fabulous in the hills.'

'I don't know,' Amber said, shrugging. 'I don't know what I'm going to do.'

'I guess you're not going to stay with the band, are you?'

Amber glanced over to Venetia and Karl. Venetia was so close to Karl that she was almost sitting on his knee, a position Amber remembered being in the first time she'd met Karl back home. It seemed a million years ago. Which of them had been shallow and stupid, she or Karl, she wasn't sure.

'I don't know,' she said to Saul now. 'I don't know what I'm going to do.' But she knew she couldn't just go home alone, could she?

Amber didn't bother telling Karl she was leaving the party.

She hitched a ride in somebody's Humvee back to the hotel and she wasn't surprised when she woke the next morning to find herself alone. It seemed he and Venetia were now an item, except he hadn't had the courage to tell her. Never mind, Amber thought, she had enough courage for both of them. She was going to move out, she wasn't going to hang around where she wasn't wanted.

When reception rang to say there was a delivery of flowers for her downstairs, Amber wondered what it could be. Flowers with a goodbye note from Karl? She almost laughed at the thought. That's probably how he'd do it, with roses and a card that said, 'Bye and won't be seeing you soon, Karl.'

She pulled on her jeans, a T-shirt and some flip-flops and made her way down to the lobby. She was just about to approach the concierge desk when, out of the corner of her eye, she saw a movement that was instantly familiar. She turned, and there, halfway out of her seat, was her mother. Comforting, familiar and utterly welcome.

'Amber,' said Faye, and there was no escaping the pure joy on her face. 'Amber, it's so good to see you.'

Amber's first instinct was to run and hug her mother, so that was exactly what she did. It was wonderful to touch her mother, to feel loved, safe and secure again.

'Mum,' she said, burying her head in her mother's shoulder.

'Darling, it's so wonderful to see you,' said Faye shakily.

'You too, Mum. I'm sorry, I'm really sorry, how it all happened,' Amber muttered, holding tight.

'Hush,' said her mother. 'Hush. It's OK now. I've missed you so much.'

'I've missed you too, Mum,' Amber said. 'Come on, come back to the room. We'll talk and we can have breakfast,' she added eagerly. 'I just have to pick up a delivery.'

Faye grinned.

423

'The delivery was from me,' she said. 'I said they had to be given to you personally, which is why they rang up to your room.'

She gestured behind her to the table beside the armchair where she'd been sitting. A small posy of wildflowers sat in a basket on the table.

'They're beautiful.' Amber felt teary again. She loved wild-flowers.

'I wasn't sure if you'd want to see me,' Faye went on and Amber felt the weight of guilt. How awful that her mother had had to adopt such a ruse.

'I'm sorry,' she said. She ran over and picked up the flowers, then ran back, linked her arm through her mother's and said: 'Come on, we'll have breakfast and we'll talk.'

They might as well have one last big blowout on Karl, she thought, leading her mum back up to the room.

They sat on the small balcony with coffee, pancakes and fresh fruit salad in front of them and barely touched anything in their eagerness to talk. Faye wanted to hear everything that had happened and Amber was amazed to find her tongue rushing away with her, as she described the hotels they'd stayed in, the misery when the band's deal had fallen through and how everything had turned up trumps in Los Angeles. She didn't mention a word about her and Karl though. Not one sentence about how they'd moved so far apart that you could drive a car between them. She was too proud for that.

'This is a beautiful hotel,' Faye said, when she'd recounted her fear at seeing the awful Arizona Fish Hotel and realising that Amber had had to stay there. 'I've been so worried about you. You couldn't imagine all the scenarios that came up in my head. I just kept thinking of all the . . .' she paused, 'all the trouble I'd got into when I was your age and in love.'

Amber looked at her curiously. What trouble had her mother got into?

Faye could see the question forming in her daughter's eyes. Amber looked so well, she thought, with that faint tan. Her daughter really was beautiful. Beautiful, clever, intelligent and a grown-up. She should have told her the truth a long time ago.

Ever since Grace had phoned with news of where the band were staying in LA, thanks to locating their manager, Faye had been practising what she was going to say to her daughter. She'd had a month to think about it but it was only when she knew for sure where Amber was that she allowed herself to have that mental conversation.

In her mind, she'd thought maybe they would drive to the beach, walk on the sand and talk there. Amber had always loved the sea and maybe if they walked side by side and let the wind ripple through their hair and the waves crash in beside them, she could tell her story and Amber would understand.

But now, sitting on a small, sheltered balcony overlooking a beautiful pool, unable to do anything except drink cup after cup of coffee, Faye knew that it didn't matter where she told Amber the truth.

'I want to apologise,' she said first. 'That's what I came here to do, not to drag you home, which is what you probably think I am here to do.'

'You're not here for that?' Amber said, startled.

'No,' Faye said. 'You're an adult, you're right, I'm sorry. I've treated you like a child for so long I didn't know how to treat you any other way. I can understand that when you wanted to leave you thought you had to do it brutally, because I wouldn't understand it any other way. That's only part of what I'm apologising over. Remember one of the things I said before you went?'

That last row was engrained in her memory, but she wasn't sure if Amber would remember.

'I said I knew because I'd been there and you didn't believe me.'

Her daughter nodded. At the time, she'd thought it was a stupid statement, just another ploy to get her to stay because how could her mother have any clue what real life was like?

Faye took a very deep breath.

'I lied to you about your dad. We weren't desperately in love and he didn't die in a car crash,' she said bluntly. 'He was just some guy in a bar from a horrible life I lived and I didn't want you to ever know about it.'

Amber stared at her mother.

'I know it's awful to hear this after eighteen years of hearing a different story about your father. I just didn't know how to tell you without you hating me.'

'I'd never hate you,' Amber said weakly, trying to process this new information.

'You could hate me because I lied to you about your birth, your father and my life before you were born.' Faye stopped.

That was the hardest thing to say: that she'd lied to Amber about everything.

'I tried to bring you up to be truthful and honest, yet I spent your whole life lying to you. I hate myself for that.'

'What really happened, then?'

Faye poured more coffee she didn't want and began to talk.

Amber sat opposite her and didn't flinch as her mother's story unfolded. It was incredible to hear all this for the first time. It was as if her mother was another woman, a woman she'd never known.

'I didn't value myself or respect myself,' Faye said finally. 'I ran with the pack, I did things because other people did them, I didn't stand up for myself. I tried to fit in. You see, all the things I spent years telling you not to do, I did every single one of them. Are you shocked?'

'No.' It was a lie. Amber had never been so shocked in her life. Her mother didn't look like her mother any more. She was still the same: the neatly tied back hair, the plain loosely cut T-shirt, the slick of lip balm the only sign of make-up. But her eyes, they were different. Her expression was different.

'I . . . I can't imagine you like that, you're so strong now,' Amber said. 'I can't imagine you letting anyone walk on you.'

'Walk on me! They walked all over me,' Faye said sadly, 'and I let them, because I didn't know who I was or what I was and that's what I was ashamed of.'

Amber tried to keep her expression neutral. All these years her mother had convinced her she was the epitome of the conservative, working mum. And now, here she was, telling Amber that she was just the opposite.

'I never told you the truth because I didn't want you to grow up being ashamed of me and I didn't want you growing up being the same sort of person I was. So I thought that if I invented this new me who didn't let anybody near, then you would grow up like that. I'm really sorry, Amber,' Faye said, and she began to cry. 'I've let you down, I'm so sorry about your dad, so sorry. All these years lying to you, telling you we were in love and . . .'

It was all too much to take in.

'Did he even know about me?' Amber interrupted.

'No,' said Faye. She might as well tell the whole truth while she was at it. 'I went to see him once, when you were a baby, but he was out of it, on drugs, and I never went back. He was on heroin. I couldn't cope with that, it wasn't what I wanted for you.'

'Wow, heroin. Right, so he could be alive or dead, you don't know,' said Amber. It didn't feel like her mother was talking about her. She felt remarkably distant from the whole thing. She'd grown up without a father, so she'd never felt

427

the loss of one. But now there was the possibility of a father after all, a man she might have known, and her mother had kept him from her.

In the background, Amber heard a click, the click of the door opening.

She turned to see Karl coming into the suite. She leaped to her feet and ran over to him. 'Hi, darling,' she said brightly and loudly.

Karl looked at her in astonishment. They'd been co-existing in the suite for the past couple of days and she hadn't run to welcome him for a long time.

'My mother is here,' she whispered, her mouth close to his. 'Try to pretend we are still together, for me, will you do that for me? Just for today and then we can go our separate ways.'

'What do you mean "separate ways"?' he said, his face going suitably blank.

'Get real, Karl,' she snapped back at him. 'Do you think I'm blind as well as stupid? I saw you and Venetia last night. I know what's going on. I'm getting out of your hair tomorrow, but I want my mother to go home thinking it's OK between us. You can do this for me, I've given up a lot for you.'

'Sure, OK. Is she angry with me?' Karl asked anxiously.

'She should be,' Amber whispered, 'but she's not. Lucky you. I'm bloody furious with you but that's a discussion for another time, you bastard.'

She turned around, smiling.

'Mum, meet Karl.'

He was every bit as good-looking as Faye had imagined: handsome, sexy, charismatic. She could imagine Amber falling in love with this gorgeous man, wrapped up in his talent, watching him on stage.

'Hello, Karl,' said Faye, trying to be civil although it was

428

incredibly difficult not to yell at this man who'd stolen her daughter and put her through hell for the past month. She'd do it for Amber's sake and she just hoped that Karl Evans would treat her daughter with love and respect, because if he didn't, he would have Faye to answer to. 'Nice to meet you, at last.'

When Karl had showered and gone off again at high speed, Amber took her mother down to sit in one of the cabanas by the pool.

In her white T-shirt and a pair of cream chinos that did nothing for her figure, Faye was aware that she probably stood out like a sore thumb amid all this LA glamour, but she didn't really care. She was with Amber, that was all that mattered.

They talked about Summer Street and home. How Faye had spoken to Ella, who was delirious that the exams were over.

'She sends her love,' Faye said, 'and wants you to phone her soon, or email her.'

'I will,' said Amber, guiltily. 'I just felt so bad when such a long time had gone by and I hadn't talked to her. Do you think she'll forgive me?'

'Of course she will,' her mother said. Faye went on to explain how she'd made friends with Christie Devlin and Maggie Maguire and the plans to demolish the pavilion and put up an apartment block.

'They can't do that!' Amber said, outraged. She didn't want bits of home being ripped up while she was away. But she changed the subject quickly, because she didn't want to talk about her going back to Summer Street, repeating her exams or going to college.

Her mother never mentioned these things either. It was as if they'd tacitly agreed that their rapprochement depended on avoiding the question of Amber's future.

It was only when evening arrived, and they walked down the street to a little trattoria, that Faye had the courage to bring up Amber's return.

'Are you going to stay here long?' she asked. 'Or are the band coming home soon?'

Amber had been holding it together all day. She felt like a boat on stormy seas, rocked by both Karl's defection and the story that her mother had hidden for so long. She'd tried to be calm and non-judgemental, but her composure finally shattered under the weight of the two blows.

Karl had cared for her, but not enough. She'd been the one to make all the sacrifices for him. He wasn't what she'd thought he was and neither, it seemed, was her mother.

She wanted to lash out at someone in hurt.

'Mum, I'm doing my own thing now, OK!' she shrieked. 'I don't know when I'll be home. I'll stay in touch but there's no point hanging around here waiting for me. I don't need that. I can make my own decisions!'

It was said as much for Karl as for her mother, except that Karl wasn't there and Faye took the brunt of Amber's anger and shock.

'I'm sorry,' she said, chastened. She should have known that she couldn't tell Amber her history and expect her daughter not to be hurt. 'I'm not going to hang around. I'll fly home but I've got some money for you.' She dug out the envelope filled with dollars and handed it to Amber. 'I know you don't want hand-outs but I worry about you. Please stay in touch.'

Amber nodded, clutching the envelope.

'Mum, dinner's a bad idea. You should go. The band have an event to go to and I have to go too.' She hadn't planned on going but it made a good excuse. Right now, she needed to be alone to think.

They stopped on the street and stood awkwardly, at arm's length.

'I love you, Amber,' Faye said, reaching out to touch her daughter tentatively. Amber looked as if she was about to break down and Faye wanted to hug her, but didn't know if this new Amber would allow that. Things were different now: the time apart and all that had happened had changed them both. 'Don't forget that. I'm sorry I lied. Our home is always there for you, please remember that. It'll always be our house, not mine. Never be afraid to come home or to call me if you need me.'

'Thanks,' said Amber. She kissed her mother quickly on the cheek because if they hugged, she might break down and tell Mum everything. And she couldn't. There were too many lies around, too many people not telling her the truth. She felt so hurt, raw.

'I have to go, Mum. I'm sorry. I need to think,' she added shakily before turning and running back down the street to the hotel.

She was more like her mother than Faye knew, but Amber couldn't say that now.

Behind her, Faye watched until her daughter was out of sight. She felt as if her heart was being ripped out of her chest and jumped on. This was almost worse than the time Amber had run off because then, she hadn't known all the facts. Now she did.

This was Faye's punishment for all the years of lying: Amber couldn't forgive her. She had to give Amber space, even though she wanted to forcibly drag her on to a plane and fly her home to Summer Street. Walking away was the hardest thing she'd ever done, but she had to do it.

CHAPTER TWENTY-EIGHT

Shona threw open the door to her Galway apartment and dragged Maggie in with a giant hug.

'Maggie, I've missed you!' she yelled happily.

Maggie hugged her back. 'Me too,' she said. She dumped her small holdall on the floor and looked around Shona's apartment where she'd once spent so many happy hours. 'New curtains?' she asked, instantly spotting the thick creamy ones that had replaced the old beige paisley drapes. 'And new cushions, too.' She picked up a fluffy fake-angora cushion. 'I love these cushions,' she sighed.

'Shows how long since you've been here,' Shona said, excitedly. 'Wait till you see the kitchen. Paul painted the units and Ross and I picked the cutest china handles for the doors.'

Shona hadn't changed in the weeks Maggie had been away, she thought fondly. Her friend was still as effervescent as ever and had squealed down the phone when Maggie had rung to say she was coming to Galway to take the rest of her stuff from the apartment.

'You'll stay with us,' she insisted.

'Thanks,' Maggie had said. She couldn't bear to stay in

her old apartment with Grey, not even for one night. It represented the past and the person she used to be. And she was still close enough to that person to want to distance herself.

When Maggie had admired the new-look kitchen, they sat at the tiny breakfast bar having tea and Maggie filled Shona in on Ivan, her job in the children's library, and how she'd talked to a lawyer about selling her share of the Galway apartment to Grey.

'I want to do it now,' Maggie said. 'The apartment's the last bit of that life and I want it removed, surgically.'

'I'll miss you, though,' Shona reminded her. 'It's not the same in work without you and it'll always be different now with you living in Dublin and us here.'

'I know,' Maggie said apologetically. 'I'll miss you too, but it's not as if I'm emigrating to the moon or anything. We have email, the phone and cheap flights to Dublin.'

Shona nodded, looking as if she was about to say something else, but had thought better of it.

'Come on, let's go out and liven up this town,' Shona said. 'I fancy a French pastry in Delaney's, or maybe a slice of double chocolate cake.'

They took the stairs. pausing briefly by Ross's door on the floor below. Loud music could be heard through the door.

'Is that "I Will Survive"?' Maggie asked. Ross had had so many break-ups, it was his anthem.

''Fraid so,' said Shona. 'He's very cut up about it, says he's going to emigrate to somewhere where men are allowed to wear pink velvet and kiss on the streets.'

'You mean San Francisco?' grinned Maggie.

'He's got his heart set on Edinburgh. I know, I've told him Edinburgh isn't known for men wearing pink velvet or kissing each other wildly on Princes Street, but he says he looks so much better in winter clothes that Edinburgh's got to be the place.'

They both pondered the workings of Ross's mind.

'The end of a love affair does strange things to a person,' Shona went on. 'I said I couldn't bear to lose him too. What will I do if both you and Ross are gone?'

'He'd never leave Nureyev,' Maggie pointed out. 'Can rabbits get a pet passport?'

'That's the only sticking point, but if Nureyev can't go, Paul and I are going to adopt him.'

'We will be hearing the patter of tiny feet around your apartment!' teased Maggie.

Shona didn't respond to the joke.

'Tiny feet, get it?' said Maggie.

'Mmm, funny,' muttered Shona.

'Have I put my foot in it?' Maggie asked quickly, alarm bells ringing. The day Shona didn't laugh like a drain at even the feeblest joke, you knew there was something wrong.

The phone and emails were great for keeping in touch but there were some things that you had to be present to feel – what if Shona had received bad news about the possibility of her having children?

'I didn't mean to upset you,' Maggie said earnestly.

'You didn't, you big nelly,' said Shona. 'I was waiting to get you sitting down in Delaney's to tell you. I'm pregnant. Paul and I are going to be parents! A baby and possibly a rabbit too! We're thrilled.'

'That's wonderful,' Maggie said, giving her friend another hug, then pulling away anxiously in case she squashed Shona's belly.

They both looked down there.

'It's still flat,' Shona said, patting her waistband. 'I've been into a maternity clothes shop where they have a cushion you stick up your jumper to envisage being five months pregnant so you can buy your clothes in advance. Actually, I keep going in. I can't afford to buy the clothes but the cushion is so realistically baby-like, I genuinely look pregnant with it and I love looking at it under my jumper. They're sick of the sight of me there.'

'Let's go there!' insisted Maggie. 'I want to see what you look like five months pregnant too.'

She held Shona's hand as they went down the last flight of stairs and out on to the street.

'I didn't know how to tell you though,' Shona admitted. 'You know, it's like we're so happy and Paul is nearly doing a dance of joy, while Grey is up for bastard of the year award and I feel so bad for you.'

'Bastard of the year award? I love the sound of that,' Maggie said. 'Really, I don't know if anyone will approve, but I think it adds something to college life.'

'You're not upset, though?' Shona asked as they crossed the street and arrived at Delaney's café.

'Shona, I am thrilled for you both. This is the most incredible bit of news ever. Why would it upset me?'

'Well . . .' Shona paused, while they waved hi to the waitress and squashed on to a little table to one side of the door. 'You were going through so much. I felt so sorry for you and I didn't want to land my joy on top of you. You know, when you're feeling bad, it can be hard to take other people getting everything they ever wanted.'

Maggie digested this bit of information. In all the years she'd known Shona, Shona had never implied that she wanted kids or even thought about it; in fact, Shona and Paul seemed like two kids themselves, happy to lurch along in their lovable way, having fun, throwing parties, buying rollerblades, going to Euro Disney on their own.

'I'm thrilled,' she repeated. 'Absolutely thrilled. How could you ever think I'd be otherwise? Just don't feng shui me out of your life when junior comes along. I'm your friend and I want to keep on being your friend. I've

435

done plenty of babysitting in my time. I can be a good auntie.'

'Thank you,' said Shona tearfully. 'I am so happy. Paul is so happy. It was a surprise, I can tell you. We weren't trying, we don't know how it happened.' Maggie opened her mouth to explain but Shona got there first. 'No, well, we know how it happened but, you know, really happened.

'Then I felt guilty because Paul said he'd love us to have a baby and I kept thinking of you and Grey, how you never seemed to think about kids either and I thought my being pregnant would remind you of that.'

Maggie shook her head.

'Stop feeling guilty,' she said. The issue of children was one of those great unmentioned subjects between her and Grey and surely if you loved someone and they were the one, you'd have the conversation, wouldn't you? But there had been times as she'd neared thirty that she'd begun to think about children.

'Grey and I never talked about it,' she said, bluntly.

'I didn't think so,' Shona said sadly, 'so I never talked to you about kids or even the thought of having them because it might . . .'

She stopped.

Maggie filled in the rest of the sentence. '. . . Because it might make me realise the difference between you and Paul and me and Grey. You thought he was wrong for me when we were going out, didn't you?' she said, not wanting to hear that Shona, whom she felt so close to, had thought he was the wrong person for Maggie.

'Hey, I loved Grey,' Shona insisted. 'Honestly. He's sexy, funny and charming, what's not to like? Paul, well, he was never really into him. I just told him to shut up. You were our friend and we couldn't hurt you.'

Maggie thought of all the nights they had spent together as a foursome and cringed.

'It's not that he's wise after the event and realised that Grey was a two-timer under all the gloss,' Shona went on quickly. 'They just didn't gel. Paul thought that Grey was a bit, you know, pompous, intellectual, trying to prove how smart he was and you know Paul hates that sort of stuff. He thinks Simone de Beauvoir was a French singer and Nietzsche was an astronaut.'

Maggie burst out laughing. 'It's good to be back,' she said. 'Let's cut to the chase, Shona, and order something full of cream.'

The next morning, Maggie left Shona and Paul's apartment a little after nine and walked a couple of blocks to the book-shop-cum-coffee shop where Grey liked to sit reading the paper and enjoying his breakfast of double espresso. During term time, it was a favoured hang-out of the political students and would-be intellectuals, a spot where many an admiring student had sidled up to Grey and Maggie as they enjoyed coffee and said a shy 'hi' to Dr Stanley.

She hadn't wanted to visit him in their apartment and neither had she wanted to phone him. She didn't want him prepared for this meeting with ready arguments all laid out. Instead, she had an armful of legal documents from her newly hired lawyer relating to selling their jointly owned apartment.

She pushed open the door of the bookshop and made her way upstairs to the tiny coffee shop. He was there, lounging elegantly on a chair, coffee cup held in long artistic fingers, gazing at the paper earnestly.

'Hello, Grey,' said Maggie.

He looked up from his newspaper and she could see that he was astonished. 'Maggie!' he said, delight in his voice. 'How wonderful to see you.'

The way his eyes roamed over her made her sure he was pleased to see her. She had made an enormous effort with what she was wearing, and had abandoned her jeans for a long cotton skirt with slits up the side that showed off her legs and a soft aqua shirt that tied neatly around her slim stomach. She looked good, better than good, she looked great.

The morning affirmations and the book of self-confidence – which she'd read for a third time – were working. After all, there was no point in being the only person who thought she looked like Quasimodo's younger sister.

'Can I sit down?' she said.

'Please do,' Grey said suavely, taking the rest of his morning pile of papers off the other chair.

Maggie sat, feeling strangely relaxed, but Grey didn't look relaxed at all. He glanced nervously at his watch as if he was worried about the time. Was he waiting for another woman maybe? Maggie tested to see how much that would hurt, Grey waiting for another woman. She bounced the idea around in her head and found that she didn't care. It hadn't been that long, she knew, since they had split up, but so much had happened. She'd got over him, she thought. She'd tried so hard to keep him by being what he wanted that she wondered if the real Maggie had loved him at all or he her.

'I didn't expect to see you here,' Grey said. 'I didn't think you were coming back to Galway.'

'And how was I going to move the rest of my stuff out of the apartment then?' Maggie asked calmly.

'I thought maybe Shona would do it.'

'You mean you thought I couldn't face coming back,' she said.

'That too,' he said. 'I'm sorry, Maggie,' he began.

'Let's stop all this "I'm sorry", Grey. We've gone through it so often it's becoming boring. It's over between us, it was over the first time you lied to me, except I don't know exactly when that was.'

'The only thing Shona wasn't able to find out,' he said, bitterly. 'That woman should work for Interpol, she's so good at ferreting around for information.'

'It's called keeping an eye out for your friends,' Maggie said evenly. 'Shona understands that I wouldn't want to be married to a man who could cheat on me, and lie about it. We might have had some chance if you'd been honest but . . .' She thought about it. 'Actually, no,' she said. 'Strike that. We wouldn't have had a chance whether you'd told me about the other women or not, Grey. I'd never trust you again. And I couldn't respect a man who'd make love to me, and still manage to screw other women without feeling in the slightest bit guilty. So no, it wouldn't have worked out. But I'd have appreciated the honesty, I'd have respected you more.'

'There's no going back, then?'

She shook her head.

'Are you coming back to Galway to live?'

'I don't think so, I've made a new life for myself, I'm busy.'

'I noticed. I saw you in the paper, you and your mother, the heroines of Summer Street.'

Maggie grinned, where once she would have been embarrassed at the thought of such publicity.

'They used that picture of us on the steps of the pavilion because you're gorgeous and I'm not too bad for an old bird!' her mother had said proudly at the time and Maggie had stared at her in astonishment. Her mother was saying she was gorgeous. Maggie didn't remember anyone saying that when she was growing up, but maybe they had and she just hadn't noticed. Her own insecurities and the emotional pain of the bullying had stopped her hearing the words. She'd been loved and adored; of course they would have told her she was beautiful.

'There was a stunning photo of the pair of you on the steps of that old building,' Grey went on.

'My mother loves that picture – she says we're gorgeous in it,' Maggie said proudly. She was able to say such a thing without wincing and was almost beginning to believe it. Men didn't look at her in the street because she had her jeans on backwards or her hair was stuck to her head, they looked at her because they thought she was attractive.

'Beauty sells,' agreed Grey morosely, staring at her. 'Are you going out with anybody?' he asked. 'It's just you seem happier, happier than you were with me.'

'I am, as a matter of fact,' Maggie said, unable to hide the broad smile that lit up her face at the thought of Ivan. 'He's a good man. Kind, handsome, very sexy.' She couldn't resist adding that, just to show Grey that he wasn't the only one who could hook up with members of the opposite sex. 'And he's older than me, by a few years,' she added.

'Not a twenty-year-old student, you mean,' Grey snapped.

'Exactly.'

'He makes you happy?' He looked as if he would prefer to hear that this man didn't make Maggie happy.

'He makes me very happy,' she said softly. 'I can be myself with him.'

'You were yourself with me,' Grey insisted.

'No, I wasn't,' Maggie said, determined to say what had to be said. 'I was what I thought you wanted me to be. We did things you wanted to do, because I wanted you to be happy. Not things I wanted to do. Not that it was all your fault, I had my own issues,' she said, 'but you didn't help. You wanted a certain type of person as your girlfriend and I was pliable enough to fit perfectly into the role.'

'I loved you,' Grey said defensively.

'Loved me enough to have four affairs while we were together?' Maggie asked sharply. 'That's not love, Grey. That's selfishness masquerading as love. If you'd really loved me, you wouldn't have needed anyone else.'

'What a cliché,' he said in irritation. 'I don't know why women buy into all that romantic bullshit. All the same, all wanting fairytale marriages and white dresses and happy-ever-after. Life isn't like that.'

'It can be,' Maggie stated. 'It can be if you want it to be, and I want it to be. And if the man I'm with is unfaithful to me, then I'll leave him too. Do you understand?' she said. 'I don't want happy-ever-after romance. I want real love and respect and I'd prefer to be on my own than be with someone and without it.'

Grey wasn't listening. He was staring, like a goldfish, at someone approaching from behind her.

Maggie turned to see a slender young blonde girl, mid-twenties at the most, standing awkwardly a few metres away from their table.

'Er . . . well . . .' stammered Grey, no doubt anticipating seeing the remains of his coffee landing on his clothes.

'Relax,' Maggie said. 'You're a free agent, Grey. See who you like.'

She got to her feet, handed him the sheaf of papers and held out her hand for him to shake it. 'Let's sort this out as soon as possible,' she said.

He took her hand and shook it.

Then she turned to face the blonde woman.

'Hi,' Maggie said. 'I'm just leaving. He's all yours.'

Then she walked down the bookshop stairs, head held high.

For old times' sake, she took the bus out to Salthill and walked along the beach. The vastness of the Altantic always awed her. She'd loved walking here when she'd first come to Galway, loved the knowledge that centuries of women had walked along here, thinking about their lives and loves when there were no amusement arcades in the background, just the stretch of the bay encircling them.

She'd like to share this place with Ivan. But perhaps not just yet.

As she walked, Maggie realised that she didn't want to make any big decisions yet about her and Ivan. She'd tried to get other people to fix what was wrong with her. And it hadn't worked; it couldn't. Only she had been able to fix herself. She didn't want to make that mistake with Ivan.

If they ended up together, it would be for all the right reasons, she promised herself that. Smiling, she turned and headed back along the beach.

CHAPTER TWENTY-NINE

The office looked exactly the same as when Faye had left it. The 'Flipper Does Dallas' painting still dominating the reception area, the arrangements of flowers on the tables in reception looking unchanged, and Grace's stilettos still crackling as she ran across the reception floor.

In a stunning cream suit with a nipped-in waist and buttons like golden golfballs, she was the epitome of the corporate madam.

'Welcome back!' Grace said delightedly. 'I love your hair!'

Faye laughed and kissed Grace on the cheek.

'I've been away for a month, I've gone through all sorts of torments and the first thing you mention to me is my hair?' she demanded in mock disgust.

It was very different. The brown ponytail was gone, to be replaced by a jaw-length feathery bob which really suited her.

'It's only a haircut, Grace,' she added, although she knew it was more than that. Asking for a new look hadn't just been chopping off a lot of hair. It was making an effort, albeit a small effort, to step back into the world.

'It's fabulous though,' said Grace, giving Faye's hair a

professional once-over. 'All you need is for Ellen to come in and maybe do something about your clothes.'

'Grace!' warned Faye as they stepped into the lift. 'I like my clothes and it's only because you're an old friend that I allow you even to mention them and my lack of interest in them without killing you.'

'Sorry,' said Grace unsubdued. 'It's just, you have had that suit quite a long time and there is a sale on in Debenhams.'

'Point taken.'

'Fine.' Grace put up her hands in resignation. 'It's lovely to have you back, even if . . .' She stopped herself.

'Even if Amber isn't with me?' Faye said.

'Sorry, I don't know what to say. I wish I knew how to console you but I suppose there is no making it better. At least you found her and talked to her.' Grace wasn't entirely sure if Amber had any plans to come back because she hadn't wanted to ask Faye such a tough question, but whatever had gone on in California between the two of them, Faye was actually looking better than she had for years. It wasn't just the hair. That was only a surface thing, Grace knew.

But Faye genuinely looked different – not content exactly, because Grace knew that Faye could never be content when Amber was away from her – but strangely more comfortable, less uptight, as if a weight had been lifted from her shoulders.

'The whole office has missed you.' Grace changed the subject. 'Personally and professionally. Little Island can't cope when you're gone. You better not have any holidays again,' she said, teasing.

'No, not ever again,' agreed Faye. 'Although I'm thinking of taking a month in September to visit Amber.'

She hadn't discussed this with Amber, not sure how her daughter would react to the news that her mother was going to fly out to LA to spend a month there. Faye realised that if Mohammed wouldn't go to the mountain, then the mountain would have to go to Mohammed.

'The month of September, that's fine,' Grace said evenly. 'Are you free for lunch? We've a lot to talk about. Neil has been driving me mad, driving Philippa mad too. You know what he's like when he gets involved in the business.'

Faye did know. Grace's husband, Neil, was not one of life's instinctive people managers. He could start an argument in an empty room.

'Of course I'm free for lunch,' she said.

When Grace had gone, Faye had sat down and glanced around at her office, thinking it was odd to find it looking the same as ever when so much had changed within herself. Her desk looked exactly as she always left it, with the phone and the stapler precisely at right angles to the top of the desk; even the cleaners knew to leave it that way, because Mrs Reid insisted upon everything just so.

God, she was anal, Faye realised ruefully. She reached over and moved the phone, the stapler and the lamp. There, just a little bit of chaos, a smidgen of unpredictability. It was probably better that way. She didn't know what she was going to do next with her life – that was unpredictable, too, but as she mulled this over she decided it could be rather exciting. She'd muted herself for so long in order to be the perfect mother and, instead, had turned into a controlling person who'd lost sight of the real Faye.

Now it was time to work out who the real Faye was and to enjoy life again. She'd punished herself enough for the past.

Amber looked around her new home, a tiny studio apartment in west Hollywood, and grimaced. Compared to the hotel – where she'd been staying in one of the cheapest rooms after moving out of Karl's suite – it was nothing much to look at and definitely needed some serious cleaning products. Her mother's weak bleach solution might do the trick. Still, it was furnished, in a reasonably safe building with security doors, an intercom system and she was on the second floor rather than the ground.

Number 2F contained a kitchenette, a tray-sized balcony overlooking the apartment block next door's pool and a minute shower room. It hadn't taken her long to move in. All she had were a lot of clothes, some nice hotel toiletries and that was it. She made a list of all the stuff she needed, like groceries, cleaning products, washing powder, some plants to brighten the place up, and headed off to find a shop.

It was Syd who had helped her find her new home when she'd told him she was leaving Karl.

'You can't –'

'– Leave?' said Amber. 'Syd, you know I have to. I can't hang on to Karl's coat-tails for ever, not when he doesn't want me. I have some pride, you know.'

'I know,' he'd replied.

So Syd had talked to Michael Levin about Amber and asked for his help in getting her a job and a place to live.

Karl, on the other hand, had done nothing.

He'd barely spoken to her since the day after her mum left.

He'd come home in the morning as usual to find Amber packing up her stuff.

'You're going,' he said flatly.

'There's nothing for me to stay for.' Amber shrugged, still packing.

'What will you do?'

'There's a street corner on Sunset Boulevard for me,' she replied sarcastically. 'Since you've been treating me like little more than a prostitute, I might as well go the whole hog and make money from it. Hopefully, Richard Gere will see

446

this Pretty Woman and rescue her, although I forgot – you already rescued me from my boring life. Nobody would be so lucky to have it happen to them twice.'

'Amber, don't talk that way,' Karl said. 'It wasn't meant to happen like this, but it sorta did. I've got to think of the band . . .'

'You're thinking of Karl,' Amber shot back, 'as usual. Number one. Nobody else gets in the way. I was useful when I was your muse but as soon as another muse came along, I was history. I hope somebody tells Venetia that you run through girlfriends pretty quickly. Although she'll probably last longer than me. She's more useful.'

'It's not like that,' he said. 'Don't be bitter, Amber. You had a blast. Nobody forced you to come.'

She glared at him. 'You did.'

'Did I hold a gun to your head and make you get on the plane at Dublin airport? No. So don't go all "you made me, Karl"! Right?'

There was no point talking to him.

'You're right, Karl. It was all my fault. I should have known better. I will in future,' she said.

She was quickly running through the money her mother had given her, and for the past few days had been working as a receptionist in a hairdressing salon close to the Beverly Center, although she guessed that her entire wages were less than the tips some of the stylists got from their wealthy clients. Because she was working illegally, she'd been lucky to find such a job. Most illegals ended up chambermaiding and cleaning but Amber's Irish accent had touched a chord with the salon owner and he'd hired her on the spot.

The salon staff were friendly and Syd seemed determined to keep in touch every day, inviting her to parties and gigs so that she felt as if she had some social life in LA. He'd also given her some more money.

'I can't take this!' she said. 'It's the band's money.'

'You were a part of the band, Amber,' Syd said sadly. 'I feel bad about the way Karl's treated you. I've known him a long time, I should have warned you. I thought it was different with you because you're not his usual type, you're smart.'

'That's something.' She grinned.

'I told him not to make you leave Ireland in such a hurry, but you know Karl, once he sets his mind on something, he does it.'

'You said that to him?' she asked.

'It's important to think things through,' Syd muttered.

'I wish you'd said it to me,' Amber replied. 'But I wouldn't have listened, would I?'

She thought about home a lot: her mother, Ella, Gran, the life she'd left behind. The longer she was away from home, the more she wanted to go back.

But after the way she'd run off, nobody would want her there, would they?

And then Saul came back into her life.

He'd simply turned up at the salon one day as they were closing, and said, 'Hello, Amber.'

She stared at him in shock, remembering that it was at his beautiful house, at his party, that she'd finally realised Karl didn't love her after all.

'We're closing, sorry,' she said. 'Do you want to make an appointment?' Pen poised like the professional she was, she smiled at him.

'I don't want an appointment. I wanted to talk to you, Amber. Syd told me you were here,' Saul said. 'I've a proposition for you.'

It took ten minutes before Saul managed to convince Amber that he wasn't a sleazy guy trying to take advantage of her now that she was penniless and alone. They sat in a health food café nursing smoothies while Saul explained.

'You know I'm an art collector and I think you have great talent,' he said. 'I'd like to invest in your talent. No strings attached,' he'd added for what had to be the tenth time. 'You know I'm a collector: you saw the paintings in my house. I'm interested in your talent as an artist. If you spent a year out here or in New Mexico, just think of the work you'd produce. I've still got the picture you drew in my house. You left it behind that night. It's only a sketch but it's more vital and alive than a lot of the work that's going for thousands of dollars in local galleries. So, what do you think?'

Amber was speechless.

'You still want to paint, right?' Saul asked. 'You don't have to go to art college to do that. You could make a damn good living right now.'

Still, she said nothing.

'You could go home and do the art college thing too, and then come back,' Saul went on. 'We'd have to hire a lawyer to sort out your immigration status first, though. There's nothing stopping you from making it. You've certainly got the talent.'

In her head, Amber repeated his words 'there's nothing stopping you'.

There was nothing stopping her – except her pride and fear of facing the people she'd hurt. What she really wanted to do was go home, be with the people she loved and go to art college. And she could do that. All she needed was her plane ticket.

'Thank you for the vote of confidence,' said Amber earnestly, 'but I'm going to learn my trade first. You need to learn how to paint an apple straight before you can paint it abstract. I want to go home. Then, I'll be able to paint.'

James had been gone over a week and Christie, who'd often thought that her beloved dogs were the best companions in

449

the world, found that Tilly and Rocket's adoration didn't mean quite as much when James wasn't around.

She tried hard to be her old self, but it was almost impossible. Her hands shook sometimes for no reason, as if her body was trying to express the shock she was desperately trying to suppress. She felt exhausted every evening and fell into bed early, drifting into a heavy sleep and then waking in panic in the middle of the night. She could never go back to sleep and lay alone in the big bed she and James had shared for so long, her whole chest aching with sadness as the dawn rose. She couldn't even cry. Tears weren't enough to express what she felt.

During their married life they had spent so little time apart.

James had gone off on a few fishing trips and she'd gone away on school trips a couple of times, but all added up together, it wouldn't account for more than a few months apart, over thirty-five years. She told nobody what had happened, she felt too ashamed and embarrassed.

Shane and Ethan still knew nothing, for which she was eternally grateful. At least James hadn't decided to destroy her totally by telling their sons how she'd cheated on him with another man. But Christie knew that if James never came home, the boys would have to learn someday. Which was the scariest thought – James never coming home or Ethan and Shane learning about Carey Wolensky?

Ana had dropped in unexpectedly one day, smiling as usual, full of chat about what she and Rick were up to.

Christie hugged her longer than was necessary, feeling the familiar remorse at how she'd betrayed her sister. If Ana ever found out ... Christie paled at the thought of that. She'd lost her husband, please let her not lose her sister too.

Citing James's working too hard and ignoring her was not a valid excuse for what she'd done to Ana. She hoped she would never have to tell her. Living with the guilt of it was punishment enough.

'Rick says we should downsize,' Ana was saying as they walked up to the Summer Street Café. Ana was mad on the new lemon muffins there. 'The house is big and so's the garden, but it's got character. Not as much as your house, but still, I don't fancy moving into something characterless, even if we made money on the move.'

Christie ordered coffee and cake, although her mouth was so dry she might as well have been eating ashes.

'Did you ever go ahead with seeing Carey Wolensky?' she asked finally.

Ana gave the irrepressible grin that reminded Christie of what she'd been like as a child, with her fair hair tied in pigtails, a dimple on either cheek.

'No,' admitted Ana. 'It was wishful thinking really. It's not as if we ever had anything to say to each other when we were going out, so what would we say now, twenty-five years down the line? And I saw a photo of him in the papers. He looks about a hundred now, you know. I suppose you always have a thing for the ones who dumped you.' Ana took another bite of her muffin and looked thoughtful. 'And he gave me a great bit of advice.'

'What did he say?' asked Christie lightly.

'That I should stop going out with men like my father, tough, controlling ones, and find a decent, nice man who'd appreciate me.' Ana beamed. 'He hit the nail on the head there – that's what you used to say to me too. But you were both right. So I went off and before long I met Rick, who turned out to be the love of my life and still is. And there aren't many people my age who can say that, now, are there? Well,' Ana added, 'apart from you and James, obviously.'

*　　*　　*

With an absence of anyone to talk to and with no work, now that school was closed for the summer, Christie did the only thing she could do under the circumstances. She set up her easel on the terrace where the pergola gave her shade and began to paint. She'd planned to do one of her botanical pictures, the detailed representations of irises and orchids she had always loved to draw, but found she couldn't concentrate on them. Perhaps she could only work on them when she was happy. So she gave up and began painting a portrait instead.

For her, painting was like therapy: as she painted, she thought of the mistakes that had brought her to this point.

She and Carey had had two days of a love affair. Two days of pure, joyful pleasure when they made love on the day bed, and curled up afterwards talking, Carey smoking the unfiltered cigarettes he adored, the ones Christie hated.

It was like being in a dream, one where none of her actions could hurt either herself or anyone else. A lovely dream from which she would awaken with a pleasurable memory and no guilt.

'If I were your husband, I would wonder where you were every day,' Carey murmured in the late afternoon of that second, glorious day.

'My husband hasn't even noticed I'm not at home every day,' Christie said bitterly. 'It's as if I don't exist for him. Right now, he's only interested in his work. I'm just someone to look after his children and cook dinner each night.'

'Is that why you did this? To get back at him?' Carey asked, like a scientist probing a rat in an experiment.

'No,' said Christie. 'That's not why. He never notices me these days, but you do. That's why I wanted to be with you . . .' Saying it out loud make the words sound feeble. Her husband was busy so she'd betrayed him.

It was more than that, wasn't it?

'We need to talk,' Carey said. 'I am going to London next month. I have an important commission, it could make me rich. Christie, leave, come with me. Bring your little boys. I can love them too. I love their mother.'

It was talking of the future that made Christie's daydream crumble. The future. Life without James, life ferrying her beloved children back and forth between them. Anger, hurt, betrayal. Ana hating her. James hating her more.

The dream shattered and she felt the iron grasp of guilt around her soul. What had she done? She must have been mad.

'No, Carey,' she said, getting up. She was naked, and she found her clothes where he'd thrown them on the floor after ripping them from her in the heat of desire.

'I can't. This was a mistake. I have to go. I can't see you again, sorry, but it has to be that way.'

Shoes, where were her shoes? She couldn't see them for tears.

'You don't mean this?' he demanded, uncurling his body from the day bed and grabbing her by both arms. 'You have to come with me. We were meant for each other, you know that. This is not tawdry sex between an artist and his model, this is real love, true passion. I've never felt this way about a woman before,' he said, almost in wonderment. 'You can't go.'

'I can,' said Christie wildly. 'I've got to. I'd lose so much, I'd lose all the people I love if I go with you. I'm sorry.'

She found her shoes, put them on, flung her coat over her shoulder and went to the door. She made herself take one last look at him standing there, looking bewildered and hurt, and so devastatingly attractive. 'I'm sorry,' she said again.

'You'll be back,' he snapped.

'I won't,' she said.

*   *   *

When she'd emptied her head of all the tumbling thoughts, Christie painted quickly and furiously.

The next day, she was outside, standing putting the finishing touches to her painting when she heard footsteps in the hall, moving into the kitchen. The dogs, who'd never been much good in the watchdog department, leaped to their feet, yapping happily and ran into the house. She could hear a man's voice, James's.

She could imagine him bending down, petting Tilly's ears, rubbing Rocket's soft belly. But Christie stayed where she was. He mightn't want to see her, he might have just come to pick up more things.

'Christie?' came his voice.

'I'm in the garden,' she called, not knowing what to expect. She put her brush down and sat down on the chair. She thought she might need to be sitting for this. James walked over towards her, then hesitated. The easel stood between them.

'How are you?' she said tremulously, her eyes glued to his face. He looked tired, pale.

James gazed back at her steadily, and Christie wished she knew what was in his heart. Please, she prayed, please.

'I've been thinking,' he said.

'Me too,' she answered quickly.

'Thinking about our lives then. How hard I was working, how hard you were working. It must have been difficult, with me so busy and you coping with the children and work and everything at home. We had no time together, no time at all. I wasn't the best husband ever at that point.'

Christie held her breath. He hadn't said, *Goodbye, I've come to pick up my stuff.* There was some hope.

'I don't know if I can ever forget what happened between you and him.'

Again, he didn't say Carey's name and Christie felt her spirits sink at his words.

454

'But,' James went on, 'I could try.'

'You could try?' Christie asked. 'Try to forget? Try again?'

He nodded. 'I love you, Christie. You're my whole life, you always have been, ever since I met you. That's what hurts, to think that there was a time when I wasn't your whole life, to think that we've been living a lie.'

'But we weren't,' Christie pleaded. 'It only happened for a short time, it was stupid, and then it was over. It didn't rewrite our history, it doesn't negate everything we had, our love, our children, our life together.'

'I know that,' James said. 'Doesn't make it any easier to handle, though. I kept imagining you and him –' He stopped. 'I can't bear to think of that, Christie. And then, when you left the pictures for me to see, I was so angry and hurt. All I could think was you were trying to show me how much he loved you, because he'd been able to paint you. I don't understand art, that's your world and I was never a part of it. But I felt bad because I'd never tried to be a part of it and, at the same time, furious with you for having him, having that other life.'

He was being so honest and it was so heartbreaking that Christie wanted nothing more than to get up and to put her arms around him. But she couldn't. She had to let him speak his piece. That was his right. She'd done what she thought was right, now it was his turn.

'When you showed me the pictures,' he went on, 'I thought you'd done it for a reason: that you wanted to be with him again. When you said it wasn't that, that he was dying and that he wanted to see you one last time, I don't think I believed you. I still thought you must be trying to hurt me.'

'I'd never hurt you, not intentionally,' she said. 'Although I have hurt you, I didn't mean to.'

'I didn't go fishing,' he said. 'I took some time off to think. I stayed in the B & B beside the lake, but I just walked and walked every day. I couldn't bring myself to actually fish,' he said ruefully. 'And I realised I couldn't let the past destroy us. We're stronger than that. You're an honest person and that's why you told me, I know that now. You could have left me in the dark and I would never have known and some day, a hundred years from now, someone would put two and two together. You'd be named as the dark lady and I'd be the fool, the cuckold, the man who never knew. I don't want to be the man who never knew, that's not what I married you for. I can't say I'm glad you told me, but now that you have, it's not going to end our marriage.'

'Oh, James,' said Christie and she ran to him.

He held out his arms and pulled her into his embrace.

'Thank you,' she sobbed, 'thank you. I couldn't ring you or try to get in touch with you, I knew you had to do this on your own. I never meant to hurt you, not twenty-five years ago, not last week, not ever, you know that. I just don't want there to be any more secrets. I've lived my life frightened that this would come out and destroy what we had. I just couldn't live with that any more.'

He held her close, saying nothing, stroking her hair, her head burrowed into his shoulder.

'I missed you,' he said. 'That's what made me come back. Thinking of a life without you, what it would be like to live on my own. We'd sell this place, split the money and both of us live out lives of quiet misery because of my pride, because of something that happened twenty-five years ago. And no, I didn't want to do that,' he said. 'Carey Wolensky nearly took so much away from me, he wasn't going to take you away again.'

And Christie stood in his embrace and prayed thank you to whoever was watching over them. They stood there for a while, until the dogs got tired of sniffing around their feet and lay down and fell asleep. It was nice just to stand there and be held by the man she loved most in the whole world.

'What are you painting?' asked James, eventually.

Christie moved back and wiped her eyes with her hand.

'I started doing one of my flower pictures,' she said with a sniffle, reaching into her cardigan pocket for a tissue. She wiped her eyes and blew her nose. 'But I couldn't concentrate on it, couldn't concentrate on anything really, I was just waiting for you. And then, I found this old photo and it came to me that's what I should be painting.' She led James around the other side of the easel and stood while he stared at the picture. In her own style, she'd copied an old family photograph of when the boys were young. Shane and Ethan sat on a couch and behind them, leaning over the back of the couch, smiling, arms around each other, were James and Christie. It was a beautiful family shot, hidden in an album for far too long, and she'd captured the joy on their faces perfectly.

'It's a family portrait,' James said.

'Because my family is what's important to me,' Christie said. 'You're what's important to me.'

He put an arm around her waist and squeezed.

'I know,' he said.

CHAPTER THIRTY

Autumn on Summer Street came very slowly. The gently curved road was a sheltered place and, by September, the leaves of the maples that lined the pavements were only tinged with the most delicate hint of gold. The Japanese maple in Una Maguire's front garden, however, had turned a startling dark crimson attracting admiring glances from passers-by. Christie Devlin's soft white blousy roses were losing their petals daily, except for the creamy climbing rose that crept up over the wall and wrapped tendrils around the ever-open gate. That still bloomed, sending a heady rose scent on to the breeze and making people talk of an Indian summer.

But in spite of the good weather, the summer indolence of barbecues and sitting out sunbathing on front steps was over.

There was a sense of business about the whole street, the feeling of a new start. Holidays were over and the new school term had arrived.

At the Summer Street Café, Henry took in all but two of the little tables that stood on the pavement. His customers were drifting indoors now, preferring their coffees looking out over Summer Street. He liked autumn with its sense of renewal; it reminded him of being a kid going back to school with a bagful of clean new copy books, ready to be filled with wisdom.

'I think you were always a wise man,' teased Xu. She'd really come out of her shell, Henry thought proudly, feeling a certain responsibility for that. He and Jane had done their best to welcome her warmly, and her growing friendship with Maggie Maguire had helped integrate her into their community too.

Xu was a lot different from the shy woman who'd come to work for them at the start of the year. She was a big part of Summer Street.

Xu herself was excited that her mother was coming from China to visit her.

Henry and Jane had insisted that Xu's mother stay in their spare room.

'You've only got a tiny bedsit,' Jane pointed out. 'There won't be room to swing a cat there.'

'She doesn't have a cat,' Xu said gravely, then laughed. She loved being able to make jokes in English now. Everyone assumed her to be so sober and serious that they didn't expect her to make jokes.

'We've taught you too well,' smiled Jane. 'You'll be as bad as Henry soon with the jokes.'

'I told you the Irish and Chinese were similar,' said Xu. 'We have the same sense of humour, except it's more hidden in my people.'

'It's not hidden now,' said Jane cheerfully. 'Come on, you pair, let's get those chairs in or the customers will be tripping over them.'

At number 34, Christie Devlin was getting ready for another teaching year, her last, she'd decided.

'Are you sure you want to do this?' James said to her the night before school started. 'Don't do it just because of me.'

'I'm ready to retire,' said Christie. 'Think of all the places we can go then, the things we can do together.'

Although James could stay another two years before retirement, he'd decided to go early. He'd stop working when Christie did the following summer. They had already amassed a collection of brochures about long holidays abroad for the adventuresome spirit. Christie particularly liked the sound of the trip around India, although Ethan and Shane had been a bit anxious when they had seen the brochure.

'A month?' said Shane, the brochure opened to the fares page. 'For this price, you're hardly going to be staying in old maharajahs' palaces,' he said doubtfully. 'And what about the food, what if one of you gets sick?'

James and Christie looked at each other and laughed.

'If we get sick, we get sick!' James said cheerily. 'We'll bring plenty of medicine to bung us up from each end. We're grown-ups, you know,' he added, 'we're not ready for the nursing home yet.'

'That's not what I meant,' Shane explained.

'I know, I know,' said his father.

'But why now?' said Ethan. 'Why did you never go on these sorts of holidays years ago? You could have taken the time off.'

Christie and James exchanged another look, a private look.

'This is time for us now,' she said. 'You're all settled, you've got your own lives, your own families, it's time for us to be selfish.'

'Yeah, but what if we need you, with the baby and everything?' Shane said, sounding briefly like a child and not like an adult with a wife and a first child on the way.

'The baby will be fine,' Christie said, and she knew he would be.

She'd seen a healthy little boy in the future, to be followed, hopefully, by two more. She and James had given Shane and Janet some money for their new arrival and to help them buy a house.

'We promise we'll do double babysitting duties when we

get back,' she added. 'You can always email us, we have a hotmail account.'

'I don't know,' joked Ethan, 'parents these days: they're crazy and want to travel the world and don't care about anyone else.'

The whole family laughed at this.

'You're right,' James said. 'It's like we're in our second childhoods.'

At number 48, Una Maguire was back on her feet and had taken up yoga.

'Flexibility is the key to taking care of yourself,' she told everyone who'd listen. 'If I'd done yoga years ago, who knows, I mightn't have broken my leg after all. Your father and I have a bet on about the lotus position. I said I'll be in it by Christmas and he says never. I'm going to win that tenner from you, Dennis.'

Maggie laughed at her mother. It was brilliant to see her on such good form. Una Maguire was one of life's strong people. No matter what life threw at her, she threw it right back with her own peculiar topspin. Maggie had stopped obsessing about how she'd turned out so different from her mother and had begun to appreciate her differences.

She was a bit more like her dad really. Quiet and shy, but with enough of her mother's strength and fire, if required. The developers involved in trying to destroy the Summer Street pavilion had certainly learned that to their cost.

The holiday season had meant that both the plan to knock down the pavilion and the campaign to save it were at a standstill. But the fact that no bulldozer had entered the park in the dead of night and ripped the pavilion to pieces was down to Maggie's work. She'd given so many interviews with newspapers and radio stations about the pavilion that she could recite her points in her sleep. And it seemed newspapers liked using her picture too.

461

'The pavilion may be crumbling and need a fortune to restore it, but it's a beautiful building,' Ivan said, looking at the picture everyone liked best, the full-colour one of Maggie and her mum sitting on the pavilion steps: two radiant redheads, smiling at the cameras with the Save Our Pavilion posters in the background. 'But having two beautiful women in the picture certainly helps,' Ivan went on.

'That's the type of thing Shona would say,' Maggie teased him, but she didn't contradict him either.

He said she was beautiful ten times a day, and he meant it. What was more, Maggie was beginning to appreciate her own worth. When there was nobody else around, she'd examined her photo in the paper, trying to be objective about her own face, and realised that people hadn't been lying to her when they said she was beautiful.

She didn't think she would ever totally see it herself. There'd always be that core of self-doubting somewhere, the doubt that made Maggie so lovable and vulnerable. But she was growing stronger and more confident every day. She had become slightly more adventurous when it came to clothes and had just purchased several new bikinis for the holiday she and Ivan were going on in November. They planned to tour Croatia and then spend one week in Dubrovnik mixing culture and the seaside all in one glorious package.

Going on holiday with Ivan wasn't the only momentous event in Maggie's life. He'd asked her to move in with him. Actually, he'd asked her to marry him, but she'd said it was too soon to think of all that.

'It's a wonderful idea and I'm honoured you've asked me,' she said, sitting on his lap, her arms around his neck. 'I just don't want to rush into anything, Ivan.'

'It wouldn't be rushing,' he said. 'But OK, I understand. I won't push you.'

'Thank you for that,' she said. 'You know I'm crazy about you.'

'How crazy?' he asked.

'Oh, this crazy,' she said, leaning forward and hungrily catching his mouth with hers.

At number 18, Faye Reid had decided that there was no point letting her savings sit miserably in the bank for ever and had employed a landscape gardener to transform her back garden.

'I love sitting in yours so much,' she'd said to Christie. 'It's so peaceful and lovely with the pergola and the scent of all those roses, and I thought why am I killing myself trying to make my little square of grass look attractive? I don't know anything about plants and, without professional help, it'll always be a disaster of a bit of lawn, loads of weeds and a few hardy shrubs that can survive my hopeless horticultural skills.'

'Brilliant idea,' Christie said. 'You need a little haven.'

With Christie's help, Faye had come up with the template for her own garden and although the flowers and plants would need a good year to settle in properly, it was a different place already. Now, down the bottom of the garden, she had a new shed which would take her gardening equipment.

'You have to actually do some gardening now,' Christie teased. 'But I promise to help.'

In front of the shed was a bed filled with large rambling plants that screened the shed, then a path that curved in an S shape around the tiny lawn, a lawn that was now sinuously rounded at the edges with beds of flowers cut into it. There were plants clustered amid rocks, beautiful grasses lazing in a raised bed filled with gravel and a cluster of pots with herbs brimming out over the top. Closer to the house was a trellised wall and a pergola, with honeysuckle and fledgling roses planted at the base waiting to spread. Finally, there was a small terracotta paved terrace graced by the new garden furniture she'd bought.

'This is a perfect place to relax,' Christie said when she saw the finished product. She sat down with a glass of wine to admire the handiwork.

'Who needs to go on holiday to get the sun?' added Maggie, sitting back on a lounger with her eyes closed and a glass of wine in one hand.

The evening sun filled the terraced corner.

'I love it,' said Faye proudly. 'I don't know why I didn't do it years ago, but I was always saving money for Amber.'

She talked about Amber all the time now with Maggie and Christie. At first she'd found it hard to mention her daughter's name to others in case she cried. Amber hadn't come home. And although the lines of communication were firmly open and Amber – who had her own US cell phone now – rang frequently but only ever briefly, there was always a sense of sadness and failure in Faye's heart. But she had to move on. Sitting still waiting for Amber was not how she was going to live her life.

It wasn't fair to herself and it wasn't fair to Amber, because one day if, God willing, Amber did come home, she wouldn't want it to be to a mother who sat anxiously watching her every move, balancing her own hopes on Amber's slender shoulders, expecting Amber to be everything to her. That was wrong. The realisation that this was what she'd done before had shocked her.

She was determined to be different. And she'd phoned Grace's makeover friend, Ellen, for that reason. She knew that Ellen didn't want to transform her with red lipstick, blonde streaks and high heels – she hoped she'd gain some of Ellen's wisdom about life and about not being invisible any more. It was time to trade in the Faye Reid who'd hidden herself for eighteen years.

'Amber would love this,' Faye said now to Christie and Maggie, looking out over the beautiful garden. 'She always used to wonder why I wouldn't spend money on things and I told her we were broke, that work didn't pay me that much and, in fact, I was just saving it for her future. Crazy really, obsessively saving so that she'd have everything and I didn't see that wasn't what she wanted.'

Christie reached over and held Faye's hand gently.

'She'll come home one day, Faye: I'm sure of it.'

'I hope so,' Faye said sadly. 'I hope so.'

A mile away, Amber sat in a small traffic jam and half listened to the taxi driver telling her all the news since she'd been away. He was very informative and clearly listened to talk radio at length, because once she'd mentioned that she'd been away from Ireland for over three months, he went into great detail to fill her in on the goings-on in the corridors of power.

'That's terrible,' Amber muttered at intervals, glad of his conversation because at least then she didn't need to think about reaching Summer Street and what sort of reception she'd get.

It was all she could think of since she'd decided to come home. Would her mother hug her the way she'd hugged her that day in the hotel in LA? Or would she feel that Amber had pushed her too far by staying away so long, and that by so doing, had sliced a division between them that could never be healed?

If that was the case, she'd say she had come home because American immigration was very efficient and she could easily be deported. But if her mum hugged her, then Amber would admit the truth: she missed her mother more than she could say.

It was all very well being wild and carefree when you had one special person to share that dream with. But when that person turned out to be nothing like you'd imagined, then the dream turned sour pretty quickly. She was working illegally in the US, relying on her tips, while the so-called love of her life was with another woman.

Amber thought back to the day she and Saul had sat in the health food café and talked about her career as an artist.

She remembered that feeling of freedom she'd experienced when she'd realised that the only thing stopping her going home was herself.

She could go home if she wanted to.

'If you want to go back to Ireland, that's great,' Saul said. 'But keep in touch, right? I still want to invest in your talent.'

He'd been about to leave and had casually said that he thought her family must be proud of her.

After spending so long pretending that everything was fine, all the pent-up misery had come tumbling out and Amber had burst into tears.

'My mum and my gran are my family and they were proud of me, and I threw it back in their faces,' she sobbed. 'I didn't understand how much Mum loved me, I just hated the fact that she expected so much of me.'

'That's parents for you,' Saul pointed out. He sat back down at the table and gazed at her seriously. 'Only they don't stop being proud of you.'

'You think so?' Amber asked. The tears kept pouring out. She'd suppressed her sadness for so long. She couldn't be miserable or tearful at work: the glossy LA women came to the salon for pampering, not to stare at the red eyes of a young receptionist who had life problems. Glossy LA women didn't do problems.

'Hey, Amber, get real here. It could have all turned really bad for you,' Saul said. 'Your ex is no prince, that's a fact, and this isn't a city where you want to be broke and alone. But it didn't turn out bad because you're a strong woman, and clever enough to walk away at the right time. You could have hung on with Karl and you didn't. I admire that.'

Amber nodded and dried her eyes with her sleeve.

'I don't know your mom, but I'd say she taught you well and I'd also say she'd be proud of you if she knew.'

Amber thought about it all. 'You're right,' she said, suddenly pleased with herself. 'I am a strong woman. And my mum did teach me well. I'm just like her, in fact.'

The taxi driver dropped Amber and her bags outside number 18 Summer Street.

'Thanks,' he said, when she paid him and gave him a decent tip.

At least she had money now, Amber reflected. She hadn't spent much of her earnings and she had refilled the envelope of cash her mother had given her. Mum was getting that back. The rest could go towards household expenses. If she was going to repeat her final year in school to do her exams, then she was going to be a paying member of the household.

She took a minute to fluff up her hair – even more tawny blonde now thanks to free mesh highlights at work – fix the collar on her sleeveless shirt, and adjust the tiger's-eye pendant around her neck. Her hand stilled around it, caressing the smooth stone. How many times had she touched this and thought of her mother? How many times had it felt like a talisman of her past life?

And now it was going to be part of her future, she decided, shaking back her mane of hair.

Dragging her bags to the front door she stood listening. There were sounds of music and laughter coming from around the back of the house. As the end of the terrace, number 18 had a tiny side passage, and Amber left her bags and walked curiously along it, pushing open the gate at the end and walking into a garden she definitely didn't recognise.

It was so pretty, full of plants and curves and . . . there

467

was a terrace with sun loungers and sitting on them were her mum, Mrs Devlin and a beautiful red-haired woman that Amber thought might be Mrs Maguire's daughter.

Nobody noticed her approach. They were too busy talking and laughing, and the music – Mum's adored Billie Holiday – was playing loudly. Mum's hair was different too – short and flicky, lovely. She looked so happy, so content.

Amber felt tears well up. Everything was different. What if her mum didn't want her back, what if she'd found other people she wanted to be with?

'Amber?' Faye stood up. She couldn't quite believe it. It had to be a mirage, but it wasn't: it really was her beloved Amber standing awkwardly at one side of the garden, watching.

'Amber!' she roared.

Christie and Maggie watched the two women embrace so hard it must have crushed their bones.

'Mum!'

'Amber!'

They were both sobbing and hugging, and saying sorry at the same time.

Christie got to her feet. 'I think I'll go home,' she whispered to Maggie.

'Me too,' agreed Maggie.

They both slipped out of the side gate, leaving mother and daughter in their own little world.

It was a beautiful evening and the sun was low in the sky now, with a hint of deep pink soaring up from the horizon, bathing Summer Street in its rosy glow. Across the road, children played in the park, dog owners walked slowly as their pets danced along happily, and a teenage boy and girl sat on the pavilion steps talking quietly, their arms around each other.

Christie walked home slowly, thanking all the stars in heaven that she lived in such a special place.

ACKNOWLEDGEMENTS

There are so many people to say thank you to but first on the list are the three men in my life who are simply the loves of my life: John, Murray and Dylan.

There's nothing nicer in the world than being 'Mummy Cathy', as Murray calls me, in our family. I love you three guys.

Very little would be possible without the help of Mum, who can still make me roar laughing in the middle of a crisis. An enormous, grateful thank you to my darlings Lucy and Francis, amazing and talented people who are always there for me; thanks to Anne for being an inspiring mum, and a big hug to Laura, Naomi and Emer, to whom this book is dedicated. Thanks to Sarah for so many things, and to Lisa for inspiring phone calls.

Thanks also to Annabel, David, Justine, Andrew, Jessica, Luke, Adam, Emily and John for our friendship.

Thanks to Margaret for kindness and for cool unflappability in every crisis; thanks to Marta for being a warm, funny and inspirational person; thanks to the kind and enviably long-legged angel Brenda Doody without whom this book wouldn't have been even started, and no, do not buy me a

KitKat, Brenda, my body is a temple . . . Oh well, OK. You go, girl! And huge thanks to Liz for all your kindnesses.

Heartfelt thanks to Marian Keyes for being there when it mattered; to Kate Thompson for being one of those people who shine like a bright light in your life; to Kate Holmquist for an incredible friendship that was meant to be; to Lisamarie Redmond for being the funniest person I know; to Fiona O'Brien, a beautiful kindred spirit with talent in abundance; to Cathy Barry for endless encouragement; thanks to Susan Zaidan and Barbara Stack, my fellow twin mummies who agree that we're blessed,

To Tricia Scanlan who is an angel herself; to Sheila O'Flanagan, the sharpest, wittiest woman in books. Thanks to my friend, the amazingly wise Maureen Hassett (without whom this book really wouldn't have been finished); to Beccy Cameron for the incredible yoga advice when I needed it; thanks to the gorgeous Amanda Cahill for the fun on Wednesdays; thanks to SuzyMcMullan for hilarious emails; to Ber Kelleher-Nolan for great fun on nights out; to fellow writers Colette Caddle and Suzanne Higgins for the laughs; and to Angela Velden for being such an inspiration.

Enormous thanks and hugs to the marathon-running genius, the kind and lovely Jonathan Lloyd at Curtis Brown. Huge thanks to all the Curtis Brown team, especially the always kind Camilla Goslett, Diana Mackay, Carol Jackson and Sarah Thursby for the exquisite hand-knits that will be family heirlooms. Thanks to Louise Page for utter professionalism in every moment of hilarious panic, and for her marvellous sense of humour. And much thanks to lovely Deborah Schneider for everything she does, all accomplished with style and charm.

Thanks (and really, thanks begins to stop sounding like a useful word and becomes hopeless as it doesn't say enough)

470

to my family at HarperCollins. When I get into Fulham Palace Road, I want hours to rush around, meet everyone and hear all your news.

First, a huge thanks to the always exquisite Lynne Drew who is simply a marvellous friend and is as wise as she's wonderful; thanks to the über-talented writer and editor Rachel Hore who has such vision that I can hear her voice in my head when I'm doing something daft, and who's taught me how to self-edit; an enormous thanks to Amanda Ridout for being dynamic and making it clear that us small women are a force to be reckoned with. And I'm sure I'm taller . . .

Thanks to the elegant Victoria Barnsley; thanks to Maxine Hitchcock for being an utter darling; thanks to Alice Russell, Fiona McIntosh, Lee Motley, Anne O'Brien, Damon Greeney, Wendy Neale, Clive Kintoff, Lucy Vanderbilt, Katie Espiner, the whole incredible sales and marketing team, all the gang in Glasgow (never let me into the book room again!), gorgeous Anita who lights up the reception, and everyone else in the HC family.

Last but certainly not least, especial thanks to the Irish superheroes: Moira Reilly and Tony Purdue.

Thanks to HarperCollins Australia and New Zealand, who make tours such a joy. (I say tours, but really, we have fun and go to restaurants and manage to shop. Can I live in Alannah Hill's shop?) For all of that, thanks to supermom Mel Caine, my dear friend Karen-Maree Griffiths, Christine Farmer, Louisa Dear, Jim and Pandi Demetriou, Lorraine Steele, Tony Fisk, Anne Simpson and Chris Casey. Thanks also for the welcome to Shaunagh O'Connor and Bron Sibree.

Thanks to my US family at Simon & Schuster: the ever kind Lauren McKenna, Megan McKeever and Anne Dowling (good luck, Anne).

Thanks to my fantastic worldwide family, particularly Anna Bajars at Gummerus and all the lovely team there, and thanks to everyone at Random House, Kontinents, gorgeous Empiria, Presses de la Cité, Sonia Draga, Eksmo and The House of Books and forgive me if I leave anyone out.

Thanks to Mary O'Reilly for sterling work and telling me she was enjoying it as she went, which matters a great deal; thanks to Carol Flynn of Nanny Solutions for giving me information on recruitment firms (naturally, my fictional creations are entirely from my own mind) and who will definitely be entrepreneur of the year any moment now.

Thanks to Jenny Turner, boutique-owner extraordinaire in Enniskerry, for giving me such helpful advice for *Always & Forever*, not to mention showing me lovely clothes to admire when I drop down to the village for a litre of milk ...

Thanks to Helen, Ming and Ethan Xu who are so brave and clever and a wonderful inspiration to me; thanks to Erin Estrich (beautiful inside and out) who will always have a special place in our hearts; thanks to Mary Walsh; to Jill Ross; to Carmel Ruttle; to darling Camilla Carruth; and thanks to one of the most spiritual people I've ever met and who's an amazing mum, Jana. I can't wait to see darling Lili.

Thanks to the lovely person in Dundrum Town Centre who found my Sony digital tape recorder and handed it in with all my notes in it.

A thanks that could go on forever to all the wonderful readers who make sense of what I do. Thanks for all your letters and emails: without you guys, none of it would work.

Thanks to my lovely friends in the bookselling world who are such fun to be with and love book gossip just as much as I do and who are the other vital part of what I do.

Finally, thank you to UNICEF Ireland for giving me the chance to become part of their team. I feel so privileged to be one of their ambassadors and for the chance to go into the field to meet wonderful people who, simply because of where they're born, don't have access to the same education, civil rights and medical help we do. My first trip to Mozambique was both humbling and life-changing. You can't see the work UNICEF do in conjunction with local people and not be changed for life. Remember: these people want a hand up, not a hand out.

So thanks to the UNICEF team: Maura Quinn, Thora Mackey, Grace Kelly, Julianne Savage, Ann Marie Foran, everyone in the UNICEF Ireland office and the incredibly hard-working committee who all work so hard to make a difference. Thanks also to Stephen Rea for being a brilliant travelling companion.

For a television interview once, we worked out how many children would have developed HIV in the time the interview took. Julianne did the maths for this book and the numbers are scary: if it takes you four days to read this book, then 5,700 children will have died from AIDS in that time and 7,014 children under 15 will have become infected with HIV.

The overwhelming majority of these children will have been infected through their mothers at birth. It would have cost around $5 for drugs to cut this infection rate by 50% but these mothers, like so many women in impoverished countries, wouldn't have access to either the drugs or the information about them. That's what UNICEF is about: changing lives for the better.

Once *in a* Lifetime

Cathy's new bestseller out in paperback
September 2009

Life is always better when
a friend lends a hand ...

Ingrid Fitzgerald is flying high. A successful TV presenter, she's happily married with two wonderful children. But as they fly the nest, she's about to discover a secret that will shatter her world.

Natalie Flynn is falling in love – but the secrecy surrounding her mother's past still troubles her. Dare she ask the questions that could help her make sense of her life?

Charlie Fallon loves her family and her job at Kenny's Department Store, but her eccentric mother is growing more demanding. Could now be the time to fight for her own happiness?

The woman with the power to help them is free spirit Star Bluestone. Experience tells her that the important things in life must be treasured and the chance for real joy comes only Once in a Lifetime...

www.cathykelly.com

Save 10% when you buy direct from
HarperCollins –
call 0870 7871 724.
Free postage and packing in the UK only.